THE STORM'S BETRAYAL

First published 2021 by Solaris
an imprint of Rebellion Publishing Ltd,
Riverside House, Osney Mead,
Oxford, OX2 0ES, UK

www.solarisbooks.com

ISBN: 978 1 78108 876 0

A CIP catalogue record for this book is available
from the British Library.

Designed & typeset by Rebellion Publishing

Printed in Denmark

THE STORM'S BETRAYAL

CORRY L. LEE

SOLARIS

To Scott –
I miss you, little bro.

CHAPTER ONE

CELKA SEES THE *blow coming before Pa does and screams warning. The truncheon arcs down, and Pa turns slowly—too slowly—and Celka's running, weeds slapping her shins, mud slipping beneath her feet, slowing her, but she has to get to him has to save him has to help.*

Crack. The first blow, sharp as a gunshot, twists Pa to the side.

"No!" she screams, still meters from him when a hand catches her upper arm, fingers closing like a steel trap.

Celka twists, panicked, struggling to tear free. She has to get to Pa. Another truncheon lands with a sick crack, and Pa cries out. Celka's shoulder wrenches, but she snarls and hits and screams. "Let me go, letmego!"

Pain—a bright starburst across her face as the Army captain gripping her arm strikes her. Celka lands hard—hands and knees hitting the mud, weeds and circus tents smearing.

The crack of blows brings her back. The Tayemstvoy, still beating Pa.

Head swimming, Celka surges to her feet. But the Army

captain—Captain Vrana—grabs her by the hair, wrenching her to the side when she tries to run to Pa. Tears blur Celka's vision, and she grabs Vrana's wrist, trying to claw open her grip, but it only tightens until she cries out, until she can only stumble beneath the woman's hold, gasping, desperate, hearing the sick crack of wood and hobnailed boots on flesh as the Tayemstvoy keep beating Pa.

Celka, remember your high wire? *The voice slices through her horror, not making sense.* Celka, you're safe.

She's not. Vrana shoves her to the ground. Celka gasps, digging her fingers into the cold mud, struggling to crush down her terror enough to turn back. She has to fight. Has to save Pa.

Vrana catches her chin, grip bruising, wrenching Celka's face up to hers. Her question ratchets Celka's fear. When Vrana doesn't like her answer, her fist smashes into Celka's cheek.

On the ground again, Celka tastes blood. The Tayemstvoy, Vrana, they want to make her small, make her give up. But she won't. She claws her hands into the mud. Looming over her, Vrana smells like gun oil, a slippery darkness that makes Celka bare her teeth.

Celka. Celka, look at me. *The voice again, the one that doesn't belong.* Can you hear the circus band?

Celka lifts her head, ears ringing from Vrana's blows, from Pa's cries and the crack of truncheons. She has to save Pa. Nothing else matters.

But a figure catches her eye, yanks her attention off Vrana. Wavering, they glow the red of fresh blood. Celka stares, drawn inexplicably.

Pa cries out. Vrana's voice menaces.

Celka blinks and the figure's closer—crouched, reaching out.

Heartbeat loud in her ears, Celka lifts a muddy hand. The figure smells of blood, of mud, of gun oil—of Celka's pain and terror and desperation, all of it so sharp that the rest of the world fades.

Celka touches their hand. It's insubstantial, a haze of blood, yet the figure grips her palm and the scents sharpen.

Pa! *Celka wants to scream, wants to snatch the pistol from Vrana's hip and defend him—but she can't make herself release the ghostly hand.*

The figure's red glow pulses in time with Celka's panicked heartbeat. Then blue like a summer sky slashes the blaze. Celka gasps, wanting to recoil. She's falling. The hand still grips hers, but she can feel Vrana looming behind her.

Remember your high wire? *The figure is too faint to see their lips move, but Celka's certain the voice is theirs. She wants to tear away. The high wire is a dream, a memory from before the Tayemstvoy attacked.*

Pa. *She wants to choke the word aloud, but doesn't dare. Wants to rip Vrana's pistol from its holster.*

You don't have to fight. You're safe. *The cracks of blue in the figure's red blaze deepen, sending an ache through Celka's chest that doesn't match the pain of Vrana kicking her with hobnailed boots.* Your costume glitters with green sequins, and your sleeves float like emerald smoke. *The words remind Celka of someone she trusts, but she can see her arms even as she can't tear her gaze from the figure rippling red and blue, their pulse slowing, tongues of purple and green flickering across them. She* doesn't *wear her high wire costume— of course she doesn't. She's in the back lot, where she was practicing with Pa before Vrana came, strutting at the head of a Tayemstvoy squad.*

"Dust dances in the spotlights around your high wire." *The figure's voice is growing stronger, the acoustics wrong for the weedy, open lot.* "Can you hear the band? They play fluting and tense as you walk the high wire. You're so confident."

Celka's stomach lurches at the familiar sensation of the steel cable pressing against the soles of her feet, though she still stands in mud. But the figure glows more blue than red now, and instead of blood and mud and gun oil, Celka smells boiling cabbage and horse manure. She wavers, unsteady. Pa. I have to save Pa. *But her desperation is fading.*

Pa is gone, dragged away by the Tayemstvoy.

"You don't need a weapon to be strong, Celka. You're strong when you walk the high wire." The words echoed, doubled by memory. Gerrit told her the same thing—when? Why?

Celka struggled to remember details, frowning to find herself on the practice wire, the steel cable live beneath her feet, the springtime sun bright like spotlights as evergreen trees cast patches of shadow.

The glowing figure still stood before her, smelling of horses and cabbage, rippling with color that echoed the circus band playing off-key. Celka gripped their hand, and it felt more solid than it had before.

"You're safe, Celka. It's just the two of us. We're alone. There's no need to fight." The voice was so soothing that Celka almost believed it. With the practice wire beneath her feet, she could finally breathe. "You lost yourself. Your sousednia warped and you lost true-life. But you're safe now. Come back."

The words buzzed almost beyond her understanding, but the picture they painted—that the practice wire and circus back lot were somehow not real—made Celka want to understand.

The figure reached one ghostly hand to stroke Celka's cheek, and Celka flinched—it felt real. *So real.* Closing her eyes, she concentrated on that touch and the feel of someone's hand warm in hers.

A new reality bled into her senses.

She lay on something hard. The air smelled of old stone and acrid sweat.

"Come back, Celka," the voice said. "Return to true-life."

Opening her eyes, Celka found herself lying on the floor, staring at a gray stone ceiling, a single electric lightbulb hanging from it, caged. She held a stranger's hand, their beige skin tanned from the sun, blond hair cropped short, eyes the same gray as the rough stone walls. The stranger wore gold lightning bolt earrings, studded with purple stone. That she wore a *pair* of earrings gave Celka her pronouns. That they were lightning bolts, suggested this woman was a storm mage—a bozhk.

Celka dropped the bozhk's hand and scrambled back. She tried to get to her feet, but stumbled, flinging a hand out to catch herself against the wall. The cell wall. Leaning hard against it, Celka willed her legs to support her. Her frantic glance landed on a heavy, steel-banded door—closed and no doubt bolted. She was a prisoner.

Breath harsh in her throat, Celka turned back to the bozhk who hadn't moved from where she'd knelt beside Celka. Not just a bozhk, a soldier. The young woman wore olive green battledress trousers and a khaki shirt. No jacket, so Celka couldn't tell her name or rank.

There was a cot at the soldier's back, a chamber pot in one corner. The bozhk soldier blinked like she was having trouble focusing on Celka, and slowly raised her hands, weaponless. "I'm Hedvika," she said, her voice the one that had broken Celka from the memory fugue of Tayemstvoy beating Pa. "I'm a strazh mage. I'm here to help you."

Celka swallowed, her mouth dry, throat raw from screaming. She understood a little better now, memory piecing back together: the circus back lot wasn't entirely real. It was the neighboring reality, *sousednia*, the place of needs and ideas where she shaped magic.

This cell was real, was true-life. And Celka was locked inside.

"Would you like some water?" Hedvika asked.

At Celka's nod, Hedvika reached beneath the cot.

She held out a metal cup. "Come sit down." Hedvika's sousedni-shape bled through from the neighboring reality, color rippling over her khaki shirt and pale skin. Despite the fear twisting Celka's stomach, that blue-red glow calmed something within her. Scents of cabbage and horses wafted from Hedvika, sousednia tangling with true-life, carrying an off-key rendition of the circus band. It made Celka feel... not safe, exactly, but safe enough that she edged forward and took the cup.

She didn't want to sit and leave herself vulnerable, but her muscles shivered with exhaustion. Lowering herself to the edge of the cot furthest from the bozhk soldier, Celka drank, the cool water a relief.

Something about the moment felt familiar, and Celka knew before Hedvika said anything that the other woman was going to hand her a cold bowl of porridge. She knew how it would taste, lumpy and flavorless, but so welcome in her stomach's gnawing emptiness. Celka expected Hedvika to sit on the far edge of the cot, and she did.

The porridge helped Celka's hunger, but her stomach felt queasy in a way that she didn't remember from before, and her jaw throbbed. "What happened?" Celka asked.

"You don't remember?"

Celka frowned, trying to shake the memories free.

She'd been in a different cell, a Tayemstvoy officer circling her, asking her question after question. Celka had tried to answer. Had tried to stay calm. She'd tried to speak the truth that she and Gerrit and Filip had hastily worked out before turning themselves over to the State. But memory had overwhelmed reason. She'd smelled blood and mud and gun oil as a desperate need to fight—a combat nuzhda—welled back up.

"You're safe now." Hedvika's soothing voice startled Celka from the memory, the touch of her hand on Celka's wrist making her flinch. "Shhh." Hedvika edged closer, blues and reds rippling bright over her uniform. "You're safe."

"I'm in a cell," Celka choked, though Hedvika's words helped, draining the red haze from her vision. "I'm not *safe*." She balled one hand into a fist, struggling to slow her breathing. How long had she been a prisoner? How many times had she lost herself in a combat nuzhda fugue?

Hedvika slid her hand down to cover Celka's, and her lips tightened. "Combat-warping won't help."

Celka forced herself to focus on her bowl of kasha, scraping the last bites of porridge from the sides and making herself swallow. "Will *anything* help?" She'd been here for days, at least—long enough that she'd lost track.

Hedvika sighed. "I wouldn't be here if..."

Celka frowned up at her. If what? If the State didn't think Celka would be useful? Celka was an imbuement mage, capable of creating new magic. It made her valuable— valuable enough, she'd thought, to keep her safe despite the Tayemstvoy she'd killed.

But if the State really believed her value, why was she still locked in a cell? Why did they repeat the same questions over and over, trying to catch her in a lie, making her relive her memory of the blood-soaked print shop until it overwhelmed her tenuous grounding in true-life and left her snarling violence?

Every interrogation since they'd brought her to this stone-walled dungeon had ended with her losing control. Her combat nuzhda flaring, she saw only threat, attacking her interrogators—attacking armed Tayemstvoy—and of course they struck her and threw her to the ground. Celka rubbed her wrists, bruised and aching from fighting against handcuffs. She was sleeting lucky the Tayemstvoy didn't use her violence as an excuse to tear off her fingernails or burn her with hot irons.

Not quite meeting Hedvika's gaze, Celka asked, "Are you Tayemstvoy?" She knew better than to ask questions of her captors; Grandfather had taught her how to survive interrogation, taught her to stare at her feet and speak meekly and only when questioned. But Celka had already sleeted that up—so many times. Yet still Hedvika sat with her, brought her food and water and didn't hurt her.

"No," Hedvika said. "I'm—" She hesitated, and Celka found the bozhk studying her, wary. She realized that Hedvika's eyes were a blue so pale they only looked gray in the slate-walled cell. "I'm regular Army, a sub-lieutenant." She said it cautiously, smelling like hay and cabbage while a nuzhda like the summer sky rippled over her skin.

Celka's stomach clenched—but at least Hedvika wasn't secret police.

Hedvika slipped her hand into Celka's. "I'm here to help."

Celka didn't believe her, but she wanted to. Today wasn't the first time Hedvika had pulled her back from a combat fugue.

The memory of panicked desperation closed like a fist around Celka's throat, and she squeezed Hedvika's hand—a lifeline. Being locked in a cell was hardly a comfort, but anything was better than being trapped inside her desperate horror, fighting to save Pa, doomed to fail.

"Thank you," she whispered, just as the cell door banged open on two uniformed Tayemstvoy. Celka's stomach clenched.

"Celka Prochazka," the Tayemstvoy said, "you'll come with us."

CHAPTER TWO

FATIGUE LEFT GERRIT Kladivo's eyes gritty as he followed his Tayemstvoy escort into the heart of his father's regime. He'd dozed on the train to the capital, but hadn't had a good night's sleep since he and Celka and Filip had handed themselves over to the State a week ago. Storm Gods, he hoped Celka was safe. Hoped her treatment had been no worse than his.

Filip caught his gaze as they left the motorcade that had brought them from the train station. Worry crinkled the corners of his eyes, strain that felt so familiar since the bozhskyeh storms' return two months ago—a return that carried the possibility of creating new magic for the first time in seven decades.

Magic Gerrit had finally learned to imbue—while hiding in the circus with Celka.

Climbing the steps of the gray stone government building, the circus' trumpeting, joyful chaos had never felt so distant. In the regime's heart, the only colors were blood red and olive drab. Red shone from Tayemstvoy shoulder tabs and flapped from the second-story banisters, Tayemstvoy flags announcing the might of the regime—his father's regime. Today, Gerrit would face Supreme-General Kladivo, the mighty Stormhawk. The hail-eating murderer.

Gerrit had come *so close* to escaping, *so close* to using his magic to strengthen the resistance at Celka's side. But instead, he was back in uniform, muddy and sore from days on the road imbuing weapons to prove his worth to his lying, storm-forsaken father. Because his only chance now was to convince the Stormhawk of his unwavering loyalty. He couldn't flinch, couldn't hesitate, or he and Celka and Filip would all be killed—eventually, once the Tayemstvoy finished torturing them to extract everything they knew about the resistance. And Celka, at least, knew plenty.

As their hobnailed boots rang across the marble foyer, Filip touched Gerrit's elbow. "You'll do fine. Your imbuement today was impressive." An edge to his voice and the warning in his eyes shook Gerrit.

If Filip could tell he was unsettled, the Stormhawk would know too. His father didn't know him the way Filip did, wouldn't be able to read him so casually, but the Stormhawk's personal guard, the Yestrab Okhrana, were almost all mages, equipped with the best imbuements stolen from the breadth of Bourshkanya. If Gerrit faced his father full of righteous rage, the Stormhawk might not immediately realize Gerrit's disloyalty, but the Yestrab Okhrana would.

So Gerrit nodded silent thanks to Filip and focused on his breath. On a slow inhale, he let true-life's ring of hobnailed boots fade into his sousednia's howling alpine wind. He expected Filip to shimmer aubergine and carmine at his side, pulling against Gerrit's core nuzhda to give him an anchor, but Filip appeared a mere heat-shimmer in sousednia, not pulling against any nuzhda.

A nuzhda was the desperate need a mage used to create

or activate an imbuement. But everyone had their own core nuzhda, reflecting who they were when calm. That core nuzhda shaped sousednia for any mage strong enough to see the neighboring reality, and Filip often helped Gerrit return to his own core when emotion—or magic—carried him away. But Filip had a role to play in what came next. As Gerrit's strazh mage, he'd be watched just as carefully as Gerrit.

Because they weren't in the circus anymore. Gerrit couldn't afford to show emotion or lose control. He had to be strong, unremorseful, unrelenting. He forced himself to think the way his father would expect: Gerrit was the Stormhawk's son and Bourshkanya was his birthright. He was a powerful imbuement mage and had proven himself many times over. The fact that he'd needed to escape into the circus to do it wasn't his problem; if the Storm Guard Academy's leadership had been competent, he could have learned to imbue within their bounds. They'd failed *him*, not the other way around.

By the time Gerrit had passed through two checkpoints, he'd settled his regime mask into place. He hated it. Hated thinking like his father, hated that he *could*. But their survival depended on him playing this role perfectly.

Supreme-General Kladivo sat behind a broad, polished desk, annotating a file, yet his likeness glowered at Gerrit from a massive portrait on the wall. Even painted in oils, the Stormhawk's gaze pierced him, making Gerrit want to drop to his knees, filled with awe in the presence of such greatness.

Gerrit struggled to keep his breathing even, his expression as solemn and respectful as he'd practiced. Visible from their sousednia bleed-through, the lines and colors of dozens of active imbuements crisscrossed the room, emanating from the pair of Yestrab Okhrana guards still as posts behind his father and another pair at Gerrit's back. Some of those imbuements were the reason for his awe and overwhelming desire to please. The fact that those imbuements made him want to grovel boded ill for this meeting; when the Stormhawk was in a good mood, he had his guard dispense with most of the emotional punch.

Fighting to maintain his own authority and entitlement, Gerrit saluted. "All hail the Stormhawk!" He spoke with unironic fervor. *All hail Father* or *All hail you* did not appeal to the Stormhawk's sense of humor. He *had* no sense of humor.

The Stormhawk continued writing, and Gerrit counted his breaths, keeping his focus on true-life. The Stormhawk did not like having the imbuements that protected him studied, even by his children. If today was like any of the other times Gerrit had been called before his father, one of the guards standing behind him was probably storm-blessed and therefore able to see sousednia and tell how deeply Gerrit focused on the neighboring reality. They would report to his father using hand signals. Gerrit could allow nothing to go wrong.

Eventually, the Stormhawk set his pen down and looked Gerrit over. A frown tugged at the corners of his mouth. Gerrit had come straight from imbuing in a muddy village, and dried muck clung to his chestnut leather kneeboots and spattered his olive uniform. He felt dirty and exhausted, and his father's habitual distain, combined with his imbuements, made Gerrit feel painfully insignificant.

He kept his head high and held the Stormhawk's gaze.

"At ease," the Stormhawk finally said, and Gerrit dropped his salute.

In his father's silence, Gerrit felt a welling urge to tell his father everything, to throw himself on his knees and beg for mercy. He locked his jaw, swallowing the words. His father had no mercy, and this urge rose from another imbuement. The bozhk who held it stood just past the Stormhawk's right shoulder. Gerrit hated that imbuement, but he'd dealt with it before—back when he'd been younger and weaker. He knew this game. He could wait his father out.

The Stormhawk folded his hands and leaned back, comfortable in his padded leather chair. Finally, he said, "There's an issue of discipline I've been considering. Perhaps you could give me your take on it, Son."

"With pleasure, sir." Gerrit kept his voice calm, confident. Once upon a time, he might have believed this conversation anything but a trap.

"There's an officer cadet who caused a fair amount of trouble recently," the Stormhawk began, and Gerrit's hope that this wasn't about him vanished. "He left his post and cost the State considerable resources to recover. But he may still be useful, and he claims extenuating circumstances. Still, a blatant disregard for regulations and a month-long absence should not go unpunished, don't you think?"

"No, sir."

"So?" The Stormhawk opened his hand, gesturing for Gerrit to go ahead. "What punishment would you suggest?"

Gerrit drew a slow breath, willing his voice not to shake. "Do you envision a public or private punishment, sir?"

"There's nothing to be gained from putting this man's mistakes on display."

Gerrit exhaled, but quashed his relief. He hated being publicly humiliated, but a private punishment could be harsher. A dispassionate part of him understood keeping this matter private. The Stormhawk had turned Bourshkanya upside-down searching for him, but had never revealed his identity. The Stormhawk would look weak if he couldn't control his own child.

"Have him beaten." Gerrit managed to say it like they were talking about someone else.

"Just him? His disobedience led to punishable offenses from

another soldier, and led a civilian into armed action against the regime."

Gerrit swallowed hard, suddenly very aware of Filip standing a meter behind him, deliberately ignored by his father. Whatever happened next, he couldn't let this punishment fall on Filip or Celka. The Stormhawk didn't care about them; he wanted to make sure that *Gerrit* knew his place. And Gerrit did. It was in the resistance, tearing apart his father's regime. But until he could get there, he had to make it look like he wanted his own place at the Stormhawk's side—and the Stormhawk's son could not be weak.

"It sounds like the others followed your officer cadet into disobedience. That means they'll follow him into loyalty, so long as they have no reason to fear it. Make the extent of the offender's mistakes clear—have his people watch, if you see fit—but punish only him."

The Stormhawk seemed to consider it, and Gerrit wanted to drop to his knees and beg his father to leave Celka and Filip out of whatever cruelty he'd devised. But the Stormhawk's son would never grovel. "And if the punishment is too severe for one person to bear? Why gather subordinates, if not to share the burden of mistakes?"

Gerrit's blood curdled, but he made his voice flat. "If the crime is so severe that its punishment cannot be survived, perhaps you should simply stage an execution." This had to be a test. The Stormhawk could not seriously be considering discarding him. Just today, he'd imbued a sniper rifle that would make miraculous shots a straightforward matter of bozhk training and skill.

The Stormhawk inclined his head. "You've grown, Son."

Gerrit straightened. "I understand what's important now. I understand my power, and how to use it to support the regime." He dared a step forward, placing his hands on the Stormhawk's desk and leaning in as though they shared some bond grown out of blood and unity of purpose. "I can give you the Storm Gods' power, Father. I'm ready to step into *my* power at your side. What I imbued today is only the beginning."

The Stormhawk rose to his feet, mirroring Gerrit's posture, holding his gaze with eyes colder than glaciers. "You ask for power after you ran like a *coward?*"

Gerrit had expected this jab. "There's no dishonor in a retreat that gains advantage. Colonel Tesarik's methods were flawed. That field gun that he forced my classmate Branislav Ademik to imbue, how useful is it to the State?" Colonel Tesarik, the Storm Guard Academy's Tayemstvoy overseer, had driven Branislav deliberately storm-mad, thinking it would make him create more powerful weapons. Gerrit refused to let himself remember his friend raging and snarling in a cell, fighting things that existed only in his mind.

Bringing up Branislav's imbued field gun was a gamble. It was powerful, and Gerrit hadn't been able to learn whether it could be used. But he could guess. When Celka had nearly gone storm-mad imbuing out of control, she'd had no concern for creating an object that another mage could safely activate.

"The weapon was retired." Disappointment tinged the Stormhawk's voice at the waste. "The two bozhki who attempted to fire it had to be relieved of service."

Gerrit tried not to imagine those two mages snarling vacantly in their own cells. Or perhaps they'd been put down like rabid dogs. "And the process used to create it?" An edge crept into Gerrit's voice. A squad of armed soldiers had beaten Branislav during a storm to 'encourage' his combat imbuement—at Colonel Tesarik's orders. Branislav had pulled down too much Gods' Breath, and it had locked him into a combat fugue, completely dissociated from true-life. Celka had combat-warped nearly as badly; Gerrit struggled to crush his fear that, since they'd been separated, the Tayemstvoy had made that warping worse.

"Some risks fail to pay off," the Stormhawk said.

Gerrit had to focus on his current problem. He couldn't help Celka if his father decided to execute him. "Thus the strategic retreat."

The corner of the Stormhawk's mouth lifted in what might have been a smile, and he settled back into his chair, steepling his fingers. "The techniques you learned while... on your retreat, could you teach them?"

The question caught Gerrit off guard, but he covered it, considering his answer. He could, he was certain. The thought of helping the rest of Bourshkanya's storm-blessed mages successfully create weapons for the regime, however, made him nauseous. But those mages would figure out how to imbue sooner or later, whether or not he helped them, and he needed to stay alive to escape into the resistance. "I think so. Though it may take longer for the older bozhki to learn."

"Good," the Stormhawk said. "You want your own command, Son?"

"Yes, sir!" Being given command of storm-blessed mages would give him power, maybe even access to information he could feed to the resistance. And it would mean leaving this office with a commission rather than a death sentence. He'd be able to protect Filip and Celka. He'd be able to find Captain Vrana and escape into the resistance.

But his father's gaze was flat and hard, no hint of leniency, and Gerrit realized what was coming the moment the Stormhawk opened his mouth. "Strip to the waist. Put your hands on the desk."

Fear landed like a gut-punch. Gerrit's throat tightened, and he had no idea how he managed to force out a "Yes, sir." His hands betrayed him, shaking as he undid the buttons on his uniform jacket. Still, he managed to keep his spine straight as he laid his jacket over the back of a chair and folded his shirt and undershirt neatly. He left his storm pendant around his neck, the lightning worked skillfully into gold; maybe this gift from his mother would give him her strength.

He wanted to stall, fuss with the folds of his shirt, catch Filip's eye and lean on his best friend for support—find any reason at all not to turn back to his father's desk. But he could not show weakness, so he made his face impassive and met his father's gaze. The Stormhawk held a wooden cane the width of Gerrit's smallest finger. Gerrit's chest went shuddery, but at the Stormhawk's cold nod, Gerrit leaned his palms on the desk's polished wood. One of the Yestrab Okhrana came forward and took the cane, before stepping behind Gerrit.

Gerrit broke out in a cold sweat. He'd been caned before for disobedience, a few lines of searing pain, the bruises beneath aching for weeks. He could handle this.

But never, since he'd joined the Storm Guard Academy at age seven, had he been beaten before his father. Never had the Stormhawk watched him with his predatory gaze, awaiting Gerrit's screams. Gerrit hadn't just disobeyed one of his instructors' stupid orders this time, and suddenly all of his feigned confidence crumbled. His vision grayed with terror.

The first strike came without warning. The line of fire stole his breath, but he fought to hold his father's gaze, determined not to look weak.

The cane landed again, and Gerrit hissed air out through clenched teeth.

He wanted to beg, wanted to take back every self-assured word he'd spoken. How had he ever talked about this beating as though it would happen to someone else? Some desperate, animal part of him wanted to scream for Filip to be dragged up here with him, taking half the blows so Gerrit could escape them.

The cane fell again.

No matter his own fear, Gerrit wouldn't throw Filip before this onrushing train. Gerrit alone had chosen to escape the academy, had chosen to hide in the circus and learn to imbue. Filip had come after him, yes, but on Captain Vrana's orders. Again.

Gerrit pressed his fingers into the desk's sleek wood, willing himself to endure, willing himself to keep the hatred for his father off his face. He was a loyal soldier. He wanted to imbue to strengthen the State at his father's side.

The cane landed again, and twice more. Gerrit realized he'd squeezed his eyes shut and forced himself to meet his father's gaze.

The Stormhawk held up a hand, and Gerrit shuddered with relief. "You serve *me*, Gerrit. Not your own whim."

"Yes, sir," Gerrit said, fervent, his back burning.

The Stormhawk measured him with his cold gaze, then clenched his raised hand into a fist.

The cane landed hard, and Gerrit cried out, unprepared for fresh pain.

"Let's ensure you remember that," the Stormhawk said, and the cane fell again.

The Yestrab Okhrana gave him no reprieve now, just agony as the cane struck his back over and over. Gerrit clamped his jaw shut and fought not to cry out. He leaned hard on the desk, struggling to keep his feet under him. But eventually, his legs buckled. The shock of his knees hitting the ground revived him momentarily, sharpening his senses enough to see his father watching. Gerrit clutched the edge of the desk, vision graying as the blows continued.

Helpless, he screamed.

When darkness finally folded over him, he welcomed the reprieve.

CHAPTER THREE

SILENCE DESCENDED ON the Stormhawk's office like an artillery shell, unconsciousness cutting off Gerrit's screams. Filip kept his hands locked behind his back, knuckles aching from how tightly he clenched his fists. The Yestrab Okhrana sergeant who'd beaten Gerrit stepped back, looking to the Stormhawk for instructions. Filip struggled to keep his face impassive, staring straight ahead—just another soldier at attention. He wanted to touch his storm pendant, send his prayer upwards with a spark: *please let this be the end.* But he knew better than to hope. There were ways to wake an unconscious prisoner.

The Stormhawk's gaze landed on him like a physical blow. Filip's knees wanted to buckle. He wanted to beg that the Stormhawk beat him instead of Gerrit. He made himself keep staring at the wall, just a little to the side of the Stormhawk's portrait. He was nothing, just an Army sub-lieutenant who'd followed orders.

"Sub-Lieutenant Cizek, you're dismissed." The Stormhawk's voice rang like a gunshot.

Filip yes-sirred and saluted. "All hail the Stormhawk!"

He forced himself to march to the door, abandoning his best friend unconscious on the floor, the Yestrab Okhrana still looming over him.

Another of the Stormhawk's guards led Filip to a sitting room and told him to wait. He sat on the hard chair like he stood at attention and silently sang all fifty-seven verses of the Song of Calming in his head as he watched the door.

Several hours had passed by the time it opened.

Gerrit stepped inside, and Filip leapt up, swallowing his cry of relief, forcing the emotion off his face. A Yestrab Okhrana private stood just outside the door.

Gerrit wavered on his feet. His naturally pale skin looked disturbingly gray, but he wore a full lieutenant's three stars on each shoulder rather than the pips of a senior Army cadet. His knuckles were white where he clenched a thin folder beneath one arm. "We're taking the train to Solnitse. I'll brief you en route." His voice sounded rough at the edges.

Filip poured him a glass of water from the carafe on the table, offering it without comment. Gerrit drank it in one go, then nodded curtly, hiding his thanks.

On the train, after a stiff, silent luncheon, they returned to their cabin. Hoping he'd finally get answers, Filip locked the door and drew the blind over its small window. It didn't necessarily give them privacy. The Tayemstvoy could be listening through the walls or with imbuements—just as Filip had, so many times, while he'd shadowed Gerrit in the circus.

Gerrit shrugged out of his uniform jacket, breath hissing through clenched teeth.

Filip decided to throw his best friend's pride to the wind. "Let me help."

Gerrit shut his eyes, clutching the rail of the sleeper car's closed upper bunk with bloodless knuckles. He jerked a nod.

Once Filip had gotten Gerrit's shirt off, he pointed to the

sofa. "Sit." He took off Gerrit's boots. Training exercises in the Storm Guard Academy were often brutal, and usually Gerrit managed some quip to shrug off whatever they'd endured. That Gerrit said nothing left Filip cold. Gerrit eased himself onto his stomach, and Filip made himself look at his best friend's back.

Where the flesh wasn't swollen and red, it was nearly black with bruises. Gerrit hadn't bled, but it had been a near thing. Telling himself it could have been worse, Filip dug in his satchel for the pot of analgesic cream he'd bought while they'd waited for the train.

He touched Gerrit's back as lightly as possible to spread it, but even that made Gerrit's breath quicken with pain.

"You should have let him beat me," Filip said, low in the hopes that they might not be overheard.

"No," Gerrit said, and Filip was relieved to hear the steel in his voice. "You didn't do anything wrong. You followed orders."

Filip's jaw worked as he spread the next dollop of cream in silence. *You followed orders.* Was that meant as a recrimination?

Captain Vrana had requisitioned an imbuement that hid Filip's sousedni-shape so Gerrit wouldn't accidentally spot him—so that Celka, who Gerrit had apparently run away with, wouldn't realize he was a bozhk. Captain Vrana had ordered Filip not to make contact with Gerrit or even reveal his presence unless necessary to protect him. He was to hide until Gerrit imbued a Category Three or higher combat imbuement. For a month, Filip had pretended to be a knife thrower in the circus sideshow, performing for the amusement of others while Gerrit risked his life imbuing without a strazh.

Convinced Gerrit had deliberately abandoned him, Filip had hated every moment of it. He'd been desperate to talk to his friend, to assure Gerrit that he wouldn't let him lose true-life. But at the same time, he'd blamed Gerrit—hated him—for casting him aside while he ran off to train with a rogue imbuement mage who'd somehow hidden her storm-affinity from the State. Filip hadn't understood how Celka was there, how Gerrit had found her, but as he watched, as he flirted and charmed his way into the circus performers' confidences, it became clear that Celka wasn't an untrained civilian. She was involved in the resistance.

At first, Filip had told himself that Gerrit had figured it out. Gerrit was using her and collecting intelligence that would buy his way back into his father's good graces and deal a blow to the hail-eaters who worked against the State.

Then Filip had made the mistake of getting to know Celka.

He hadn't wanted to like her. She'd lured Gerrit away, had involved him in treason and put the Tayemstvoy on his trail. But she was clever and funny and had a spark of that same intensity that Filip loved in Gerrit. And Celka hadn't fallen for Filip's flirtatious smile. She'd brushed him off until he'd told her the truth about who he was—as much as he could while following his storm-forsaken orders. And only then, only after he'd admitted how alone and empty he felt cut off from everything he loved, did she open up. Worse, he found himself wanting to spend time with her. He'd even helped her get an illegal pistol from her resistance contacts, careful to learn as little as possible in case he was questioned.

He'd told himself he was doing it to protect Gerrit. If Celka was caught, Gerrit would be too. All of his best friend's clever excuses wouldn't save him if he was found printing resistance leaflets in the circus's snake trailer.

But Filip knew himself well enough to see it for a justification. He'd spent time with Celka because he liked Celka. When she imbued out of control and attacked a Tayemstvoy squad, Filip had stopped being able to follow orders. He'd revealed himself and tried to ground her back in her core nuzhda—and it had all gone wrong. In the aftermath, Gerrit had told him they were leaving for the resistance. Gerrit Kladivo, the Stormhawk's son, was fleeing into the resistance—and Filip just couldn't. Couldn't keep up the lies, couldn't pretend it wasn't the stupidest, most suicidal idea his best friend had ever had.

So his flirtatious Ctibor-the-knife-thrower mask had slipped, and Celka had panicked. She'd nearly imbued combat a second time, all her hard-won grounding shattered. Gerrit had saved her, and Filip had saved them both, but it had cost precious time.

If Filip had followed orders and stayed out of that print shop, Gerrit and Celka might have escaped into the resistance.

They would have been caught by now, Filip was certain—almost certain. And then they'd really have been tortured. What the Stormhawk had done to Gerrit today would have been just the beginning if Filip hadn't delayed their escape long enough for a Tayemstvoy platoon to surround the print shop. Boxed in by Tayemstvoy, their only way out had been for Gerrit to stop hiding and reveal his identity as the Stormhawk's son.

Yeah, Filip had followed orders. Until he hadn't. And because of it, Gerrit was alive and had a lieutenant's stars, and Celka would be safe too—soon, if she wasn't already.

Filip had no idea if his best friend hated him for it. Celka probably did.

He never would have believed that Gerrit could betray the State. But when Gerrit had asked Filip to join them in the print shop, he'd sounded deathly serious. They'd stood surrounded by Tayemstvoy corpses and Gerrit had gripped Celka's hand like he'd finally found purpose.

You followed orders.

Filip and Gerrit had spent most of their lives training together, and the Tayemstvoy were always watching, always listening. They'd learned to communicate without saying the important things aloud. But now, when it really mattered, Filip didn't understand.

"I have your back," Filip finally said. He screwed the lid on the pot of analgesic. "I always will."

Gerrit pushed himself up enough that he could crane around and search Filip's expression. His jaw tightened.

Filip wished he could trust that they were unobserved and ask what in sleet-storms was going on. Was Gerrit still harboring resistance loyalties? If so, *why?* Celka believed in the resistance, sure, and Gerrit was clearly smitten with her, but Gerrit understood the State's might. Today's beating was a love peck compared to what the Stormhawk would do if Gerrit betrayed him.

They were headed to the Storm Guard Fortress because the Stormhawk had given Gerrit command of a platoon of imbuement mages. All his life, Gerrit had wanted this authority. He'd proven his ability to imbue, and his father respected that—even if he'd needed to demonstrate the cost of disobedience. He'd beaten Gerrit's back to pulp, but he'd handed him a prestigious command. If Gerrit acquitted himself well, he'd have his father's trust; he'd rise through the ranks as quickly as his brother and sister—more so, perhaps, because he was the only one of them who could imbue new magic.

Gerrit was about to get everything he'd always wanted—and Filip was too. He'd be his best friend's strazh again, protecting him during every imbuement, working with him to develop and understand new magic. They'd have authority and respect. Filip wouldn't have to worry about his mother or sisters; the State would keep them in comfort.

Yet a dark edge to Gerrit's expression warned Filip that he shouldn't get comfortable. Whatever had brought Gerrit and Celka to a resistance forger during a bozhskyeh storm, whatever had made Celka imbue and murder a squad of secret police, it wasn't over.

CHAPTER FOUR

THE TAYEMSTVOY GUARDS led Celka to a cell with two chairs on either side of a scarred and stained wooden table. They pointed to the chair opposite the door and ordered her to sit. Pulse loud in her ears, she obeyed.

You're safe. She tried to make herself believe Hedvika's lie. Shifting her focus to sousednia, she concentrated on the feel of the practice wire beneath her feet, the back lot empty and smelling of cabbage and horses. But she glanced at the cook tent, expecting Captain Vrana to stride around it ahead of a Tayemstvoy squad.

Instead, the cell door banged open, and Celka started. Two Tayemstvoy entered, one stopping just inside the door. The other, a captain who'd questioned Celka before, approached the wooden table and hooked out the empty chair with her foot.

Gold lightning bolts adorned the captain's collar, marking her as a storm mage who'd passed the State's highest bozhk qualifications. As she sat, the cell's dim light glinted off her matching gold lightning bolt earrings. She'd been the calmest of Celka's interrogators, but her every word had exuded menace by the end. Celka wasn't sure how much of that had been her runaway combat nuzhda coloring everything with threat, but seeing the captain again, she gripped the wooden seat of her chair, struggling to quell her rising panic for another interrogation that would lock her back inside a combat fugue. To distract herself, she tried to remember the captain's name. It had been something generic, so she glanced at the nameplate on the captain's chest.

Her heart seemed to stop. Today, the nameplate said *Kladivo*.

Celka's gaze snapped back up to the captain's face, searching for a likeness—to Gerrit and the Stormhawk—that she hadn't noticed before. Captain Kladivo held perfectly still, calm and predatory. She and Gerrit shared the same pale skin, as well as something in the shape of their cheekbones and the line of their foreheads. Celka had never met the Stormhawk, but his portrait adorned every shop and home; the icy evaluation in Captain Kladivo's eyes was a dead match.

"Captain Iveta Kladivo." Gerrit's sister extended her hand as if they were just meeting.

Swallowing hard, Celka shook it. Gerrit had talked about his ruthless sister. Iveta was several years older than him, storm-touched rather than storm-blessed—so able to use existing magic, but unable to create new imbuements. She and Gerrit had overlapped at the Storm Guard Academy, Iveta the darling of all her instructors, Tayemstvoy and Army alike. Most Storm Guard cadets became bozhk Army officers, but Iveta had commissioned with the Tayemstvoy, following her father's blood-drenched footsteps into the secret police. Gerrit had always sounded bitter when he talked about his sister— bitter, and a little afraid.

Captain Kladivo's grip was firm but not crushing, and Celka tried to keep breathing.

"I'm forming an imbuement company," Captain Kladivo said, "bringing together storm-blessed bozhki like yourself. Sign this, and I'll have you placed under my command—and released from here." She flipped open the file she'd brought, pushing it toward Celka and handing her a pen. The page was dense with text.

Celka made herself read. Grandfather had warned that the Tayemstvoy would beat you and convince you to sign a confession to make them stop. Then they'd send you to a labor camp or you'd disappear into another cell, no longer able to even protest your innocence.

Captain Kladivo's papers weren't a false confession. They would make her an Army private, committed to a four-year tour. The page said nothing about imbuing, about Celka having already created more new magic than anyone alive. She stared at the paper, Grandfather's advice to be meek warring with everything she'd learned from Gerrit about his time in the Storm Guard Academy. The State respected strength as much as it demanded obedience. What if this was a test to see if she deserved a place in the Storm Guard? Crushing down her terror, she met Captain Kladivo's icy stare. "Gerrit promised I'd be made a Storm Guard officer."

"Was that before or after you murdered a Tayemstvoy squad?"

Cold sweat slid down Celka's sides, the scent of blood and mud hazing the cell. She fought to feel the practice wire beneath her feet, fought to hold Captain Kladivo's viper gaze. "I've explained what happened."

Captain Kladivo leaned back in her chair, expression softening. "Look, Prochazka, I understand your concern. Gerrit probably believed his promise, but officer training takes years and teaches irrelevant skills. The bozhskyeh storms returned decades early, and we don't have many storm-blessed mages. You should be out imbuing. No one wants you leading troops into battle."

It sounded reasonable, but of course the Tayemstvoy would make any trap sound sweet. "This says nothing about imbuing."

"True. Your arrival here is... irregular enough that you can consider this enlistment a trial period. I'll have you assigned to my company and, *once* you prove that you can handle being out there"—she gestured vaguely to the ceiling—"you'll get your bozhk bolts and a promotion. Prove your loyalty, and you'll have an official pardon for your crimes."

Celka looked down at the enlistment papers, hating that she had to take it all on the captain's word. With that, hatred welled the sense-memory of her imbued pistol warm in her hands, each shot splitting the air like a thundercrack as she fired at Tayemstvoy after Tayemstvoy. Captain Kladivo had a Stanek pistol on her hip. Celka could feel it, a hum in the back of her mind that made her want to leap for the gun.

She pressed her hands against the tabletop, struggling to focus. No storm raged overhead; if she got Kladivo's pistol, she couldn't imbue it. And even if she did, the cell door was closed and locked. Fighting would not save her.

"What about my family?" Celka tried to keep her voice level. Through all the interrogations, she'd avoided asking about them, terrified that anything she said would only make things worse. She remembered the printmaker screaming as the Tayemstvoy ripped off his fingernails before she'd imbued that pistol; too easily she could imagine her cousin Ela in his place. Her family had been arrested, she was certain.

"As your station rises, so will theirs." The set to Captain Kladivo's jaw made clear she understood exactly what Celka was asking.

Celka pressed her palms harder against the wood, the red haze worsening, the crack of blows echoing across sousednia.

Breath quick, she uncapped the pen and signed her name on the line. *You don't need to fight*, she told herself, though it felt like a lie. *This paper will get you out*.

"Welcome to the Army, Private Prochazka." Captain Kladivo took the paper and stood. "I expect you'll do your family proud." Celka thought she said it without menace, but her red Tayemstvoy shoulders carried menace enough.

The cell door banged closed behind the captain, and Celka flinched, the sound like a truncheon on bone. *Pa*. Squeezing her eyes shut, Celka struggled to feel the practice wire beneath her feet. In sousednia, she made herself turn her back on the Tayemstvoy beating Pa, struggling to imagine the back lot empty, the only sound the clang of hammers on tent stakes and the laughter of roustabouts.

Hobnailed boots crunched on stone, startling her eyes open. Celka leapt to her feet, seeking a weapon. The chair crashed to the ground behind her.

Hedvika raised her hands, empty and open. "You're safe, Celka," she said, her wavery sousedni-shape beginning to glow blue.

Celka exhaled a breath that was almost a sob. Behind Hedvika, the cell door was open, two uniformed Tayemstvoy in the dim stone corridor.

"Do you feel the high wire beneath your feet?" Hedvika asked.

Celka struggled to slow her breathing, finding the steel cable beneath her feet in sousednia. She opened her arms for balance in the back lot's chill, springtime air.

The blues of a concealment nuzhda in Hedvika's sousedni-shape gained protection's purples and hunger's greens, and the scents of boiling cabbage and horse manure wafted off of her, along with a trill of trumpets. Celka gave up on seeing true-life, letting Hedvika's complex nuzhda call her back to herself.

After a time, her balance came easier, and Celka managed to turn on the practice wire, surveying the back lot. She stood alone but for Hedvika's colorful shimmer and the fainter smoke-forms of the two mundane Tayemstvoy guarding the door. She inhaled cabbage and horses, and a chill traveled down her spine, like she was forgetting something. She frowned, surveying her sousednia, wondering what she was missing.

"That's better," Hedvika said, and Celka blinked her eyes open in true-life. Hedvika wore her uniform jacket, a sub-lieutenant's pair of three-pointed stars on each olive shoulder. Her nameplate said *Bur*. "You ready to get out of here?"

Celka nodded, gaze flinching to the Tayemstvoy at the door.

Hedvika held out her hand, and Celka rounded the table and took it. She told herself she shouldn't—that Hedvika was a regime soldier and as much an enemy as the guards. Worse, she couldn't imagine Gerrit needing to hold someone's hand to keep from losing control. But she wasn't Gerrit, and Hedvika might be the enemy, but she was the only thing keeping Celka from succumbing to a combat fugue. As much as it might make Celka look weak, holding Hedvika's hand made her feel a little stronger—a little more like herself.

Hedvika squeezed her hand and smiled, not showing her teeth. She led the way out of the cell, past the armed Tayemstvoy, and out of the dungeon.

She brought Celka to a washroom, staying reassuringly close while Celka cleaned up and dressed in an Army uniform. The khaki shirt scraped Celka's freshly scrubbed skin, and the stiff brown ankle boots were too large. Celka locked her jaw and pulled the laces tight, determined not to complain, struggling not to panic as she wrapped her calves in puttees, each piece of the uniform making her feel more and more like the enemy. *It's camouflage*, she told herself sternly, taking her new uniform jacket from Hedvika, the olive wool scratchy and stinking of dye, a private's single silver pip on each shoulder.

Pa had promised that if the State found her, the resistance would get her out. In his letter, delivered by a resistance supporter the day before Celka's arrest, he'd also warned that her only ally in the regime would be Captain Vrana. The impossibility of it had choked her, but Pa had explained that his brutal arrest had been an act to convince the State that Celka's father was Storm Guard deserter Leosh Kratochvil, who was shot for treason. In reality, Vrana had helped Pa escape to lead the resistance.

Pa's real name was Jaromir Doubek, the Hero of Zlin, and everyone already thought he was dead. Celka had been about to join him in the resistance when everything had gone wrong—or, not join him, exactly. Pa was going storm-mad, losing true-life with each passing day, leaving Vrana to run the resistance. In his letter, Pa had told her goodbye, but he was still alive, and Captain Vrana knew where.

Celka had made a mistake getting caught by the State, but she would wrest some good out of it. For all Captain Vrana led the resistance, everyone believed her regime façade. Vrana had been Gerrit's imbuement instructor in the Storm Guard, which meant Celka could find her and ask where Pa was hiding. Then it was just a matter of holding out, feigning regime loyalty until the resistance extracted her, and she'd finally get to see Pa again.

That goal firmly in mind, Celka followed Hedvika down tangled corridors and out into a bright summer day. Squinting, Celka tilted her face to the sky and inhaled. Storm Gods, *sunlight*. The fresh air and birdsong washed over her like a balm.

She had no idea how long she stood there before Hedvika said, "Lunch?"

Celka almost smiled as they left behind a fortress of gray stone, following a path across a lumpy lawn toward a red-roofed outbuilding. Inside a busy mess hall, the cook staff scooped barley porridge into bowls. Celka's mouth watered. Sleet, were those turnips and field greens in the kasha? It smelled *incredible*, and the portions put her prison rations to shame.

Hedvika glowered some bozhk cadets out of a corner table, and Celka sat with her back to the wall, relieved to discover that her Tayemstvoy guard had vanished. Soldiers and cadets crowded the tables, but few had red shoulders. Celka looked like she fit in.

Clinging to the idea of *camouflage*, Celka dug into the porridge, finding it deliciously salty, the turnips giving the kasha a spiced earthiness. She'd made it through half the bowl when two people in uniform slid into seats across from her—surrounding her.

A gust of impossible wind carried the stink of blood and gun oil, and Celka gripped her spoon, wishing it was a knife.

Hedvika laid a hand on her shoulder. "Relax, they're friends."

Still strangling the spoon, Celka struggled to slow her breathing.

"I hear that your sousednia's a high wire," one of the newcomers said, and it shook Celka from her spiraling desperation.

Why did everyone assume her sousednia was a high wire? She'd performed on the high wire for the Slavni Cirkus, her family famous for the act, but her sousednia was the circus back lot. She stood on the practice wire, only a meter off the ground. Should she tell them?

Before she could decide, the bozhk grinned and stuck out their hand. A single earring signaled his gender. "I'm Yanek—Sub-Lieutenant Kysely. Hedvika's been telling us about you. It's nice to actually meet."

On reflex, Celka shook his hand. Yanek looked about her

own age with coppery brown skin, broad shoulders, and short, tightly curled hair. His earring was a dangling trio of teardrop glass beads vibrant as gemstones—red, blue, and purple. Each perfectly matched the glow of those three primary nuzhdi—red for combat, blue for concealment, and purple for protection.

She wondered if he'd tested for his gold bolts in those nuzhdi—frequently bozhki could control only one or two. A glance at his uniform proved otherwise. Military bozhki wore insignia showing their nuzhda competencies: enameled bars above the left breast pocket that proclaimed their prowess with the desperate needs at the core of magic. Yanek sported all six, each colorful enameled bar outlined in gold, showing that he'd passed the State's highest qualifications not just in one—which would have been enough for the gold bolts on his collar—but all six nuzhdi. An impressive feat that Celka realized with a start both Hedvika and the other newcomer had achieved.

She was surrounded by gold-bolt Army officers who could control every type of magic it was possible to create. Celka, herself, knew only how to pull against three nuzhdi—combat, concealment, and hunger—and she'd never taken any bozhk exams, her whole life spent hiding her storm-affinity from the State.

The other newcomer stuck out their hand. "Lieutenant Lishak—call me Dbani." They were maybe a dozen years older than her, slender and bird-like with pale skin crisped red. An earring high in one ear indicated neutral pronouns.

"They're both strazhi," Hedvika said. "We'll be part of the same squad."

"I'm going to have *three* strazhi?" Celka looked between them, overwhelmed. Gerrit had talked about strazhi; they were strong bozhki who dedicated their lives to protecting imbuement mages. Gerrit had *one*—Filip.

Celka would *not* think about Filip.

Hedvika snorted. "No. *I'm* your strazh. We have two more imbuement mages in the squad—you'll meet them later."

"They're probably eating *real* food." Dbani poked at their kasha.

Celka glanced down at her empty bowl, cheeks heating that the bozhk officers thought this food beneath them.

"You sound like His Lordship." Yanek deliberately took another mouthful, his bowl already half empty. "It's not *that* bad."

Dbani raised a brow and pushed their untouched bowl toward Celka. "Have as much as you want."

Yanek's hurt 'what about me?' face made Celka laugh.

"*You* are not a tvoortse." Dbani's hauteur sounded feigned, like he was mocking someone.

Yanek rolled his eyes.

"A what?" Celka wasn't sure whether she should be insulted.

"It's an old word for an imbuement mage who's successfully imbued," Hedvika said. Lowering her voice, she added, "I just learned it yesterday. Wasn't really relevant until, well, you."

Despite being surrounded by regime soldiers, a warmth bloomed in Celka's chest. She focused on Dbani's kasha, discomfited by how easy it was to feel comfortable around bozhki who kissed the Stormhawk's boots. *Remember they're your enemies*, she told herself, but the thought perfumed the air with blood, and she shuddered. Before truncheons could crack the air, she blurted, "Where are we?"

The others frowned at her, like they didn't understand the question.

"I mean, what city are we in? I..." Celka shut her mouth, realizing that Yanek and Dbani might not know she'd spent the last however many days locked in a cell.

"The Storm Guard Fortress," Hedvika said, pride in her

voice, "in the hills above Solnitse."

Celka struggled to keep her face impassive even as her pulse thundered. She darted a glance around, reevaluating the cadets and soldiers while trying not to grin. The Storm Guard Fortress was where Gerrit had trained—with Vrana. It meant that everyone in this elite academy would be boot-lickingly loyal to the regime, but it also meant she'd come straight to the heart of the resistance. Captain Vrana had spent years here, decades, maybe, plotting an end to the Stormhawk's rule.

Hedvika elbowed Celka in the ribs. "You think this is impressive, wait until you see the officers' mess—or our suite in Usvit Hall."

That startled Celka's attention back to her table companions. "Our suite?"

Yanek grinned. "We're roommates. Our whole squad. It's supposed to make us a *team*." He eyed Dbani sidelong.

Dbani spread their hands. "Don't look at me. *I* have no objection bunking with junior officers and an enlisted... tvoortse." Their hesitation made Celka wonder what they'd been about to say.

"Is there a problem?" Celka's excitement collapsed back into the reality that she was surrounded by regime-kissing Army officers.

Hedvika shook her head. "You're not inferior just because you went to some no-name school and spent your summers preening for money." She sounded like she thought this was reassuring. "Our squad will get on *fine*."

Yanek shot her an incredulous look. "Beautifully put, Hedvika."

Celka snorted.

Hedvika wrinkled her nose. "That came out bad? What I mean is, Celka, you're storm-blessed. You've imbued. Maybe you don't have the kind of control you would if you'd trained alongside us, but we're here to fix that. Everyone will see that you've earned your place."

Not terribly reassured, Celka focused back on her kasha, eating until she was full for the first time since her arrest. But with her hunger's retreat, a new worry bubbled to the surface. Tvoortse. She had imbued, multiple times, but what came next... Setting down her spoon, she said, "I don't think it's safe for me to imbue again. Not yet."

They stared at her, and Celka wondered if that admission would get her locked back in a cell.

She hurried to explain. "I'm worried that in a bozhskyeh storm I would—"

Hedvika laid a hand over hers. "Hey. No one's sending you into a storm. Not yet. You're combat-warped. We all know that. I'm here to help you recover your core nuzhda. That's why Captain Kladivo assigned you the *best* strazh."

"Modest, Hedvika, as always," Yanek muttered.

"It's only right for her to know," Hedvika said with an edge that hinted at rivalry. To Celka, she said, "The State will take care of you. And so will I."

Celka's stomach churned at Hedvika's fervor, but she gripped the other woman's hand, feeling oddly safer. "I thought strazhi were just important for imbuing?"

Hedvika wrinkled her nose. "Yeah. Usually." Her brows drew down, and she turned to Dbani. "Can you explain this?"

Dbani perked up, pulling out a notebook. "You're right that a strazh's primary job is to ground a tvoortse during imbuements. *Once* you've recovered from your combat-warping, you'll go out in a bozhskyeh storm. While you're shaping an imbuement's weaves, Hedvika—or whoever's acting as your strazh—will form their own weaves. Strazh weaves don't create new magic, they just siphon off storm energy if you pull too hard on the bozhskyeh storm."

While Dbani talked, they doodled in their notebook, sketching two people standing beneath a cartoon cloud. One held a knife in their outstretched hand, and Dbani labeled them *tvoortse*; the other, they labeled *strazh*. The strazh mage had their hand on the imbuement mage's neck. Dbani fell silent, scribbling a twisting pattern around and through the knife and labeling it *combat weave*. The similarly styled strazh weave twined down from the imbuement mage's neck, through the strazh's arm and body, to extend like tree roots into the ground. Then Dbani drew a bolt of cartoon lightning striking the imbuement mage on the head, labeled *Gods' Breath*.

Yanek peered sideways at the drawing. "Wow. I didn't know you were an artist."

But Dbani wasn't done. "People typically refer to the lightning strike itself as 'Gods' Breath' and the magical... current, if you will, that comes from getting struck by it as 'storm energy.'" They added neat arrows of storm energy to the drawing, flowing from where the Gods' Breath struck the imbuement mage, down through the mage's torso and into the combat weave around the knife.

"Huh," Hedvika said. "I thought the terms were interchangeable."

Dbani shrugged. "Does that make sense?" they asked Celka. She nodded. "And when we're not imbuing?"

"Then it's a question of being your anchor." They tore off their drawing and slid it to Celka, revealing a blank page. "The stronger a person's storm-affinity, the deeper their connection to sousednia. You and other tvoortsei, or imbuement mages, are storm-*blessed*, meaning you can see sousednia." They paused to check that Celka was following. She nodded; she'd learned as much from studying scripture. "The rest of us, merely storm-*touched*, have weaker storm-affinities; with training, we can still pull against nuzhdi and activate old imbuements, but since we can't actually *see* sousednia, we can't shape the weaves necessary for creating new imbuements."

"Wait," Celka said, "how can you create strazh weaves, then? Aren't they nuzhda weaves?"

"In a sense," Dbani said. "They're less complicated than the kind of weaves you make, because they're not designed to *do* anything. Think of it like a grounding line for a house." They doodled a house as they spoke, adding a lightning bolt from a storm overhead. "The metal creates a path for the electricity from a regular lightning strike to flow safely into ground and not burn up the house, but it doesn't matter what shape that metal takes. It could be a water pipe or a steel cable or intricate wrought iron—or a combination. Strazh weaves are similar. All we need to do is make a path from you to the ground for any excess storm energy."

"So glad I spent years learning how to do something so *trivial*," Hedvika said.

"Right, it's not actually that simple," Dbani said.

"Especially since we can't see what we're doing," Yanek said, "to tell if we've actually made... well, I think of it like interlocking links on a chain. And all the links have to connect and be 'conductive'—if you want to use Dbani's analogy. Which means—"

Dbani held up a hand. "She's not here to become a strazh."

"Fine. Please continue, *Lieutenant*." Rolling his eyes, Yanek scraped up the last of his kasha.

Dbani tore off the drawing of a house, tapping their pencil against a fresh page. "So, an anchor. As a storm-blessed bozhk, your mind's already pretty deep in sousednia, but you have to go deeper, I'm told, to shape an imbuement. Any storm energy you pull down, which doesn't get contained by and crystalized into your nuzhda weaves, overflows into your mind."

"Unless I have a strazh protecting me," Celka said, relieved to have finally met someone who could explain things. Gerrit was great, but he was *not* a natural teacher.

"Exactly," Dbani said. "So if you imbue without a strazh—like you did—that storm energy pours into your mind and crystalizes the closest thing to nuzhda weaves, which is the nuzhda you were pulling against to create the imbuement. In your case, you imbued combat and overflowed, which means the storm energy burned the combat nuzhda into your mind. We call it 'nuzhda-warping.' It's like you've made a groove in a phonograph record, and the needle of your thoughts keeps slipping back into it. The worse the warping, the deeper the groove and the harder it is to erase. Often, a nuzhda-warped bozhk won't be able to see true-life at all, or if they can, it's colored by the nuzhda."

"Which is why you kept attacking Tayemstvoy officers with your bare hands," Hedvika said, low so her voice wouldn't carry. "You're not *actually* an idiot, just combat-warped."

Celka swallowed hard, the kasha like a brick in her stomach. "How do I erase the groove?"

"It's a matter of practice," Dbani said, "training your mind not to slip into the nuzhda-warping, and getting out as fast as you can if it does—to minimize how much you reinforce the groove."

"So Hedvika's not so much your anchor right now," Yanek said, "as your lighthouse. She's been practicing pulling against your core nuzhda—we have, too, but not as much, so Hedvika will be the one to watch."

Celka nodded, but then realized—"Wait, how does Hedvika—how do any of you—know how to pull against my core nuzhda?" She hadn't met any of them until after she'd already combat-warped imbuing the pistol.

"Gerrit and Filip wrote up reports," Yanek said. "We're guessing based on those. But you're not attacking us, so it seems to have worked."

Hedvika clapped Celka on the back. "Lucky you have such a good strazh."

Before Yanek could sprain something rolling his eyes, he leapt up, waving to get someone's attention. "Filip! Hey!"

Celka jerked around to find Gerrit and Filip rounding a table of younger cadets. Breath catching, she leapt to her feet. "Gerrit!" She remembered herself before launching into his arms. They weren't in the circus anymore. She didn't know what had happened to him—or to Filip, though that thought carried an edge that sounded like truncheons on flesh.

Gerrit reached out, but his expression was neutral, warmth only in his eyes. She clasped his hands hard.

A spark like storm energy burst up her arms at the contact, and she drew a sharp breath. Stormy skies, it was good to see him. She searched his expression for some explanation of what had happened while they'd been separated, not wanting to say the wrong thing in front of so many regime ears.

"It's good to see you," Gerrit said.

"You too." She wanted to wrap him in her arms and never let go. Bleed-through from sousednia left the air bright with the pine and glacier scent of him, and Celka shut her eyes, breathing him in.

"Nice stars," Hedvika said from behind her, and Celka snapped back to herself. "Didn't expect you to come back a full lieutenant."

Celka made herself look at Gerrit's uniform, noting the trio of stars on each of his jacket's shoulders. "Did you skip a rank?" she asked. Gerrit's identification folio—when he'd finally showed it to her and admitted to being the Stormhawk's son—had said he was a cadet.

A muscle in Gerrit's jaw tightened, but he nodded. She expected him to look embarrassed about it, but instead he straightened, and all the soft edges and relief at seeing her vanished beneath his soldierly front. "I'll be leading an imbuement platoon. The captain and I still need to work out the details, but I wanted—" He faltered, gaze searching Celka.

She felt a tug from sousednia and shifted her focus, the mess hall fading into the springtime back lot where she balanced on the practice wire.

Gerrit's sousedni-shape never wore his uniform jacket or khaki shirt; instead, his short-sleeved undershirt revealed the lean muscle of his arms, his beige skin cut with shadows subtly wrong for the sunlight in Celka's sousednia. He'd told her before that he stood in a mountain clearing, ankle-deep in fresh snow, sun beating down from a noonday sky. The scents of evergreens and crisp, cold air strengthened around him, and she tightened her grip on his hands.

He searched her with his golden brown eyes, and she wanted to ask how much danger they were in—but dozens of bozhki surrounded them. Though the others appeared as insubstantial as heat rising off baked sand, someone could be using an imbuement that let them hear sousednia, or a storm-blessed mage could be nearby, hiding their sousedni-shape. In the circus, Filip had made her believe him a simple mundane with such an imbuement.

Surrounded by regime mages, she could trust nothing and no one—except Gerrit.

«We'll speak later,» he said, voice a caress in sousednia before he focused back on true-life.

Celka followed him back to the mess hall, vaguely aware of Yanek talking to Filip, of Hedvika shifting beside her, irritation tightening her square jaw. Dbani had nodded greeting, but now focused on their notebook, giving them space; Dbani could have been a decade older than Celka, so maybe they didn't know Gerrit or Filip well.

"Celka," Gerrit said, solemn, "you're not wearing your high wire costume in sousednia."

Hedvika straightened, as if this was a shock, but Celka scowled. "Of course not." Why would she get her costume sweaty and dirty during practice?

"You should," Gerrit said, his earlier warmth transformed into intensity. "Are you walking the high wire beneath the big top?"

Where was he going with this? She glanced to the side, finding Hedvika focused on her, her gaze a little distant, like she was staring through Celka. Yanek and Filip, too, paused in their conversation, and even Dbani leaned in.

"Your core sousednia is the high wire," Gerrit said into her silence. He cut a sharp glance at Hedvika. "Make sure she finds it."

"Gerrit, what is this—?" Celka started, but Gerrit just gave her hands another squeeze.

"I need you to listen to Hedvika." He released her hands. "I have meetings now, but I'll see you tonight." He jerked his chin to Filip, then strode away.

Filip started to join him, but hesitated. Turning to Celka, he said, "I missed you." His voice was the same deep, lion-purr velvet that had made her feel so comfortable in the circus— back when she'd known him only as Ctibor, the circus knife thrower with a secret past in the Army. He'd changed his earring from the simple stud he'd worn in the circus, and the gold lightning bolt glinted against his deep brown skin. Full lips curving in that private half smile he'd used when they were alone together, Filip reached out a hand, palm up—an invitation.

Celka tensed. She'd loved spending time with Ctibor, but

Ctibor was a lie. Filip had been hiding in the circus to spy on Gerrit. She didn't know if he'd ever cared about her, or if she'd been only a means to an end. Part of her shouted that she wasn't being fair—that Filip would never have covered for her resistance activities if he'd only been using her to stay close to Gerrit—but the memory of him bursting in after she'd murdered the Tayemstvoy squad, his storm-touched sousedni-shape appearing after she'd spent weeks convinced he was a mundane... it made her want to hate him.

If not for Filip, she and Gerrit would have escaped after she'd shot those Tayemstvoy.

If not for Filip, she would be free.

So she beat down the flutters in her belly and stared at his hand like he'd offered her a cold pile of sleet. Making her voice flat, she said, "You look good in uniform. You must be glad to be back." It's what he'd wanted, after all.

Because not everything he'd told her in the circus had been a lie. She could read truth and lies from a person's sousedni-cues. But she couldn't tell if they'd cleverly omitted key details. Filip had said he'd trained to be an elite guard but had made a mistake on his first mission and got sent to the circus. He'd let her believe it was a punishment, him throwing knives to drive Army recruitment. He'd said nothing about the Storm Guard, about being Gerrit's strazh. He'd buried those omissions in the truth of how badly he wanted to return to his old life.

Filip's smile vanished. He dropped his hand back to his side. He covered it well, but her blow had landed.

Part of her was glad. "You should go. Gerrit's waiting for you."

Filip's jaw tensed. "Take care of yourself, Celka." The edge to his voice said, *clearly that's what you're good at.* It stung.

CHAPTER FIVE

GERRIT HARDLY SAW the Storm Guard Fortress as he hurried to the main keep. Celka was alive, unharmed, and it made him want to collapse with relief. Her face looked gaunt, light skin pale and drawn, but her spark was undiminished by whatever she'd endured since they'd been separated—though her combat-warping churned his stomach. She'd balanced like usual in sousednia, feet in a perfect line like she walked the wire, but she'd dressed like a laborer, and the shadows on her had been wrong. It made him want to stay at her side, work with her and Filip until she danced across her high wire, wrapped in glimmering sequins that matched the emerald gleam in her eyes. But the Stormhawk's son would have different priorities.

Hedvika was a good strazh—for all she was the last person in the world he would have chosen for Celka. Gerrit would have to trust her to pull Celka back—if only until this evening.

Climbing steep stone steps into one of the keep's towers, his back's painful throb returned, warning him not to get overconfident. His father had given him a commission and a command, but it was not without strings.

Inside her office, his sister stood with her back to the door, pointing to something on a small conference table as she conferred with junior officers. While she wrapped up their discussion, Gerrit studied her, trying to predict how this meeting would go. Iveta had been a lieutenant when he'd last seen her, and memory of that day—the day the Tayemstvoy had driven Branislav storm-mad—made his throat taste of bile.

Dismissed, Iveta's staff strode past Gerrit, and he shook himself, snapping off a crisp salute. "All hail the Stormhawk!"

"At ease." Iveta's expression softened. "It's good to see you again, Gerrit."

A snide *I doubt that* leapt to his lips, but he swallowed it— and several other, less charitable replies.

When he'd come to, bruised and aching on the floor of his father's office, the Stormhawk had ordered him to attention and presented him with his lieutenant's stars and a mandate: to lead Bourshkanya's imbuement mages in preparing the country for war. Only later, reviewing the written details, had Gerrit learned he'd be reporting to his sister.

He'd railed against the idea but, like anything coming from his father, he had no hope of altering his circumstances, so he'd decided to make the best of it. Iveta would jockey for power, would take every chance to rub his nose in his mistakes and failures, but the fact remained: Gerrit was storm-blessed and could create new magic; Iveta could not.

Besides, Gerrit only needed to play the regime-kissing commander until the resistance could extract him and Celka. He could endure his sister's overbearing superiority that long.

"Have you eaten?" Iveta asked.

He shook his head, setting his hat on a sideboard. "We came straight from the station."

She focused past him to Filip. "Sub-Lieutenant Cizek, have

food sent up from the officer's mess—and avail yourself to a meal. You can rejoin us when you're finished."

Once the closed door offered an illusion of privacy, Iveta waved Gerrit to a seat at the conference table. "Unless you're more comfortable standing?" It could have been a casual comment, though an edge to her expression suggested otherwise.

Gerrit refused to let his sister see weakness. Moving as naturally as he could toward the table, Gerrit set down the folder with his preliminary notes on the imbuement platoon. Filip had rubbed more analgesic into his back before the train had pulled into Solnitse, but every motion still scraped fabric against his raw flesh, and he felt every beat of his heart in the bruises. He tried not to favor the wounds as he sat, careful not to lean against the chair back.

Iveta hooked out the opposite chair with her ankle. "I know Father had you beaten," she said softly.

Gerrit made his voice emotionless. "He had to ensure discipline."

Her lips thinned. "You should stop by the hospital—"

"I'm fine," he snapped. He didn't need his commanding officer intimating that he couldn't handle a little physical discomfort. He held her gaze unflinchingly, willing her to see him as a peer for once, and not as her disappointing little brother.

She sighed. "You don't always have to fight alone, Gerrit. Your success with this platoon is my success too. We're not in competition." Clearly she could still lie with a perfectly straight face. They'd always been in competition; and she'd always been determined to win.

Teeth grinding, he broke the staring contest to open the folder he'd brought. "Would you like to see my thoughts on the platoon?"

"I would," she said, like she hadn't heard the edge to his voice, "but there's something else first." She crossed to her desk, opening a locked drawer. "Father wants us preparing Bourshkanya for war, but there's more to a successful campaign than imbued weapons. And—in the absence of active hostilities—it makes sense for us to look into imbuements that also have peacetime applications."

Gerrit frowned before he could think better of it, and struggled to wipe away the expression. That sounded reasonable—too reasonable for his Tayemstvoy sister. "I'm listening."

She returned to the table and slid a single printed sheet across to him. Written bold across the top,

The Storm-Blessed Turn from the State

The mimeographed page had the stamp of a running wolf at the bottom—the resistance's signature—and a skilled drawing of a young civilian being struck by lightning. She held a pistol and stood with one boot on the back of a dead Tayemstvoy, whose blood pooled at her feet. She wasn't a dead match for Celka, but the artist clearly had her description. *The Storm Gods bless those who stand against State brutality*, the caption read. *Each day, more civilians imbue, wresting power from the Tayemstvoy. Join the Resistance, and embrace the Storm Gods' blessings!*

Gerrit's mouth went dry. He wanted the resistance to fight, but this seemed like throwing oil on a fire. Civilians weren't equipped to go up against the Tayemstvoy, and this would damage his and Celka's efforts to convince the regime of their loyalty. Keeping his voice calm and cold, he asked, "Where did you find this?"

"They turned up in several cities a few days ago." She watched him carefully. "It's not the first of its kind."

Gerrit raised his eyebrows. "There are more stupid, suicidal civilians?"

She inclined her head as though he'd made a good, if worrisome point. "Civilian unrest in increasing." She took the leaflet back, locking it away inside her desk drawer. "Before Prochazka, civilian imbuements have mostly been what you expect—congregations singing for the Storm Gods' miracles over baskets of grain or the terminally ill. But there've been a few other combat imbuements. You can be certain there are plenty of questions about how that"—she jerked a thumb over her shoulder to indicate the leaflet—"managed to be so accurate."

"Her imbuement storm-marked the floor. People—"

Iveta held up a hand. "I'm not *questioning* you. That leaflet isn't my problem. It's not even my problem that towns have started rioting, or that factories are missing their quotas because of worker unrest. The Tayemstvoy, I have been *assured*, have it under control." She leaned toward him across the conference table, her already quiet voice dropping further. "But Bourshkanyans—regular civilians—are paying the price for rabble-rousers throwing themselves at an opportunity." She shook her head, intense gaze locked on his. "Within Father's mandate, we have a chance to *help*. But to do that, we need to work together—a team. I need you on my side, not thrashing against my authority or maneuvering for your own."

He sat back, angry at how well she'd strung her trap. The motion pressed his back against the chair, and he flinched. Iveta was good at her job, he'd give her that. If he didn't click his bootheels to her every order now, he'd look like he didn't care about Bourshkanya's civilians—or worse, supported the resistance.

Iveta's expression darkened. She glanced at the still closed door then back at him. Spreading her hands on the table, palms flat against the wood, she drew a slow breath, as though marshalling her calm. "Look, Gerrit, I know we've never been close and that you've seen me as a rival. But—"

"You think that's supposed to change?" He blurted it out before he could think, but maybe it was better they hash this out now. "All my life, you've poisoned Father against me, pointing out my failures, locking me out of family business. Now you want me to open up like you're not about to stab me in the back?" He shook his head. "You want to *use* me and my imbuements to further your own career—that's fine, it's what I expect. But don't pretend it's anything else. You'll gleefully report my every misstep—just like you always do."

Iveta ran her hands through her short, sandy blonde hair. "That's fair." She paced to the window before turning back, searching him with eyes so like their father's. "It makes sense that you'd see it like that—and maybe you're even right. But we were *children*. I did want Father's attention. And he demanded that I be perfect. He married Mother to give his line a storm-affinity, and since Artur was a mundane, that pressure fell on *me*. You think I didn't want to quit sometimes? You think I didn't want to lash out at my instructors? I know how your back feels right now, Gerrit, because Father made very clear to me *many times* that failure was never an option.

"But *you*—you wouldn't stop talking back to your instructors, you kept challenging the rules, antagonizing older cadets." An angry edge cut her voice. "You *never* should have been at the Storm Guard Academy. You had the makings of a brilliant engineer or a scientist—your inquisitive mind, your disregard for convention. But Father was determined you follow the mold. 'Discipline' is Father's answer for everything.

"So, yes, I cut you out, I outshone you. I did my sleeting best to draw his attention so he didn't grind you into dust trying to make you into someone you weren't." She searched his expression, and Gerrit didn't know how to respond. She seemed... genuine.

Iveta spun her chair around and straddled it. "I'm *glad* you're coming into your own, Gerrit. You look good—strong. Like you've started to figure out what's important. That fiasco with the circus and Prochazka... it could have gone very differently. But you stood up to Father. Maybe even earned his respect. You're right that he doesn't trust you yet, and why should he? But I'm not your babysitter. Neither of us want that."

Shaken, he asked, "Then what do you want?"

"You're right that I want to *succeed*. But I want *you* to succeed, as well. It doesn't have to be one or the other. Someday, our father will be too old to run this country. Our brother would like nothing better than to see us tear each other apart before that day. *Artur* sees us as competition, and you know what he's like."

Gerrit frowned. Their brother Artur was three years older than Iveta and had trained at a military academy since before Gerrit could remember. Gerrit recalled myriad torments at Artur's hands during school holidays, but he also remembered Iveta as part of them.

Except... Iveta had often come late to those torments, dismissing Gerrit as too young, drawing Artur off for more interesting sport. He thought back, trying to peel away childhood assumptions.

Iveta hadn't been there when Artur had tied Gerrit to a bench, making him watch while he eviscerated a twitching squirrel, slapping Gerrit with a bloody hand whenever he shut his eyes, snarling that he not be such a coward. Iveta had only come later, firing a pellet gun from across the garden, a sniper shot that ended the squirrel's agonized screams in a spray of gravel, leaving Artur chasing after her, swearing vengeance.

Maybe she'd saved Gerrit from more than he'd realized as a child.

"He's a sadist," Gerrit finally said.

Iveta inclined her head. "I believe 'ruthless and efficient' is the term Father prefers."

Gerrit kept the grimace off his face, but it twisted his insides. Still, their brother's proclivities didn't excuse Iveta everything. "I've heard the same applied to you. You were *Tesarik*'s attaché, after all." Iveta had stood at Tesarik's side as he'd given the order that shattered Branislav's true-life grounding. "How big a part did you play in Branislav's storm-madness?"

Iveta's jaw muscles clenched. "That was Tesarik's scheme. There's a reason he's not here anymore."

Surprised, Gerrit said, "He's not?" Tesarik had supported their father since before the war; Gerrit had assumed he was untouchable.

"I convinced Father that Tesarik's leadership was untenable."

That stunned Gerrit speechless. He hadn't thought it possible to convince the Stormhawk of anything. Maybe he had something to learn from Iveta after all. And maybe, if she was telling the truth about wanting him to succeed—which Gerrit was starting to believe, despite himself—she could get him into their father's council, get him access to intelligence that could benefit the resistance. "All right," Gerrit said. "I'm convinced." He couldn't believe he was saying this, but it felt surprisingly good. "Let's be a team."

Iveta smiled. Gerrit wasn't sure he'd ever seen a genuine smile from her before. Then a knock came on the door, and the smile vanished. "Come," Iveta called, crisp and military.

She said nothing while two servants laid out plates of holubky—'pigeons' made from cabbage leaves stuffed with ground beef and rice, swimming in a fragrant sauce. Gerrit's mouth watered. A month eating only what he or Celka stole from the circus's already meager rations had left him permanently hungry. He snatched up knife and fork, tearing into the holubky before the servants had even left.

When they were alone again, Iveta said, "Let's talk about your plans for the platoon."

Gerrit nodded, pausing in wolfing down his food to flip open the folder he'd brought. Except... "Wait." He shut the folder, swallowing to clear his throat, stomach churning on fear that he was about to push Iveta's newfound sympathy too far. "I want in. If we're a team, I need you to stop undermining me with Father."

"Of course."

His chest tightened with the childhood certainty that her easy agreement meant he'd walked into a trap. He tried to crush it down, grabbing a slice of rye bread, slathering it with butter. Trap or not, he needed more than empty reassurances. "When's the next family dinner?"

"In a few days. You're welcome to join us." The corners of her mouth tightened, like she didn't like making the offer. She soaked up some of the holubky's garlicy tomato sauce with her bread, but didn't eat. "Gerrit. You don't..." She set the bread down, dabbed her linen napkin against her lips. "You don't have to get involved in family business. You could focus on imbuing, on helping your mages succeed. You'll still garner Father's respect, but avoid the... more unpleasant aspects of his rule."

"What, you finish dessert by torturing political prisoners?" Gerrit said.

Iveta's lips thinned. "More often than you'd think."

The holubky sunk like a rock in his stomach. He'd meant it as a joke. His blood roared in his ears, and he reached for his water glass to buy himself time to think. Before today, he would have railed at her implication that he wasn't strong enough to join them in whatever Father deemed necessary, but he didn't think Iveta was playing him. He could too easily imagine the Yestrab Okhrana delivering some gaunt, desperate prisoner to his father's study, the Stormhawk offering 'helpful' critique while Artur made them scream. The idea of standing by— or worse, being expected to take part, like they were playing some sick parlor game—made him want to vomit.

But if pretending to be like his father was the price of getting intelligence that could destroy the regime, Gerrit would just have to get better at wearing a mask.

He set his water down and met Iveta's gaze. "I'm not a child anymore. It's time I took my place at Father's side."

CHAPTER SIX

HEDVIKA LED CELKA up a steep staircase inside the Storm Guard Fortress's main keep, the stair risers worn to bowls by centuries of feet. Seeing Gerrit and Filip safe but in uniform had made Celka as angry as it had been a relief. She and Gerrit needed to get out, which meant Celka needed to talk to Captain Vrana right away.

Rallying her courage, Celka had asked Hedvika if it'd be possible to speak to the captain, citing Gerrit's claims that Vrana had been one of his best instructors. "Maybe she'll know more about how I'm supposed to regain my core grounding."

Hedvika had frowned, but Dbani had cocked their head and said, "She'd be worth talking to, at least. She invented most of our training."

Celka had never been very good at covering her surprise.

"Strazhi are a pretty new idea," Yanek had explained. "Even last storm cycle, it wasn't very common to—"

Hedvika had interrupted. To catch Captain Vrana in her office, they had to go now. Which brought them to the unending stairs. When they finally stopped at a landing, Hedvika hesitated, dropping her voice to a whisper, "Captain Vrana... she's the Hero of Zlin, right? Don't expect sunshine and puppies."

She's no hero. The thought rose with a snarl, the edges of Celka's vision hazing red.

Her heartrate sped, panicked, as the scent of blood wafted across sousednia. Coming here was a terrible idea. Why hadn't she thought about Dbani's warning that combat-warping was like a phonograph groove *before* asking to see Vrana? Already she saw threat at the first crunch of a hobnailed boot, yet she was about to face the woman who'd haunted her nightmares for years.

But Hedvika had already opened Vrana's office door, and she frowned over her shoulder at Celka's hesitation.

Vrana's your ally, Celka told herself sternly. *Pa told you they were friends.*

In sousednia, she put her back resolutely to the cook tent and struggled to hear the distant strains of the circus band. The practice wire pressed into the soles of her feet. Vrana was the only person who could get her to Pa. Celka needed to have this conversation. She couldn't afford to slip into combat-warping.

Hands balled into fists, Celka followed Hedvika inside.

Vrana sat behind a desk, her face impassive but for the skeins of light and shadow twisting across her walnut skin and olive uniform, a nauseating bleed-through from Vrana's sousednia. "Sub-Lieutenant Bur," Vrana said with a nod. "Private Prochazka." Her voice carried banked menace, but that was probably just Celka's combat-warping.

"We were hoping to talk to you about core grounding, sir," Hedvika said, deferential. "If you have a few minutes?"

Vrana inclined her head, her sousedni-shape sharpening.

A hint of acrid smoke rolled off her, and Celka focused on sousednia to see the nightmare of her childhood—*Pa's friend, the resistance leader*—more clearly. When Vrana had come to arrest Pa, Celka had clung to true-life as hard as she could, weakening her sousednia bleed-through, trying to hide her storm-affinity—for all the good it had done. After beating Celka until she couldn't stand, Vrana had spoken Celka's name—her real name, Celka Doubek. It had terrified her.

Today, Celka clung to her new understanding, struggling not to let memory overwhelm her. Vrana had known Celka's name because she and Pa had been friends; they'd built the resistance together.

Vrana is your ally.

In sousednia, Vrana sat on a simple wooden chair at the end of Celka's practice wire, on a post that had widened to a platform. Snakes of sunlight and shadow rippled her uniform, almost covering the bloodstains. A combat helmet covered Vrana's short hair, and her shoulders sported only a lieutenant's three stars. Her earrings were tiny, incongruous yellow flowers.

"Tell me what you see in sousednia," Vrana said, her voice almost gentle.

Celka pressed her lips together and shook her head. She was barely keeping the back lot under control as it was; if she started talking about it, the memory from four years ago would surge back up.

Vrana steepled her fingers and sighed. "Very well. Do you know what happens when an imbuement shatters?"

"Its storm energy explodes," Celka said, not sure if she was using the right terms. When she and Gerrit were learning to imbue, he'd filled his weaves wrong once and a hunger imbuement had exploded, tearing her from true-life, hunger-warping her sousednia.

"The crystalized nuzhda stored in its weaves does, yes," Vrana said. "For this reason, we are careful not to activate imbuements once their weaves are frayed and close to shattering. The result is similar to what you're experiencing."

At Celka's side, Hedvika straightened, as if hanging on Vrana's words.

Celka frowned, trying to figure out how that helped her. When Gerrit's imbuement had shattered, she hadn't realized anything was wrong. She'd been ravenous, though they'd just eaten lunch, and it wasn't until Gerrit noticed that her sousedni-shape was wrong and coaxed her back to seeing her sousednia as a... The thought slipped away and she shook her head. Her sousednia was the circus back lot. It was fine. The scent of blood and gun oil had faded back into the natural smells of mud and cooking cabbage.

"During the war," Vrana continued, "we were not so careful. I shattered a high-Category imbuement and lost my core grounding."

Celka lowered herself into a seat facing Vrana. "How did you come back?"

"My friend, Jaromir Doubek, knew my core sousednia well."

Celka struggled not to react to the casual mention of Pa's name.

"He could see that my sousedni-shape had changed, and reminded me of what it had been." Vrana leaned forward, her gaze locking Celka's—just as it had that horrible spring day. But today, Vrana's expression was softer. "Your sousednia will never *feel* wrong, this is the curse of nuzhda-warping. To escape it, you must trust those around you to guide you back. Gerrit Kladivo and Filip Cizek wrote detailed descriptions of your core nuzhda—they will be limited by what they could see and what you told them, but those reports will light the path back to yourself. I'll ensure you're given copies. Read them—as often as you can—until nothing in your sousednia disagrees. You must learn to be vigilant. Memorize what your sousednia *should* be, and seek signs that it is not. You will be tempted to ignore the inconsistencies or explain them away." Vrana's lips tightened, the snakes of light and shadow lashing fitfully over her sousedni-shape. "Nuzhda-warping twists your perceptions to protect itself."

Celka's hands had gone sweaty, her fear no longer for facing Vrana, but at the thought of losing herself and not knowing it. "What about Hedvika? My strazh?"

Vrana nodded, a honeyed warmth rolling off her in sousednia—a sousedni-cue that smelled like approval. "She's used those same reports to reproduce your core nuzhda. It's unlikely to be exactly right, since she's never seen your un-warped core, but it—even more than Kladivo and Cizek's words—should draw you toward yourself. You must learn to trust her and follow her prompts. I was fortunate to have a dear friend to draw me back. Sub-Lieutenant... Bur must become that for you."

Celka wondered at Vrana's hesitance before Hedvika's family name. If Vrana had taught the strazhi, shouldn't she know their names? She brushed aside the concern. Vrana was telling her that she needed to trust a regime boot-licker— Vrana, the resistance's Wolf.

Searching Vrana's expression, Celka tried to decide if it was safe to ask her real questions. When she'd been intent on getting to Vrana, she'd never considered that she'd have no way to talk safely.

"Sub-Lieutenant Bur," Vrana said, not breaking from Celka's gaze.

"Yes, sir?" Hedvika said.

"Go to the records office and secure copies of Kladivo's and Cizek's reports."

"Shall I send a runner, sir?" The edge to Hedvika's tone suggested the task was beneath her.

Vrana raised an eyebrow at Hedvika, a cool waft of icy air rolling off her in sousednia, like the chill of disappointment. "Your rank will cut through the bureaucracy, Sub-Lieutenant. Prochazka needs those reports promptly."

Hedvika straightened as though slapped. "Yes, sir!" She snapped a salute and hurried from the room.

"Until she returns," Vrana said, "join me in sousednia. I'll do what I can to guide you back to yourself."

When Celka focused on sousednia, Vrana bared her teeth, sweat standing out on her brow. The snakes of light and shadow vanished. She stunk of sweat and smoke, of things not meant to burn, then the summer sky-blue of a concealment nuzhda burst over her skin.

It happened so fast that Celka barely had time to flinch.

Vrana met her gaze impassively. The blue concealment glow flared, and Vrana's form doubled.

Celka squeezed her eyes shut in sousednia, opening them in true-life. Vrana still sat casually at her desk, only her single light-and-shadow sousedni-shape superimposed over her true-form.

Back in Celka's sunlit circus lot, however, Vrana's second sousedni-shape stood. She jerked her chin behind them, then vanished, reappearing five meters away. In true-life, that put her on the other side of the office wall.

It was an invitation, Celka realized as Vrana's other sousedni-shape began talking about the high wire and the big top's spotlights. Somehow, Vrana had doubled her sousedni-shape to hide a clandestine meeting. Which meant that speaking normally in sousednia was not safe.

Celka hesitated. She didn't know how to double her sousedni-shape. If whoever Vrana was worried was spying on them could see sousednia as well as hear it, by following Vrana, Celka could reveal their treason.

Vrana reappeared at Celka's side. Her double said nothing, but the air gained a verdant freshness, like after a spring rain. Vrana's ghostly double met Celka's gaze and, deliberately, pointed over her shoulder to where she'd previously disappeared. Then, once more, she vanished.

Celka didn't give herself time to deliberate. Vrana's reassuring sousedni-cue had been an invitation to trust—and Celka needed Vrana's help.

Closing her eyes in sousednia, Celka reached out with her thoughts until she found that scent of spring rain. Ignoring the version of Vrana who described the circus band, Celka shifted her sousednia. The change needled an ache into her temples as she put five meters between her true-form and her sousedni-shape.

When she opened her eyes, she faced Vrana, her own feet still perfectly aligned on the practice wire.

Without her true-life senses, Celka had only the vaguest idea of the true-life space in which they stood. It felt cold, cramped, and dusty. Vrana inclined her head, her sousedni-cues shifting again, subtly, warming Celka as though from a close friend's embrace.

Approval from this soldier who still haunted Celka's nightmares made her shiver, and she tried to cover the reaction by looking around. The weedy field warped and darkened, and suddenly, rough stone walls enclosed them—a cell like the one Celka had been locked in beneath the fortress. Instead of the practice wire, Celka found herself standing on cold stone. The ceiling crowded so close she could almost touch it.

Panicking, Celka spun in place, searching for a way out. The cell couldn't have been more than a meter and a half square—with no windows or doors. She was trapped—with Vrana.

«Calm yourself.» Vrana's voice echoed oddly, filling Celka's mind, drowning her.

Could Celka pull against a nuzhda and shatter whatever Vrana had done to her mind?

«*Don't* try it,» Vrana said. «Here, we can speak freely. Though not for long.»

Fighting for calm, Celka searched Vrana's face, finding her eyes tight with strain. Around her, sousednia smelled like fire, but rather than the warmth of woodsmoke, it carried the crackling wrongness of burning hair, flesh, and metal.

«Out there,» Vrana said, «even in sousednia, we can be overheard. This is for our safety. Do you understand?»

Celka licked dry lips but nodded, struggling to ignore the cell's close confines. She had never tried to affect someone else's sousednia, had never even considered it might be possible. She wanted to ask Vrana to teach her how, but first, she needed to know, «Where's Pa?»

«Somewhere safe. Which you are not.»

«I need to see him.»

«You *need* to reclaim your core grounding. Return to yourself and prove you can imbue combat without slipping, and I'll see about getting you to him.»

«That's not good enough.» Celka struggled to keep her voice low, not sure how well Vrana's defenses worked. «Pa said he's been losing true-life. I need to see him before it's too late.»

«And I need a trained army.» Vrana's voice was deathly calm. «You get me what I need, we'll trade.» The stench of a battlefield thickened around them, filling the cell with the bloat of rotting bodies and the stench of shit. «I *gave* you an opportunity. I gave you and Gerrit a way out, but you couldn't control your nuzhda well enough not to *slaughter* a Tayemstvoy squad. You nearly got Lucie killed and your family's no longer useful.»

Celka felt like she was falling. «Are they hurt? Are they—?» She couldn't speak her worse fears. Dead? Tortured? Starving in a labor camp? Gerrit's sister had claimed they were safe, but she should have known better than to trust a Tayemstvoy officer.

«Your family is safe, but they'll be closely watched. Lucie managed not to get caught. Your recklessness put many things in jeopardy.» Vrana drew a slow breath. The scents in the cell muted to an acrid tang over old stone. «Your father and I disagreed about your involvement in our work. If you want me to risk resources for you again, prove it's worth the investment. Right now, you are a liability, *not* an asset.»

Celka wanted to cower but made herself hold Vrana's icy gaze. «What about Gerrit?»

«What about him?» Vrana's battlefield stench roiled.

Celka bit her lip, terrified of how Vrana would react. But she didn't know when she'd next get a chance to talk to the Wolf—and she would be a terrible rezistyent if she withheld important information. «I showed him Pa's letter.» The same letter that had revealed Pa's true identity, called Vrana out as his co-leader of the resistance, and accused the Stormhawk of starting the Lesnikrayen war to gain power.

The blow came out of nowhere, Vrana's palm connecting with Celka's cheek, the force flinging her to the side. Celka cried out and would have lost her sousedni-dislocation, but Vrana caught her mind in an iron grip, locking her in that stone cell. Grabbing Celka's shoulders, Vrana jerked Celka to face her. «Who else did you show?» The shadows and snakes of light in her flesh seemed to burn, crackling like flames.

«No one else,» Celka whispered.

«Does Cizek know?»

«I didn't tell Filip anything.» Celka's voice shook. «Gerrit asked him to join us in the resistance after I shot the

Tayemstvoy squad. He doesn't know about you or Pa.»

Vrana's jaw tightened, but she released Celka. She turned her back, silent for several long breaths. Celka's cheek throbbed. When Vrana finally spoke, her voice was smooth like ice. «How convinced was Gerrit?»

«He's not his father,» Celka said.

Vrana faced her, the war zone scent welling again, yet subtly changed. It carried the stench of blood and antiseptic, urine and bodies too long unwashed.

«He wants to control his own life,» Celka said, «make his own choices.»

«That's not an answer.» Exhaustion seemed to overwhelm her, the snakes of light tearing apart her face.

«Gerrit trusts *me*. I said the resistance could keep us safe.»

Vrana made a derisive noise. «You're powerful and attractive. He's a teenage boy interested in girls.»

Celka started to deny it, but realized Vrana could sense lies as well as she could—better maybe. «That's not the only reason. He *cares* about Bourshkanya. He saw—he *understood* that the Stormhawk and the Tayemstvoy are crushing us. He wants to make it right. He's on our side. I trust him.»

Vrana studied her for what felt like an eternity, as if trying to uncover a lie. Finally, so low Celka almost didn't hear it, she said, «Children make fools of us all.»

«What does that mean?» Celka asked, but Vrana's sousedni-cues had vanished.

When Vrana spoke again, her voice had gentled. «Your father was right about your ability to read sousedni-cues—and keep yours hidden. I'm glad to see it. While you're here, maintain that secret, and hide your sousedni-dislocations. The other bozhki don't realize they're possible.»

«Gerrit knows,» Celka said. «We practiced dislocations together.»

«How much can he do?»

«Maybe a meter or two. He can't read sousedni-cues.»

«Don't teach him.»

Celka frowned.

«Stop hiding your cues from me,» Vrana said, and Celka dismissed the wind she usually kept blowing. «Good. I never intended for you to end up here, but you're dangerously combat-warped and what I said out there is true: you must learn to trust your strazh in order to recover—but trust her *only* in this. Hedvika is skilled, but Captain Kladivo chose her because of her regime loyalty.» Vrana held her gaze until Celka nodded. «If you understand nothing else, understand this. *Everyone* here is your enemy. Trust me and the people I send you. No one else.»

«What about Gerrit?»

The snakes of light and shadow lashed across her face. «I'll deal with Gerrit.»

Celka's stomach clenched. *Deal* with him? What in sleet-storms did that mean?

Before she could protest, Vrana said, «Your father cares deeply for you. I owe him my life, so I will do what I can. But I will not risk the resistance. If you want to leave this place, regain your grounding and prove you're *worth* extracting.»

CHAPTER SEVEN

LEAVING IVETA'S OFFICE, Gerrit's mind churned with mingling fear and excitement. Iveta had reviewed his plans for the imbuement platoon, and her suggestions had been solid. She really wanted them to work together. A team. He shook his head, still struggling to believe it.

Rounding a corner, a servant collided with him. The motion shot pain through his back. He put a hand on the wall, steadying himself, expecting the servant to grovel. They just ducked their head with a muttered apology and dashed onward. Teeth gritted, Gerrit scowled after them.

Filip watched him sidelong, his unasked 'are you all right?' hanging in the air.

Gerrit shook his head, dismissing Filip's concern and the servant, both. Only then did he recall the servant's touch on his hand and feel the paper now balled in his fist.

He nodded for Filip to continue ahead, and unfolded the note. It specified a meeting place in the hills outside the fortress. His breath caught, and he glanced back down the corridor. The servant had vanished.

Stupid. Of course they'd vanished. Captain Vrana—or one of her supporters—must have arranged this meeting. Gerrit needed to learn not to be so obvious.

Catching up to Filip, Gerrit said, "I need to get some air. Meet me in an hour." He didn't specify where; Filip would find him.

Outside in the evening's long shadows, he made for the western gate, signing out at the guard post. He knew the labyrinthine trails through these hills well from his time as a cadet. He'd circle around to the meeting point, ensuring he wasn't followed.

At the specified junction, however, he found himself alone. Edging into sousednia, he searched his alpine clearing for other presences. Failing to find anyone storm-blessed, he looked closer, seeking a storm-touched bozhk's heat-ripple or a mundane's faint smoke-form. As far as he could tell, he was alone. A closer inspection of true-life revealed a slip of paper mostly hidden beneath the stones of a rock cairn. A hand-drawn map marked a point several kilometers away. After double-checking that he was still alone, he took off at a jog.

«Take the trail ahead on the left,» a voice whispered in sousednia once he'd arrived. «Into the trees.»

Increasingly paranoid, his back throbbing from the run, Gerrit followed the instructions. He almost missed the trail—more of a game trail than an actual path—and his back protested ducking branches and pushing through undergrowth.

Finally, the trail opened into a clearing. Captain Vrana sat on a downed log, jacket tossed casually aside, shirtsleeves rolled up. She wore a pistol in a shoulder holster, her sousedni-shape crisply focused on the neighboring reality. "Beautiful evening, isn't it, Lieutenant?"

"A little warm for my taste." He sloughed off his own

jacket, sharpening his attention on sousednia, searching again for other presences that might be able to overhear—though presumably Captain Vrana had chosen this location carefully, the subterfuge designed to enable a candid conversation.

"Come." She stood. "You should see the view." She waved him toward a gap in the trees, gesturing for him to precede her. He found another game trail, worse than the last, and managed to suppress a sigh. Maybe this was his punishment for not escaping into the resistance the way she'd planned.

A couple of meters ahead, the underbrush gave way, opening on a magnificent view across the valley. Sunlight glinted off a distant river, and forested hills rolled away to the horizon. "It's magnificent." Then he looked down and realized he stood at the edge of a sheer cliff.

Gerrit recoiled, but pain lanced his back—a sharp stab from the muzzle of Captain Vrana's gun.

«Step to the edge.» Her voice in sousednia yanked his attention to the neighboring reality.

He half turned in true-life, opening his mouth to protest. Her expression stopped him cold. Gerrit raised his hands in surrender. «I'm on your side,» he said in sousednia.

«Then you won't have any trouble obeying my orders.» Her tone was as reassuring as her pistol's dark gunmetal. «Face the view and put your hands in your back pockets.»

Breath harsh in his throat, Gerrit obeyed. Hands sunk into the deep pockets of his battledress trousers, he'd be slow to react if she shoved him in the back—probably too slow to save his life. All his Storm Guard training urged him to attack preemptively, knock aside her pistol and fling her from the cliff before she could shove him over. He might manage it. He was younger and probably stronger, maybe faster. If she was planning to make his death look like an accident, she might hesitate to fire. Might.

But he believed in the resistance, he *supported* the resistance. This had to be a test.

He heard a scrape that could have been her reholstering her pistol, but didn't dare turn to check. In sousednia, Captain Vrana stepped up beside him, casual as could be, hands in her pockets as if they were merely two friends enjoying the view. So sharp was her sousedni-shape that Gerrit edged back into true-life to double-check she wasn't there. Her hand closed on his collar, firm against his back, holding him one good shove from certain death.

Sousednia contracted, squeezing tighter, stone walls replacing the distant gleam of snowcapped mountains until he stood with her inside a space smaller than an interrogation cell. «Tell me what you know,» she ordered.

Fear had swept his mind blank, but he struggled for words, doubting she'd give him a second chance. He admitted everything he'd learned from Celka and realized during his time with the circus. «I know Celka and I were supposed to escape. We sleeted that up—but I'm still *loyal*. To you. To the resistance.» He searched her expression, desperate for some sign she believed him.

At her continued silence, he said, «I figured out what you meant, when you asked how our attackers knew where Mother and I would be four years ago.» Shortly after the Storm Guard had realized that the bozhskyeh storms were returning decades early, Gerrit had gone to visit his mother for the winter holidays. She'd picked him up from the train station in a motorcar, and they'd detoured to look at the view. «No one should have known the route we'd take—no one but family. Father ordered her murder.» He turned to Captain Vrana again in sousednia, giving up on keeping a stoic face. «Mother never agreed with Tayemstvoy repressions. I think she was working with you and the resistance. Celka told me everything she knows, and I haven't breathed a word of it to the State. You know that. Neither of us would be here if I'd talked. I never knew how the rest of Bourshkanya was suffering under my father's boot, but I do now. Let me *help*.»

«I gave you a chance,» she said. «You failed.»

Gerrit squeezed his eyes shut, trying to forget how close he stood to the edge. «I know. Everything happened too fast, and Celka lost control when she realized who Filip was.» He glared at her then, angry that she'd threaten him when they could have escaped if she hadn't given Filip such limiting orders. «If I'd known Filip was there, if I could have worked with him, if Celka could have known—»

«You never would have opened your eyes,» Captain Vrana said. «And if you'd sleeted up anyway, we'd all be dead.»

Gerrit ground his teeth, hating that she might be right. «So what now? Can you get us out? Doubek implied you could.»

«You assume you're worth the risk.» Beneath the snakes of light and shadow lashing her sousedni-shape, he saw cold evaluation in her gaze.

He swallowed hard. «The resistance needs imbuement mages.»

«Are you willing to escape without Celka?» Captain Vrana asked. «She's no good combat-warped.»

«So we wait for her to recover.» Gerrit tried to make his voice unequivocal.

«You assume she will.»

His stomach lurched as though she'd pushed him, and he rocked back reflexively on his heels, Captain Vrana's knuckles digging like stones into his injured back. «She can come back. She has to.»

«You think you're in love with her.» It wasn't a question.

«That's not why.» Gerrit dug his fingernails into his palms, hands still obediently stuffed in his back pockets, his heart still hammering in panic. He wanted to pace, but he didn't dare move. «I believe that what my father's doing to Bourshkanya is *wrong*. I believe that you wouldn't risk everything to lead the resistance if you didn't have a good chance at succeeding. I don't want my friends to die in a war only to give my father more power. He'll just send the Tayemstvoy out to ruin more lives. But I'm also not willing to abandon Celka just because she lost control in a single storm. She's better than that, stronger than that, and if it means I stay here longer and pretend to be loyal, that's what I'll do. I can get you intelligence. I'm working on getting closer to my father. Iveta wants me on her side, which means I can learn things you can't.»

«And your father can give you the power you've always wanted. He can convince you that everything he's done was *necessary*.» Captain Vrana gave the word a cruel twist.

Gerrit shook his head. «He might try, but I've seen through his mask. He's tearing Bourshkanya apart, not strengthening it.»

Captain Vrana studied him, impassive in sousednia, hand still gripping his collar in true-life. «There might be something you can do.»

«Anything,» Gerrit said.

«Kill him.»

All the air went out of Gerrit's lungs. He gaped at her, trying to imagine—kill his father? Assassinate the Stormhawk? The Stormhawk was a mundane, but that didn't matter when paranoid guards armed with Bourshkanya's best imbuements surrounded him. «It's not possible. People have tried—they always fail.» Fail, and get tortured to death.

«You just told me you had unprecedented access,» Captain Vrana said, reasonably, as if they were discussing anything else.

Gerrit felt like he was drowning. «Not that kind of access. *No one* has that kind of access.» He doubted even his step-mother was ever alone with his paranoid father.

«You're clever, Gerrit,» Captain Vrana said, «and you just explained how motivated you are to protect Bourshkanya. You want to stay and help Celka recover? *This* is how you serve the resistance.»

«And if I say no, you push me over the edge?» The thought shook him less this time. Compared to dying after months of torture, at least a hundred-meter fall would be quick.

Captain Vrana raised an eyebrow, and it felt painfully like her making him work out an answer in imbuement practicum.

He squeezed his eyes shut, part of him desperate to return to Storm Guard training where he knew what was expected. But he'd never been content following the rules, as Iveta had been so quick to point out. He'd always done better when he could think for himself, make his own mistakes. It was just... if he sleeted up trying to kill his father, his punishment wouldn't be a simple caning. «If I try, but don't manage it, can the resistance—*will* the resistance get me out?»

«Our resources are finite,» Captain Vrana said.

«So you'd leave me to die in an interrogation cell if it cost too much to free me?»

«Yes.»

He looked away, focusing on the true-life view before making himself stare down at the drop. If he turned his back on this assignment, it would be the same as turning his back on the resistance. He knew far too much for the Wolf to let him live. Maybe he should just step over the edge right now, take control of his life if only to choose his death. The moment the thought crossed his mind, he dismissed it. «I'll do it. I'll find a way.» He focused back on sousednia, meeting her iron gaze. «But if we can't do it before Celka recovers her core grounding, you'll get us out.»

Making demands of the Wolf while she dangled him above certain death seemed about as smart as leaping in front of a machinegun, but Gerrit wouldn't allow himself to be trapped—and he wouldn't give Captain Vrana the opening to leave Celka to rot in Iveta's imbuement company just because he failed to assassinate the unkillable Stormhawk. «Agreed,» Captain Vrana said, and Gerrit released a breath he hadn't realized he'd been holding. The tight stone walls confining sousednia wisped away and, in true-life, she let go of his collar. "Come away from the edge, Gerrit, it's starting to look unstable."

Gratefully, he retreated, following her through the undergrowth into the sun-dappled clearing.

«What about Cizek?» Captain Vrana asked as she picked back up her jacket. At Gerrit's frown, she asked, «Do you trust him?»

Gerrit opened his mouth to say yes, of *course* he trusted Filip, but the word wouldn't come. Finally, he said, «I don't know.»

Captain Vrana raised an eyebrow and crossed the clearing for the game trail. «Figure it out.» She disappeared into the bushes.

Gerrit waited until he couldn't hear her footsteps any longer, then collapsed onto the downed log, shaking all over.

CHAPTER EIGHT

FILIP'S STOMACH CHURNED as Gerrit strode toward the fortress's gate. *Getting some air, my ass*, he thought angrily, wondering who Gerrit was meeting, hating the idea that he'd meet them alone. *One hour*, he told himself. In one hour, he'd find Gerrit and demand answers.

Until then, he needed a distraction.

Scowling, he turned back to the fortress. Maybe he could at least do some good.

He expected to find Branislav still locked in a dungeon cell, had steeled himself to see his old friend chained to a wall, filthy and stinking because how much care would they really give to a storm-mad mage they'd forced past the point of recovery? Instead, Filip's enquiries led him to a small, aggressively bland room in the fortress's hospital.

A sign on the door told visitors to leave weapons and uniform jackets outside. It gave Filip hope that his friend might still be able to see true-life, that maybe Branislav wasn't utterly lost—even as the warning recalled too vividly Bran's snarling. Branislav had broken with a combat nuzhda—like Celka had.

Struggling not to think about Celka, Filip shrugged out of his jacket. Maybe her dismissal of him in the mess hall had been more a factor of combat-warping than her true feelings. He scrubbed a hand across his jaw, hating how badly he wanted it to be true.

He needed to focus. He was here to check on his friend, to help remind Branislav of who he'd been; Branislav didn't need Filip's baggage.

Drawing a slow breath, Filip closed his eyes, concentrating on his own core grounding. He imagined himself in the fortress's restricted library, surrounded by centuries of knowledge. He hummed the Song of Calming under his breath, its rhythm soothing the day's strain.

Careful of sudden motions or sharp sounds that could trigger a threat response, he entered Branislav's room. A single cot filled most of the space, Branislav propped half-upright with pillows, staring vacantly at the ceiling. He didn't move, didn't even blink at Filip's arrival. But Branislav wasn't alone.

Yanek sat in the tiny room's single chair, his back to Filip, hands on Branislav's cheeks. At the sound of Filip's bootfalls, Yanek turned. It took him a minute to focus, blinking back from the intense concentration that Filip knew so well from his own efforts to lure Branislav back to his un-warped core nuzhda.

Filip crossed to Branislav's other side, greeting his old friend like Bran had some chance of hearing him. Even before the Tayemstvoy had forced him to imbue while already storm-mad, Branislav had barely tracked true-life.

Once Yanek focused fully on him, Filip asked, "How is he?"

Yanek took Branislav's limp hand from where it rested on the gray wool blanket. The gesture had the look of familiar companionship, but Branislav didn't stir. "It's good of you to come."

Filip took Branislav's other hand, but studied Yanek. They'd trained together the last three years, but when pairing with imbuement mages, Branislav had usually worked with his own strazh, Jolana Kohout. "I didn't know you two were close."

Yanek shrugged. "I've been working with him since they transferred him here. The other strazhi too. It doesn't..." He searched Branislav's slack features, shaking his head, unwilling to speak the truth that echoed so clearly through the tiny room: it didn't help, but they tried anyway. "Sometimes we just come here to talk, try to give him some true-life normalcy. There's another chair in the hall if you want."

Filip went to get it, returning to take Branislav's hand. "Where's Jolana?" Colonel Tesarik had stopped Jolana from doing her job during either of Branislav's imbuements, but she should have been here if anyone was.

"She was reassigned," Yanek said, an edge to his voice. "No one's heard from her in weeks."

"Reassigned where?" Filip asked. All of Bourshkanya's promising storm-blessed mages with any sort of affinity to combat had been assigned to Iveta's imbuement company. Jolana was a strazh. Reassigning her elsewhere didn't make sense unless... Filip swallowed hard. "How was she—before she left?"

Yanek's grimace was subtle, just a tightening of his lips.

Filip felt his own calm cracking. Gerrit and Celka had come sleeting close to storm-madness after he'd showed up in that print shop. He'd managed to ground their out-of-control imbuement, but it had been a near thing. Sitting next to Branislav, it was all too easy to imagine Gerrit in his place. Too easy to imagine being crushed under that failure. Worse, the Tayemstvoy hadn't even let Jolana *try*. "Is she still on active duty?"

"I heard she was assigned to some border patrol," Yanek said. Which was a waste of someone with Jolana's skills and training. It meant the regime had washed their hands of her.

Filip swallowed hard.

Yanek caught his hand across the cot, and Filip turned, startled. Yanek said nothing, and after a moment, Filip returned his grip. A shuddery exhale left him hollow. Minutes stretched, but Yanek kept hold of his hand, the silence soothing.

Eventually, Yanek turned Filip's hand over, revealing the starburst scar from where he'd gripped the back of Gerrit's neck during their imbuement. Yanek rested his thumb on the central branching point and met Filip's gaze, a silent question. When Filip nodded, he stroked the branching tendrils, following them down Filip's palm and up his wrist to where the scars disappeared beneath his shirt cuff. Warmth bloomed outward from his touch and, this time when Yanek looked up, Filip's breath caught.

"How far does it go?" Yanek asked.

"Further," Filip said, and Yanek stood, tugging Filip with him toward the door.

They collected their jackets and weapons in silence, then Filip followed Yanek into the shade and relative privacy at the back of the building. They dropped their gear, and Yanek caught his hand again, stepping close.

He touched Filip's cheek, fingers like butterfly wings. "I'm glad you're back."

Filip opened his mouth to say that he was, too. But the words wouldn't come. He wanted to believe that his life had gone back to the way it had been before the storms' return, but Celka's simmering anger and Gerrit's tension told another story—one he hoped he was misreading.

Yanek's thumb stroked Filip's cheekbone, his fingers curling around the back of Filip's neck. Filip closed his eyes, leaning into his touch. He wanted to take Yanek up on his invitation, leave duty behind and remind himself that he was home, that the month of terrifying uncertainty was over—he was done wearing a false face, worried every day that the Tayemstvoy would find Gerrit and that Gerrit would do something stupid to make everything worse.

But Filip wasn't a cadet anymore, though Yanek's strong hand on his face made him want to forget the stars on his shoulders.

Pulling away, Filip slipped out the gold pocket watch Gerrit had gifted him for his birthday two years ago. His hour was nearly up. "I have to meet Gerrit." Regretful, he stooped to collect his gear.

"You don't owe him your every breath."

Filip frowned at the edge to Yanek's voice. "He's my commanding officer. He'll be yours, too, soon." From Gerrit's meeting with Iveta, it was clear that all the imbuement mages and strazhi in Iveta's company would report to Gerrit.

Yanek's jaw tightened. "And he'll never *see* you. Not the way you want him to."

Filip paused. "That's not..." He hesitated, swallowing his denial. Yanek was a good strazh, and strazhi trained to see hidden depths. Filip buckled his knife and pistol back onto his belt, but left his jacket off, even the summer-weight wool stifling. "He's my best friend," he told Yanek finally. "And I'm his strazh." That had been enough, once. He'd never thought to wonder if it still was.

Yanek stuffed his hands in his pockets and nodded unconvincingly. "I'll be here if you want to talk."

The conversation lingered like a stone in his boot as Filip headed for the fortress' northern gate, following the faint tug in his chest that pointed in Gerrit's direction. He and Gerrit had created the strazh bond in an arcane ritual two years ago. Filip had dug up and translated the original text from the Storm Guard's restricted library, and Captain Vrana had agreed to oversee the process—before swearing them to secrecy on the technique and its results. Too dangerous and costly for weaker mages to attempt, she'd said. Given that Filip had passed out during it and had only scattered memories of what had happened after they'd shattered the old imbuement to create the bond, he believed her.

Still, the risk had been worth it. Beyond letting him sense subtle changes in Gerrit's core nuzhda, it gave him a compass-like read on his best friend's location. Useful for clandestine meetings that, Filip hoped, would finally lead to answers.

He hoped they were answers he wanted to hear.

When he finally found Gerrit, Filip was sweaty and irritated. Gerrit had tucked himself away off the trail and, much as Filip had wanted to crash through the underbrush following their bond's magical pull, he couldn't risk drawing attention to their meeting. So he'd followed dead-end game trails and backtracked a dozen times before finally stepping into a clearing to find his best friend sitting on a downed log, looking for all the world like he was peacefully contemplating troop deployments in the evening sun.

Filip stepped on a branch, and Gerrit flinched around at the *crack*.

Pain washed over Gerrit's face. "Filip, hey." He moved more carefully to sit straight, and Filip's irritation sublimated. If Gerrit had hidden himself away this well, he must have done it to ensure they could speak openly.

Giving Gerrit time to search sousednia for presences, Filip studied the familiar lines of his best friend's face, letting the forest fade as he listened sideways for the murmurs that were all he could sense of sousednia. Gerrit felt like the howl of icy wind and the slippery sharpness of pine needles crusted with ice. That familiarity grounded Filip, and he breathed a little easier.

"I had a meeting," Gerrit said, and Filip swam back to the clearing. "With a new... ally."

An *ally?* Filip's calm popped. Was Gerrit meeting resistance dogs *here?* Hands balling into fists, he made his voice flat. "A friend of Celka's?"

Gerrit shook his head, but the denial felt like a lie.

"I followed you into the middle of nowhere, Gerrit. *Talk* to me."

"What I told you of our plans in Bludov hasn't changed," Gerrit said.

It felt like a gut punch. Bludov, where Gerrit and Celka had gone to get forged identification papers before vanishing into the resistance—abandoning Filip. No, that wasn't what mattered. Gerrit was supporting the sleeting *resistance*. It would get him killed. But if Filip just said that, Gerrit would clam up, so instead, he forced out, "Why?"

Very softly, Gerrit said, "My father started the Lesnikrayen War to gain power. He assassinated the king himself, blaming it on Lesnikrayen spies to stir up popular support. The supposed 'resistance' supporters who attacked me and my mother four years ago, they were disguised Tayemstvoy, operating on *his* orders. Mother had begun to support the resistance, and Father decided that I'd be more useful to the regime if my core nuzhda were grounded in combat."

Filip recoiled, but Gerrit was still talking, no longer looking at Filip but staring off at the trees.

"All his power still isn't enough. My mandate to get the imbuement mages producing? He wants me to imbue field guns—like what Doubek used to win the war at Zlin. He wants to start an aggressive war—he wants an *empire*—and he doesn't care who he kills in the process."

Filip had expected some sob story about how Celka wanted to help starving civilians, Gerrit determined to trail behind her. This... Filip swallowed hard.

The Stormhawk was Bourshkanya's heart and mind; he'd rallied Bourshkanyan troops to turn the tide on what had nearly been a crushing defeat in the Lesnikrayen war. Since their victory, the Stormhawk had revived Bourshkanyan industry, pulling the country up by their bootstraps after the old nobility's criminal neglect. The Stormhawk had leapt them technologically decades ahead to match their less storm-favored neighbors, so no one would dare attack again. The Stormhawk *was* Bourshkanya. And he was Gerrit's father.

"You must have seen it when we were with the circus," Gerrit whispered, "the way he's crushing Bourshkanya. People are starving and terrified. We have the resources to feed them, but he's stocking it away to feed soldiers. Our *imbuements* could help people, but all he wants are weapons."

"He's your *father*." Stormy skies, what did Gerrit think he was doing?

Gerrit crossed the distance, catching Filip's arms. "He is." His voice simmered with hatred. "And everything good we've learned about him is a lie."

"The *resistance* told you that." Filip spat the word. Suddenly, the fact that he'd helped Celka smuggle an illegal pistol through Tayemstvoy checkpoints sickened him. He'd committed treason for her—to keep her and Gerrit safe. What had it bought him? Celka had twisted Gerrit's loyalty, made him side with the *enemy*. "*Why* would you believe them?"

"They're good people—*smart* people—who know the truth my father buried."

Smart people. Gerrit wouldn't say that lightly. Filip tried to keep the sudden attention off his expression. Gerrit had met someone high enough up in the resistance that he trusted their intel and was willing to back their plans. Sleet. "Who?" Filip tried to make the question casual. If he could rip the ground out from beneath the resistance leadership, maybe Gerrit would see reason.

They couldn't fight the State—even if they wanted to. And Filip didn't.

Gerrit shook his head. "It's safer for everyone if you don't know."

Filip balled one hand into a fist, almost as annoyed that he'd failed to extract a name as relieved that Gerrit was smart enough not to tell him. He pulled free, striding to the downed log. His back to Gerrit, he tried to think. If Gerrit thought he could trust the resistance's leadership, Filip needed a plan to stop him—fast. "What are you planning to do?" He turned, studying his best friend, trying to read the answer in the tense lines of his jaw. "You'll run away again?"

"Not yet. Not until Celka's grounded."

Which meant that whoever Gerrit had met knew enough about imbuement mages to know how close Celka had come to storm-madness. The resistance must have its claws in the Storm Guard, though it was hard to know how deep. "*Will* she recover?" Filip wished he didn't care so much. Celka had set Gerrit on this path; it would serve her right if she wound up locked in a combat fugue. The thought made him sick. Whatever her mistaken loyalties, Celka was a good person; he didn't want to see her hurt.

"I don't know," Gerrit said, voice tight. "But she's strong."

Filip turned, pacing, thoughts circling the memory of Gerrit holding Celka's hand while surrounded by Tayemstvoy corpses, blood on his face but eyes bright, asking Filip to join them in the resistance. "You're doing this for Celka." Filip made it a statement, wondering how much of it was true.

"No," Gerrit snapped.

Filip didn't believe him, not entirely. The story about the Stormhawk killing Gerrit's mother had clearly turned him against the State—sleet, it couldn't be true, could it?—but Filip needed to knock a hole in Gerrit's suicidal drive to commit treason. Gerrit's crush on Celka might be exactly the weakness he needed.

"You're in this for Celka," Filip pressed. "Are you sure she's in it for you?"

Gerrit crossed his arms. "Celka made her choice."

Filip stuffed his hands casually in his pockets and shrugged, as if to say, *believe what you want.* "You're the Stormhawk's son, and we were handing ourselves to the Tayemstvoy. She needed your protection." Filip let a fond smile tug at his lips, gaze slipping off Gerrit. "But she wasn't thinking about you when she kissed me—not over loupak and coffee, not in the print shop."

Gerrit rocked back like he'd been gut-punched.

"Where do you think she was when she wasn't with you?" Filip pressed. "Who do you think taught her to shoot? We were flirting with each other for weeks before we finally kissed." And Filip had been trying and failing to ignore his own attraction to her. But physical contact helped ground an imbuement mage, and when Celka had nearly imbued to fight off an aggressive Tayemstvoy patrol, Filip had given in. Celka had melted deliciously against him and he'd wondered what in stormy skies had taken him so long. He tried to shake the thought.

His own feelings for Celka didn't matter. He needed to turn Gerrit from this path before it got him killed. Filip kept his voice smooth, almost that flirty tone that had lured even suspicious circus performers into his confidence. "You lost your chance, Gerrit. The only reason she 'chose' you, was to recruit you for the resistance." He let his voice harden, hoping to remind Gerrit of their duty, their training. "At your father's side, you're strong. The resistance doesn't want that." He closed the distance between them. "Celka's using you."

Gerrit shook his head. "That's not true."

"She did the same to me, batted those beautiful butterfly eyes, and I ushered her through Tayemstvoy checkpoints, helped her get that pistol she imbued." It was a lie, the causality reversed, but sounded plausible. "I trained her to use it when I knew sleeting well it was treason. The resistance is *smart*, Gerrit, you said so yourself. Smart enough to manipulate even us." Saying it, Filip realized it might be true. He didn't think Celka had deliberately played either of them, but if Gerrit was meeting resistance leadership here, then maybe the unlikely chain of events that had brought them to Celka hadn't been coincidence. Celka was passionate and fierce—the perfect trap for them both.

Before Gerrit could shake free of his doubts, Filip said, "Don't let the resistance undercut your power. You thought you had to run before—fine. That's in the past. Whatever the resistance's plans, you figured out how to imbue and we're back now, back where we *belong*. You're stronger than you were when the storms returned—you said that to your father, and he listened. Maybe he did terrible things in the past—or maybe that's another resistance lie—but you have a chance to make a difference *now*.

"If you don't like what he's doing to this country, tell him. Face your father like you did this morning. Make him see you. Make him *change*."

"He won't listen to me." But Gerrit no longer sounded so sure.

"You're wrong." Filip gripped Gerrit's arms, willing his best friend to understand. "He didn't listen to you as a child, but you're not a child anymore. If you care about Bourshkanya, seize your power. Celka and the resistance are trying to tear you away because they know how *strong* you can become. They want to destroy the State, not save it."

Frowning, Gerrit pulled away. Filip let him retreat, though Gerrit didn't go far, peering across the clearing toward the trampled leaves of another game trail. Gerrit scrubbed a hand through his hair and shook his head. Quietly, he said, "Destroy it?" He turned back to Filip, eyes haunted. "Maybe that's the only choice. Maybe the State's too corrupt to save."

"No." Filip put command in his voice. "The resistance wants you to believe that, but it's a lie." He held out his hand. "Together we can make changes. I have your back, Gerrit, I always have. Together, we're strong. Don't let Celka—or the resistance—tear us apart."

Gerrit stared at Filip's hand for a long time, the struggle raw in his face. His gaze flicked up to Filip's face—for one heartbeat—then he turned his back.

Filip rocked back on his heels. *Don't do this*, he wanted to scream. Instead, he made his voice low. "She's using you."

Returning to the downed log, Gerrit picked up his jacket. Caught in a shaft of sunlight, he met Filip's gaze. "This is bigger than me now. Bigger than my own power." He started for the trail back to the main path, pausing until Filip joined him. "I'd hoped you would understand."

But Filip didn't. All the long walk back to the Storm Guard Fortress, he kept remembering Gerrit in the Stormhawk's office, falling to his knees as the Yestrab Okhrana made him scream.

CHAPTER NINE

"MAYBE THEY'RE WRONG," Celka told Hedvika, frustrated. "Gerrit and Filip—they've never seen my sousednia. They're just guessing. They could be wrong."

Hedvika frowned at her, crouched in a shaft of evening sunlight. She couldn't seem to just sit in a chair, but was always moving, circling Celka, her sousedni-shape glowing multi-colored in a way that definitely didn't make Celka magically appear on the high wire.

Celka braced herself for the other woman's objections, for the strained way Hedvika would suggest, again, that they keep trying. But Hedvika stood fluidly and held out her hand. "Let's get out of here."

Wary, Celka looked between Hedvika's proffered hand and her face, but the strazh's expression was serious and her sousedni-cues were uselessly swamped by the scents of manure and boiling cabbage roiling off of her from the nuzhda she pulled against, trying to remind Celka of her supposed core.

When Celka didn't immediately take Hedvika's hand, Hedvika shrugged, stuffed her hand in her pocket, and started for the door. "Come on. I have an idea." She strode out of the practice room, and Celka scrambled after her. She didn't trust Hedvika, but she trusted everyone else in the Storm Guard Fortress *less*.

Hedvika led her across the fortress's outer yard to the stables—though the horses seemed to have mostly been replaced by gleaming motorcars. "What are we—?" Celka started to ask, but Hedvika waved her silent, motioning to one of the stable hands who vanished and returned wheeling two bicycles.

Belatedly, Hedvika turned to her. "You know how to ride, right?"

Not well, but Celka nodded. If this meant getting out of the Storm Guard Fortress—or even just riding around the perimeter wall, it was sleeting better than struggling to change her sousednia. She grimaced at the thought. She would regain her core grounding, she would. But she felt like she'd been slamming her head against a wall for hours.

Hedvika mounted her bicycle with a tiger's grace, and Celka wobbled behind her along the dirt road hugging the fortress's outer wall. As they neared a guarded gate, Celka's stomach churned, but Hedvika just dismounted and pulled out her identification folio, handing it casually to a Tayemstvoy guard. Celka mimicked her, her own folio a bright, military red like Hedvika's and so crisp from being made this morning that it felt fake.

The guard took their folios and wrote in a logbook while Celka tried to keep breathing. Any second, they would match her name to a list of people not allowed to leave. The other red shoulders would slap their rifles into their hands and order her back inside, a gun to her back. What had Hedvika been thinking trying to take her out of the fortress?

But the guard handed back their folios, saluted Hedvika, and waved them through.

Hedvika mounted her bike, and Celka hurried to follow, wobbling worse as she forced herself not to look over her shoulder at the Tayemstvoy guards. Still, she kept imagining a rifle shot—or at least a shout—calling them back.

When Hedvika slowed to ride at her side, Celka started to hear her voice. "You ever been to Solnitse?"

Breathe, she told herself, keeping her eyes on the road so she wouldn't lose her balance. "Last year," she said. "With the circus. But we always stay in the fairgrounds. I've never been into town." Pa had always 'fallen sick' when they played in Solnitse, and had warned her to keep out of sight as much as possible—worried someone would spot her sousedni-shape. That he'd played sick only to sneak out and secretly meet Vrana, Celka hadn't learned until recently.

"You missed out," Hedvika said. "Solnitse's small, but it's nice."

Hedvika had a destination in mind, and Celka didn't question it, glad for the fresh air. As the kilometers from the Storm Guard Fortress grew, she found herself breathing easier. She could almost imagine this was just a rest day between performances, that instead of Hedvika, she rode at her cousin Ela's side, escaping chores for a bit of window shopping. The imagining drove an ache through her chest, but Celka made herself breathe past it. Ela and her family were safe, and soon Celka would regain her core grounding and see Pa.

"Here we are." Hedvika leaned her bike against the white stone wall and led Celka inside a tailor's. Hedvika asked after someone by name and tossed a silver striber to one of the assistants, telling them to send their bikes back to the fortress.

Celka almost protested—a full striber to leave them without a ride home seemed ludicrous—but maybe a striber was nothing to Hedvika. Pressing her lips shut, Celka recalled Vrana's advice: Hedvika was her strazh because of regime loyalty. Celka couldn't forget that.

Soon another assistant beckoned them into a back room, and an older person spoke quietly with Hedvika before digging through bolts of fabric. Celka stayed near the door, hands in her pockets, trying to disappear. If Hedvika wanted to run errands with Celka in tow, at least it got her out of the fortress and away from the maddeningly pointless exercises to restore her core grounding.

Once she got back to the fortress, she needed to find a way to see Gerrit. What he'd written in his report on her core nuzhda couldn't be right. It made no sense that her sousednia was a high wire, and she couldn't imagine wearing her high wire costume out in the back lot. He had to be mistaken.

"How about these?" Hedvika asked, and Celka started to realize her strazh was talking to her. Hedvika motioned her toward a large table, where the tailor had laid out several bolts of green cloth.

Celka frowned at Hedvika. "What about them?" Was her strazh asking for fashion advice? One glance at the fabrics showed them all to be finer than anything Celka had ever owned. She was careful to keep her hands in her pockets.

"Do any remind you of your high wire costume?" Hedvika asked.

Celka flinched back, shaking her head, but Hedvika wrapped an arm around her shoulders like they were old friends.

"I'm sure they're not perfect, but are any close? Even just the color or the texture?" The warmth in Hedvika's voice made Celka focus on the fabric despite herself.

They were all wrong, satins and silks too fine for her costume's sturdy bodice, yet too weighty for the gossamer sleeves. And yet... Celka slipped forward, reaching out before she could catch herself and touching hesitant fingers to a corner of emerald silk.

"I can imagine you dressed in it," Hedvika said from behind her. "Brilliant and glittering up on your high wire. So confident as you balance far above everyone."

Celka shuddered, chest tight like she was about to burst into tears. Distantly, she heard Hedvika order a pocket square cut from the material, and even as the tailor went to work, Celka couldn't tear her eyes off the cloth. She felt a warmth behind her, like the humid heat of the big top in the summer sun, dust motes swirling in the spotlights. But the smells were wrong, and Celka shook her head, searching for something—not cabbage or manure, something lighter, fresher. But she didn't know what.

Then the tailor pressed the pocket square into her hands and Celka startled back into the close dark room, dusty and cool, bolts of cloth a muted rainbow along the walls. Clutching the square of silk, Celka shook her head, turning to Hedvika. "I can't pay for this," she said, meaning to hold the square back out but finding herself hugging it to her chest.

"It's nothing," Hedvika said.

But it wasn't. This little scrap of cloth, too soft in her hands, felt like falling, like flying. It felt like the future and like escape. It terrified her. Tears beaded in her eyes but didn't fall. She clutched the fabric, staring through blurred vision, and it sounded like laughter and the warmth of her family crowded around the phonograph player in their sleeper car's small sitting room.

Hedvika and the tailor were speaking, and Celka followed their instructions without really hearing them, shrugging out of her uniform jacket and shirt, letting the tailor attack her with measuring tape and a sharp gaze. They moved her body, and she felt like a marionette as she clutched the green silk. In the corner of Celka's eye, Hedvika glowed, her sousedni-shape flickering like blue sky and rainbows.

By the time they left the shop, a tune had started in the back of Celka's mind, a fluting melody drifting up from beneath her, filling a vast open space. She walked in a daze down Solnitse's cobblestone streets, well-dressed civilians spinning around her—too close for the spectators she sensed below. Her boots crunched on the cobbles, dissonant, and she changed her pace to match the rhythm of the band. When Hedvika steered her to a bench in a public garden, she shook her head and, instead of sitting, pulled off her boots and climbed onto the bench's wooden back, balancing too easily, but at least the perspective was closer. The pocket square flapped in the breeze as Hedvika talked about her family's high wire act.

If the words were a little stiff and repetitive—like something Hedvika had memorized—Celka hardly noticed. Because even as sousednia carried the cold bite of spring and the rotten-egg stink of boiling cabbages, Celka could almost—*almost*—see a different world. One where the big top's canvas fell into shadow and the audience gaped up at her in anticipation and wonder.

Standing atop a park bench holding a square of green cloth, Celka's world changed. Like a sigh, the back lot fell away, and the cable beneath her slippered feet gained a springy liveness, so unlike the shorter practice wire that hung too close to the ground. The cook tent's smoke wisped away, replaced by a sawdust freshness, and dust danced in the spotlights.

Open-handed, Celka crossed the high wire toward the platform at the end, her family invisible in the darkness, but their presence felt—a warmth, a welcoming that calmed her breathing. The distance stretched and blurred, the steel cable spooling out ahead of her, the platform staying perfectly distant as she reveled in her freedom, in power and control.

Despite everything, she felt the back lot looming, the soldiers pacing behind the cook tent, twitchy fingers tapping truncheons. But here, in the big top's reaches, she could almost forget them, almost breathe in a way she'd forgotten was possible. So she did. She breathed. She walked the wire. And evening shadows crossed the park and slipped into the darkness of streetlamps.

A hand on her arm startled her, and Celka blinked away the high wire to find Hedvika smiling in a streetlamp's golden glow. "You want to get some honey cake?"

Celka frowned at the question, trying to connect it to the world beneath her big top or her suddenly swooping memory of questions and uniforms and stone interrogation cells.

"Come on." Hedvika offered her hand. Celka hesitated, but made herself take it, jumping down off the back of the bench. "My treat."

If Hedvika noticed her hesitation, she didn't comment. Medovnik's delicate honey flavor filled her like the warmth beneath the circus big top. As they climbed the hill toward the Storm Guard Fortress, Celka's mouth still decadently sweet, Hedvika's hand slipped into hers, solid and steadying as any balance pole.

BY THE TIME Celka and Hedvika returned to the Storm Guard Fortress, exhaustion weighted Celka's limbs. Hedvika had mentioned sharing a suite, and Celka blotted out the Army and Tayemstvoy uniforms striding past by imagining a bed. Usvit Hall turned out to have gleaming wood bannisters and plush burgundy rugs, brass detailing polished to a mirror shine.

The feeling that Celka didn't belong rushed over her, but Hedvika didn't let go of her hand, and Celka struggled to crush the feeling down, clutching the green pocket square.

"Here we are," Hedvika said, but a Tayemstvoy corporal

barred their way, and Celka's pulse roared in her ears like the crack of truncheons.

"Lieutenant Kladivo—Gerrit Kladivo," the corporal said, "would like to see you." They gestured to the room across from where Hedvika had been leading her.

Celka's heart leapt, but Hedvika squeezed her palm. "I can come if you want."

Celka shook her head, hurrying to the door, praying her strazh didn't insist. Inside, she discovered a spacious sitting room with two wingback chairs arranged before a broad widow. A brightly tiled fireplace occupied one wall, faced by a writing desk, the wood polished to mirror shine. Gerrit sat at the desk, back straight, dressed in a finely tailored uniform, gold bozhk bolts at his throat and a full rainbow of gold-banded nuzhda competencies across his chest. His single gold and ruby lightning bolt earring screamed wealth and influence.

When he met Celka's gaze, she wavered on her high wire, truncheons cracking over the circus band. He looked like the Stormhawk's son. That cold appraisal, the solemn, commanding set to his jaw. How had she missed it before?

He stood, and Celka flinched, her hands balling into fists, the big top cracking open, gusting a springtime chill. Then he opened his arms and strode toward her, the command melting into relief. "Celka." His voice was soft, vulnerable the way he'd only revealed after weeks in the circus. He caught her arms lightly, as though to pull her into an embrace, but stopped. "How are you?" Sousednia smelled of pine and glaciers, and it was so utterly the Gerrit she'd trusted that Celka flung her arms around him.

He stiffened with a gasp.

Celka released him, edging back, terrified she'd misread him. His jaw was clenched, but it wasn't a return to the sharp-edged officer—but pain. "What's wrong?" Celka asked before she could think who might be listening. She shifted into sousednia, searching his wavery form and the tangle of urine and cold stone that twisted through his alpine scents. «Are you all right?»

His sousedni-shape solidified, his strong lean arms bare despite the icy air around him. «I'm fine.» But the urine scent of the lie strengthened. «I just—» His jaw tensed and he looked away. «It's nothing.»

She searched his expression, unwilling to call him on the lie if it was something he couldn't discuss without revealing disloyalty. It clearly wasn't nothing.

Finally, he sighed and, with a grimace, returned to true-life. She followed him back to the gilt and polished sitting room, and found him unbuttoning his shirt. "My father," he said, voice almost emotionless, quiet as a breath. He shrugged out of his shirt and braces, not quite covering a grimace. Meeting Celka's gaze, he seemed to steel himself. Turning his back to her, he breathed out sharply and pulled his undershirt off.

Celka gasped. "Gerrit—"

He faced her suddenly, holding out a hand to stop her from saying more. His jaw muscles worked and he shook his head. "I'll be fine." The words came out tight, a warning.

She swallowed hard.

He took her hands. A buzz like storm energy brightened true-life, bringing sousednia closer. He held her gaze, matching it with that tiger's intensity she loved. "Did they hurt you?" he asked.

"No," she said quickly. "Not like—" She searched his expression, wondering what he'd done that his father had had him beaten so brutally. But of course she knew. He'd run away. He'd hidden in the circus with her. Her fractured memories of the Tayemstvoy knocking her down and handcuffing her wrists when she attacked them in a combat fugue paled in comparison. She hadn't been tortured, *he* had. Sleet. The Stormhawk's *son*. And she'd been angry he hadn't protected her. Nauseous, she looked away.

"Hey." He touched her cheek lightly. She met his gaze. "I'm glad."

Shaky, Celka exhaled, and he put his arms around her. She laid her cheek against his chest, arms awkward at her sides as she didn't know how to hug him back without hurting him.

He pressed his face against her hair. «It's so good to see you,» he whispered.

«You too,» she said.

«You found your core sousednia?» he sounded hopeful but uncertain. «You're wearing your high wire costume, at least.»

«Hedvika helped me.» She fingered the silk pocket square.

Gerrit tensed, almost imperceptibly, sousednia wafting urine and old blood.

She drew back, frowning.

His jaw tightened, and he shook his head. «I was so worried when I saw you earlier, still warped.»

Celka didn't know how to respond to that, didn't know how to explain that she hadn't been worried at all, that she hadn't known anything was wrong. Looking out across sousednia, she frowned at the mud and weeds of the back lot, balancing awkward on her practice wire, feeling exposed in her high wire costume. Vrana had told her she wouldn't know if anything was wrong, but she would, wouldn't she? If she didn't have this steel cable beneath her feet, if her costume shifted away from the pocket square's green.

Gerrit stroked her hair and she sighed, leaning against him, the steady lub-dub of his heart making it easier to breathe. She had work to do to erase the groove of combat-warping, she could feel it—the Tayemstvoy lurking just around the cook tent's grimy canvas—but she was strong. She'd return to herself, and she and Gerrit would get out.

Maybe some things had changed, but not him. Gerrit was still Gerrit, still the boy who'd made her laugh, who'd helped her print rifle training manuals with an illegal mimeograph machine in the snake trailer. She trusted him. They were in this together.

«I met with my old imbuement instructor today,» Gerrit eventually said, voice quiet beneath the back lot's background clamor. «Captain Vrana—I mentioned her?» He managed to say it like Celka might not know who he was talking about, like Captain Vrana was just some bozhk instructor and not the Wolf herself. «I'll probably be working with her some, figuring out how to get the older mages imbuing.»

«I met her today, too,» Celka said. «To ask her about grounding. She's... scary.»

Gerrit choked. «You have no idea.» Shakily, he exhaled, drawing her away and crossing to the writing desk. Celka couldn't help but stare at the purple and red mess of his back. If she didn't hate the Stormhawk already, she would now. She couldn't believe Gerrit was even walking around, let alone acting almost normal. Now that she was looking, she could see the ginger way he bent over the desk as though trying not to use his back muscles. What kind of parent would torture their child like that?

Gerrit was talking, saying something about the imbuement platoon and his sister commanding the larger company of 'bolt-hawks'—Tayemstvoy who were also bozhki. Celka joined him at the desk and tried to concentrate past her own exhaustion.

Then Gerrit lifted his pen and slid a piece of paper over for her to read.

She wants us to assassinate my father.

Celka stared at the page, at the stark line of text. She re-read it, sure she must have misunderstood. Then she stared at Gerrit. Jaw tight, he nodded.

"We're still working out the composition of the imbuement squads," he continued like he hadn't written the most treasonous, brilliant thing. "But my sister seems pretty insistent on keeping your squad as-is. She hand-picked them, apparently, for you." He sounded annoyed by it, but all Celka could see was the mission.

"That's great," Celka said, looking back at the paper. She waved for Gerrit to give her the pen, and wrote, *How?*

"I didn't expect you to... be all right with them," he said, snatching up a pencil. *We have to figure that out. It won't be easy. He has imbuements. He's survived attacks before.* "They're not exactly easy to get along with... especially Havel. He's—"

"We'll work it out," Celka said quickly, wondering who Havel was—probably one of the imbuement mages she'd yet to meet. *You must know his imbuements, right?*

No, Gerrit wrote. *His guard is secretive.*

So we need to get in and study them, she wrote. *And we need a better way to talk. To plan.* To cover their clandestine conversation, she asked, "What about us?" Her throat suddenly closed off, stomach lurching in a way that had nothing to do with Vrana's mission. "Will we... see more of each other?" Before they'd turned themselves over to the Tayemstvoy in Bludov, Gerrit had kissed her, convinced that his importance as an imbuement mage would be enough to protect her from his father, even if the Stormhawk knew how much they cared about each other. Given Gerrit's beating, Celka doubted he still believed that.

I'm working on it, Gerrit wrote. He hesitated, not meeting her gaze. "Do you want to?" he finally asked. "If you've changed your mind about me—about us..."

"No! I just—" She gestured at his back.

His nostrils flared, a cold edge appearing in his expression and just as quickly suppressed. "No. That was a... reminder of authority. It has no bearing on you." He spoke low, voice clipped. Taking the paper with their treasonous conversation, he crossed to the hearth, striking a match and letting the note burn to ash. He stirred the ash around, ensuring the note was entirely destroyed. When he turned back, his expression has softened, uncertainty poking through like crocuses in snow.

He approached, sousedni-shape sharpening as he focused on the neighboring reality. She met him on her springtime back lot, brushing aside the practice wire to clasp his hands on solid ground. Touch sharpened both realities, igniting her nerves and making her viscerally aware of the sharp-fresh smell of him. Her gaze found his mouth, so often locked in a soldierly line, hiding all his spark and brilliance.

«You kissed Filip in the print shop,» he said, voice wooden.

Celka frowned, retreating half a step but unwilling to let go of his hands. She almost denied it, but something stopped her... a fractured memory of pain burning down her back and darkness pressing close, hazy and red. A strong hand at her waist and another cupping the back of her neck. Her body weighing too much and nothing at all.

She remembered warmth drawing her back from the darkness and pain, a softness. Ctibor's deep brown eyes catching hers, then his lips. His kiss had been a gasp of fresh air, an embrace that snapped her back into her body, driving back the darkness—if only for a moment. «I... did,» she whispered, throat tight, but a flutter in her belly. She crushed the flutter down. She hadn't kissed *Ctibor*, but Filip. A boot-licking bozhk who'd been lying to her with his every breath.

She drew back from Gerrit, needing to feel the practice wire beneath her feet, even as her balance fought her. «I didn't...»

She met Gerrit's gaze, finding his hurt and uncertainty poorly hidden. She could imagine him snapping that military command back into place, turning his back on her. She shook her head, refusing to allow it. «I didn't kiss *Filip*, I kissed Ctibor because... I don't know. The world was falling, but he was real.» Catching her balance, she reached for Gerrit's hands. He didn't take them. «Ctibor helped ground me, I think. But *Ctibor* was a lie.» Even thinking about him, truncheons cracked against bone, and she felt the Tayemstvoy swarming Pa just past the edge of her vision. «Filip is a—» She swallowed her words, suddenly aware that, should they be overheard, she could hardly be caught calling a Storm Guard sub-lieutenant a hail-eating boot-licker. But Gerrit knew her; she'd have to hope he understood what she couldn't say aloud. «Everything in my world changed when *you* came into it, Gerrit.» He finally took her hands, and sousednia sharpened, the pine and ice scent of him blowing away some of the stench of blood on the wind. «If there's any way we can make this work, I want to be with *you*.»

Hope brightened his expression, and the pine-scented breeze wiped the back lot clear. They stood alone, Celka balancing on the wire, Gerrit on the post that anchored it. «It might be difficult. My family... I'll have responsibilities. I won't always be able to include you.»

She nodded, squeezing his hands. It didn't matter. All of this would be temporary. Just until she regained her core grounding. Just until they assassinated his father and escaped into the resistance.

He pulled her to him, thumb brushing her lips in both realities. «If we do this, I want us to be exclusive.»

That sent a shiver through her belly. She'd never been in a relationship serious enough to become exclusive, had never found someone she'd consider giving that kind of focus in her life. «Yes,» she said, and Gerrit's concern melted into a smile.

Standing on her toes, she kissed him.

Gerrit returned the kiss, cupping her face in his hands. Both realities flared bright and vibrant around them, even as everything but the sweet taste of his lips fell away.

CHAPTER TEN

CELKA HAD NEVER attended one of the Stormhawk's rallies before. She'd studied his speeches in school like any child, but hearing one in person was different. His voice filled the city square, rich and commanding, thanks to an imbuement. He used *so many* imbuements—or rather, the Yestrab Okhrana did.

Even if Celka had attended a rally in the past, she never would have gotten this close to the Supreme-General. She hated the part of her that thrilled at it, that felt special and wanted to tell her cousin Ela and her friends that she'd stood a mere twenty rows from the Stormhawk. He was almost close enough to touch.

When he'd mounted the dais after red-shouldered boot-lickers had warmed up the crowd, the applause had been thunderous. Around Celka, people thrummed with excitement, listening with bated breath as if the Stormhawk really was great, as if being here was an event they'd relate with pride to their children and grandchildren. It shook Celka. She'd expected a few rabid supporters and many more who attended because they worried the Tayemstvoy would notice their absence. She'd expected a crowd cheering because they feared the consequences of silence.

Celka struggled to focus. She wasn't here to bask in the reflected glory of Bourshkanya's brutal dictator. She was supposed to be studying emotional imbuements wielded by the Yestrab Okhrana.

She wished she understood why.

A bolt-hawk had brought Celka and Hedvika to Gerrit's rooms this morning, and he'd explained that Celka's unusual imbuement style might give her insight into creating imbuements that could manipulate emotions. The Stormhawk's personal guard would be using them on the crowd during the rally, and Gerrit and Iveta wanted Celka to study them and report on whether she could create more. Oh, and could Celka ensure the Okhrana didn't suspect what she was doing? The Stormhawk had classified the existence of these imbuements, and would not be pleased to have them studied. Gerrit's grim expression had sent a chill down Celka's spine, and Hedvika had shifted uncomfortably beside her.

All during the morning train ride, Celka had churned over the mission. Did Gerrit think emotional imbuements would help them assassinate his father? Celka wished she'd had some way to ask. It seemed dangerous getting Hedvika involved if so, but during the rally, surrounded by the Stormhawk's supporters, Celka was glad to have Hedvika at her side. Maybe the emotional imbuements were a ruse—an excuse for getting Celka close enough to the Stormhawk to unravel his magical defenses.

Though she couldn't, at the moment. The crowd left sousednia smelling thick and soupy, their enthusiasm swamping details. She could certainly *see* the Stormhawk's imbuements, though, and maybe that would teach her something.

A candyfloss web of color spread from dozens of Yestrab

Okhrana guards on or near the dais. But, unable to smell the imbuements, Celka could intuit only basic function from their nuzhdi glow. Each of the six fundamental nuzhdi glowed a distinctive color and, around the Stormhawk, she saw the full rainbow—even the spinach green of a hunger nuzhda, which surprised her. Protection's purple and strengthening's orange made sense. And of course the Yestrab Okhrana used blood-colored combat imbuements and the summer sky blue of concealment. She almost missed the rippling gold of healing nuzhdi; those imbuements seemed inactive, presumably carried by the guards in case of attack.

Not that Celka could imagine attacking the Stormhawk here. Her determination to unravel his imbuements faded as his speech drew her in. The bozhskyeh storms had returned as a blessing upon the regime, he claimed, the great forces beyond humanity stirring as they never had in response to Bourshkanyan determination.

"Should foreign nations threaten us, should those *cizli* seek to take by force what the Storm Gods have given us for our faith, we will not stand passive. They have connived to make us weak, but we are *strong!*"

The crowd cheered, and Celka added her own voice alongside Hedvika's. Grinning, Celka found her strazh's eyes bright with the same fervor Celka felt—yet something deep within her recoiled.

From the corner of her eye, Celka caught a flicker of blue, brighter than the embroidery on the few civilian kaftans and sarafans that peppered the sea of Army and Tayemstvoy uniforms this close to the dais. When she turned, it vanished.

Frowning, Celka edged into sousednia, the sun beating down from the blue, springtime sky above where she stood on the practice wire. Nothing seemed wrong. She wanted to return to true-life and focus on the Stormhawk's speech, but she resisted. Gerrit's orders were to study the Yestrab Okhrana using emotional imbuements on the crowd—but Celka hadn't spotted any. Whether or not those orders hid a secret plan, she needed something to report.

The crowd made sousednia smokey, the hazy forms of mundanes plus the occasional heat-shimmer of a storm-touched bozhk blurring the circus back lot. Though their forms were somewhat translucent, searching through them for active imbuements—besides the ones blaring from the Stormhawk's dais—was a challenge. About to abandon the effort as fruitless, Celka grimaced up at the sky. It pressed close, the blue flickering in time with her excited pulse, driving her to return to the Stormhawk's speech.

Resisting the urge, Celka peered more closely. Skeins of orange and violet rippled through... sleet, it wasn't just the sky. Threads of nuzhda—strengthening's orange and protection's violet—wove through the blue base nuzhda of concealment. Celka wrinkled her nose. Most imbuements were constructed out of a pure nuzhda, and trying to understand something created out of a muddy mixture wouldn't be easy. Even Celka, with Pa's unorthodox training, used pure nuzhdi.

But this imbuement was all she had to work with, so Celka had to make the best of it. The glow fanned overhead, and she followed the loops and whorls of crystalized storm energy, tracing them to the originating imbuement a few meters away.

Squinting through mundane smoke-forms, Celka spotted the bozhk holding the imbuement. In true-life, she craned past heads and shoulders to discover a person dressed in an embroidered sarafan, the colors a little faded and some of the embroidery fraying. They could have been a shop owner or minor bureaucrat, and Celka double-checked whether she'd made a mistake in sousednia—they looked so ordinary. But no, they definitely held the imbuement.

Was she mistaken that they were Okhrana? Could this be someone's personal imbuement? She shook the thought. The Stormhawk had gathered up all imbuements after the war, redistributing them to his worthiest supporters. Even if someone had treasonously hidden an imbuement all these years, they wouldn't be fool enough to trot it out during the great leader's rally.

Something about those thoughts seemed wrong, but Celka struggled to think past the Stormhawk's rousing speech, trying to follow Gerrit's orders and disentangle the imbuement's scents from the crowd's excitement. It was like trying to hold her breath despite her lungs screaming for air.

Then the Okhrana pulled the imbuement off of her, like sweeping a cloak away to another section of the crowd. Celka expected her awe to burst, but she still strained to catch the Supreme-General's every word. She wanted to cheer his commanding presence and bold, decisive gestures.

Had another Yestrab Okhrana cloaked her in a fresh imbuement?

No, the air around her in the circus back lot was clear. The emotional imbuement's effects must linger, like nuzhda-warping. Drawing deep breaths of mud and boiling cabbage, Celka concentrated on the steel cable pressing into her feet. She was dealing with her combat-warping, she could deal with this.

Tightening her grip on Hedvika's hand in true-life, Celka described the Yestrab Okhrana. "I'm going to get us closer. I think the imbuement creates a feeling of awe."

Hedvika frowned at her, glancing back at the dais as though she struggled to turn away from the Stormhawk's speech. But she cut Celka a nod and followed as Celka wove them through the crowd.

When Celka neared, the disguised Yestrab Okhrana

narrowed their eyes. Celka's pulse pounded over the Stormhawk's amplified voice, and she returned her attention to the dais. After a moment, the Okhrana relaxed, their gaze going distant the way Hedvika's did when she focused on imitating Celka's core nuzhda.

True-life gaze still on the dais, Celka edged back into sousednia.

Based on the Okhrana's wavery shape, they were only storm-touched, so they shouldn't be able to see Celka studying them from the neighboring reality. Celka hoped it was true. She didn't want to rely on Gerrit's protection if she got caught studying the Stormhawk's classified imbuements.

When the Okhrana didn't immediately call her out, Celka breathed a little easier. The awe-imbuement's nuzhda cloak spread outward from the Okhrana's hand. Celka dared a glance in true-life, discovering a thick gold ring. Unlike the Okhrana's modest costume, even unimbued, the ring would be worth a fortune.

In her circus back lot, the ring glowed a bright, shifting puzzle, the blue of a summer sky smudging into a rich purple before twisting to the orange-red of sturdy roof tiles. Concentrating on the nuzhda made it a little easier to ignore her rabid enthusiasm for the Stormhawk, and Celka studied the imbuement's flickering lightshow for a minute, hoping it would give her insight into the weaves. But she'd never had to *understand* old magic before.

Sure, she'd activated the simple, Category One combat knife that Pa had left her, and the concealment imbuement Gerrit had brought into the circus. But activating an imbuement was so much simpler than creating one. You just had to pull against the right kind of nuzhda, then connect that nuzhda to the imbuement.

That said, Celka wasn't clear *how* she'd connect to this

imbuement. The glow of Pa's old knife or Gerrit's concealment stone had coalesced, creating a single point that had called to her, tugging harder the more she pulled against the right kind of nuzhda. Connecting to those imbuements had been intuitive.

Even when Gerrit held an imbuement active, like the Okhrana was doing now, the activation points had glowed like pinpricks, the nuzhda bleeding from them into Gerrit like ink into water. She sought those points on the Okhrana's hand, squinting in sousednia, expecting the twisting blue-orange-purple to sharpen. It didn't.

Except... there. A point coalesced then vanished again, and Celka shook her head, wondering if she'd imagined it. The multi-hued glow shifted, tangling and untangling, rippling—not like a normal imbuement's base rhythm, but like the whole fabric of the imbuement was alive.

She squeezed her eyes shut. Maybe she was going about this wrong.

Celka didn't pull on nuzhdi by imagining the right color, but by reaching into her past for the visceral memory that embodied that need. The Okhrana had draped the imbuement over yet another section of the crowd, and Celka tugged on Hedvika's hand, pulling her along as she moved to the Okhrana's other side. She noticed, as she did it, that the imbuement's active glow touched the Okhrana only where they wore the ring—the nuzhda cloak arced up from their hand and outward across the crowd. When they shifted which section of the crowd they draped in its magic, they moved their hand, as if careful the nuzhda didn't touch them.

She didn't blame them. Bad enough that they had to pull against some weirdly complex nuzhda to activate the thing; how much worse would it be if they also felt like licking the Stormhawk's boots? Though, Celka realized, they might want to anyway—they were Yestrab Okhrana, after all, fervent believers trained to trade their lives for the Stormhawk's.

She shuddered, putting a little space between herself and the Okhrana. *They won't realize what you're doing*, she told herself. Though if she kept circling them to stay within the imbuement's active zone, they'd be an idiot not to. Which meant she needed to make the best of this opportunity to—

Celka's focus on sousednia slipped, her attention snapping back to the Stormhawk like falling from the high wire.

"Since you entrusted me with power, Bourshkanya's industrial economy has grown from one of the weakest on the continent, to amongst the strongest." His powerful voice echoed through her chest, making her stand taller. "We strengthen ourselves not to threaten others, but to embrace the greatness of Bourshkanyan spirit."

Celka leaned forward, wishing she could throw herself down at the Stormhawk's feet. Bourshkanya was *great* because the Stormhawk was *great*. How had she ever thought to fight him? He was power made manifest. Without his leadership, Bourshkanya would crumble.

Her stomach churned as she remembered coming here to uncover his weaknesses. How could she possibly want to assassinate him? How could she *dare*?

Beneath these thoughts, a small part of Celka resisted. It shouted that she faced a despot, a villain. But that voice came out a whisper.

Struggling to understand, Celka dragged herself into sousednia. She needed to silence the voice—*she needed to listen to it*.

The air pressed close, a stunning blue cut with orange and violet like an aurora's winter display. Celka's chest squeezed and she wavered, disoriented as sousednia blurred, two different realities struggling for dominance: one the practice wire rigged across the back lot, the other the big top's performers' entrance. In the first, the air smelled vaguely like cabbage and horses, but that sousednia was fading, smudging away until she stood beside Grandfather, his dry, calloused palm in hers as they gazed upwards, watching the trapeze artists perform a perfect catch. The air felt charged beneath the rippling blue-orange-violet sky, a thunderstorm's sharpness filling Celka's lungs along with the tearing, spitting sound of a lightning strike on a jutting storm tower—the air alight before thunder drowned the world.

Over the circus band, the Stormhawk's voice boomed. He could have been a Storm God, himself, he was so magnificent.

Celka's grip on sousednia slipped, and she stared at the dais in the Stormhawk's thrall.

Slowly, like water draining into sand, her awe faded. The Stormhawk's speech still commanded her attention, but she no longer yearned to reveal all her traitorous plans.

Blinking, she swam back into sousednia to find the back lot smelling of cabbage and horses. If she squinted, she could make out trapeze artists flying above her and taste the sharp-fresh thrill of the thunderstorm, but it was fading. The blue-dominated nuzhda-glow still rippled the sky, but not so strong as when she'd started questioning her own treason.

Could the imbuement's spread be controlled—condensed into a stronger, pinpointed effect or opened into a broader, subtler one? The thought churned her stomach, and she barely managed to avoid looking over her shoulder at the Okhrana wielding the imbuement. Had they suspected her and deliberately hit her with the imbuement's full force? She glanced at Hedvika, wondering if her strazh had felt it, or if the Okhrana had focused specifically on her. Did she and Hedvika look suspicious? Celka in her factory-standard uniform still stinking of dye, Hedvika in tailored upper-class finery with gold bozhk bolts and a full rainbow of nuzhda competencies? Did they look like they'd stolen the uniforms?

Celka shoved aside the thought. Whether out of suspicion or happenstance, the Okhrana had given her an opportunity. That blast of awe had given her the scents she needed to tease out of the crowd. With its intensity diminished, she had a chance to understand how those elements fit together— because they did fit. The heart-stopping gasp of a trapeze artist's catch was looped into weaves that draped across a person's shoulders. Celka saw it now, the weaves repeated, looping across the crowd. They were complex, unlike anything she'd seen before, but they also made sense in a way Gerrit's weaves hadn't. The way her imbued pistol interfaced with its mage, these weaves infiltrated other peoples' perceptions.

Was that the trick? Did she just need to turn her own weaves outward?

The Stormhawk's speech receded as she concentrated more deeply on sousednia. These weaves carried a complexity that hers had lacked, but if she squinted, they almost... *almost* made sense.

By the time the rally ended, Celka's knees were weak with exhaustion. The square emptied out around them, and Celka leaned on Hedvika's shoulder. Once the Okhrana moved away, following the crowd as though they were just some innocent civilian, Celka dared ask her strazh what she had felt.

"There was a moment," Hedvika said, "when everything came into perfect clarity." She stared at the now-empty dais, wonder softening her expression. "We're so blessed to have such a powerful leader."

Celka nodded and, in the emotional imbuement's wake, it didn't even feel like a lie.

CHAPTER ELEVEN

ARTUR SAUNTERED INTO the parlor before dinner the night of the Stormhawk's rally, appraising Gerrit and Iveta with haughty insouciance. A major's star and bar glinted from his red shoulders, and he looked Iveta over before visibly dismissing her, turning his edged smile on Gerrit.

Gerrit tensed. Nothing good ever came after that smile.

"Brother." Artur sounded almost warm in his greeting. Then he slapped his hand down on Gerrit's back.

Gerrit stumbled under the force, vision bleaching in agony. He nearly cried out, but caught himself with a stifled gasp. Struggling to twist his expression back into stone, he straightened and made himself face his older brother.

"Done with your little vacation in the circus?" Artur asked before Gerrit could recover enough to speak.

Gerrit's back pulsed in pain in time with his heartbeat, but he looked Artur in the eye and said, "I learned to imbue magic absent from our world for decades, if that's what you mean." He made his tone neutral, as though this were just an ordinary conversation in an ordinary family. "What have you done this summer?"

Artur's lips tightened fractionally, and Gerrit prepared himself for another blow. Instead, Artur said, "Pity you needed a traitorous *civilian* to teach you how." The word dripped with contempt.

A hot defense of Celka leapt to his lips, but Gerrit swallowed it. Winning an argument with Artur was never an option; the goal was to survive it. "We all have our strengths." He tried to put hard finality in his tone.

Artur smirked, sweeping Gerrit in the same lazy assessment that had earlier dismissed Iveta. "Some more than others."

Before Gerrit could retort, the Yestrab Okhrana at the door stepped forward. "Dinner is served."

Their father was already seated at the head of a modest oval table. Place cards put Gerrit directly opposite him, at the table's foot, Iveta and Artur at his left and right hands. Gerrit stopped before his chair and, when the others had as well, snapped to attention. "All hail the Stormhawk!" The three spoke in almost perfect unison. Whatever their differences, they knew better than to disrespect their father.

The Stormhawk studied them each in turn, gaze lingering long on Gerrit, as though he could see straight to Gerrit's traitorous heart. Gerrit held his salute, keeping his attention on his father in true-life, ignoring the dozen Yestrab Okhrana with rippling sousedni-shapes.

As they'd entered the dining room, Gerrit had spotted a storm-blessed Okhrana amongst his father's guards, though she must have been strongly focused on true-life, keeping her sousedni-shape almost as translucent as a storm-touched bozhk's. Gerrit hoped it meant she wouldn't be paying close attention to sousednia but, more likely, she'd been angling for him not to notice her storm-blessing—the better to secretly observe him from sousednia during the meal. That she'd been stationed at his back was further evidence the Stormhawk wanted him watched. It made Gerrit's shoulders crawl.

Finally, the Stormhawk said, "Sit." Servants flooded in, bringing appetizers, filling glasses.

Gerrit made himself breathe.

When the servants had vanished, the Stormhawk raised his glass and said, "A toast. To family reunited." His voice carried pride but no warmth.

Gerrit raised his own glass, struggling to act honored that he was dining with a murderer. When his father drank, Gerrit touched his glass to his lips. He didn't drink alcohol often, and had no intention of dulling his faculties when a misstep could reveal his disloyalty.

When the Stormhawk dug into his herring salad, Gerrit edged cautiously into sousednia. Balancing his attention in both realities, he took a forkful of the salted herring with beets and sour cream while lifting his sousedni-gaze to the Okhrana just behind his father's right shoulder.

The guard rippled faintly violet with a walled-off protection nuzhda that matched access points in a shield slung across their back. They must be holding the nuzhda but not connecting it into the imbuement in order to minimize the wear and tear on the magic. They'd have trained to activate the imbuement at the slightest provocation.

Barely tasting his herring, Gerrit focused through the Okhrana's heat-shimmer, trying to gain a sense for the imbuement's purpose. Gold-bolt bozhk exams had demanded similar analysis, requiring an accurate description of an imbuement's capabilities within a limited time. But in testing, he'd always been alone with the object and the examiner, only a single imbuement in the room. He hadn't counted on how much more difficult it would be with dozens of imbuements drumming their competing rhythms.

Protection typically sounded to him like the scrape of a dull knife on thick, hempen rope, and Gerrit listened for that, finding it echoed around the room—faster or slower, louder or faint depending on the strength of the imbuement. He stabbed another forkful of herring in frustration, wishing he dared attempt a sousedni-dislocation that would bring him closer to the imbuement in question. But he couldn't risk it—especially beneath the gaze of a storm-blessed Okhrana.

Instead, Gerrit made himself draw slow, deep breaths, trying to tunnel his focus down to the shield, letting the rest of his alpine clearing fall away until the shield filled his awareness. The hurried scrape of dull steel on rope took on a resonance, bleeding the edges of his sousednia toward the panicked memory he used to pull upon a protection nuzhda. Gerrit refused to let the memory coalesce, instead feeling into the rhythm even as he studied the shield's rippling nuzhda glow. The imbuement was powerful—Category Four, at least—and he wished he had a notebook to draw up a detailed weave description. But he didn't need to understand the weaves well enough to reproduce them; he just needed to figure out what they did.

That understanding came slowly, in the angle of the brightest pulse in relation to the base rhythm; in the shape of the expansion weaves that provided an area effect. This imbuement created a barrier of some sort, its effective area tenfold larger than the shield's surface. Deeper in the weave, tight knots of nuzhda would absorb sudden, point-force impacts, though they'd be vulnerable to a sustained, heavier force. This shield, then, would protect from bullets or swords, but wouldn't save his father in an artillery barrage, especially if they could bring the building down on him.

"You haven't attended a rally in some time," the Stormhawk said, and Gerrit realized with a start that his father was talking to him. Gerrit looked up from his nearly empty plate of herring salad as the Stormhawk asked, "What did you think?"

Gerrit had watched the rally from a second story window above the dais, Iveta at his side, whispering commentary. Still half-focused on uncovering weaknesses in his father's defenses, Gerrit's first thought was, *You preyed on the crowd's hopes and fears. You gave them platitudes when they need real change.* He clamped down on the thought. He needed to get this right. "I was impressed at how you enflamed the crowd's passion. You shaped their patriotism into a drive to defend Bourshkanya—while at the same time warning foreign observers that they not push us into battle. You skillfully implied that if there was war, the other nations would have no one to blame but themselves."

"Implied? You don't believe it?" the Stormhawk asked.

Careful, Gerrit could almost hear Iveta whisper. Not that he needed the warning. Any question his father posed was a double-edged sword. "I believe," Gerrit said, "that Bourshkanya is a great nation. And that our borders were once far larger." He scraped up the last of his salted herring, the plate bloody from the beets.

The Stormhawk grunted, waving servants forward to clear their plates.

In the bustle of their next course's arrival, Gerrit returned to sousednia, discovering another protection imbuement carried by the bozhk Okhrana at the Stormhawk's other flank. He couldn't make the object out clearly—something rectangular, carried in a plain wooden case across the Okhrana's back like a rifle. This guard held a protection nuzhda active, like the other Okhrana, but hadn't connected to the imbuement.

As Gerrit attempted to bring the individual weaves into focus, Iveta spoke. "I'm surprised you didn't address Kralovice's current unrest. The protests during the rally—"

"Were dealt with," Artur interrupted.

"—indicate a growing systemic problem," Iveta continued as though he hadn't spoken.

Gerrit tried to maintain his focus on the protection imbuement, but his thoughts slipped to the rally when, midway through the Stormhawk's speech, several dozen people in work clothes had converged at the back of the crowd, unfurling placards demanding increased wages and reduced hours. Gerrit hadn't been able to hear their chanting above the Stormhawk's magically amplified voice, but Iveta had speculated they were metalworkers. She'd had reports of them agitating in Kralovice even before their arrival.

The Tayemstvoy had converged on the protestors, and Gerrit had expected blood to fly from their truncheons, but the protestors had gone peacefully. Gerrit had hoped—naively, it seemed—that that had been the end of it.

"A problem," Artur said, "that the Tayemstvoy are more than equipped to deal with. Those workers will keep their heads down after today."

Gerrit's jaw felt hard as steel hearing his brother's smug dismissal of what had, at best, been a brutal beating of people just trying to make their demands heard. He faced the sharp-edged slice of holodets on his plate, the jellied meat, which he normally enjoyed, turning his stomach. He made himself take a forkful. *You have to play along*, he told himself fiercely. *You're not here to critique your brother's abuse of power—or your father's.* He needed to unravel the Stormhawk's defenses and, so far, that was proving more of a challenge than he'd expected.

"*Those* workers may no longer be a problem," Iveta said, as though the cruel edge to Artur's tone was unremarkable. "But Kralovice has other disaffected metalworkers and, across Bourshkanya, industrial output is in decline."

Gerrit tried to push the conversation aside, returning to

the protection imbuement slung across the Okhrana's back. Another high-Category imbuement, with its own expansion weaves. Their design was subtly different from the shield's but, when Gerrit pushed past the flourishes particular to the imbuement mage who'd created the object, he found expansion weaves superficially like those in the shield. The deeper weaves, however, were bottom-heavy loops, each far larger than the tight knots in the shield. They appeared almost floppy at first inspection, though energy feeds like thorns sprouted from them. Gerrit puzzled over them, trying to keep one ear on the dinner conversation.

"This," Artur said, "is exactly why we need a clear, brutal demonstration of State power. We've grown *soft*, and the maggots think that makes us easy meat."

The thorns weren't energy feeds, Gerrit realized with a start—not like he was used to thinking of them. They didn't channel energy between other parts of the weave, but rather dumped physical energy—heat or pressure, maybe—out of the weave structure entirely. They must lock into the ground, somehow. Oh, that made sense. They could—

"Gerrit"—the Stormhawk startled him from sousednia—"what do you think?"

Panic tightened Gerrit's chest, and he thought frantically to recall the details of the discussion he'd nearly lost track of in his study. Artur, exhorting their father to a violent demonstration to curtail worker protests. He swallowed hard. Agreeing with Artur would be safest, but ran counter to everything Gerrit believed. But would any other response satisfy his father?

Iveta had talked about peacetime imbuement applications, and Gerrit thought she might have been about to disagree with Artur's brutal stance, but even so, she was likely a long way from Gerrit's newfound sympathies for Bourshkanya's hardworking labor class. And even if Iveta did oppose Artur in this, Gerrit could only guess that the Stormhawk fell closer to Artur's position on challenges to his authority.

Gerrit needed to cement his loyalty during this dinner and get his family's attention off of him so he could continue searching for weaknesses in his father's defenses. And yet Filip's insistence that his father had listened to him—that the Stormhawk might finally respect him enough to consider his opinions—made Gerrit want to do more than toe the oppressive party line. Maybe he would fail to find a weakness the resistance could exploit. Wasn't it his duty to use his presence in this room to try and make Bourshkanya better?

"I think workers are starving," Gerrit said before he could talk himself out of it.

Artur's expression darkened, and the Stormhawk's attention sharpened like a rain of ice.

Gerrit rushed to find an analogy that would hold them—and make his nearly treasonous statement palatable. "If you feed a horse too little, you can't expect it to pull a plow. If you beat it, it might struggle onward, but the work you'll get from it will pale in comparison to that of a healthy animal. This past month, I moved invisibly amongst our people. They are as hardworking and determined as you credited them in your speech today, Father. But they are also hungry."

"Hardworking?" Artur sneered. "The rabble are lazy and spendthrift. They see the regime's wealth and want our comforts without any understanding of our responsibilities. Give them more, and they'll just—"

"It would be simple enough to evaluate." Iveta tipped her attention to their father. "Audit the cost of food and living quarters along with the weekly take-home pay of laborers across the nation. But use *independent* auditors—with no connection to the factory and mill owners, so we can ensure accurate information."

"How like you, Iveta," Artur sneered, "to propose emptying our treasury to discover what we already know. The laboring classes cannot be trusted to—"

"We could begin in a handful of locations where factories have already reported shortfalls," Iveta said. "Spot-test the problem. Easy enough to divert a few bureaucrats."

Sweating beneath his formal uniform, Gerrit turned back to his meat jelly. When the Stormhawk allowed Iveta and Artur to continue sparring, Gerrit shifted his attention once more to the protection imbuement. Its weaves came together like a kick in the chest, and Gerrit realized it perfectly addressed the weakness he'd discovered in the shield's magic. This imbuement, which he now recognized as a sturdy, unremarkable board inside its tooled-leather case, would hold up tonnes of stone or brick as easily as Gerrit lifted his fork. If they brought the entire building down on the Stormhawk's head, his Okhrana need merely activate this imbuement to create a pocket of perfect safety.

Gerrit felt his teeth grinding.

"If they manage to concoct some shortfall," Artur said, "what then? You order factory owners—who, need I remind you, sister, are loyal, regime supporters—to raise wages? You'd prioritize the rabble over the strength of Father's regime backing? How does that benefit Bourshkanya?"

"With sufficient evidence," Iveta said, "I'm sure they'll come around. If they're really so loyal as you say."

Another time, Gerrit might have enjoyed Iveta's barbed smile or the way Artur's lip twitched as he realized he'd walked into her rhetorical trap. But dinner was progressing too quickly, and Gerrit had dozens of imbuements left to study—for all the good it would do. He struggled to hold off a swooping hopelessness. Even the two imbuements he'd studied so far made the Stormhawk practically unkillable. If he drew a gun right now, he might manage to shoot his father before the Okhrana at his flank could activate the shield—maybe, though Gerrit wouldn't guarantee it. In a more exposed situation, he suspected the Okhrana would hold the shield active, reducing even that slight window of opportunity.

But Gerrit had thought his future bleak before and had wrested it back under his control. He wouldn't give up so easily.

CHAPTER TWELVE

LIGHTNING STRUCK THE train, blinding in the storm's looming darkness. Sparks rained from the railcar's metal sides, and a metallic bitterness soured Filip's mouth. He flipped his belt knife over his fingers, back and forth, back and forth, struggling to clear his mind.

The region's storm speakers had predicted that today's bozhskyeh storm would break late in the afternoon, leaving the imbuement platoon plenty of time to rendezvous with Gerrit and Iveta in Chodsky Uzhezd. Instead, outside the railcar, lightning already arced through the clouds. The storm speakers had been wrong.

It shouldn't have mattered—storm timing was hard to predict—and normally, the mistake would have rolled off Filip like water from an oilskin coat. But he'd tossed restlessly in his bunk last night, the strazh bond that connected him to Gerrit thin as spider silk. He'd tried to convince himself that Gerrit haring off to dine with the Stormhawk was a sign that Gerrit had heard his arguments; but that wouldn't have required bringing Celka to the rally beforehand. Gerrit had some plot in mind, maybe even direct orders from the resistance, and fear had raked nightmares across what little sleep Filip had managed.

He'd given up well before dawn, climbing to the Storm Guard Fortress's isolated prayer tower to make his obeisance—and to pray that for once in his life, Gerrit listened to him.

Today's early bozhskyeh storm left Filip's shoulders crawling, like Tayemstvoy lurked around every corner, watching for Gerrit's disloyalty. Filip grimaced at his hubris to think that the Storm Gods had shifted this storm as a warning, but he couldn't shake the chill down his spine.

When coppery lightning lashed the sky, Filip gasped as though at a lover's nails skating down his back. He fumbled the knife.

"Gods' Breath," Masha Yedlichka whispered, and Filip turned to the storm-blessed artillery lieutenant. She wasn't looking at him, but staring out the window—at the exact spot where Filip had seen the coppery flash.

Stomach churning, Filip turned back to the sky. More lightning licked the clouds, but it looked different—actinic white—and while it forked beautifully, it stirred nothing in him. "What about that one?" he asked, after its thunder had faded.

"No," said Captain Rostislav Havel, the other storm-blessed bozhk who would fill out Celka's squad. Filip knew Havel primarily by reputation; he'd graduated from the Storm Guard Academy in Filip's first year, but his entitled arrogance had cast a long shadow. His family was old nobility, their massive assets strengthened by shrewd investments—and support of the Stormhawk—during the war. Why Gerrit's sister had put Havel in Celka's squad, Filip had no idea; and Filip didn't envy Dbani the job of being his strazh.

Masha, Filip knew better. She'd been two years ahead of him in the academy, and they'd spent a couple of years on the same squad. She was thoughtful and more technically-minded than most, which had led to a number of spirited discussions over the years. Deliberate and meticulous, not to mention powerfully storm-blessed, Filip expected she'd be one of the first to imbue. No surprise, then, that Yanek had been assigned as her strazh.

As storm-blessed, it made sense that Masha and Havel could distinguish Gods' Breath from regular lightning. But Filip was storm-*touched*, unable to see sousednia. He couldn't imbue. Bozhskyeh storms didn't call to him. He shouldn't be able to spot Gods' Breath—and he'd never been able to before. Except...

No. He shut down the thought.

Maybe his prayers this morning had given him a sensitivity. Maybe the Storm Gods really were trying to warn him.

He swallowed hard, not sure that was better.

Yanek, seated next to Filip, bumped his shoulder. "You all right?" he asked, low enough that the rain hissing on the window and the clack of train tires nearly drowned his voice.

"Fine." Filip sheathed his belt knife; a strange buzz in his fingertips made the blade too dangerous. "Just worried how the storm will affect the platoon." The words came easy, not entirely a lie. Though the imbuement platoon was Gerrit's, Filip was his second-in-command, tasked with the training and preparedness of the platoon's strazh mages and responsible for giving orders in Gerrit's absence. Two of the platoon's four squads were on the train today: Red Squad—except for Celka and Hedvika, who were safe at the fortress—and Yellow Squad. The strazhi were all technically capable of building strazh weaves, though Yanek was the only one Filip would trust to ground Gerrit. Dbani seemed solid, though they'd been pulled into active service only after Filip had gone after Gerrit in the circus, so they hadn't trained together. Yellow Squad's strazhi were all green, their weaves coming together only after long minutes of effort. A bozhskyeh storm would make those weaves more challenging to build and easier to break.

Another bolt of coppery lightning snapped Filip's head up like someone had yanked on his spine. Yearning tightened his chest.

"That one was Gods' Breath," Masha said.

Filip scrubbed a hand across his jaw, barely avoiding continuing the motion to rub the back of his neck. When he'd first stood in a bozhskyeh storm, Gods' Breath had blinded him. What had changed that it now drew him like a moth to flame?

In Chodsky Uzhezd, the imbuement platoon deployed inside the train station, the bolt-hawks spreading out to secure the exits and drive back onlookers. As Filip led the imbuement squads to Gerrit, his vision smeared just as thunder cracked overhead. He stumbled but recovered, even as worry lodged like a splinter in his mind. Was he so underslept that he'd be a liability to Gerrit in this storm?

He shook the concern. He just needed to focus.

Gerrit acknowledged Filip's salute and called the imbuement squads to attention. Filip tried to read some hint of what had transpired during his family dinner but, except for underlying tension that could have come from the storm, Gerrit spoke with confidence and authority, reminding the storm-blessed mages to hold their sousednia empty of all nuzhdi, as they'd begun practicing with their strazhi. "Your most important skill is control during a bozhskyeh storm," Gerrit said. "Whether or not you imbue today, if you keep control, I'll consider this exercise a success."

Somehow, it was exactly the right thing to say. The tense postures of the imbuement mages relaxed, and the strazhi straightened with determination. Filip hid his smile behind a neutral expression, but when Gerrit turned to him, tipped his head in approval. This was the leader he knew his best friend could be.

"I'll imbue combat outside with Sub-Lieutenant Cizek," Gerrit continued. "I'm working with experimental weaves, so we'll work on the other side of the square to minimize the risk in case something goes wrong. Watch us from sousednia as best you can. Once we're finished, I'll demonstrate the hunger imbuement you'll all get a chance to attempt on turnips. Any questions?"

"Why hunger?" Masha asked. "Our strongest affinities are with combat."

"It's a good question," Gerrit said, including the rest of the platoon in his response, as they'd likely all been thinking it. "Your most difficult imbuement will be your first. While you're learning to imbue, you'll make mistakes that result in failure. That may mean your weaves fail to crystalize, leaving the object inert. But you're just as likely to overfill or improperly construct your weaves, which can make the object unstable. Sometimes, it'll explode—both physically and in sousednia. Exploding turnips are far less dangerous than exploding weapons. And hunger burn-in won't make you a liability to yourself or the platoon."

"Just the mess hall," Yanek quipped.

Gerrit quirked his lip in a half smile rather than reprimanding him. "A risk I'm much more willing to take."

The squads chuckled, and Gerrit caught Filip's gaze, the tilt of his chin ordering him to fall in as they headed for the train station's main entrance.

Bolt-hawks handed them metal-topped storm helmets, padded enough to protect from small hail, and Filip buckled his on in place of his cap. He strapped on storm-gauntlets before releasing their grounding lines to unroll, creating a safe path to ground for electrical lightning. Even so, Filip disliked stepping outside beneath a storm. It made him feel cizii—foolish and imprudent in his disregard for the Storm Gods' power. He buried the discomfort and strode at Gerrit's flank into the driving rain.

Out in the square, the grounding lines' spiked chains caught and tugged on weeds growing between paving stones. He tried not to take it as a sign that he shouldn't be out here. Sleet, what was wrong with him? He'd strazhed beneath open skies before; it hadn't been a problem.

"How was your family dinner?" Filip asked as Gerrit directed them to the howitzer unlimbered in the center of the square. Rain drummed a cacophony on his metal-topped helmet, though the air seemed oddly dry with the faint, reassuring scent of old books.

Gerrit's jaw tightened. "Delightful as always." An edge seemed to imply more than his usual family strife.

"I'm glad you went," Filip said, deliberately neutral.

The glance Gerrit cut him said, *you really shouldn't be*, though he smoothed the expression away fast—as if he could fool Filip. "I'm sure it won't be the last." A dark undercurrent to his words carried the stink of diesel fumes and the thud of fists on flesh.

The light from another flash of Gods' Breath saturated Filip's vision, washing the gray square improbably in autumn sunlight. He faltered, taunts and insults echoing distantly—yet somehow drowning out the rain.

"I took your advice, over dinner." Gerrit's voice startled Filip back to Chodsky Uzhezd. They'd reached the howitzer, and Gerrit spoke facing the artillery piece, turned so no one in the train station would be able to read his lips. "I spoke to my father about starving workers."

Surprised, Filip asked, "Did he listen?"

Gerrit's grimace was just a slight tightening around the eyes. "He might have. At least enough to investigate wages and cost of living. Iveta backed me—or I backed her? Both, I guess."

"That's great." Maybe he'd been wrong to read the early storm as a warning. Perhaps, it heralded good news.

"Yeah." But Gerrit's expression was grim. Cutting a glance toward the train station, he said, "Let's teach these bozhki how to imbue."

Filip nodded, holding his attention on his best friend despite the coppery Gods' Breath overhead. Gerrit might not have believed him about Celka, but he had listened. If the Stormhawk acted in response to Gerrit's suggestions, maybe Gerrit would abandon the resistance's suicidal lure.

When Gerrit pressed both hands flat on the howitzer's barrel, Filip rested his palm on the back of Gerrit's neck and focused sideways, struggling to tease out details of Gerrit's growing combat nuzhda. A great clamor of blows erupted around him, tangled in air too cold for the summer thunderstorm. As Gerrit began to shape his combat weaves, Filip worked to discern purpose and form out of the growing rhythm.

A pattern emerged fitfully, playing in the thud of wood on flesh, in cries of pain. Filip listened and kept his own breathing slow, the Song of Calming humming in the back of his mind as he tasted the synesthesia around his friend. The rhythm's complexity fit with a Category Three imbuement, but the clamor of blows and grit of motorcar exhaust overwhelmed it.

When Gerrit signaled he was done, Filip said, "Your nuzhda's too strong."

Gerrit tensed beneath his hand. At first nothing changed, then the chaos subsided until the rhythm stood out clearly, the size of the nuzhda matched to the weaves' complexity.

"Good." Filip glanced back at the train station, only then registering the bruising sting of hailstones as big as the last joint of his thumb. He opened his mouth to shout for the strazhi to pay attention as he built his own weaves, but his vision blurred, the scent of motorcar exhaust from Gerrit's combat nuzhda twisting into the crunch of autumn leaves.

Rather than fight it, Filip turned the nuzhda's momentum to his advantage, following the chill of autumn into the memory of—

—*skidding to a stop, the crackle of dry leaves giving away his position. A younger Storm Guard cadet is already on the ground, just a glimpse between the legs of their older tormentors. Several glance Filip's direction before dismissing him—Filip alone, unarmed, younger than most of them, though older than their victim, who's lifting their head, blood bright like Tayemstvoy shoulders streaming from their nose. Filip's pulse hammers in his ears, telling him to run, fetch an instructor, but he doesn't move. The cadets' voices tumble over one another with insults and goading. If the scrawny child would just stay down, the older cadets would kick them in the ribs a few times and lose interest, unwilling to risk punishment for marginal amusement, convinced they'd cowed a member of a competing squad.*

But the child doesn't stay down, won't—Filip knows it even though he's barely met Gerrit Siroteh, new to the academy, freshly assigned to Filip's squad amidst their grumbling at being saddled with the year's weakest and youngest recruit.

Snarling, Gerrit launches to their feet.

Filip doesn't think. He sprints into the fray, attacking the cadets at Gerrit's flank. Then they're fighting back-to-back, but the cadets were right to mock the younger child. Gerrit has had some training but they're small, their technique sloppy. Filip fights harder—for both of them—not knowing why he's taking blows meant for the younger cadet, only certain that it's important.

When Gerrit goes down and tries to get back up, Filip pushes them into the dirt. "Stay down," he hisses, stumbling beneath blows. He's good, but he's not good enough, and when Gerrit miraculously listens, Filip dives for a break between the older cadets, fighting half a meter past before they close on him, ignoring Gerrit for the more entertaining target. The cadets know better than to maim, but their blows hurt, and before Filip knows what's happening he's the one chewing dirt, pushing himself stupidly up, inviting more blows to protect a cadet he barely knows.

Clinging to the taste of blood in his mouth, Filip shifted his focus, reaching for another memory nearly as fuzzed with youth. Reaching out, he—

—wraps his hands over his sister Lenka's larger ones, trying to stop them from shaking so badly. She cups a handful of soil, pale white roots tangling through the dark earth. The sprout shakes like it's buffeted by stormwinds, and Lenka snarls, frustrated. But Filip keeps his hands wrapped around hers, singing the Song of Calming and fixing in his mind a vision of her from before she broke with a combat nuzhda during her silver-bolt test.

They've already dug the hole for this seedling, and Filip steers her hands toward it, head splitting from how hard he's believing the impossibility of her old self. For an instant, her gaze focuses on him. Confused, she blinks, snarl fading.

Locked into a fugue of both moments, Filip concentrated on the Song of Calming, slipping its soothing notes into both fugues like the finest thread. He stitched the disparate memories together, knitting his combat nuzhda seamlessly into protection. That shifting nuzhda flowed from his hand gripping the back of Gerrit's neck, down Filip's arm and body, through his feet and down into the earth. At Filip's hand, the taunts of older cadets and the pain of fists and boots landing blows meshed perfectly with the brutality of Gerrit's combat nuzhda. Traversing Filip's body, however, combat's violence edged toward protection's hope and anguish before plunging into the ground at his feet, the soil beneath paving stones like the rich dark earth of Lenka's garden, where Filip had toiled week after week to return her to herself. Beneath him, the earth's vastness swallowed the Song of Calming and the last, wriggling tendrils of his protection nuzhda.

Strazh weaves complete, Filip walled off the entwined nuzhdi, envisioning garden walls of old stone covered with waxy-leafed vines. Goldcrests hopped and flitted through the vines, the tiny birds' twittering calls shielding Filip from the Gods' Breath that would burn through his weaves if Gerrit made a mistake.

"Ready," he told Gerrit—Kladivo or Siroteh, his family name had never mattered. As Gerrit pulled Gods' Breath down into himself, Filip held, unflinching, as storm energy lit his best friend. The coppery flame buzzed across Gerrit's skin, shifting crimson as his weaves funneled power into the howitzer. Flickers of storm energy rebounded off imperfect connections, lashing up Gerrit's arms, burning into Filip's hand.

He gritted his teeth, but the pain was nothing like Bludov. A mere trickle of storm energy burned into his strazh weaves and quickly faded.

When Gerrit straightened, solemn in his accomplishment, the howitzer flickered crimson behind him. Then Gerrit grimaced, noticing the hail. "Let's get inside," he said.

Filip nodded, focusing sideways to check Gerrit's core grounding as he followed his tvoortse over hail-slick paving stones back toward the train station. He expected to hear the howl of icy wind and feel the chill warmth of winter sun around Gerrit, and he did, but tangling with that, he caught the spicy warmth of chicken paprikash, and his stomach rumbled.

It wasn't yet noon, and he'd eaten a full breakfast in the officer's mess. Were some of the storm-blessed in the imbuement platoon pulling on a hunger nuzhda already, overeager or out of control? Beneath the mouth-watering scent, Filip heard the dull thud his fist had made on the testing room door, heard the rawness in his own voice as he screamed to be let out, to be given a bowl of the stew whose scent wafted, tantalizing, beneath the cell door.

But as Filip entered the train station and two bolt-hawks shut the doors behind him and Gerrit, the scent faded, like his instructors taking the stew away because he'd again failed to pull hard enough on a hunger nuzhda. Keeping the frown from his face, he leaned close to Gerrit as he pulled off his storm gauntlets. "Is anyone pulling against hunger?"

He handed his storm gear to one of the bolt-hawks while Gerrit assessed the platoon. "No," he said. "Why?"

"You don't feel it?" Filip asked, realizing he didn't anymore, either.

Gerrit shook his head minutely.

Could the nuzhda have come from Gerrit? Filip focused on his best friend, finding only the shush of blowing snow and the crunch of boots breaking through a scrim of ice into powder. "You feel grounded." But the phantom hunger nuzhda nagged at him. "Permission to step back outside?"

"Granted." Gerrit cut a glance toward the waiting squads. "I'll demonstrate the weave I want them to attempt. Will that be a problem?"

"Give me a minute?" Filip asked.

At Gerrit's nod, Filip stepped outside, glad for the building's shelter. He pulled the door closed behind him and, even before he shifted his attention sideways, he felt it. No—heard it. Singing.

Holding his breath, he listened. The hail had faded to a misting rain and, distant, Filip caught the stuttering rhythm of the Song of Feeding. As he shifted his focus sideways, the Song, rather than fading, intensified until he caught snatches of the chorus. He reached automatically for his storm pendant, pulling it out from beneath his shirt, the brass warm from the heat of his skin, seeming to pulse with the desperate rhythm of his fist pounding the testing room door in time with the Song. The scent of chicken paprikash swelled, and he scanned the skyline past the square, seeking—there—a storm tower's jutting spire.

Suddenly, the distant singing made sense. As in scripture, the congregation must have come together around donated food. In small miracles of old, the people sang the Song of Feeding, gathered together, building the resonance that would imbue to feed their needy.

Filip's tension faded and, his back to duty and the imbuement platoon, he smiled. He rubbed his thumb across his storm pendant, no time to charge it for a proper prayer. "May I feed those who are hungry," he whispered the traditional Feeding prayer, hoping the congregation would succeed. Then he ducked back inside, feeling lighter than he had in days.

Inside the train station, Gerrit demonstrated his weaves, and the rhythm of his hunger nuzhda built, strong and focused. From everything Filip had read and learned in storm temple, community miracles were slow, low-Category imbuements, requiring the entire congregation in focused Song, sometimes for hours. They might achieve a doubling of the nutrition in their food, or save someone's life with a healing miracle. The imbuements of trained mages were like aeroplanes compared to donkey carts, and here, Filip had a job to do.

He reported his conclusions to Gerrit, then strazhed for him as he imbued a weak, Category One hunger imbuement into a turnip. Overflowed storm energy barely pricked Filip's palm and, when Gerrit finished, he called Masha up, handed her a turnip, and ordered everyone back. Gerrit had allowed the imbuement squads to cluster around to better watch while he'd imbued, but he wasn't risking them to Masha's untested capabilities.

Standing a little apart from the squads while Masha hunched over her turnip, struggling to pull against a hunger nuzhda, Filip told Gerrit, "You're a good leader."

Gerrit turned to him with a start, the hint of a frown tightening his brows as though he wasn't sure if the compliment was genuine. Filip nodded minutely to say that he was. "Thanks." Gerrit sounded off-balance. He focused back on Masha, but Filip could feel his attention lingering. "It feels good," Gerrit admitted, low so as not to be overheard. "Especially with hunger. Something I know can help people."

The innocent remark sent a chill down Filip's spine, reminding him too much of Gerrit's vehemence in the woods: their imbuements could help people, but the Stormhawk wanted only weapons. "It's smart starting them with hunger." Though it would be difficult. Even Masha was struggling. Everyone in the platoon had grown up privileged, their bellies always full except during testing and fasts for the Feeding Miracles.

"At least Iveta understands that," Gerrit said, voice tight.

Masha completed her weaves, and Yanek built his own, more capable with hunger than Masha. Still, by the time his weaves were ready, Masha's had begun to destabilize. She got them back under control, but pulled too weakly on the storm. Gods' Breath struck her, but barely skated over her skin. At least the turnip would still be edible, if no more nutritious than it had begun.

Her jaw was tight while Yanek ensured her core grounding,

her frustration palpable as she returned to stand with the rest of the squad. Gerrit assured her that failure was part of learning, that she'd be better equipped to succeed next time, and called Havel forward. His imbuement proceeded similarly, though he didn't even manage to call down Gods' Breath, his weaves and Dbani's coming only after long struggle and destabilizing too quickly.

Filip expected Gerrit's calm to fracture at their failures, but instead, he congratulated them on their control, on building weaves during a bozhskyeh storm. "You'll get there," he told them. "I have complete confidence."

But while Gerrit remained an impeccable commander, Filip's own control crumbled. As one of the Yellow Squad mages yanked too hard on Gods' Breath and exploded their turnip, Filip yearned forward, barely keeping himself from reaching for the coppery flame. His mouth watered, and he found himself fantasizing about tender meat in creamy, red-pepper sauce. He could almost taste the perfectly chewy dumplings.

While another of Yellow Squad's storm-blessed stepped up, Yanek nudged Filip with his elbow. "You're sparking," he whispered.

Filip frowned, struggling to concentrate on the train station. He wasn't a mundane to be overwhelmed by emotion in a storm, but Yanek wasn't far off; whatever was happening, Filip wasn't in control. He swallowed hard, but still tasted paprikash's rich flavor. "How's Masha doing?"

"She's not used to failure," Yanek said. "She'll be all right."

Filip felt Yanek's gaze and the unasked question in it. *Will you?*

He wished he knew how to answer.

CHAPTER THIRTEEN

CELKA PUNCHED THE pad Hedvika held, wishing it wasn't between her and her strazh's face. She hit harder, her knuckles sore despite their wrapping, her wrists aching. Teeth bared, she threw her weight behind each punch, as if the pad was one of the Tayemstvoy beating Pa.

"Wait!" Celka stumbled as she pulled a punch just short of the bag. "Wait. My sousednia's wrong." She retreated a pace, then two, even as every instinct screamed at her to *keep fighting*, to shove the pad aside and hit Hedvika. Neither of them wore their uniform jackets or long-sleeved uniform shirts, but Hedvika was still a soldier, an enemy bozhk and even if she didn't have red shoulders, she reported to them.

Celka shook her head, struggling to focus on the forest clearing. The grass was trampled from their boots—they'd circled the space as the shadows moved throughout the day. *You're safe*, Celka told herself as Hedvika tossed the pad aside.

"What should your sousednia look like?" Hedvika asked, and Celka struggled to strip away the menace in her voice. *You're just hearing the combat-warping.*

But blood flew from Tayemstvoy truncheons and Pa fell beneath their blows. Celka balled her hands into fists, seeking a weapon, seeking a target. "A high wire," she said, but her voice didn't sound like her own, and the fir trees encircling her began to feel like a cell.

"That's right, a high wire," Hedvika said. "And your costume? You have the pocket square. Use it."

Celka struggled to think past the desperate need to fight. *Pocket square.* She repeated the words, reaching into her hip pocket and pulling out the too-soft green cloth. A small, animal noise escaped her as she held it up, and she stumbled another pace back from Hedvika, back from the Tayemstvoy beating Pa.

"Turn your back." Hedvika's voice was almost soothing— though Celka could too, too easily read it as cruel.

Clutching the pocket square, a bright emerald splash even in sousednia, Celka wrenched her gaze from Pa. She put her back to him without turning in the forest clearing.

In true-life, Hedvika held her hands out, glowing the blue of a summer sky. "Now find the practice wire." They'd learned through trial and error that Celka found her grounding faster if she started by climbing on the practice wire already in her combat-warped back lot. It didn't require changing sousednia and, on it, she usually found it easier to think past the haze of rage and desperation.

With the steel cable beneath her feet, Celka draped the green pocket square over her arm, trying to make its color bleed into her clothes, transforming them into gossamer and sequins. Shifting all of sousednia was a strain, but her clothing was not such a large thing to change.

Hedvika stood on the support post at the end of the practice wire, purple and green joining the blues chasing her wavery form. From within that nuzhda glow, the circus band fluted.

"The air smells of sawdust and horses," Hedvika said, those scents spooling from her. Practice had deepened Hedvika's understanding of Celka's core nuzhda, and her efforts to recreate it no longer stunk of cabbage and mud.

Closing her eyes on the forest, Celka reached for those scents and the fluting band. She felt into the wire beneath her feet and, at Hedvika's urging, imagined the dark expanse of the big top around her.

"Can you see the spectators far below?" Hedvika asked, and Celka dared open her eyes.

She wavered above the open space, her muscles stiff from fighting, from Vrana's blows as she dragged Celka away from Pa. But the spotlights caught the sequins on her bodice, and Celka's balance held. Far below, Army and Tayemstvoy soldiers filled the audience, watching too attentively, waiting for a misstep. Celka forced herself to face straight ahead, toward the platform where she could sense her family's outstretched arms, where Hedvika stood, heat-shimmer rippling with sawdust and open space. Ignoring the threat below, the threat she knew lurked around the cook tent outside, Celka fixed a performer's smile to her face and stepped along the wire.

Allowing true-life to track sousednia, Celka approached Hedvika with a measured step and took her strazh's hands. Contact sent a ripple of fear through her, the distant crack of blows sharpening before Celka shoved them aside. Hedvika might serve the State, but for now, she was Celka's ally.

"Describe it," Hedvika said, and Celka focused on sousednia, detailing the high wire and open space. She kept her gaze forward, afraid to check if the seats were still filled with red shoulders, afraid to tell Hedvika if they were. When she ran out of things to say, Hedvika squeezed her hands companionably. "You're getting faster."

Celka blinked into the clearing, chasing away sousednia to

focus on true-life. The shadows had lengthened into evening, their picnic dinner long-devoured, and the air had cooled enough to make the humidity almost cozy. She released Hedvika's hands and meticulously folded away her pocket square, fingers lingering on the silk. With nothing left to do, she shoved down her exhaustion and turned to her strazh. "What's next?"

They'd been out here all day. Celka had learned to field strip and clean a bolt-action rifle, had practiced pulling against concealment and hunger nuzhdi, and had learned basic hand-to-hand fighting. No matter the exercise, at some point, Celka always slipped from her core grounding, sousednia twisting into the circus back lot, Vrana and her squad of red shoulders striding around the cook tent to brutalize Celka and Pa. At first, Hedvika had been the one to call her out, and Celka had resisted, violence flaring. But, as the day wore on, it had started to get easier—not to notice, exactly, because sousednia always felt right, but to... remember. Like Vrana had counselled her, Celka was starting to look for the high wire, for her costume, for the big top's vastness. Even when those things felt deeply wrong, Celka made herself call out their lack.

"Want to meet the rest of the squad?" Hedvika asked.

"They're back?" She'd seen Yanek and Dbani at breakfast, but they'd left right after, off to chase a storm.

"I saw a convoy come up the road." Hedvika nodded to where they could just make out the entrance to the Storm Guard Fortress through the trees.

Celka stuffed her hands into her pockets and made herself nod. "Sure." Though the thought of meeting more regime bozhki—and storm-blessed ones at that, made her struggle for balance. She touched the silk square in her hip pocket, imagining its vivid green.

Hedvika slung an arm around Celka's shoulders. "It'll be great. You'll like Masha. Havel... well. Don't let him under your skin. It's not personal. He's like that to everyone."

"Like what?" Celka asked, but Hedvika just packed their gear.

Walking back down the forested path, Celka realized that if her squad was back, Gerrit should be too. The dread that had dragged at her evaporated, and she quickened her pace. She hadn't seen him since before yesterday's rally. He'd expected to join his family for dinner and, with luck, he would have uncovered the weakness they needed to kill the Stormhawk.

Back inside the gleaming Usvit Hall, however, no one answered when she knocked on Gerrit's door. When Hedvika got impatient, Celka steeled herself to meet her squad.

Inside their suite, Celka and Hedvika crouched to remove their boots, and Celka bit her lip as she unwound the puttees from around her calves. Her squad's sitting room was a larger version of Gerrit's, a pair of wingback chairs facing broad windows that overlooked the surrounding countryside. A stranger sat in one, maybe a decade older than Celka, wearing an ornately patterned silk dressing gown. Ankle hooked over their knee, they didn't look up from the slender book they were reading. A wood-burning stove tiled in elaborately enameled blues and greens brightened one corner, and a writing desk much like Gerrit's sat against another wall. Four doors opened off the space, one a water closet. Celka and Hedvika had bunked in one of the three rooms last night, the rest of the squad due to move in today.

"Hey, Red Squad," Hedvika called. "How was the storm?"

The person in the wingback chair gave an aggrieved sigh and snapped their book closed. Unfolded from the armchair, they were tall and lean. As they looked down their nose at Celka, she spotted a single ornate earring. It climbed the man's whole ear and cascaded gold and pearls nearly to his shoulder—and probably cost more than Celka's family earned in an entire season. The man's black hair was long enough to show a slight curl, his skin tawny gold. Celka edged into sousednia to get a clearer sense of his sousedni-shape, surprised to discover that he appeared only weakly, a hint of jacket and riding breeches barely distinguishing him as storm-blessed. Presumably this was Havel.

Before Celka could figure out if she was supposed to introduce herself, Yanek bounded out of the room Celka and Hedvika had shared the night before. "Hey!" he said, grinning. "You're back. How's your grounding coming?"

No matter how she told herself that these people were regime boot-lickers, Celka found it impossible not to return Yanek's smile. "It's"—she shrugged—"better."

"That's great." He clapped Celka's shoulder like they were old friends.

Dbani emerged from another room, nodding a greeting. They wore a dressing gown almost as fine as Havel's, though in a subdued gray.

"Welcome to Red Squad." The voice, from the other side of the room, startled Celka. It belonged to a person with warm bronze skin, their long black hair hanging loose about their shoulders, still wet from a shower. Simple silver studs glinted from both the woman's ears. "I'm Lieutenant Masha Yedlichka. A pleasure to meet you." The welcome didn't quite reach her voice, her dark eyes behind thick glasses more evaluative than warm. In sousednia, her lips curved in a contented smile—a stark contrast to her solemn evaluation in true-life. "Call me Masha."

"Celka Prochazka," Celka said. "Um, Private Prochazka. It's nice to meet you too." She glanced back over at Havel who was looking her over like she was a three-legged, toothless horse someone was trying to swindle him into buying.

To Hedvika, Havel said, "You let them put her in a factory-produced uniform?" He sounded like he'd found more palatable imbuement mages smeared on the bottom of his boots. "Bad enough they threw her into the enlisted ranks."

"I'm working on it." An irritated edge clipped Hedvika's voice.

Havel rolled his eyes. "At least we won't be travelling with her anytime soon." He finally deigned to focus on Celka. "Your combat-warping hasn't miraculously healed, has it?"

Celka lifted her chin and tried not to hate him. Hedvika, she might be able to forget was a regime boot-licker. Havel's refined accent and superior bearing screamed that she never dare.

As the silence grew awkward, Hedvika charged in like a bull into a glass shop. "How was the storm?"

Havel inspected his fingernails, a picture of boredom. "Instructive."

"Frustrating," Masha said. "We were supposed to imbue simple, Category One hunger into turnips."

"And?" Hedvika asked.

"We all failed." Tension cut Masha's voice.

Yanek crossed to her and laid a hand on her shoulder. "You heard Lieutenant Kladivo. You kept control, which was all he asked. That's not easy in a bozhskyeh storm." He pulled a face. "My own nuzhdi certainly blew up, and I was only building strazh weaves."

Masha pressed her lips into a thin line, but the nod she gave him seemed grateful.

"What about Gerrit?" Celka asked. "Did he imbue?"

"Twice," Masha said, like it was an affront.

"Category Three combat—some experimental weave in a howitzer," Yanek elaborated. "And he demonstrated the hunger imbuement he wanted the storm-blessed working on."

Celka nodded, biting her lip to avoid asking if he was all right. Of course he was all right. Even in Bludov, he'd imbued with control. She was the one who couldn't control herself in a storm.

A knock at the door startled them, and Celka jumped. Hedvika opened it on two servants and a large wooden crate. "Delivery for Filip Cizek," one said, and Celka's stomach flipped. She expected Hedvika to tell them they had the wrong room, but she just craned over her shoulder and bellowed Filip's name.

"Set it over there." Hedvika pointed to the third door inside the sitting room, just as it opened.

Filip stuck his head out. "I'm not deaf, Hedvika." His gaze cut to Celka, and she swallowed hard.

Then the servants passed between them, lugging the crate, and Celka shook herself. Freezing sleet, why was Filip in their suite? Usvit Hall was enormous, surely there were other rooms.

She turned her back, marching determinedly to the room she'd shared with Hedvika. She froze inside the bunkroom, wondering if they'd changed who slept where. She and Hedvika had slept in facing bunks, sharing the spacious room with a single enormous armoire. The room now contained two sets of bunk beds and a second armoire. Even so, it was still a thousand times more spacious than her family's sleeper car on the circus train, but if they'd moved her while she was out, she wasn't about to go barging into a regime bozhk's space.

In the sitting room, she found the others clustering around Filip's crate—except for Havel, who feigned disinterest over by the wingback chairs.

"Did our room move, Hedvika?" Celka asked, just as Filip pulled the top off the crate.

Hedvika leapt back with a shriek, drawing her belt knife. "What in sleet-storms, Cizek?"

Celka's breath caught, truncheons cracking across sousednia. She gripped the doorframe with bloodless knuckles.

Dbani and Masha startled back as well, though they managed to look merely wary.

Only Yanek tipped his head, more curious than concerned. "It's imbued," he said.

The comment, as much as the casual way he said it, dampened the crack of blows. Steadying herself against the doorframe, Celka edged into sousednia, climbing onto the practice wire and squinting past her squadmates' sousedni-shapes to see what had caught their attention.

In true-life, Filip pulled a three-meter-long python out of the crate, looping her chestnut and black-spotted body over his shoulders. On Celka's circus back lot, the snake glowed a bright, rippling rainbow, dominated by combat red.

Recognition crashed over her, a wave of panic and ease that smelled of blood and turpentine, sawdust and icy pine boughs. "Nina." Celka crossed the room, reaching for the snake.

Hedvika caught her. "Stay back."

"She's just a little snake." Filip adjusted Nina's coils on his shoulders in a way that made Celka ache for her sideshow snake charmer act.

"That is *not* a little snake!" Hedvika snarled, barring Celka's approach.

Yanek coughed to cover a laugh. "Filip, your sense of scale might be off. It's hardly *little*."

"She won't hurt anyone," Celka said. Belatedly, she realized that might no longer be true. Nina the python wouldn't have hurt anyone—so long as she got enough rats. Nina the imbuement... despite Celka's role in creating the snake's magic, she didn't understand it.

"Bur's right. This is no place for an *animal*." Havel's voice was imperious, though he pointedly didn't move any closer.

"It's a Category Seven imbuement," Filip said.

"I can see that, sleet-licker," Hedvika said. "It still doesn't get to live in our rooms."

"She's really tame," Celka said, surprised at how glad she was to see the python. She tried to edge around Hedvika, but her strazh pressed her back. Nina's thick, ropy body twisted, and she gazed at Celka with unblinking eyes. Celka stared back, finding color churning behind the snake's vertical slit pupils.

"I have authorization to study it," Filip said.

"*Study* it?" Hedvika said. "You don't even know what it does?"

"No," Filip said. "It's been classified low-utility."

"That's not the same as *safe*," Hedvika snapped.

Staring at the snake felt like peering at her reflection in a rippling pond. Something in Nina's nuzhda glow felt... familiar. Pressing against Hedvika's hold, Celka tried to edge closer, a tug in her sternum making the distance between her and the snake uncomfortable.

As though from far away, Celka heard Hedvika calling her name, but she couldn't look away from the snake.

Hedvika grabbed Celka's arm and jerked her around, breaking her eye contact with Nina.

It felt like a slip on the high wire, the panicked swoop of her stomach as Celka remembered the ten meters of open space beneath her. Gasping, she reached for Nina, but Hedvika dragged her back, away from Filip.

"Get it out of here," Hedvika told Filip as Celka tried to escape her strazh's iron grip. "I'm not joking."

"It's not a problem," Celka told her strazh as Hedvika pulled her to the opposite side of the suite.

"No offense, Celka, but you were kicking up a nuzhda resonance with that thing." She leveled her hard gaze on Filip.

"Celka's fighting a combat-warping. You should know better than to strut around with a combat-adjacent imbuement. Especially one that can"—she shuddered visibly—"move on its own."

Masha jerked her head toward the door out of their suite. "It can catch rats in the basement."

"I'm not throwing a Category Seven imbuement in the boiler room," Filip said, but a line of worry crossed his brow as his gaze slipped to Celka. "I'll keep my door closed." He kicked the crate ahead of him into his room.

Celka wanted to chase after him and pull Nina from his arms. She didn't want to worry Hedvika—though privately, it made her feel a little better that her martial, ass-kicking strazh wasn't *entirely* fearless—but the idea of letting Nina out of her sight made something in her chest shuddery. It didn't make sense. In the sideshow, she'd begrudged Nina's weight, missing the freedom and distance from the crowd that she'd known on the high wire. But maybe now, with the rest of her life torn away, Nina was the last familiar thing to remind her of the circus. She balled one hand into a fist and tried again to pull free of Hedvika. This time, her strazh let her go.

She edged a little closer to Nina, though Filip's door blocked her from true-life view. In sousednia, the door posed no barrier, and Celka wanted to dislocate her sousedni-shape toward the snake. Recalling Vrana's warning stopped her.

At this distance, Nina's pull weakened. Celka inhaled, studying the complex interplay of scent and sound and light from the python's imbuement. Something in it was familiar. At first, she passed it off as a simple resemblance to her pistol's weaves. She'd imbued the snake—well, joint-imbued her—after all. But the resemblance ran deeper. The snake's magic recalled the emotional imbuement she'd studied at yesterday's rally. Nina's weaves were a tangled mess compared to the precision of the Okhrana's awe-inspiring imbuement but, in the way a child's cake of sticks and mud resembled the spongey, honeyed sweetness of medovnik, something in their shape matched.

Filip stepped out and banged his door closed, startling Celka back into the common room. He dusted his hands in a manner that seemed somehow challenging and met Hedvika's gaze. "Satisfied?"

"If that thing gets out," Hedvika said, "I swear I will *kill* it."

"You'd stab a Category Seven imbuement?" Dbani sat in the wingback chair across from Havel's. "That would be unwise."

"I don't care. It's not *living* with us."

"I'll get her a cage," Filip said. "She can't open doors."

With a sleet-eating grin, Yanek said, "So far as we know."

Hedvika gave him a withering glare. "This goes no further than these walls."

"Wouldn't tell a soul," Yanek said.

Havel sighed, settling back into his chair as though supremely bored. "Prochazka, perhaps you can settle an issue we were discussing on the train." When Celka didn't object, he said, "What does a storm-scar from imbuing look like?" Havel still sounded bored, but his expression gained a subtle intensity. Maybe he wasn't so different from her after all.

Celka glanced around, found the others watching eagerly.

"Only if you're comfortable showing us," Yanek said.

Celka bit her lip. She wasn't comfortable with them—with anything inside this fortress. But she'd be sharing bathing facilities and a room with them; they'd see it eventually. Besides, it might help them to see her as a peer. She might not come from an elite family but, unlike them, she had *actually* imbued. Shrugging like it was no big deal, she pulled the tie out of her hair, sweeping it up from the back of her neck to reveal her storm-scar.

"That reminds me," Masha said, "you need to wear your hair in a regulation style."

"Or cut it off," Hedvika said.

"Remind you too much of a snake?" Yanek asked.

"You're lucky I never learned to throw knives," Hedvika said.

Celka bit back a smile, turning away so Hedvika wouldn't see it, and opened the top buttons on her shirt so she could pull the collar down in back. Filip joined them, and Celka made the mistake of meeting his gaze, finding his familiar mahogany eyes framed by long, dark lashes. For a moment, none of the others existed.

"It's more thunderclap than I expected," Yanek said, and Celka turned abruptly from Filip, craning around as though to look at her own back.

Filip is not Ctibor, Celka told herself. *Ctibor was a lie.*

"It's more like a tattoo than a scar," Hedvika said.

"'Gods' Breath inscribed on flesh,'" Dbani quoted scripture.

"It's beautiful," Masha said.

"How big is it?" Havel asked.

"Down most of my back, I think." Celka's gaze snared again on Filip. Her stomach flipped, and she imagined him stepping closer, his strong hands pulling up the hem of her undershirt, brushing her skin in the softest caress.

Sleet. Stupid hormones.

Angry that he could be so distractingly handsome while also a hail-eating liar, Celka yanked her undershirt off over her head. She didn't honestly know what her scar looked like. The mirror in their bathroom was too small. But in Bludov, she'd felt storm energy burn all the way down her back.

Arms held out in front of her, the storm-scars traced fractal, fernlike patterns down from both her shoulders. The right scar twined down to her wrist.

Havel whistled. "How big was your largest imbuement?"

"Category Seven, I guess. The snake." Filip had mentioned Nina's strength, or Celka wouldn't have known.

"*You* imbued the snake?" Hedvika asked, as if Celka had just admitted that she enjoyed eating kittens. "*Why?*"

Celka's gaze flicked up to Filip and, this time, her stomach could have been filled with vipers. The edges of her vision flared red. Struggling for control, she said, "It was a mistake."

Filip's expression hardened.

Struggling to feel the practice wire beneath her feet, Celka said, "I combat-warped imbuing a pistol. I was about to imbue again, but Gerrit... changed the nuzhda—or reshaped my weaves? We joint-imbued, and *Filip*"—she snarled his name—"grounded us."

"Wait, Gerrit did what?" Yanek sounded incredulous. "He *modified* your weaves?"

She flinched from glaring at Filip to frown at Yanek. "Yeah. I guess. I don't really remember."

"He did," Filip said, grim. "Celka had already begun to pull down Gods' Breath. Gerrit—" His jaw worked like he was trying not to yell. Celka was used to him being so calm—but maybe that was part of the Ctibor lie. Filip looked dangerous, like he wanted to punch something—her, maybe—and Celka tensed.

Hedvika stepped to her side, cutting Filip a warning scowl.

Some of Filip's violence ebbed, but his anger at Celka stayed sharp. "Gerrit nearly got himself killed saving *your* life. Grounding you wasn't a *choice*. Not if I wanted Gerrit to survive."

"Good to know you wouldn't have risked your precious self for *me*," Celka snapped.

"Right." Hedvika caught Celka's arm, bulling over Filip's retort. "Put on your shirt. We're going for a walk." Not giving Celka a chance to do anything but obey, she dragged her out the door.

CHAPTER FOURTEEN

WHEN THE DOOR slammed shut behind Celka and Hedvika, Filip spun, striding for his room, too angry to think. He kicked his bedroom door shut. Nina coiled on his bed, and he glared at the snake like it was her fault. He wasn't even sure who he was most angry at, but it felt good to abandon his tightly held control.

Not that it helped.

Filip had almost managed to convince himself of the story he'd spun for Gerrit up in the hills, that Celka was bait in a resistance trap, using them both. But that narrative crumbled upon seeing her. For a moment, when her eyes had locked on Nina, he'd felt a tug in his chest like when they'd trained together in the circus, but more visceral, more like the strazh bond he shared with Gerrit. He'd wanted desperately to cross the room to her, wished they stood alone. When he'd stepped close to see her storm-scar, he'd felt it again, but more physical, reminding him of their kiss outside the bakery in Bludov—and how much more he wished they'd had a chance to do. For a moment, he'd been certain she felt it too.

Then she'd remembered who he was. Not that he'd saved her life when she'd been on the edge of storm-madness, no. She remembered only that he'd lied to her—about his name and his storm-affinity, and apparently that was enough to make her hate him. Even though Gerrit must have lied just as badly.

In no world would Gerrit have admitted his family name to Celka early on. He'd lied just as much as Filip had, but apparently *his* lies were forgivable.

Filip scrubbed his hands over his face, pacing his small room with its writing desk and single bunk. He'd never expected the luxury—the isolation—of a private room this early in his career. But he was Gerrit's strazh, and the family name came with perks—even for a lowly bodyguard. He let the title cut, wondering if that's all he'd become. You expected a bodyguard to take a bullet for you; you didn't listen to their advice.

Tearing his knife from his belt sheath, Filip flipped it over his fingers. But he didn't want to challenge his dexterity, he wanted to throw the sleeting thing. He wanted a target he could see. An enemy he could kill.

While he'd been convinced Celka was merely resistance bait, he'd been able to tell himself that she didn't matter. Filip's job was to protect Gerrit, to serve the State. But Celka tangled everything up. Despite himself, Filip cared about her. Gerrit clearly did too. That Gerrit mattered to Celka had been obvious in the mess hall. Whether she had any feelings for Filip besides rage and betrayal, he didn't know.

What that meant for the future left Filip pacing. No matter which way he looked, someone got hurt—or killed. If Celka convinced Gerrit to follow her into the resistance, they'd both get killed and, at best, the Tayemstvoy would question Filip but leave him to strazh for someone else. If Filip managed to change Gerrit's mind—and how likely was that really?—then either Celka escaped alone, or she stayed and hated Filip for it. But at least in that case, they'd be alive and Gerrit would have a chance to use his power to better Bourshkanya. Was there any way he could convince Celka it would be best?

Filip dropped onto the bed, head in his hands. If he and Celka kept tugging Gerrit in opposite directions, he knew who would win. Gerrit had rarely heeded Filip's advice when they were cadets; now, choosing between Celka's hot-burning passion and fervent belief in the resistance and Filip's admonitions to stay the course—it wouldn't matter that what Filip advocated had once been Gerrit's greatest dream. All that had been before Celka, before Gerrit had decided that the only way to save the State was to burn it down.

A knock on his door startled Filip, but he couldn't imagine talking to anyone right now, so he ignored it. The door opened anyway, and Yanek slipped inside.

Filip met his gaze, ready to tell Yanek to leave him alone. But he didn't want to *be* alone.

He expected Yanek to say something—Gerrit would have—but Yanek just waited, leaning against the closed door. Finally, Filip dropped his head back into his hands.

Yanek sat beside him, their thighs brushing.

Filip exhaled a breath that felt like a sob.

"What happened between you and Celka?" Yanek asked.

Filip shook his head, not knowing how to explain without revealing treason on all sides. But Nina nosed up against his hand, and Yanek waited, patient. Soon, Filip found himself talking. Even skirting their treason, there was still so much to say, an entire month spent pretending to be someone else.

When he reached the end, he told Yanek about the print shop filled with corpses, the Tayemstvoy shouting ultimatums, threatening to gas them and come in shooting. Despite the imminent threat, Gerrit and Celka had taken the time to kiss, staring into each other's eyes like idiot lovers. And when they'd parted, Gerrit had barked orders at Filip to ensure he understood the chain of command. It left Filip nauseous and hollow.

"He's a Kladivo," Yanek said once Filip's words had dried up. "They're not like the rest of us."

A laugh choked in Filip's throat. "You'd think that." When had Gerrit become so unlike his family that he'd throw in with the resistance? Except, maybe it wasn't unlike them, after all. Intent on power, certain they knew what was best for everyone else. "Gerrit's different." Filip needed to say it.

"Is he?" Yanek asked.

Filip looked away, wishing he knew how to defend his best friend. Wishing they could go back to what they'd been before the bozhskyeh storms had returned. Gerrit had chafed at the academy's structure, but Filip had thrived in it. This world of shifting loyalties left him unmoored. He'd thought he'd found his compass, thought that if he just followed Gerrit, everything would be all right.

Yanek stroked his back, rubbing circles that eased a little of his tension. "I see why you're so angry with her."

"Do you?" Filip asked. He wished he could be sure, himself.

"Gerrit knew her for one month, but he chose her over you."

"I'm still his strazh," Filip protested.

"But you were more. Or you wanted to be."

Filip stared at his hands. The only future he'd ever imagined had been at Gerrit's side, just the two of them. Imbuing, discovering new magic. Gerrit would rise in the regime, and Filip would stay at his side. There'd never been anyone else.

"Is that why you were... off today in the storm?" Yanek asked.

Filip tensed, shoulders going hard as steel. His lack of focus early in the storm, the blurring vision, the tug of coppery Gods' Breath—he might have been able to dismiss it. But Yanek had been right that he'd been sparking, pulling unconsciously and without control on a hunger nuzhda. Something was wrong, and he couldn't imagine bringing it to Gerrit. He needed Gerrit to trust him, needed to make Gerrit listen.

So he turned to Yanek, terrified to reveal a weakness that could compromise his ability to do the one thing that had ever mattered to him. But Yanek was one of the best strazhi in the Storm Guard—and Filip sleet-sure wasn't going to talk about this to Hedvika. Exhaling a shaky breath, he said, "I've started seeing Gods' Breath."

Yanek tipped his head, studying him. "Seeing it—like you can tell the difference?"

Filip nodded.

"I thought that was a storm-blessed thing."

"So did I."

"Wait," Yanek said. "Started? You couldn't always?"

Filip shook his head.

"When did it start?"

"Today." But Filip grimaced, realizing that wasn't entirely true. The tug on the back of his skull had been worsening since Bludov, but he'd been so on edge when strazhing for Gerrit while surrounded by Tayemstvoy that he'd hardly looked at the sky. "Maybe earlier. Maybe since grounding that sleeting snake."

Yanek searched his expression then slid off the bed, crouching to put his face level with Nina. "There was something..." He glanced briefly up at Filip before focusing back on the snake. "Give me a minute. I think..."

The air around Yanek seemed to ripple as he focused on the snake. Filip blinked to clear his vision.

When Yanek didn't look back up, Filip sunk to the floor at his side, letting their knees touch as he stretched his focus sideways to better hear Nina's weaves. Most imbuements carried a regular rhythm, their complexity increasing with their power, but the underlying beat still discernible. Nina's imbuement sounded like the chaos of a city street. It smelled like blood and sunshine and desperation. The snake had travelled with them for a while after Bludov, and Filip had studied the imbuement to keep his mind off of how everything might fall apart. Sometimes he thought he'd caught a refrain, but it always vanished beneath the tumult.

Quiet, Yanek asked, "What does it do?"

"Nothing." Though his own skepticism showed. The imbuement might have been 'low-utility,' but Filip could have sworn the snake had warned him and Gerrit of the Tayemstvoy outside the print shop.

Yanek turned, clearly not believing him.

"It... talked," Filip finally said. He expected Yanek to laugh, but he didn't. "And I think"—Filip lowered his voice, mouthing the words more than speaking them—"that I heard Gerrit in sousednia."

Yanek straightened, surprised, but he didn't dismiss it. Instead, he focused back on the snake. "What does Gerrit say about it?"

"He doesn't know. Celka was shaping combat weaves. She had a pistol—trained on *me*." Filip snapped the word, struggling to push past the memory. "Gerrit shifted the nuzhda, dragged it closer to his core. I see his core nuzhda in the snake, sometimes, but it's not *just* his core. Maybe Celka's? I don't know." He scrubbed a hand across his jaw. "It doesn't make sense." Crimson and cobalt rippled over Nina's scales when he wasn't focused directly on her. "Neither of them know what they did."

"I can't believe you survived it," Yanek said.

Filip rubbed the storm-scar that still twinged across his chest. The imbuement still sounded like chaos, rage tumbling over laughter. It gave him a headache, and he squeezed his eyes shut, concentrating on his own breathing.

When he opened his eyes, Yanek was watching him with eyes like the night sky reflected in still water. "You joint-imbued it," Yanek said.

"*They* joint-imbued it," Filip said. Yanek was usually more precise. It was one of the things Filip liked about him.

Yanek shook his head. "I don't think that's true."

Filip stood, pacing. "I know what they did. I sleeting grounded them."

Yanek held his hands up in surrender. "I'm not questioning that. But I think the imbuement's built from core nuzhdi. Celka's, Gerrit's... and *yours.*"

"That makes no sense. I'm only storm-touched." But as Filip said it, he recalled a ripple of green sequins as he'd lifted Celka onto his shoulders to carry her out of the print shop. And, when he'd looked at Gerrit, he'd caught the too-bright glare of sunlight off snow. He swallowed hard. "I can't see sousednia," he said, as if saying it could make it true. "I *can't* imbue."

"Show me your storm-scars," Yanek said.

Stomach churning, Filip pulled off his undershirt.

Yanek inhaled sharply. "Freezing sleet." He touched Filip's chest where the scars from his arms crossed and merged. The brush of Yanek's fingers was the scrape of a knife, the warmth of a cat's purr. Hand on Filip's shoulder, Yanek circled him, tracing the burning lines across his shoulder blades and down his spine. Filip closed his eyes, focusing on the other man's touch, trying to ignore the scar's lingering pain.

Standing close, Yanek swept one hand up the muscles of Filip's back, up his neck to the base of his skull. There, he paused, thumb kissing Filip's spine, just beneath the line of his hair.

"What is it?" Filip didn't want to hear the answer.

"I've heard that a strazh's storm-scar originates from their hands, where they touched the imbuement mage."

"But a tvoortse's grows from their storm-thread." Filip felt like he was falling. "At the base of their skull."

Yanek's hands slipped down his neck and around to rest on his bare chest. In a whisper that Filip felt more than heard, Yanek said, "You imbued."

Filip shuddered, leaning into Yanek's hold as the room spun. "For years, Gerrit tried to speak to me in sousednia. It never worked."

"Was that before or after you joint-imbued a Category Seven imbuement?" Yanek asked.

Filip struggled to breathe.

As though his silence was natural, Yanek said, "We know storm energy changes people. The children of desperate civilians who imbue are more likely to have storm blood." He turned Filip gently so they stood facing. "Mundanes imbue by singing the Songs, but sometimes, when they're desperate enough, they imbue on their own." He cupped Filip's cheek. "What Gerrit did should have failed. You were desperate to save him."

Filip squeezed his eyes shut, shuddering at his memory of the imbuement's terror. Yanek pulled him into an embrace and Filip leaned against him, breathing against Yanek's neck, struggling to hold himself in the moment.

When Filip could make his voice work, he said, "Don't tell anyone, please. I need to work through this."

"It's not my secret to share." Yanek stroked a hand down his back, and Filip let himself melt into the caress, remembering the storm yanking against his spine today. Was that what an imbuement mage felt in every storm? No, he *wasn't* storm-blessed. Maybe his storm-affinity was stronger now, that was fine. Real storm-blessed mages fell into sousednia; they needed help and training to escape it. He'd seen a hint of Gerrit's and Celka's sousedni-shapes, that was all. A second reality had never torn him from true-life.

He was still a strazh, still merely storm-touched. He just needed to get used to what storms felt like now, and he'd be able to do his job just as well as before.

Assuming Gerrit stuck around long enough to need him.

Pulling himself from Yanek's embrace, he said, "I need your help learning to activate the snake." Through Nina, he'd heard Gerrit in sousednia. But something about the connection, about the way the snake had spoken... it felt more personal than how Gerrit described conversations in the neighboring reality. Maybe even more secure. If Filip could get Nina working, he might have a chance to actually *talk* to Gerrit. To make Gerrit listen.

CHAPTER FIFTEEN

WHEN GERRIT RETURNED from his evening meetings, he found Celka and Hedvika on a bench in front of Usvit Hall. Celka was speaking, hands moving in emphatic frustration, Hedvika uncommonly still. They hadn't yet seen him, so Gerrit slowed, edging into sousednia, checking that Celka wore her high wire costume. She did. To his surprise, Hedvika's sousedni-shape was a colorless shimmer; he'd expected them to be working on Celka's grounding, but Celka was already grounded—at least so far as he could tell.

As he neared, Celka's voice sharpened, the way it did when she was trying not to yell. "—if he hadn't been lying to me in the first place!"

"Am I interrupting?" Gerrit asked.

Celka startled like she hadn't noticed him approach. Hedvika nodded silent greeting.

"Gerrit!" Celka leapt to her feet, anger evaporating as she searched his face, eager for answers about the Stormhawk's defenses. She wouldn't like what he had to say.

"How about we go for a walk." He'd been fantasizing

about pulling off his boots and collapsing into bed, but this conversation couldn't wait—and they couldn't have it here. He pulled Celka close, losing himself in her bright enthusiasm to manage a faint smile. "We can watch the sunset together."

"I'd love to," Celka said, and they left Hedvika behind.

At the eastern guard post, they signed out, and Gerrit led her into the hills, wishing he could enjoy the hike and her company. He didn't notice anyone following them—from true-life or sousednia—but couldn't take chances this close to the fortress. "I'm sorry we didn't get a chance to talk in Kralovice," he said, so their silence wouldn't seem suspicious if they were being watched. "What did you think of the rally?"

She managed a few minutes of innocent commentary before describing her awe in the Stormhawk's presence. «I've been thinking about the weaves since,» she said, switching to sousednia. «The way my pistol's weaves interface with the mage, I think I can turn those weaves outward. Hedvika and I have been practicing with concealment nuzhdi, and I'm starting to be able to shape them. I don't know how to do awe, exactly, but I think I might manage something like calmness.»

«That's fantastic,» he told her, though a calming imbuement wouldn't have a clear enough military application to satisfy his father.

«I also...» Celka glanced back over her shoulder in sousednia, then grimaced, like she'd realized it made her look suspicious. «Today, when *Filip*»—she said his name with an angry snap—«brought Nina into our rooms, I realized something. I think she *is* an emotional imbuement. I don't know what she does, exactly, but the way she affected me and the shape of her weaves, they're similar to what I saw at the rally.»

It surprised him, but it felt like it shouldn't. He squeezed her hand. Her anger at Filip felt like he'd swallowed a heavy stone, but the part of him that still flinched at the memory of them kissing in the print shop was glad. «Does this mean you think you can shape one next time you're in a storm?»

She chewed her lip, shoulders hunching as they walked. «How soon will that be?»

"How's your grounding coming?" he asked, moving the conversation aloud, since he'd be expected to ask it.

"Better. But I'm not ready yet." She sounded wary.

"No one's saying you are." Gerrit realized he'd failed to keep the edge out of his voice. At Celka's frown, he said, "Iveta understands the importance of you being grounded before your next storm. But..." He edged into sousednia, uncomfortable saying the next words aloud. «But the State needs weapons, and you've proven you can imbue them. Not everyone will accept keeping you from storms.» He imagined trying to convince Artur that Celka wasn't ready yet to imbue, and his back throbbed in remembered agony. At least today's storm had helped his wounds; the burst of healing from pulling down storm energy had cleared the worst of the pain, though deep bruises still ached when he moved.

Gerrit focused back on the current problem. «That's one reason I suggested emotional imbuements. Besides that you're likely the best person to figure them out, it could mean creating uniquely valuable magic *without* imbuing combat.»

She searched his expression, walking at his side as the path widened. *Is that the only reason?* her emerald eyes seemed to ask.

When Gerrit gave her hand a warning squeeze, she sighed and focused on the trail, her gaze going distant. She seemed to be stewing on something, and he let her have silence, not sure they could discuss whatever had given her expression an edge.

Eventually, she said, "Filip thinks we wouldn't have survived imbuing Nina without him. He acts like he's some sleeting hero, but I wouldn't have even lost control if not—" She bit off the words, but he didn't need her to finish the sentence—*if not for Filip revealing his storm-affinity.*

She'd surged ahead of him on the trail, and Gerrit hurried to catch up. "Maybe we wouldn't have imbued Nina, but you might have imbued again. You were dangerously combat-warped. If Filip hadn't been there, whatever happened next could still have set you off." Meaning: *if we'd run, if we'd tried to disappear from that print shop into the resistance.* He hadn't thought about it before, but it seemed likely they would have encountered more Tayemstvoy during their escape. The bozhskyeh storm had raged for hours after they'd turned themselves in. Chances were good that Celka, volatile from combat-warping, would have imbued again. "If we hadn't had Filip"—if Filip had stayed out of the print shop or hadn't followed them into the resistance—"we might not have survived." As much as Gerrit hated being back here, Filip might have been right. The other options could have been worse. "You could be storm-mad."

Celka stumbled over a tree root. He reached to catch her, but she'd already caught herself, was already turning to him, arms hugged around her waist, eyes haunted. "I might have ended up like—" She stopped herself. He moved to wrap her in his arms, but she stepped back, uncurling, eyes brightening with enthusiasm. "That's it. Sleet-storms, Gerrit!" She caught his arms. "An emotional imbuement. It might help storm-madness."

Gerrit shook his head, not following.

Grinning, Celka caught his hand and pulled him onward down the path. He met her in sousednia, surrounded by the wail of icy wind, her glitter and gossamer utterly incongruous in his alpine clearing. «When the imbuement at the rally hit me hard, it changed my sousednia,» she said. «Storm-madness is nuzhda-warping, at least in part. What does nuzhda-warping do? It changes sousednia. Gerrit, if I can get this working—and I think I can—I might be able to shift someone's sousednia, even if they're deeply nuzhda-warped.»

«Like Branislav,» Gerrit said, in case anyone was following their conversation, though as they got further from the Storm Guard Fortress, still with no pursuit he could detect, that grew increasingly unlikely.

«Right.» Celka almost managed to sound like that's who she'd been thinking of, certainly not her storm-mad father whom everyone believed was already dead.

«That's wonderful,» Gerrit said.

Celka gripped his hand hard, her enthusiasm carrying a calculating edge. Captain Vrana knew where her father was hiding, and he could imagine Celka dangling the hope of reclaiming his true-life grounding as a lure. Captain Vrana had built the resistance with Celka's father; getting him back would be an enormous boon.

«It could work,» Gerrit said.

«I might need to study one of the emotional imbuements,» Celka said. «Everything I'm doing, I'm just guessing.»

He grimaced. «I'll see what I can do, but it won't be easy.» He switched their conversation aloud. "Keep working on it with Hedvika. You've imbued impressive magic by guessing."

The tension creasing her forehead smoothed, and she gained a mischievous smile. "Such confidence in me, Lieutenant. Or are you just complimenting me so I'll kiss you?"

"Ulterior motives, me?" He tried for innocence. By her laugh, he missed.

At a fork in the trail, she said, "Are you sure you know where you're going? I haven't seen this promised sunset."

"Such little faith. Come on, this way. Though it's a bit of a scramble."

Further down the trail, he turned them onto a rarely used

path before slipping onto the game-trail that led to Captain Vrana's cliff. They edged up to the sheer rock face, sitting in the undergrowth well back from the edge. To sell their cover story in case anyone *had* followed them, he leaned close to Celka and kissed her jaw.

At first, he thought she'd pull away, but she smiled. Turning to meet his kiss, she deepened it.

A few minutes later, Gerrit said, "We're missing the sunset."

She chuckled against his mouth and he trailed kisses down her throat. Eventually, as the sky bloomed red, she said, "It's pretty up here."

Without Captain Vrana's gun to his back, Gerrit had to agree. Slipping his arm around her shoulders, he hugged Celka to him as they watched the clouds burn.

«How was seeing your family?» Celka eventually asked.

Gerrit dipped into sousednia, sweeping aside true-life obstacles, straining to the limits of his perception. As far as he could tell, they were alone.

«Artur's a hail-eater,» he said, telling her about his 'friendly greeting.' «If it were up to him, Tayemstvoy power would be limitless.» He shook his head, trying to enjoy the sunset rather than feel Artur's venomous stare as their father dismissed him and Gerrit before leading Iveta off for a private conference that had lasted hours. «On the train this morning, Iveta told me I'd lucked out, that dinner had been 'tame.' Apparently, Father and Artur went easy on me.» Iveta had said it like he should find it reassuring, and she'd complimented him on making his case to their father about hungry workers. «The entire dinner, I was certain they were going to realize my...» He hugged Celka close, unwilling to speak the word *treason* even though they were truly alone.

«But they didn't,» Celka said, like that meant anything more than a stay of execution.

«I don't know if I can do it again. When I look at my father, I see a monster. Everything he says is wrong and cruel. That veneer of justified power can't hide the rot, and I don't know how to keep saluting him like it does.»

«So we focus on the mission,» Celka said.

The colors in the sky had faded to gray, and Gerrit felt cold, dark water closing in over his head. He struggled to breathe, to make his voice level as he said, «He's too well protected.»

«I don't believe that. He has a weakness, a flaw. He must.»

Gerrit had hoped that would be true, and maybe Celka would see something he missed, so he detailed the Stormhawk's imbuements. But as he spoke, all the evening's beauty faded. They couldn't kill the Stormhawk with a bullet or a collapsing building. And several of the healing imbuements eliminated the possibility of poison.

«What about something new, a poison that didn't exist during the last storm cycle?» Celka asked.

«I asked Iveta about poison on the train,» Gerrit said. «With all of us eating together, it seemed like an easy way to take out our whole family line, so I figured I could get away with asking. She wasn't concerned. Father's staff uses an imbuement on the food, eliminating poisons. Iveta has one, too, as does Artur. She said she'd make sure her people start screening my meals. Father's apparently survived a dozen poisoning attempts, and I doubt it's just because his assassins chose old poisons.»

Celka grimaced, but didn't relent. «What about contaminated water?»

«If they're screening food, they'll screen everything he drinks, too,» Gerrit said.

«So we need something they can't eliminate,» Celka said. «Like a disease that we can, what, spit on him? Inject?»

«One new enough his healing imbuements couldn't protect him from it?» Gerrit said, skeptical.

«When the Tayemstvoy surrounded us in Bludov, they threatened to gas the building if we didn't come out,» Celka said. «Could we use gas to disable him and his guards long enough to... I don't know, take their imbuements? Force them to deal with one threat while we surprise-attack in a different way?»

«Wait,» Gerrit said, surprised he hadn't thought of it before. «Poison gas. That's our answer.»

Celka frowned. «I didn't think it was deadly?»

«What the Tayemstvoy use isn't, but I've heard about new gasses they're developing for war. Ones that would kill. And the imbuements wouldn't protect against it, because it would attack his lungs.»

«And you can't screen poison out of the air,» Celka said appreciatively. Then her gaze sharpened. «Can you?»

«No,» Gerrit said. «An imbuement like that, they would have had to hold it active. I would have sensed it. I'll talk to the Wolf. We'll need to learn more, but I think we have a real chance.»

CHAPTER SIXTEEN

WHEN CELKA GOT back from the showers a few days later, she discovered a brown paper-wrapped parcel on her bed. "It's for you," Hedvika said, dressed in a silk bathrobe, toweling off her short hair.

"From who?" Celka asked. Masha hopped down off her bunk, and Yanek came around to peer over her shoulder.

"Me, sort of," Hedvika said.

"How do you sort of give someone a present?" Celka asked, tearing it open.

"I ordered it," Hedvika said. "Gerrit paid for it."

Soft olive wool greeted Celka's fingers, and she lifted it, discovering a new uniform jacket. Across sousednia, truncheons cracked on bone, and the big top's dimness shattered into springtime sun. Squeezing her eyes shut, Celka held herself motionless, drawing a deep breath and concentrating on the feel of the practice wire beneath her feet. It felt right, but she knew it was wrong. Knew the wire should feel more alive; knew her costume should glitter in the spotlights. Hedvika stepped up behind her, touching cool fingers to the back of Celka's neck, and the back lot faded.

When Celka stood again on her high wire, she set the jacket down on her bed, and looked at what lie beneath it. Soft uniform shirts and trousers. She set her jaw, unable to smile.

"You don't like it." Hedvika sounded like someone had stolen her puppy.

"No, it's…" She balled her hands into fists, but that made the crack of truncheons and the scent of blood filter even into the high reaches of the big top. "I do," she made herself say, but it didn't come out very convincing.

"I thought you'd feel more like you belonged." Hedvika chewed her lip. "And it should fit better. It's tailored. You won't look like a dirt-scrubber anymore."

"Nice, Hedvika," Yanek said, "insult her. That'll help."

"I didn't—but she's *not*." Hedvika took Celka's hands. "You're *not* a dirt-scrubber. Not anymore, is what I meant. You're one of *us* now. Like family."

The words felt like a blow, like Vrana's strong hand connecting with Celka's cheek when she'd been only a child. Celka tried not to stumble as blood roared in her ears.

"Look." Hedvika shoved aside the Army shirts and trousers, revealing a gorgeous blouse of the same emerald silk as Celka's pocket square. She held it up. "I got you civilian clothes, too. It's like your high wire costume, but better, right? Maybe we can wear it out dancing next leisure day."

"She got you a whole outfit," Masha said, holding up a beautiful pair of slim, dove-gray trousers and a richly embroidered belt while Celka struggled to strip the threat from their voices.

Allies, she told herself as she turned her back on Vrana in sousednia and climbed onto the practice wire. *You're not one of them, but you can pretend. It's an act. Just long enough to kill the Stormhawk.* The thoughts steadied her, as did the steel cable beneath her feet.

"And silk underclothes," Hedvika said. "You can dress like you belong here. Because you *do*."

Apart from the handkerchief Hedvika had bought her, Celka had never owned silk. As the crack of blows faded, she fingered the hem of the emerald blouse. Its delicate softness tightened her throat, the scent of blood gusting on the breeze. People across Bourshkanya were starving, yet the State bought her silk finery as a bribe. *We'll end this*, she told herself, and the strength of that belief shattered sousednia's spring sky. The big top's canvas settled around her, and Celka smiled a performer's smile. "Thank you." She made herself meet Hedvika's pale blue eyes, made herself embrace her strazh. "It's beautiful," she told her, and it was true. "It'll be nice to fit in."

Wearing this uniform wouldn't make her a traitor to the resistance, it would help her blend in—a snake in the grass, waiting to strike. The fine, tailored wool didn't mean she'd be here forever, but it could be weeks or even months before she got out. Gerrit had told Captain Vrana about their idea to use poison gas on the Stormhawk, and the Wolf's people were investigating the options. But even once they had the gas, Celka didn't know how soon they'd be able to act. While they waited for an opportunity, Celka needed to reclaim her grounding and her ability to imbue. And the State needed to trust her if she and Gerrit were going to get close enough to the Stormhawk to end him. That meant making her squad trust her. It meant acting like one of them. The right costume would help.

Drawing back from Hedvika, Celka smiled at Masha and Yanek.

Masha stroked a skein of damp hair from her face. "You're part of our squad," Masha said. "We take care of each other."

Yanek touched her shoulder, echoing a trill of the circus band as he pulled weakly on her core nuzhda. "Like family."

Longing for her real family hit like a gut-punch, but Celka pushed down the homesickness before it could threaten her grounding. In sousednia, she felt her family's love, their warm support from the platform just outside the spotlight. They were safe. Being here, playing the loyal soldier kept them safe. Turning away from her squad, Celka dug through Hedvika's gift to the silk underclothes. "It's a lot, still," she said as she pulled them on. "Being here."

"I know something that can make it better," Hedvika said, pulling on a fresh uniform.

"Stealing Havel's dessert?" Yanek suggested.

"I heard that!" Havel shouted from the common room.

"Ears like a bat," Yanek muttered.

"Face like one, too," Hedvika said.

Celka wrinkled her nose as she buttoned up her new uniform shirt, the soft linen a caress. "Nah, bats are cute."

Hedvika snorted laughter.

"Heard that, too," Havel shouted.

It made Celka's smile feel a little less like a performance, and she pulled on the new trousers, impressed despite herself at their quality.

When she was dressed, Hedvika pulled something out of the depths of her armoire with a flourish. "Boots, too." She presented them as though upon a silver platter. "Ones that fit."

"Sleet-storms, *yes*," Celka said, not having to feign her enthusiasm. Apparently, joining the Army meant more running than she'd ever endured in her life, and her too-big ankle boots had given her messy blisters.

"Come on, there's more." Taking her hand, Hedvika pulled her out into the common room.

From the wingback chair, Havel clapped sardonically. "You actually look like a tvoortse now."

Hedvika saved Celka having to reply, dragging her out and down the corridor. "Sorry, I lost track of time. Come on, we don't want to miss it!"

"Miss what?" Celka asked, but Hedvika didn't answer.

On the ground floor, Hedvika pulled Celka inside a small room with a black telephone. "It's for you."

Curious, Celka pressed the receiver to her ear. Leaning toward the microphone, she said, "Hello?"

"Celka? Is that really you?"

Celka's stomach did a flip. "Ela?" An echo and noise on the connection made it hard to be sure, but that voice sounded like her cousin. Celka glanced up at Hedvika, who winked then slipped out, shutting the door behind her.

Ela laughed, dispelling any doubt. "See, I told you she'd recognize my voice! These things are the future, Mom."

Celka gripped the handset with desperate strength. "Ela, are the others with you? Is everyone all right?"

"We're fine," Ela said, light and earnest. "Well, Demian enlisted, so he's not here, and Dad took Aunt Vaclava and Grandma back to Mirova to help get them settled back in, but Mom and Grandfather are here."

"Where's here? Where are you? What happened—are you all right?"

Muffled, as though at a distance, Celka heard Aunt Benedikta say, "Give me that." Then her voice came clearly. "Foolish child. Celka, we're well. We're back in the circus."

"And tonight we're staying in a mansion!" Distance from the microphone distorted Ela's voice.

"The mayor of Loket is hosting us for tomorrow's rest day," Aunt Benedikta said, and Celka could imagine the disapproving scowl she used to drive Ela back.

Celka sunk into a chair, overwhelmed.

"Child, are you crying?" Aunt Benedikta asked.

"No," Celka said. "Yes. I'm so glad you're all right." She wiped her eyes on her fancy new sleeve. "Is anyone..." She hesitated, not sure she wanted to hear the answer. "Was anyone hurt?"

"No, though Demian is probably hurting by now. Basic training will not be as easy as he thinks." Aunt Benedikta sounded smug. She'd been an infantry sergeant during the war; she would know. "How are *you*?" The sudden solemnity in that question balled all of Celka's words up in her throat. "They told us there was an... incident during the storm in Bludov. That people died, but that you did your duty."

"I enlisted, too." Celka felt small, and Aunt Benedikta barked at her to speak up. "I'm learning to control my storm-blessing." Celka tried to think what else she could say without endangering her family. "It's hard, but I'm all right." Masha had encouraged her to write her family letters, had lent her paper and pens, but Celka hadn't known what to say—still didn't know what to say. She'd iced up in Bludov, put them all in danger.

A crackle sounded over the phone, and Celka feared the line had been cut. Then Grandfather's voice came through, stern and unyielding. "The State is watching out for us, so you take care of yourself. Do what you need to succeed. You made an impression on them, that's certain."

Celka swallowed hard, easily imagining the warning in Grandfather's ice-blue eyes. He knew Vrana had helped Pa disappear to lead the resistance; he was telling her to do what the resistance needed and get out if she saw an opportunity—no matter the consequences to her family.

"They bought us new clothes," Ela said, and Celka could just imagine her cousin pulling the handset from Grandfather's hands, bouncing on her toes, hair done up in an elaborate braid, gleefully wearing the State's bribe. "I've never worn a dress this fine. I can't *wait* for you to see it."

"I'm sure it's beautiful." Celka fingered the fine linen of her khaki shirt before Grandfather shoed Ela away and reclaimed the handset. Would she ever see her family again? "Are you really well, Grandfather?" They might have been ordered to lie, but she'd grown up hearing Grandfather speak the right words while implying the truth.

"Benedikta got in a fight with the guards." Grim disapproval weighed his tone. "She has always had a temper. But we were not hurt—though I will appreciate sleeping in my own bed tomorrow, no matter how fine our rooms at the mayoral residence. Change does not come so easily to your elders." Which meant they'd probably been kept in cells as barren as Celka's, maybe starved, but not tortured. And now the State kept her family close, their status risen as bribe and warning.

"I'm sorry," Celka whispered.

"Child, the Storm Gods blessed you. You have nothing to apologize for." He paused, as though listening to something the telephone did not pick up. "It is time for us to dress for dinner. Take care of yourself, Celka. We're proud of you."

The operator came on, and Celka returned the receiver to its hook. She stayed long minutes in the chair, staring at the telephone. They were safe. If—when—Celka and Gerrit killed the Stormhawk, her family... No, she couldn't think about what would happen. Grandfather must have a plan.

When Celka finally emerged, she found Hedvika doing push-ups in the corridor. She leapt to her feet, her sousedni-cues the spicy, honeyed sweetness of hot sbiten on a winter's night.

When Celka didn't say anything, Hedvika's sousedni-cues lost their warmth. "The dinner bell will ring soon," she said softly. "I heard there'll be honey cake for dessert."

"Sounds delicious." Celka wondered if her family would eat as well with the mayor of Loket. Wondered how many people would go hungry so she could eat medovnik in her beautiful new clothes. She shoved the thoughts aside. "You arranged the call?" It couldn't have been easy. The circus train had no telephone.

"I pulled a few strings." Hedvika still didn't show her teeth when she smiled, though Celka had realized it was because her big front teeth embarrassed her. "I figured, family's important. Did it help?"

Celka's throat tightened. "Yeah."

Hedvika hesitated a second, then said, "I know we're not... really family. But—"

"Do you miss yours?" Celka asked, hoping to escape another well-meant insult.

Hedvika nodded. "Especially my little brother Lubomir. He's training to be a doctor, like Dad—though he's not a bozhk."

"Do you have a big family?"

"Five children and my fathers." Hedvika led her to Usvit Hall's main entryway, passing up a nook with fine upholstered armchairs to sit on the carpeted stairs. "We're all pretty close in age—a bunch of war orphans. My fathers adopted us all around the same time." She smirked and shook her head. "I can't imagine what it must have been like for them to suddenly have five children running around screaming." She shrugged. "But they wanted to start a family. The war was over—and we sure lucked out." Her gaze went distant, troubled. "Not everyone did."

"How old were you?"

Hedvika sat on the step behind Celka and started braiding her hair. "Five. The war'd been over three years. My birth parents were both bozhk doctors; Dad knew my mom, so when he found out they were dead, he came looking for me. Apparently, the hospital where they worked got shelled late in the war, and they didn't evacuate fast enough."

"Why'd it take him so long to find you?"

"Bourshkanya was a mess back then. Doubek and Vrana won the war at Zlin, but the Lesnikrayens *devastated* the country."

Hearing Pa's name spoken casually made Celka start, but Hedvika kept braiding her hair like she hadn't noticed.

"I was lucky, I had a bed at the orphanage—even if I had to share it. A lot of kids were out on the street. Half the buildings in my city were rubble. Even if my fathers had started looking for me the moment the truce was signed, it might have taken them that long to find me—but they didn't even meet until after. Father got badly burned in the Battle of Oleshka. His battalion stayed behind, harrying the enemy while our main forces retreated to Zlin. He could have evacuated like most of the other officers, but he stayed to fight. Got pinned in a burning building. One of his soldiers dragged him out— barely got him out alive. Dad was his doctor in a burn unit after the war." She shrugged. "So I guess they came looking when they could."

"Your other siblings, are they...?"

"Children picked up here and there. I'm the only bozhk. Lubomir was at the orphanage with me—scrawny little kid. I looked out for him when it was just us, and made sure when my fathers adopted me that they took him too."

"That's brave," Celka said. "They might have chosen a different kid—if they only wanted one."

Hedvika shrugged, tying off Celka's braid with a piece of string. "It never really seemed like a choice."

CHAPTER SEVENTEEN

WHEN THE TROOP transport rumbled to a stop inside the Storm Guard Fortress's outer walls, Filip was the first to leap out. The instant his boots hit the ground, he was moving—not running, not quite—striding to the fortress's isolated prayer tower. Everyone else would disperse back to their quarters, cleaning up after the day on the road, dressing for dinner. But Filip wasn't hungry.

Rather, the taste of chicken paprikash lingered on his tongue and his stomach growled desperate counterpoint, but he couldn't imagine sitting at Gerrit's side in the opulent officer's mess listening to barbed politicking from regime elites after what he'd seen today. A skipped meal wouldn't hurt *him*.

He'd fast. And he'd pray.

He barely noticed the three-story climb to the disused prayer room, his hobnailed boots echoing on the stone. The heavy wooden door was closed, the room it opened into silent. He circled the hexagonal space, throwing wide the shutters to admit fresh air and evening light, before turning to the six-sided stone altar built into the room's center. He was trembling.

Swallowing hard, Filip ignored the altar's Protection Aspect—his usual starting place in prayers—kneeling instead before the Feeding Aspect. He pulled his storm pendant off over his head, fumbling open the charging sack to withdraw the faded square of gray wool. Voices and the crunch of boots on stone filtered up from the fortress's yard, and Filip stared at the carving of lean, hungry peasants around a sheaf of wheat, struggling to see the altar and not the Tayemstvoy surging into the storm temple where they'd imbued today.

He shook his head, as if it could shake the horror, and gripped his storm pendant by its insulating leather cord, rubbing his charging cloth over the etched brass as he began to sing the Song of Feeding. He shouldn't have started with Feeding, he knew that; he'd struggled not to pull against a hunger nuzhda all afternoon. But he couldn't help himself. He was too angry to sing Calming, which is probably what he needed; too incensed to sing Protection, which would have been almost as good.

The Song worked its magic anyway, his rage draining through the ritual motion of charging his storm pendant. He rarely sang more than the base verses of the Song of Feeding—he'd never had much affinity to the Storm Gods' Feeding Aspect—but today he sang until the small hairs all up his arm stood on end from his storm pendant's charge. Before he could lose the spark to accidental discharge, Filip made himself set the cloth on his knees, fixing the traditional prayer in his thoughts: *May I feed those who are hungry.* He touched his pendant to the iron spike protruding from the top of the altar. A spark leapt between them but, rather than leaving him cleansed, it left him feeling unworthy.

How could he call himself devout, how could he come here and pray as he did every day knowing that, when people had needed him, when people had been *hungry* and the Storm

Gods might have answered their call, he'd stood aside and let their chance at a miracle be ripped away?

Instead of shifting around the altar to pray before the next Aspect, Filip picked up his charging cloth and returned to the Song of Feeding. Barely had he gotten past the first verse when the prayer room's iron banded door creaked open. Filip's fingers slipped, skin touching brass, dissipating the building charge. He swallowed a grimace and the urge to shake out his fingers, and started the Song from the beginning.

Normally, he was alone here. Most chose to pray and be seen doing so in the fortress's official storm temple. Few even knew this room existed, and it probably would have been converted to storage long ago, except that the massive stone altar had been built into the floor.

Filip sang a little louder, trying to get swept away by Feeding's hitching rhythm—and encourage whoever had interrupted to leave.

He never used to mind who came or went during his prayers. His focus had been a sniper's unwavering attention, cradled in prayer's meditative calm. But in the circus, there'd been constant interruptions, and he'd had only a single-faceted altar before which to pray: cloudy tin mounted on wood, it carried a traveler's prayer for protection. It shouldn't have mattered; the Storm Gods would forgive him singing each Aspect before a single facet, but few others were so devout, and it made him feel more an outsider when already he didn't belong.

Today's interloper said nothing, motionless until Filip had released his prayer. The spark seemed to burn his fingers, despite his pendant's insulated leather wrap.

Jaw tight, he began the Song again.

Hobnailed boots scraped the stone floor behind him. "You're going to miss dinner," Yanek said.

Filip cut him a glance before focusing back on the altar. "I won't be the only one." It came out barbed, though he wasn't angry at Yanek—not really, though he had been beneath the storm.

Instead of leaving, Yanek sighed and knelt beside him. "Do you mind if I join you?"

"You'll miss dinner," Filip turned Yanek's words back on him.

"Then I'll be in good company." The tightness to Yanek's voice suggested he didn't mean Filip.

Filip tore his eyes off the altar and found Yanek scowling as he pulled a charging cloth of white rabbit fur from the pouch next to his pendant. "I didn't think you cared," Filip said, low. They were alone in the prayer room, but it never paid to speak too freely.

"You couldn't have stopped it," Yanek said.

They'd been standing together at one side of the storm temple's massive outflung doors, watching Havel and Dbani attempt a hunger imbuement next to the storm tower. Behind them, inside the temple, the congregation had been singing the Song of Feeding since the storm had broken. Iveta had wanted to stop them, concerned the Song would distract their imbuement mages, but Gerrit had argued to let them sing. If anything, hearing the Song of Feeding would attune the platoon's mages to hunger, making the nuzhda easier to access.

It should have stopped there. The platoon's mages should have imbued—or not—and the congregation should have achieved a minor miracle on their collected barrel of grain—or not. But as Havel pulled his weaves together for a simple, fourfold increase in his turnip's nutrition, the pounding of infantry boots had surrounded the temple. A full company of Tayemstvoy had converged on the modest temple, truncheons in hand, ordering the congregation to silence. They'd shoved the storm speaker to the ground and done the same for anyone who tried to continue the Song. Gerrit had stepped forward, mouth opening as if to protest, but Iveta had touched his shoulder and shaken her head. She'd said something Filip couldn't make out over the shouts and stomping boots, and when Filip had moved to demand that Gerrit stand up for the civilians, Yanek had caught his arm.

Kneeling in the prayer tower, Filip said, "Gerrit might have listened to me."

"Over his commanding officer?" Yanek asked, rabbit fur rubbing over his ornate storm pendant.

Filip had abandoned his own prayer. "Neither of them are devout. Maybe they didn't realize—"

"They're Bourshkanyan," Yanek said. "They know what that prayer meant."

Filip wanted to argue, but Yanek was right. On the train back to Solnitse, Filip had pulled Gerrit aside, asked what Iveta had told him. "It's not our jurisdiction," Gerrit had said. "Iveta thought it would be unwise to interfere." Filip had wanted to know if it was an isolated incident—local Tayemstvoy high on their own power, thinking to step between the people and the Storm Gods. Gerrit hadn't known, had agreed to find out, but his expression was one Filip knew too well—his best friend preparing to turn his back on something unpleasant he couldn't control.

"You can't let them do this," Filip had told Gerrit, meaning, *You can't let them do this again*—because they had already allowed it. Two and a half platoons of bolt-hawks and bozhk officers had let bullies with red shoulders steal the grain collected by hardworking laborers, held up before the gods as offering and hope.

In the prayer tower, Filip gripped his storm pendant so hard that the brass cut into his palm. He stared at the Feeding Aspect, feeling unworthy even to pray.

Yanek set his charging cloth down, silent for a moment before he touched his pendant to the altar's spire. Sitting back on his heels, he turned to Filip. "You talked to Gerrit. He'll look into it. You've done what you can."

It didn't feel like enough.

Yanek studied him as Filip fingered his charging cloth, feeling powerless. He'd been taught that the Tayemstvoy were necessary—brutal when they had to be to ensure Bourshkanya's safety. But those civilians had threatened *nothing*. They'd said nothing against the State, merely called upon the Storm Gods to fill their aching bellies. And even if they had accused the State of taxing them too harshly or their employers of paying them so little that they couldn't afford enough grain, would that have been so wrong? Talk like that could get even a Storm Guard officer dragged away by the red shoulders, but why? Was the regime so fragile that it couldn't face the truth? Or was it an excuse for bullies with red shoulders to crush people beneath their boots?

The only way to improve was to listen to feedback—even if that criticism hurt. But the State silenced criticism. The Tayemstvoy silenced it. The Stormhawk silenced it.

Filip rubbed the prickling storm-scar at the back of his neck, disturbed that he could even think that level of treason. But he *had* thought it. And maybe it wasn't wrong.

Could Gerrit and Celka be right that the regime was rotten?

"Let's go to the shooting range," Yanek said, tucking his storm pendant away.

Relieved for the distraction, Filip's restless energy urged him to agree, but he said, "Let's work on Nina." He slipped his storm pendant back over his head and closed the prayer room's shutters.

"I'd have thought your focus was shattered."

Filip snorted. "It is. But yours isn't."

Yanek pulled a face and, despite himself, it tugged a smile to Filip's lips. "Sure, make me do all the work."

They started down the stairs together. Struggling to put the day behind him, Filip reached for his flirtatious mask. "Gives me time to check out your ass."

Yanek raised his eyebrows and slipped his arm around Filip's waist. "I can think of better ways for you to do that."

"Activate Nina, and we'll talk."

"You're a cruel taskmaster," Yanek said.

"I can be," Filip said, low and suggestive. "If you want."

By the time they reached his room, Filip had almost forgotten his helpless rage. Yanek pushed him back against the closed door and trailed strong fingers down his chest to his belt, mischievous smile on his lips. Filip's breath caught, and Yanek stepped close, twilight sinking the burnished brass of his eyes into darkness.

Catching Yanek's face, Filip kissed him.

Yanek drew out the kiss even as he leaned into Filip, strong body pinning Filip against the door, hands clutching his hips. When he drew back, the absence left Filip gasping.

"I thought we were here to play with your snake," Yanek said.

Filip laughed, but when he tried to kiss Yanek again, the other man slipped away. Grinning, Yanek crossed the small room to Nina's cage, lifting the lid off the python's crate while Filip tried to catch his breath.

"You were the one who wanted to work," Yanek said, pooling Nina on Filip's bed. With a sly glance, Yanek tossed aside his uniform jacket before beginning to unbutton his shirt. "Wouldn't want to disappoint you."

As Yanek's fingers slipped downward from button to button, Filip couldn't tear his eyes away. When he finally tugged the hem of his shirt out from his trousers, his undershirt slid up, hinting at his muscular, coppery brown stomach and the divots of his hips. Yanek dropped his khaki shirt on the floor, and Filip crossed the distance between them before he could think.

Catching Yanek's hip, he said, "Maybe the imbuement can wait."

"Are you sure?" Yanek worked open the top button of Filip's shirt. "You seemed awfully concerned about duty."

Filip slid his hand up under Yanek's undershirt even as he tried to think. But the frisson of the other man's skin hot against his palm made it hard to care about whether Nina would let him communicate securely with Gerrit. Even with the snake, he had no guarantee his best friend would listen. Yanek's hands undid his last button, and Filip's breath quickened as Yanek pushed his uniform jacket and shirt down off his shoulders.

Dropping them both on the ground, Filip pulled his undershirt off, then lifted Nina back into her crate. "Sorry, snake."

Yanek chuckled and pushed Filip back against the bed.

After they were sweaty and spent, Yanek propped his chin on Filip's chest, gazing at Nina's crate in the corner. "You still want to try and activate the snake?"

Filip smirked. "I think you already did."

Grinning, Yanek rolled to sit across Filip's hips. He danced his fingertips across Filip's chest and over his shoulders, but his expression had sobered.

"What is it?" Filip asked.

Yanek hesitated, on the verge of words, but instead leaned forward, capturing Filip's mouth in a long, slow kiss. When Yanek drew back, Filip kept his eyes closed, feeling more grounded than he had in days, content in a way he couldn't remember.

When Yanek rolled off him, he reluctantly opened his eyes. His undershorts landed on his face, and Filip sat up, sputtering.

Yanek laughed. "You going to laze in bed or come figure this thing out?" He'd pulled the lid back off Nina's crate, his own shorts hiding his distractingly fine ass.

"I thought I was supposed to be the taskmaster," Filip grumbled, twitching the comforter over his rumpled sheets so Yanek could deposit the snake on his bed.

Yanek swept his hand across Filip's waist and stole a kiss. "Next time," he promised before his expression grew serious. "You have paper?"

Filip pulled out a notebook, and Yanek stole his desk chair to start scrawling weave diagrams on his knees with his feet propped on Filip's bed. Filip grabbed his own notebook, sitting next to Nina. But unlike Yanek's, his page remained stubbornly blank. Looking at Nina, he still flailed to find any stable structure in the weaves.

Frustrated, he gave up and went to look over Yanek's shoulder. He touched the base rhythm Yanek had diagramed. "Where do you even see this?"

Yanek blinked vaguely for a moment, shaking his attention back to true-life to see what Filip had indicated. "Do you see the access points?" Yanek asked rather than answering, and Filip slipped his attention sideways, focusing back on the snake.

"Not really." He held two fingers out, pointing. "There's something here, but it's complex—Celka's core nuzhda, maybe."

"I think you're right." Yanek took his hand, shifting it to point at a tangled mess of color that gusted glacial wind. "This is Gerrit's."

Somehow, having Yanek point it out, it made sense.

"Except, it isn't him." The access point shifted, growing and folding back in on itself, stinking of diesel smoke and gun oil, echoing like blows.

"It's a combat nuzhda," Yanek said, "with multiple access points *inside* Celka's and Gerrit's core nuzhdi. I think it's a staged imbuement—you have to activate one to activate the other, but it's like they're looped; not like a normal, sequential staged imbuement."

"How do you activate it, then?"

Yanek grinned at him. "You want to try it?"

"No." Filip said, a crawling feeling down his spine.

Yanek snorted. "Activate your part, at least."

"You say that like I know what my part is."

"It's the base rhythm," Yanek said.

"The snake doesn't *have* a base rhythm," Filip said. But Yanek still had his hand, and ran it through the air, looping to trace the snake's coils.

"It's not an access *point*, it's... more like an open line. And it's harder to see because... I think you're already half activating it."

"If it's my core nuzhda, shouldn't I automatically activate it?" Filip said, though obviously if it worked that way, he already would have. "Like schoolchildren ringing a hunger nuzhda bell after fasting for a Feeding Miracle."

"I thought that at first too," Yanek said, "but look at this." He held up his weave diagram, and Filip shook himself out of his sideways investigation of the weaves to study the lines and symbols Yanek had scrawled, connecting loops of energy, the imbuement so complex that the lines seemed to tangle, thick with descriptive symbols.

"A protection nuzhda?" Filip asked.

"It makes sense, right?" Yanek said. "Protection's close to your core, and you're used to building strazh weaves out of it.

I think you integrated your strazh weaves into the imbuement, but somehow made them more than what we think of as strazh weaves. It's another staging loop—but this time with your core nuzhda and protection."

Filip grimaced. "So if I pull against protection, it'll activate?" It sounded too simple.

"Only one way to find out."

"Unless we activate it wrong, and strain the weaves so it explodes."

"It won't," Yanek said.

"You can't just make that true by fiat."

Yanek chuckled. "No, look here." He pointed at the diagram where he'd drawn a dozen tight symbols for nuzhda buffers. "This means you can hit it with as strong a nuzhda you want—pretty much—and it'll just swallow it."

Filip squinted at the snake, trying to disentangle the buffers from the cacophony of sound. He knew Yanek had tested for his gold bolts young; he hadn't known he was this skilled. "Unless you're wrong."

Using his hold on Filip's wrist, Yanek pulled him around to sit on the bed. "You were the one who wanted to get it working. What's stopping you?"

"Even if I activate my portion, I'm only one third of what it needs." Filip's stomach churned, remembering the agony of the imbuement, the way it had shredded his mind, leaving him clawing through ash and darkness, struggling back to the print shop only to find Celka slipping from true-life.

"I can pull against Gerrit's core nuzhda pretty well, still, from training. It might not work without Celka, but we can try it."

"And it could blow up and tear us from true-life," Filip said, wondering why he hadn't worried about the problem before now.

Yanek squeezed his knee. "I think the risk's manageable. Trust me."

"You've studied this thing for one evening."

"I got a good look at it a few days ago. And I've been listening to it every night. Category Seven's not exactly subtle, and your room's not far from mine."

"Fine." Filip said, reasonable protests exhausted. If he wanted to talk Gerrit out of getting himself killed for the resistance, the sooner he got this working, the better.

Laying his hand on the snake, Filip dove into memory, returning to Lenka in the garden to pull against protection. As he did, the snake's weaves sharpened, and the access line that Yanek had indicated flared like sunlight through amethyst. Filip reached for it, but it was like trying to climb with the handholds all out of reach. He strained, but couldn't touch it.

"You need a stronger nuzhda," Yanek said, and Filip tried not to be annoyed that he'd realized it first.

He sunk himself deeper into memory, cutting open his pain and fear of losing his sister, of never again having her laugh and point out the names of flowers as they circled the storm temple's gardens. The pain felt like heartbreak, like running into the cell where they had her restrained after she'd first broken in testing. Felt like seeing her snarl at him, not recognizing him for her brother. But Filip grasped that pain, twisting it into hope the way he had as a child, refusing to give up on her.

«*Hey, little brother,*» the snake said in Lenka's voice, and Filip recoiled. He glanced at Yanek, wondering if he'd heard, but found only a chaotic swirl of crimson and aubergine, threaded with gold and ultramarine.

Then Yanek's heat-shimmer form seemed to double, stepping away from the vivid glow of Gerrit's core nuzhda. His second form flared crimson, a pure combat nuzhda, and the snake lifted her head.

«There,» she said. *«Now you understand.»*

"Sleet!" Yanek yelped, flailing backwards, tripping over the chair he'd sat in and tangling with it, falling on his ass as he recoiled. The combat nuzhda winked out, but the snake still felt just as alive and vibrant.

"What is it?" Filip asked, though he had trouble tearing his gaze from Nina.

Yanek's response was cursing as he scrambled back against the far wall, swiping vaguely at the air in front of him. Filip shook his attention from Nina, hastily walling off the protection nuzhda—though it had dampened, somehow, after he'd activated the snake. To connect to her access points, he'd needed to pull against a Category Five protection nuzhda; now, it couldn't have been more than Category Two.

Garden walls shielding his mind, Filip crossed to where Yanek pressed himself back against Filip's bookshelf, teeth gritted, chest heaving. "Are you all right?" When Yanek didn't respond, Filip touched his cheek. "Yanek? Look at me." But Yanek's gaze was fixed on the snake. Only when Filip stepped between them, capturing Yanek's chin so he couldn't dodge around, did Yanek's attention snap to his face.

Filip felt a jolt through Nina. The room dimmed, and Filip reeled. But then Yanek caught his face in both hands, eyes wide and desperate, and Filip tore apart his protection nuzhda, wrenching himself free of Nina to focus on his friend.

"What happened?" he asked Yanek.

"Calming," Yanek begged. "Sing Calming."

Frowning, Filip did as Yanek asked, starting with the chorus that everyone learned as a child. He could sing the Song of Calming without conscious attention, so he focused sideways on Yanek, finding him still glowing vaguely crimson and violet, sounding less like Yanek and more like... Gerrit. "You're still pulling against his core nuzhda," Filip said.

Yanek shook his head. Before Filip could protest, he realized that Yanek wasn't disagreeing—he was fighting it, like he'd gotten locked in a nuzhda fugue but remained somehow aware.

Abandoning the Song of Calming, Filip started the Song of Protecting, which was closer to Yanek's core nuzhda. Since Yanek was a strazh, Filip had never tried pulling against his core nuzhda before, but they'd trained together long enough that he had a vague sense for it. Yanek's family was in glassworks, and he'd told Filip once about spending long winter months in his family's house, siblings and cousins and aunts and uncles and grandparents all crowded into the winter rooms, everyone but the smallest children working to polish glass beads. He'd warmed talking about it, and Filip tried to imagine the scene, the joyful, shouting, grumbling chaos, the glitter of firelight through a kaleidoscope of glass, every surface sparkling crystal.

Slowly, Yanek's breathing calmed, his desperate grip on Filip's face easing. Filip walled off the nuzhda-imagining, and studied Yanek, seeking hints of ice-crusted pine and howling wind. But Yanek had returned to himself.

"Thanks," Yanek said shakily. With a wary glance at Nina, he righted the chair he'd knocked over and dropped into it.

"What happened?" Filip asked.

"It amplified my nuzhda—*Gerrit*'s nuzhda. Reinforced it somehow. And when I tried to disconnect, it... locked me in."

Filip returned to the bed, thoughts spinning. Suddenly, the tangle of Nina's weaves—the way they wrapped and folded over each other—began to make sense. "It reinforces Gerrit's and Celka's core nuzhdi. To ground them."

"And it talks."

Filip snorted. "Heard that, did you?"

Yanek laughed like a bottle shattering, then scrubbed his

hands over his face. "Sleet. You imbued a talking snake." He cut a glance sidelong at Filip. "I'm never activating that thing again. Hedvika was right. It's a menace." But his tone was amusement as much as relief. When he sobered, he said, "Do you think this could help Celka?"

Filip's gut reaction was, *of course*. But he hesitated. They'd all been out of control or nearly so when imbuing Nina, acting out of instinct and desperation. The imbuement took more than their core nuzhdi to activate, and the complexity of its activation points made Filip wonder if part of that was from Celka and Gerrit being ungrounded when they'd pulled Gods' Breath. What if activating it with Celka pulled her further off her grounding? What if it undid all the progress she'd recently made?

"How is Celka's grounding coming?" Filip asked.

Yanek leaned the chair back on its rear legs, propping his feet on Filip's bed. "Pretty well. She hasn't been slipping into a combat fugue very often, and when she does, she's usually the first to notice it."

"Can she pull herself back?"

"Sometimes. She's gotten better at that, too, and seems to listen to Hedvika."

Filip shook his head. "Minor miracle."

Yanek dropped his chair legs back down. "Yeah. Not who I would have assigned as her strazh. But I guess that's why I'm not the captain." He grimaced at the door and stood. "Masha's probably looking for me. She'll want to practice hunger weaves some more." He made a face, but Filip was still thinking about Celka.

"Are they going to put Celka in a storm soon?" Filip asked.

"Probably." On his way to the door, Yanek trailed his fingers across Filip's chest like a promise.

Once Yanek had gone, Filip crouched before his bed. Nina

nosed up to him. If Celka went into a storm soon, she might prove her grounding to the resistance's satisfaction—and Filip would lose both her and Gerrit.

He understood Nina's weaves better after tonight. He just needed to figure out how that translated into using her for secure communication—while making sure he didn't accidentally reinforce Celka's core grounding. Guilt twinged him at withholding a tool that might help her, but he didn't *know* that it would. It might make her worse. He clung to that doubt, hating that it felt like a justification.

CHAPTER EIGHTEEN

GERRIT PACED HIS sitting room, glancing at the clock on the mantle as it ticked past midnight. The note folded into his napkin at dinner tonight had said only *leave your window open* and the time. A time that had passed. «They're late,» Gerrit whispered in sousednia. Captain Vrana had latched onto the possibility of poison gas with an edged delight that must have made her utterly terrifying during the war, but in the intervening week—with no resistance contact—Gerrit's doubts had grown. What if tonight's note hadn't been for him? What if Captain Vrana's contacts had been captured? He and Celka could be about to meet an undercover Tayemstvoy operative who'd get proof of Gerrit's treason before turning them both over to the Stormhawk for months of brutal interrogation.

«Relax,» Celka said, slouched diagonally across a wingback chair by the open window, her bare foot kicking over the chair's arm. «They'll be here.» But tension cut her voice.

A scuff sounded outside the window.

Gerrit drew his pistol, pressing himself against the wall beside the window frame as a pair of slender brown hands gripped the sill. As the newcomer pulled themselves up, Gerrit cocked the gun. They froze, head and shoulders through the window.

He almost missed their earrings at first, the pair of simple, blackened steel lightning bolts dim in the darkness. The woman's gaze flicked from Gerrit's gun to his face. "You planning to shoot me or let me in?"

"Lucie!" A grin sounded in Celka's whisper, and she waved Gerrit's gun away, offering their contact a hand into the room.

"Easier than leaping onto a moving train," Lucie said, "but only just." She glanced at Gerrit. "They could have assigned you a lower room." She dusted her hands on dark trousers, flexing her fingers. "Sleet." Gerrit leaned out the window, assessing her climb—it wouldn't have been easy. He shut the window, latching it to prevent their voices from carrying on the night air.

Celka wrapped Lucie in a fierce embrace, which the other woman returned. "Lucie brought me that letter I showed you," Celka told Gerrit. The one from her father, Major Doubek. "We can trust her."

Gerrit holstered his pistol, waving them away from the window.

"What's the imbuement?" Celka asked, staring at Lucie's throat. Only then did Gerrit notice a blue glow beneath Lucie's collar—some sort of necklace. He would have expected a concealment imbuement to hide her, but it didn't seem to affect his perceptions—unless it was altering her appearance?

Suspicious, he edged into sousednia as Lucie said, "It dampens voices. As long as we stand close and don't shout, no one should be able to hear us outside this room."

The weave's resonances matched her description and, in sousednia, a shimmery blue dome covered the three of them. "That's a neat trick," he said.

"Yeah. Too bad we only have one," Lucie said.

Something in her voice sounded familiar and, as she moved into the lamplight, recognition slammed into him. "Byeta?"

Her head snapped around, and their eyes locked for a long second during which Gerrit wasn't sure he was breathing. Then her intensity softened, a smile melting away the intervening years. "Hi, Gerrit."

He caught her hands, searching her face. "You're alive." He could barely believe it.

She snorted. "So far."

"You cut your hair."

She raised a hand, slipping her fingers into her short, spiky black hair. She shrugged. "Easier when you don't know if you'll have a bed."

"How many years since they expelled you?" he said, still searching her face. "You're all right? *Really* all right?" In the years since they'd kissed behind the stables, Byeta had grown even more beautiful. She moved with confidence now, as though she'd settled into her skin in a way he didn't remember from their days in the academy.

She held his gaze, light humor falling away, more than a few years aging her face. "A lot's happened." She glanced over at Celka. "We should get started. We don't have much time."

"Of course." Gerrit shook himself, glancing at Celka and realizing he still held Byeta's hand. He opened his mouth to explain.

Celka beat him to it. "She's the girl your father disappeared to teach you a lesson?"

The punch of that memory hit Gerrit again, and he managed only a nod.

Byeta rolled her eyes. "I'm Lucie now," she told him. "Just a black-bolt servant in the fortress. I get to clean your rooms— lucky me."

Gerrit gaped at her, but Celka smiled. "Is that how we'll communicate?"

Byeta—Lucie, sleet, he didn't know if he could think of her as anything but Byeta, but he needed to—nodded. "I'll slip notes inside your pillowcase as a dead drop," she told Gerrit. "But for tonight, I've been doing some research on your idea."

Gerrit shook himself. As thrilled as he was to discover Byeta still alive, he couldn't let it derail them. They had an assassination to plan. He glanced toward the door—wary, despite the silencing imbuement, of speaking treason aloud.

"The main possibility I could dig up is chlorine gas," Byeta said—no, *Lucie* said—pulling a page out from a pocket in her jacket. She held it out, and Gerrit and Celka converged to read it. "In high enough doses, it can kill within minutes. Keeping him in place for it, though, and getting a high enough concentration will be a challenge." The page had technical specifications: the concentration at which a person could detect the gas, and some notes about tests on rats.

"He'll be able to smell it," Gerrit said.

Lucie made a face. "Yeah. I got a whiff at a low concentration, and it *stinks*. Even that whiff was enough to tear up my eyes. He'll know something's wrong right away—and so will his guards."

"So we'll need to get him into a closed room," Celka said. "No windows, no chance of anyone coming in or pulling him out."

"And he'll *want* to get out," Lucie said.

"So we have to barricade him in?" Gerrit didn't like it. He'd assumed—naively, it seemed—that poison gas would be subtle or would kill fast enough that they could release a grenade of it and run.

"Or get him to barricade himself," Lucie said. "We could launch a conventional attack at the same time, lock down the building?"

Gerrit scrubbed a hand through his hair. "Do we have the resources for that?"

"Sounds like it would get a lot of people killed," Celka said.

Lucie nodded to her. "It probably would. Which is not ideal, but if it *works*, it'd be worth it."

"There has to be a better way," Celka said.

"Can we sedate him?" Lucie asked.

"Unlikely," Gerrit said. "His imbuements would neutralize anything in his food or drink. Unless we could hit him with a sleeping gas first? Is that possible?"

Lucie shook her head. "Not that I've found."

"What about sedating his guards?" Celka asked.

"We've investigated that," Lucie said. "The Yestrab Okhrana operate on a complicated rotation that ensures that they don't all eat or drink from the same sources. We might be able to give a mild sedative to half or two-thirds of them, but even that would have to be pretty light or they'd raise the alarm. No way to hit them all with something stronger."

"What if we do just take out half of the guards?" Celka asked. "Kill them or knock them unconscious with poison? Could we do it at the same time we attack *him*—make sure they couldn't respond to get him out?"

They fell silent, thinking it through.

Gerrit said, "It wouldn't be enough. The Okhrana with him would still be alert—and so would he. The second we opened that gas canister, they'd get out."

Celka paced the perimeter of the silencing imbuement's dome, tugging at her long hair. "So we make an exit impossible." She rounded on Gerrit. "You mentioned artillery, being able to smash whole buildings. You said he'd survive it, but could he get out quickly? What if we brought the building down on him and *then* triggered the gas canister?"

"The civilian casualties—" Gerrit started.

"Is it *possible?*" Celka asked. "If so, we could find a way to evacuate—something. Keep the civilians safe."

"Or sacrifice them," Lucie said, grim. "For this, we would."

"There *has* to be a better way." Gerrit hated the idea of civilian casualties, though he acknowledged that they might have to make the trade-off. "Blowing up a building is hardly precise. Even if we knew exactly where he'd be and we could set charges ahead of time, the way the building collapsed would be hard to predict. Unless he's down in a basement? I guess if he was on a low enough level and we brought down several stories on top of him, then there'd be little chance that the rubble would leave air-gaps. If we made sure that the only way he'd survive would be from his guard holding up the building with imbued force."

"How would we ensure that the gas canister was in there with him?" Lucie asked. "How would we open it once the building came down?"

Celka pulled over Gerrit's desk chair, perching on its back, her feet on the seat. "We need a better gas."

"We don't *have* a better gas," Lucie said. "There's tear gas—the Tayemstvoy have experimented with using it to quell riots, but that'd just blind him and his guard."

"And the moment they tear up," Gerrit said, "they'd throw up all their imbued defenses and call for backup." Gerrit paced, wishing the confines of Lucie's silencing imbuement didn't box him in. Poison gas had seemed perfect. They couldn't get this close only to fail because it sleeting *smelled* bad.

"What about using chlorine as part of another attack?" Celka sounded dubious. "If he and his guard run out of the room, coughing and choking, could we have someone ready as a doctor? Get them to give him some supposed treatment that finishes him off?"

"He has a personal physician," Gerrit said. "We'd have to take them out first."

"Can we poison them?" Celka looked to Gerrit, but he didn't know.

Lucie shrugged. "I don't know if we've looked into that. He travels with the physician and an assistant, and given the Yestrab Okhrana's paranoia, it wouldn't surprise me if they have precautions in what they consume."

"There has to be a weakness we can exploit," Celka said. "Can you learn more?"

Lucie's lips tightened. "I don't know. We don't have much access. The Okhrana are paranoid as sleet—and more vicious than the worst Tayemstvoy."

"And I can't exactly go asking questions," Gerrit said. "Not unless I can make it sound relevant to my own growing importance and paranoia."

"Your sister might know," Lucie said.

Gerrit blew out a breath, nodded. "She might. I get the sense she's been setting up her own little empire." He rolled his shoulders, suddenly tense. Iveta was smart; he'd have to be careful in what he asked to avoid arousing her suspicions—especially if he wanted to come out of this attack without the blame falling on him. "I'll talk to her, try to learn what she's modeled after Father's setup."

Lucie nodded. "I'll keep digging on the gas, see if there's anything else." She swept them with a solemn gaze that seemed older than her years. "Be safe." She was out the window and gone before they could respond.

CHAPTER NINETEEN

"YOUR THROW." HEDVIKA handed Celka the stick they were using as a lightning bolt in their game of cizii myesto. A few meters down the farmyard, Masha and Yanek's 'little houses' were roughly cylindrical chocks of wood filched from the farmhouse's firewood supply and chopped to size, the confines of their 'city' formed with lines kicked in the dirt. Celka tested the lightning bolt's heft and balance, eyeing the distance. She'd never been great at cizii myesto, but Hedvika insisted it would be a good distraction while they waited for the bozhskyeh storm to break.

Celka threw, the lightning bolt pinwheeling through the air. She managed to topple a house, sending it skittering close to the boundary... but not over. The house wound up far enough from the others that it would probably require its own throw to knock out.

Hedvika managed not to sigh too audibly. She clapped Celka on the shoulder. "You'll get better."

Celka doubted it. Already, the building storm tugged against her spine, leaving a taste of dry leaves in her mouth.

Her stomach churned with worry about being beneath a bozhskyeh storm, and she obsessively checked her sousednia. She balanced on her high wire, spotlights glinting off her costume, the air smelling of sawdust and horses with only the faintest tang of blood. She was grounded, just like she'd been all morning. She could do this. She had to.

Today's storm wouldn't just prove her grounding to Vrana, it was her chance to save Pa. Practicing with Hedvika and the rest of her squad, she'd figured out how to turn her weaves inside-out so they'd act on someone else. Rather than forcing people to tremble in awe, she'd designed this imbuement to give them calm clarity—she thought. Celka wasn't used to planning the shape of her imbuements, so her weeks of practice with Hedvika since the rally had felt... stilted. She hoped that was just because she'd been building nuzhda weaves beneath clear skies, and not that she'd been building them wrong. Hedvika had been encouraging, but she hadn't understood the awe-inspiring imbuement well enough to tell Celka if she was getting it right.

She had to get it right. Pa was going storm-mad. He needed her help.

Celka's gaze settled on Hedvika, lining up for a powerful throw that would destroy Masha and Yanek's city, and cold clambered down her spine. Hedvika released the bolt, her casual violence shattering the city who, in irreverence to the Storm Gods, failed to properly ground their buildings against lightning strikes—that's what the name meant: cizii myesto, irreverent city. Celka tried to picture Hedvika as a Storm God, the way she always did when playing cizii myesto with family or friends—but it didn't fit.

Overhead, the bozhskyeh storm darkened, the pull on Celka's storm-thread a near-constant burn down her storm-scar—though no lightning yet streaked the sky.

If Hedvika wasn't a Storm God, this couldn't be an irreverent city, and they were just throwing sticks at more sticks. Except... cizii meant foreign, too, not just irreverent. Suddenly, today's game made an ominous kind of sense. The bolt they threw was not lightning from the Gods, but humanity's pale reflection of that power—an imbuement. The city they attacked was not some foolish group of Bourshkanyans too lazy to properly ground their homes; it was foreign, one of many to be crushed beneath Bourshkanya's machine of war.

Celka swallowed hard.

Hedvika leaned close, pointing to the 'house' Celka had nearly rolled free of the city's bounds with her throw. "If you can get that one, I can win with my next throw."

Of course Hedvika could. She was the perfect instrument of State expansion—brutal and capable. That Celka had learned to trust her made this worse, not better. Was Celka really helping the resistance if she attacked cizii homes at Hedvika's side?

My imbuement will help people, she told herself as she hefted the bolt. Whether or not it brought Pa back from the brink of storm-madness, calm clarity could save people from violence in storms, it could help them resolve problems. Maybe it could even make the Tayemstvoy reasonable. She shuddered at the memories of Major Rychtr questioning her in the circus and the Tayemstvoy lieutenant tearing off the printmaker's fingernails in Bludov. *Cizii myesto is just a game.* But the stick felt dangerous, Hedvika's grip on her shoulder as threatening as the bozhk Tayemstvoy surrounding her squad.

Sousednia shuddered, the high wire bucking beneath Celka's feet, truncheons cracking, the air gusting blood and mud. Gripping the cizii myesto bolt in true-life, Celka willed the high wire to stillness, imagining the air bright with a sawdust freshness.

"Come on," Hedvika said, "throw. You can do it."

Jaw set, Celka flung the bolt. As she released it, Gods' Breath flashed overhead, yanking against her storm-thread. The stick went wide. Yanek yelped, barely dodging.

"Sleet." Masha lifted her face to the sky. "There it—"

Thunder drowned her words. Then the sky opened, and rain sheeted down. Hedvika grabbed Celka's arm, cursing enthusiastically, dragging her toward the farmhouse, cizii myesto pitch forgotten.

As Celka leapt up the steps onto the farmhouse's broad covered porch, her hobnail boots clacked against the wood, so like those of the red shoulders keeping watch from the door, from across the farmyard, from the troop transport trucks down the drive. Those red shoulders had evicted the farmers from their home, vanishing them who-knows-where so the imbuement platoon could use their farm as a base.

Masha leapt up onto the porch beside her, slapping water off her flat cap. Yanek grinned, leaning on the railing to peer up at the sky flashing with lightning. Then Gods' Breath slashed the heavens and Celka saw instead two gold-bolt Army officers, pistols on their hips. Her hands tightened to fists.

"Maybe cizii myesto wasn't such a great idea," Hedvika said, a distant clarion. In the farmyard, rain had erased the foreign city's boundaries, the houses washed away. Hedvika draped her arm over Celka's shoulders. "We'll never know who would have won." Her tone could have been amusement, but it exuded menace.

You trust Hedvika, Celka told herself, the words automatic from practice, and she reached into her pocket, pulling out the green pocket square. The soft silk grounded her, the high wire wavering back beneath her feet even as the bozhskyeh storm yanked on her spine.

With Gerrit in the circus, Celka had learned to reshape her sousednia into a featureless plain, clearing it of all nuzhdi—even her core—in order to escape the bozhskyeh storm's tug. Closing her eyes, she concentrated now, but her recent practice gripping her core sousednia made it difficult to sweep the landscape clean.

"You're in control." Hedvika laid her hand on the nape of Celka's neck. Rainwater trickled down Celka's spine, and her strazh's calm eased some of the storm's insistent pull. Over the circus's scents of horses and mud, Celka caught the sharp odor of a dirty child, the feel of strong small arms wrapping her, protecting her even with the whole world against them.

The familiarity of Hedvika's protection nuzhda settled sousednia, the scent of mud fading into fresh-dry sawdust, the circus band trilling the high wire act's tense anticipation. From there, Celka pressed the big top into the ground.

With sousednia a pristine field of green grass stretching to the horizon, Celka opened her eyes in true-life, focusing on her strazh's familiar face. Hedvika might kiss regime boots, but it was hard, sometimes, not to think of her as a friend. "Thanks," Celka said, and Hedvika nodded.

The rest of her squad had gathered beneath the porch along with the six imbuement mages and strazhi from Yellow Squad. Gerrit stood before them, Filip at his side, official and serious while the storm crashed overhead and wind sprayed them with rain despite the porch roof. Tayemstvoy circled them, alert but no more threatening than usual. Celka moved next to Masha, not quite at attention, but attentive, and Hedvika's hand slipped into hers.

«Do you see your high wire?» Gerrit asked her in sousednia.

«I pushed it away,» she said, feeling calm, the storm raging overhead but not yanking on her. «I'm in my featureless field. I'm ready.»

A smile tugged his lips, though in true-life his expression was solemn. "Private Prochazka," he said aloud. "Show us what you can do."

She traded her cap for a steel storm helmet, releasing its grounding lines to thunk down to the wet planking. Hedvika at her side, she stepped into the drenching rain, the grounding lines catching in the churned weeds and tugging against the helmet's leather chinstrap. With only the farmhouse and its outbuildings for shelter, Gerrit had decided the imbuement-strazh pairs would work beneath open sky, putting a safe twenty meters between the active imbuement attempt and the rest of the platoon.

Out past the demolished remains of their cizii myesto pitch, Celka pulled a thin brass oval punched with a simple lightning bolt from her pocket. Hedvika had bought it for her. An object had to fit an imbuement's weaves, and a storm pendant seemed perfect to quiet someone from a raging nuzhda or powerful emotions.

Gripping the pendant as if in prayer, Celka slipped into sousednia, checking that her grassy field remained featureless. Satisfied, she reached for the memory that would drive her concealment nuzhda.

The angle of the sun shifted, her shadow lengthening as the verdant field sprouted the back lot's tents, dirty white canvas rippling as the summer air carried the dusty golden smell of ripe barley. In true-life, Celka clasped Hedvika's hand, but in sousednia, the figure shifted until Pa grinned down at her.

Pa winks as they near Clown Alley, the tent where the clowns change out their props between acts, and Celka stifles laughter. Sunlight saturates the sky's blue as they press their backs to tent canvas. Loud on the other side, a clown whose wig they drenched in cheap perfume grouses to the others. Pa presses a forefinger to his lips, eyes twinkling mischief.

Celka cradled that moment in walls of tent canvas, protecting it from the outside world as she shifted into true-life, focusing on the brass storm pendant before pulling it into her concealment-warped sousednia. The pendant gleamed blue from her nuzhda as she wrapped stifled laughter and floral perfume around it. The weaves she'd designed were tricky, and the nuzhda fought her, trying to shove her through the tent canvas to tickle the grouchy clown from sousednia, intent on innocent mischief rather than deep, calming breaths. But she'd practiced these weaves over and over in the Storm Guard Fortress. The nuzhda giggled and writhed, almost alive beneath the bozhskyeh storm, but she prevailed.

By the time she settled the weaves around the pendant, strain quickened her breath and an ache needled into her temples. In true-life's rainstorm, Hedvika's hand warmed the back of her neck. "Ready?" Celka asked her strazh.

"Ready." Strain clipped Hedvika's confident voice, and Celka returned to sousednia, walling off her concealment nuzhda and weaves with tent canvas.

Stepping outside those canvas walls, however, blood and the crack of blows gusted over her, the springtime back lot tangling with the sawdust-scented stillness beneath the big top. Pa cried out as a Tayemstvoy truncheon landed, but Celka remembered Hedvika asking how the high wire felt beneath her feet. *The high wire is your true sousednia*, Hedvika seemed to say, though, at the moment, she was a purple and blue ripple at Celka's back, her strazh weaves ready.

«I stand on a high wire,» Celka said in sousednia, even as the combat nuzhda buffeted her, concentrating on believing it. Slowly, the cook tent and practice wire faded, until Celka balanced in the spotlight.

Slipping her attention back through tent canvas into her concealment-warped sousednia, she double-checked her weaves. They'd slipped as her core-sousednia demanded her attention, and she wrested them back into shape, even as she desperately wanted to tickle someone. Then, gripping all three realities—her core sousednia's high wire, true-life's rain-soaked farmyard, and her concealment nuzhda's sunny laughter—she grasped her storm-thread and *pulled*.

Gods' Breath leapt to her call, euphoric agony sluicing her spine, lashing along her arm and into the concealment weaves she'd wrapped around the pendant. She cried out, the pain worse than she remembered, and her control shook, the rush of storm energy nearly tearing through the careful, calming loops of nuzhda. But she held, *held*, clinging to laughter.

Red-gold Gods' Breath shifted to a blue like the summer sky above Clown Alley, settling into her weaves, a trickle searing the back of her neck before soaking into Hedvika's hand.

Knees weak, Celka wavered. Hedvika caught her, tilting Celka to lean against her chest.

Imbuement complete, the tent walls surrounding Celka's concealment nuzhda faded into the earth, the nuzhda dissipating with them, until only two realities pressed in on her. In sousednia, she wavered on her high wire, the scent of blood thick in the air, while true-life's rain slicked her skin.

Hedvika described Celka's high wire in words that had become routine, but Celka swiped water from her eyes to see the storm pendant. "It worked." But the words felt wrong, and her stomach twisted with fear. Her weaves had shaped Gods' Breath, converting it into a crystalized concealment nuzhda, but the imbuement felt broken. In sousednia, Pa cried out.

The imbuement couldn't have failed. Pa was counting on her.

Ignoring Hedvika, Celka marched back through the rain toward the farmhouse, scowling at the storm pendant. It pulsed summer-sky blue, but felt somehow restricted, like its weaves were locked in a too-small box.

Struggling not to panic, Celka dove back into memory, activating the imbuement with summertime mischief. Or she tried to. Nothing happened.

Stopping a few meters from the porch steps, she asked Hedvika, "Do you feel anything?" But she didn't need to hear her strazh's answer. Hedvika felt nothing, because there was nothing to feel. Celka could connect into the imbuement's access points, but the imbuement did *nothing*.

Weeks of training and practice for *nothing*. Pa was going storm-mad. He needed her and she'd *failed*.

Snarling frustration, Celka flung the pendant into the mud. She'd thought that finally she'd found a way to help him—just like she'd thought she and Gerrit had found a way to help the resistance. But poison gas was a dead-end. They weren't going to be able to kill the Stormhawk. She wasn't going to be able to help Pa. Gerrit wanted her working on emotional imbuements so she could avoid building weapons for the State, but maybe she *should* be imbuing weapons.

Maybe she should imbue the artillery gun in the farmyard and turn it against these regime boot-lickers so she and Gerrit could escape into the resistance where they could do real good.

Turning her back on the house, she strode toward the massive artillery gun the red shoulders had wheeled into the farmyard. She'd warn Gerrit in sousednia before she fired, and they'd scythe down the rest of the Tayemstvoy and escape in one of the troop transports. She'd been a fool in Bludov to let them get captured; she wouldn't make that mistake again.

Sousednia cracked with blows. Hedvika caught her arm, shouting, and Celka didn't know how she'd ever trusted the bozhk. She remembered another bozhk officer in the circus, pretending to be her ally, telling her to answer Tayemstvoy questions so she wouldn't be hurt. But Celka *had* answered their questions, and they'd hurt her anyway.

She remembered Major Rychtr looming over her in the tack trailer, hitting her, pinning her to the ground and snarling threats. He'd been trying to find Gerrit. Celka had been an innocent civilian, and he hadn't cared. How had Celka been so naïve to expect a calming imbuement to do any good? The Tayemstvoy understood only violence. Major Rychtr had threatened to lock her in a cell and torture her for months. Threatened to make her watch while he made Ela scream. Celka's cheeks still throbbed from bruises, and she could feel the steel handcuffs biting into her wrists as he slammed her to the ground.

"Remember your high wire," Hedvika was shouting, but she was a regime toad just like Major Rychtr, just like Captain Vrana, just like the Tayemstvoy beating Pa. She'd worn a friendly face to twist Celka into a boot-licker, but Celka was through letting the regime dictate her moves.

The smell of blood and mud thickened the air, and Celka shaped her rage to fit the barrel of the artillery gun she'd drawn into sousednia's back lot. She turned it, aiming for the Tayemstvoy beating Pa. True-life had blurred, and someone had grabbed her arm, wrenching her to a stop before she could reach the gun.

She bared her teeth. It didn't matter where the artillery gun was in true-life. With the imbuement, she'd shell the farmhouse full of her enemies. No one would stop her.

CHAPTER TWENTY

FILIP FROWNED AS Celka neared the farmhouse porch, clutching the imbued pendant. Hedvika trailed her, glowing the colors of Celka's core nuzhda. He told himself she could handle it, but his stomach churned like when he'd burst into the print shop and found Celka surrounded by Tayemstvoy corpses. "Something's wrong," he told Gerrit.

Celka snarled and flung the pendant aside.

"Celka, no!" Filip vaulted the porch rail as Celka strode back into the farmyard.

Hedvika started at his voice and lost precious seconds looking back at the farmhouse and then at the imbuement in the weeds. Filip couldn't spare her more attention.

Flaring crimson, Celka sprinted for the unlimbered howitzer, the ghostly overlay of her high wire costume shifting into rugged work clothes like she'd worn around the back lot. As Filip ran, he fumbled open a pouch on his belt, snatching out the glass ampoule he'd started carrying for emergencies. The sedative was a risk—it had been designed to be fast, but he didn't know how fast, and if it shattered Celka's control after she pulled Gods' Breath, it would be worse than nothing—but if she imbued again, and combat... he didn't know if she'd come back. And Gerrit was too far away for another miracle.

Behind him, Hedvika shouted grounding-cues as she ran. Filip tore off the needle's cover and plunged the syringe into Celka's shoulder. Hedvika caught Celka's arm, wrenching her to a stop, flaring bright with Celka's core nuzhda.

Celka cried out and twisted, tearing the now-empty syringe from her shoulder. She threw a punch, and Filip blocked. She grabbed for the pistol at his hip.

He caught Celka's wrist, pinning her hand against his chest so she couldn't reach the weapon. "Celka! Celka, you're safe." But as he said it, he knew the words wouldn't matter. She hadn't listened to him before, and she'd been used to trusting him then. "Ground her!" he ordered Hedvika and, abandoning words, Filip dove into memory.

Blood tastes coppery bright in his mouth, the autumn sunlight blinding as the older cadets loom over him.

The combat nuzhda flared hard beneath the storm, and Filip scrabbled after control, struggling to contain the desperate urge to fight so he could shift it into Celka's core nuzhda once he caught her attention.

Behind the Storm Guard Fortress, Filip pushes himself to his hands and knees, ribs and jaw aching from blows, and Celka turns. She glows like a hot coal, her expression fierce. She catches his hand, pulls him to his feet. «We'll kill these sleet-lickers,» she says, and Filip wants to say yes, wants to stand back-to-back with her and fight.

«No.» He barely managed the word, clawing back to the muddy farmyard. He had Celka's attention, he needed to—

«We have to fight,» Celka snarls. «I won't let them kill Pa.» She's still looking at him, but he can feel that she wants to look past him, at the Tayemstvoy in her sousednia.

Filip clutched her hand where he pinned it against his chest, struggling to tear free of his own combat nuzhda. He needed to see Celka as she had been in the circus, imagine her sousednia as he had when they practiced dry-firing her stolen pistol. But the vivid imagining he'd used resisted him—like straining against a heavy weight with atrophied muscles.

He refused to give up. Locking away the part of himself that fought behind the fortress, Filip dove into the hay and sawdust smells that had swirled around her during their long afternoons together in the circus. He dragged against his memory of the big top's hush as the band began to play for her family's circus act, and imagined the high wire as though he stood level with it. The image wavered, threatening to decohere. He'd never stood on her family's high wire platform, looking out across the steel cable glinting in spotlights, but he refused that knowledge. He'd stood on the high wire, he stood on it *now*, the steel cable digging into his bare feet.

Filip threw himself fully into that belief, echoing it back to Celka as loudly as he could and forcing his own combat nuzhda to disperse.

Standing on Filip's imagined high wire, Celka blazed crimson—but he refused to believe her rugged clothing. She wore her high wire costume, she stood on the high wire with him, light with purpose and grace.

"No!" Celka screamed, and she swung at him, her hook punch too fast for him to block.

Her fist caught him hard across the jaw. Pain burst his vision red, but he clung to her core nuzhda, pinwheeling his arms on the imagined high wire.

They stumbled together, Hedvika gripping the back of Celka's neck, her heat-shimmer tangling crimson and violet as she scrambled to build strazh weaves.

Celka slammed her knee up, aiming for Filip's groin but

missing. The burst of pain in his thigh shouldn't have mattered, but it made him taste blood, and when Celka's hand on his chest became a claw as she grasped for focus, those contact points burned like fire. The taste of blood strengthened, gritty like he'd been thrown face-first into the dirt.

The high wire shuddered, autumn sunlight cutting through rents in the tent canvas. Filip tightened his grip on Celka's wrist, desperate to fight even as he struggled to see the big top's open darkness around him.

Pain flared at the base of his skull, and a prickling, static charge yanked on his spine.

Then her claw hand spasmed, and her knees buckled. She collapsed against him, eyes rolling up, crimson combat nuzhda draining like water into sand.

With it, the charge drained from the air. Filip gasped, stumbling beneath Celka's deadweight. Hedvika swooped in, catching Celka as true-life reeled, the space around Filip expanding and contracting as he teetered on the high wire, as he stumbled to his feet in the autumn sunlight with blood streaming from his nose.

Gerrit grabbed his shoulder, pushing between him and Celka. "I've got her."

Filip's foot slipped on the wire. Stomach lurching, he flailed out—but he caught nothing. He plummeted into open space.

Impact was a jolt, wet and squelching—just mud, not a dozen-meter fall. Filip's breath came hard, and one of the older cadets kicked him in the ribs. He swallowed a cry, blood hot and metallic in his mouth, and lurched to his feet. He had to keep fighting, had to keep the cadets' attention off Gerrit—except Gerrit knelt next to Celka, wiping rainwater from her face.

"What did you do?" Gerrit demanded.

"Tranq." Filip's jaw ached from the older cadets' blows.

Gods' Breath flashed overhead, yanking on his spine. The back of his neck burned, and he struggled to focus. "Did she imbue?"

"No," Hedvika said, slinging Celka up over her shoulders to carry her to the farmhouse. Gerrit followed her, shouting for the company medic.

One of the older cadets punched Filip, a hard blow up under his solar plexus, stunning his diaphragm. He folded, fighting for breath. Yanek caught his elbow, and Filip staggered forward, trying to escape the follow-up punch that would drive him into the dirt.

"Are you all right?" Yanek asked.

Filip tore from his grasp, certain his hold preceded a punch. Why? No one was fighting him. He turned on Yanek, swimming through rage and desperation. "You said she was grounded!" He dodged a blow and surged forward, catching up to Hedvika as she climbed the porch steps. "You said she was safe to be out here!"

"You're sparking." Yanek caught his arm, jogging to keep pace.

"I'm not a sleeting mundane," Filip snapped.

"How big was the dose?" Gerrit demanded as they shoved through the farmhouse door, Hedvika arrowing for the bedroom, depositing Celka atop a faded quilt.

"Big." Why was Filip fighting with only his fists? He had a knife at one hip, a pistol at his other. Breathing hard from the fight—*what fight?*—he struggled to think. This was his platoon, not the enemy. They'd slushed up, and he'd sleet-sure dress down the strazhi, but he didn't need to fight. "It was dosed for *you*." He snarled the word, angry to see Gerrit crouched beside Celka, angry that Gerrit hadn't realized she was unsafe to be in the storm. How was he such a lousy partner that he missed her lingering combat-warping?

Hands open in surrender, Yanek said, "We slushed up." He stepped closer, gaze snaring Filip's. "We'll talk about it later, all right?"

"No, it's not—"

Yanek cupped Filip's jaw in his big hand, and Filip's words failed him. The taste of blood sharpened. The dim farmhouse bedroom flared into a hidden corner of the Storm Guard Fortress's training yard.

Autumn leaves crunch under Filip's boots as he pushes himself back to his feet, jaw throbbing. Stay down, *he tells young, scrawny Gerrit.* Against his own advice, Filip, blood gritty in his mouth, turns to the older cadets.

But when he throws a punch, his fist wisps through his attacker like they're smoke. Stumbling, he smells ancient ink on a breeze that draws him up, out of the fortress's yard. He blinks, trying to clear his vision. He must have taken a harder hit than he realized.

One of the older cadets lunges, and Filip tries to parry, instead sweeping a book aside, sending it arcing for the floor. He dives to catch it before it can hit the ground and crack its ancient binding. Ruin a book, and he'll lose his precious access to the restricted library. Already they didn't want to grant it to someone so young.

He catches the book just in time, impact bruising his elbows on the stone floor.

The pain is nothing compared to his relief. Cross-legged on the gray stone, Filip smooths the book's rumpled pages. Beside him, the desk where he'd been working. But his jaw still throbs. Disoriented, Filip peers down the row of tight-packed shelves, the air heady with ink and knowledge, quiet like nowhere else in the fortress.

A figure stands before him, glowing violet, the protection nuzhda *tangling with gold and crimson, slashed by azure.*

Cradling the book to his chest, Filip stumbles to his feet, drawn to the figure. Setting the book down, he touches—

—Yanek's face.

They stood in a small bedroom, dim with the shutters closed against the storm. A bolt-hawk lit a gas lantern, holding it over Celka who lay on the bed, the company medic taking her pulse, Gerrit concerned at her side. Disoriented, Filip frowned around. On a stump that served as a bedside table, a small, framed daguerreotype of strangers stared back at him. The rain must have slackened, because he couldn't hear it on the roof anymore, though the shutters shook in a way that suggested hard wind. The room was strangely silent.

Yanek still glowed with a complex nuzhda. Only then did Filip realize he was still touching Yanek's face, as though they were lovers alone together—or an imbuement mage and his strazh.

Filip stumbled back, releasing Yanek's face. It was harder to tear his gaze away, but he managed, forcing himself to the window. Fine mist sprayed him as the shutters rattled—silently still—on their hinges. "The storm?" he asked as Yanek came up next to him. Distantly he heard conversation behind him.

"There's hail on the roof." Yanek spoke louder than necessary given how close they stood and the room's utter silence.

Filip shook his head. Hail, he'd hear. He rubbed the back of his neck, his storm-scar a hot brand.

Then Gerrit was calling to him, and Filip jolted, following him back out onto the porch. Gerrit gripped his arm and thanked him for grounding Celka, a concerned frown wrinkling his brow before he smoothed it away and ordered one of the other imbuement mages to attempt their hunger imbuement.

Pea-sized hail coated the farmyard like snow, more

bouncing to the ground all around them, but still Filip heard nothing. He scrubbed his face with one hand, struggling to concentrate, struggling to keep his breathing level. Gerrit had described the world going quiet after he imbued, but Filip hadn't—couldn't—imbue; and the tranq had stopped Celka. What was happening to him?

CHAPTER TWENTY-ONE

CELKA FADED IN and out, vaguely aware of someone glowing beside her, singing the Song of Calming off-key, mumbling the words. Twice, Celka vomited, twisting over the side of her bed just in time, her body feeling like it belonged to someone else. Eventually, she recognized Hedvika, and her stomach twisted, the scent of blood strengthening before fading as Hedvika rippled with the circus band's fluting.

In Celka's hand, she clutched the green pocket square. Hedvika held her other. Celka's memories cut like shrapnel. Pa. Failure. Tayemstvoy with blood-stained truncheons. Hedvika called her name.

Flinching from her strazh, Celka pressed her eyes shut.

When consciousness next retuned, something had changed. The singing voice at her side was richer, the words clearer. The tune, too, had shifted, Calming's drone replaced by the Song of Concealing's twittering scales.

Eyes closed, she reached into sousednia, surprised to find herself laying on the high wire platform. Beside her, a figure glowed the sky-blue and violet rainbow of Celka's core nuzhda, the band's tremulous fluting coming less from below and more from—Filip, she realized, recognizing his vibrant heat-shimmer, or maybe the way he pulled against her core nuzhda. From him, the scents and sounds felt... more right, in some indescribable way.

Part of her wanted to reach for him, even as anger snarled for her to turn her back. She forced her eyes open. "Hey," she tried to say. It came out a dry croak.

Filip stopped singing and offered a glass of water. She struggled and failed to sit up, and he put an arm around her shoulders, mounding pillows behind her back.

Celka made herself take small sips of water, hoping to settle her stomach. Avoiding looking at Filip, she glanced around the bunkroom. They sat alone, the sky outside graying. Dusk, she wondered, or dawn? "How long was I out?" her voice was rough.

"It's evening," Filip said. "The same day."

"Where are the others?"

"I sent Hedvika to get some air. She's been with you all day. The rest of your squad is out celebrating. Masha imbued."

Emotion twisted through Celka—happiness for Masha; worry about the weapons she'd create; betrayal that her squad would leave her behind, unconscious. They'd claimed to be family. She didn't believe it, but... she'd convinced herself they cared.

"Gerrit ordered them not to wait for you," Filip said, as if he could hear her thoughts. "They wanted to be here."

"Why?" she asked.

"He wasn't sure it would be wise to have them here when you woke." Filip searched her face, gaze defocusing. "Seems like Hedvika mostly pulled you back, though."

"Mostly?"

Strain tightened his eyes. "There's something I want to try. I'll be right back."

Filip returned carrying Nina, the python looped over his shoulders. Like when he'd first unpacked the snake, a hook lodged under Celka's sternum, tugging her toward the python. When Filip sat at her bedside, Celka ran her hand down the snake's smooth, cool coils. A buzz like raw storm energy tingled her skin, and mesmerizing colors twisted across Nina's scales.

Sometime between leaving her room and returning, Filip had stopped pulling against Celka's core nuzhda. Now, his heat-shimmer shifted, crouching, hands cupping something. Before she could puzzle it out, a violet protection nuzhda burst across him. He brightened like a flare before reaching into Nina and—

Celka gasped, her fingers prickling. She felt like she was falling—not down, but *up*.

She meant to jerk her hand away, but her body resisted, gripping Nina. The python shifted on Filip's shoulders to catch Celka's gaze. Combat's red flickered through the snake's eyes, tangling with other colors. As Celka stared, Filip's sousedni-shape shifted again, rolling away, fighting—before he burst red with combat nuzhda. This, too, he connected into the snake, and the hook beneath Celka's sternum yanked harder.

She gasped, true-life falling away. Instead of laying on the high wire platform, Celka balanced on the steel cable, spectators far below. Out of habit, she avoided looking at them, instead inhaling hay and sawdust, the humid air close like her family's embrace.

«Can you activate the snake?» Filip asked. She could swear she heard him in sousednia.

She frowned to find Filip, sharp and real, seated on the high wire platform in the chair her family used for their four-person pyramid. His khaki sleeves were rolled to mid-forearm, muted light glinting off his gold lightning bolt earring. Nina coiled about him, as bright and colorful as in true-life. Around Filip, the air smelled like when she'd known him in the circus—old books and oiled steel, though beneath that cut a garden freshness and the bright iron taste of blood from his walled-off protection and combat nuzhdi. Looking at him now, she would have said he was storm-blessed—though his sousedni-shape blurred and sharpened as though she adjusted the focus on a pair of binoculars, fading back and forth into a storm-touched heat-shimmer.

Tearing her gaze off him, Celka pushed aside the mystery of his storm-affinity. He'd wanted her to activate Nina. Could she?

Squinting at the snake, Celka discovered bright points of light—activation points—that glowed the blue-violet rainbow of her core nuzhda. They seemed to draw her in—that hook beneath her sternum—and she reached out, pressing the sawdust and horse smell of sousednia into them. Nothing happened.

She pressed harder, focusing on the feel of the high wire beneath her feet. Something resisted, like a barrier had formed between her and those alluring points. But she strained harder and—with a *crack*—the barrier shattered. Her vision flared white, brightness painful and crushing like being swept away in an avalanche, and a hush fell over the crowd—even the band going silent. Gasping, Celka flung her hands up to shield her face, but nearly lost her balance. Shooting her arms out to the sides, she crouched to lower her center of gravity on the high wire, wavering dangerously, squinting through eyes streaming tears.

The light sharpened, tightening to a single line—the steel cable beneath her feet—then dampened, the cable's dull metal braid gaining a depth of texture that tightened her chest with joy. Before, she'd felt her family reaching for her in the platform's darkness, but now their love blazed around her, the summer humidity bright with suppressed laughter, with Aunt Benedikta's shouting, with Grandfather's strong embrace.

The band started up, its notes crisp and pure in a way she hadn't realized they'd been muddied before. She strained, expecting another sound beneath the band, the constant drumbeat of blows, painful and dissonant. She heard only music.

Above her, the big top's peak stretched upward, hazy in dust from the spotlights, and Celka felt like she was flying. Only now did she realize how much her balance had fought her before, her body aching from Vrana's blows. Spreading her arms, she balanced effortlessly on one foot. Stretching her other leg back along the line of the wire, she tipped forward to soar like a bird.

A cheer rose from the crowd and, despite herself, she glanced down. Instead of Army and Tayemstvoy soldiers, civilians filled the crowd, colorful embroidery and bright sarafans joyful in the dimness.

«*Welcome back, little lightning rod,*» Nina said, and it felt like Pa wrapping her in his arms.

On the platform just ahead, Filip sat with Nina around his shoulders, sharp as any storm-blessed mage. His expression had softened—hopeful, relieved—but when she met his gaze, his became guarded.

«Thank you,» she said in sousednia.

Some of his wariness eased, and Celka arched her back, reaching over her head to clasp her ankle. Stretching upwards, she balanced on one foot, the strain narrowing her focus. She was strong. She remembered Gerrit saying it in Bludov, calling her back to this place. How had she forgotten? How had she let it twist away?

Releasing her ankle, Celka settled her feet back into a perfect line. Gazing around the big top, she searched for other storm-blessed presences. Finding none, she dared a small dislocation, pirouetting on the wire and taking several steps away from Filip, reveling in her newfound balance.

Each breath tasted so right, and Celka felt strength deep within her muscles, a strength that drew from the steel cable's bounce, that misdirected her audience with a smile. She carried combat within her, for certain. Pa had guaranteed that by having her watch the Tayemstvoy brutalize him. But Pa had also taught her to smile through strain, to make the near-impossible look easy. She didn't need to lose herself in a combat fugue to be strong. Didn't need to flinch at the sight of regime uniforms.

Pa had led the resistance for years, and no one had ever seen him holding a gun. Destroying the regime meant more than imbuing weapons. She would make it a dance, a performance—and the Stormhawk wouldn't realize she was coming for him until it was too late.

Sensing Filip's gaze, she turned back to him, studying him across several meters of high wire. Between them, the air shimmered, as though from a thin film of oil on water, diffracting rainbows. The distortion concentrated between them, fuzzing out into the darkness beyond, pulsing like Nina's imbuement.

Closing the distance, Celka touched the snake still coiled on Filip's shoulders. «She grounded me,» she said in sousednia. «*You* grounded me.»

Filip lifted his chin in acknowledgment, still wary.

Saying it, though, she realized that depiction of Nina was incomplete. Inside her coils, Celka sensed another access point, one that smelled like old books and oiled steel—like Filip. She reached for it, and the moment she touched it, her sense of Filip intensified in a way that seemed to blot out everything else. «*It lets us... communicate?*» she asked, not quite speaking in sousednia, but rather pushing the words through Nina.

«*It did in Bludov,*» Filip said, his voice tinny through the snake. «*I've been studying the weaves. I think it's secure.*»

Peering into Nina's weaves, Celka realized something else. «*We can reach Gerrit through her, too.*»

«*I haven't gotten it to work,*» Filip said. «*Yanek and I activated her for the first time last night.*»

«*Yanek can hear us too?*» Celka asked, suddenly worried. Filip's claim that Nina could make their conversation secure felt right; but she wouldn't have expected Yanek to be able to use her.

«*No. He had to drop the imbuement. It reinforces your and Gerrit's core nuzhdi. It nearly overwhelmed him.*»

«*But not you,*» she said.

«*I helped imbue it.*» He said it like fact.

Celka searched his expression, but the anger she'd felt every other time at seeing him never flared. He'd lied to her, yes, but she'd been lying to him too—about her own storm-affinity, and Gerrit, and the extent of her resistance involvement. She'd been planning to leave without telling him. He'd interrupted that escape, but not to drag her before the Tayemstvoy; he'd risked revealing himself to save her from storm-madness. Shifting back into true-life, she reached for him, hesitating just short of touching his knee. "Thank you for saving my life. Today, and in Bludov."

"Just doing my duty," he said, wooden.

She shook her head. "You did more. What you said in the circus, about being a guard...? That was true, wasn't it."

Filip nodded, still wary. He stood, piling Nina at the foot of Celka's bed.

"Was..." Celka bit her lip, not wanting to ask her next question because she was afraid of the answer. "Was what you said to me true too? That I wasn't just an excuse to keep an eye on Gerrit?"

Jaw tense, Filip glanced at the door like he was considering his escape.

Celka hugged her arms around her middle, trying to blame the nausea on the sedative.

With a sigh, Filip flipped the chair around to straddle it backwards, making the wooden chairback a barrier between them. "It was true."

"Was?" The past tense stung.

He shook his head. "Is? I don't know." His rich mahogany eyes flicked over her face, and Celka felt a tug that seemed to come from sousednia.

She resisted it. "You've been avoiding me."

"You've hated me."

She swallowed hard and twisted the pocket square. "Are you Ctibor?" She darted a glance at his familiar face that had become a stranger's—or maybe she'd just told herself he was a stranger.

His knuckles whitened on the chair. "No."

"Not even a little?" She searched his expression, breathing deep in sousednia, trying to understand him—to understand them, together. She'd trusted him when she thought he was a mundane, but never enough to share all her secrets.

He stood, pacing like he was caged. *«I won't let you get Gerrit killed.»* The snake's imbuement stripped some of the richness from his voice.

She glared at him, but he smelled like lilacs and turned earth over a fear stink of piss and antiseptic, and her anger faded. *«That's not what we're doing.»*

«You don't know anything,» he snapped. The tug in sousednia was stronger this time. When she followed it, she found Filip standing on her high wire platform, edges as

crisp as Gerrit's ever were. «*Maybe you believed you could fight the State while hiding out in the circus, but* not here. *This is our world—mine and Gerrit's—and whatever you're planning, whatever these emotional imbuements are for, the Tayemstvoy will figure it out and they'll take you apart. Slowly. You'll wish you were dead a thousand times. And they'll do the same to Gerrit.*»

«*And to you? Is that what you're afraid of?*» Celka asked.

«*This isn't about me! Freezing hailstones, why won't* either *of you see it? Gerrit could do so much—be so much—if he wasn't chasing after you.*»

Disgust curled her lip. «*You want him to be like Artur? That's what the Stormhawk wants. A whole army of Arturs.*»

«*That's not what I meant.*»

«*No?*» Celka left her true-form behind, putting her face right up in his. «*What do you think happens to him if he stops fighting? If he gives up and becomes what the Stormhawk wants? You knew him before he met me, so maybe you think that's what he should return to—crushing down his compassion, justifying brutality that sickened him because it was the only way he knew how to survive. Gerrit's more than that.*»

Filip held her gaze despite the fact that he shouldn't have even been able to *see* her in sousednia. «*At least he* will *survive. If you run again? If you try to strike first? The Tayemstvoy will murder him.*»

«*You're wrong. The resistance is stronger than you know.*»

His nostrils flared. «*Stronger how?*»

She shook her head. He might have saved her life; that didn't mean she could trust him with treason.

The iron taste of bloody noses and the sharp pain of blows wafted across sousednia. «*I won't throw his life away for a glittery daydream.*»

She snorted. «*Is that what you think I am?*»

He held her gaze, unflinching. «*That's all you were to me.*» His voice was a knife, but sousednia gusted the lie, acrid like burning hair.

She studied him, trying to understand. She'd convinced herself that his flirtation had been a ploy to keep close to Gerrit, but sousedni-cues didn't lie. Slowly, she brought her hand up to touch his cheek. He tensed but didn't pull away, and the air gained a cardamom sweetness even as something cold and sterile coiled beneath it. When she spoke, she managed no more than a whisper. «*Why* have *you been hiding from me?*»

Pain tugged at the corners of his eyes, and he shifted like he wanted to retreat. «*You muddle everything.*»

She shook her head, not understanding, wishing they stood this close in true-life so she could feel the solid warmth of him. She'd missed this—missed him.

Voice rough, Filip said, «*I followed you in the circus— helped you get that pistol and train with it. But I can't follow you now. Gerrit can't. It's too dangerous—and it won't change anything. Gerrit has a chance to make a real difference here, as his father's son. Please.*» He touched her face, the sensation only a fraction of what it could be in true-life. «*Please listen to me. I know you think the resistance is the only way, but you haven't seen Gerrit the way I have. He's a good commander. The Stormhawk is starting to listen to him and Iveta—*»

«*Filip.*» Celka pressed her fingers over his lips, his rich brown skin contrasting with her paler fingers. «*We're doing this.*»

«*Why?*» The anguish in his expression was so raw, Celka couldn't convince herself he was just a regime boot-licker. He cared—about Gerrit and duty, yes, but maybe also Bourshkanya. Maybe also her.

Twice, Filip had saved her life at the risk of his own. Maybe he'd done it for Gerrit the first time, but in the farmyard today, Gerrit hadn't been in danger. If they succeeded at killing the Stormhawk—and the possibility seemed precarious now, though no longer so impossible as when the bozhskyeh storm had swept her way—then she and Gerrit would be alone, strazh-less in the resistance. Unless she could bring Filip over to their side.

But admitting their plan to assassinate the Stormhawk was too big a risk to leap into alone. If anyone knew how Filip would react, Gerrit would.

So instead of answering, Celka reached into Nina's weaves, stretching her thoughts into the space that felt like Gerrit.

The pine and ice scents of him sharpened. Carried on a burst of confusion, she heard his voice, more distant than Filip's. *«Celka?»*

Holding Nina's Gerrit-scented weaves, Celka touched the threads that smelled of old books and steel, including Filip in their conversation. *«Can you come to my room?»* she asked Gerrit. At his agreement, she filled him in on Nina's ability to keep their conversation secure. Then, dropping Filip, she tried calling Filip's name, double-checking that she understood how to remove him from the conversation. Filip didn't react, so she focused on Gerrit as he crossed the fortress yard to Usvit Hall. *«I think we should tell him, persuade him to join us.»*

«You assume we can,» Gerrit said, grim.

«He doesn't want to lose you. We just have to make him understand that he won't.» When Gerrit acquiesced, Celka released the link and focused back on true-life, on Filip frowning, the chairback still a barrier between them. She reached for the water glass, and he handed it to her, their fingers brushing. She wanted to catch his hand, keep him close. "I've missed you," she admitted aloud.

Filip grimaced like the admission hurt. Staring at the

wallpaper's elaborate curling lines, he spoke in a voice that could have been a confession extracted by the Tayemstvoy. "I've missed you too."

This time she did clasp his hand. He tensed at first, but eventually, his fingers curled around hers.

CHAPTER TWENTY-TWO

HOLDING CELKA'S HAND felt dangerous, but it also eased a tightness in Filip's chest. Part of him wanted to flee before Gerrit could stride into the bunkroom. He hated feeling cornered, was certain they were going to try to convince him to join them in some terrible scheme. Easy, too, to imagine the jealousy on Gerrit's face, so Filip tried to drop Celka's hand. She tightened her grip, clever green eyes snaring him. "Stay," she whispered.

Filip swallowed in a throat too dry. Including Gerrit in their link through Nina felt natural now that he'd felt Celka do it. *«I'm not a traitor.»*

«Neither are we,» Celka said. *«The Stormhawk betrayed Bourshkanya. We haven't.»*

«Treason isn't an opinion,» Filip said, frustrated.

When Gerrit entered, his gaze landed on their entwined hands, and Filip tensed. But rather than erupting with jealousy, Gerrit sat on the edge of Celka's bed, taking her other hand when she abandoned the silk pocket square. Gerrit reached his other hand out for Filip's.

Filip fought himself, wanting to take Gerrit's hand, wanting their connection to be like it had been before the storms— back when the world and his place in it made sense. But Filip wasn't a traitor. Still, he'd never been able to resist when Gerrit reached for him.

He took Gerrit's hand. His best friend's touch—and Celka's warm palm in his other hand—made the wobbling world briefly seem right.

Before Filip could manage words, Celka asked through Nina, *«How long have you been seeing sousednia?»*

Gerrit's attention sharpened, his posture straightening in surprise.

Filip wanted to deny it, but whatever his protests before, when he'd activated Nina, he'd seen Celka, resplendent in her high wire costume, incongruous amongst the restricted library's bookshelves. *«I can't,»* he said, *«not always. But since Bludov. Yanek thinks we joint-imbued Nina, the three of us.»*

Celka tipped her head, a tiny crease between her brows as if she struggled with memory. *«What about today, in the farmyard?»*

«Yanek saw... not quite Gods' Breath, but a glow almost like it—around us. Or just me, maybe?» Filip pulled free of Celka's hold to rub the back of his neck.

Gerrit said, *«It wasn't a strike, more like a... nimbus. I dismissed it as part of Celka's combat nuzhda, but it might have been more.»*

«My storm-scar's been burning.» Filip focused back on Celka. *«It doesn't make sense. You didn't call the storm.»*

«I started to,» Celka said. *«Before the drug took hold, I reached for it. The thread slipped from my fingers.»*

«Hedvika's weaves didn't catch anything,» Filip said. *«She thought Yanek imagined the flare. I was pulling against your*

core nuzhda, but afterwards, I was combat-warped. Yanek pulled me back.»

Gerrit gaped at him. *«Freezing sleet. After Celka collapsed, you were—sleet. Yanek was grounding you? I could tell something was off, but I thought you were just angry.»*

«I was angry,» Filip said. *«Celka shouldn't have been in that storm.»*

«I thought I was grounded.» Celka bit her lip, looking to Nina at the foot of her bed. *«But with Nina, I feel different. I haven't felt this... free since the print shop.»*

Gerrit nodded, a tenderness in his expression that Filip didn't recognize. To Filip, he said, *«No wonder you've been more volatile during storms. Have you told anyone? Captain Vrana would be able to give you exercises.»*

Filip shook his head. *«I'm not storm-blessed.»* He couldn't say it with as much conviction as before.

«Maybe you are now,» Celka said.

Filip released their hands to pace away, crossing to the window to peer out at the darkened fortress. *«I thought I could handle it.»*

«You don't have to handle it alone,» Celka said.

He turned back, hating how easily she said it. *«Who's going to help?»* Filip asked them. *«You're both too busy plotting treason to have even noticed that I'm seeing Gods' Breath.»*

Celka and Gerrit exchanged a look, and Filip felt a ripple in Nina's imbuement, as if they'd dropped him from the connection. He spun away, leaning hard on the windowsill, glaring out at the night, discarded as always.

«We're planning to assassinate my father,» Gerrit said.

Filip's heart seemed to stop. He turned back, open-mouthed. He shook his head. *«You can't.»*

Celka lifted her chin in defiance.

«He's unkillable,» Filip said. All the horrible deaths

he'd imagined for Gerrit since his best friend had admitted resistance sympathies paled in comparison to what he imagined now. «*The Yestrab Okhrana will tear you apart.*»

«*We won't get caught,*» Gerrit said, a hard edge to his voice.

«*Of course you'll be caught,*» Filip said.

«*Our odds are better if you help us,*» Celka said.

Their hubris was unbelievable. Filip felt like he was being buried under the earth, the air crushed from his lungs. «*Imbuements protect him. How can you possibly—?*»

«*Poison gas,*» Gerrit said. «*I studied his imbuements. Nothing cleanses the air, and the weapon's new; none of the old healing imbuements should be able to repair his lungs.*»

Filip returned to Celka's bedside, spinning the chair around and sitting so his knee pressed against Gerrit's. He wanted to tell Gerrit he was being an idiot, but it sounded... plausible.

«*But we have a problem with the gas,*» Celka said. «*Chlorine. It smells terrible. We don't know how to get him a long enough exposure.*»

«*Why don't you use phosgene?*» Filip asked before he could think not to.

«*Phosgene?*» Gerrit asked, both his and Celka's attention sharpening.

Filip recoiled, realizing he'd made himself complicit in high treason. He shook his head, wishing he could take the words back.

But Gerrit reached out and gripped his shoulder. «*What is phosgene? Is it another gas?*»

Reluctantly, Filip nodded. «*It's supposed to be colorless and odorless—or close.*»

«*But it kills?*» Celka asked.

Again, Filip nodded. «*It's more deadly than chlorine, but it's a slow death.*» He frowned, trying to remember what he'd heard or read, wondering where he'd learned the details.

«I saw reports on testing it on rats. The lungs fill with fluid after a day or two, and there's no way to stop it. The fluid suffocates its victims.»

Gerrit shifted on the bed, looking queasy, but Celka's expression brightened with determination. *«This is perfect,»* she said. *«Thank you, Filip.»*

Filip struggled to swallow, feeling like a grenade had caught in his throat. Had he just helped them assassinate the Stormhawk? To Gerrit he said, *«He's your* father. *You can't really—»*

«The resistance needs this,» Gerrit said. *«And I'm the only one with access.»*

«But why?» Filip asked. *«You told me he listened to you. You have access—influence.»*

«I looked into your question,» Gerrit said, solemn, *«about civilian Songs during storms.»*

The grenade dropped to Filip's stomach. He moved to pull away, but Gerrit's grip on his shoulder tightened.

«For now, it's unofficial. Though there've been memorandums encouraging the Tayemstvoy to disrupt 'civilians agitating' during storms. Father doesn't like anyone imbuing outside his control. He thinks it weakens the regime— especially since our platoon is hardly producing imbuements by the train-full. And the resistance is growing bolder; leaflets keep boasting of civilian imbuements, shouting that the Storm Gods have turned their backs on the State.»

«So tell the resistance to stop before the Tayemstvoy crack down,» Filip said.

Gerrit shook his head. *«I don't have that kind of influence.»* Beside him, Celka's lips pressed thin. *«It's only a matter of time before Father makes the order official.»*

The very idea choked Filip. The Storm Gods' blessings were Bourshkanya's foundation. To deny people a connection to the gods, especially when those people were starving—to make it a crime to pray for help when the Storm Gods' had awoken to hear people's pleas... He shook his head. «*He can't outlaw Singing during storms. He wouldn't.*»

«*He will,*» Gerrit said. «*Nothing matters to him but his own power.*»

Filip dropped his head into his hands, subsumed by the memory of Tayemstvoy shoving the storm speaker to their knees, truncheons driving people to the ground as the congregants sought to defend their barrel of grain and continue their Song. He remembered the taste of chicken paprikash thick in the air outside the train station after Gerrit's imbuement, his own joy at knowing regular people Sang in prayer and hope.

Celka touched his shoulder. «*The regime is rotten, Filip. I know you hoped to make changes from within, but it's too late for that. We have to start over, and that means killing the Stormhawk.*»

Filip lifted his head, but flinched from her fervent belief. Instead, he found Gerrit's gaze, solemn and sure. «*If you do this,*» Filip asked, hating that he was even considering it, hating that the State he'd sworn loyalty to could make him even consider turning his back, «*what happens next? If you kill him, Artur will step in. If anything, he's worse.*»

Gerrit tensed, the tightening of his eyes suggesting he hadn't thought that far ahead. Of course he hadn't. Gerrit never thought through the consequences.

Celka squeezed Gerrit's hand, a conversation passing silently between them. Before Filip could chafe at being excluded again, she said, «*We'll find out. You're right that we need to know.*»

«*You don't have to run,*» Filip told Gerrit. «*You said that you and Iveta supported each other at dinner. If you kill the*

Stormhawk, you and Iveta could take power—could force *changes.»*

Gerrit frowned, thoughtful; but Celka snapped, *«She's Tayemstvoy. We're not killing the Stormhawk just to put another despot in his place.»*

«Are you sure?» Filip asked, mind whirling. *«That could be exactly what the resistance is planning—but their own despot. If this starts a civil war, innocent people will die. A smooth transition of power, one Kladivo to another, could prevent all that.»*

«No,» Celka said. *«Bourshkanya doesn't need another Stormhawk.»*

«Unless that's why the resistance wants Gerrit out of the way.» Filip met Celka's gaze, no longer flinching from her ferocity. *«How better to ensure that their own people claim power than to convince him to hide in the woods, imbuing weapons they can use to slaughter people who are just trying to do their duty? You don't know.»*

«I trust the Wolf,» Gerrit said.

Filip turned to him, agape. *«You know the resistance leader?»*

Gerrit nodded. *«I'll find out their plan. Can we count on your help?»*

Filip almost said *yes* on reflex. He'd always followed Gerrit into danger, always watched his back. But they weren't talking about sneaking out after curfew or disobeying stupid orders. And when Filip swallowed that reflex and actually thought— he shook his head. *«I don't know.»*

«You care about Bourshkanya,» Celka said.

«I do.» Filip stood, his proximity to them too dangerous. He'd always followed Gerrit, but Yanek's admonition that he didn't owe Gerrit his every breath made him wonder, maybe for the first time, *why*. Did he owe Gerrit his loyalty? And

if Gerrit was turning his back on everything they'd been taught, what did loyalty even mean? *«I care enough,»* Filip said, backing away, *«not to throw everything away in blind obedience.»*

Gerrit leapt to his feet, reaching out. *«We're not going in blind. I'll find your answers. Until then, I'm asking you to trust me.»*

Filip stared at his best friend's hand, at the hand he'd always taken before leaping into the fire. But this time, Filip shook his head. *«I need answers first.»* Before Gerrit could break through his wavering resolve, Filip severed his connection with Nina and strode from the room.

Celka called after him, but he kept walking, out the common room and across the fortress yard, his step quickening like they chased after him. He wanted to run, and if any light had been left in the sky, he would have taken to the hills, exhausting himself to escape his churning thoughts. But he wasn't fool enough to risk the forest paths in darkness, so he sought instead the prayer tower's tight confines.

Leaving the shutters closed, Filip lit the gas lantern hanging near the door and fell to his knees before the altar's Protection Aspect. His mind galloped. He pulled his storm pendant free, but instead of reaching for his charging cloth, he tipped his forehead against the altar's carved stone. The bas-relief pressed lines into his skin, and Filip squeezed his eyes shut, the earth seeming to close over him, squeezing his chest tighter and tighter, crushing out his air.

Part of him wished he'd never activated Nina, wished he'd never gotten involved. But that was a child's wish, to pretend the world was simple, that his place in it hadn't changed.

Eyes closed, he looped on Gerrit reaching out, asking for his trust. Never before had Filip turned his back. Not like that, not when it mattered. He reeled to discover he could.

Struggling free of that moment, he told himself to think, to plan. He needed to act. But he knew too little to choose a course. Gerrit or duty. Treason or his oaths.

Maybe he shouldn't wait to learn more. Maybe he should report Gerrit and Celka now—it was probably the only way to save himself. But even as he thought it, he dismissed the idea. He might be unwilling to join Gerrit in treason, but he would never throw his best friend to the red shoulders.

That certainty steadied him a little, finding a line he would not cross. Maybe choosing his path forward was just a matter of finding those lines. But in the morass of uncertainty, any other line he sought ended in questions to which he had no answers.

The scrape of the prayer room door opening came as a relief.

Filip turned, expecting Gerrit. Instead, Yanek stood in a civilian kosovorotka and trousers, the long shirt's asymmetrical collar and cuffs richly embroidered, tied with a brocade belt. Filip struggled to keep the disappointment off his face. Why had he thought Gerrit would seek him out? He always had to be the one to find Gerrit.

"I came to see if you were all right," Yanek said when Filip didn't manage to speak.

Sitting back on his heels, Filip shook his head. He wasn't, though not for reasons he could voice.

Yanek crossed the prayer room, feet nearly soundless in soft leather boots. He crouched at Filip's side, the lamplight glinting off his earring; the glass beads were faceted teardrops of spinach green, perfectly matched to a hunger nuzhda's glow. His necklace centered a violet cabochon, strung with seed pearls, and he'd layered it with two strands of faceted green beads that matched his earring. Filip wasn't used to seeing him in anything but a uniform, and the sight pulled him from some of his worries.

"This is new." Filip brushed his fingertips over the earring's dangling beads, not quite touching Yanek's throat.

Yanek's lip quirked. "I just don't wear it often. Hunger." He shrugged. "But it seemed appropriate for tonight."

"How was the party?" Filip asked.

"Would have been better with you there."

Filip couldn't quite manage a smile. "And Masha?"

"Drunk on success. Which is better than Havel, who's just plain drunk. Dbani and I had to carry him home."

"Up the hill?" Filip had overheard Masha talking as they headed into Solnitse.

"All those airs, you'd think he'd be lighter," Yanek said.

Filip managed the smile this time, but the humor vanished quickly. He stood. "Let's get out of here." Praying left too much room to think, and that was the last thing Filip needed right now.

Yanek stood. "And go where?" His tone walked the line between suggestive and simply friendly, letting Filip choose which way to take it.

Filip caught Yanek's hand, tugging him out of the prayer room, blowing out the gas lamp as he went. The stone staircase opened into a disused corner of the fortress's yard, but the moon was high and nearly full. "I never got a chance to properly thank you for grounding me," Filip said.

"Properly?" Yanek asked, definitely suggestive.

Filip grinned, catching Yanek's belt. "Properly." He glanced over his shoulder, then pushed Yanek back into the alcove at the base of the stairs. Yanek caught his face, guiding their mouths together in the darkness, and Filip ground his hips against Yanek's, desire finally overwhelming his churning mind. He deepened the kiss, and Yanek's teeth caught his lip, making him gasp.

Edging back, Filip slipped his hands between them to undo Yanek's belt.

"Maybe you should lose control in a storm more often." Yanek's words faded into a groan as Filip slipped a hand into his pants.

"You'll be the one losing control tonight," Filip said, kissing him once more before dropping to his knees.

BY THE TIME Filip and Yanek crossed the fortress yard, returning to Usvit Hall, Filip's lips felt deliciously bruised from kissing, the knots in his shoulders undone by Yanek's pleasure.

Yanek looped his arm through Filip's and, as they came within view of the officers' barracks, said, "Do you mind if I sleep in your room tonight?" The low rumble of his voice startled Filip almost as much as the request.

Filip stopped dead in his tracks. What had he done? He realized his mistake as Yanek faced him—two nights in a row. Filip's stomach clenched. He'd gotten sloppy, misled a friend. "This was just a tumble," Filip said. "I'm sorry if I implied anything more."

Yanek rocked back, arm slipping from Filip's. A gas lamp on the path showed his contentment burst into confusion. "Wait, *what?*"

Filip's jaw tensed. "You *know* me. How is this coming as a surprise?" He liked Yanek, but he didn't get involved. He *never* got involved. He never *had*. He didn't need a relationship to distract him—especially not now, when he couldn't control himself in a storm. He had duty, and Gerrit. That was enough.

The thought sent him spinning back to their conversation in Celka's room, to treason and the uncertain future. He stretched his neck, the knots in his shoulders returning like icepicks.

Yanek just stared at him, moonlight silvering his eyes, shadow making the beads of his earring look black. He stepped close, and Filip felt like a fish caught on a line. "I *do* know you, or I thought I did." Yanek searched Filip's face, and Filip told himself to back away, told himself to close his expression the way he did when he knew the Tayemstvoy were watching. But he couldn't. Around Yanek, he felt raw and open. It terrified him. "Don't you want us to be more?" Yanek asked.

Filip shook his head. "I don't—?" His voice betrayed him, less denial than question.

Yanek cupped Filip's cheek with one hand. "Don't you?"

Everything in Filip wanted to lean into Yanek's touch. He jerked away, retreating two paces so he could breathe. "I don't—I don't get involved."

Yanek's expression shuttered. In the academy, he and Filip had been in different squads, in competition outside of strazh training. Yanek's expression now was the one he wore on the battlefield. "Fine," he said. "My mistake." He turned on heel and strode away.

As if he'd landed a perfect punch, Filip failed to draw breath. Yanek made it three steps before Filip surged after him. "Wait!" He caught Yanek's arm, pulling him to a stop. Yanek froze, but didn't turn. "Don't go," Filip managed.

"Why not?" Yanek asked, all his earlier sympathy scrubbed away.

What was Filip doing? Yanek was *leaving*, just like he wanted. Filip didn't want a relationship. He needed to focus on grounding himself, on doing his duty, on trying to stop Gerrit and Celka from getting killed. "I think, in the storm today, Celka and I almost joint-imbued." It wasn't what he wanted to say, wasn't what he needed, but in the absence of the right words, it bubbled up, and he realized it was true. The way his nuzhda had twisted out from under him, the swooping brightness, and the pain at the base of his skull.

Yanek turned, his face all hard lines. "Why are you telling

me? Go tell Gerrit. He's the one whose opinion you actually care about."

Filip flinched but didn't release Yanek's arm. "We're not—" He didn't know how to finish that.

"What? You and Gerrit are fighting, so you come to me? You want comfort and a tumble, but never anything more, is that it? Did you ever think that *I* might want something else? You're not the only one having a hard time right now." Yanek wrenched his arm from Filip's grasp but stepped closer, lowering his voice.

"Ever since Gerrit took command of this platoon, my tvoortse's been tearing her hair out from her failure to imbue, keeping me up late every night for extra practice. And when I'm not bone-tired from holding strazh weaves in a storm, I've been trying to convince Celka that we're not the fanged monsters she imagines every time she sees someone in uniform." Yanek moved even closer, their bodies almost touching, his voice a cold whisper in Filip's ear. "I'm trying to act like Hedvika sleeting *Rychtr*"—Filip flinched to hear the name aloud, but Yanek bowled on, giving him no space to object—"is just innocent, friendly Hedvika Bur; someone that a civilian found up to her elbows in Tayemstvoy blood could absolutely trust to pull her back to her core grounding. Captain Kladivo made it *very* clear that my role in this squad is to make everyone work together—so my success is riding on a sleeting lot more than just Masha's imbuements.

"So I'm sorry Celka drove a wedge between you and Gerrit," Yanek continued. "I'm sorry you're finally realizing that he's just as power-hungry and ruthless as everyone else in his family, and that it's somehow coming as a shock. And, yeah, it's weird you almost joint-imbued with the nearly storm-mad civilian, and I'm sure it's hard, but I'm not *selfless*. I *like* you, Filip—or I thought I did. But if you just want someone you can call up whenever you want a tumble and then toss aside—maybe you should talk to Hedvika. I'm sure she keeps a detailed list of which servants are amenable."

When he finished, the creaking of the massive linden tree just off the path was the loudest sound in the fortress. Filip struggled to make his voice work, gutted by the only person who'd seen him struggling since his return to the Storm Guard. Finally, Filip managed, "Are you done?"

"I don't know," Yanek said. "Give me a minute, I could probably come up with more."

Filip stared down at their feet. Yanek's civilian boots looked wrong, like he was facing a stranger. "I'm sorry. I was so caught up in my own problems, I never thought about what you were facing."

"Yeah." Yanek shoved his hands in his pockets, jaw tight.

"I didn't realize Hedvika liked servants."

"You learn a lot about someone sharing a room." Yanek's voice didn't soften. "Especially when they're keeping secrets from their tvoortse."

Filip flinched at the reminder, but Captain Kladivo had ordered them to use Hedvika's secondary family name—and he wasn't entirely sure she was wrong, even if he hated lying to Celka. "Is Hedvika... respecting her partners? Giving them a choice?"

Yanek cut a glance behind him, toward Usvit Hall, before shaking his head. "I don't know. She says she is. But Sub-Lieutenant Hedvika Rychtr?"

"Stop saying her name," Filip snapped. He didn't see Celka, but this would be a terrible day for her to discover that her strazh was Major Rychtr's daughter.

Yanek's nostrils flared, but he just said, low, "Who turns her down without worrying the hawks will pay them a visit?"

Filip tightened one hand into a fist, recalling all too easily when Major Rychtr had come to the circus hunting Gerrit. He'd questioned Filip, too, not recognizing him—but Filip had known what to expect. The interrogation had been light compared to some days in the Storm Guard Academy, yet still it had made an impression.

But he and Yanek couldn't be overheard implying that the Tayemstvoy were brutes. "What servant wouldn't want a patron with elite regime connections?" He tried to say it like he believed it—the way Hedvika would.

"Celka won't like it when she learns we've all been lying to her," Yanek said.

"At least she'll be grounded by then." Filip said, hoping it was true. "If you keep your mouth shut." That came out with a snap Yanek didn't deserve.

A muscle in Yanek's jaw flexed.

Filip kicked the paving stones. "I'm sorry," he said, meaning for more than his harsh words. "What happened today—" He shook his head, storm-scar burning at the base of his skull. But there he went again, focused on his own problems. "How are *you* doing? Did Masha overflow when she imbued?"

Yanek's soldierly mask slipped into disgust. "You're unbelievable. You think you can ask that now? That it *fixes* anything?"

Filip spread his hands. "What do you want me to ask?"

"I want you to *answer*," Yanek said. "Are we done? Because if all you want is a tumble, I'm out."

Filip swallowed hard. The answer should have been easy—it always had been before. But when he imagined Yanek striding alone down this path, imagined them working side-by-side in the imbuement platoon but never kneeling together in prayer, never touching, never laughing, the image hurt. Finally, low because he didn't want to say it, couldn't believe he was saying it, Filip said, "I don't want you to go."

They still stood close enough that Filip heard Yanek's breath catch. Yanek searched his face, the soldierly mask crumbling into quiet yearning. "We don't have to be exclusive," Yanek said. "I don't care about that." His fingers touched Filip's cheek, soft as butterfly wings, and Filip found it impossible to breathe. "I do care about having *all* of you. Having a partner."

"I don't know how," Filip whispered.

"Yes, you do," Yanek said. "It's what you've been for Gerrit. He just hasn't reciprocated."

Filip shook his head. "I'm his strazh."

"And I want you to be *my* partner."

The prospect of agreeing felt like leaping off a cliff. But maybe falling was better than standing still. Trembling, Filip said, "I'd like that too."

CHAPTER TWENTY-THREE

IN TRUE-LIFE, GERRIT asked Captain Vrana's advice about training the platoon's weaker storm-blessed mages. They sat in her office, and as soon as Gerrit shifted into sousednia, his alpine clearing twisted, walls crashing in, leaving him and Captain Vrana alone in a close stone cell. There, he told her about phosgene.

«An important development,» she said with grim approval, «but one for your dead drop, not for me.»

Chastened, Gerrit said, «There's more. I need to know what we're working toward. Once Celka and I succeed, what next?» When Captain Vrana's expression hardened, he added, «I think we can get Filip to join us, but he needs to know we're building toward something—and so do I.»

Captain Vrana studied him, and Gerrit tried not to squirm. Just as he grew certain she would refuse to answer, she said, «Your father has been grooming Artur to take his place. He will fling himself into power, and much of the regime will follow—but not all. Artur is young and has a reputation for... excessive force. Many of your father's supporters agree with using the Tayemstvoy as a hammer to solve any problem, but some will balk. It will cause cracks in the regime, and as Artur implements increasingly extreme policies, more people will turn to the resistance.

«Following the assassination, we'll extract you and Celka—and Filip if you persuade him to join us. There, you'll help build our army. The pieces are already falling into place, but your imbuements, and the powerful symbolism of storm-blessed leadership, will give us an edge. The fight will be difficult, but we are prepared to win it.»

«And once we do?» Gerrit asked. It was a pretty speech, but Captain Vrana was planning a civil war. Filip would balk at it, and even Gerrit, committed to the cause, hated the idea of pitting Bourshkanyans against each other. «You take power as the next Stormhawk?»

Captain Vrana shook her head. «I have no desire to lead a country. We'll build a council of representatives—not just from the military and wealthy elite, but also from the laboring classes. Some of your father's rhetoric is justified; before he took power, the old nobility had turned their backs on regular Bourshkanyans, focused on augmenting their own wealth and privilege. Our industry was weak, and people were suffering.

«There are no easy solutions. People with wealth and power always scrabble for more. But we have deep thinkers in our ranks, and I believe that this council could lead our country. To make way for something new, however, we must first purge the current regime. I have no guarantee that what we build will succeed, but it will not fail in the same ways.»

The conversation galvanized Gerrit, though he churned over Captain Vrana's ideas as he led his imbuement platoon through weave-building exercises. He'd been taught that only the elite were fit to lead, but of course those who clung to their own power would insist they were the only ones who could wield it.

By the time he met Iveta that afternoon, he was convinced.

Once they got through the mundane business of adjusting the platoon's deployments based on updated weather forecasts, Iveta dismissed the rest of her staff.

"Father has become more insistent on seeing 'real progress,'" Iveta told Gerrit, her confident demeanor falling into worry. "He's displeased that you're still the only tvoortse making weapons."

Gerrit opened his mouth to parrot the same justifications he'd given her when they'd first set up the platoon—that the older mages hadn't been trained to imbue, that starting with hunger imbuements was safer long term, that bozhskyeh storms risked a mage's control—but Iveta waved him off.

"You don't need to convince me," she said, and fear landed like a blow. "I'm sending you to the capital. Convince Father."

Gerrit swallowed hard. He'd asked for Iveta to include him in family business, asked for her trust. He could hardly beg her to shield him now, especially on a matter so tied into his own command. Struggling to press down his fear that the Stormhawk would see straight through his justifications and realize that starting the platoon with hunger imbuements was, in part, an effort to delay how soon they could begin building weapons, Gerrit realized he might be able to turn this encounter into an opportunity. "With your leave, I'd also like to request an emotional imbuement for Celka to study."

Iveta's lips tightened. She'd hoped that Celka would imbue something that they could parlay into greater access to the Stormhawk's tightly held emotional imbuements.

"I'm confident she can make one," Gerrit said, "but she'll do it faster if she has an example to help understand where she went wrong."

"You'll have to walk a fine line with him," Iveta said. "He's already displeased with our progress, and current events have left him feeling far from generous." She opened her locked drawer, sharing classified reports on worsening civilian unrest, especially in the north. Food and weapons shipments had vanished, and riots were closing factories. The Tayemstvoy tightened its grip, and still the resistance slipped through.

Gerrit managed to keep his expression grim. It wasn't hard. He would have been pleased to see the resistance's growing influence if not for the promise of confronting the Stormhawk when his power already seemed threatened.

That night, he managed only a few bites of dinner before retreating to his rooms. The idea of requesting access to the Stormhawk's most secret magic throbbed pain through his healed back like a phantom heartbeat.

Gerrit could not count on this encounter being 'tame' like the last family dinner. To get Celka the imbuement she needed and keep his and Iveta's command of the imbuement company, Gerrit needed to play into the Stormhawk's thirst for power and stand unflinching before his disregard for civilian lives and freedoms.

Pacing his room, Gerrit tried to settle into his mask of loyalty, experimenting with openings in his head, imagining his father's responses. But even in the best cases, where he convinced the Stormhawk to part with an imbuement for Celka's study and give him space to get his platoon imbuing, he could all too easily imagine his father bringing him to a filthy cell, proudly ordering the Yestrab Okhrana to demonstrate an emotional imbuement on a prisoner. Perhaps they'd trot out the imbuement that nearly brought Gerrit to his knees, ready to spill his secrets and beg forgiveness. His father would want more of those, and stronger, and he would enjoy demonstrating its effects, ensuring that Gerrit understood what he was to make—ensuring, too, that Gerrit would not flinch from 'necessary' violence.

He tried not to shudder at the thought. Tried, and failed.

Before he'd met Celka, he'd endured interrogation training with Tayemstvoy instructors. He'd never been skilled, but he'd passed his practical exams. But back then, he'd believed his father's narrative.

Now, he knew Bourshkanya's real enemies. His father, Artur. The Tayemstvoy governors and factory overseers living in luxury while paying their workers barely enough to buy moldy grain. Civilians were right to protest. Everything Gerrit had read in resistance leaflets was true—so how did he pretend it wasn't? How did he pretend to be a monster—and not become one?

The room thickened with shadows as the night wore on. He needed to sleep so he could be in top form for tomorrow's performance, but still he paced. How could he match wits with his father and come out ahead? He kept circling the question and flinching from the answer. Because to have any chance, he needed to be the person he'd been before he met Celka.

The thought jerked him to stop. At his washbasin, he pulled the cord on the electric light above his mirror, and stared at his reflection.

He needed to become the Gerrit Kladivo who believed in the regime.

He remembered riding a troop transport into his first bozhskyeh storm, convinced that imbuing would give him everything he'd ever wanted: his father's respect, power, a voice of his own in the regime. It seemed like years separated him from that boy, but only a few months had passed. Just a few hidden facts revealed, a few assumptions questioned, and he'd become someone new.

Could he do it again, this time deliberately? Gerrit had spent his entire childhood learning to wall off fragments of his mind. If he could lock away a raging combat nuzhda or a desperate hunger, why not facts? Why not a few small memories?

Staring at his reflection, he swallowed in a mouth gone dry. It seemed so simple, but something deep within him recoiled. Central to Storm Guard training had been the warning that the more you fractured your mind, the deeper the cracks would grow, and the less stable you'd become. It was why they were required to carefully reintegrate their minds after pulling against even the weakest nuzhda, ensuring that the cracks—held open by mental walls—healed. Even the most skilled bozhki often grew unstable late in life. Years of missed hairline fractures grew and spread until it became all too easy to convince yourself that the painful, exhausting process of reintegration wasn't necessary.

Gerrit shook his head and splashed water on his face. He knew how to reintegrate. He was careful. Besides, the danger he faced tomorrow wasn't some nebulous threat in his distant future; if he couldn't play the loyal son, he would—in the best case—lose Celka the chance to save her father, as well as losing the Stormhawk's respect and the access they needed to assassinate him. In the worst case, the Stormhawk would discover his treason.

He needed to be ready for anything the Stormhawk would throw at him. He needed to be certain he wouldn't flinch.

After toweling off his face, Gerrit leaned close to the mirror, as if it would show the doubt and weakness behind his eyes. Where did he start? He couldn't wall off his every experience in the circus and leading up to it; he didn't even know if it was possible to excise memories from his consciousness, let alone carve off months of experience.

What then? Could he lock away knowledge? He'd have to hide from himself the knowledge that his father had ordered his mother's murder, that their attackers had been Tayemstvoy, and that the Stormhawk had killed her for her resistance sympathies. But Gerrit had pieced that puzzle together over weeks, turning his memories over and over, following the clues Vrana had laid out for him.

So he'd start with something easier: the knowledge that the Stormhawk had started the Lesnikrayen war to gain power. He'd learned that from reading a letter written by Celka's father.

Concentrating, he returned to the muddy alley behind a Bludov storm temple, Celka staring at him, wide-eyed in the rain, as he admitted that the Stormhawk was his father. The memory coalesced, his fear tangling with hope as he silently pleaded for her to look past his family name, for their growing trust to survive.

As if manipulating a nuzhda, Gerrit locked himself in that moment, Celka gripping his identification folio, staring at him as though she faced a monster. He built walls, just as he would around a nuzhda and, as he did, the light glinted strangely, refracting off his weakness. The Stormhawk's son wouldn't crave Celka's acceptance, wouldn't care whether this rezistyent saw him as worthy.

Stomach churning, he fortified the walls then opened the memory up, running time forward but also back, excising both the cancer of wanting her approval and Major Doubek's accusations. Locking away this memory would remove his early knowledge of Captain Vrana as the resistance's Wolf, weakening his belief that the resistance could stand against the State.

By the time he'd finished, sweat beaded Gerrit's brow. But, as he returned to true-life, the face in the mirror seemed stronger.

Next, he walled off his recent conversations with Captain Vrana, locking away his future role in the resistance and his orders to assassinate the Stormhawk. Then he reached further back, to when Captain Vrana had sown the seeds of his realization that the Stormhawk had ordered his mother's murder.

When he faced his reflection, he still retained the knowledge of what his father had done, but its impact was blunted.

Finally, he pared away the events in Bludov, walling off his urgent desire to escape into the resistance and leaving behind only the cold, bloody facts as he'd related them to the Tayemstvoy.

Staring into the mirror, he felt fractured, but also lighter. The fear that had haunted his expression was gone. As he considered facing his father tomorrow, he squared his shoulders, more determined and confident. Yet part of him still quailed at what he might be forced to do.

Drawing a deep, steadying breath, Gerrit forced those emotions down, pressing his fear behind walls of granite. As he undressed for bed, he felt taller, stronger. Doubt edged in as he slipped beneath his satin duvet, a worry that his mental walls might not hold—even as a more distant part of him worried they'd hold too well. He shrugged aside those doubts as easy as tossing away a coat that no longer fit. He was tired. He needed sleep so that tomorrow, he could be at his best.

CHAPTER TWENTY-FOUR

GERRIT NEEDN'T HAVE worried. Standing before his father in the very spot where the Stormhawk had had him beaten, Gerrit explained that, while Celka could not yet produce weapons due to her lingering combat-warping, her unorthodox training made her perfectly suited to emotional imbuements. She needed only an example to study, and Gerrit would unlock for his father an entirely new class of magic. As for the other imbuement mages, the Stormhawk had seen—in Branislav— what came of rushing their storm-blessing.

The Stormhawk studied him, searching for weakness.

Memories locked behind impenetrable walls, Gerrit held his gaze, unflinching.

Eventually, the Stormhawk said, "Next time you come to me, I expect progress, not excuses. Pray that Prochazka's efforts are more successful than those of your other mages." He ordered one of his guards to fetch a low-utility emotional imbuement and waved Gerrit from his office.

The abrupt dismissal rankled, but Gerrit pushed the emotion aside, following his Yestrab Okhrana escort to a waiting motorcar. An Okhrana sergeant soon joined him, opening a polished wooden box inside the motorcar to reveal an intricately carved stone owl. Its plumage rippled with crystalized nuzhda—concealment's blue and strengthening's orange, shot through with yellow and violet. "It grants calm rationality," the sergeant said. "I'll accompany it to Solnitse."

"That's not necessary." Gerrit held his hand out for the darkbox that hid the imbuement's magical signature.

The sergeant snapped it closed and tucked it into their satchel. "I have my orders, sir." Their voice softened, and they said, "I'm to ensure its safety en route, and I imagine your mages will have questions about these imbuements."

Gerrit nodded approval. He didn't like thrusting Celka before the Okhrana, but if the sergeant understood these imbuements, their insights could be valuable.

Before they rolled away from the government building, a Yestrab Okhrana captain flagged them down. Gerrit's chest tightened, a tremor of fear escaping his granite walls, but the captain only climbed up front next to the driver. Gerrit recognized Captain Kochevar vaguely and nodded greeting. "Just catching a ride to the station," she said before facing front and ignoring him.

At Gerrit's side, Corporal Shimunek, a copper-bolt Tayemstvoy whom Iveta had assigned as his attaché, shifted. Catching Gerrit's gaze, she cut a deliberate glance at Captain Kochevar before twisting one fist in a sign Iveta used with her guards—Gerrit was not to trust Kochevar. At the compound's gates, another Yestrab Okhrana hopped onto the running board. No one remarked it.

Gerrit crushed his rising concern. The Yestrab Okhrana reported directly to his father; the Stormhawk had granted Gerrit's request; perhaps this was nothing more than Captain Kochevar said—a convenient ride to the station.

It became easier to believe as the motorcar progressed through the city. But as the modern train station of iron and glass came into view down a long avenue, the driver turned abruptly off the main road.

"Where are you going, Private?" Gerrit demanded as the motorcar left behind populous streets.

"Just following orders, sir," the private said.

"Whose orders?" Gerrit asked.

The private didn't respond, and Gerrit repeated the question with a snap.

After a silence that made clear the private had no intention of answering, Captain Kochevar said, "Mine."

Silent, Gerrit debated his options. Captain Kochevar outranked him, so he had no chance at ordering the driver to return to their original route. The detour could be routine—the Okhrana were tight-lipped at the best of times, so it might mean nothing that the captain felt disinclined to explain. But the Stormhawk's abrupt dismissal combined with Corporal Shimunek's warning made that innocent explanation unlikely. Gerrit had gotten off easy in his father's office—too easy.

The question then became, what were they heading into? The Okhrana obeyed the Stormhawk, but Shimunek wouldn't have warned him about Kochevar if the Okhrana's captain's loyalty were so simple. Then who? The answer tensed the muscles all across Gerrit's shoulders: Artur.

The motorcar pulled inside a warehouse, shadowy figures slamming the large wooden doors behind them. In the darkness, Captain Kochevar said, "Lieutenant Kladivo, you'll come with me. Your attaché can wait in the car."

Crushing down his panic as he left the motorcar's questionable safety, Gerrit squinted to make his eyes adapt. A door opened in the far wall, lamplight shining through. Captain Kochevar strode towards it without a backward glance, confident Gerrit would follow.

He hesitated. Crates filled one wall of the dirt-floored room, and figures moved in the darkness. As his eyes adapted, he caught the gleam off brass buttons and the unmistakable shape of a truncheon swinging from a belt.

"Coming, Lieutenant?" Kochevar's voice echoed like a gunshot.

Whether the figures were Okhrana or merely Tayemstvoy, Gerrit was penned in and surrounded. The only way out was through. Making his face expressionless, he followed.

The scent of blood hit him as he walked through the door, but Gerrit had only the fleeting impression of open space before Captain Kochevar's fist drove hard into his gut—the blow stunning his diaphragm. Gerrit folded, unprepared.

But he was no rookie cadet. His lungs spasmed, failing to draw breath, but Gerrit pushed past the animal panic and dove forward, hitting the dirt with his shoulder, turning it into a roll that brought him, gasping, to his feet. But he and Kochevar weren't alone. His dive escaped Kochevar but, without a chance to assess the room, he came up from his roll right in front of a uniformed Tayemstvoy. As he straightened, their fist cracked into his jaw. A third assailant slammed their truncheon down hard on his kidneys.

Gerrit's knees buckled. He stumbled back up, viscerally aware of the danger of being caught on the ground. A truncheon cracked his ribs as his hand closed on the butt of his pistol. Pushing past the pain, he freed the gun and fired. Someone cried out.

He didn't manage a second shot. A truncheon slammed down on his wrist, and the gun dropped from nerveless fingers, his arm alight with pain. He kicked out, aiming to break his attacker's knee, but another blow to his back threw his balance. He stumbled, and one of them struck him at the base of his neck. His legs folded, his vision flaring white, and another blow drove his face into the dirt.

This time when he tried to rise, he barely made it to his knees before they beat him back to the ground. The pain he'd shoved aside earlier swelled and burst as their hobnailed boots landed in his ribs and back. The painful flare of each blow smeared into an agony of red and black as he tried again to fight to his feet, only to be kicked back down. Darkness threatened to subsume him. Surrounded and outnumbered, he abandoned the fight, curling to protect his internal organs, forearms up to shield his face. The blows kept coming.

Just as the pain overwhelmed him, a voice snapped, "Enough."

The pain crashed and dulled, and over the rasp of his breath, Gerrit heard boots crunch the dirt near his head. Someone nudged him in the shoulder, none-too-gently.

"You planning to stay there all night?" This time, the voice was unmistakably Artur's.

While the animal part of Gerrit screamed at him not to expose his soft underbelly, Gerrit knew better than to play possum. He also knew better than to leap to his feet and try to give Artur a taste of his own violence. The Tayemstvoy Artur had called away would happily swoop back in if Gerrit proved insufficiently cowed.

Slowly, Gerrit uncurled, the pain of cracked ribs sharp as he pushed himself to hands and knees. When he moved to stand, Artur placed his hand pointedly on the truncheon hanging from his belt.

Gerrit froze, debating the utility of making another stand, of meeting Artur face-to-face only to be beaten down for his impudence. If his father had meted out this punishment, he might have done it. But standing up to Artur would win Gerrit nothing. It would only make this worse.

Swallowing his anger and his pride, Gerrit stopped on his knees. Teeth gritted, he struggled to slow his breathing and hold absolutely still to minimize the pain in his ribs and back, forearms and thighs. He told himself to make some pithy greeting, but it took all his will to strip the agony from his expression. By Artur's smug smile, he'd failed.

"Do you know why you're here?" Artur asked.

Deep beneath his mental walls, Gerrit shook. If the Okhrana had discovered his disloyalty, the Stormhawk could have given him to Artur to take apart. Gerrit crushed the fear beneath his walls, managing to hold Artur's gaze, hardening his expression to match the granite containing his memories. After a minute, he broke from their staring contest to spit out a mouthful of blood. "Enlighten me."

A truncheon landed hard across his shoulders, flinging Gerrit forward. He caught himself on hands and knees, barely swallowing a cry.

"Come now, brother," Artur said as if they chatted casually over drinks. "You're weak and naïve, but not entirely stupid."

Gerrit pushed back up to his knees. He wanted to surge to his feet, punch the smug smile off Artur's face. But Gerrit knew his brother's games, and his mental walls let him push aside his pride. Artur would leap at any opportunity to beat Gerrit back to the ground.

Forcing a neutral tone, Gerrit said, "Maybe you overestimate me."

Artur's cheek twitched.

Gerrit imagined the ground beneath his mental walls as permeable as sand. He drained all his pain and rage into it, leaving behind calm clarity. "But I imagine you intend to teach me a lesson." He said it like Artur had come to him in good faith with brotherly advice.

Artur drew his truncheon, the motion slow as molasses,

dripping menace. But Gerrit's terror flowed beneath his walls, and he held his brother's gaze without a flinch. As though demonstrating the move to a pupil, Artur brought his truncheon in a leisurely arc down to kiss Gerrit's cheekbone. There, Artur applied just enough force to make Gerrit either turn his head or let the hard wood dig into the bruise from an earlier blow.

Gerrit held his ground, not breaking from Artur's gaze despite the pain swelling across his face.

Artur's lips thinned and his weight shifted, a subtle prelude to drawing the truncheon back for a bone-shattering blow.

Gerrit turned his face aside, just enough to end the staring contest. There, he held motionless, Artur's truncheon still pressing into the bruise on his cheek. Staring at the rust-colored dirt, Gerrit breathed the sweet-rot scent of old blood. He didn't know if his gambit would be enough, but his mental walls let him keep his breathing steady, his terror distant.

"At dinner in Kralovice," Artur finally said, not lifting his truncheon, "you spoke out of turn."

"Father asked my opinion," Gerrit said, still facing the dirt. The position bared his neck to his brother, an uncomfortable reminder of his powerlessness. Except that Gerrit wasn't powerless, not entirely. A Yestrab Okhrana captain had led him into this trap, but if Iveta knew of the captain's split loyalties, then the Stormhawk likely did as well. Artur could order him beaten, but as long as Gerrit displayed no disloyalty to his father, the Okhrana would stop Artur from inflicting lasting harm—Gerrit hoped.

"Your *opinion*." Artur twisted the word, as if Gerrit were shit beneath his boot. "You're a *tool*, Gerrit. Tools don't get to have *opinions*." The truncheon pressed harder, forcing Gerrit's face further to the side, twisting his neck uncomfortably. "But a tool should be cared for." The pressure suddenly released and Gerrit lifted his chin to see Artur clip the truncheon back to his belt. "Iveta sold you some line about working together." His voice was cold, his hand still casual on the truncheon. "You support her, she ensures your rise in the regime." His lip twisted as though he'd found maggots in his meat. "You believed her at the time, but I think you're smarter than that. You just needed a reminder of what real power looks like to understand that Father will have only one successor. *Me*. Don't make the mistake of grasping above your station. You're useful to Father's rule, and you'll be useful to mine. So long as you keep your attention on imbuements, we'll have no need for further *lessons*, don't you agree?"

Memory thrashed beneath Gerrit's walls, a certainty that Gerrit could not restrict his purview merely to imbuing. But he'd spent years training with raging nuzhdi; while chips cracked from the granite, his mental walls held. "You've made your point loud and clear."

Fingers tapping on his truncheon, Artur searched his expression, hunting insolence or defiance. Finding none, he turned on heel and strode out.

When a door had closed behind him, Captain Kochevar spoke as though nothing more than a conversation had transpired. "Don't want to miss your train, Lieutenant."

CHAPTER TWENTY-FIVE

CELKA FIRED AGAIN, but her shot barely clipped the edge of the target.

"Take a break," Hedvika said, and Celka let the barrel of her rifle drop with relief. "Here." Hedvika took it, snapping in a new clip. "Shake out your arms," she reminded Celka, voice muted by Celka's beeswax earplugs. Then she raised the rifle to her shoulder and fired, nimbly working the bolt to punch five quick, neat holes in the center of the paper target.

While Celka shook out her trembling arms, Hedvika reloaded. She took her time with the next series of shots, aiming at targets further down the firing range. Celka had to squint to make out the holes—not that she needed to. Of course Hedvika's aim was excellent.

"How's your sousednia?" Hedvika asked once she'd finished murdering the distant targets.

Celka shifted her focus, drawing a deep lungful of sawdust freshness. She executed a lazy spin on the wire, perfectly balanced. "Good," she said, but Hedvika made her describe it anyway. As she spoke, she glanced at Nina, coiled at the feet of a bolt-hawk private a few meters back. Since activating the snake with Filip, her grounding hadn't slipped once.

Hedvika followed her gaze in true-life. She twitched, almost raising the rifle, but caught the reaction and turned away instead, jaw tight. "That's good," she said when Celka finished her description, her voice only a little strained. Since learning that Nina reinforced Celka's core grounding, she hadn't protested the snake's presence. She always ordered Nina's bolt-hawk minder to station themselves on the opposite side of any room they worked in, but her stern determination to ensure Celka's grounding had made it easier for Celka to push past her failure in the bozhskyeh storm. If Hedvika could work with the giant python just a few meters away, Celka could figure out what she'd done wrong with her emotional imbuement—especially if Gerrit actually managed to bring her back one to study.

"How are your arms?" Hedvika asked, glancing again at the snake before resolutely facing the firing range.

"Tired," Celka said.

Hedvika's nod carried understanding but no promise of relief. "You can work on your aim with the gun supported. Stack those sandbags." She pointed, and Celka swallowed her sigh, heaving sandbags into place before taking the rifle back from Hedvika.

When she crouched behind the barricade as Hedvika had taught her, her strazh laid a hand on Celka's shoulder. "You're doing well," Hedvika said, and warmth flushed through Celka. Shifting to line up her rifle's sights, she told herself not to care what this regime boot-licker thought. But despite her best efforts, it was hard not to think of Hedvika as a friend.

Barely had she gotten two shots off—her aim slightly better when she didn't have to steady the rifle's weight—when a bolt-hawk trotted up to her. "Lieutenant Kladivo requests your presence immediately."

Celka handed her firearm to one of the cadets on duty at the range and followed the bolt-hawk back into the fortress grounds. By the time they reached the meeting room, Filip and the rest of Celka's squad were already there.

Barely had they gotten seated when Gerrit strode stiffly in, flanked by an unfamiliar Tayemstvoy in a strange uniform—the trousers red instead of olive drab, red braid decorating the jacket's cuffs. Celka guessed they were some high-ranked officer, important enough to flout the standard uniform, but their red shoulders sported only a sergeant's pips. Gold bozhk bolts gleamed on their collar, and their nuzhda competencies showed the full rainbow.

Gerrit introduced the Yestrab Okhrana sergeant, and suddenly the uniform made sense. Uncomfortable, Celka reached into their link through Nina, «*What's going on?*» Only then did she notice the bruise purpling his cheek in what she'd earlier taken to be a shadow. «*What happened?*»

«*Later.*» A cold snap to Gerrit's voice ended the conversation. She knew that tone—he was pretending to be a tiger, and that meant she should too. She'd get answers when they weren't watched by a Yestrab Okhrana.

The Okhrana sergeant opened a polished wooden box, the imbuement inside flaring bright as they cracked the darkbox's seal. "This Category Two imbuement grants calm rationality," the sergeant said. "One of our lowest-utility emotional imbuements. Its safe range is two meters." Their gaze swept the squad with cold menace. "'Safe' means that under no circumstances should you attempt to stretch the imbuement's range further." The consequences of straining or shattering the weaves hung unspoken. "Beyond that, know that emotional imbuements are difficult to activate and more difficult to hold active. They respond as though higher-Category than their weave- and nuzhda-Category suggest.

I recommend fully understanding it before you attempt the activation—to prevent any... *mistakes*."

Celka swallowed hard, clutching fistfuls of her battledress trousers beneath the table to keep her hands from shaking.

"The sergeant has about an hour before returning to the capital," Gerrit said. "If you have any questions for someone who's worked with emotional imbuements, ask them now." He swept them all with a hard gaze, and even Havel paid attention. "These imbuements are classified at the highest levels. No one outside this room is to learn of their existence. Understood?"

At their chorus of "Yes, sir," Gerrit nodded and swept out. He covered it well, but his stride was off, and Celka could have sworn he was limping. She glanced at Filip. His jaw tightened, but he focused pointedly on the imbued stone owl.

Filip and the others pulled out notebooks, settling in to study the imbuement while the Okhrana sergeant glowered. They scrawled lines that made no sense, annotating them with symbols Celka vaguely recognized from Hedvika's efforts to teach her rudimentary weave theory. After a few frustrating sessions, Celka had convinced her strazh that Storm Guard methods would only muddy her ability to imbue, and Hedvika had abandoned the attempt.

Now, Celka didn't try to follow as they talked about inflection points and energy flow, internal connections and base rhythms. Instead, Celka tried to ignore the watching Okhrana, focusing on sousednia, letting the conference table take up space on her high wire platform, the imbuement at its center.

The owl glowed a bright shifting puzzle, a summer sky's blue smudging brown as it twisted into the orange of autumn leaves. Had the Stormhawk or his Okhrana deliberately chosen an emotional imbuement made with an impure nuzhda for them to study? Were they trying to sabotage her efforts? In sousednia, she clenched one hand into a fist. Gerrit's bruise and limp suggested that she be grateful she'd gotten anything at all, so she needed to make the best of this. And whether they'd thought to sabotage her or not, 'calm rationality' seemed close to what she'd need to create in order to help Pa return to himself.

Determined, Celka focused on the imbuement's complex flicker, breathing deeply through her nose. Getting a sense for it was harder than when the Okhrana at the rally had hit her with the full force of their imbuement's trembling awe, but Celka teased out a feeling like a fresh, cool breeze cutting through summertime languor. With it came the sharp scent of sweat and dry grass, the sound of Grandfather correcting her work on the low wire. As she narrowed her focus, she felt a low ache in her muscles as if from long practice with her family, a clarity of her body and mind fully aligned, fully intent on the problem at hand.

As those sensations strengthened, the imbuement's nuzhda glow condensed, sharpening to two, multi-faceted points of light at the stone owl's eyes. But even as those points grew clear, they were never static. The nuzhda shifted and pulsed, the colors tangling—except... tangling implied chaos, and as she breathed, as she reached deep into that feeling of control on the practice wire, of trust in her family, the shifts of color became... not ordered, but predictable. As if she couldn't imagine them being anything else. As if the nuzhda's complexity wasn't an accident.

Shaking herself out of sousednia, she drew a steadying breath and lifted her gaze to the Yestrab Okhrana sergeant. "The other emotional imbuements, are they all made with complex nuzhdi?"

The sergeant's gaze sharpened, light glinting from their—

his—single Tayemstvoy hawk earring. Celka wanted to shrink before his scrutiny, but forced herself to hold his gaze. Gerrit had said they could ask questions of the Okhrana, and she wasn't going to waste this chance. "Yes."

Filip set his pencil down, head cocked like this gave him an idea.

But Yanek was the one to ask, "Do you have more than one created by the same mage?"

Celka frowned, not sure where the question was headed, but Filip nodded, like it was a logical follow-up.

"Several," the sergeant said.

"For those made by the same mage, are the nuzhdi different?" Filip asked.

"All the imbuements have different nuzhda admixtures," the sergeant said. "Those with similar purposes have similar compositions, but no two are identical."

Yanek leaned forward, eager. "And those with similar purposes, are they created by different tvoortsei?"

"Often, but not exclusively," the sergeant said.

Filip and Yanek looked at each other, a brightness to their expressions and sousedni-cues. If not for the Okhrana in the room, Celka thought they'd be grinning.

"Explain," Havel snapped.

Yanek rolled his eyes at Havel's hauteur, but Celka was glad he'd asked. She felt like their questions almost unlocked something for her, but she couldn't quite grasp the shape of it.

"The nuzhdi harmonize," Hedvika said, blinking out of that distant 'I'm trying to see sousednia' gaze, and they all turned to her.

"Is that supposed to make sense?" Havel asked.

"Ah, it's like a core nuzhda," Dbani said, and turned to Havel. "The mix of nuzhdi in someone's core harmonizes, becoming something more than its parts. The elements of this imbuement's nuzhda fit together in a way that a random mixture wouldn't."

"The ones we saw—" Hedvika bit off the comment, gaze cutting to the Okhrana. "Sergeant, could you step outside." Her tone made it an order.

The Okhrana sergeant raised his chin, but when Hedvika didn't back down, finally left the room.

Once the door had shut, Hedvika said, "When Celka and I... happened to notice an emotional imbuement at the Stormhawk's rally, its nuzhda was similar. The components harmonized just like a core nuzhda."

"But we know it's not a core nuzhda," Filip said, "since multiple, different imbuements have been created by the same tvoortsei."

"And it's not just a case of poorly trained mages mixing their nuzhdi," Yanek said, "because *all* the emotional imbuements use complex nuzhdi."

Nodding, Celka edged some of her focus back into sousednia where the nuzhda, itself—not even the weaves— echoed that competent clarity of training with her family. "The nuzhda has to fit the emotion, has to be built with the right emotional... resonance." She snapped her attention back to her squad. "That's why Nina works, even though her weaves are sloppy. Maybe for an emotional imbuement, the nuzhda's just as important—or *more* important—than the weaves, themselves."

CHAPTER TWENTY-SIX

"DID YOU KNOW?" Gerrit asked Iveta when they were alone in her office. He spoke low, voice as flat and cold as when he'd faced Artur from his knees. His body ached, every breath painful from cracked ribs, but he held her gaze unflinchingly.

"No." At least Iveta didn't insult him by asking what he meant. Corporal Shimunek would have reported to her and, though his attaché hadn't been in the room for Artur's 'lesson,' the details wouldn't take much imagination. "Though I should have expected he'd try something. I'm sorry I didn't prepare you—that I couldn't shield you." The comfort was cold, but her grim tone made him believe her. "I have a bozhk physician on my staff. I'll send them to you."

"I won't strain imbuements for this," Gerrit said, though he wanted to. "There's a storm tomorrow. I'll imbue—that should handle the worst of it."

She rounded her desk, stopping before him as though she might clasp his shoulder or pull him into an embrace. He held her gaze, unwilling to show how much he craved her sympathy. He shoved that weakness down, beneath granite walls with the rest. Quietly, Iveta asked, "What will you do?" Worry tugged at her expression, though she nearly mastered it. "He wants you to turn your back on me." It wasn't a question. "Will you?"

"I'm not a coward," Gerrit said.

"*I* never said you were." Her emphasis was subtle but unmistakable.

Emotion thrashed against his walls, but they held. "I'll work out my platoon's deployments for tomorrow and send them to you for approval." He kept his voice hard. "If there's nothing else?"

She searched his expression, eyes narrowing as she sought— what? But she just gave him a curt nod. "Dismissed."

Gerrit locked himself in his room and sat at his desk, shoving aside the throb of his injuries, reviewing the day's reports and writing the details of tomorrow's deployment. He had the sense that he was missing something, and a distant, cold knowledge that he should dissolve the granite walls in his mind. He shoved those concerns aside, focusing on his work. Only when nothing remained to distract him, did the worry grow.

Reintegrate, a voice in his mind whispered. He didn't know what lurked behind those walls, but the pain that cut his sides with each breath and throbbed in time with his heartbeat carried a conviction that whatever those walls hid was far worse than what he'd endured at his brother's hands.

Gerrit stood and paced. Stiff from sitting at his desk, the motion worsened his discomfort. He leaned into it, letting pain sharpen his mind, hone his anger. Artur could not be allowed to become the next Stormhawk. He'd known it before, but today's demonstration made it agonizingly clear. He was crueler even than their father, his methods an end in themselves. At least the Stormhawk believed he did what was right for Bourshkanya; Gerrit could no longer pretend that Artur cared for anything but himself.

If anything happened to the Stormhawk—Gerrit's searched his memory, convinced that something would, and soon, but his memories were hazy, the certainty unmoored from knowledge that supported it—no one would stand between Artur and his cruelest imaginings. Gerrit couldn't allow that to happen. But what could he do?

A knock at the door startled him, and he strode for his desk where he'd left his weapons belt, reaching for his pistol even as he heard Filip's voice. "It's me. Can I come in?"

Gerrit reholstered his gun, flicking aside his irritation that he thought himself so vulnerable. He was in his rooms inside the Storm Guard Fortress, a bolt-hawk guarding his door. He was safe.

When the door had closed behind Filip, Gerrit felt a tug in his mind that tasted of bloody noses and crushed autumn leaves. Nina was distant, back wherever Celka was, he supposed, and connecting into her imbuement took long minutes of effort. But once he managed it, Filip seemed closer, and speaking to him through the link was a simple exercise of will.

«What happened?» Filip asked through the snake.

Gerrit hesitated, loath to reveal that he'd been trapped and vulnerable. *You need Filip's help*, urged the voice that insisted he reintegrate, and he relented.

"It sounds like you handled yourself well," Filip said when he finished. "Here." He pulled out a paper packet with two small, white pills in it. "Thought you might want this." *«Should help with the pain.»* Not giving Gerrit a chance to refuse them, Filip went to the washbasin and poured Gerrit a glass of water.

Gerrit downed the pills with a nod. *Tell him the rest*, that same voice urged. *Explain your walls*. Gerrit grimaced at the pills' bitter taste. The walls weren't a problem; and Filip might not understand.

«*Your core nuzhda feels... off,*» Filip said through Nina.

Tell him. Gerrit glanced out the window. Summer was quickly slipping into fall, the long days already just a memory. «*I started pulling against combat,*» Gerrit said. *Tell him the truth.* «*I may not have fully released it.*»

A frown creased Filip's forehead, his gaze defocusing. He opened his mouth as if on a protest.

«*Help ground me,*» Gerrit said before Filip could pull at the loose threads of his lie. «*Pull against my core; that should be enough.*»

The worry didn't leave Filip's expression, but he nodded, stepping close and laying one hand on Gerrit's unbruised cheek. He hesitated, his other hand coming up automatically but failing to find a place to settle. Gerrit took it, gripping hard.

You can do this, Gerrit told himself, slipping into sousednia. But when he laid his palm against the rough gray granite rising out of his mountain clearing, fear choked his throat. *I can't*, he wanted to scream. *I won't.* But Filip had already begun to glow, and the howl of the icy wind steadied him. He'd reintegrated a thousand times after pulling against painful nuzhdi. He could do this. He had to.

Gritting his teeth, Gerrit shattered the granite walls.

Agony and terror crashed over him, riding on memories of his father's betrayal and the Wolf's plans for the future. Gerrit cried out, falling to his knees. Impact shook him, the force like the crack of truncheons against his flesh. Childhood terror—that Artur would follow through on his threats, that he'd carve Gerrit open and leave him to die slowly in the woods—tangled with the fear that if he didn't obey his brother now, Artur would see everyone Gerrit cared about hurt.

Beneath that, almost as raw as his fear for himself and his friends, was the cold calculation in Captain Vrana's gaze as she explained that Artur would claim power and make Bourshkanya worse, that Captain Vrana would use the people's suffering to fuel her rebellion. He wanted to fight it, wanted to argue, but he drowned in powerlessness—the feelings of helplessness he'd shoved aside during his confrontation with Artur; the fear that his father's drive for weapons would force Celka back into a storm before it was safe; the terror that his own treason had been discovered.

A sob tore from his throat. Filip caught him, cupping his chin despite the bruises, holding Gerrit against him, both of them on their knees, Gerrit on the verge of collapsing further.

He told himself to endure, to ride out the emotions with a stoic face as he'd learned to do in Storm Guard training, but a nuzhda fugue—even one held for hours—had never subsumed him like this. Numbly, he realized that throughout the full night and day that he'd held these walls, he'd shoved every inconvenient emotion, every perceived weakness beneath them—as if it were a solution, as if his escape could be permanent. But, locked behind his walls, the emotions echoed, amplifying instead of diminishing, fighting to make themselves heard. Now, released, they crashed over him all at once, an ice storm that left him flayed.

Slowly, the echoes receded, torn apart by his sousednia's howling wind, the deep furrows where the granite walls had sat filled in by blowing snow. His breath came ragged, his face wet with tears he'd been helpless to hold back. He leaned heavily on Filip's shoulder, and his best friend's arm slipped around his back. The hold hurt—everything hurt—but Gerrit didn't flinch away. Without Filip, he would have collapsed to the ground, curled in on himself as though still cowering from vicious kicks.

But this was worse. Physical pain, he knew how to endure. It flared, and it healed.

This... Gerrit choked down another sob. He'd joined the resistance to make things better, to save Bourshkanya. But the Wolf wanted to let a monster loose to pick off a few stray dogs.

«There has to be a better solution.» He'd said it through Nina before he knew he was going to speak.

Filip tensed, the question in the coil of his muscles. But his breathing slowed again, his body relaxing, waiting like still water for Gerrit to tell him.

Gerrit hesitated, his own breathing finally slowing as his terror and helplessness settled. Gerrit didn't like Captain Vrana's plan for the future; if he told Filip now, his best friend could turn his back completely. The thought of losing Filip, now of all times, felt like he'd fallen beneath Artur's merciless Tayemstvoy once more.

As the silence stretched, Filip said, *«That wasn't a combat nuzhda.»*

Gerrit lifted his head, meeting Filip's deliberately calm gaze, but couldn't make himself speak the truth. *«No,»* he managed. *«Thank you.»*

«Talk to me, Gerrit.»

Clasping Filip's shoulder, Gerrit used his best friend's strength to steady himself as he got to his feet. His head felt clearer now, his memories sharp as broken glass. If he wanted Filip's help, he needed to be honest with him. Filip was the smartest person he knew. If anyone could help him find a better way out of this mess, it would be Filip. *«The Wolf intends to let Artur become the next Stormhawk,»* he said, explaining Captain Vrana's justification. *«She's building an army, and wants us to help lead it.»* At the narrowing of Filip's eyes, Gerrit realized he'd slipped up with the Wolf's pronoun, revealing more than he'd intended. But the damage was done. *«There has to be a better way. It could take years for the resistance to overthrow him, assuming our revolution even succeeds. Artur could do terrible damage during that time.»*

Filip scrubbed his hands over his face, pacing before the cold tiled stove.

«She wants to weaken the regime,» Gerrit said. *«If we assassinate Artur, maybe the high-ranking generals will fight over who takes power.»* But if it were that simple, surely Captain Vrana would have thought of it.

«Artur's a bully,» Filip said softly, staring at the stove's brightly patterned tiles. *«Bullies are afraid.»*

Gerrit frowned; Filip was two steps ahead of him like usual, and he couldn't follow the leap.

«He attacked you because he's worried Iveta has a chance,» Filip said. *«You and she worked together at the family dinner and your father listened. Artur wants to ensure it doesn't happen again because he feels threatened. That threat might be real—or at least, you can make it real.»*

«I'm not turning my back on the resistance,» Gerrit said.

«I'm not telling you to.» Filip scrubbed a hand across his jaw, grimacing like he chewed lemons. *«Not anymore. I think... you're right: the regime's rotten. Your father encouraged Artur to become what he is. Those Tayemstvoy that beat you are no different from the ones attacking storm speakers and civilians singing prayers.»* He swallowed visibly. *«But what the Wolf said makes sense. If you can get the regime to tear itself apart, that war will happen with few civilian casualties—far fewer than in an armed rebellion.»*

Gerrit finally understood. *«If I can bolster Iveta's standing, get the Stormhawk to start favoring Iveta publicly, then when we kill him, Iveta and Artur can split the loyalties of regime elites. She's already thinking about it—some of the things she's said to me, and the way her people knew about Captain Kochevar. I just need to help her gain influence faster. I need to make sure that the right people see her as a contender—and a better option than a power-hungry sadist.»* Gerrit gripped Filip's shoulders, hopeful for the first time since his walls crashed down. *«This will work. I can convince the Wolf, I'm certain. We might have to delay the assassination, but maybe not that long. How's Celka coming with the emotional imbuement?»*

Filip shifted beneath his grip, clearly uncomfortable, but said, *«Well, I think. We've had some breakthroughs. We were planning to try activating it this evening, but I... didn't want to leave you alone.»*

Gerrit nodded. *«I appreciate it.»* He searched Filip's expression, trying to understand his reticence. *«Will you help us?»*

Filip's jaw muscles flexed. *«No more secrets.»*

«Some details—»

«I'm not asking the Wolf's identity,» Filip said, voice clipped.

Remembering the tide of fear and helplessness as his walls crashed down made Gerrit swallow a grimace. But the walls were gone now; they'd done what he needed. If it became important, he'd tell Filip about it later. *«No more secrets,»* he agreed.

Wary, Filip nodded. *«Then I'll help.»*

Relief subsumed him. "Thank you," Gerrit said aloud. He gripped Filip's shoulders, already feeling stronger. Through Nina, he added, *«I never wanted to do this without you.»*

Filip nodded again, but a tightness to his expression carried the words he didn't voice: *but you would have.*

CHAPTER TWENTY-SEVEN

AFTER FILIP LEFT to find Gerrit, Yanek offered to explain to Celka what he understood of the stone owl's weaves. She was skeptical. He'd torn out a dozen pages from his notebook and spread them across the table like a magical map, replete with symbols and equations, arrows indicating energy flow and nuzhda density. But the others were game and the scary Okhrana sergeant had left, so Celka decided to try and follow along. Yanek was patient and clear and, with the help of a few well-illustrated analogies from Dbani, his depiction of the calming imbuement actually helped her understand it. By the time the dinner bell sounded, she was exhausted and her head felt stuffed to bursting. For once, she didn't begrudge the idea of an opulent meal. She was hungry, and she needed a break.

Beneath crystal chandeliers while serenaded by a string quartet, red-shouldered privates brought the soup course. Havel's horror shook Celka from her exhaustion. "What *is* this?" He poked the bread basket with his knife, as if he couldn't bear to touch the lumpy rolls. "Were the cooks taken out and shot?" His tone suggested that perhaps they should be. "This is unacceptable."

One of the privates muttered apology. "It's like this for all the tables, sir. Even the high table."

Disgusted, Havel waved away the soup.

Celka was not so foolish. The soup was watery and flavorless compared to their usual fare, but she'd eaten worse. Beside her, Masha shrugged and tucked in. The others barely managed a few bites.

Dbani split open a roll and grimaced. "I think they left maggots in the grain."

Masha raised her eyebrows. "More nutritious that way."

"Oh, goodie," Havel said. "The field officer is right at home."

"I've eaten worse," Masha said.

"I'd rather *not*." Havel threw down his napkin. "At least I can get some answers, if not a decent meal." He stalked away from the table.

Hedvika sighed. "As much as I'd rather not agree with Havel..." She pushed back her bowl.

Dbani glanced around before leaning in, as if reaching for another roll. "There's been word of food riots. If this is the soup, I can't imagine we'll get better for mains."

"Riots?" Hedvika asked, surprised. "Why don't the Tayemstvoy just put them down?"

"They'd have to be organized to impact the supply line this deeply," Dbani said. "I'm sure the fortress stocks grain."

"And we're eating it." Yanek swiped the roll off Dbani's plate. "Why else would the bread be so... earthy?"

"Bugs, Yanek," Hedvika said. "You're taking a second helping of *maggot* bread."

Celka glared at her. Hedvika's description was *not* helping. "Could you not?"

Yanek shrugged. "It's food. I'm hungry."

Masha sighed and set her spoon down, bowl still half full. "Maybe this is an opportunity."

Everyone stared at her, uncomprehending. Havel slid back into his seat, expression pinched.

"We're working on hunger imbuements," Masha said. "I managed one a few days ago despite myself, but maybe this"—she waved a hand at the modest fare—"can help. I've been trying to get myself to skip dessert for weeks."

"I suspect the cooks will have made that choice for you tonight," Dbani said.

Everyone looked at Havel.

"Dbani wins a prize," he said dryly. "No dessert. Main course is some sort of kasha with what looks like grass. All they'll tell me is 'rationing.'"

"Which is nicer than saying 'riots,'" Yanek said.

"Especially when *people* can hear," Dbani said, warning.

Hedvika shook her head. "I still don't understand why the Tayemstvoy don't restore order."

"And do what?" Celka asked, irritated at her strazh's bootlicking naïveté. "Arrest the starving masses? Send them to labor camps to starve there instead?"

Masha laid a warning hand on Celka's arm, before glancing pointedly over her shoulder.

Celka lowered her voice. "If the riots are shutting down food *here*, it's not a few malcontents."

Hedvika narrowed her eyes. "Are you saying people are *justified* attacking the State?"

A few weeks ago, Celka would have shrunk from the implication and worried the red shoulders would drag her away. Worse, she probably would have lunged for a weapon. But in sousednia, she balanced on the high wire with perfect ease. "I'm saying they're probably *hungry*, Hedvika. Something *you* should understand."

Hedvika pressed her lips together, but looked away.

As the silence got awkward, Dbani said, "With luck, it's mostly a problem of distribution. Even before I left, the Agriculture Ministry had run into some... setbacks."

"Like what?" Yanek asked. "Havel's parents stole all the cream for their estate?"

Havel rolled his eyes.

Masha frowned in mock severity. "Havel's kittens *need* cream."

"Seriously, Yanek," Dbani said. "Those kittens have *standards*."

The whole table cracked up, though Havel tried to cover his laugh with a cough.

When the main course came out, Celka was glad she'd eaten her soup. The kasha was as much rock as buckwheat, and she suspected Havel had been right about the grass. She watched Dbani surreptitiously as she ate, wondering what else they knew. The circus bought its food stores day-by-day, but the Storm Guard Fortress should have plenty of food stockpiled. How long had the shortages been going on before trickling up to the officers? How isolated from the rest of the country's problems were they?

Celka cast around for Vrana, wondering if the resistance was building its own reserves somewhere. But if the Wolf was in the officers' mess, Celka didn't spot her. Instead, she found Filip, an amused grin on his face, leaning back from the high table. Their eyes met, and the moment stretched.

Through Nina, the paper and steel scent of him strengthened. Celka reached for it, her sense of him sharpening. *«Is Gerrit all right?»* He sat stiffly across from Filip, nodding seriously to some high-ranked officer Celka didn't know. They must have come in late. Celka hadn't seen either of them when her squad arrived.

«He is now,» Filip said. *«Or mostly. Ask him about it later.»* He'd turned back to his dinner, and Celka did likewise, not wanting to draw attention.

«And you?» Celka knew Gerrit had spoken to Vrana yesterday, but with his trip to the capital, he'd dodged sharing the resistance's plans with Filip.

Nina carried more than just words, the antiseptic scent of Filip's worry wafting through the big top. *«I'm with you.»*

She couldn't help herself, she looked back up at the high table, grinning relief. *«I'm so glad.»*

Filip cut her barely a glance past the people between them. *«Yeah. Me too, I guess.»* He didn't sound glad.

«We'll win this. We'll make Bourshkanya better.»

«I hope you're right.»

After dinner, they gathered in the suite's sitting room, Filip's concern smoothing into intense concentration. They understood the imbuement well enough to try activating it and, after some debate, that honor fell on Filip. Havel, Masha, and Dbani all excused themselves, but Yanek perched on the arm of Filip's wingback chair, and Hedvika straddled the desk chair backwards, leaving Celka the other wingback. They clustered close, conscious of the imbuement's limited range.

Celka expected activating it to be... not straightforward, exactly, not with so complex a nuzhda and its shifting access points—but relatively fast. Instead, Filip cupped the carved owl in his hands started singing the Song of Calming.

Five verses in, Hedvika got up to pace, keeping well away from Nina's corner, even though the snake was back in her crate. "I thought Calming only had two verses."

When her path brought her close to Celka's wingback, she whispered back, "Pretty sure he made that last one up."

"He didn't." Yanek gave them stink-eye. "Now, shhh. Let him concentrate."

Hedvika rolled her eyes and started doing push-ups.

Tamping down her own restlessness, Celka watched Filip as he sang, eyes closed. At first, the Song didn't seem to do anything—though Filip at least had a beautiful voice. With little else to concentrate on, she found herself admiring more than just his voice. Forgiving Filip had left her more aware of his presence and the flutter she felt when he walked into a room. Too easily, she remembered kissing him—his soft lips and strong hands, and the way she always felt more like herself when he touched her. Cheeks heating, she shook the thought. She and Gerrit were exclusive. She shouldn't be thinking about Filip.

Imbuements. She needed to understand this imbuement. She needed to create something like it, but better and stronger if she was to save Pa.

Clinging to that intention, she focused on sousednia, trying to understand what Filip thought the Song of Calming would accomplish. As he continued with verses that Celka swore she'd never heard before, Filip seemed to... diminish. She wasn't quite sure how to describe it, because his sousedni-shape remained—though he appeared a mere heat-shimmer at the moment—but it was like he took up less space, like he vanished into the background even when she was looking right at him.

Confused, she peered around, wondering if he had activated a concealment imbuement—or if they'd just misunderstood the owl's weaves. But it wasn't an imbuement. Somehow, the Song of Calming just made Filip... calm, she supposed. So calm that he became like still water, perfectly reflecting the world.

"Are you seeing this?" she whispered to Hedvika and Yanek.

Hedvika scowled, but Yanek nodded, gaze slipping briefly

off Filip. "He's gone quiet," Yanek whispered, which was absurd since Filip was still singing—but also exactly right.

When Filip eventually exhausted the Song's verses—or maybe just decided it was the right time to stop, Celka didn't know—he sat in silence for a long minute, head tilted as though studying the imbued owl, though his eyes were still closed. Just watching him made Celka feel calmer, and she slipped back into sousednia, wondering if he'd activated the imbuement without her realizing it.

But no, he just sat motionless.

Though as she watched, he flickered. She wouldn't have noticed it if she hadn't been so intently focused on him. His sousedni-shape didn't move, yet it also... did. As though a sliver of him had split off, slipping sideways in a sousedni-dislocation. Knowing what she was looking for, Celka discovered more slivers—always faint, and she never quite knew where they'd appear. They stood, crouched, or knelt, sometimes a blur of motion. As those slivers flared and vanished, Filip began to glow.

His nuzhda built in fits and starts, and twice the rippling colors faded so much that Celka worried he'd lost it. But Filip seemed undeterred, his eyes open now in true-life, studying the carved owl as if none of them existed. He must be modifying the nuzhda as he built it, Celka realized, those ghostly slivers a manifestation of... what? Memories that he called upon to create the need? And when he faded, he must be letting elements go, having determined, somehow, that they weren't right.

Time flowed in the strange, stretched-taffy way of walking the high wire, and Celka would have believed hours or only a few minutes had passed by the time the owl flared in Filip's hands, its glow vanishing from true-life.

In sousednia, Filip cupped a brightly glowing, orange and blue ball. Then he made an unfolding gesture, and rain seemed to fall around him, shimmering with the nuzhda's colors. Celka shivered, a bracing chill travelling down her spine. Hedvika and Yanek straightened. Filip spent another moment focused on the imbuement, subtle shifts of attention changing the pattern of nuzhda-rain. Then he blinked them all back into focus.

"You did it," Celka said. It came out less excited than she expected, more a statement of fact. Already, she evaluated his methodology, breathing the feel of the active weaves.

"Nice work." Hedvika betrayed none of the impatience that had pulled her repeatedly up from her chair. She flipped open a notebook and, squinting at the imbuement, starting scribbling more technical notes that Celka couldn't interpret.

"What can you tell us?" Yanek asked Filip.

"The nuzhda feels like it's breathing with me," Filip said. "Like it's alive in a way I've only felt with Nina." He stroked his thumb down the back of the carved bird's head. "I envision the nuzhda as the tower prayer room, but it's expansive. The walls are gone, and the acoustics are perfect. The air is fresh with the slightest breeze, and it's silent, but I'm surrounded by friends.

"It's more than that, though," he continued. "It echoes with a storm speaker's sermon. With the trained competency of a farrier making horseshoes. It feels like a farmer plowing moist, rich earth; and a magistrate, making a fair decision. I didn't build those elements into the nuzhda, they... grew, like echoes, as I created the base. There's more, multiplying— reaching into the distance, like possibilities or... choices." He shook his head, the gesture more wonder than disbelief. "But until they grew out of my nuzhda, I couldn't connect into the imbuement."

Cradling that description, Celka sought the imbuement's effects on her sousednia. At first, she thought it too weak to affect the neighboring reality. With the awe-inspiring imbuement, she hadn't noticed changes until the imbuement's full force had hit her. But she *felt* calm, clearheaded like she studied the problem from a new angle. Within that calm, she started to notice little things. The smell of sawdust and horses beneath her big top had faded, replaced by what at first seemed odorless air, but she eventually discovered was a springtime freshness, bright with possibility after winter's long nights. Normally, humidity pressed in on her, almost cloying, dust in the air tightening her lungs. Now the air felt light and clear. She balanced even more effortlessly, making smaller corrections, her muscles strong and sure.

The changes were subtle, but she realized that made sense. She was already grounded, her sousednia solid in her truest self. Would it pull her back if she nuzhda-warped?

"I want to try something," she said. "Keep the imbuement active."

She got up from the wingback chair, crossing to the other side of the sitting room before pulling against a concealment nuzhda. She didn't wall it off, but let it hold her sousednia warped. Then she moved back within the imbuement's active range.

Pa's grip on her hand wavered, the summer sunlight fading. As she focused on the memory of back lot mischief, she found she could still experience the moment from her nuzhda fugue, but it felt like stepping out of a house into the rain. With little effort, she could step back inside and let the nuzhda go.

It wasn't perfect. She had the sense that if she'd attempted more than a Category One nuzhda, the calming imbuement wouldn't do as much. But it meant that this imbuement was close to the one she needed to make—close to what she needed to save Pa.

CHAPTER TWENTY-EIGHT

GODS' BREATH DRAINED from Gerrit into the prototype gun. He struggled to control it, already fatigued from an earlier combat imbuement in the same storm. Storm energy slipped his control—a burn at the base of his spine, soaking into Filip—but he gritted his teeth and held, forcing the weaves to cohere.

Imbuement complete, he wanted to sag against Filip, but forced his spine straight. He met Filip's gaze, waiting for his strazh's confirmation of his grounding before marching back into the storm temple's shelter. He handed the weapon off to one of the bozhk engineers who'd machined it, and she grinned like he'd given her the best gift. Iveta caught his eye and nodded approval.

Filip got him a chair, and Gerrit sunk gratefully into it as the rest of the imbuement platoon—minus Celka—attempted their imbuements. At least the aggressive imbuing schedule had let him pull enough storm energy to heal the last of Artur's injuries. Fatigue was much easier to handle when it didn't ride atop bruises and broken bones.

Today's storm had broken close enough to Solnitse that he'd mustered all four of his imbuement squads, driven by Captain Vrana's acceptance of his plan to increase Iveta's influence with the Stormhawk. The prototypal weapon was part of that initiative. Masha had come to him weeks ago with the idea of giving engineers leeway to design weapons based around magical components, completely circumventing problems in traditional weapons. Rather than making incremental magical advancements on conventional weapons, she theorized that they could revolutionize Bourshkanya's armory by starting with a magical foundation. Originally, he'd mothballed the idea, worried it would work too well, but now it seemed a perfect way to impress the Stormhawk. If it paid off.

Hence imbuing twice in the storm. Once to fortify a regular howitzer, a second time to give the engineers a small-scale test of whether their new design would work.

When first taking command of the platoon, he'd planned to have the tvoortsei imbue hunger several times before moving on to combat, but that, too, he had accelerated. Once with a small imbuement, to test their control safely; twice to expand the weave and learn to wield greater storm energy. A tvoortse's third imbuement, he now ordered to be combat.

Masha succeeded nicely today with a pistol, her weaves meticulous, control impeccable. Havel imbued a simple weave in a turnip, which meant he'd be creating weapons by the end of the week. Only one of the other squads' imbuement mages managed a stable hunger imbuement, but more were close.

On the train ride home, Gerrit sat with Iveta in a private compartment, her bolt-hawks guarding the door. "I'd like to put the imbuement platoon on half rations," Gerrit said as the tires clacked a soothing rhythm. The supply problems that had affected the officer's mess had cleared, last night's dinner a return to its usual quality. "They can return to the officer's mess once they've managed their first stable imbuement."

Iveta tapped her steepled index fingers to her lips, considering the idea. "There'll be grumbling, but it's a good idea. Although, do they risk weakened control? Everything but pulling against the nuzhda must be harder when you're hungry."

"It's not like they'll starve," he said, thinking of the gaunt townsfolk who'd watched from the storm temple's depths as they'd imbued. He scrubbed his hands through his hair, though, and sighed. "But it could be a risk. We could try it for half the squads."

"Agreed," Iveta said.

"There's another thing." Gerrit moved one hand in the signal she'd taught him for a private conversation, and Iveta sent her guards to ensure they wouldn't be overheard. A week had passed since she'd asked whether he'd stand with her against Artur; Gerrit wasn't sure how much time they would have to build her power base, but it was time to make the best of it. Still, he needed to tread carefully to ensure she didn't suspect his treason. "Artur's lesson got me thinking. He wouldn't be so concerned with my... sibling allegiances if he didn't consider you a threat to his eventual power."

Iveta crossed her arms, her iron gaze revealing nothing.

"It seemed, from the family dinner, that Father was open to your suggestions about investigating worker pay. Has anything come from that?"

"It has," she said. "He forced factory owners to the negotiating table with workers in Kralovice. They increased wages. Hard to know the impact yet, but initial factory output is promising. Father sent investigators to other industrial cities. We should have their reports by the end of the week."

Gerrit nodded, struggling to hold her gaze. "Celka thinks she's close to being able to create an emotional imbuement;

and Masha's suggestion to work with the engineers is showing good progress. I expect that Father will soon have reason to laud our work here."

She tipped her head in acknowledgment, but volunteered nothing more.

Gerrit resisted the urge to squirm. "Corporal Shimunek seemed to have intelligence on Captain Kochevar's loyalties. I had assumed, mistakenly it seems, that the Okhrana reported only to Father."

"Father demands their absolute loyalty," she said. "If Okhrana are found reporting to anyone else, they're dealt with severely. We're the only exception. So long as the Okhrana report their dealings with his children, Father allows us to... solicit their allegiance. Artur has a considerable head start."

"But you're not without resources?" Gerrit said.

"Did Artur ask you to spy on me?" Iveta asked.

"No. I doubt he thinks that highly of me."

She snorted. "Then he's a fool."

Warmth flooded Gerrit, but he tried not to show it. Time to make his gambit. "If something were to happen to Father, would you oppose Artur?"

Her expression betrayed nothing but a calculating intensity. Gerrit focused on his breathing, on the icy wind howling across sousednia, letting the silence stretch as though he hadn't just implied a possible coup against their brother. "Father is healthy and well-protected," she finally said, "but no one lives forever. I would not like to see our brother take power."

"And if something were to happen... soon? Unrest is spreading like wildfire."

A muscle in her jaw flexed. "If Father were to die tomorrow?" She shook her head. "I'm not ready."

He nodded, the motion slight, acknowledging the situation, but doing his best to imply he thought that scenario unlikely.

"I'd like to continue imbuing twice in every storm. But"—he'd thought about how to phrase this, to give deniability to the idea that they were building their own power base—"two combat imbuements in a row isn't sustainable, even for me. Protection or strengthening, though. And it seems only logical that we maintain control of some of the imbuements. With unrest increasing, the imbuement mages are a clear target. Father should understand arming *your* bolt-hawks with imbuements as well as rifles."

She tipped her head. "No sense in imbuements languishing in a vault somewhere."

He nearly smiled. "Exactly."

"We could strengthen alliances—in Father's name, of course—by loaning out certain imbuements to selected supporters." She nodded to herself. "Bozhki especially, or those with strong bozhk ties, would appreciate seeing a bozhk... advisor close to the Stormhawk."

Gerrit rubbed his hands together, glad she saw merit—and a clear path forward—from his suggestions. "Then let's talk imbuements. Beyond the weapons Father wants, how can we best"—he met her gaze and held it pointedly—"serve Bourshkanya together?"

GERRIT RETURNED TO the Storm Guard Fortress energized from his conversation with Iveta. *«This will work,»* he told Celka and Filip through Nina as they waited for Lucie to climb through the window that night. *«Though it may mean delaying the assassination to let Iveta secure enough influence.»* He expected Celka to balk, but she only nodded, grim.

«So long as it doesn't delay me using the—» She cut off abruptly, tensing as though she barely avoided glancing

at Filip. *The calming imbuement*, she'd been about to say. Though Filip had demanded no more secrets, they hadn't told him about Celka's father. The link between Doubek and Vrana would be an easy leap for Filip; or at least, that was Gerrit's justification. He suspected Celka just wasn't ready for anyone else to know.

Dropping Filip from the link, Gerrit asked her, «*Do you think it will? Presumably Vrana had some way to coordinate with him before the storms returned.*»

«*We'll find out once I make it. I'm close, I think. I started being able to manipulate the calming nuzhda today without it fraying.*»

Before Filip could question their sudden silence, Lucie heaved herself over the windowsill.

Gerrit hugged her, still so relieved she was safe. Filip gave up his place in the second wingback chair, pulling over Gerrit's desk chair and straddling it backwards. Celka settled cross-legged on the floor, leaning against Gerrit's knees.

"Phosgene"—Lucie nodded to Filip—"is exactly what we need... sort of." She made a face. "It's colorless and practically odorless. My contact said it smells like moldy hay—so depending on where we deploy it, it's easily missed."

"So what's the bad news?" Gerrit asked.

"Getting it. Delivering it." Lucie said. "The stuff's brand new, so it's hard to make."

"Which means expensive," Filip said. "The resistance can't be rich."

"It's worse than that," Lucie said. "It takes *time* to make and we—or, the people working on it, rather—don't know much about it."

"Like how much it takes to kill someone?" Gerrit asked.

Lucie grimaced. "They've done... calculations for scaling it up from rats."

"We're going to trust our future to guesses." Gerrit's stomach churned. Celka reached back and squeezed his knee, but her lips pressed tight with worry.

"Or aim for massive overkill," Lucie said.

"You said delivery was a problem," Filip said. "A problem how?"

"It's a gas," Lucie said, "so we'll get it compressed into a metal cylinder. Probably a pretty big one, so we need to figure out how we get it into position. But the scientists think phosgene's density is a problem. It's hard to get it to spread out, I guess."

"It's denser than air?" Filip asked, making connections quicker than Gerrit, as usual.

"That's what they said. Um." She patted her pockets before coming up with a paper that she passed to Filip. "Chemical formula," she said in answer to Gerrit's frown.

Filip looked it over, considering. "We'll want him in as small a room as possible." He handed the page to Gerrit. It didn't mean much. Chemistry wasn't one of his strongest subjects. "If we could get him down on the ground, it would help."

"Why?" Celka asked.

"The gas is heavier than air," Filip said. "That means it'll sink."

"So we're back to a conventional attack?" Lucie asked. "Get his head down and then gas him?"

"We can't risk breaking windows and letting in fresh air," Gerrit said.

"Better if there are no windows, right?" Celka said. "No chance he'll open them."

"So we scare him and his guard down into a bunker room where we've hidden the gas canister?" Gerrit said. "How do we open the canister once he's in the room?"

"How do we ensure he goes where we want him to?" Celka

asked. "With the Yestrab Okhrana's imbuements, there's no guarantee he'll care about physically hiding, right?"

Gerrit cursed. "You're right. He could as easily wade into the fight and make a big show of being unkillable. Take out the attackers bare-handed in a show of might and the Storm Gods' blessings." He gave the words an ironic twist, wondering how he'd never seen through his father's glorymongering propaganda before.

"What if he's asleep?" Filip said.

"He's not going to sleep on the ground," Gerrit said.

Filip rolled his eyes. "It still puts him lower than if he's standing."

"Would that be enough?" Celka asked, looking to Lucie.

"If we get enough gas in the room," she said.

They considered it.

"Bedroom's a good idea," Gerrit finally said. "He won't be as heavily guarded compared to when he's out in public or in private meetings. And if it's the middle of the night, even the guards should be sleepy. They're well-trained and motivated, but they're still people."

"How do we hide a gas canister in his bedroom?" Celka asked, craning up to look at Gerrit. "His guard must search it before he goes to sleep."

"A concealment imbuement," Filip said.

Lucie shook her head. "Won't work. We'd need a mage right there with it. They'd be in the room with the gas. It'd be suicide."

Gerrit activated their link through Nina, *Could you do it with a sousedni-dislocation?* he asked Celka. He trusted Lucie, but if Captain Vrana wanted Celka to hide the ability, he knew better than to discuss it, even with an ally.

Celka glanced up at him, considering it. To Lucie, she said, "I can do it."

"No!" Lucie said. "Did you just—"

"*Without* it being suicide," Celka said firmly.

Lucie shook her head, not understanding.

"I can… separate from my true-form." Celka made a pulling apart motion with her hands. "If we can find me somewhere safe nearby in true-life, I can hold the imbuement active from a distance."

Lucie narrowed her eyes. "How large a distance?"

Celka bit her lip. When they'd trained together in the circus, Gerrit had seen her do a dozen meters, but she'd been hiding the ability since coming here, and he didn't know how quickly the strength to dislocate atrophied. "How far do we need?" she asked.

"Does direction matter?" Filip asked.

Celka shook her head. "It shouldn't."

"So you could be in the room below," Gerrit said. "Or above."

"I could probably do two stories if we needed," Celka said. "Or one story and sideways."

"Practice it." Gerrit squeezed her shoulder. "We can work on it in my rooms so no one notices." Another thought occurred to him. "We'll need something to hide your sousedni-shape, though. The guards could be storm-blessed."

He realized the answer as the words left his mouth. Celka reached the same conclusion, turning to Filip. "The ring."

Filip nodded and, at Lucie's frown said, "There's an imbuement that diminishes sousedni-shapes; it should make her look like a faint mundane. It's here, in the fortress's imbuement library. Captain Vrana got it issued to me when I deployed to find Gerrit."

Lucie looked pensive, not reacting to Filip casually dropping Captain Vrana's name, though he suspected that she knew Captain Vrana was the Wolf. It gave Gerrit a jolt of much-needed confidence. Lucie was good. "We should be able to make that happen."

"We still need a way to get the canister into his bedroom," Gerrit said.

"You said it'd be big," Filip said to Lucie. "How big?"

She shook her head. "I don't know."

Gerrit sat back with a sharp exhale, and glanced at Filip, wondering if he was about to propose something stupid. "Can one person carry it?" he asked Lucie.

"Subtly?" Filip amended, catching on.

Lucie frowned, looking between them. "Maybe. Why?"

Celka squeezed Gerrit's knee, worried. "You think you can bring it in without getting caught? To his bedroom?"

Could he? "We'd have to do it while he was travelling—but we'd want that anyway. No matter how many guards he brings, any location will be less secure than when he's at home. Next time I see him for family... business—" He scrubbed a hand through his hair, stomach churning not just at having to face his father, but also Artur. Throwing in with Iveta was the right thing to do, but imaging Artur's next 'lesson' left his throat tasting of bile.

Celka perched on the arm of his chair. "But his bedroom? From what you've said, I wouldn't have thought he'd see you anywhere... unofficial?"

"He'll allow it if he's impressed with me." He glanced at her, realizing what that meant.

She figured it out and shook her head—not in denial, he thought, but discomfort. "An emotional imbuement. A 'useful' one."

They'd talked about possible ways to weaponize the imbuements, imagining complex, violent nuzhdi—though they'd made no progress creating them. Gerrit nodded. "I'd just need to come up with some question. Something I could have forgotten to ask him—or tell him. Then I walk in, drop the canister, ask my question and leave."

"And if it leaks?" Celka asked. "If it goes off prematurely and you breathe in the gas?"

He turned to Lucie. "How likely is that?"

"I don't know," she said. "I can try to find out."

"Do that." Gerrit made the words an order. When he faced Celka, though, his bravado crumbled. "Do you have a better idea?" When Celka didn't, he looked hopefully to Filip, who just shook his head.

"Does Gerrit have to start the gas release, too?" Filip asked.

"Good question," Lucie said, scribbling notes. "I'll find out."

"If so, we need another plan," Celka said.

Gerrit grimaced. If they couldn't come up with another plan, it might come to that.

"We *can't* expose you to the gas," she insisted. "We just finished talking about how we have no idea what a lethal dose is. We're just going to pump in as much gas as possible and pray it kills him ten times over. You can't walk through that."

He sighed. "You're right. Lucie, what about a timed release?"

Lucie nodded, taking more notes. "I'll look into that too."

After Lucie disappeared out the window, Gerrit bid Filip and Celka good night.

Celka bit her lip, still perched on the arm of his chair, and slipped her hand into his. "I thought maybe I could stay." As the door closed behind Filip, she slid onto Gerrit's lap. Her cheeks colored, and she said, "Unless you have work to do, or...?"

Breath quickening, Gerrit slipped his hands around her waist. "Nothing that can't wait until tomorrow."

She smiled, a little hesitant. "I was thinking maybe... I

could stay the night? We could do more?" They'd shared long kisses, hands slipping over clothes and beneath each other's shirts, but one or the other of them had always stopped there, churning over responsibilities and core grounding, magic and expectations. That, or he'd just been beaten to sleet and couldn't manage more than a kiss.

"I'd like that," Gerrit said.

Her fingers went to the buttons of his shirt, her smile turning playful. "I was wondering if you might want to show me your bedroom." She tugged his shirttails free in front, but they caught in the back. Catching her hips, he stood, holding her against him. She *eeped*, then laughed, squirming to be put down.

When he released her, she caught his lapels, pulling him close enough to kiss before her hands slid up beneath his undershirt. He shrugged out of his shirt, and she played her fingers down the line of his suspenders before slipping them off his shoulders so she could relieve him of his undershirt. When she kissed his throat, he tipped his head back and sighed. His breath caught as her fingers ran down his bare chest to the waistline of his trousers.

She tugged at his belt, and he caught her hands. "Wait," he said, breathless. He cupped her face, drawing her into another kiss. "Let's focus on you," he said, trailing a hand down her chest and the swell of her breasts. "Teach me to make you sing."

"I have a terrible voice."

He tugged her shirt free of her waistline. "I very much doubt that." He unbuttoned her shirt and slid it off, waiting for her nod before pulling her undershirt up over her head.

She caught his beltloop, pulling him behind her to his bedroom. There, she ran a hand over the satin duvet, a flicker of uncertainty in her gaze when she turned back to him. He cupped her cheek, kissed her gently. «*What is it?*» he asked through Nina, activating the link second nature by now.

Hesitant, she said, «*You're really willing to leave all this luxury?*»

He drew back. «*You still doubt that?*»

She shook her head, tossing back the duvet, exposing the satin sheets. «*No, it's just a lot.*»

«*And none of it matters,*» he said when she turned back. He took her face in both hands, holding her gaze, hoping she'd read his sincerity from sousednia. «*You matter. Saving Bourshkanya matters. All this*»—he swept a hand across the handsomely carved and polished furnishings—«*how am I supposed to enjoy it when I know people are starving?*»

His words softened her expression, and she pulled him to her, her kiss hungry this time. «*You're so sexy when you talk about revolution.*»

She swallowed his chuckle and when she gave him space to breathe, he rained kisses along her jaw and down her throat. Clasping her waist, he kissed the line of her breast band. She made a frustrated noise and he drew sharply back, worried he'd done something wrong, but she only freed the fabric, letting it fall away. He ran splayed fingers up her ribs and around, cupping her breasts, thumbs brushing her tented nipples in the softest caress. She moaned, and the sound felt like the ecstasy of Gods' Breath.

«*Maybe it's for the best,*» she said, voice through Nina clear even as her breath caught in true-life, «*what happened in Bludov.*»

He paused, frowning.

"Don't stop," she said aloud, touching his hand.

«*What do you mean?*» he asked through Nina, struggling to concentrate on words.

«*Turning ourselves in,*» she said even as her back arched

deliciously. «*Here, we have a chance to do so much more. We'll kill the Stormhawk, and I'll save Pa. We couldn't have done any of that if we'd gotten away.*»

«*So you're not mad at Filip anymore?*»

She cracked one eye open, even as her hips ground against his. «*I'm certainly not thinking about Filip right now.*»

It startled a laugh from him. «*I'm glad.*»

She caught his face, lips nearly brushing his. "*I'm glad I'm here,*" she whispered, her breath the softest caress. "With you. It's like we said in Bludov. Together, we're powerful." She kissed him, her spark bringing true-life and sousednia into perfect balance, her hands on his face and his chest like burning brands that made him ache for her.

When she drew back enough that he could look her in the eye, he said, "You're magnificent." He trailed kisses down her stomach and along her waistline. On his knees, he reached to unbutton her trousers, but paused, meeting her gaze, waiting for her to urge him on.

"Yes," she said, and slowly, he undid the buttons, slipping her trousers down off her hips. Everything else in his life felt rushed right now. But with Celka, he wanted to get everything right.

CHAPTER TWENTY-NINE

A BOZHSKYEH STORM was predicted in Solnitse less than a week later. Celka wasn't ready, but she was close. Maybe close enough to make imbuing safe.

Hedvika didn't want to risk it. She wanted to take a train south before the storm could break, flee the building tug against Celka's spine like they had twice before when bozhskyeh storms risked Celka's grounding. But since she'd activated Nina, Celka's balance on the high wire had held steady.

"I'm ready," Celka insisted. Hedvika had dragged her to Gerrit's sitting room to protest the orders to deploy with the rest of the platoon. Through Nina, Celka added, *«Pa doesn't have time for me to keep training. I need this. You need this.»*

"Celka can barely control her weaves beneath clear skies," Hedvika said. "Rushing into the last storm nearly destroyed her grounding. What's the hurry, sir?"

In the end, Gerrit had sided with Celka, and she felt triumphant as she joined the full imbuement platoon parading through Solnitse. It reminded her a little of when the circus came to a new town, how they loaded onto trailers and marched the animals from the railyard to the fairgrounds, eager townsfolk cheering them on. But today's parade had little else in common with the circus's joyful enthusiasm.

Storm Guard Cadets marched in formation, followed by the imbuement platoon and ranks of Tayemstvoy. Flags flew high, military bands playing patriotic marches. The recent civilians amongst the imbuement and strazh mages rode in troop transport trucks or gleaming motorcars, and Celka had been confused by that choice before she saw the soldiers all marching in lock-step. She would have screwed that up for certain, and it wouldn't do for the regime to reveal that its imbuements mages were anything less than perfect cogs in the State's military machine.

The parade ended at one of the most elaborate storm temples Celka had ever seen. Most of its copious onion domes were tiled in glossy red, though the largest gleamed gold, its sheen barely diminished beneath thickening storm clouds. The temple's asymmetric main roof left the high-ceilinged storm face open to an elaborate wrought iron tower, its tip spearing the clouds. Unlike most temples Celka had visited, the storm face was fully enclosed with glass windows, protecting the congregants from the elements as they watched lightning strike the storm tower. Elaborate stained glass around the edges illustrated scenes from the Fighting Miracles, those same miraculous battles wrought in iron on the tower.

Though Celka had started to feel at home in Usvit, she shifted uncomfortably as the storm speaker acclaimed the platoon before the wealthy congregation. When the storm broke, she was relieved to concentrate on holding her sousednia as a featureless plain.

But as much as she'd insisted she was ready for today's storm, Celka's hands sweated when it came her turn to imbue. Beneath the weight of hundreds of regime eyes, her storm-thread felt like a live, snarling thing, and she wondered if she had been a fool. Hedvika's entire job was to ensure her grounding, and Celka had bulled past her objections. What if she lost control of her nuzhda? What if storm energy tore through Hedvika's strazh weaves and ripped them both from true-life? She wanted to save Pa, yet she might end up just like him.

Celka's hands shook as she buckled on her storm helmet. Once they'd stepped out into the driving rain, however, Hedvika's warm calloused hand slipped into hers. "You're going to do great."

For all she'd objected this morning, Hedvika's sousedni-cues smelled confident. Her determined gaze made it a little easier for Celka to pull out the new storm pendant and cross the rainslick paving stones to keel before the storm tower's spire.

The position put her back to the congregation in their gold-thread embroidery and gleaming jewels. Rolling her shoulders, Celka pretended that was an accident. *You're a performer. An attentive audience is a good thing.* But her assurances rang hollow. She'd never had an audience while practicing a new stunt for the circus. Her family always rigged a wire in the back lot or in a field outside their winter quarters, raising it higher day by day as they grew more comfortable with the new act.

But the platoon's every imbuement had become a performance for the State, the Stormhawk struggling to prove that the Storm Gods favored the regime. She'd be a part of that today, and the thought shook her tenuous confidence.

Only until we kill him, she promised herself.

Exhaling a shaky breath, Celka gripped the pendant in cold, wet fingers and eased into sousednia. *I'm coming, Pa. Hold on just a little longer.*

In sousednia, the high wire steadied her, the patter of rain against her steel storm helmet fading into the audience's held-breath anticipation. Here, she knew how to perform. Hedvika a shimmer at her back, Celka stepped across the wire. Balancing, she breathed sawdust and manure, the humid heat beneath the big top a comforting weight on her skin.

From that point of grounding, she reached out, expanding her awareness. The big top's tent canvas bounded her world, creating a universe of glitter and spectacle. But her core nuzhda couldn't create this imbuement, so she shifted outside the big top, leaving her body behind.

Floating, Celka rises higher, higher, the big top receding as though she gazes down from a mountain peak, the circus's other tents and bright-painted trailers fading into the ground. Below stretch fields and forest, golden ripples of ripe grain contrasting with the blue-green expanse of conifer forests and the glint of sunlight off rivers. From here, problems feel small, disagreements unimportant. Here, she can breathe. She can simply be.

Holding tight to that feeling, Celka reclaimed awareness of her body, letting herself float weightless yet perfectly supported. The wind blew fresh and cool across her face, and Celka drew the air into her lungs, exhaling deep calm onto the storm pendant cupped in her palms.

Her breath shimmered lilac and amber, wended through by a river of golden sunlight. The blue of calm water swirled around and through the other nuzhdi, concealment the thread that wove together protection, strengthening, and healing. The air rippled and pulsed, alive and shifting as she tried to shape it. Her first try didn't work, the nuzhda draining from her cupped palms. But calm suffused her, made the failure a fact rather than a frustration, and she tried again.

This time, when she exhaled, she didn't grip so hard, instead cupping the nuzhda gently as she shaped loops and twists of will. Its pulse sloshed against the bowl of her hands, threatening to overflow, and this time, she didn't fight but shifted along with it, her body following its ebb and swell.

Once that rhythm became natural, she risked returning to true-life. Or she tried.

She remembered gray slate paving stones and an intricate storm tower, but the knowledge was abstract, like she'd read it in a book. When she reached for that reality, she found only distant fields and forests.

Fear tightened her chest, but it ebbed as quickly as it swelled, lulled by the calming slosh of her weaves and the fresh, clear air around her. She returned her attention to the weaves wrapping the plain storm pendant, their clarity making so simple an object beautiful. The storm tugged on her spine, Gods' Breath urging her gaze upwards. The sky was a pristine blue, but her storm-thread felt thick as rope. She need only reach...

An itch in the back of her mind stopped her.

True-life.

The idea recalled a body, heavy and awkward, wet with rain, stomach tight with nerves. The thought of returning to that felt like contemplating a dive into sewage.

Yet distantly, she heard a voice—Hedvika's voice, describing the gray slate beneath her knees and the lightning streaking the sky. Celka didn't want to hear her, but practice had trained her to listen, to follow the descriptions even when they repelled her, to feel cold fingers of rain sliding beneath her collar and Hedvika's hand warm on the back of her neck.

The plaza's gray and the amber and gold of autumn flowers seemed vulgar in the bozhskyeh storm's bruised light, so Celka tilted her head up, tracing the storm tower's ornate spire into a sky streaked with lightning. "Ready?" Her voice sounded flat, but she'd practiced this, too, so asked it despite herself.

"Ready." Hedvika sounded fierce and determined. She'd had to learn to pull against the calming nuzhda, too, to build her strazh weaves. But her experience with the complexity of core nuzhdi seemed to give her greater control.

The cold rain was enough of a shock to remind Celka what she was doing—*what she risked*—so she clung to a sliver of this blunt, vulgar reality even as she released true-life's gray from her awareness. She wanted desperately to return to open skies, but forced her thoughts back beneath her big top, searching to verify the cues she'd memorized: high wire, green costume, circus band, sawdust and horses. She wanted to rush the assessment, but clung to control. She needed to get this right to save Pa and continue fighting for the resistance.

Satisfied, she opened her thoughts back up, calm washing over her. Color pulsed and rippled across the storm pendant, the complex rhythm and weave of scents exactly what she'd practiced beneath open skies—yet also more. Drawing a deep, confident breath, Celka reached for the storm and *called*.

Gods' Breath lashed down her spine, blinding agony pouring into her cupped palms. Storm energy's pure red-gold exploded, prismatic through the storm pendant, and Celka cried out, the energy snarling between protection's violet and strengthening's orange, lashing out in burning tendrils of healing's gold and concealment's blue. The nuzhda that had seemed perfectly harmonized crackled and split, the components flaring and condensing, searing her hands, her arms, her mind.

Pain clenched her muscles, the struggle to control the storm energy locking her hands in rictus. Her body shuddered on the paving stones, shaking with her agony of will. Never before had storm energy fought her like this, never before had it taken all her strength to keep it from tearing apart her weaves.

Yet as she struggled, Celka realized that this fight felt like struggling to control the nuzhda. And she had only managed to shape the nuzhda when she'd *stopped* fighting—when she'd met the nuzhda as it was, coaxing it, guiding its natural curve and weft. Maybe the storm energy tore at her mind because she was gripping too hard. Maybe she'd only succeed at this imbuement if she abandoned her struggle.

Or maybe abandoning the fight would tear her from true-life.

Beneath the storm tower, Celka cried out, the agony of live storm energy burning her storm-scars, boiling her blood. She couldn't control it much longer. She needed to choose.

Everything she'd learned screamed at her not to let go. The storm energy had already overflowed her weaves. If she released her desperate grip—

The sliver of her mind that touched true-life felt the weight of Hedvika's hand. If she let go, Hedvika would protect her.

Forcing an exhale, Celka released her grip on the storm energy.

It exploded, a snarling rainbow tearing outward from the storm pendant in a brilliant shockwave, flaring across sousednia's wide open sky. Celka gasped, focus riding that explosion, senses stretched to tearing. Then the storm energy snapped back, snarling violet-amber-blue-gold contracting tighter and tighter like a vice squeezing her mind until—with a sigh that echoed like a gunshot—it condensed into the pendant.

Celka collapsed to her hands and knees, the pendant clutched in her fist.

As Hedvika called to her, as she spoke about a high wire and emerald sequins, Celka slumped on the wet paving stones and opened her palm. A complex pattern of violet and amber, blue and gold shimmered over the pendant, flaring and condensing, smelling of open skies and calming breaths. Celka turned her face up to the sky, grinning.

She'd done it. She could save Pa.

CHAPTER THIRTY

FILIP SHED HIS weapons outside Branislav's hospital room, strangely reluctant to be rid of them with the storm still tugging against his spine. Celka fussed with the sleeves of her uniform jacket where she'd hung it, motions jerky with tension. Filip didn't understand why she was nervous, didn't understand why they were here at all. Trying the calming imbuement on Branislav made sense, but the urgency with which Celka had charged up the hill from Solnitse didn't. Nor did Gerrit's easy dismissal of them from the pomp and circumstance of imbuing.

Hedvika didn't seem bothered or suspicious, her expression the same solemn determination she'd shown all day—so long as she didn't glance toward Nina. The bolt-hawk private carrying the snake got strange looks and wide berths from the nurses, but one had still been bold enough to approach Filip, warning them not to release Branislav's restraints. Already the doctors were considering sedating him for the duration of the storm.

"You ready?" Hedvika asked Celka.

"Yeah." She bit her lip, but followed her strazh as they

entered Branislav's room, Filip at their heels. The bolt-hawk and python stayed outside.

Leather straps buckled Branislav to the narrow hospital bed at shoulders and waist, wrists and ankles, and he thrashed against them. When they entered, he briefly stilled, sniffing the air, wide eyes flashing in animal desperation before he snarled and flung his weight against the restraints. The bed lurched to the side and Celka recoiled.

Her retreat stumbled her back against Filip, and he caught her, steadying himself against the doorframe so they didn't both end up on the ground. Filip's mouth tasted of dirt and blood, the air suddenly bright with an autumn crispness. He struggled to ignore the sensations, focusing on Celka. Her already rapid breath had gained a panicked edge, and she half turned, as though contemplating escape.

He laid a hand on her shoulder. "It's safe, he won't hurt you." He spoke low and calming, the tone as much for Branislav as her, though he doubted Bran would hear it. "But we could come back later, after the storm."

Celka made a soft, distressed animal noise but shook her head and, straightening, forced herself around to face Branislav.

"Take a seat," Hedvika urged her, standing behind the room's single chair. Celka edged forward and, when she sat, gripped the wooden seat with white knuckles.

Filip grabbed the other chair from the corridor, settling it on Branislav's other side. He tilted his chin to offer it to Hedvika, but she shook her head, silent sentinel at Celka's side, her hand on Celka's shoulder.

"You don't have to do this now, if you don't want," Hedvika said. "They can just sedate him."

Celka shook her head, lips set in a thin line. Shoulders tense, she stared at Branislav. "Is he always like this?" Once again, the fear in her voice didn't fit.

"Only during storms," Filip said when Hedvika looked to him. "Usually he's... mostly catatonic in true-life."

Celka's gaze flicked to his, then she set her shoulders, resolute, her green-costumed sousedni-shape brightening as she focused on the neighboring reality. Filip wondered what she saw. He caught flickers of Branislav's bloodied and charred sousedni-shape from the corner of his eye, but couldn't see him as clearly as he could see Celka.

Or maybe he just didn't want to.

Keeping the grimace off his face, Filip let his gaze rest on Branislav's snarling, thrashing face and drew a slow breath. He started singing the Song of Calming, ignoring Hedvika's eye roll. Calming never helped Branislav, but then, nothing helped Branislav—and it wouldn't hurt.

When Filip had gone to Captain Vrana to ask about controlling his apparent storm-blessing, she'd told him to begin by learning to see sousednia at will. The first step was to calm his mind, and Captain Vrana knew him well enough to suggest he do it through prayer. With his eyes closed, she'd told him to look around, to reach into the darkness and feel the space as though trying to understand an imbuement's weaves. It didn't always work. Or, rather, he struggled to control it—the restricted library's narrow stacks coalesced then fuzzed out when he tried to see more detail, slipping like water through his fingers.

Today, after only two verses of Calming, he let his attention slip sideways, as though to hear and smell the hints he'd gotten of sousednia in the past. His ears popped, and the lingering scent of feces and industrial cleanser from Branislav's hospital room vanished.

The bed and Bran's snarling face blurred into overcrowded bookshelves and the smell of old ink. Dustmotes lazed in a shaft of sunlight from the imbued false-window above a small desk.

At Filip's elbow, an ancient manuscript sat on the polished desk, a near-perfect replica of his favorite reading nook in the Storm Guard's restricted library. Near-perfect, because the real nook was cramped now that he'd grown tall, and the suit of imbued armor behind him probably didn't even exist.

A buzzing energy yanked against his spine, and the books sharpened until he could almost feel brittle, ancient paper beneath his fingertips. The storm called to him, tugging harder than in true-life.

But even as he touched the back of his neck, probing fingers finding a solid cord growing from it, a figure dove to the floor, cursing as he rolled to his feet, throwing punches at attackers Filip couldn't see. Filip leapt to his feet on instinct, toppling his chair, reaching for his belt knife, ready to defend his friend. «Branislav,» he called, before remembering that his friend wouldn't hear him.

Branislav cursed, not quite managing words, and stumbled back as someone Filip couldn't see punched him in the face.

Past Branislav's shoulder, Celka had begun to glow, her high wire costume fading into a swirl of gauzy fabric that rippled the violet-sienna-azure-gold of her calming nuzhda. Another time, he would have watched her, but Branislav cried out and staggered beneath an invisible blow.

Filip decided that it didn't matter if he could see his friend's attackers. He lunged, a knife suddenly in his hand though a small part of him remembered leaving it outside. He plunged the blade into what he saw as open air but, judging by the angle of Branislav's motion, had to be one of his friend's attackers. Filip expected resistance, like stabbing someone cloaked in a concealment imbuement—but there was nothing, just air. He slashed down and back, in case the enemy had retreated, and Branislav straightened, gaze meeting Filip's for an instant before he turned, struggling to defend against someone else.

«Bran, it's me,» Filip said, still surprised that speaking in sousednia felt just like speaking; though the memory that he was in sousednia—that none of this was real—shook the library, the stacks fading for a moment before Filip focused back on his friend, putting his back to Branislav's, slashing his knife through the air to buy Branislav some space in his combat-warped sousednia. «How many people are attacking us?»

He felt Branislav's attention, but his friend just grunted beneath another blow. Filip tried to defend him, but he couldn't tell what he was doing, and maybe he wasn't doing anything, because Branislav's invisible assailants drove him to the ground.

«They're not really here, Bran,» Filip said, crouching over his friend, gripping his shoulder as Branislav folded to protect himself from kicks. «Look at me.» Filip started to pull against his own combat nuzhda, trying to attract Branislav's attention like he would if Gerrit wound up in a combat fugue.

Breathing hard, Filip skids to a stop before a group of older cadets.

The memory crashed over him, and the library vanished. The scent of autumn leaves sharpened, shouted insults loud in the crisp pale sunlight. The nuzhda-memory was always vivid, but this felt real in a way it never had before, and Filip panicked.

He flinches back, but flails, arms pinwheeling as he slips on mud. Several of the older cadets turn to him, sneering, and it's Branislav they kick while he's down, even as it's Gerrit.

The rope yanking against Filip's spine flared agony down his spine and he *needed* to pull it, *needed* a weapon, *needed* to fight.

He remembered: his knife. He'd left it outside the hospital room. Though he couldn't see that space, he felt the blade.

Felt it flipping over his fingers, felt its weight and balance as he drew it from his sheath and aimed at his target. That knowledge condensed the blade in his hand. Branislav-Gerrit's attackers weren't invisible; why had he thought they were? They surrounded his friend, cowards kicking him while he was down.

Not this time.

The air around him reddened with his fury. He'd charge into the fight, but *this time*, he wouldn't just survive. He would *win*.

Then the moment snapped.

Like a bubble burst, Filip stood in the restricted library. His hand was still raised to throw the knife, but the knife had vanished. Why did he have a knife? Confused, he peered down the narrow aisle between bookshelves. Celka sat on a chair, scarves of nuzhda smoke condensing into her high wire costume, Hedvika a colorless ripple at her side. Between them, on the floor, Branislav curled on his side.

«Bran?» Filip crouched, laying a hand on his friend's shoulder. Branislav flinched at his touch, but Filip repeated his name. «You're safe.» Never before had he believed that so fully. His storm-thread still tugged at his spine, but its pull felt like spider silk. Lifting his head to meet Celka's gaze, he asked, «What happened?»

«I activated the calming imbuement.»

Filip frowned around them, wanting to argue. Nothing felt out of place. Except... distant, almost like an echo down the long row between bookshelves, he heard Lenka's laughter. Joyful, utterly free of the strained edge that had haunted her since she'd broken in Storm Guard testing. He felt Gerrit behind him, proud and trusting, and could sense Yanek, just around the corner, ready to poke his head around the stacks with a grin and wink to draw Filip out of study.

Slowly, Branislav uncurled, lifting his head from where he'd sheltered behind forearms. «What...? Filip?»

«Bran.» He tightened his grip on his friend's shoulder. «Hey.»

«Where's...» His eyes darted around them, seeking threat, but he pushed himself up to hands and knees. «Jolana?»

«She's been reassigned.» Filip tried to break the news gently. «She'd be here if she could.»

Branislav lurched to his feet, snarling. He blocked and dodged, then threw a punch at open air. Filip surged up beside him, catching his friend's shoulder, turning him. But Branislav struck his hand away, following it up with a jab Filip barely parried.

«Branislav! Bran. You're safe,» he said, retreating, hands up, weaponless. «It's not real.» But he could tell Branislav wasn't hearing him. Already, Branislav had spun back into the fight he never won, and Filip recoiled.

The hospital room crashed down around him like a fist to the jaw, and he stumbled, tripping over his true-life chair. He fell, jamming his shoulder against the chair leg, narrowly avoiding cracking his head on the wall. For an instant, Branislav wavered in and out of focus, snarling as he fought and dodged.

Filip squeezed his eyes shut before focusing on Branislav thrashing against the restraints in true-life. Branislav had seen him, spoken to him. Maybe there was still hope he could come back.

"You all right?" Hedvika asked, arms crossed where she stood behind Celka.

"Pull against his core nuzhda. I think—" Filip struggled to figure out what to say. Celka and Gerrit thought it dangerous to reveal his growing storm-blessing until he had a better handle on it, and Captain Vrana had agreed. "I think Celka's imbuement helped."

Hedvika scowled but didn't argue, and Filip righted his chair, trying to follow his own advice. He was a strazh. He didn't know how to help Branislav in sousednia, but maybe, under the influence of Celka's calming imbuement, he could lure his friend back to himself the way he'd done before the storms.

Hours later, Branislav still thrashed and fought.

"It's not working," Celka said, voice thready. When Filip and Hedvika agreed, she dropped the calming imbuement, squeezing her eyes shut, Hedvika gripping her cheeks as she reintegrated. Tears glinted bright in Celka's eyes, but she locked her jaw and they didn't fall.

Reaching into Nina, out in the corridor with her bolt-hawk minder, Filip asked, *«Why is this so important to you?»*

Celka swallowed hard and focused back on Hedvika, thanking her strazh, grimacing as her gaze flicked to Branislav. They left Bran in his room, Hedvika gripping Celka's hand, and Filip tried to tamp down his frustration. Gerrit had promised no more secrets, but this was clearly more than it seemed.

The storm had grumbled off to the south, and the sky above the fortress yard swam with bulky white clouds, free of lightning. Gerrit would return soon with the rest of the imbuement platoon. Filip should check in with the strazhi, ensure there hadn't been any problems. Balling one hand into a fist, he glanced at Celka only to find her waving Hedvika off. As Hedvika retreated, Celka looped her arm through Filip's. "Let's walk," she said. "I need to clear my head."

The bolt-hawk fell a little behind, giving them the illusion of privacy as Celka directed them to one of the more highly trafficked paths into the hills. As they walked in seemingly companionable silence, Celka picked up their link through Nina. *«It's my father,»* she said. *«He's going storm-mad. I want to save him.»* The tightness to her voice was back.

«I thought—» Filip cast back through everything she'd told him and all the reports he'd read. *«The State arrested him. Executed him.»*

«It was a ruse. He set it up.»

«With Captain Vrana?» That came out incredulous. Captain Vrana had been the one to track down Celka's father; had signed his arrest papers.

«Yes.»

Filip opened his mouth to argue, but snapped it shut again, mind whirling. Captain Vrana, Hero of Zlin, had falsified Celka's father's death. *«Why?»* he asked. *«How?»* But Celka squeezed his arm a little tighter, and Filip felt the pieces falling into place.

«They were friends during the war,» Celka said.

«Freezing sleet,» Filip said. Captain Vrana was the Hero of Zlin, but she wasn't the only hero. In all the stories, there were two names: Captain Vrana and Major Doubek. No one knew what Doubek had done to win the war, a Miracle, it was said, but that shouldn't have been possible during the bozhskyeh storms' off-cycle. Still, somehow, they'd won the war. But it had cost Major Doubek his life. Unless it hadn't. *«Major Doubek is your father.»*

«He is,» Celka said, and he felt her gaze—though in true-life she stared off into the trees as though this walk was perfectly innocent.

It explained certain things. Major Doubek had been powerfully storm-blessed, and whatever he'd done at Zlin would have only strengthened his storm-affinity before he passed it along to Celka. And if her father was Major Doubek, and Captain Vrana was willing to commit treason to hide that he was still alive... Filip stumbled to a stop, the pieces slamming into place.

Gerrit had met with someone in the resistance leadership

here, at the Storm Guard Fortress. He'd referred to the Wolf as 'she.' Captain Vrana had sent Filip after Gerrit into the circus with strangely limiting orders and an imbuement that the resistance now thought it could acquire to aid their assassination plot. On the trail, Filip stared at Celka, even as he told himself that he needed to keep walking, needed to make this walk look innocent. Instead, he clutched her arm, feeling like the ground shook beneath him. «*Captain Vrana is the Wolf.*»

«*She is now,*» Celka said, as though the admission wasn't world-changing. «*She and Pa built the resistance together. Until the storms returned.*»

Filip scrubbed his hands over his face in true-life, making himself murmur something about Branislav so the gesture and his sudden emotion would seem plausible. «*Hailstones.*» Captain Vrana and Major Doubek—Heroes of Zlin—had built the resistance. All his life, he'd looked up to them— one as a role model, the other as an ideal. Knowing they led the resistance, that they stood against the State, it changed everything. No wonder Gerrit thought they could win this fight. They weren't blindly following untested civilians. Doubek and Vrana had saved Bourshkanya once. Maybe they could do it again. «*Thank you,*» Filip said, «*for telling me.*»

Celka met his gaze, wary. «*I'm sorry we kept it from you.*»

Filip scrubbed a hand across his jaw. Part of him wanted to argue that if they'd trusted him with this, he might have sided with them sooner. They could have worked together ever since Bludov. But he understood their silence. «*It was dangerous,*» he said. «*Even telling me now—anyone who knows is a risk if we're captured.*» He caught her hand. «*I understand.*»

She squeezed back, fierce. Aloud she said, "I'm sorry we couldn't help your friend."

He grimaced.

«*It might not matter,*» she said, picking back up their conversation through Nina. «*The calming imbuement didn't pull Branislav back. It might not save Pa.*»

«*Branislav imbued while storm-mad,*» Filip said. «*Your father...?*»

«*I don't know,*» Celka said. «*He shattered imbuements during the war. He was fine until recently, I think.*»

Filip nodded, trying to make it confident, for her sake. «*Then you have a chance.*»

Tears welled in her eyes, but she pressed her lips together and just nodded. «*I need to talk to Vrana. Can you cover our conversation? Ask her about what happened in the hospital room?*» She hesitated, searching his face. Aloud, she said, "You were flaring combat. I think you almost called the storm."

Filip swallowed hard. "Is that what happened?"

She grimaced. "I think so."

"I'll talk to Captain Vrana," he said, wishing it was just an excuse and he hadn't felt so desperately out of control. "Will you come with me? I think you might have a better shot at explaining what happened."

CHAPTER THIRTY-ONE

Dawn roused Gerrit from sleep in an unfamiliar room. The storm-scar along his back prickled, and he stared at the room's crown molding, the wallpaper's gold leaf glinting in the day's new glow. He tried to remember the name of the town where they slept, where he'd imbued the day before, but gave up, distracted by Celka's soft snores.

She sighed and rolled over, hand finding his chest, heavy with sleep. The morning light brushed her chin, playing over her collarbone and across her camisole. He watched her, spellbound. He'd grown accustomed to sleeping in unfamiliar places; he didn't think he'd ever get used to waking at Celka's side.

Not wanting to disturb her but unable to fully resist, he skimmed his fingers across her stomach where her camisole had risen to expose a line of bare skin.

Her eyes blinked lazily open, and she smiled. Stretching exposed more skin and his hand slipped up her ribs.

They still hadn't had intercourse, though they'd gotten bolder, exploring each other's pleasure with lips and tongue and hands, checking each other's comfort, careful not to push too far. It was a relief, to take his time. Everything else in Gerrit's life felt rushed, forced, other people defining their timeline, his father careening them headlong towards war. With Celka, he could move slow and listen, he could make sure that every time he touched her, it was because she wanted him to.

Gerrit wasn't like Filip. Sex had never been a casual, physical release for him, like diving into a lake on a hot summer's day. With Celka, Gerrit had finally began to understand that what he wanted was for someone to *want* him—all of him, not just for a tumble, not just fumbling, grasping, hot-slick bodies. He wanted to imagine creating a future together. With Celka, he thought—maybe—they could.

In the morning light, she hovered half asleep, her eyes fallen closed again like a cat in the sun. He wanted to let her sleep as much as he wanted to slip his hand just a little to the left, find the swell of her breast and spend the morning exploring the soft sounds of her pleasure.

But his conversation with Iveta after yesterday's storm returned like cramped muscles after a day locked in the stocks, and he rolled over, grabbing his pocket watch from the nightstand to check the time. He snapped the watch closed more forcefully than it warranted and dropped his head back on the pillow, grimacing over at Celka. Reveille would sound in fifteen minutes. They were out of time, and he should have had this conversation with her last night.

Leaning over, Gerrit kissed the base of Celka's jaw.

She blinked her eyes more fully open. "Is it morning already?"

At least he had something to bring her more gently to wakefulness. From beneath his pillow, he pulled a small, polished wooden box. "I have something for you."

She frowned, propping herself up on one elbow. "This better not be new insignia."

He'd promoted her to Specialist and given her four gold-banded imbuement competencies after she'd made the calming imbuement. He snorted. "Open it."

She wrinkled her nose, but took the box. He watched her face as she lifted its lid, and caught the moment when her expression softened with wonder. She hesitated, then reached into the box, stroking one finger delicately over the earring. "It's beautiful." She glanced up at him before the gift drew her gaze again. She shook her head. "But I'm not—I haven't tested with all nuzhdi. I don't even know how to pull against half of these."

"It doesn't matter." He lifted the earring from its velvet nest. A gold lightning bolt formed its center, but smaller lightning bolts, each enameled a different color, hung off of it on a dozen fine chains, attached to a gold earcuff. "Most aren't even pure nuzhdi." The six pure nuzhdi were there, of course, larger than the rest, but the other bolts glinted and gleamed outside the simple rainbow. "It reminded me of you," he said, "of the circus." He placed it in her hand, watching the play of emotion across her face as she fingered each lightning bolt in turn. The earring's mate remained in the box, a plain gold bolt that wouldn't detract from the primary's majesty.

He couldn't be sure, but he thought tears glinted in her eyes. "Thank you," she whispered, and started to replace it in the box.

Gerrit caught her hand. "You could put it on."

Her exhale shook. "What if I... break it? Or lose it? Gerrit, this must have cost a fortune."

He touched her cheek, drew her into a gentle kiss. "It's nothing. Celka, I'd buy you the moon."

"But—"

He smiled. "But nothing. It's meant to be worn."

She shook her head again, tracing the delicate chains as she held it sparkling in the air. He felt the tug of Nina's imbuement from where the snake had spent the night in a nearby closet. *«It feels like a bribe,»* she said through the imbuement. *«This is Kladivo money—regime money. I don't...»* "Gerrit, it's beautiful, but..."

His stomach clenched as she laid it back in its box. *«It's not a bribe, it's a gift.»* He caught her hands to stop her from closing the box. *«My money is more Skala than Kladivo— from my mother's side.»* He dropped their link through Nina, needing to say these words aloud, let them fill the air between them. "Let me do this for you. I know it's not what you're used to, I know it must feel... wasteful. But I care about you, Celka. I wanted to get you something beautiful, something that captures even a little bit of your brilliance." *«It's not a bribe, Celka, because I don't want to change anything about you.»* "I just wanted to show how much you mean to me."

She sat cross-legged on the bed, searching his gaze, and he tried to leave himself open the way he had when they'd been together in the circus. It felt unnatural now, dangerous, but he stared into her beautiful emerald eyes and tried to let her see him—the real him, the man that cared enough about her that he'd risked everything to ground her out-of-control imbuement, the man that loved her enough—loved Bourshkanya enough—that he'd agreed to murder his own father.

Finally, Celka's hand on the box relaxed. She stared down at the earrings for a long time before setting the box on her lap and pulling out her own simple enamel studs. She had to fiddle with the ear cuff to get the cascade of rainbow bolts to hang right, but when she had, she asked shyly, "What do you think?"

"I think it pales in comparison to its wearer."

Her cheeks flushed at that, and she smiled, shutting her old earrings away. Then she kissed him, and for a few minutes, he let his worries fall away.

The reveille bell startled them apart like cadets caught kissing after curfew. Celka scrubbed a hand through her long hair and laughed. Gerrit traced the line of her jaw, wishing he didn't want to dampen the morning's enjoyment. But already, his thoughts churned ahead.

She frowned. "What is it?"

He sighed and sat against the headboard. "Your imbuements aren't working." They'd travelled almost continuously these past two weeks since she'd created the calming imbuement, and in each storm she'd attempted an emotional imbuement more aligned with the Stormhawk's agenda. Each time, her imbuement had failed.

"I know." She flopped back onto her pillow, staring up at the ceiling. Her sousedni-shape paced in a fluid, high wire walk to the other side of the room. She'd gotten good at dislocations again, a single room no longer a challenge. "I don't know why I can't get them to *do* anything. Maybe I need to study another one. Figure out what's different."

Iveta had taken Gerrit aside yesterday, after the bozhskyeh storm had faded. Father had sent a courier to express his displeasure, and the framing stunk of Artur's influence. Rather than praise for Celka having created a new emotional imbuement or nearly every mage in the platoon now being capable of imbuing, the Stormhawk was displeased that they were letting a mage, who'd imbued the most useful combat imbuement of the cycle, 'waste the Storm Gods' blessings playing like a child in the sand.' *I've allowed you leeway to command the imbuement company as you see fit,* the Stormhawk had written Iveta. *But I expect results, not excuses.*

They needed something to show the Stormhawk soon.

"I talked to Filip." Gerrit watched Celka closely. Her lips tightened and, for just a moment, she froze.

Her shrug managed to look almost nonchalant. "And?"

"He thinks you're using the wrong nuzhdi."

"Maybe he should try it himself," she said with the venom of an old argument.

"Hey." Gerrit slid back under the sheet with her, rolling onto his side to put them face-to-face. She glared over his shoulder. "He may just be a strazh"—they could be overheard, after all—"but that doesn't mean he's wrong." He took her hand, half expecting her to snatch it away. She tensed at first, then melted into the bed, looking exhausted.

"I don't know how," she whispered, finally meeting his gaze. "I've tried. I know Filip's trying to help—and he's probably right. But the nuzhdi he pulls on..." She shook her head, lost.

He brought her hand to his lips, kissing her knuckles. "You can do this."

But she shook her head again, and he realized he'd misunderstood her expression. She wasn't lost—she was afraid. Frowning, he activated Nina. *«What is it?»*

She rolled over, putting her back to him, curling into herself. He hugged her to his chest, slipping his arm under her head, so he could hold her close. *«It's the nuzhda,»* she whispered. *«I can't.»*

«I don't understand.»

«These aren't like other imbuements. These nuzhdi... you have to live them in a way that pure nuzhdi pale in comparison to. Calming, I could do. It was... nice. Strange, and hard to wall off, even though it was only Category Two, but nice. What you're asking? These military nuzhdi? I barely came back from a combat imbuement. What if... if I make one of these, what if I never come back?»

«Do you want to abandon the project?» he asked.

«No. Yes. I don't know. I don't want to lose myself.»

He stroked a hand down her hip, mind racing. Aloud, he asked, "What if we joint-imbue?"

She turned abruptly, shifting in his arms, wriggling around to face him. "What if that makes it worse?"

"It never has before," he said. When they'd joint-imbued in the circus, it had been so much easier—so much more *right*— than imbuing alone.

«You don't know how to shape emotional weaves,» she said, picking the conversation back up through Nina.

«But you do.» They'd worked together seamlessly in their other imbuements, compensating for each other's weaknesses.

She searched his face, desperate, like she was trying to find some way to say no. *«There has to be another way to increase Iveta's powerbase.»*

«Would you rather imbue howitzers?» It wouldn't be as revolutionary as emotional imbuements, but if she couldn't get them working soon, fortress-breaking weapons were at least something the regime elite would understand.

«No.» The speed of her response seemed to startle her. She closed her eyes and nestled against his chest. *«No,»* she whispered, *«I don't.»* She breathed shakily for a minute, and he held her, biting his tongue, giving her space. Finally, she said aloud, "Let's try it."

Gerrit sent Celka on to breakfast without him, claiming he needed space to pull his thoughts together on a nuzhda he'd been considering. The idea had come in the depth of night, when sleep had escaped him. Filip talked about building core nuzhdi by imagining the landscape that would create the scents and sounds he intuited from a person's core, and then pushing that imagining, brightening it until it became reality. And Filip, who'd worked with Celka on emotional imbuements almost as closely as Hedvika had, thought the problem stemmed from her creating the wrong nuzhda.

Sousednia was a realm of needs and ideas, and for an emotional imbuement to work, it followed that its intention had to fill sousednia. At his urging, Celka had been trying to develop an imbuement that would drive the enemy to paranoid violence, turning them against their own. As Gerrit had stared at the ceiling last night, trying to imagine the necessary nuzhda, the idea had sickened him. All his life, Gerrit had trained for war, but in battle, the enemy was clear. The enemy was *other*—not standing at your side.

Celka's fear this morning made sense if you had to live that reality. And so did her failure. Which meant that for Gerrit to succeed where she had not, he needed to believe that violence absolutely necessary.

Striding across the bedroom, Gerrit sought his reflection in the mirror above the washbasin. The man he'd shaped himself into before facing his father, who'd held Artur's gaze and refused to play his game, that version of himself wouldn't flinch from this nuzhda.

It seemed the perfect solution, yet he hesitated. The memory of the person he'd become after his mental surgery chilled him. Becoming that regime-kissing brute again—becoming it every time he needed to imbue... what if he stopped being able to reintegrate? What if he stopped wanting to? He'd barely managed it last time, able to talk himself out of it for hours. Bozhskyeh storms raged across Bourshkanya. Traveling by rail, he could imbue nearly every day. How long could he wear a mask without that mask becoming him?

But Iveta needed their father's respect if she was to split regime loyalties after his death. And Gerrit needed the Stormhawk's regard in order to get close enough to kill him. Gerrit might not believe in knifing your friends in the back, but he *believed* in the resistance. If saving Bourshkanya meant crushing down his compassion, well, he could be ruthless.

Locking away these memories would not be permanent. He was still figuring out how to create emotional imbuements. Walling off his weaknesses was a crutch, just something he'd use while learning to shape the required nuzhda. Once he'd practiced pulling on the nuzhda and imbuing with it, he should be able to recreate it without partitioning his mind.

And if not... he'd deal with that problem if the time came.

As dawn brightened into a crisp autumn day, Gerrit walled off memories, one by one.

It was easier than the first time; the walls he'd initially built seemed to retain their foundations, and cold granite grew up around those moments of weakness as if it had been simply awaiting his command.

When he finished, he tested his thoughts, considering the imbuement he needed to create.

He shied from it still, flinching into memories of holding Celka against him, of her fear that the nuzhda would consume her.

Remorseless, he walled that memory off, then locked away their more tender moments for good measure. He couldn't afford to be soft, and the uncertainty in her emerald eyes made him waver. To the growing space behind his mental walls he added his memories of assassination, of plotting, his joy at discovering Byeta still alive and vibrant in the resistance. Then he carved away his discussion with Filip after Artur's beating. He needed to believe what he'd told Iveta—that he supported her fully and intended to stand with her against their brother.

By the time he felt only cool detachment when contemplating driving the enemy to self-slaughter, the imbuement platoon had gathered in the country house's drive, milling impatiently. He'd penned a quick note to Iveta, that he was working on something important for the day and would be along shortly, but the minutes had passed quickly.

Stomach rumbling, he threw on his jacket and hurried out the door.

On the train, he drank bad coffee and imagined a sousedni-landscape of shadow and threat where no one could be trusted. He failed at first, and had to interrogate his preparations, walling off more memories of the circus and his friendship with Filip. But by the time they arrived in Mrach, storm clouds just beginning to bulk overhead, he was ready.

CHAPTER THIRTY-TWO

THE TOWNSFOLK WHO attended the imbuement company's parade in Mrach looked lean and hungry. Filip watched from the corners of his eyes while he marched behind Gerrit, their route winding up cobblestone streets from the train station to the Temple of Overflowing Grain atop a hill in Mrach's historic city center. The temple, like the city, had been beautiful once. Onion domes gleamed with fresh paint that, even beneath a darkening sky, couldn't cover years of neglect, and the temple's storm face showed remnants of expansive windows mostly replaced by utilitarian shutters. A local band trotted at the head of their column, blaring "The Stormhawk's Victory March" a little off-key, while local red shoulders prowled the bystanders. The townsfolk, rather than watching with awe or even curiosity, seemed nervous and resentful.

As the parade neared the temple, the spectators grew more vibrant, the local elite turning out the appropriate State fervor along with fine clothes and colorful embroidery. Their faces and bodies were fuller, but even here, Filip caught bitter glances and tight lips. The imbuement company was not welcome, and Filip wondered whether it was due to their storm-blessings or their obvious comfort.

Even Mrach's mayor looked nervous when they shook Gerrit's and Iveta's hands on a raised platform before the storm temple's outflung doors. They had a major's star and bar on each red shoulder, so should have enjoyed the implied favor of a visit from the Stormhawk's children—unless there was more to Mrach's recent trouble with broken-down factories than in the official briefing.

Not his problem, Filip tried to tell himself. Every bozhk in Gerrit's imbuement platoon was outnumbered two-to-one by Iveta's bolt-hawks. Any unrest, they would deal with it.

So when Filip slipped out of formation into the temple's depths, he told himself it was only to make his obeisance before the storm.

At the alcove housing the temple's Protection Aspect, he knelt and sang, barely aware that Yanek had joined him until after he'd released his spark to the altar. They brushed fingers as they moved to the next alcove and joined voices for the Song of Fighting. As they moved on to Strengthening, Filip leaned close. "Something's off." The benches inside the temple had begun to fill as the speeches outside wound down, and a few others sang before the aspects. But the tangle of voices sounded wrong, prickling Filip's spine even as his storm-thread began to thicken. The bozhskyeh storm would break soon.

Yanek nodded, but said nothing.

Given the crowd outside, Filip expected the alcove for Feeding to be packed with bodies. Instead, it was empty, Tayemstvoy menacing on either side, rifles in hand. Filip ignored them, singing the Song of Feeding while his shoulders crawled.

The icon for the merged Storm Gods was worn but, furthest

from the temple's storm face, retained some of its colorful paint and original grandeur. As Filip and Yanek sang the Song of Calming, an older person in a storm speaker's long robes knelt at Filip's side.

"I've warned the congregation," they said, voice a papery whisper by Filip's ear, "but people are hungry and desperate. They were frightened into silence last storm; I worry your arrival has turned their fears outward."

Filip kept facing the icon, but when the speaker reached out to pat his arm, he caught a flash of white in the corner of his eye. Pausing only briefly in charging his storm pendant, he placed his hand over theirs. They gave his arm a reassuring squeeze, then withdrew their hand, leaving behind a folded sheet of paper. Filip tucked it into a pocket without looking, continuing the Song of Calming.

Only after he'd released his spark and slipped his storm pendant beneath his shirt did he unfold the page. A skilled artist had sketched an exultant figure in worker's clothing being struck by lightning. A caricatured Tayemstvoy cowered. The blotchy, mimeographed type said,

> *The Storm Gods see you suffering beneath the regime's boot. Sing as scripture teaches and reach for the sky. Thousands of ordinary Bourshkanyans have already imbued.*
>
> *No matter how the regime tightens their grip, we will remain free.*

A running wolf stamped the bottom.

Yanek drew a sharp breath when he read it. Filip tucked the leaflet away. "I need to bring this to Gerrit," he said, but the words tasted sour. Something had been off about Gerrit since he'd emerged from his room late this morning, a confident snap to his bearing. It had worsened on the train, a pall descending over him as he'd practiced building the complex, violent nuzhda that he and Celka would attempt to joint-imbue with today.

Filip tried to shrug off that concern as he had on the train. He had a duty to warn his commanding officer of the building unrest. But Filip also wanted the people to succeed. They deserved the Storm Gods' blessings more than anyone in Gerrit's platoon.

Surveying the filling storm temple, however, Filip discovered too many red shoulders who weren't from Iveta's company. Maybe the presence of local hawks would keep the civilians from reaching for Gods' Breath—or maybe the people's resentment and resistance-fueled regime hatred would take on its own resonance beneath the storm.

Already, Filip tasted blood and grit in his mouth when people glanced his way. He tried to slow his breathing, but a flash of Gods' Breath tore apart the calm he'd won through prayer. By the time he reached Gerrit's side inside the meager shelter of one of the open storm face's doors, the restricted library overlaid true-life with ghostly bookshelves.

Gerrit cast Filip a hard look that asked, *Where were you?*

When Filip passed him the leaflet and shared the storm speaker's warning, his expression darkened.

"Bring this to Iveta," he said, clipped. "We can't allow any foolishness today."

The edge to his tone worsened Filip's unease, and he glanced at Celka whose lips were pressed in a thin line. On the train, Filip had concentrated on learning to reproduce Gerrit's brutal paranoia nuzhda well enough to integrate it into strazh weaves, using that focus to push aside his concerns. But he realized now that some of his dread came not just from resentful citizens, but from a subtle wrongness around Gerrit. Shifting his focus sideways, Filip tried to verify his best friend's grounding. But barely had he caught the whisper of wind over ice when it transmuted into the gentle scrape of a turned page. Instead of pine and ice, he smelled ink and steel, and the restricted library sharpened.

"Cizek," Gerrit snapped. "I gave you an order."

Filip blinked back into the storm temple to find Gerrit's expression as edged as his words.

"Bring this to Iveta." He thrust the resistance leaflet at Filip. "And warn the platoon."

CHAPTER THIRTY-THREE

GERRIT LET SEVERAL of his tvoortsei imbue first, hoping their relatively minor combat imbuements would shift civilian unrest into appropriate awe without enflaming the discontent that resistance dogs clearly wished to exploit. But even as Masha succeeded in imbuing new weapons components before ceding the space beneath the storm tower to one of the tvoortse from Green Squad, Gerrit itched to call the storm.

He checked his sousednia. In his snowy mountain clearing, the sun had nearly disappeared over neighboring peaks, the snow at his feet blue with shadow, the valley in darkness. Behind him, a granite cliff rose high above the clearing, its stone regular, almost quarried—like a wall. The last of the day's sun hit the granite, and it glowed, almost translucent. He turned quickly away, discomfited, preferring the familiarity of the cold breeze, its cry reminding him of his mother's last breaths after resistance dogs had stabbed her.

The rain he'd coaxed from the evening sky to drown out the howl of his core nuzhda had slackened, which probably explained his impatience. But, rather than restart it, he nodded to Celka. "We'll imbue next."

True-life's cold wind carried rain edging toward sleet, warning that winter would soon tighten its grip. Deep gutters funneled water past the feet of the crowd gathered at the edges of the square. The storm temple had not been large enough to contain the crowd that had turned out for their imbuements and, with Filip's warning, Gerrit had worried that they would resist as bolt-hawks pressed them back from the storm tower, creating a safe buffer in case his people made mistakes. The precaution seemed largely unnecessary at this point; both Red and Green Squad's tvoortsi had gained excellent control.

As if to prove his point, Gods' Breath lashed down from the heavens, limning the tvoortse from Green Squad. The storm energy drained neatly into the rifle he aimed at an empty roof, the nuzhda crystalizing.

Catching Celka's hand, Gerrit strode into the rain, the wind a brisk slap, refreshing after the temple's humid stink of close-pressed bodies. Celka's brows were drawn, shadowed beneath her storm helmet, her expression as tense as it had been since Gerrit had first demonstrated the paranoid violence nuzhda on the train. But whatever her concerns, Gerrit was confident they could imbue together. Gaining his father's regard was critical. Failure was not an option.

Beneath the storm tower, two starburst storm-marks bleached the paving stones. After the platoon moved on, the lightning filigree would be a sign of pride for the town, a reminder of the State's storm-blessing.

But Gerrit was not creating some minor imbuement, so he climbed up onto the dais, stepping with Celka onto a polished slab of wood that, once storm-marked, would go to one of his father's supporters. Celka positioned herself across from him, Filip and Hedvika falling in at their backs.

"Together, we're strong," Gerrit told Celka as he drew his

belt knife for them to imbue. He'd released her hand as they climbed onto the dais, and made no move yet to recapture it. "Build a combat nuzhda," he ordered her before transitioning into sousednia.

Staring into the valley's shadow, icy wind whipping the snow around him, Gerrit reached for the narrative he'd developed on the train. Resistance dogs had hidden in the woods to ambush him and his mother four years ago, but betrayal was worse when it came from people you trusted. And all trust was an invitation to betrayal.

Locked on that belief, Gerrit imagined a dark, terrible moment, feeding it until it cut more sharply than reality.

Celka grips his identification folio in the rain, speaking his name in horror. "Gerrit Kladivo." Her lips curl. "You're his son." She flings the folio aside, in its place holding a pistol aimed at his chest.

At the scrape of hobnailed boots on paving stones behind him, Gerrit turns to see Filip stalking toward them. "A gunshot would be too loud," Filip says, drawing his belt knife. Catching Gerrit's arm, Filip yanks him off-balance and drives his blade up between Gerrit's ribs.

Catching the memory-hallucination, Gerrit froze it as his best friend knifed him in the chest. Breath harsh, pain bursting from the steel between his ribs, Gerrit focused back on his shadowy mountaintop. There, his own combat knife sharpened, clutched in numb-fingered hands. In the mountain clearing, he felt only a grim determination even as, behind a new granite wall, he knew exactly what to do with this knife.

Filip was fast, his betrayal unexpected, but Gerrit could be faster. Everyone would turn on him if he gave them a chance—so he wouldn't. He would act first.

Slipping back into the invented memory fugue as it restarted—

—Gerrit turns at the scrape of Filip's hobnailed boots. "A gunshot would be too loud."

But this time, as Filip catches his arm, Gerrit's ready. He twists away and, drawing his own belt knife, Gerrit drives his blade up into his traitorous best friend's heart.

One threat eliminated; but he's not safe yet. Celka still holds a gun on him.

Abandoning the knife lodged in Filip's chest, Gerrit trips Filip into her. Disarming Filip as he dies, Gerrit uses Celka's surprise to strike the pistol from her grip. With Filip's knife, he slits her throat.

Celka collapses to the cobblestones in a spray of blood, landing next to Filip's corpse. His supposed friends dead at his feet, Gerrit is finally safe.

Gods' Breath lashed the sky overhead, red as Celka's blood on the knife—though, as Gerrit transitioned back to true-life, the knife-edge glinted silver. Granite walls locked away Gerrit's paranoid violence nuzhda yet, beneath Mrach's storm tower, he itched to spin and plunge his blade into Filip's chest.

He forced his true-form to stillness. Rain pinged against his storm helmet, and Celka—*your enemy*—faced him, skin glowing with combat nuzhda. Filip—*the traitor*—stood behind him, hand on the back of Gerrit's neck—*the perfect position to stab you in the back.*

Teeth gritted, Gerrit focused past the paranoid nuzhda-murmur. "Now, Celka." He extended his hand with the knife and, posture taut with suppressed violence, she clasped her hand over his so both of them could grip his knife.

Contact jolted him, a sharpening of all three realities—true-life, his core nuzhda's shadowy mountaintop, and his nuzhda fugue of violent betrayal. A crimson echo rippled through the realities like a gunshot, and the granite walls on Gerrit's mountaintop trembled, chips of stone raining like blood onto the snow.

Muscles straining, Gerrit focused back through the wall surrounding his paranoid nuzhda, facing Celka as she tossed his identification papers aside and drew a gun. Gerrit spun at the crunch of Filip's bootsteps, chest tight with betrayal as he drew the knife he'd pulled with him from true-life, refusing to go down without a fight.

In true-life, Celka made a strangled cry.

Before she could pull away, he clapped his free hand over hers, locking her hand between his on the knife. "Build the weaves," he snarled beneath the rain, beneath her betrayal—and felt sousednia shift.

Instead of Celka holding a gun on him in sousednia, now—

—*Hedvika draws a gun, aiming at Celka who stands at Gerrit's side, even as the crunch of Filip's hobnailed boots echoes off the alley's looming walls. Gerrit still holds Celka's hand between his, both of them gripping the knife. «We have to strike first,» Gerrit says, feeling Celka's resistance. «They want to kill us.»*

Gerrit didn't know what Celka saw in her sousednia, didn't fully understand the connection that let them joint-imbue, but her nuzhda had warped his in Bludov, so he strengthened his certainty that their friends would betray them unless they struck first. A combat nuzhda had already brought Celka to the brink of violence, the bozhskyeh storm yanking against them both, urging that violence to take form.

«We have to fight.» Gerrit's voice is a snarl as Filip closes on them.

"A gunshot would be too loud," Filip says, and Hedvika holsters her pistol, drawing a knife.

«We have to fight,» Celka echoes, a whisper. When she meets his gaze, her lips peel back in a snarl. «They betrayed us.»

«They deserve this.» Gerrit snarls the words.

Around Celka, the air that had rippled crimson began to

shift, chased through with cobalt and aubergine, laced with burnt umber. Weaves Gerrit hadn't known how to shape exploded like ghostly futures: a glimpse of himself plunging the knife into Filip's chest; Celka, the knife's grip reversed, slashing the blade across her strazh's throat. A hundred possibilities spooled out faster than he could follow—death, bloody death, but *always* he and Celka struck first.

The air thickened like taffy, and the part of Gerrit that stood on his shadowed mountaintop nearly cried warning. The nuzhda was too big; if they imbued this, they'd lose themselves. But he clamped down on the words. Celka had warned that the nuzhda would seem out of control, that it was a fact of emotional imbuements, a danger. They had to lean into the nuzhda's all-consuming intensity. Only when they stopped fighting it, would they be ready to imbue.

Despite her warning, as the fragment of his mind grounded in his mountain clearing diminished, crushed between granite walls, Gerrit panicked. He wanted to tear away from her, fling the knife aside. The wall at his back, glowing with sunset, cracked, a rockslide tumbling from its summit. His father's esteem wasn't worth his sanity.

Now Celka's hand was the one to clench over his, her grip in true-life making him wince.

"We fight," she snarled beneath the rain. "We win." Her sousedni-shape glowed so brightly that he couldn't see her expression in true-life. She drew him like a moth to flame. In his paranoia-warped sousednia, they had no choice. Their friends had betrayed them. They had to strike first or they would die.

His uncertainty vanished.

The air smells of blood and shit and desperation. «That's right,» he snarls at the traitors who'd pretended to be his friends, «you should be desperate. You betrayed us.»

The words echoed as the nuzhda-futures thinned, ghostly forms still slashing and stabbing, but the air no longer choked by them. Celka met his gaze across the knife. «Ready,» she said, not asking, echoing the word aloud to their strazhi. Neither Filip nor Hedvika had gotten the paranoia nuzhda quite right on the train, but they'd come close enough that their strazh weaves would at least do some good.

Gerrit had no time to worry about the risks of that misalignment. The violent nuzhda reflected in Celka's eyes and, as they reached together for the storm, Gerrit was glad that Celka, at least, had not betrayed him.

Gods' Breath came at his command, slicing through him, bloodying the back alley and its brutal betrayal. He screamed—in rage, in defiance—and drove his blade into Filip's chest, barely locking himself motionless in true-life. The lightning's coppery carmine poured into his hands, flaying him as it twisted into combat's crimson slashed with a deep purple swath of self-protection and cobalt whispers of betrayal.

The pain was worse than he remembered from joint-imbuing, the euphoria that usually chased it reduced to a trickle that only intensified the agony, but Gerrit gritted his teeth and rode it out.

As the nuzhda-haze faded along with the agony, Gerrit heard Filip's voice, distant and edged with betrayal. "Drop the nuzhda, Gerrit." Filip still gripped his neck. Too easily, Gerrit could imagine a knife in his best friend's hand. "The imbuement's complete. You command the platoon. We're in a crowded public square. Iveta's watching. You've done well." Not Filip's usual words, and part of Gerrit read treason in the change—even as it was exactly what he needed to hear, focusing him on the threat to his reputation if he lost control, the threat to his platoon if he frightened the civilians into rioting.

Celka's hand slipped from between his, and she folded over her knees, retching on the storm-scarred wood at their feet. Her reaction startled him.

He needed to reintegrate. Plunging into sousednia, he struggled to expand his shadowy mountain clearing. The paranoid violence nuzhda fought him, catching like a grappling hook, scoring a deep, painful line through the snow before it shattered.

On the dais, he leaned over his knees, struggling to catch his breath, still gripping the pulsing, imbued knife in one hand. Rain slid cold down the collar of his jacket, contrasting with the warmth of Filip's palm, his fingers digging too hard into Gerrit's neck. In the eerie, post-imbuement silence, Filip's breath rasped loud and fast. When Gerrit lifted his head, he found strain pinching Hedvika's expression.

The four of them retreated beneath the storm temple's shelter, and Gerrit ordered the weakest tvoortse from Green Squad to imbue. She was still working on a simple hunger imbuement in a turnip, and Gerrit hoped that any nuzhda charge from his and Celka's imbuement would fade from the crowd by the time she finished.

With half an ear, Gerrit listened to Filip's grounding cues, and the lingering itch between his shoulder blades that insisted his friends were about to knife him in the back faded.

With the Green Squad bozhk pulling against hunger, Gerrit didn't immediately realize that the Song of Feeding rose from elsewhere in the square. Only after Gods' Breath struck and successfully crystalized the woman's first imbuement, did Gerrit wonder at the frenzied heartbeat rhythm. Instead of fading, it built, and Gerrit cast about the square, finally discovering an elder in a faded sarafan kneeling over a woven basket beside where one of the storm tower's grounding wires anchored into the earth. Gerrit shouldn't have been able to hear them at this distance, especially as the rain blew harder, but their voice carried, pure yet anguished, skipping through the Song of Feeding. He could sense that their basket contained grain—a relative fortune of it, if the elder's hollow cheeks matched their means.

"Havel, you're next," Gerrit ordered, still watching the elder, trying to decide what to do. Imbuements by solitary civilians were rare—despite the resistance's growing claims and the State's concerns—but given how the Song rippled the air, this one had a chance.

Desperate, exultant, the elder lifted their face to the sky. Hunger nuzhda pooled spinach green over their skirts. Gerrit didn't know who they needed to feed, but he could sense that their desperation was not for themself. A pity they'd come to attempt their imbuement here, just as the regime flexed its muscles, just as two of the Stormhawk's children demonstrated the *State's* storm-blessing.

Signaling to a nearby pair of bolt-hawks, Gerrit pointed to the elder. "Stop them," he ordered.

Filip caught his arm, grip bruising. "What are you doing?"

On the dais, Havel put the sniper rifle he intended to imbue to his shoulder, aiming up at something outside Gerrit's view—nowhere near the crowd, no reason for them to feel threatened. Already Havel rippled with combat nuzhda, Dbani at his back, glowing violet.

Filip's grip on his arm tightened.

Gerrit shook it off. Low, he said, "This is a State operation. You know that. Don't make a scene."

The bolt-hawks he'd sent approached the elder casually, moving as though they just happened to be walking that way. But they weren't alone. A knot of local Tayemstvoy converged from the west. The elder saw none of them, intent on their Song, on their grain, on the rain streaking their face like tears. Their hunger nuzhda pulsed, settling into a steady heartbeat.

At Gerrit's side, Celka said, "These people are on edge. You can't send the red—the *hawks* to stop an elder *Singing*."

Sleet, she was right. What had he been thinking? If the elder imbued, the people would rejoice, and their mood might calm. If the Tayemstvoy mishandled this—and chances were they *would*, given that the local hawks hadn't even thought to inform him or Iveta of the resistance leaflets—the people might riot.

Stepping out into the square, Gerrit called, "Tayemstvoy, stand down."

From the corner of his eye, he caught Iveta's frown. She shouldered past her people to reach him, but Gerrit ignored her, striding toward the civilian, though he wouldn't reach them before the local hawks. The Song of Feeding's quick rhythm thickened the air with the scent of grilling meat. "Tayemstvoy, stand down! That's an order."

Iveta's bolt-hawks stopped. The local Tayemstvoy didn't.

Gerrit broke into a jog. "Stop them!" He pointed at the local hawks.

One of Mrach's Tayemstvoy turned and met his gaze. Misunderstanding his urgency, the sergeant jogged the last few paces and smashed the elder across the face with a closed fist. The elder fell backwards, and another local hawk struck them with the butt of their rifle.

Lightning flashed. The basket tipped. Barley cascaded across the paving stones.

The thud of boots on flesh as the sergeant kicked the elder in the side shattered Gerrit's post-imbuement silence, and the world erupted in noise.

Screams. Shouting. The crack of a truncheon. Thunder.

"Stop!" he shouted. "Tayemstvoy, *stand down!*"

Then singing. Across the square, rising from the tangle of side streets, a new Song filled the hole left by the elder's melody. Instead of Feeding's empty, gasping desperation, the Song of Fighting marched to the cadence of Tayemstvoy blows. It tore across the crowd like wildfire, and lighting struck the storm tower, blinding, tendrils of white fire wriggling down the grounding lines, hissing into the earth beneath a deafening crash of thunder.

Instead of drowning the voices, the thunder amplified them. Gerrit's heart hammered in his ears, his pulse aligning to the Song's rhythm. Coughing, he tasted diesel smoke from the stalled motorcar in his icy, combat-flared sousednia.

In an effort of will, he wrenched his sousednia back to his mountain clearing and anchored himself in true-life.

Beneath the storm tower, Havel glowed crimson, Dbani's own weaves merging crimson to violet—both nearly ready to imbue.

Crimson smoke wafted through the square, weaving through the crowd in sousednia. Again, lightning struck the storm tower. The civilians kept singing. Any minute now, someone in the crowd would imbue. Then singing would become fighting—would become a riot.

"Captain Havel, stand down!" They needed to get out, not imbue and fan the fire. "Imbuement platoon, *retreat!*" Even as he shouted, Gods' Breath ignited the square, Havel at its core.

Gerrit couldn't spare the attention to watch. All around the square, Songs that had begun at different times with different tempos converged into a single resonance like an enemy army boxing in Gerrit's platoon. Tayemstvoy—both local and from Iveta's company—struggled to keep the civilians out of the square, already coming to blows. The local hawks weren't singing, but their snarling faces showed them to be sparking as bad as the civilians. This would end in blood—and Gerrit refused to let it be his platoon's.

Filip skidded to a stop at Gerrit's side, the rest of the imbuement platoon on his heels. "Retreat to the train station." Gerrit had to shout over the civilians' Song.

A gunshot cracked the air. A Tayemstvoy lieutenant stood, pistol raised to the sky, shouting. People screamed. The singing crescendoed.

Gods' Breath stabbed into the crowd, the thunder instantaneous. Gerrit turned, even as the mob cringed away. The air tasted of blood and frozen earth over the half-flooded town square and, despite the chaos, Gerrit spotted the civilian who'd called the storm. The youth snarled and swung a glowing crimson pipe at one of the still-cringing Tayemstvoy.

Their head exploded in a spray of gore.

The Song of Fighting faltered then swelled, and any restraint the Tayemstvoy had shown evaporated at the youth's attack. Gunshots echoed off buildings, and sung rhythms built and fell, twining into resonances that strained to coalesce into weaves.

Even in the field during Branislav's catastrophic imbuement, the air hadn't been so charged with combat nuzhda.

"Strazhi, protect the storm-blessed," Gerrit shouted as Filip pulled him toward a side street slightly less teeming with angry townsfolk. Dbani had grabbed Havel's arm, pulling him down from the dais, sprinting toward them from the central square. As they reached the crowd in the side street, a phalanx of bolt-hawks joined them, creating an armed wedge to push the imbuement squads through. "Weapons are a last resort," Gerrit ordered, screaming to be heard as they fought their way through sparking civilians and snarling local Tayemstvoy. "These are Bourshkanyans, not the enemy!"

To Sergeant Mares, one of the bolt-hawks, Gerrit asked, "Where's Iveta?" But the sergeant just shook his head, driving civilians back with merciless blows of his truncheon.

Iveta could handle herself, but Gerrit twisted back toward the central square anyway, scanning the crowd. He watched not the details but the ebb and flow of people, the way Iveta had taught him during the Stormhawk's rally, trusting Filip and the bolt-hawks to keep him from harm. As they pressed into the side street, he spotted her—Iveta's familiar heat-shimmer clustered with a handful of bolt-hawks. She was pinned by civilians wielding improvised weapons that glowed crimson.

"Filip, with me!" Gerrit called, no time to think, only react. "Sergeant Mares, get the imbuement platoon to the train station!" Then he was running, dodging and twisting between sparking civilians and Tayemstvoy, trusting Filip to have his back.

But even in the chaos, he could tell that the mob between him and his sister was too large, too violent. The bolt-hawks who had been standing moments before were beaten to the ground, weapons torn from their grasps. He wouldn't make it in time.

"No!" Gerrit screamed, drawing his imbued knife and diving into imagined memory.

Imbuing with Celka, it had taken long minutes to imagine his closest friends' betrayal. Now, gripping the knife, breathing its nuzhda, already desperate, the imagining snapped into realism like the shock of diving into icy water. He threw the imbuement's rippling crimson-cobalt over the crowd between him and Iveta. Then, thanking Celka's training, he split his sousedni-shape from his true-form, sprinting forward, closing the distance without regard for the crowd. He managed only three meters before agony drove him to his knees in true-life, but it was enough. He cast the imbuement's paranoia about, flinging it over the heads of rioting civilians.

Already sparking with violence, they turned on one another.

Gasping, Gerrit lost the dislocation as Filip dragged him to his feet. But the civilians had stopped attacking them. Gerrit sheathed the imbued knife and shouted for Iveta. She punched through, dodging blows no longer meant for her, blood streaming like combat nuzhda from her nose. Five bolt-hawks followed her, limping and barely keeping their feet.

"Over here!" Gerrit called, casting the paranoid violence imbuement out to clear a path.

Iveta reached them, breathing hard, eyes darting to the civilians tearing into each other. "Your imbuement?"

He nodded, already cutting through the riot. Near them, the Song of Fighting had faltered, the civilians too intent upon their friends' betrayal to Sing cohesively.

Filip caught his arm, pointing to an opening. "This way."

Together, they ran.

CHAPTER THIRTY-FOUR

ALL AROUND CELKA, people fought and died. At first, the imbuement platoon's military bozhki and the bolt-hawks fought hand-to-hand, obeying Gerrit's orders, treating the rioting civilians like fellow Bourshkanyans. But there were too many. Boxed in, they paid for every meter of forward progress in blood. The Song of Fighting surged through the mob, Gods' Breath making ordinary objects deadly and their wielders combat-warped and desperate.

Celka saw only one solution. "Hedvika!" she shouted.

"Don't worry!" Hedvika screamed over the riot, her face bloody. She drew the pistol at her hip. "I'll keep you safe! Just keep moving forward."

Celka grabbed her arm, shoving the gun down before she could fire. It got both of them slammed against a brick wall by the person she'd been about to shoot, and Celka took an elbow to the side of her head that left her ears ringing. Hedvika cursed, smashing the pistol across their attacker's face, a whirlwind of fists and boots, fighting to make space for Celka to right herself.

The mob pressed in, breaking through their defensive lines. Instead of fighting side by side, Celka's friends now fought alone or in pairs.

Gods' Breath struck the crowd, and someone rammed an imbued broom into Dbani's chest. It drove through them like they were made of paper, erupting out the other side in a spray of blood. Havel screamed as Dbani collapsed.

"Ground me!" Celka shouted, not waiting for Hedvika's answer, her focus already on sousednia.

From the high wire, Celka pinwheeled into the sky, circus tents receding like she'd been fired from a cannon. She grasped at the fresh, cool air, shedding her fear and panic like layers of wool and fur coming in from winter's cold.

She was safe. Everything would be fine.

Beneath a cloudless summer sky, the breeze blows distant birdsong and bountiful harvests of golden grain. Here, she can breathe, can relax and let the sun warm her face. Here, she can listen to what others have to say, can speak her mind. Can be herself. Be calm.

That calm pulsed around her, quiet and rational, river-blue and gold like summer wheat. Green fields lent their nuzhda glow, and the lavender that kissed the air was for the protection of others, the protection that came from listening, from considering.

In true-life, she heard the sound of blows distantly, but she focused on the feel of the storm pendant Pa had given her—the pendant she held when she prayed, when she sat calm and peaceful, when she clung to hope.

People were shouting, but she felt Hedvika nearby. "I'm ready," Celka called, hoping her strazh would hear, but prepared to imbue without her.

"I'm here," Hedvika said, her hand cold and wet as she clasped the back of Celka's neck. "Go."

Reaching into the darkness above her spotlit high wire, Celka grasped her storm-thread and *pulled*. Gods' Breath blazed into her, her whole body a torch. The storm pendant's edges bit into her palm, and Celka gasped like drawing fresh air after swimming deep at the bottom of a lake. Storm energy poured into her pendant, and barely had the weaves crystalized when she threw their power outward.

She hadn't paid attention to the strength of her imbuement, desperate only to imbue as fast as possible, but the nuzhda-cloth flung wide—it reached both sides of the narrow street, extending a full house-length ahead and behind. Holding it so outstretched left her heart racing, sweat mingling with the rain streaming down her face. Hastily, she retreated to her core sousednia, strengthening the tent walls to hold the calming nuzhda apart from herself. Then, unsteady on her feet, she swam back into true-life.

Everyone had gone still. The fighting had stopped.

Lightning lit the street in staccato flashes, glinting off eyes and weapons.

Havel dropped to his knees at Dbani's side. No one else moved.

"What's happening?" someone asked.

"Please," another called, "I need help." Pain sounded in their voices, but not fear.

Celka stumbled toward Havel, heart in her throat. So much blood pooled around Dbani.

Hedvika caught her. "Stay back."

Celka opened her mouth to argue before realizing that Havel glowed like he sat in golden sunlight. Around him, the air smelled fresh and violins played like a summer breeze.

She tore her gaze off him, finding Yanek several meters away, helping Masha up off the ground. "Yanek," she called. "Ground Havel!"

Yanek turned with a start, but didn't question her. He rushed to Havel's side. Havel's nuzhda was powerful, and Celka's chest squeezed despite the calming imbuement cloaking them. She'd never seen anyone imbue healing before, knew nothing about how to shape those weaves. Havel had a full rainbow of nuzhda competencies, but Celka thought healing took special training.

Past him, a bolt-hawk with a sergeant's pips—Sergeant Mares, Celka thought—wrenched the imbued broom from the unresisting youth's hands before issuing orders with calm command. He sent the bolt-hawks to form a perimeter around Havel and Dbani, pushing the civilians outside it—though keeping them within the calming imbuement's sphere. He joined Celka with a respectful nod. "We need to move out. Can you hold that active while we march?" At her nod, he ordered two bolt-hawks to carry Dbani.

"Wait," Celka said. "Havel's imbuing."

The sergeant scowled. "There's no saving Lishak. We're still surrounded. We march to the train station." He turned away, mouth opening on more orders.

Celka caught his shoulder. "No." The violins had formed a stable rhythm, and Yanek's strazh weaves bled yellow to violet. "Havel only needs a minute."

Hedvika stepped to Celka's side, arms crossed, and the sergeant swallowed his protest.

Inside the range of Celka's imbuement, the civilians and handful of local red shoulders were helping each other up, supporting the wounded, rain washing away the blood. But at the edge of their pocket of calm, people still fought and screamed, and the air shook with thunder.

Then Gods' Breath hit Havel, and Celka bit her lip, casting a desperate prayer to the Storm Gods.

The scarf he'd pressed to Dbani's chest flared golden, Havel's weaves crystalizing for just an instant before the magic drained away. On her knees, Masha cradled Dbani's head as they convulsed. Celka surged forward, Hedvika at her side, closing in on Dbani, grief choking her throat to see the scarf nothing more than blood-soaked cloth.

She'd thought Havel had had a chance.

As Celka clustered helplessly with her squad, grief shook her tent canvas, her calming nuzhda close to shattering. Desperately, Celka wished she knew the first thing about healing imbuements.

Then Dbani coughed.

Face twisted in pain, Dbani rolled onto their side and hacked blood on the cobblestones.

"Dbani?" Havel repeated their name, urgent, and Dbani caught his hand. They spent a moment gasping for breath, then pushed themself up to sit, wiping blood from their lips. "What...?"

Masha's laugh sounded hysterical. "You're all right?"

Dbani patted their chest. Blood darkened their uniform, a ragged hole where the imbued broomstick had punched through but, beneath it, the pale glint of unbroken skin. As they gripped Havel's arm, Celka struggled to understand. The scarf didn't glow. The imbuement had failed, hadn't it?

"Never thought I'd be so impressed by a one-shot," Hedvika said, crouching to squeeze Dbani's shoulder, and suddenly Celka understood. The imbuement hadn't failed. It had done exactly what it was meant to do—save Dbani's life. Now the scarf was nothing more than bloodstained cloth.

"Thank you," Dbani said to Havel, voice shaky.

Pale, Havel helped them to their feet.

"We need to move out," Sergeant Mares snapped. "This location is not secure."

As he said it, the sounds of the fight filtered through Celka's post-imbuement silence. Screams. The sick crack of violence.

With sudden conviction, Celka said, "We can't go. People are dying."

"Lieutenant Kladivo's orders are to retreat to the train station," the sergeant said, unequivocal. "Everyone move out!"

"Stand down, Sergeant." Command weighted Havel's voice. His gaze darted around, assessing, his too-pale fingers locked on Dbani's arm. "Prochazka, we need you to clear a path through the riot to the train station. Sergeant Mares will secure it with the bolt-hawks and Green Squad, while Red Squad returns to quell the riot."

The sergeant opened his mouth, but Havel's glare snapped it shut.

"Prochazka." The snap to Havel's voice pulled Celka's attention off the screams. "Let's move."

They didn't have far to reach the edge of the riot, Celka's imbuement cutting a path of calm through the chaos. When they broke through the mob, Sergeant Mares seemed to expect Celka to accompany Green Squad all the way to the train station. Havel set him straight, ordering Green Squad and the bolt-hawks ahead. His command faltered when he turned to Dbani. "You should go with them."

Dbani shook their head. "I'm fine. Let's go save more lives."

Havel straightened, ordering Red Squad back the way they'd come, his decisive confidence making it easier to plunge back into the riot. Celka had never expected to be grateful for his entitlement and rank.

Mind soaring in the blue sky above the circus, Celka jogged back toward the sound of gunshots and fighting. The street she'd calmed had emptied, but not as much as she'd expected. "Go home," Celka called, "tend your wounded." The rest of her squad took up the cry, and Celka focused on fanning out the imbuement.

The central square was worse than Celka had feared.

The singing had stopped, so combat nuzhda no longer rippled the air. Instead, people fought each other with fists and knives, broken chair legs and shards of glass. The cobblestones ran red with blood, and people had fallen and been trampled. The division of civilian against Tayemstvoy had broken, people turning on each other, desperate with rage that didn't care who it destroyed. The Song of Fighting had given the crowd a determined ferocity, a purpose, an enemy. Now they simply boiled with hatred and fear.

Celka threw all her strength into her imbuement, her whole body vibrating with its nuzhda as she stretched its weaves to their limit. The nuzhda overflowed into true-life, and she sang the Song of Calming, the melody resonating with her imbuement's pulse. Her squad took up the Song, and Yanek began to ripple amber and blue—he had her smaller calming imbuement.

Where her imbuement touched, Celka expected the fighting to cease, as it had in the alley. Sometimes it did. Civilians stumbled and shook themselves, peering around as if waking from a dream. Some took longer to react, sunk more deeply into the violence, launching themselves at the people Celka had calmed. Others just kept fighting.

All around her, people took up the Song of Calming, and Celka forced herself to keep moving. The square was huge, and it seemed like the entire city had turned out to riot. Fighting spilled into the side streets, Tayemstvoy who'd come to quell the violence enflaming it anew, squeezing desperate civilians between the enemy in the square and the enemy cutting off their retreat. They had no choice but to fight, the storm still raging overhead, sparking their violence. Every now and then, a bolt of Gods' Breath would streak from the heavens, creating another weapon, stealing more lives.

Celka trusted her squad to determine their path, forming a determined wedge of olive drab. They quartered the square first, quelling the worst of the violence before moving into the main street packed with rioters. By the time they returned to the square, the violence had flared anew, and Celka's squad circled the storm tower, singing and calming, before arrowing off down another road.

By the time they reached the end of the last street, Masha and Hedvika were supporting Celka under her arms, and Celka had no voice left to sing.

As they limped back toward the square, Hedvika said hoarsely, "Drop the imbuement."

Celka wanted to protest, but her vision was blurring and her friends supported nearly all of her weight. She stumbled to a stop, wavering, and struggled to dispel the summer sky and golden wheat. Eventually, grounded back on her high wire, Celka reached the storm temple.

The temple had been transformed into a hospital, people lying on the floor and benches, bleeding and moaning. Celka's chest tightened to see Tayemstvoy and civilians side by side, fearing more violence, but even as the fading bozhskyeh storm licked the sky with Gods' Breath, the only Song she heard was Calming. People in uniform and out moved amongst the casualties, bringing water, cleaning and bandaging wounds. Others merely sang or hummed, the calming cadence rising and falling.

"Sit," Masha said, and Celka realized they'd steered her toward one of the open storm walls, and someone had found her a chair.

"Someone needs this more than I do," Celka said, but Hedvika lowered her into it, and she didn't have the strength for another protest.

"Rest," Havel said. "You've earned it." He looked

exhausted, but some of his color had returned. He caught Dbani's hand with a wan smile.

Yanek flopped, boneless at Celka's feet, flinging an arm over her lap, head on her knee. His brown skin had faded gray, and Masha sat at his side, stroking his head. The calming imbuement he'd used had been smaller, but he didn't have the advantage of having imbued it, so holding its complex nuzhda for so long would have been a strain.

Hedvika moved behind Celka, relieving her of her drenched cap and finger-combing out her wet hair. Celka suddenly remembered blood on Hedvika's face as she'd fought in the street. But when she asked if her strazh should find a doctor, Hedvika just said, "I'm fine. Rest," and started braiding Celka's hair.

Celka let her head flop back, soothed by Hedvika's touch and Yanek's weight on her knee.

After a silence that stretched and blurred, she realized their group had shrunk. Fearing Havel's magic hadn't fully healed Dbani, she asked, "Where are Havel and Dbani?"

"Wrapping bandages," Hedvika said, settling on the ground at Celka's side, no more hair to braid.

That surprised Celka, and she craned around, finding Havel's haughty figure, his wavy hair matted with blood, gently washing the wounds of a middle-aged person in ratty homespun. Tears leapt to Celka's eyes and, exhausted, she couldn't push them back.

Masha passed her a handkerchief—it was damp.

"Don't worry," Masha said, chuckling at Celka's grimace, "it's just wet from the rain."

Celka kept expecting a platoon of Tayemstvoy to march up and start making arrests, but whenever red shoulders arrived, Havel put them to work. Celka wasn't naïve enough to believe no arrests would be made, but it was nice, for the moment, to see the hawks working alongside civilians, caring for people instead of hurting them.

Occasionally, someone would ask Celka's blessing, and a few children ran up, begging to see her storm-scar. But mostly the townsfolk let her rest, a few self-appointed citizens steering would-be supplicants on their way. "What happens next?" she asked her squad.

They just shook their heads, watching Havel and Dbani move amongst the wounded. Carts and the occasional motorcar drove through the blood in the square to transfer people to the hospital.

After the storm faded, someone brought them clay cups of water, then bowls of weak soup. Celka drank both gratefully, then rallied herself to move. "We should go." She didn't have the strength to help as Havel and Dbani did, and someone could surely make better use of her chair.

Hedvika nodded, but Masha laid a hand on Celka's knee. "They need this," she said softly. *And so does the State,* Celka heard in an echo beneath her voice. "You saved them. Let them see you." *Let them see you wearing that uniform.*

Celka tried to shake the undertone of State propaganda—maybe all Masha cared about was giving the people hope and a connection to the Storm Gods. But even if that was all *Masha* intended, Celka knew the regime would use her presence, soggy uniform jacket draped over the back of her chair, for their own ends.

Barely had she thought it when two gleaming motorcars rolled up. Gerrit and Iveta climbed out of the first, followed by Filip and a few bolt-hawks. A cluster of Tayemstvoy emerged from the second carrying a large camera.

Gerrit's approach filled Celka with dread.

Frozen in her chair, she searched his expression for horror or remorse—or even some acknowledgment that this disaster had been his fault. Instead, she found the same cold, hard lines as she'd met on the train ride here. Something had changed in him this morning, allowing him to pull against a crueler nuzhda than she'd ever imagined, and the dead bodies surrounding her were the result.

"Specialist Prochazka," he said, cool like he was no more than her commanding officer. "Thank you for calming the riot. You're a great credit to the regime."

The words felt like a slap, and she remembered Dbani's wide eyes, mouth opening on a scream, as the broom plunged into their chest. *You started the riot,* Celka wanted to scream at him, but instead she reached into sousednia, finding Nina inside the storm temple, where she'd been forgotten in the violence.

Activating the snake felt like climbing onto the high wire with a raging fever, but once she did it, the python's imbuement steadied her. Easily, she connected with the thread that felt like Filip, but when she activated the one that smelled of Gerrit, nothing happened. She frowned up at him, wondering whether he was deliberately ignoring her—or if whatever he had done this morning made connecting through the snake impossible.

«*Can you reach Gerrit through Nina?*» Celka asked Filip privately.

«*No.*» His worry tinged the air with an antiseptic, chemical scent.

But Celka had no time to interrogate the problem because a Tayemstvoy lieutenant set about arranging photographs. The storm speaker looked on, tight-lipped from the shadows, as the crew arranged Celka and her squad with Gerrit and Iveta and wounded civilians for a seemingly endless parade of photographs.

By the time the State propagandists released her, Celka

looked around for Gerrit only to find him already gone. Her stomach twisted, and she wasn't sure if she wanted to scream or crumple with relief. Despite the steady stream of hospital vehicles, wounded still lay everywhere.

"Things will change after today," Hedvika said. In her voice still gravely from their efforts to quell the riot, it sounded like a threat.

CHAPTER THIRTY-FIVE

FILIP ENTERED GERRIT'S room without knocking. Gerrit and Iveta had been in close conference ever since the riot, but now, he was alone.

Gerrit had one of the larger rooms in the governor's mansion, the bed wide enough to easily accommodate both him and Celka. Not that Celka was here. She'd retreated to Hedvika and Masha's room, exhausted and heartsick, Hedvika's arm around her waist. Filip didn't think she'd spoken to Gerrit. Filip certainly hadn't. But going to bed without having this conversation would be cowardice, so he'd squeezed Yanek's hand and gone to find his tvoortse.

"Hey." Filip shut the door softly behind himself. He'd expected—hoped—to find Gerrit slumped on the bed, but his best friend stood at the window in a fresh uniform, hands clasped behind his back like he watched a parade. All afternoon Filip had been trying to get Gerrit to activate his end of Nina's imbuement—trying and failing.

He expected Gerrit to say something as he approached, but Gerrit stayed silent. The reports were still coming in, the riot's death toll already over two hundred. How many of those deaths were Gerrit's fault?

"You didn't have to use the paranoia imbuement." The words slipped out before Filip could stop them. They shouldn't have this conversation aloud, but he couldn't wait any longer.

In Mrach's city square, pushing through the rioting crowd, everything had happened so fast. Filip had been singularly focused on protecting Gerrit as they pressed toward Iveta, and when he'd realized what Gerrit had done... Filip swallowed hard. At the time, he'd told himself that Gerrit knew what he was doing. Filip's job was to support him, get him out of that mess alive. He'd focused on that job to block out the carnage, but the horrors had been everywhere.

"You didn't have to *keep* using it." Filip kept his voice low, but couldn't strip away his anger. He wasn't even sure who he was angrier with. Gerrit, for using the imbuement; or himself, for not trying to stop him.

"I saved Iveta's life." Gerrit's voice was cold, remorseless. "Those civilians never should have been singing. I did what was necessary."

Filip caught his arm, dragging Gerrit around to face him. "They have as much right to the Storm Gods' blessings as we do." *More,* he wanted to say, *because they need the miracles.*

"Not anymore." Gerrit handed Filip a telegram from his jacket pocket.

Filip's pulse pounded in his ears as he forced himself to read. The edict he'd been dreading had come through: singing any Song but the Song of Calming during a storm was now a crime. Feeling like all the air had been sucked from the room, Filip whispered, "You have to change his mind." He'd seen drafts of the newspaper articles the propagandists were preparing, blaming the riot on sparking civilians, claiming the death toll would have been higher but for the State bozhki whose magic had calmed the crowd. They blamed the riot on the Songs—not on Gerrit ordering a Song silenced, not on Tayemstvoy brutality.

"I'll pretend I didn't just hear you speak against the Stormhawk," Gerrit said.

Filip caught Gerrit's arms, barely stopping himself from shaking his friend. "What's wrong with you?"

Gerrit's expression gained a warning edge, and Filip released him, barely managing not to step back. He'd seen Gerrit wear this face before, but it had always felt temporary, a mask he knew his best friend would remove as soon as it was safe.

"Your core grounding's off," Filip said, wondering if it was true, hating that he could no longer tell. Gerrit felt *wrong*—but not wrong enough to be nuzhda-warped. The wind sounded slightly different as it howled around him, but the air still smelled of icy pine boughs. If only sousednia didn't press on Filip's senses, maybe he'd be able to understand. Maybe he would already have *done* something instead of standing by while Gerrit got innocent people killed.

Gerrit's cheek twitched. He turned back to the window. "I'm fine."

"You're *not*," Filip insisted, Gerrit's too-quick denial strengthening his conviction. Shifting his perception sideways, trying to ignore the ghostly library, Filip asked, "What did you do this morning?" The space around Gerrit felt enclosed in a way that didn't fit with an expansive mountain clearing, and Filip realized with a start that Gerrit felt like he had after returning from the capital, bruised from Artur's sadistic powerplay. Somehow this all fit together; he'd figure it out and get his best friend back. "How did you figure out the paranoia nuzhda?"

Gerrit tensed. Before Filip could press him on it, Gerrit turned abruptly to face him. "Help me reintegrate."

Filip opened his mouth to object—Gerrit wasn't holding

a nuzhda. The almost imperceptible shake of Gerrit's head silenced him. Swallowing his confusion, Filip placed his hands on Gerrit's cheeks. Pulling against Gerrit's core nuzhda was harder than usual—harder than he could blame on simple exhaustion. But when he managed it, Gerrit trembled.

Like after Artur's beating, Gerrit's breath quickened as though with panic. He tensed, about to pull away, before a low cry tore from his throat. He caught Filip's face and leaned into his support, their foreheads touching. Gerrit's fingers dug hard into Filip's cheeks and his shoulders shook, but he made no further sound.

When that death-grip loosened, Filip led him to the bed and they sat side by side. Gerrit clutched his hands like Filip was a lifeline, his gaze fixed, unseeing, on the middle distance. Filip kept pulling against Gerrit's core nuzhda, letting the icy wind scour him. Ivy-covered walls locked away a tiny space within him, the restricted library compressed until Filip nearly vanished inside his own mind.

Beside him, Gerrit's breathing changed, the panicked stutter giving way to deep, gasping draughts and, slowly, he released his grip on Filip's hands.

A new sensation tickled Filip's mind, howling like alpine wind and warming him with winter sunshine. He almost dismissed it as coming from within himself, but it scraped against his mental walls.

His own thoughts were slow with so much of his mind walled off, echoing Gerrit's core nuzhda, but his best friend sat straighter in true-life, so Filip risked pressing his mental walls outward, letting some of Gerrit's core nuzhda dissipate. As he started to be able to think again, Filip recognized the soft scrape of Nina's imbuement. Releasing more of Gerrit's nuzhda, he pulled against protection and then combat, fully activating the snake.

As their link through Nina flared, Gerrit gasped, jerking

upright. Filip searched his best friend's face, strengthening his mental walls around the various nuzhdi, trying to interpret Gerrit's sousednia. He felt... right, Filip thought, like pine needles slick with ice, and a frozen scrim that crunched as Filip's boots broke through the snow's icy surface.

Sweat rolled down Filip's temples from the exertion of holding so many disparate nuzhdi. He tugged open his collar and scoured his mind of Gerrit's nuzhda. The release left him dizzy. He wanted to flop back onto the bed, but he made himself focus back on Gerrit sitting next to him.

«*What was that?*» Filip asked through Nina, shaky with relief that Gerrit had finally activated the snake. «*What happened today?*»

Gerrit dropped his head into his hands. «*I can't keep doing this.*»

«*Doing what? Talk to me, Gerrit.*»

Gerrit's jaw tightened, but he lifted his head enough to search Filip's face, his golden-brown eyes catching the cold, electric light. «*You'd tell me to stop.*»

Filip felt the words as a physical blow, but forced his voice through the imbuement to stay calm. «*Just tell me.*»

Fast, like Gerrit wasn't sure he could get it out otherwise, he said, «*I'm walling off memories.*»

Filip stared at him, not understanding. «*Memories?*»

«*So I can play the part.*» Gerrit straightened on the bed, squinting into the distance as though struggling to remember something he'd learned long ago. «*So I can...*» He hesitated, visibly struggling. «*...can support Iveta. So I can ensure that Artur won't become the next Stormhawk.*» He turned abruptly to Filip, as though the pieces had snapped into place. When he spoke again, his sudden conviction carried an edge of desperation. «*I have to do this. But I...*» He launched to his feet, pacing like he was caged. «*I'm taking an early train* *to the capital tomorrow. To see my father. He'll want me to demonstrate»*—his voice choked—*«the paranoia imbuement. Filip, I can't do this without walls.»*

Sickened, Filip realized what Gerrit was saying. *«You're somehow locking away memories. And it changes you.»*

Gerrit met Filip's gaze as though expecting him to tear into him for it. *«I know it's dangerous. I didn't see any other way.»*

«How much did you hide?»

Gerrit squinted again, as though struggling to recall. *«A lot, I think. More than before. Creating that nuzhda...»* He scrubbed a hand through his hair, his already pale skin going ashy. *«But I had to. Didn't I?»*

Filip's first reaction was to take his best friend's hands, tell him that he'd done what was necessary, that they'd find a way through this. But Filip couldn't move from the bed, couldn't close the distance. *«You ordered the Tayemstvoy to stop an elder singing the Song of Feeding. They would have imbued. They deserved to imbue.»*

Gerrit swallowed convulsively.

«You used the paranoid violence imbuement on the crowd.*»* Now Filip did stand, his stranglehold on calm slipping. He wanted to scream the words aloud in Gerrit's face, and it took all his control to force them through the imbuement. *«You turned innocent civilians against each other. You made them slaughter each other. Two hundred people are dead! You started the riot. You made it worse!»*

Gerrit rocked back like Filip had punched him, but he didn't retreat, didn't even look away. Filip closed the distance between them, unable to keep the rage off his face—rage, because it was better than horror, better than the desperate, clawing feeling of falling that lurked just beneath it.

«Two hundred people,» Filip repeated in a whisper, the rage slipping away, darkness swallowing him with the memory

of that sleet-cursed telegram and its order silencing civilian Songs. «*And now...? You've stripped the right for people to sing to the Storm Gods. You did all that. Your walls... you could have been Artur.*»

He half expected Gerrit to retreat back into his remorseless mask, but Gerrit looked raw, the horror in his eyes a mirror to Filip's own. Low, barely a whisper through Nina, he said, «*If Iveta had died in the riot, Artur could have stepped unopposed into power. Was I wrong to save her? Artur's policies will be worse even than Father's.*» He gripped Filip's upper arms as though desperate for answers that Filip didn't have. «*And this imbuement? I couldn't have created it without my walls. The Stormhawk will be impressed. Iveta and I will gain favor. Was it worth it? Maybe we'll save thousands by putting her in power.*»

«*And maybe not,*» Filip said.

Gerrit searched his face, a prisoner seeking a stay of execution. «*This imbuement won't be the last. Until we can kill my father, Celka and I will have to keep producing. Each day we strengthen the regime, we strengthen Iveta. We weaken the resistance's enemies. And I need access to my father to deliver the phosgene.*»

«*And if the cost is too high?*» Filip said. «*You can't wall yourself off again. You* can't *return to the person you were today.*»

«*Maybe to win this fight we have to be ruthless.*»

«*No,*» Filip said. «*Your father is ruthless. Artur is ruthless. You can't become like them. That's the whole point of joining the resistance!*»

Gerrit looked away, jaw tight, fingers still digging into Filip's arms. «*I have to play the part.*»

«*Then play it like you used to. As a cadet you weren't—*»

«*As a cadet I was* weak. *Father didn't listen to me.*»

«*So what? Tell Iveta you can't go. She offered you an out—*

take it. *Let* her *deal with your father. Your imbuements can give her the influence she needs to buy regime loyalty. We'll find a way for you to imbue without the walls.*»

«*It's too late.*» Gerrit dropped his hands from Filip's arms, pulling himself straight as though facing inspection. «*I'm committed. I can't back out now.*»

Filip shook his head, but Gerrit spoke aloud before he could marshal another argument. "You'll return with the imbuement platoon to Solnitse tomorrow. Get some rest, Filip, and make sure Celka does, too."

Filip searched Gerrit's face, catching the faintest chill from sousednia, as though the sun on Gerrit's mountaintop had begun to set. «*You're doing it again, aren't you?*» he said through Nina, the link feeling tenuous. «*You're walling off memories.*»

Gerrit lifted his chin in the barest acknowledgment. «*Just until I return. I need this, Filip. I can't face my father as myself.*»

«*You can,*» Filip tried to say, but the link had thinned to spider silk. He grasped it, flaring the combat and protection nuzhdi he'd locked behind diminishing walls. «*Don't do this,*» he tried to say, but too late. The link had evaporated. Gerrit started to turn away from him, but Filip caught his shoulders, letting his face say what he didn't dare speak aloud.

Gerrit met his gaze, already distant. "Thank you for watching my back in the square today." He laid a hand on Filip's shoulder. "Now get some sleep."

Dismissed, Filip found himself in the corridor. He was still staring at Gerrit's closed door when Yanek found him.

Yanek pulled him into their bedroom, but Filip felt like he stumbled through darkness, like he wasn't breathing air, but water.

Once they were alone, Yanek asked in a low whisper, "Does he regret it?"

"Yes." But the word choked on the memory of Gerrit slipping back into his regime mask like it was a coat he could don and toss casually aside.

"They *won't* make more, then." Yanek made it a statement, as if that would make it true.

"They will." Filip couldn't keep the pain from his voice.

Yanek had tossed aside his clothes and crawled into bed. Filip joined him in his undershorts, curled on his side. Yanek wrapped strong limbs around him, but even his warmth couldn't stop Filip from shivering.

After a long time, Yanek whispered, "Why?"

Filip shook his head, but he knew what Yanek was asking. "To save Iveta."

Anger tightened Yanek's muscles. "Sleeting Kladivos." His voice was low, the whisper barely brushing Filip's ear.

"Wouldn't you?" Filip asked into the darkness. "To save someone you love?"

"No." Yanek didn't hesitate. "And you wouldn't either."

Filip pressed himself into Yanek's embrace, clutching the other man's arm around his chest. Wouldn't he? If the mob had been about to swallow Gerrit and he'd carried that imbuement? Wouldn't he have done exactly the same thing?

"You wouldn't," Yanek said, and he sounded so certain.

But Filip just shook his head, darkness filling with the memory of people turning on their friends, imbuements cracking skulls, blood slicking the stone beneath his boots. He curled tighter into himself, shivering in Yanek's embrace. The question haunted him and he felt Gerrit's iron gaze. *I did what was necessary.* For all he'd studied complex battles and intricate magic, Filip couldn't see the path forward. He was a soldier and a guard. He was supposed to follow orders, supposed to protect his tvoortse. When had that started to feel impossible?

CHAPTER THIRTY-SIX

GERRIT SNAPPED TO attention before his father's desk. "All hail the Stormhawk!" Despite the iron gaze of his father's portrait, Gerrit felt no fear today. As his father looked up, Gerrit discovered a striking similarity between their faces.

He reported on the riot in Mrach and his joint-imbued knife as he'd been ordered, and the Stormhawk listened, leaned casually back in his chair. When Gerrit finished, his father said, "You brought the imbuement with you?"

"Your guards have it outside."

"Good." The Stormhawk stood. "Show me."

Barely had Gerrit reclaimed the knife from the Yestrab Okhrana corporal in the Stormhawk's waiting room when his father started issuing orders for prisoners to be prepared. Several Okhrana sprinted ahead, and Gerrit fell into step beside his father through the complex's back corridors.

A major in a Yestrab Okhrana uniform joined them at an iron-grilled window looking down into a grim-walled courtyard of gray stone and concrete. A dozen ragged individuals in prison scrubs were herded in and told to stretch their legs. A single bored-looking Tayemstvoy entered to watch them.

"Can you use the imbuement from up here?" the major, whose gold bozhk bolts gleamed from her collar, asked. "Or do you need to be down amongst them?"

Gerrit glanced at his father, not sure he should discuss the imbuement, despite the major's rank.

The Stormhawk inclined his head. "Major Blatnik oversees Division Three. They handle the... advanced imbuements."

"Pleased to meet you." Gerrit shook the major's hand. "Unfortunately, I need to be down there."

An Okhrana private led Gerrit to a ground-level entrance on the other side of the courtyard and handed him the uniform jacket and weapons belt of a Tayemstvoy private. Gerrit shrugged into the scratchy wool and buckled the black leather belt, the truncheon an unaccustomed weight at his side. The jacket was too large across the shoulders, too short in the arms, and his Army officer's chestnut knee-boots broke the illusion, but he supposed it didn't matter. The charade only needed to hold long enough for him to amble across the courtyard. Depending on where the prisoners stood, he might have trouble affecting them all; he hoped he could do enough.

Deep within his mind, he shuddered. If not for the walls of sheer granite enclosing his memories, the nausea that roiled his stomach might have broken free, might have made him hesitate. As it was, he didn't give himself time to speculate or imagine the scene he'd produce. He sheathed his imbued knife in place of the private's and, closing his eyes, placed his hand on its grip, envisioning betrayal.

With the Okhrana private waiting beside him, Gerrit was careful to control the imbuement's active radius, locking its seething nuzhda behind fresh walls and gripping its crimson-cobalt gossamer in his fist. Once he had the active imbuement under control, he nodded to the private, who threw the bolt to let him into the courtyard.

The prisoners tensed at his entrance, some flinching or backing away, others seeming to hold their ground through the thinnest grip on willpower. All were filthy and gaunt, a few showed obvious bruising or moved with the stiffness of recent injuries. Gerrit affected disinterest, part of him surprised at how easy it was to ignore their obvious suffering. *They're criminals*, he told himself, refusing to question further, refusing to consider their humanity.

Two stood near enough to reach with the imbuement, and he cast its crimson-cobalt over them while he swept the tense assembly. He gave it one breath, two, not sure how long the imbuement needed to enflame their paranoia. At the riot, everything had happened so fast that it had been impossible to separate the imbuement's effects from those of the storm and the mob's rage. His stomach roiled, and he swallowed hard, pushing his emotions beneath his mental walls. Crossing the courtyard, he passed a cluster of prisoners who were conspicuously silent, dragging the active imbuement over them and catching a few others before reaching the guard. He tightened the nuzhda cloth back down in his fist.

"The commander wanted to speak to us," he told the guard for the prisoners' benefit. The Tayemstvoy private nodded and banged on the door for them to be let out. They went together, leaving the prisoners alone.

The Yestrab Okhrana private who'd handed Gerrit the decoy jacket waited for them, slamming a bolt into place to lock the door into the courtyard while Gerrit shredded his nuzhda. It left behind a bitter aftertaste and a crawling in his shoulder blades. He crushed the discomfort down alongside his nausea, and changed back into his own uniform as shouts erupted inside the courtyard.

At a jog, he followed the private to rejoin his father, reaching the barred window in time to see the prisoners trading blows, accusing each other of selling them out. A smile tugged the Stormhawk's lips and the major watched with hawkish attention. One of the prisoners went down, curling beneath their attacker's kicks. Gerrit wanted to shout for them to stop, call for guards to separate them, but he made his face impassive, pressing that weakness beyond his walls.

One of the prisoners had edged away from the others, and Gerrit would have assumed them to be avoiding the fight if the major hadn't said, "There," and pointed. They'd crouched and, Gerrit realized with a start, picked something up. It gleamed dully in the courtyard's shadows, and the prisoner stood, eyes darting, edging toward the fight. They were one of the ones he'd influenced in his initial entrance, one he'd let the imbuement linger on. In a sudden scramble, they lunged, driving whatever they'd found into another prisoner's back.

"A shiv?" Gerrit heard himself say, voice emotionless.

The prisoner yanked the improvised blade out of the other's back and turned, stabbing it into another's gut, twisting and struggling to drag it out as one of the other prisoners grabbed them by the collar and drove a fist into their face. From there, it took all of Gerrit's control to hold himself motionless, to avoid shouting for the guards to end the bloodbath. Several of the unaffected prisoners panicked, banging on the doors, screaming for rescue. The others turned on each other until only one remained. That one rounded on the ones Gerrit's imbuement hadn't touched.

Soon, of the fifteen prisoners who'd entered, only one remained on their feet, their hands and tunic dripping blood. They staggered against the wall, badly injured. On the bloodslick paving stones, several prisoners moaned, not yet dead; another screamed. Others were silent, motionless.

The Stormhawk turned to one of his guards. "Clean up the mess; dispose of the bodies." To the major, he said, "Work with Gerrit, teach him to give these imbuements range." At the major's "yes, sir," the Stormhawk clapped Gerrit on the back. "I'm proud of you, Son. We'll have dinner together tonight, just the two of us. You can return to Solnitse in the morning."

Somehow, Gerrit managed to say, "I look forward to it. Thank you, sir."

The Stormhawk disappeared down the corridor, flanked by his guards, and Major Blatnik regarded Gerrit critically. "They said you weren't Tayemstvoy material." She *hmph*ed. "Clearly you've grown."

Gerrit managed to straighten, praised by someone his father so clearly trusted. Part of him wanted to scream that she was wrong about him. Instead, he said neutrally, "Thank you, sir."

Her eyes narrowed, assessing. "If you're ready to stop slogging through the mud"—a pointed look at his brown Army boots—"I imagine your father would listen. It sends a certain message to see you in a... lesser branch." She brushed at her red shoulders as though he might be unclear where she ranked the Army.

In sousednia, a tremor cracked the granite wall still lit by the setting sun, and rock chips rained down like flechettes. Gerrit pressed one hand behind his back, balling it into a fist, and struggled to breathe naturally. "I appreciate the recommendation, sir."

She jerked her chin for him to follow and started down the corridor.

You need this, he told himself as he fell into step, another tremor shaking sousednia. *You need access to your father. Don't sleet this up.*

Following the Yestrab Okhrana major through the government complex, however, his mental walls seemed wholly inadequate. He locked his jaw and strengthened his hold on true-life, blocking out the crumbling sunset clearing. His father had been *proud*. Gerrit was gaining the Stormhawk's trust, just like they needed—*for what?* part of him wondered, but he shoved the question aside. He had to learn more about emotional imbuements and that, at least, would mean immersing himself in magic, in weave theory. Increasing the imbuements' range would be useful. Next time, he wouldn't have to get close. Perhaps he could even escape the screams and the slick tear of blades through viscera.

Gerrit's work with the Tayemstvoy major left him drained, a headache splitting his temples. She left him twenty minutes before dinner, a Yestrab Okhrana corporal escorting him to a sitting room with an attached washroom. Gerrit scrubbed his face with cold water, trying to push aside considerations of nuzhda weave mechanics and prepare to face his father.

In sousednia, great chunks of granite cleaved off his mental walls. Instead of the setting sun lighting the rock face, noonday sun glowed through the wall's cracks, edged like a knife.

I can't do this.

A boulder crashed down, shockwaves in the clearing throwing Gerrit to his knees. Sunlight blinded him along with memory. Phosgene. Assassination. And murder—his mother's murder at his father's order.

In true-life, he clutched the washbasin with white-knuckled hands, stomach heaving, bile souring his throat.

«Get a hold of yourself,» he snarled in sousednia, forcing himself to stare into the blinding glare shining through memory's walls. «You don't have time to be *weak*.»

Breath harsh, he stumbled to his feet in the snowy clearing. The sunlight burned his skin, a blast-furnace roar that pushed him back even as he pressed forward. Teeth gritted, he kept walking until he reached the wall. He pressed both hands against the fractured granite and focused, making himself believe the wall back into wholeness.

I'll reintegrate once I'm home, he promised himself. *But I need this. I need to be strong.*

When the tremors ceased and his breathing slowed, Gerrit reached back into the day's events, forcing himself not to flinch from his memory of testing the imbuement. Instead, he tore the memory apart, stripping his emotions from it like tearing needles from a pine bough. The emotion, he locked behind his walls. Then he reached back to the riot in Mrach, doing the same.

Combing back through his memory, he sought moments that made him flinch or cringe, stripping them and locking the emotion behind stone. The Stormhawk wanted to be proud of him, which meant Gerrit needed to shape himself into someone Supreme-General Kladivo could respect.

When the Okhrana corporal returned to escort him to dinner, Lieutenant Gerrit Kladivo followed with a measured step, pleased to finally meet his father as an equal.

Over dinner, conversation turned to the imbuement platoon. "Artur was convinced your efforts on emotional imbuements were a waste of time," the Stormhawk said as their soup course was taken away.

"I don't see how Artur's opinions on my platoon are relevant," Gerrit said.

"They may not be," the Stormhawk said, "though while it's natural to want to outshine your competition, it may not be wise to make enemies."

"To be an enemy, doesn't someone need to have a reasonable stake in disputed... territory?" As Gerrit spoke, he realized he stood on thin ice; Artur was a mundane and Gerrit could claim that cut him out of bozhk business—but the Stormhawk had no more magic than his eldest son. "You clearly have children much better suited to use the Storm Gods' blessings."

The Stormhawk studied him over a bite of pickled herring, gaze flat and measuring. Gerrit made himself pop another forkful of fish in his mouth, returning the Stormhawk's gaze with casual confidence.

"Urging your mages to caution," the Stormhawk finally said, focusing back on his dinner as though he'd not laced the air with threat, "and starting them with hunger imbuements was an... interesting choice."

Gerrit recalled conversational openings like this from childhood, the Stormhawk spooling out rope, expecting Gerrit to hang himself with it. Today, his childhood fear seemed distant. Rope could be used for so very many useful things. "Colonel Tesarik certainly explored the other end of that spectrum." Gerrit kept his voice flat. He'd hated the Storm Guard's Tayemstvoy overseer as a cadet; now that hatred seemed petty and unimportant, as much a waste as hating someone's dog. "We don't have so many imbuement mages left, after the destruction of the war." Bozhki had paid a higher toll than the rest of Bourshkanya's citizens. Too much storm-blood lost had left the next generation with fewer mages—and even fewer strong enough to control Gods' Breath.

The Stormhawk grunted agreement around a mouthful of herring. "But hunger?" he asked when he'd finished chewing. Gerrit wondered whether the Stormhawk had ignored his explanation a month ago, or if he expected the answers would change.

"Suitable material grows on trees, and failure doesn't risk lives."

"You expected them to fail." A statement, but Gerrit decided to see it as a question.

"Everyone fails when they're learning. It seems a good commander ensures that those failures lead to success—rather than unrecoverable losses."

The Stormhawk fell silent for a time, wiping sauce from his plate with thick rye bread. When the course had been cleared, he said, "Bozhskyeh storms are fundamentally dangerous. While your caution so far is understandable, you need to prepare for losses as you push your platoon to greater heights."

A muscle in Gerrit's jaw twitched.

"It's not an easy thing to learn or to accept," the Stormhawk said, sipping a glass of kvass. "A leader must care about the people, but be willing to sacrifice individuals—or whole groups—for the greater good."

Holding his father's gaze unblinkingly, Gerrit asked, "Is that why you killed Mother?" The words were out before he realized what he was going to say and, in their wake, all the rich food he'd eaten threatened to come back up. He fought the reaction, holding himself motionless.

The Stormhawk set both palms on the table, and Gerrit imagined his expression was one few people had survived to speak of. But past his initial horror at having uttered the question, Gerrit felt no fear.

"Artur mentioned something." Gerrit kept his voice level, as though they were still discussing abstract questions of leadership. "He implied that she wasn't the hero everyone made her out to be. It got me thinking, considering coincidences of timing and location. Your search while I was learning to imbue on my own terms cast a wide net—a challenge, even for me, to escape. The resistance may be made of desperate fools, but it's hard to imagine them so utterly short-sighted to think they could hold your child prisoner for years." Gerrit placed his own hands on the table, mirroring his father. "What did Mother do that you thought execution the only choice?"

Gerrit let his words hang in the air, waiting, letting silence do the work of interrogation as he'd been taught.

For a long time, the only sound was the ticking of a clock on the mantle. When servants returned with the next course, the Stormhawk waved them sharply away. Across the empty table, the Stormhawk finally said, "She'd begun to support the resistance."

"How did you find out?" Gerrit asked, abruptly certain that his father had more than suspicions.

"A scientist who'd been captured during the war made contact," the Stormhawk replied. "I assigned Artur to lead the extraction team. The mission was top secret, but your mother knew about it. Across the border, Artur's team was ambushed. We lost all operatives—except Artur—and we only recovered him through a costly prisoner exchange. He'd been extensively questioned. We never heard from the scientist again."

"You're certain Mother was the mole?" Gerrit asked.

"I wish I hadn't been." A crack showed in the Stormhawk's icy demeanor. "But she'd been growing increasingly radical. I wanted to be surprised, I wanted to disbelieve it. But the proof was overwhelming. Artur suffered and could have been killed because of her betrayal. What sort of *parent* sacrifices their child to commit treason?" Venom laced his voice.

What sort of parent, Gerrit wanted to ask, *murders their partner in front of their child?* But the question felt distant, abstract, and he kept it to himself.

The Stormhawk shook his head, an abrupt, angry gesture, and broke from Gerrit's gaze to glare into the past. The clock on the mantle ticked, and Gerrit waited with the silence.

When his father faced him again, his expression had softened into something that might have been regret. "A public execution would have tarnished her memory, so I did the best I could for her, for our country—and for you." The lines of his jowls looked weary, and the ice Gerrit had always known in his gaze had melted. "The bozhskyeh storms were returning, yet you struggled with the more powerful nuzhdi. A person is shaped by trauma. I never wanted your mother to betray us, Gerrit, but at least in punishing her treason, I made you strong."

Gerrit nodded, feeling a sudden kinship with his father. The act had been horrible, but Gerrit was starting to understand necessity.

CHAPTER THIRTY-SEVEN

"OH, GOOD," CORPORAL Shimunek said when Celka came down the corridor toward Gerrit's room. "You're going to see him?"

Celka honestly hadn't decided. She'd heard Gerrit had returned and had slipped away from training to see him—she had to see him eventually, but she wasn't sure she was ready.

Corporal Shimunek took her hesitation as a 'yes' and pressed a tray with a tea service into her hands. "Birch bark tea. I had it sent from the kitchens. I thought it might help." She picked up a bucket at her feet. "He wanted to be undisturbed, but..." She thrust the bucket at Celka.

"What am I missing?" Celka asked, but retching sounded on the other side of the door. The bucket suddenly made sense.

"My grandparents always made birch bark tea when we were sick," Corporal Shimunek said.

"Thanks." She eyed the door, even less sure she wanted to face Gerrit now. "Has he been this way... since he got back?" Maybe she could deliver the tea and the bucket and escape. She shook off the idea. The riot in Mrach wasn't going to un-happen if she avoided Gerrit.

"He seemed fine when he went in." The corporal shrugged. "I'll send for a servant with a fresh chamber pot, too... in case."

Celka couldn't help pulling a face. "Good idea."

Inside, Gerrit looked blearily up at her from the floor where he sprawled in front of a wastebasket. The room was a mess, his boots and jacket tossed on the floor, one sock dangling from a wingback chair. It looked like he'd clawed out of his shirt, and sweat slicked his face.

"Bad food on the train?" Celka set the tea service on his desk.

"Must have been," he said, voice wavering.

Celka traded the bucket for his wastebasket, which she set outside with apologies to the bolt-hawk corporal. Door locked, she knelt at Gerrit's side on the floor, searching his expression. He looked haunted—or maybe it *was* just bad food.

Their link through Nina tugged at her with the scent of icy pine boughs, and Celka activated it warily.

«*It wasn't bad food,*» he said through the snake.

«*What, then?*» She made her voice flat. On the train back to Solnitse, Filip had explained about Gerrit's mental walls, grimly admitting that Gerrit had settled them back into place.

Now, Gerrit's knuckles clenched white and bloodless on the bucket's rim. He stared at her like he was drowning. «*Mrach.*»

«*Is* your *fault,*» she snapped.

Gerrit flinched back, and for a moment it felt *good*. She wanted to *shove* him, *hit* him. She wanted to scream in his face and detail every death she'd seen, the screams, the sobbing parents and children, the slick-dark redness of organs in gaping wounds. Dbani, falling, their chest gushing blood.

Blood had stained Celka's face and uniform. She'd tripped and would have fallen in the square, but Hedvika had caught her and Celka had realized that she'd slipped on a person's entrails spilling like sausage on the cobblestones.

«It's your fault!» This time, her voice choked.

He shook his head, lost. *«I know.»*

Struggling to lock her sob inside, she looked away, hating that he admitted it, that his hands shook and that sweat stained his too-pale skin from the same horror. She wanted him to deny culpability. Wanted to feel the same cold stare he'd given her as he pulled against that sickening, twisted nuzhda that had made her believe Filip and Hedvika and Masha had turned against her. She wanted him to be the *enemy*, because then she could hate him, and the riot that had killed hundreds of innocent people wouldn't be just some awful *mistake*.

«I thought...» He pressed a fist to his mouth. It wasn't enough, and he heaved, face shoved deep in the bucket, finally spitting up a thin stream of bile. He gasped quick breaths afterward, staring into the bucket like he stared at the carnage in the temple square. He shook his head. *«And my father—»* He wiped his mouth with the back of his hand, cleared his throat.

Celka shoved to her feet, pouring Gerrit a cup of birch bark tea, handing it to him without looking, unable to face his guilt.

He sipped shakily. *«My father was proud.»* She barely heard him through their link. *«He didn't care about the riot, only the imbuement.»*

She snapped around to face him, unable to believe it. The Stormhawk was a monster, she knew that, but *this much* of a monster? The bolt-hawks from their imbuement company had pitched in at the storm temple, boiling bandages and cleaning wounds. They had red shoulders. Corporal Shimunek with her bucket and birch bark tea had red shoulders. Celka had thought—hoped—that maybe the fear she'd carried all her life had been wrong. That her cousin Ela was right, that people could be good even in that uniform she hated.

Her naïveté disgusted her. Individuals might be kind under the right circumstances, that didn't mean the Stormhawk was anything but a monster. He'd started a war for power. He probably laughed at the idea of civilians dying in a riot his own son had started.

«*He had one of his top bozhki teach me more about emotional imbuements. I think I understand the weaves now, enough to give them range.*»

It took a minute for his words to penetrate. It seemed wrong to talk about magic right now, in the wake of so many deaths, but part of her reached for a problem she could understand and solve. «*Range, like holding the effect at a distance?*»

He nodded, steadied a little by the discussion or the tea. «*So we don't have to be right next to the people we...*» He swallowed convulsively and set his teacup on the floor, eyeing the bucket again.

«*You want to make more of them,*» she realized in horror. She grabbed his arm, hard enough to make him grimace and *glad*—not caring if she hurt him, *wanting* to hurt him. «*How can you even talk about that right now? How can you* ever *want to touch that nuzhda again? I can't believe I helped you. I can't believe I let you manipulate my sousednia into becoming...*» Horror choked her voice, but she clawed through it. «*And you want to do it again? Wasn't the riot enough? Or are you just like your father?*» She shoved him back and he fell.

Gerrit lay on his side, staring wide-eyed up at her, panting.

«*Get up!*» she screamed. «*Say something! Tell me we won't ever make one of those again! Tell me you're not like him.*» Tears streamed down her face and her fingernails cut into her palms. «*Get up!*»

He didn't. «*I'm not,*» he whispered. «*I'm not like him.*»

Celka's rage collapsed, and she crumpled to her knees, hands over her face, sobbing as she remembered Dbani collapsing in a spray of blood.

Gerrit reached over, touching her knee, and Celka flinched. He withdrew, and her chest tightened. She pulled her hands from her face, wiping tears and snot on her sleeve, and reached out.

Warily, he took her hand, fingers cold and shaky.

With a cry, Celka threw herself into his arms, burying her face against the slick skin of his neck, sobs wracking her throat. He clung to her, chest shaking with silent tears, face pressed against her hair, holding her so tight that she could barely breathe, but she clung to him even harder. Together, they held each other and cried.

AFTER CELKA HAD gone, Gerrit cleaned up. Still shaky, he made himself bathe and dress. When he emerged, he discovered a bowl of fermented cabbage soup and a slice of rye bread waiting on his desk, along with another pot of birch bark tea and a stack of reports. He shoved the reports aside and sipped the soup, stomach twisting as he tried to face the idea of leaving his room.

The tale of food poisoning gave him an excuse to curl up in bed. He wanted to. Wanted to pull the eiderdown over his head and hide from the world. But mostly, he wanted to hide from himself.

When the knock sounded, he groaned, ready to send them away. A servant entered with a clean chamber pot and fresh linens, and he opened his mouth to chase them off before recognizing Lucie. "Fine." He waved her in, letting Shimunek close the door. When Lucie's silencing imbuement shrouded them, he asked, "Is there news?" It came out desperate, and he scrubbed his hands over his face and stared at his tepid soup.

"Some." Lucie handed him a sheet of paper.

A gas canister had been sketched, along with its dimensions and an estimated weight. He released a held breath—it'd be heavy, but he should be able to carry it without attracting suspicion. At least, if he didn't have to be athletic.

"It's not ready yet." She nodded at the diagram. "But I got some of our answers."

He memorized the details, then returned the diagram to Lucie. "Celka's getting good at her sousedni-dislocations," he said. "But the sooner you can get us the imbuements we need, the better shape we'll be in. We're asking a lot of her to hold the gas canister invisible."

"I'll see what I can do. As far as the canister"— she tucked the paper away—"we shouldn't have any problem with leaks unless the canister's damaged in transport. And if it is, we'll know it before you go in—the ol' sniff test—and can abort. Or not, if it's not leaking too badly. A small exposure shouldn't be a problem. They claim. Though scientists are always cavalier with deadly stuff."

"And starting the gas flow?" Gerrit asked. "Will I have to do something?"

"They're working on some sort of timer. They wanted to use a fuse and blow the top off it, but I figured that'd attract too much attention."

Gerrit snorted. "You think?"

"So, still working on that," Lucie said, wry.

More delays. Some rational part of him was glad. It gave him and Iveta more time to build influence, which would help the resistance. But the thought of pulling against the paranoid violence nuzhda again churned his stomach. Contemplating what his father would do with a more powerful version of that imbuement made his soup nearly come back up. "How soon?" he whispered.

Subdued, Lucie said, "I don't know. I conveyed our urgency,

but science and engineering run on their own time. It doesn't help that we can't work on this openly."

The bedroom walls seemed to collapse, and Gerrit struggled to breathe. Flailing into sousednia, he tried to let the alpine wind scour his thoughts. But although the noonday sun beat down on the clearing, something about the shadows stretched too long, the clearing choked by walls he couldn't see.

Sensing motion beside him, Gerrit jerked back into true-life. Lucie crouched and took his hand. "What happened?" she asked. "I heard about the riot, and that you were in the capital...?"

Gerrit swallowed hard, staring at their clasped hands. He'd planned to talk to Celka about it, but the way she'd screamed at him through Nina and Filip's horror last night had shaken him. He told himself he wasn't like his father, but was it a lie? *He'd* activated the imbuement—no one had forced him to. *He'd* stood by as prisoners slaughtered each other, doing nothing to help them. If he told any of that to Celka, he was terrified she'd flinch from him again—and maybe this time she wouldn't come back.

Gripping Lucie's hand, he studied her, remembering her serious and intent in classes and field exercises. They'd endured the same training and had survived. She'd been forced away from that life and he'd broken with it, and they'd ended up back on the same side. Maybe, out of everyone he knew, Lucie would understand.

So he told her about Mrach, about the imbuement and the riot, about deploying paranoid violence on civilians to save his sister's life—and then again on caged prisoners. He told her what the major had said, about how he deserved to wear a Tayemstvoy uniform. When he finished, Lucie stared at him, wide-eyed, but without revulsion.

"Freezing sleet, Gerrit, that's awful. How are you even..."

She gestured to him, as if she found it miraculous he was even dressed and upright. Then she lowered her voice and asked, "How did you do it? How did you wear the mask so convincingly?"

"Mental walls," he told her before he could talk himself out of it, explaining how he'd partitioned off his memories and emotions. "I know it's dangerous, but I didn't know how else to play the role."

"That's brilliant," she whispered.

He choked a laugh.

"No, I'm serious. It really works?"

He nodded. "I held it for two and a half days." He'd left some of the walls down after Filip helped him reintegrate in Mrach, but everything he'd put in place after studying with Major Blatnik, he'd held strong until this afternoon. He glanced at his wastebasket—a new one, vomit-free—and swallowed hard. "Reintegrating was... brutal." Filip had helped him again, and it had been worse than either of the previous times. In part because Gerrit hadn't reintegrated fully in Mrach. Afterwards, Filip had wanted to stay, but supposed food poisoning didn't require his strazh's care. Or maybe Gerrit just hadn't wanted to face Filip's insistence that he never build the walls again. "I knew I was holding things back, suppressing my reactions. But when I reintegrated, everything hit. At once. All the violence and death I'd caused..." The bile rose again and he struggled to swallow it down.

"You made a mistake," she said. "It was an accident."

"And people died. I can't just shrug that off."

She squeezed his hand. "And you shouldn't. Because you're a *good* person. You're *not* like your father."

He couldn't look at her. "Thank you for saying that."

"I mean it," she said.

He nodded, throat too tight.

"But, sleet, two and a half *days?* That's a long time with walls. How are you doing now?"

"How do I look?" he asked with grim humor.

She shook her head. "No, I mean, your mind." She dragged over a wingback chair, perching on the seat with her knees pulled in. "I held a concealment imbuement active for two days once," she said. "There was a Tayemstvoy raid and some of my contacts were captured." The emotion drained from her voice, her eyes going flat and distant. "They locked the town down, searched house-to-house. They had dogs. Sleeting *dogs.* I *hate* dogs. Snarling teeth and—" She wrapped her arms around herself, silent for a time. "Anyway, I hid, catching a few minutes of sleep here and there, in a tree, a root cellar. Nowhere was safe. They arrested everyone from the local cell—and a few innocents for good measure because they're sleeting *Tayemstvoy.*" Her venom made Gerrit intensely glad that the major hadn't insisted on getting him that lateral 'promotion.' "I was nearby while they interrogated the prisoners. I couldn't get out, I just had to *hide.*" Her throat worked, but no words came out.

Gerrit pulled his chair close to hers, touching her shoulder. She tensed but didn't pull away. After a minute, she shot him a grateful look.

"Once I did get out, once I was finally *safe*"—her voice shook on that word—"I reintegrated. It's the hardest thing I've ever done in my life. Harder than hearing those interrogations, harder than being convinced I was about to die. It was like... it *felt* like dying. I hadn't realized it, but I'd spent those two days reinforcing the walls. Tearing them down and letting that horror out..." She stared at the ceiling, shuddering.

"On the train back here this morning, I almost convinced myself to leave them up," Gerrit said. "Just never reintegrate."

She nodded. "You know that testing cell, where they train the concealment nuzhda?"

"I hate concealment." Even talking about it reminded him of the cell where he'd been bound, waiting for the door to slam open and a pair of Tayemstvoy to enter, ready to whip him again.

"You know that clock that hung on the wall?" she asked.

"Counting down until the Tayemstvoy returned for the next beating." No matter how you screamed or begged, the only way out of that cell was to ring a nuzhda bell, to be so desperate to hide that you *believed* yourself invisible.

"I still hear it ticking sometimes," she whispered. "If I'm in a quiet room, I hear it. I reintegrated as well as I know how, but I still hear that clock."

He caught her hand, and she returned his grip with crushing strength. "Stormy skies, that's..."

"I see them, too, the Tayemstvoy." Lucie glanced at him, then back away, staring into nothing, her muscles tense. "Out the corners of my eyes. When no one's there."

"My sousednia feels wrong." Saying it aloud felt dangerous, like the words would make it true. "It looks just like I remember, but I feel like the walls are still there."

She finally turned to him. "You have a strazh. You can work with Filip, get his help."

"I..." What she said made sense, and yet he resisted. Was it the same resistance that made nuzhda burn-in so hard to fight? "I don't know if I should. When I first built the walls, it was painstaking. The second time, it was like I knew exactly where they needed to go, like the material was already there, waiting." Cold clambered down his spine, though he was sweating. "We're not out of this yet. Until we kill him... Before this gets better, it's going to get worse."

CHAPTER THIRTY-EIGHT

Overnight at Potokovy Manor. For Celka.

Celka read the note three times, trying to make sense of it, struggling to contain the giant wellspring of hope in her chest. She met Gerrit's gaze and asked, through Nina, *«Do you think it's about Pa?»* When Celka had told Vrana about the calming imbuement's effect on Branislav, the Wolf's eyes had lit. But three weeks had passed, and Celka was starting to worry that Vrana would never come through.

«I doubt they're researching phosgene at my family estate,» Gerrit said, frowning.

«Wait,» Celka said, *«your what?»*

He took the note back from her, burning it at the fireplace. *«Potokovy Manor. It's where I grew up—apart from here. It's been on the Skala side of my family for generations.»* His mother's side, then, which made Celka breathe a little easier. *«But why would...?»* He trailed off, eyes darting.

«What is it?»

«A couple years ago, my grandmother converted the estate

into a retreat for war veterans. Do you think—?»

«*Pa.*» Celka's uncertainty vanished. «*It must be where he's... while he's going storm-mad.*»

Gerrit dusted ash from his hands and stood, but after one step toward her, he hesitated. They'd hardly touched since Mrach. Every time he reached for her, she remembered him crushing her hand over the knife in Mrach, her combat fugue twisting until he made her believe her friends were about to betray her. Every time he stepped close, she smelled shit and viscera, and heard screams—so she flinched away. Finally, he'd stopped reaching. She didn't know whether or not to be glad.

She looked toward the fireplace where the resistance note had crumbled to ash, and her chest squeezed. «*I'm going to save Pa,*» she said through Nina, but the words came out small. She bit her lip. She'd been so hopeful when she'd created that first calming imbuement, but Branislav had barely spoken, and she'd been so naïve about the good they could do dressed as regime soldiers.

When she met Gerrit's gaze, she found her own uncertainty and fear echoed, and it made it possible to cross the gulf between them. She stepped close and, for the first time since sobbing together on the floor, let him enfold her in his arms.

«*What if it doesn't work,*» she whispered, barely able to press the words through Nina. «*What if he doesn't even recognize me?*»

Gerrit held her against him, his shirt soft against her cheek, his face pressed into her hair. Wet lines tracked down her face, and her breath came stuttery around her fear. «*He will,*» Gerrit said, but he couldn't know. «*Your new imbuement's powerful, and your grandfather told you your father was holding on. Captain Vrana wouldn't risk bringing us to him if there was no hope.*»

His words soothed her, and it felt good to be held. Part of her still flinched from him, remembering him cold and distant in Mrach, but that wasn't the real Gerrit. He'd made a mistake using those mental walls. He wouldn't do it again.

«*We'll go there for a storm?*» she asked, knowing the answer. They'd spent the last few days since Mrach at the Storm Guard Fortress, but it couldn't last. The Stormhawk's pet monsters had taught Gerrit weaves to give their emotional imbuements range; as much as she wanted to believe they could hide out here forever, she wasn't a fool.

Gerrit nodded against her hair, his whole body tensing.

«*What is it?*» she asked, not wanting to know.

He released her, taking her hands and stepping back enough to look her in the eye. «*I've tried to create the nuzhda without my walls. I can't.*»

She shook her head, not wanting to believe what he was saying. «*So we come up with a different imbuement.*» Gerrit's grip on her hands tightened, but she didn't give him time to deny it, even as the sick twisting in her stomach knew she was trying to hold back an avalanche with a snow shovel. «*We can practice together. Come up with something new. Or you can work harder, find a way to do it without walls. I did it without walls!*» Her voice was rising, but she couldn't stop herself, feeling like she was slipping on Mrach's slick, bloody cobblestones again. «*What if you make another mistake? What if you sleet up again and more people die? That nuzhda is horrible and I don't want to make it again, but I will because I know we have to. But I'm not going to hide from the consequences or pretend that creating it isn't wrong. It's wrong, Gerrit, and you didn't see it with your walls.*» Her torrent of words choked off and she stood, gripping his hands like she could squeeze sense into him, searching his face and finding only hard edges.

«I'll try,» he said, but the words rang flat. *«But if I can't get it before we leave tomorrow morning—»*

She shook her head. *«Gerrit, no.»*

«If we fail to imbue, all our plans crash down.»

«Then we find another way,» she said.

«We already have a way.» He reached into a pocket, pulling out a gray wool pouch. From it, he dumped a large steel ring that glowed concealment blue. *«We just have to play the Stormhawk's game a little longer.»*

Chest tight with unshed tears, Celka touched the ring on his palm. Filip had worn it in the circus when he'd pretended to be Ctibor, a mundane no more magical than a horse. The imbuement was low-Category, but the regime jealously guarded even weak imbuements. *«This came with the note?»* she asked.

Gerrit nodded. *«And another note that said, "soon."»*

Squeezing her eyes shut, Celka turned her face away, struggling to pull herself together. Of course Gerrit was right that they couldn't just avoid imbuing more paranoid violence. But maybe this ring meant that they'd need only imbue it once more. Maybe the phosgene was almost ready, and the other concealment imbuement they needed was, too.

Once she could breathe without trembling, Celka made herself face Gerrit and take the ring. *«Then we'd better practice.»*

Since they'd come up with the original plan for Gerrit to carry the gas canister into the Stormhawk's bedroom, Celka using a concealment imbuement to hide it from the guards, she'd been practicing sousedni-dislocations whenever she could. Even these last few days, when she'd returned to sleeping in her own bunk, she'd practiced, exploring Gerrit's rooms with her sousedni-shape while she lay alone in her bunk. She'd had to be careful. She couldn't let anyone storm-blessed spot her sousedni-shape somewhere it had no business being, and she certainly couldn't allow someone to notice her sousedni-shape unattached to her true-form, which meant she couldn't just wander the corridors or float around outside.

With the ring, she had another piece of the plan to practice. They couldn't risk one of the Yestrab Okhrana noticing her sousedni-shape at Gerrit's side when he brought the phosgene into his father's bedroom, so Celka would cloak herself in the ring's magic, diminishing her sousedni-shape to a mundane's faint smoke-form. Celka hoped the ring could do even more.

Activating it was simple. She'd gotten good at pulling against a concealment nuzhda, and the ring's access point was easy to connect into her sunny laughter. Once she walled it off and draped the imbuement's blue gossamer threads over herself, she focused on Gerrit. "How do I look?" she asked aloud, flipping her hair out and striking a ridiculous pose.

He smiled a little, and it softened him back into someone she could almost imagine kissing. Then he shook his head, and focused on sousednia.

Giving him time to search for her sousedni-shape, Celka balanced on one foot on the wire, reaching her leg out behind herself and arching her back, catching her ankle in her hands to draw up into a vertical splits. When she'd done it in the circus, it usually made Gerrit's eyes fall out of his head. Not good if she wanted him capable of rational speech, but she'd enjoyed the effect. Wavering a little on the wire—even in sousednia, it seemed she needed practice to keep her balance during difficult tricks—she glanced over at him.

His brow was furrowed and he squinted, the bright, overhead sun in his sousednia leaving his eyes in shadow. He had his hands stuffed in the pockets of his uniform trousers, his lean arms bare. He didn't look thunderstruck and, when Celka released her ankle and settled her feet back onto the wire, she saw only the faintest distortion when she waved her own hand in front of her face.

«*It's working,*» Gerrit said through Nina. «*Dislocate. See if I can spot you.*»

The idea nearly made her giggle as she imagined sneaking up behind him with a feather like she used to do in the circus. She took a few steps along the wire, feather coalescing in her invisible hand. She could get used to this imbuement.

With a start, she realized the tent walls around her concealment imbuement had thinned to the point of nearly vanishing, bright summer sunlight and the floral scent of cheap perfume filling her big top. She reached to strengthen the walls, but hesitated. She hadn't felt this light since... The sky darkened and she almost lost the concealment imbuement. Since Mrach.

Swallowing hard, wavering on her high wire, she slapped walls around the concealment nuzhda's mischief, barely maintaining enough of the nuzhda to keep the ring active.

Her big top back to smelling of sawdust and horses, Celka focused on the steel cable beneath her feet and the band fluting below, struggling to calm her breathing. *Mrach is done. You saved as many people as you could. You can't change what happened.* The words still hurt but, each day, they felt a little less like hollow reassurance.

Gerrit's hand passed through her in sousednia and she flinched from the weird shivery sensation and nearly lost her balance.

«*Here,*» he said, patting the air near her arm. «*You're here, aren't you?*»

«*Yeah.*» It came out a whisper, and she cleared her throat and tried again. «*I guess it's not perfect.*»

Gerrit shrugged, gaze focused a little to the side of her head in sousednia. «*It's pretty good, though. I was actively looking for you with no one else in the room, and it was still tough to pick you out. Unless we get super unlucky and there's not just a storm-blessed Okhrana guarding him, but they're doing a really thorough sweep of sousednia, you should be safe.»*

«We *should be safe*,» Celka said, because if the Okhrana spotted her standing next to Gerrit, *he* was the one they'd physically detain—and they'd find the phosgene canister he carried.

Gerrit swallowed hard, but after a beat managed to straighten. «*This'll work*,» he said, but not with the military confidence he used in front of the platoon. Shoulders slumping, he sighed. «*I hope.*» Celka dropped the sousedni-dislocation so she could take his hand. He smiled wanly at her, then said, «*We should practice with you walking at my side via sousedni-dislocation. You'll be out of view of our true-forms; we need to make sure you don't accidentally vanish* my *sousedni-shape in front of the Okhrana.*»

She nodded. It was a good idea. «*We need someone to keep an eye on us in sousednia, watch for me to make mistakes.*»

«*Filip,*» Gerrit said, and extended their link through Nina to ask him.

CHAPTER THIRTY-NINE

THE NEXT DAY, after the platoon concluded its imbuements, Gerrit stepped away to use the facilities, claiming enough privacy to reintegrate his mind. Despite the paranoid itch between his shoulder blades, breaking down the granite walls was easier today. He didn't delude himself that it was practice or skill. He'd built the walls on the train from Solnitse, and had held them for less than six hours. Even so, the snow of his sousedni-clearing showed deep furrows where the walls had been, no amount of blowing snow or scouring wind filling them.

He'd handed his and Celka's imbued knife to one of Iveta's bolt-hawks, glad to be rid of it, today's bozhskyeh storm raging above an unremarkable town half a day's ride from his family estate. Ridding himself of the knife had been a weight off, but not enough to dispel his coiling dread. He hadn't returned to Potokovy Manor since the attack that had killed his mother. Her funeral pyre had burned in the capital, mourners coming from across Bourshkanya to see her essence returned to the Storm Gods' realm. His grandmother had asked him to visit the estate numerous times over the years, but he'd always found some excuse, throwing himself into training, determined to never be weak and helpless again.

It seemed like sick irony that he'd be forced to return now, so fast on the heels of his father's self-congratulatory claims of necessity. That Celka would have a chance to reunite with her father should have been a balm, but felt more like the twist of a knife—a reminder that he'd never see his mother again.

Climbing into the gleaming motorcar at Novy Bidshov's small train station, Gerrit intended to order the driver straight to the estate. But when Iveta joined him, his only company save a bolt-hawk who took a guard post in the front seat, Gerrit found himself needing to retrace the route he'd followed four winters ago.

The driver knew the route without being told, and when Gerrit glanced at Iveta, she returned a solemn nod. That she'd thought of this—of him—tightened something in his throat, and he focused out the window to avoid scrutinizing the emotion.

They stopped at the overlook he and Mother had loved, and Iveta climbed out at his side. He expected the guard to trail along, but the bolt-hawk and chauffeur both remained with the car.

Away from the road, Iveta clasped her hands behind her back and stared out at the view. After a time just listening to the wind and the birds, she said, "I come here whenever I visit."

"Father said she was making me soft, bringing me out here." Gerrit couldn't keep the bitterness from his voice.

"It's not weakness to appreciate beauty," Iveta said.

Gerrit felt the weight of his storm pendant beneath his shirt, recalled Mother handing him the box in the back of the motorcar. He studied his sister, surprised to see a resemblance to Mother in the shape of her jaw.

"Do you remember when you first tested with a storm-affinity?" Iveta asked.

Of course he remembered. He'd been seven, and it had been the proudest moment of his young life. "I remember the cake."

A smile quirked the corner of her mouth. "It was a good cake." The smile fell away. "That night I found Mother crying alone in her room."

Gerrit frowned. "Mother was proud."

Iveta nodded. "But she didn't want you in the Storm Guard." Iveta tilted her head back, looking up at the clouds. "I'm surprised she talked to me about it, honestly. But I don't know, my first year was pretty rough."

"You were top of your class." Gerrit's old resentment welled up.

"Father made that expectation clear," Iveta said, wooden. Flicking a wrist to dismiss the memory, she said, "Remember those drawings you used to make? Aeroplanes and people flying to the moon on fanciful imbuements?" Her voice softened in reminiscence, then her expression tightened. "She asked me to look out for you." She faced him, strain pulling at the corners of her eyes. "I'm sorry I didn't do a better job."

Gerrit struggled to swallow in a throat too tight. He blinked quickly, eyes stinging, and stared out at the mountains. "You're making up for it."

He turned to find her extending a hand. He took it, her grip a solid strength. "I didn't get a chance to properly thank you for saving my life in Mrach," she said. "I'd be a smear on the cobblestones if you hadn't come back for me. Thank you."

"You would have done the same for me," he said, believing it.

Her lip quirked. "I never expected you'd be rescuing *me* one day."

He snorted something almost a laugh. "I think it's expressly forbidden somewhere in the younger-sibling handbook."

"Then let's rewrite the book."

His smile slipped, and he turned back to look at the view. His exhale shook him. "I miss her."

Iveta shifted to press her shoulder against his. "She'd be proud of you."

"Would she?" He fingered the empty sheath from his imbued belt knife and glanced at Iveta, wondering if she knew of their father's role in her death.

Iveta didn't seem to notice, still gazing at the mountains. "She would." Her confidence left no room for doubt.

CELKA SITS AT *dinner with her squad, light glinting prismatic from crystal chandeliers, silverware clinking over murmured conversation in the vast hall.*

Dbani leans in and says, "Those kittens have standards."

Hedvika snorts laughter, and Masha leans back in her chair, eyes bright. Yanek's laugh is full and loud, while Havel coughs, hiding his face with a napkin. Celka laughs, too, loving these people even as they take their privilege for granted.

Then, with a screech like an angry cat, the string quartet goes silent. The clink of silverware ceases. All the bozhk officers and red-shouldered servers turn at once to Celka's table.

"There." At the high table, Filip stands. He points at Celka. "She's the traitor."

Fear tightens like a noose around Celka's neck, and her squadmates follow Filip's accusing finger. Laughter and good humor vanish.

"Resistance dog." *Hedvika whips her belt knife into her hand and, before Celka can react, catches her wrist. She wrenches Celka's arm down to the table and stabs her knife through the back of Celka's hand.*

Celka screams.

"Celka, Celka, look at me." Hedvika's voice was wrong, urgent but kind, her hands on Celka's face. Celka tried to push her away, stumbling back—*surrounded, trapped*—but Masha caught her, an arm around Celka's shoulders—*pinning her so they can start torturing her right there in the dining hall*. But Hedvika glowed blue and violet, and Celka drew a gasping breath, opening her eyes with a start to see a wrought iron table beneath a linden tree clinging to the last of its golden leaves.

She flinched back again, and Masha squeezed her shoulders. "You're safe, Celka. We're at Potokovy Manor. The storm's over."

Celka's breath rasped in her throat, but spicy steam rose from three mugs set around the table, the sun bright, though the air carried the promise of winter. Her heart still beat too fast, but when she flinched up to see Hedvika's familiar face, her friend blinked and met her gaze, worried lines of her brow softening. "You're back," she said, stroking her thumb over Celka's cheek with a half smile. "How's your sousednia?"

Celka drew a shaky breath, not sure she could face the neighboring reality. Masha pressed a mug into her hands, and she sipped the purplish sbiten, spicy-sweet on her tongue. "Do you still have the pocket square?" Masha asked, and Celka breathed the warm spices as she dug into her pocket for the green silk. She hadn't needed it since first activating Nina, but she hadn't stopped carrying it.

"Can you activate the"—Hedvika shuddered—"snake?" She tipped her head toward the stone-lined path where Nina coiled in a patch of sunlight.

By the time Celka had fully regained her grounding, the sbiten was cold. Masha waved a servant over, sending them after fresh mugs. While they waited, Celka glanced around, her memory patchy since the imbuement. They sat at the edge of a manicured, formal garden, and dozens of older people moved about—presumably the veterans the retreat at Potokovy Manor now served. Many were missing limbs or wearing partial masks to hide facial injuries. One had no obvious wounds, yet stood rifle-straight, staring at the trees as if a monster of teeth and claws surged toward them. Younger people in uniform—nurses or servants—moved amongst them.

"You've been slipping in and out of a nuzhda fugue," Hedvika said when Celka glanced at her, questioning. Her lips tightened, and she gripped Celka's hand hard in both of hers. "I'll practice the nuzhda, get better at it. I still haven't gotten it right, so I didn't catch all the overflow. I'm sorry."

Celka squeezed her hand, struggling to see Hedvika, her friend, and not the regime sub-lieutenant calling her a resistance dog. "It's all right," she managed, though it wasn't.

The sbiten arrived and Celka sipped, trying to get warm, trying to forget the betrayal on her friends' faces and everything that happened next in that twisted memory-hallucination. The moment when the fugue changed and she dodged Hedvika's grasp rather than let her traitor-friend pin her to the table. The moment when Celka grabbed Hedvika's sidearm and shot every single member of her squad while Gerrit, suddenly at her side, sent a bullet through Filip's heart.

She wrapped her arms around herself. Hedvika stood and pulled the slipping pins from Celka's hair, finger-combing out the knots. Celka leaned into her ministrations, struggling to breathe. As Hedvika started braiding, Celka turned to Masha. In barely a whisper, she asked, "How do you sleep at night—after you've imbued weapons?"

Masha squeezed her shoulder. "We're not starting a war, Celka. We're just making sure we can defend ourselves."

Celka swirled her sbiten, wishing it was hot enough to burn her throat. "You don't really believe that?"

Hedvika's hands in her hair stilled.

Masha glanced quickly around before setting her sbiten down with a sigh. "Maybe not. But there are always weapons, and always war. I'd rather we win."

"But what if...?" Celka swallowed the last of her sbiten, telling herself to stop talking. The memory-hallucination could become real if she said the wrong thing. These people were her friends, but Vrana's warning echoed louder today. *Everyone here is your enemy.* But Celka wasn't walling off her memories like Gerrit. She didn't know how to keep going without someone to talk to. "What if our weapons mean we *start* a war? If we were imbuing... grain or bandages—" She touched her storm pendant beneath her shirt. At some point, she'd have to give it up. The calming imbuement was too powerful for her to keep it to herself, even if she'd imbued her personal storm pendant. But Gerrit had contrived for her to keep it this long, and after today, it wouldn't matter as much if the State took it. Somewhere inside the palatial manor or on its expansive grounds, Pa waited for her. "We could be making things to help people."

"And you *did*." Masha laid her hand over Celka's, the storm pendant warm beneath. "But we have our orders."

What if our orders are wrong? Celka wanted to ask. But she wasn't fool enough to trust their friendship that far. Grimacing, Celka rubbed her abdomen.

"What's wrong?" Hedvika's hands stilled again, voice sharp with concern.

"Nothing." Celka poked at her empty mug, glad for the distraction. "Just cramps. I think my period's early."

Masha leveled a weighty glance on Hedvika, who quickly jammed a couple of pins in to hold Celka's hair and crouched at Celka's side, looking strangely worried.

"It's fine. My cycle's always a little jumpy," Celka said. "Especially since the storms' return."

"Why are you having periods at all?" Hedvika asked.

"What?" she asked, half laughing, as if her strazh had asked why Celka needed to breathe.

"Freezing sleet," Hedvika muttered, frowning at Masha, "she's a dirt-scrubber."

Celka made a rude gesture at her strazh. "I love you, too, your highness."

"What Hedvika means," Masha said, "is have you had your plodnosti?"

Celka's confusion must have shown.

"Hail-balls," Hedvika said. "And she's tumbling Gerrit."

"What are you talking about?" Celka snapped, sick of being talked around like when she'd first enlisted. "And besides, we're not—not intercourse. Not yet."

But Masha just took her hand, serious like an older sister warning her about the dangers of intercourse. "When a person has their first menses in the Storm Guard, we're treated with one of the old imbuements. We don't have periods and we can't get pregnant. Not until the plodnosti is reversed."

Celka stared at her. No bleeding, no counting days. No worrying about sex accidentally changing her life forever? "No cramps?"

Masha shook her head.

"It'll probably clear up your acne, too," Hedvika said.

"Seriously?" Celka said, as excited by the prospect as irritated that no one had thought to mention it. "I assumed you all just had amazing skin because of the... meat or something you eat. Or dessert."

Hedvika snorted. "Dessert does *not* help."

A strand of hair had already escaped Hedvika's braid, and Celka adjusted the pins, trying, hopelessly, to contain it. "You have some secret for your hair, too?"

"Cut it off," Hedvika said. "That's the only secret."

"Or have well-behaved hair," Masha said sweetly, laughing at Hedvika's rude gesture.

"Fine." Celka shoved her chair back and stood, suddenly restless. "Let's do it. Once we're home, I'm cutting it all off. And getting that sleeting plodnosti."

Hedvika whooped, standing with fluid grace. "You won't regret it."

Masha rolled her eyes and finished her sbiten, but she was smiling.

"Wait." Celka turned back to her friends. "Why is this only a Storm Guard thing?"

Hedvika shrugged. "It's not. But imbuements don't grow on trees. There's probably not enough to go around."

Masha became suddenly focused on tracing elaborate swirls across the wrought iron with spilled sbiten.

Celka sat back down and laid her hand over her friend's. "What is it?"

"We have enough imbuements—and enough bozhk doctors." Masha stole Hedvika's mug, making a face when she found it also empty. "It's not a question of supply. It's policy."

Hedvika flipped her chair around to straddle it backwards. "Now you *have* to explain."

Masha glanced around. "I shouldn't. I only know because Anastahzie told me, and she nearly lost her medical license advocating for it, so..."

"It goes no further than us," Celka said. "I promise."

Masha looked around again, then leaned in and dropped her voice. "Back before the Lesnikrayen War, a plodnosti was standard after a youth's first menses. The medical schools made sure there were enough imbuements, and because they're so standard, they have excellent durability." She sighed. "And it's not like they got pushed to failure during the war like combat imbuements. But. Bourshkanya lost a huge fraction of its combat-aged population in the war. After the treaty, the government decreed that only people with 'high potential' receive the treatment. In practice that means—"

"Rich people." Celka sat back, eyeing the opulence of Gerrit's palatial home.

"Did it work?" Hedvika asked, and Celka tried not to glare at her, tried not to hate Hedvika for acting like they discussed strategy out of a textbook.

Lips tight, Masha nodded. "Birth rates have increased dramatically since the war."

Celka balled her hands into fists beneath the table. In sousednia, she drew a deep breath of sawdust and hay, struggling to balance.

"There were other policies, too—incentives to have bigger families, campaigns to be patriotic and repopulate Bourshkanya." But when Masha's gaze met Celka's, it slipped quickly away.

"War is coming," Hedvika said with a shrug. "We'll need soldiers. It's the sort of hard decision necessary for the good of the State." She clapped a hand on Celka's shoulder, smiling. "Don't look so grim. You're one of us now."

CHAPTER FORTY

GERRIT'S GRANDMOTHER MET him when he stepped out of the motorcar. Her resemblance to Mother shook him, but less than he'd feared. With Iveta at his side, it seemed the most natural thing that they cross the stream he'd played in as a child and visit his mother's memorial together.

Afterward, returning to the manor's formal gardens left him disoriented. Despite the late autumn chill, veterans filled the benches and paths, enjoying the last of the season's sun. In his childhood, his mother's smile had overflowed the vast flowerbeds and neat hedgerows, but the gardens had stayed empty apart from the occasional party, and the officers present at those had all dressed in uniform. Today, even the sunlight seemed gray. The horror of today's powerful paranoid violence imbuement weighted Gerrit's shoulders, and too many of the eyes around him were vacant or shadowed.

Iveta, on the other hand, brightened as they entered the gardens, greeting veterans with fond familiarity. When Grandmother left to speak to one of her staff, Iveta introduced Gerrit around.

"How often do you come here?" he asked her.

"Whenever I can." She took Gerrit's arm, waving and calling greetings. "After Mother's death, Grandmother... we helped each other, I guess." She shrugged. "Starting the retreat helped her move on, but I still like to visit."

Gerrit studied his sister as she crouched to pet a veteran's ridiculously fluffy white dog, wondering how he'd never considered the impact on her of their mother's death.

Did Iveta know about Mother's resistance sympathies? He doubted it, but he never would have imagined her laughing, either, letting a dog the size of a bread loaf lick her face.

Grandmother rejoined them, laying a hand on Gerrit's back. The top of her head reached barely to his shoulder. "I thought you might like to look through some of your old things. When I had the attic cleaned, I set some aside."

The thought of revisiting his childhood twisted like an eel through his stomach. "I don't—"

"Come." She looped her arm through his. "It'll be good for you." Her smile was a little too sharp. "Might even show your partner or Filip, hm? It's good to share these things."

As Gerrit suffered to be led away, Iveta gave him a *better you than me* smirk.

Grandmother led him through corridors that all felt unfamiliar, leaving behind the gilt and finery for a narrow servants' stair. At a ladder into the attic, she said, "I'll send Filip and Celka up." She patted his hand. "My boy. So big now. So much like your mother." She pressed a papery kiss to his cheek. "I'm proud of you."

Chest tight, he watched her go before heading up the creaking wooden ladder. In the dusty dimness, he wondered how he was supposed to find the right trunks, wondered what from his childhood could be so important.

Spotting a lantern's glow, he wove around crates and piles of old furniture. The roof sloped low enough that he had to duck, and when he came up, he was surprised to find a figure sitting with a book across their lap. When they looked up and smiled, his heart skipped a beat. Lucie.

Gerrit glanced behind him, wondering if his grandmother had known he'd find her here. He shook himself. *Of course* she'd known; the whole story about rummaging through his old things must have been a cover. His grandmother supported the resistance. The realization tightened his chest, made her pride in him all the more meaningful.

When he turned back to Lucie, Gerrit found her heat-shimmer writhing beneath the violence of a Tayemstvoy beating. Then a blue concealment nuzhda burst across her, and she tossed the silencing imbuement's blue dome over them.

Once she'd walled off the nuzhda, she said, "Took you long enough."

"I wasn't expecting you here," he said.

She stretched, her back popping. "You were a cute kid." She tapped an old scrapbook.

He started to reach for it, but couldn't make himself pick it up.

"I have something for you." She pulled the lid off the crate she'd been sitting on. A steel gray cylinder rested inside.

"Is that—?" Surreptitiously, he sniffed the air, not wanting to get too close. "It's ready?"

She pulled the cylinder out and tossed it to him. He recoiled, like she'd flung a poisonous snake, but managed to catch it. Over his pulse hammering in his ears, he frowned—the gas cylinder was lighter than he'd expected.

"It's empty," Lucie said. "It's a dummy for us to practice with. I got the other imbuement we need, and the real thing's ready as soon as we are."

Gerrit exhaled relief. "You could have told me that before throwing it."

"How would that have been fun?" she asked.

He rolled his eyes, juggling the cylinder, trying to figure out how to carry it inconspicuously. "How much heavier will it be?"

"Here." From the crate, she threw him a clacking burlap sack.

He caught it awkwardly. "Rocks?"

"For the weight." She pulled out twine, and they tied the rocks to the cylinder, making it even more awkward.

He spent a few minutes shifting it around, the bag of rocks slipping off and crashing to the floor before he gave up. "We'll figure it out when the others get here." He nestled the cylinder back in the crate, still not entirely convinced it was safe.

Lucie pulled out a pack of cards. "You want to play sedma?"

Gerrit didn't. He paced, eyeing the dusty crates and rolled-up rugs, the family album pulling him like a lodestone. "We imbued again, me and Celka."

Lucie tucked the cards back into her pocket. "More paranoid violence?"

He nodded and crouched before the scrapbook, fingers tracing uneven pages. "Celka doesn't want to do more."

"What about you?" Lucie asked, brown eyes sympathetic in the lamplight.

"Do I have a choice? We have to get close to my father to do anything with that." He nodded at the phosgene canister.

"Can you come up with a different emotional imbuement?"

"Maybe. I wish we'd started with something... less useful. Less brutal." His stomach churned, but not as badly as it had when he'd returned from reporting the original success to his father. He had a vague sense he was forgetting something, but brushed it away.

Turning his back on the scrapbook, not brave enough to face his mother even in photographs, he sat on the floor, his back against the crate. Looking up at Lucie, he asked, "Do you know about my mother?"

"I heard your father had her murdered and blamed it on us."

Gerrit pulled the old photo album onto his lap, palm pressed against its cover. "At dinner with him last week, I asked why he ordered her killed."

"You sleeting *what?*" Lucie said. "You didn't."

Jaw tense, Gerrit nodded. "He explained how she'd gone over to the resistance, gotten my brother captured by the Lesnikrayens. He spoke with *solemn regret* about how he'd done what was necessary to minimize the damage of her betrayal and used that *unfortunate* circumstance to make me strong."

"How did you sit there for that?"

Gerrit stared at the dusty floor, sickened by the memory and afraid to speak his next words. "It was easy. When he was explaining, I could almost..." He stroked the photo album, knowing that inside it, he'd see posed photographs of his parents standing side by side. "I almost understood. Almost *agreed* with him, like what he was saying made perfect sense."

In the attic's quiet, he heard Lucie's breath catch. Gerrit kept staring at the floor, half convinced she was about to invent an escape, that she would run and poison his sbiten, and tomorrow morning, he just wouldn't wake up.

"You were using mental walls," Lucie whispered. "You told me you were blocking emotions."

He jerked a nod. "I blocked a *few* memories"—well, more than a few, but the number was slippery and he wasn't interested in being generous with himself—"how could that make me take his side? He ordered the Tayemstvoy to beat her to death in front of me. I was a *child*. That's not something you can *justify*."

Lucie's boots scuffed on the rough planks, and she settled next to him, draping an arm around his shoulders. He tensed. The gesture seemed too intimate for the monster he'd admitted to being. Maybe she was about to knife him in the ribs. Maybe she should. "You're not justifying it, Gerrit. You're as horrified as I am."

"But when he said it—"

"You were in deep cover, playing a role." She squeezed him against her shoulder, and his throat closed off. "You have the hardest job of all of us, and you're performing it remarkably. Deep cover's *hard*, Gerrit. Most people are terrible at it. And no one gave you a choice."

Leaning against the crate, he stared up at the ceiling beams. The warmth of her arm around his shoulders thawed some of his self-loathing. "Still. Where's the line? People have died so I can maintain that cover persona. They won't be the last. Not until we kill my father."

"It's a revolution," she said. "People will die."

He swallowed hard, grasping after a vague sense that more people had died than he remembered. "I know. I just wish..." That he didn't have to do the killing? That his hands could be clean? That had never been a possibility, even before he'd met Celka and joined the resistance. At least now he knew enough to be disturbed by the carnage. "I just wish it didn't hurt so much."

The scrape of hobnailed boots on the attic floorboards startled him, and Gerrit scrubbed his hands over his face, wishing he trusted Filip and Celka enough to keep his defenses down.

Lucie swooped the silencing imbuement off of him, and he stood. "Filip? Celka?" He offered Lucie a hand up.

Celka's face melted into relief when she saw Lucie and, after she piled Nina off her shoulders onto the floor, she wrapped the other woman in a hug. Lucie explained about the phosgene canister and Filip—ever the focused one—asked whether the scientists had solved the dispersal problem. They had.

"How?" Filip asked.

Lucie shrugged. "They didn't give details."

Filip looked unsatisfied, but Lucie was right that it didn't matter. All they needed to know was that the gas would spread. Their job was getting the canister *into* the Stormhawk's bedroom.

"You have the ring?" Lucie asked.

Gerrit pulled out the gray wool darkbag and dumped the imbuement that would conceal Celka's sousedni-shape onto his palm. Celka took it, slipping the ring into a pocket of her uniform jacket. During their practice, she'd discovered that she didn't need to be physically touching it to keep it active, and it was too big for her to wear.

"Good," Lucie said. From the charging cloth's pouch on her storm pendant, she pulled a carved jade pendant. It glowed blue—another concealment imbuement. "This will hide an object from true-life." She offered it to Celka. "It's mid-Category, so if things go sideways on us, it'll also hide a person—two, if they're friendly."

Celka's serious expression melted into a mischievous smile as she pulled against a concealment nuzhda, and the jade carving flared blue, vanishing her hand to the elbow. Celka's expression sobered as she got the nuzhda walled off. When Lucie handed her the dummy canister, Celka pocketed the imbuement and focused, wrapping its magic around the gas cylinder. It took her a minute to manage it without vanishing any part of her body, then she extended her arms—which appeared empty in true-life—to Gerrit.

The concealment imbuement left the canister glowing blue in sousednia, the magic bleeding through into true-life. So as long as he didn't cling too hard to true-life, he could still make out the canister's shape. He took it from her.

"You want to try it with the rocks?" Lucie asked.

Celka made a face and Gerrit shook his head. "The hard part's not going to be dealing with the weight," he said. "Let's make this as realistic as possible for Celka."

Celka cut him a grateful glance.

As he shifted the canister to rest on his left forearm, half of it reappeared, and his upper arm vanished.

"Sleet," Celka muttered, focusing on Gerrit's arm. He froze and she got the concealment imbuement wrapped around the canister—and only the canister—again. "Right," she said after a minute. "Try walking."

He did, and the imbuement slipped again, but she slipped it back over the canister more quickly this time.

"You're not going to be able to see him in true-life," Filip said, disrupting Celka's focus enough that Gerrit's elbow disappeared.

Celka scrubbed her eyes with her palms, but said, "You're right. This isn't how I should be practicing." To get the gas canister into the Stormhawk's bedroom, Celka would have to hide her true-form somewhere innocuous and dislocate to keep her sousedni-shape at his side while Gerrit walked. "Let's try this." She sat on a crate with her back to Gerrit.

He focused on sousednia just as Celka appeared at his side in her glittering high wire costume. It reminded him of their practice with the ring, though this was better because he could actually see her. In the real assassination she'd have to hold both concealment imbuements—the jade carving hiding the gas canister in true-life, and the ring hiding her sousedni-shape and the first concealment imbuement's blue glow—but she was smart to practice with just the one for now. Make sure she could keep the gas canister hidden in true-life, then worry about how they appeared in sousednia.

Celka's nose wrinkled as she studied him in sousednia, staring at his arm where he cradled the now half-visible phosgene canister. Gerrit was about to tell her that she didn't have it fully concealed, but swallowed the comment. She probably knew. Disrupting her concentration would not make this easier.

But when a long minute had passed and Celka made a frustrated huff in true-life from where she sat with her back to him, he said, "Can you anchor your attention on my elbow, or something? Do it while you're looking at me so you can get the cylinder covered, and then turn away?"

She pulled a face, and it almost felt like sneaking around the circus together. In sousednia, she looped her arm through his. It wouldn't have been possible in true-life—the gas canister would have blocked her. At the scrape of her boots on the attic floor, he focused back on true-life, finding her staring at him, a meter away from her sousedni-shape. The gas canister vanished and Gerrit shifted a little, thumb hooked in his jacket pocket, trying to make his empty-armed stance look natural. She managed to hold the gas cylinder invisible for it, and when he met her gaze in true-life, she nodded and turned her back.

"You've got it," he said, his arm still empty except for the blue sousednia bleed-through from the imbuement.

"Try going for a walk," she said, and he strolled away.

In sousednia, she floated next to him. They'd figured that trick out last night: with her sousedni-dislocation, she didn't have to actually walk, she could simply shift her sousednia to remain at his side. *Simply*, because for her, such a trick made sense. Gerrit had tried it after she'd figured it out, curious if it was as intuitive as she claimed. He hadn't managed it, and had abandoned the attempt rather than waste valuable practice time.

In the attic, Gerrit rounded a heap of unused furniture, and the canister popped visible again.

«Hailstones,» Celka cursed at his side in sousednia.

He rejoined the others in true-life, setting the canister on a stack of crates. Even empty, its weight added up.

Celka snapped back in line with her true-form, rubbing her temples. "I don't know what I'm doing wrong."

Filip flipped a knife over his knuckles, seemingly ignoring them except that Gerrit knew his best friend's thinking face. "You can stay at Gerrit's side because you can see his sousedni-shape, right?" At Celka's nod, he continued, knife still pirouetting over his hand. "But inanimate objects don't extend deeply into sousednia, so you can't track the gas canister that way."

Celka's lips pinched in a *I sleeting know that*, expression, but she didn't say it.

"Gerrit's moving in unexpected ways, and you're trying to track those motions and compensate for them," Filip said. "But Gerrit's relation to the canister isn't changing."

"So I need to give her warning or something before I turn?" Gerrit said.

Filip shook his head. "Celka should be able to feel it—with her arm through yours."

"Sousednia's not that—" Celka broke off, cocking her head to the side. "Oh, that might work."

"What might work?" Lucie asked.

"Pick up the canister," Celka told Gerrit, and he did, as in the dark about her idea as Lucie.

Celka appeared at his side in sousednia and looped her arm through his again, her true-form still seated on the crate. She turned her back in true-life, and he shifted onto his alpine clearing, breathing the cold, fresh air as her sousedni-shape sharpened. Then, as it had when she'd tickled him mercilessly in the circus, the weight of her arm on his solidified.

"A sousedni-disruption?" he said.

In sousednia, she nodded, patting the space above his arm with her free hand. The air rippled, something gray and almost solid appearing under her palm. Away from her hand, it bled into the open air, fading like ink in water; but near her palm, he could almost make out the gas cylinder.

She laughed, triumphant. "All right. Try walking now."

This time, when Gerrit rounded the stack of furniture, the canister stayed invisible, Celka's phantom hold lifelike on his arm. Filip strolled along after them, watching for mistakes. When they'd crossed nearly the whole attic and made their way back, Gerrit decided to push the technique. He clambered up onto a stack of crates, awkward with the phosgene cylinder cradled in one arm. This time, it remained fully invisible, and none of his arm disappeared.

As he started to climb down, a voice called, "Lieutenant Kladivo?"

Gerrit slipped, knocking over a smaller crate, hobnailed boots slipping on the smooth wood. The gas canister slipped, and he almost lost it. Celka kept hold of his arm, but the bottom quarter of the canister reappeared. Gerrit's breath caught.

"Everything all right, sir?" He recognized Corporal Shimunek's voice as he jumped down from the boxes.

"Fine. Everything's fine. It's just a mess in here." He spoke too quick, pulse ponding in his ears. Celka snatched the canister from his arms, wrapping the concealment imbuement back over it. Gerrit straightened his shoulders, trying to settle back into his officer role. When he called, "What is it?" his voice sounded more authoritative.

Hobnailed boots clacked onto the attic floor. "The captain wants to see you, sir."

Sleet, if Shimunek saw them with Lucie...

Celka hurried around a stack of crates, footsteps too loud on the attic floor, but when Gerrit returned to where they'd been gathered, he sighed with relief to find Celka hugged up against Lucie's back, Lucie and the gas canister invisible in true-life.

"I'll be right there," Gerrit told the corporal. Through Nina, he told Celka and Filip, *«Keep practicing.»* Ducking beneath the eaves, he picked his way around to the ladder.

Corporal Shimunek hurried him down the corridors, stopping at a room guarded by two bolt-hawks from Iveta's personal guard. They opened the door without knocking, and Iveta looked up from her desk with a start.

"Lock it," she told him, an edge to her voice.

He locked the bedroom door, skin prickling with subtle wrongness. Iveta had been bright-eyed and smiling when he'd left her, but now her hair was mussed, her jacket thrown aside and shirt half untucked. "What's wrong?" he asked.

"Orders." She sounded like she wanted to punch someone. "I wanted to see if you had ideas."

Frowning, Gerrit said, "Sure."

Iveta gathered up a sheaf of papers, about to hand them to him before she instead started pacing, abandoning the papers on her desk. "We got orders for you to take your new imbuement to Zbishov to quell a factory worker revolt. Orders from *Artur*."

Gerrit rocked back, as much as at the venom in Iveta's voice as from the details. But she didn't give him space to speak.

"I dug into the situation," Iveta said. "Zbishov is an industrial city to the east. Our step-mother's family has a lot of factory holdings out there, and they've had problems meeting quotas the last couple of years. The overseers have suppressed a handful of attempts by the workers to organize, and there's been some minor violence. Two days ago, the workers in a dozen factories walked out—peacefully. The strike is ongoing and still peaceful. In a rare show of restraint, the local Tayemstvoy have refused to step in, considering it a private matter between the workers and factory management."

"That sounds like good news," Gerrit said cautiously.

"This is why we work well together," she said. "I recommended we send Celka with her calming imbuement, thinking it could smooth negotiations." She flicked a hand as though swatting a fly. "Denied. Artur wants a *demonstration*."

Gerrit felt sick. "On civilians?" He struggled to keep his voice level, fighting back memories of Mrach.

She cut him an angry nod. "Artur's been agitating for Father to make it illegal for workers to organize. This work stoppage is big enough that if it turned into a violent mess, he'd be able to use it the same way they used Mrach to interdict civilian Songs."

"So we escalate this to Father," Gerrit said.

Iveta stopped pacing and faced him, rigid. "I did."

A vise squeezing his chest, Gerrit asked, "And?"

"He told me it was Artur's operation and to follow orders."

Gerrit felt like he'd been punched in the face. He struggled to regain his composure; he was the Stormhawk's loyal son, he shouldn't balk at 'necessary' sacrifices. But his voice was choked when he said, "So I'm going to Zbishov?"

She shook her head but looked as horrified as he felt. Low, she said, "Father's usually smarter than this."

He blinked, surprised she'd say something so treasonous. "Is he?"

Her eyes narrowed, and Gerrit wished he'd kept his sleeting mouth shut. He'd gone too far. Her caged energy would lash out at him for speaking treason above hers.

Instead, her anger collapsed into a laugh that was half sob, and she dropped to sit on the edge of her bed, elbows on her knees, head hanging. "Freezing hail-balls, what a mess. Mrach was a storm-forsaken accident and they want to *repeat* it."

"Maybe the demonstration already turned violent," Gerrit said, searching for any way to justify the horror.

"So we should make it worse?" Iveta asked.

Gerrit blew out a hard breath. "No. But what can we do?"

She chewed on a hangnail, glaring at nothing. After a long time, she said, "I miss Mother."

Gerrit flinched, his own loss too raw in this place.

"You might have been too young to remember," she said, "but she and Father used to get into the worst fights. She would have stood up to him on this."

"Would she have won?" Gerrit asked.

Iveta balled one hand into a fist. "I don't know." She flopped back on the bed, staring at the ceiling, and it hit Gerrit that she was only five years older than him, just twenty-three. She'd always seemed so much older—and, recently, wiser. "She was the one who taught me to pick my battles. How to argue my case so he'd listen. Sleeting *dogs*." Her tone became suddenly venomous. "If they had to kill someone in our family—" She bit off the words.

Quietly, Gerrit asked, "Do you wish it had been me?"

She sat up like she'd been shot from a howitzer. "*No.* Gerrit, no." Her shoulders slumped. "Forget what I said." She scrubbed her hands over her face. "I'm tired. I don't even know what I'm saying." Her eyes darted to the bedroom door before she dropped her gaze to her hands. "Arguing orders over encoded telegram... Sleet. I don't like seeing Artur win." Another glance at the door, and he could practically see her wondering at the loyalty of her guards and how well the door blocked their voices. "I can't wait until someone figures out how to secure telephone lines." She ran her fingers through her short hair, succeeding only in mussing it further.

Gerrit studied her, chilled. Iveta truly cared about people and, unlike their father and Artur, saw factory workers *as* people. It should have given him confidence he was doing the right thing, bolstering her standing in the regime, but hearing her dance around treason, hearing her practically wish Artur or their father dead, Gerrit realized he had to be the one to put on the Kladivo mask today.

Artur had issued orders, and Iveta couldn't get out of them. To try would, at best, weaken their standing with the Stormhawk; at worst, call their loyalties into question, which could compromise everything the resistance had worked for. Soon, Gerrit would be in position to give Iveta her wish that the resistance had killed their father. The thought sickened him even as the orders on Iveta's desk made painfully clear why the assassination was necessary.

"Being the Supreme-General's children does *not* absolve us of responsibility," Iveta said. "If anything, it heightens it."

Afraid of what she'd say next, Gerrit spoke over her. "I'll go."

"Gerrit—*what?*"

He paced to the window, feeling like a pack of wolves chased him through a night-dark forest. "Our orders are clear. Mother taught you to pick your battles." He shook his head, wondering if one of the veterans playing cizii myesto down on the lawn was Celka's father. "We're not going to win this one."

Iveta stared down at her hands for a long time before nodding. "You're right. Except..." She stood, fitting her mask of a remorseless Tayemstvoy captain back into place. "You don't have to be the one to do this. If Father's committed to letting Artur run amok, *he* can provide the bozhki. Let some Division Three Okhrana give Artur his 'demonstration.' *You* serve the regime best by continuing to imbue."

Gerrit's relief at not having to deploy paranoid violence on civilians withered at the idea of creating another horrific weapon in the next storm. After the first paranoia imbuement, his father's sick enthusiasm had given him no choice but to create another; now, with Iveta to back him, maybe he could buy some time. Turning from the window, he met her gaze, keeping his own regime mask in place. "I think it's time Celka and I develop a new emotional imbuement." He let the weight of his words say the rest.

She stilled, studying him with a gaze that reminded him too much of their father hunting for weaknesses. But he trusted Iveta; she wasn't seeking *his* weaknesses. "You have proven your ability to produce this imbuement," she finally said, "so you can imbue more if we go to war. It makes sense to expand your repertoire." She nodded, satisfied with the justification. Stepping close, she laid a hand on his shoulder. He wasn't sure which of them needed the reassurance more. "This time, consider the repercussions if it's... *mistakenly* deployed on our own population."

CHAPTER FORTY-ONE

CELKA STARED AT the point where Gerrit had disappeared around a stack of crates even after his boots had clunked down the attic ladder, trying to convince herself she was wrong.

"It's just us again," Lucie said, invisibly touching her arm, startling Celka. "You can drop the concealment imbuement."

Celka glanced surreptitiously around, checking sousednia and verifying the silencing imbuement's blue dome still covered them. She peeled the imbuement off Lucie, then let it fall away from the dummy phosgene canister, too. Filip took the canister, saying something about practicing, but she was only barely listening. Instead, she said, "Gerrit's still holding mental walls."

Filip scowled. "You're sure?"

Lucie glanced toward the ladder, eyes narrowed.

Cold in the drafty attic, Celka wrapped her arms around herself. "He said he'd reintegrate after we imbued."

"He did." Filip's tone made it almost a question.

Celka shook her head. "I used a sousedni-disruption to hold onto him so I could keep the gas cylinder hidden. It requires... a connection to a person's core nuzhda. I'd never really thought about it that way before, but you have to create a... resonance with your target for it to work." She glanced at Filip, certain he'd love to dig into the technical details, but this wasn't the time. "Anyway. His core nuzhda's... wrong. Not by a lot, but it's there."

"He's under a lot of strain," Filip said. "Maybe it's just that. People seem different—in subtle ways—when they're feeling strong emotions."

Celka had suspected Filip of unconsciously using sousedni-cues before; this confirmed it. "I know what Gerrit feels like when he's stressed." She couldn't quite keep the irritation from her tone. "This is different. Can't *you* tell?" As his strazh, Filip should have been the one to notice the problem.

He set the canister on the floor, jaw muscles working like he fought with words. "I can't..." When he straightened, a frown had cracked his soldierly face. "I can't sense his core nuzhda very well during storms. Or before or after. Sousednia gets in the way."

"Even now?" The storm had been over for hours.

Filip sighed, scrubbing a hand across his jaw. Not meeting her eyes, he jerked a nod.

She gripped his hand hard.

He returned the pressure, looking lost. "Sleet-storms. I'm supposed to be good at this."

"I don't understand the problem," Lucie said, and Celka startled to find her beside them. "So Gerrit's hiding a few memories still. I understand it's dangerous, but it's not like he's surrounded by good people out there." She gestured vaguely to the rest of the mansion.

Anger tensed Filip's jaw as he turned to her. "If he fails to reintegrate, those walls could become permanent."

Lucie straightened to face him, though the top of her head

barely reached Filip's chest. "And if he loses his cool in front of Iveta—or one of the Tayemstvoy secretly reporting to the Stormhawk—we could all lose our heads."

"He can't keep doing this," Celka said. "It's making him a monster."

The bright enthusiasm Lucie had shown when stealing Celka's bunk in the circus had hardened into determination. "You have *no idea* the pressure he's under. This entire assassination is riding on *his* ability to play that role."

Celka started to protest, but Lucie didn't let her.

"How about you stop worrying about what Gerrit's doing, and focus on *your* part in the plot? The faster you figure out how to keep that sleeting canister invisible, the sooner he gets to stop licking his father's boots."

Celka wanted to argue, but Lucie was right. So Filip picked up the phosgene canister, and they got to work.

Her arm looped through Filip's in sousednia, Celka got to the point where she could keep the concealment imbuement reliably covering the gas cylinder no matter where he moved—so long as she held onto the sousedni-disruption that made his arm feel solid. It was exhausting, but she could build up her stamina. She could practice sousedni-disruptions on Filip or Gerrit anytime. Unlike sousedni-dislocations that split her true-form and sousedni-shape, disruptions wouldn't be noticeable to anyone but her target.

Concealing the canister once Filip crouched to set it on the floor, however, was a different matter entirely—one Celka struggled to come up with a solution for. So when Gerrit shouted up the ladder that he had something to show them, Celka dropped the imbuements with relief and arranged to meet Lucie for another practice session in the middle of the night.

«*What's this about?*» Celka asked, Nina looped around

her shoulders the way she'd carried the snake in the circus sideshow.

«I found your father,» Gerrit said.

Celka's heart seemed to stop, and she faltered mid-stride. Gerrit's smile wasn't the grin they might have shared before Mrach, but when he offered his arm, she took it without hesitation. Whatever memories he'd hidden, he clearly remembered how much this meant to her. Filip squeezed her shoulder, and she gripped his hand, thankful for the support.

Leaving behind the meticulously tended gardens, they entered a shadowed forest, a stream babbling alongside the path. Filip trailed them, the path not wide enough for all three to walk abreast. The stroll could have been wholly innocent for all Celka's heart raced. But as the path curved around a bend in the stream, the temperature plummeted, and the smell of burning undercut the green scent of water plants. Celka's eyes started to water, her throat raw as if she'd been shouting. And somehow, too distant yet entirely too close, she heard explosions—the chest-shaking, percussive booms of artillery. Beneath them, screaming.

Gerrit pulled her to a stop. *«You should activate the calming imbuement.»* He squeezed her arm. *«Grandmother said she'd make us space—I'm pretty sure she's involved in... everything—so it should be relatively safe to talk.»*

Edging into sousednia, she scanned the space ahead—blocked by trees and undergrowth in true-life. Faint with distance and her big top's shadows, a figure lunged and dodged. Balance wavering, she clutched Gerrit's arm harder. After all these years, she was finally about to see Pa. She should have been excited, but the stench of battle terrified her, and the memory of Branislav thrashing against his restraints made her taste bile.

She clawed back into true-life. "What if he's fully—" She couldn't finish the sentence. *Storm-mad.*

"Grandmother said he's not," Gerrit said. "Not quite." Through Nina, he added, *«This will work, Celka. You can do it.»*

The air pressure changed with a *pop* as Filip activated her original calming imbuement, the fresh breeze off fields and forests caressing her cheek. Celka squeezed her eyes closed, leaning into a feeling of being held. She couldn't change the past and the mistakes that had driven Pa to the brink of storm-madness. But, after everything, she'd finally made it to his side. She couldn't waste this opportunity.

In sousednia, Celka expected to peer down on the world from above, but her original calming imbuement couldn't overcome her anxiety or her core grounding—not with Nina still active. Loading the python off her shoulders to coil on the cold path, Celka released the snake's activation points. She could usually hold Nina active and still pull against moderate nuzhdi, but the calming imbuement she'd created in Mrach required throwing almost all of herself into its nuzhda. She'd have no space for clandestine conversations, and would have to trust to her own core grounding without the snake's assistance.

Exhaling, Celka squeezed her eyes shut on both realities, focusing on the fresh breeze caressing her face from Filip's calming imbuement. Building from that sensation, she reached into the sky above her big top, releasing both fear and hope and floating—up, up...

By the time she activated her own pendant's imbuement, the others' sousedni-shapes had grown as distant as the circus tents, inconsequential. She draped true-life in calm presence and, leaving the majority of her attention behind to maintain the nuzhda, arrowed her focus back into the Slavni Circus's big top.

"I'm ready," she told Gerrit, still gripping his arm.

In true-life, the undergrowth parted, revealing a figure bundled in a fur coat on a wrought iron bench, staring unmoving at the stream. Strain lined his features where a thick, graying beard and moustache did not obscure them, yet even so, recognition hit Celka like a train. Pa sat erect, tense as though only great effort held him still. Yet in sousednia, he fought and snarled.

His sousedni-shape wore a uniform not unlike her own, though it was ragged and dirty, stained with what had to be blood. He gripped a rifle, bayonet fixed, lunging and stabbing, his features blurred by sweat and grime and the shadow of his combat helmet. Cuts and burns in his uniform revealed crimson wounds, crackling with combat nuzhda.

Celka piled the calming imbuement's multi-hued nuzhda over Pa as, in true-life, she dropped to her knees beside the bench. Staring at his face, so familiar and yet so strange, she whispered, "Pa?" aloud, then again in sousednia. «Pa?»

At first, he hesitated, missing a beat in his dance of bayonet and blood. Then, as she laid a hand on his knee in true-life and settled the last of Mrach's calming imbuement tightly over him, focusing all the calming that had quieted a riot, Pa froze.

The slashing-screaming-exploding stopped. The artillery fell silent. Celka breathed laughter and musty stone corridors, dustmotes dancing through shafts of sunlight in unused rooms, and the smell of sweat and hard work beneath the glitter of sequins.

In true-life, he turned abruptly to face her, the motion as sudden as a rifle report, followed by utter stillness. Pa's green eyes roved sightlessly before fixing on a point just over Celka's ear. "Celka?" His voice scraped, rusty, the sweetest music.

A strangled cry tore from her throat, and she threw herself into his arms. He stiffened.

In sousednia, too, she tried to hug him, but he twisted away, bayonet flashing in sunlight. «You can't be here,» he said as he fought on her high wire platform. «You're not here. You're safe.» His voice sounded so little like her pa's, torn from shouting across the battlefield, staccato between lunges that drenched his bayonet in blood.

«No, Pa, it's me.» In true-life, she slipped onto the bench next to him, taking one of his stiff-clawed hands. He didn't return the pressure. «It's Celka. I'm here.»

He kept fighting, muttering under his breath.

Throat too tight for words, she looked to Filip and Gerrit in true-life.

"Try talking to him," Gerrit said, moving behind the bench to lay a supportive hand on her shoulder. "He saw you. Prove to him you're real."

Filip crouched in the decaying leaf litter by Pa's feet. "Tell me what he was like before." His voice carried the soothing tones she recalled from their visit with Branislav, and Celka struggled to forget their failure. Branislav had been fully storm-mad. Pa wasn't.

Chest tight, Celka told Filip about their life before the Tayemstvoy had dragged Pa away. She'd been a child, and Pa had been her world. But her world had been awash in the circus's bright colors, in laughter and illusions. How much of what she remembered was Pa, and how much was the role he had played—just a simple high wire walker who hadn't traded his sanity for a temporary peace with Lesnikraj?

Yet as she spoke, she echoed the words in sousednia, shouting over the battlefield clamor. Did she imagine it, or did the artillery bombardment abate? Did the combat nuzhda crackling through Pa's bloodied uniform dim?

Slowly, Filip settled a hand on Pa's knee. A tremor rippled through Pa, a hint of his sousednia's violence bleeding into true-life. But Filip was humming something, a chaotic tune that raced and slowed. Only belatedly did Celka recognize the Song of Concealing.

Pa settled back into stillness.

«I wish you'd told me what you saw in sousednia,» she said as Filip began to ripple with color, trying to pull against Pa's core nuzhda without actually knowing it. «But I know where *I* am. On the high wire we used to walk together. Do you remember it? Do you remember the hush in the big top when the first one of us stepped out? I miss seeing you and Ma dance on the wire. She always toyed with you, playing coy, though now I wonder how much of that act was your idea. You made her laugh. You made all of us laugh.» A tear traced down her cheek, but she ignored it, trying to picture them all together, crowded around the small table in their sleeper car at night, telling stories, playing cards, repairing costumes. She tried to let their happiness swell through her like she pulled against a complex nuzhda. «Even Aunt Benedicta. I forgot she knew how to laugh. She doesn't anymore.»

Pa paused in his desperate fight, not quite turning to face her. But his head cocked. Blood dripped from his bayonet, falling through the high wire platform's metal grating.

Leaving her true-form behind, seated next to Pa on the bench, Celka crossed the now broad expanse of her high wire platform to stand before him, careful not to step in front of his rifle. In his burned and torn uniform, he was clean-shaven but gaunt, his face not quite the one she remembered from when her family had been whole and the summers stretching with endless sunshine. Reaching out, Celka laid a hand on his arm. In memory, he was so much taller than her, but now, if anything, he seemed small.

«I'm here,» Celka said, gently, the way Filip had spoken to Branislav. «I finally found you. I've come to bring you back.»

Sweat slicked Pa's face, but he tipped the bayonet up, gaze darting between Celka and the enemy she couldn't see. Celka kept the calming imbuement wrapped tight around him.

«You don't need to fight anymore,» she said as Filip flickered with a complex nuzhda behind her.

Pa blinked at her, resting his rifle against his shoulder, bayonet and barrel pointing at the sky. He searched her face before his attention slipped off of her. He staggered a step past her and Celka's stomach lurched, but he didn't return to the fight. Instead, he fell to his knees before Filip, the rifle wisping away. Celka crouched at his side as Pa reached a hand out, hesitant, touching Filip's shoulder.

When he did, a shudder went through him, the tears and stains in his uniform mending, the haunted edge leaving his features.

«What do you see?» Celka asked. «What was your sousednia like before?»

Pa's exhale shook him, and he squeezed his eyes shut before sitting back on his heels. He tore his gaze off Filip as though with a great effort of will, and when he faced Celka, he finally *saw* her. «My little lightning rod.» He reached a hand out to stroke her cheek.

Tears welled in Celka's eyes, and she leaned into his touch.

«You're really here.» His voice was rough, but not as battle-torn as before.

She nodded, not trusting herself to speak.

Pa pulled her into an embrace, and Celka melted against him, tears slipping free.

«I missed you,» she choked out. «I thought you were dead.» Pa's embrace felt wrong even as she wanted to curl against him and never let go. She was too big to nestle into his arms, and his touch felt insubstantial.

Focusing back on true-life, she put her arms around him

on the wrought iron bench. He didn't react. Breathing deep, focusing on the feeling of laughter and musty stone corridors that had begun to emerge beneath the blood and grit of battle, she struggled to perform a sousedni-disruption, bringing his true-form and sousedni-shape into contact. It felt like trying to grasp a fish in a stream—each time she thought she had it, Pa's sousedni-shape slipped sideways, escaping. But she persisted. Finally, she got the two realities to align, and Pa trembled beneath her embrace.

"Pa." She drew a little back in both sousednia and true-life. "I'm here. Look at me." She gripped his shoulders, holding his gaze in sousednia even as she returned most of her attention to Potokovy Manor's shadowed streamside.

Motions stuttery, Pa turned his head in the dappled autumn light, squinting at her from his gaunt, bearded face. "Celka." His gaze threatened to slip off of hers, but he gritted his teeth and managed to focus. She let go of his shoulders to grip his hands and, this time, he returned the pressure. "You've grown. So big. So strong."

She bit her lip.

His gaze slipped off her and she was afraid she'd lost him, but he only glanced around the clearing. "You're at Potokovy?" She nodded, and Pa studied Filip for a long moment before making a satisfied sound. But when his roving gaze found Gerrit, he stiffened. "Kladivo."

"It's all right, Pa," Celka said softly. "He's with us. He's helping."

Pa's gaze snapped back to her, and he spoke in sousednia as though the effort of moving in true-life had exhausted him. «Helping? You're...? They found you.»

Guilt washed over her before flaring into anger. «You could have told me earlier. Could have warned me! Could have taught me *anything* I needed for the storms' return.»

The words came out in a rush, and Pa's grip on her hands tightened. «They dragged you away and I was terrified I'd never see you again! I wanted to fight, but Grandfather told me to hide.»

«And yet the State found you.» Disapproval edged his voice along with a hardness that reminded Celka of Vrana. Around her, sousednia's tent walls collapsed, and panic caught in her throat. But the collapse halted, leaving her in a close, dark space lit by a single flickering candle. When she looked around, she couldn't see Gerrit or Filip. Pa still wore his uniform, a major's bar and star on each shoulder, but he no longer smelled of blood and things not meant to burn. «We can speak here,» he said. «I've made it quiet.»

«You never taught me to do this,» Celka said, struggling to swallow her resentment. She had Pa back. This is what she'd wanted, what she'd dreamed of for four long years.

«I only learned as the storms neared.» He reached out and stroked her cheek, his hand no longer so large as she remembered. Once, his touch had filled her with warmth and comfort, but today it made her uneasy. «Sousednia is so much more than we knew.» His gaze slipped into the distance, a tremor shaking his form. «And so much less.»

«What does that mean?» Celka studied his face, seeking the Pa she remembered, the parent larger than life, eyes crinkling with laughter, always ready with some new prank. Pa had made everything right, but sitting beside him on a stone bench in a cramped, dark sousedni-space, nothing seemed right at all.

He focused back on her. «You've held true-life like I told you?»

Celka chewed her lip. «It's not that simple.»

He took her hand, and she expected him to reprimand her. «Nothing ever is. Is that how they found you?»

«I lost control in a storm. Imbued combat and killed a Tayemstvoy squad that was torturing Lukska and his child.» Pa clearly recognized the resistance printer's name, and Celka told him more, about Gerrit and Filip, about nearly escaping before losing control and imbuing Nina. Then she told him the rest—about regaining her core grounding with Hedvika's help, the riot at Mrach, and their plans to assassinate the Stormhawk. As she did, she searched for the Pa she remembered—the quiet reassurance, the quick smile— but he nodded, solemn, a commander taking a report from one of his scouts.

Not knowing what else to say, Celka explained her role in the assassination, concealing the poison gas cylinder while Gerrit carried it into the Stormhawk's bedroom. «I manage it just fine until he moves to set it on the ground. Sometimes I can even keep it hidden while he crouches, but the instant he lets go of it, I can't tell where the cylinder is anymore. I mean, I can never *really* tell where it is, I've just practiced where it must be. But so when they set it down...» She threw her hands up, the frustration from her practice session welling along with the gnawing disappointment that this was what her reunion with Pa had become. Her heart felt empty, like instead of saving Pa, all she'd managed to save was the Wolf— the resistance leader she'd never known.

«Dead objects don't exist in sousednia,» Pa said, as if this clarified her problem or gave her the solution.

She scowled at him. «That can't be true. Otherwise we wouldn't be able to imbue.»

Pa cocked his head, as though struggling to put his understanding into words. «It's not the object that comes here, it's the *purpose*.»

«The purpose? Like, killing the Stormhawk?»

«More specific than that. The better you understand and

can grasp the purpose—the object's heart—the more vivid it becomes. Our ties to true-life limit our understanding of sousednia. Physical space means nothing here. Sousednia is all intention and strength of will.»

Celka nodded, the idea almost making sense. «I'll try that. Thank you.»

Pa smiled sadly and took her hand again. «Thank you for coming for me. I missed...» His exhale curled him in on himself, but he managed to straighten again, searching her face. For what, she didn't know. «You've grown into such a strong young woman. I wish I could have shielded you from all this. You shouldn't have to get blood on your hands. I'm sorry.»

Her throat closed off, but she managed to say, «I wish you'd trusted me.» She searched for remorse on his face or in his sousedni-cues, but he was opaque. «You could have come back for me.»

He patted her hand. «I thought I could keep you safe. It's a parent's job to keep their children safe.»

«But you *didn't*.»

Regret tugged his lips. After a long silence, he said, «Remember when we used to make the elephant poop?»

Celka couldn't seem to get enough air. Somehow, she managed, «We'd tickle her under the chin from sousednia.»

«You were always better at it than me,» Pa said.

«Was I?» Celka couldn't remember and didn't see how it mattered.

«I think you can do more.»

«More than make elephants poop?» She laughed a little, but it wasn't the laughter she remembered. «I hope that's not the pinnacle of my life's work.»

Amusement crinkled Pa's eyes. «I love you,» he said, voice too tight.

Tears sprang to her eyes again, but she blinked hard to push them away. «I love you too.»

«My lightning rod.» He stroked her cheek again, and she leaned against his palm, trying to believe that his warmth was anything but fleeting. «I'm glad you found me.»

«I'm going to save you,» she said, though her voice broke. «With this imbuement, you'll be able to hold true-life.»

«I will,» he said. «For a time. You've given me a great gift.» He pressed a kiss to her forehead and her heart felt like a dam inside it had burst. A sob tore free. «I love you, little lightning rod. Sit with me for a while. Let's enjoy the sunlight.» He wrapped an arm around her shoulders, pulling her close in both realities, and she rested her head on his shoulder, feeling small—yet at the same time, he was the fragile one. In true-life, he wiped the tears from her cheek. "Help me stay here, with you."

"I will," Celka promised aloud, even as she heard the crunch of footfalls.

The sound snapped her around, heart in her throat, terrified the Tayemstvoy had realized who she was, who Pa was, and were about to surround them and drag them all away. But it was just Vrana, almost unrecognizable in a blue wool kaftan and fur hat.

"Calm yourself," Vrana said, her voice gentle in a way Celka had never heard. "You've done well. And now"—her gaze shifted off Celka to Pa, whose attention had sharpened, though he still gazed toward the stream—"Jaromir and I have matters to discuss."

CHAPTER FORTY-TWO

CELKA SHIVERED IN the back seat of the motorcar as it struggled along a slushy, muddy road, and Hedvika pulled her close, arm around her shoulders. The circus band echoed faintly off her, Hedvika's heat-shimmer rippling blue-violet-red as she pulled against Celka's core nuzhda. But Celka couldn't stop trembling. The cold and the bone-deep, paralyzing fear she and Gerrit had pulled against for their latest imbuement were only part of the problem.

The motorcar's engine strained, its tires slipping. Celka wished Yinovatka Manor had just sent a sleigh—though winter had not yet tightened its grip, and mud dirtied the snow, making any travel except by rail a struggle. But the Stormhawk had invited Gerrit and Celka's squad to join him at Yinovatka Manor in celebration of the Miracle of Teeming Lakes. Lucie would meet them, bringing concealment imbuements and the real phosgene canister. Tonight, they would act. The Stormhawk would die, and Bourshkanya would take its first, decisive step towards freedom.

Celka shivered again. *This'll work*, she told herself for

the millionth time. She'd gotten good at concealing the phosgene canister—though she still struggled once whoever was carrying it set it down. But Pa's advice had helped. If she concentrated on the purpose of the canister rather than its physical shape, she had an easier time holding it inside the concealment imbuement's blue gossamer.

Peering past Yanek's broad shoulders out the wind-screen, she spotted the motorcar ahead of them, where Gerrit rode. She rubbed her hands together beneath the lap furs, wishing she could get warm. Winter fought for its grip on Yinovatka Manor—today's Gods' Breath streaking through a blizzard—but the weather had been balmy compared to Gerrit's demeanor.

Celka hadn't expected him to need mental walls to pull against the complex mélange of terror and helplessness that they'd developed for this latest imbuement. *She* could certainly pull against it more easily than violent paranoia. Celka needed only to slip into her memory of the Tayemstvoy marching through the circus hunting Gerrit. She locked herself inside moments when Major Rychtr with his red shoulders snarled question after question, striking her again and again, pinning her helpless to the floor.

Shuddering, she fought free of the memory before it could consume her.

That Gerrit resorted to mental self-surgery to pull against the nuzhda made her angry. She focused on that emotion to lock out the terror that drummed her pulse and sent pain sparking along her storm-scar. Did he think this was *easy* for her? She had to pull just as hard on the nuzhda, had to shape its weaves. She didn't want to. It made her feel like sleet, but she managed it without hiding from herself.

Hedvika adjusted the furs around Celka, snuggling her closer to the warmth of her side. "We'll get you a hot bath when we get to the manor," Hedvika said. "That should help you warm up before you meet the Stormhawk."

This time, Celka's shudder definitely wasn't from the cold. The Stormhawk was pleased with her and Gerrit's emotional imbuements. He wanted to meet Celka in person.

On the train, Gerrit had coached her on what to expect. Knowing what she was walking into should have reassured her, but Gerrit had already built his mental walls, so his coaching had carried an icy aloofness. *He's just giving you a taste of what the Stormhawk will be like*, she'd tried to tell herself. But she would rather have been able to trust that Gerrit had her back.

Warmed from the bath, but still nowhere near ready, Celka strode at Gerrit's side to the parlor converted into the Stormhawk's office at Yinovatka Manor.

After a thorough search by humorless Yestrab Okhrana, they were allowed inside. Celka stopped before the Stormhawk's desk, clicked her heels, and did her very best salute. At Gerrit's sousednia prompt, they said in unison, "All hail the Stormhawk!"

Supreme-General Kladivo looked up from a sheaf of papers on his impressive desk, evaluating first his son, then Celka. Two Yestrab Okhrana with bozhk heat-shimmers stood motionless behind him, holding a rainbow of active imbuements. "At ease."

Celka spread her feet to a comfortable stance and let her hands hang neutral at her sides, trying to look the regime soldier while her pulse hammered. She stood before the *Stormhawk*. Not as one anonymous member of a supposedly adoring crowd, but in a private office with few enough guards that she could foolishly imagine drawing a gun and shooting him where he sat. Not that she had a gun. Not that she was so stupid.

Another two Okhrana stood behind her and Gerrit, more just outside the office door. When she let true-life blur, they filled the neighboring rooms. None appeared storm-blessed, though, and maybe that luck would hold when they placed the gas canister in his rooms tonight.

As Gerrit formally presented Celka, she tried to shake her regime conditioning. She stood not before some mythical, all-powerful figure, but a human being. Yet, beneath the Stormhawk's scrutiny, she struggled not to squirm. Too easy to imagine that hard gaze turned on a prisoner in irons.

Our plan will work, she told herself again. *You won't be caught.*

"You have an impressive record of imbuements," the Stormhawk said, the resonance of his voice making her feel small. At the same time, it made her want to please him. "Despite your... problematic youth."

"A child only knows what her parents teach her, sir." Celka dropped her gaze to the Stormhawk's hands, trying to appear contrite. A trembling in her chest made her want to cower, desperate for his approval. That the sensation was created by magic didn't make it any easier to bear. "I thank your wisdom for the chance to prove myself worthy of my storm-blessing."

When the silence stretched, she glanced up, finding the Stormhawk studying her. She couldn't read anything in his icy gaze. Finally, he asked, "What do you think of life in the imbuement company?"

"It suits me, sir," she made herself say. "If nothing else, my childhood prepared me for the constant travel. I'm proud to better serve the State now, though. And..." She hesitated. Despite practicing this conversation with Gerrit, she wasn't sure how much to toe the party line. "I feel like I've finally found my home. My... true family." She glanced at Gerrit as she said that, making herself recall his amused horror as she pulled out her toothbrush to scrub down a typewriter's flanges back in the circus. The memory let her smile. He would return to that, after tonight.

The Stormhawk's expression became even colder. Throat tasting of bile, she faced her boots. Had she overstepped to suggest that her relationship with his son was more than youthful amusement? She knotted her hands behind her back. The Stormhawk had destroyed Lucie's life because Gerrit had dared envision romance with her. Had that presumption been Gerrit's, or Lucie's?

Supreme-General Kladivo's chair creaked as he stood, and Celka darted a glance at him, trying to read whether he was about to order the Okhrana to beat her. "Son"—he nodded to Gerrit—"give us a minute. I'd like to get to know your young tvoortse better."

"Yes, sir." Gerrit's lips quirked in a small smile that suggested he and his father shared some great secret. It was incredibly un-reassuring.

The office door closed with a metallic click that echoed like irons snapping about Celka's wrists, and she struggled to keep breathing. Rounding his desk, the Stormhawk gestured for her to sit. He settled into a facing chair as if they were equals. As if a single word from him couldn't have her tortured to death.

"Tell me about yourself," he said, and it felt like being ordered to dig her own grave.

But Celka made herself sit. Made herself speak. Tried to pretend—but not let herself actually believe—that this was just an awkward conversation with her partner's parent.

She described the circus and her family, eliding her early bozhk training with Pa.

"Don't be ashamed of your humble origins," the Stormhawk told her. "The Storm Gods pay no heed to inheritance or prestige. To do so ourselves would be cizii. Bourshkanya did not become great by ignoring exceptional abilities in the unwashed masses." A scent of swamp and feces wafted around him in sousednia, and Celka struggled not to choke.

She'd studied his life and deeds like any schoolchild and, sure, he hadn't been born into the elite. But he'd stabbed and murdered his way into a new upper class just as entitled as the people he'd railed against in his early speeches. *Look around yourself*, she wanted to say. If family wealth and influence were so unimportant, why were the only people invited to tonight's celebration wealthy factory owners, Tayemstvoy officers, and bozhki? Why were starving laborers made to cheer his greatness from behind red-shouldered barricades? How often did the Stormhawk's jaw ache from chewing woody turnip in watery soup that barely dented his hunger?

But she had to survive this conversation, so instead of challenging his twisted doctrine, she thanked him.

When he signaled an end to their interview, Celka felt like she'd imbued a thousand times. She'd never realized how exhausting it could be to say nothing.

"I'm glad we had this chance to get to know one another," the Stormhawk said, gripping her shoulder a little too hard. "Continue your good work. You may yet be worthy of my son."

She saluted when she wanted to spit. "Yes, sir. Thank you, sir!"

He waved her out and, only when she reached the door did she realize what she'd forgotten.

She turned, clicking her heels in another salute. "All hail the Stormhawk!"

He studied her appraisingly, and she held the salute, struggling not to tremble outwardly.

Finally, he nodded. "You're dismissed, Specialist."

CHAPTER FORTY-THREE

GERRIT HAD PLANNED to reintegrate after the afternoon's imbuement but, deeply chilled, he'd convinced himself to wait until he reached the manor and could reintegrate in a hot bath. By then, it had gotten late and the Stormhawk's sycophants were already enjoying mugs of hot, spicy sbiten and appetizers that smelled divine. No sense, really, in reintegrating. He'd only have to rebuild his walls. He couldn't risk an inopportune reaction spoiling his father's regard—not when he was so close to victory.

He'd bought this opportunity to celebrate at his father's side through hard work, had paid for it in blood. Tonight was important and, when he'd erected his mental walls on the train this morning, he'd been careful not to hide the reason. Months of planning would finally come together, and his father would die. Well, phosgene took a few days to do its damage, so his father wouldn't *actually* die today. He'd be dead, he just wouldn't know it yet.

The knowledge left Gerrit oddly unmoved. The dispassion shook his mental walls, but he ignored the tremor and sipped his sbiten. He often found the drink too sweet, but the manor's chef had balanced the honey and jam against sharp spices. Non-alcoholic, it warmed him without risking his faculties. Tonight was too important to be dulled by drink.

After presenting Celka to his father, Gerrit joined Iveta, letting her introduce him to important people and compliment his leadership of the imbuement platoon. When his father emerged from his office, the Stormhawk, too, made a great show of introducing Gerrit. Celka escaped most of it; she was a tool, so far as the Stormhawk was concerned, useful and worth caring for, but only to ensure her utility.

Gerrit had planned to keep an eye on his father to know when he retreated to his rooms, but the Stormhawk spent no more than an hour rubbing elbows with his elite guests before slipping away for private meetings.

Activating Nina was a struggle tonight, but eventually Gerrit managed it—though the connection felt fragile and hammered against his mental walls. He struggled to keep the discomfort off his face, a headache already building. *«We need to find out when he's alone,»* he told Filip and Celka, hoping they'd have ideas.

«Lucie has the concealment imbuements,» Celka said. *«Maybe she can keep an eye on his rooms?»*

«I'll coordinate with her,» Filip said. *«No one's watching me.»*

Relieved, Gerrit dropped his connection with Nina.

Two hours later, the snake's imbuement tickled Gerrit's thoughts. Across the ballroom, Celka met his gaze, frowning. He headed for the stairs.

She caught up to him, looping her arm through his, managing to look relatively innocent. The pressure from Nina strengthened, and he finally managed to activate the imbuement.

«What's wrong?» she asked him.

«Nothing.» He turned down the long, first floor corridor toward the room he and Celka shared.

«You're having trouble activating Nina, aren't you?»

«It's not a problem,» he said.

Inside the bedroom, she caught his arm and forced him to face her. *«We need to know we can communicate if anything goes wrong. You have to drop enough of your sleeting walls that you can hold the link.»*

"Is something wrong?" Lucie asked, frowning between them beneath the blue dome of her silencing imbuement.

"No," Gerrit said at the same time Celka said, "Yes."

"Celka's right, Gerrit," Filip said, grim. "We need to be able to talk to you."

At Lucie's frustrated confusion, Gerrit said, "They want me to drop my mental walls."

Lucie's irritation vanished, and she caught his hand. "Can you do that safely?"

Gerrit returned her grip, relieved that she, at least, understood the pressure he was under. "I have to face my father," he said, as if that was answer enough—and it should have been.

Celka made a frustrated noise, but Lucie still held his hand. "What if you drop just some of them?" Lucie asked. "Can you carve off enough to be able to communicate?" She glanced at Nina caged in one corner.

Gerrit released a shaky breath, wanting to say it was impossible. But Lucie still held his hand, and it gave him strength. "I'll try." He made himself look from Lucie to the others. "The rest of you get ready with the imbuements."

Lucie gave his hand a squeeze but didn't let go. "Before you do, there's a problem. The Yestrab Okhrana changed the room assignments. We're no longer close enough for Celka to hide here."

Worry cut through Gerrit's mental walls, and he exchanged a glance with Celka, his irritation with her vanishing. "What about Filip's room?"

"Also too far," Lucie said. "There's a supply closet within range on this floor—we're the floor below his—but it's at the edge of Celka's range. There's a closer closet one story up, but there will be guards in the corridor." She turned to Celka. "It's your call."

Celka scrubbed her hands over her face. "How close to the edge of my range?"

"It's twenty meters to the center of his bedroom. If the canister ends up rolled against the far wall, it'll be another three or four meters. It's a stretch."

"But if I'm upstairs and anything goes wrong," Celka said, grim, "I'll be trapped in a closet on the same floor as our target and a dozen Yestrab Okhrana."

"Or more," Gerrit said. "If they suspect an attack, they'll search nearby rooms. If they open the closet door, they'll spot your true-form immediately."

"And they'll be efficient in their search," Filip said. "They train for this sort of thing."

Celka swallowed hard, whatever horror she was picturing leaving her pale. "I'll stay on this floor. I should be able to handle twenty-four meters. Sleet, I hope I don't have to, though."

Gerrit laid a hand on her shoulder. "You can do this. You're strong."

She wrinkled her nose up at him, but stood a little straighter.

Now he just had to be. Making himself release Lucie's hand, he crossed to the washbasin and stared at his reflection in the mirror. The location put him outside the range of Lucie's silencing imbuement, so though they probably discussed final details while Celka activated the two concealment imbuements, he heard only the distant roar of conversation from the ballroom.

Widening a crack in his sousednia's sheer granite rock face enough that he could slip inside his own walls was brutally difficult. Worse than pulling against the nuzhda for paralyzing fear; more of a struggle even than staying on his knees after Artur's beating.

As Gerrit slipped sideways to edge through the fissure of granite toward the blazing noonday sun on the other side of the wall, his chest constricted, as though the towering stones collapsed in on him. Panicking, desperate to retreat, he nonetheless forced himself forward. Even before he reached the other side, he started to remember. When he erupted from the stone, memory and emotion assailed him, driving him to his knees in the snow. In true-life, he barely kept his feet, gripping the washbasin with white knuckles.

Panting, he struggled to think past the tide of anguish and loathing, terror and rage. He didn't have time for this. His father had retired to his rooms. Gerrit needed to deliver the gas canister now, before the Stormhawk went to bed or decided he wouldn't accept any surprise visitors.

But on this side of the wall he was weak. He remembered wrapping Celka in his arms, kissing her and making her laugh; his mother's last words as she gasped that he never become like his father; Filip gripping Gerrit's shoulders after interrogation practicum left him vomiting in the latrines. «I can't do this,» he whispered in sousednia. If he let any of this out, his father would see straight through him.

«You can.»

The voice snapped Gerrit around, and he found Filip standing there, sousedni-shape fuzzing and blurring, as though he couldn't quite maintain his focus on the neighboring reality. But when Filip laid his hand on Gerrit's back, the touch felt real.

«We're so close,» Filip said, still in sousednia. «You wore the mask all through academy training. You can do it again for one night.»

Filip's solid presence at his side eased Gerrit's breathing and, when Filip offered him a hand in sousednia, Gerrit took it, letting Filip pull him to his feet. Then, still gripping his best friend's hand, he looked around, forcing himself to think. Standing before his father, he couldn't appear weak, but it didn't matter now how much he recalled of their treasonous plot. He was paying a visit to the Stormhawk to assassinate him, and knowing the details of all their planning would only make him more assured as he walked into his father's bedroom. Catching those memories, he pushed them through the fissure to the other side of his wall.

Then he reached for his knowledge of his mother's murder. Touching it, reliving it, the memories still hurt, but the anger it roused in him had grown cold. From the other side of the wall, he remembered his father's justification and his own heartless understanding; but he remembered, too, Lucie's fierce support. *Deep cover*, he told himself as he released those memories from behind his walls. He'd done his job for the resistance, was doing it still. He would avenge his mother's death; show his father exactly the price of thinking he controlled the lives of everyone around him.

When Gerrit faced the darker side of his granite walls, he discovered that the fissure had widened. Easily, he stepped through, a shift of perspective bringing Filip with him to stare back at the sheer rock face and the bright sunlight behind it.

Those walls still held his most precious memories, too tender and softhearted to trust with this mission. But it might be enough.

Concentrating, he repaired the gap in the walls and returned to true-life.

Staring at his reflection in the mirror, Filip behind him, his hand still on Gerrit's back, Gerrit searched for weakness. He imagined his father congratulating him on his and Celka's latest emotional imbuement, and felt pride over a cold confidence that, with this powerful imbuement of paralyzing fear, he'd bought Iveta further status in the regime. When he imagined the Stormhawk telling him about the results of Artur ordering paranoid violence deployed on peaceful protestors, he didn't flinch from his gaze in the mirror. Instead, Gerrit thought: *Artur made a mistake thinking he could attack innocent people without consequences. I won't let him do it again.*

Satisfied, he caught Filip's gaze in the mirror and nodded.

The tug in his chest that sounded like whispering pages and ringing steel blossomed, and Gerrit reached for Nina's imbuement. It took him a minute to connect—a new arrangement of walls in his mind let him imitate his old core nuzhda—but when the imbuement flared, it didn't hammer against the sheer granite cliff as painfully as before. Instead, Nina's magic felt like a friend's voice luring him toward the terrifying drop from Captain Vrana's cliff. Straightening his shoulders, he glanced one last time at his reflection before turning back to Lucie and Celka. *«Let's get this over with,»* he told Filip and Celka through the link, just to prove he could.

Inside the dome of Lucie's silencing imbuement, Celka raked him with a wary gaze, but only said, "I've activated the imbuements. I'm ready."

On sousednia's twilit mountaintop, Gerrit checked. Her sousedni-shape was the merest ripple barely visible even when he looked directly at her.

Lucie went to the phosgene canister on the bed, and activated its release timer. "I set the timer for an hour and a half," she said, bringing the gray metal cylinder over to Gerrit. "We rendezvous here after that. I'll take the imbuements back and disappear into the night. I'll contact you again for your extraction."

"An hour and a half?" Gerrit frowned. "We planned on the middle of the night. He might not even be asleep by then." He turned to Celka. "I thought you could hold it invisible longer."

Celka's lips pressed into thin lines. "No, Lucie's right. At that distance, even an hour and a half will be a strain. If we push it longer, I might not be able to keep the canister hidden."

"Freezing sleet," Gerrit muttered. But they couldn't do anything about the room assignments. He took the phosgene canister from Lucie. It was heavier than the empty cylinder, but less awkward than the bag of rocks. He settled it into the crook of his arm.

"Good luck." Filip's voice was strained. He would return to his room and provide an alibi for Celka, claiming they were alone together while Gerrit returned to public view after dropping off the canister.

Celka looped her arm through his in sousednia with a realism that had him checking true-life, expecting her to be standing at his elbow. Instead, she waited by the door, intense concentration on her face. The phosgene canister vanished from true-life when Celka dropped the concealment imbuement over it, flaring blue in sousednia. Then Celka extended the magic from the concealment ring—the one that hid her sousedni-shape—and the canister's blue glow in the neighboring reality winked out.

As far as Gerrit could tell, he looked natural, his left arm crooked, thumb looped casually through his weapons belt in true-life. He turned to Lucie and Filip for confirmation.

Lucie adjusted his uniform sleeve, shifting it beneath the canister so it wouldn't appear flattened, then squeezed his free hand. "You'll do great." Her confidence warmed him. Filip had his back and Celka's burning intensity had set him on this course, but Lucie was his anchor. She understood what he'd sacrificed, understood the brutal necessity of all they would accomplish.

"See you soon," Gerrit told Lucie, looking forward to building the resistance's army at her side.

Out in the corridor, Filip strolled casually at Gerrit's side while they trusted Celka to keep pace in sousednia. Her true-form stayed behind in their shared room—until they could ensure that the true-life path to the closet was clear. In the low light on sousednia's mountaintop, Gerrit couldn't even see her, but her sousedni-disruption made her arm feel heavy in his.

When they reached the stairs, Filip said through Nina, «*The corridor's empty, Celka. Now's your chance.*»

She left the bedroom with a surreptitious glance over her shoulder, then Gerrit turned the corner out of view. Losing sight of her made his shoulders itch, but he shoved the worry behind his mental walls. They'd spent weeks practicing for this. He had to trust that she could handle getting her true-form to a closet while keeping pace in sousednia.

Despite his mental walls, Gerrit wanted to hunch around the phosgene canister. Though he couldn't see it, its weight made him feel dangerously exposed.

CHAPTER FORTY-FOUR

CELKA STRUGGLED TO see enough of true-life to navigate the corridor as she kept her sousedni-shape anchored at Gerrit's side. She hadn't expected to need to move her true-form, so had concentrated her practice on sousednia. Using a sousedni-dislocation on Gerrit let her sweep along at his side, true-life's staircases and corners mattering only in the increased focus demanded by the distance. But that focus left little for true-life.

«*Wait, give me a second,*» Celka told Gerrit when she neared the closet, needing more true-life attention to open the door and get inside. In her haste, she barked her shins on something and swallowed a curse. Door pulled shut, she fumbled to light a match, using its tangerine glow to sit on the floor where she wouldn't cascade mops and brooms if she startled.

The match burnt out, and she returned her attention to sousednia.

She took a second to reorient back on Gerrit. His sousedni-shape wavered, translucent with most of his attention on true-life. She couldn't see true-life, though the play of spotlights on her high wire platform echoed the confines of the space, dustmotes hinting at the corridor walls, disturbed here and there by decorative vases or lamps or tables. Gerrit was his usual self, dressed in olive drab trousers and short-sleeved undershirt, though the shadows on his face were wrong—as they so often were these days. He still smelled of pine and ice, but another scent wove beneath it, the chill of stone, echoing the crunch of hobnailed boots. She pushed the worry aside. Once they killed the Stormhawk, he'd have no more excuse to not fully reintegrate.

«I'm set,» she said, *«let's go.»*

Silent, he started walking again, nearing two heat-shimmers spaced like they stood on either side of a door. He stopped before them, and Celka struggled to hear what he said, but sousednia didn't work that way.

She expected fear to coil off him, a smell of urine and damp stone that she knew from their resistance activities in the circus. But, apart from the chill of his warped sousednia, his conversation with the guards didn't seem to affect him. She wanted to ask what they were saying, but bit her tongue. She couldn't afford to distract him when an overly suspicious Yestrab Okhrana might wonder at his lapse.

One of the guards shifted, and Celka tensed—though what could she do but ensure the phosgene canister remained invisible? They moved away, into what must be the Stormhawk's room. She tracked them, true-life walls only forming a barrier in sousednia when she let them. Beyond, in the Stormhawk's room, she discovered another bozhk, this one sharp-edged, storm-blessed, the violet glow of a protection imbuement spooling off them across the room. Celka touched a hand to the pocket in her true-life jacket, the one holding the iron ring that rendered her sousedni-shape faint as a mundane's. In sousednia, she edged slightly behind

Gerrit, hoping his brighter sousedni-shape would conceal hers.

Near the storm-blessed bozhk, Celka discovered another bozhk heat-mirage, limned red from a combat imbuement. More searching revealed the fainter smoke-forms of two mundanes, one of them presumably the Stormhawk.

Celka shared what she'd learned, figuring that Gerrit knowing what he was walking into was worth the risk of distraction.

Minutely, Gerrit nodded. As they waited, she expected him to shift nervously, but he faced straight ahead, casual, one thumb looped in his belt the way he'd practiced holding the dummy phosgene cylinder. Celka tried to mirror his calm, tried to draw deep slow breaths, but couldn't help chewing her lip. Was the Stormhawk about to send Gerrit away?

The guard returned and, after an anxious moment, Gerrit stepped into the room.

Celka exhaled relief then redoubled her focus. Now was her most critical moment. As soon as Gerrit saw an opportunity, he'd set the canister down. She had to make certain the concealment imbuement continued to hide its physical shape, and had to stay close enough to it that Filip's iron ring would hide the magic's blue glow as well as masking her own sousedni-shape.

As Gerrit walked deeper into the Stormhawk's rooms, Celka kept his sousedni-shape between her and the storm-blessed Okhrana. Gerrit sat, and Celka crouched at his side where he held the canister. Waiting, waiting for... there. He leaned down as though to scratch at his ankle, discretely slipping the canister from his arm to the floor.

In practice, they'd found that the concealment imbuement muffled sound, and Gerrit had been reasonably confident he'd be able to set the canister on a rug. Celka hoped the combination would be enough, unable to spare the focus to check whether the guards had reacted. With the dummy canister, this had been the moment when she'd most often failed.

Already a headache needled her temples from the massive sousedni-dislocation, and the high wire platform wavered around her as she attempted to hold onto the phosgene canister. *The poison gas will choke its victim, fill their lungs with fluid. The canister compresses it, holding it in a tight prison of metal.* Celka let the object's purpose fill her mind.

«*Can I risk kicking it across the room?*» Gerrit asked through Nina after a moment that had probably involved conversation with his father. «*The bedroom is through a door. If they close it off, the gas won't even reach him. I think I can get a good angle to roll it through and up against the wall.*»

Celka licked dry lips. If he kicked the canister and she lost her sense of it, it could blink visible and expose their entire plot. If he left the canister where it was, all their planning might do no more than kill a couple of guards. «*How far will you have to kick it?*» Celka asked. Focused on phosgene's murderous purpose, she could almost feel the canister's dull steel beneath her hands on the high wire platform, but her record at keeping hold of it wasn't great when he'd tried kicking it in their practice sessions.

«*Four meters, maybe,*» Gerrit said.

«*Sleet.*» Celka drew a deep breath, grounding herself not only in the gas canister's purpose but the remembered feel of it in her arms—its weight, its texture, the softly ticking mechanism of its timed valve release, the sound barely covered by her concealment imbuement. She shifted her crouch so that she pressed her sousedni-hand against the cylinder's flat bottom. The concealment imbuement, she draped over it like a blanket, wishing she could spread it to the limit of the imbuement's weaves, but she was limited by the iron ring's ability to hide the concealment imbuement's glow. *«Can you point out where you're going to kick it?»*

Gerrit didn't respond immediately, and she waited, pulse pounding in her ears. Finally, he shifted on what she saw as a simple wooden chair on her platform, but which was probably ornate and richly upholstered in true-life. His gesture might have been a casual stretch, but one finger arrowed away. When Celka breathed deep of the space, she could sense an opening in the fall of dustmotes and the sweep of spotlights, a darkness behind true-life's open door.

«All right,» she said. *«Ready when you are.»*

A moment passed. She struggled to split her focus between the feel of the canister and Gerrit's sousedni-shape, focused on his legs, trusting him to keep his sousedni-shape tracking his true-form so she'd see it when he kicked out. He scuffed his boot on the platform grating, and Celka tensed, ready to move. But he didn't make contact with the cylinder—she didn't think. Then he did it again and she felt it, a dull metal clunk that echoed through her big top louder—she hoped—than the sound in true-life. The cylinder began to roll, and she crab-walked along beside it, insubstantial fingers brushing the canister's murderous sousedni-echo as it rolled.

When it stopped, Celka dared look around herself, trying to orient to where she was in the physical space. It didn't feel like she'd made it through the door.

«Gerrit? I'm at the cylinder. Is this where it's supposed to be?»

«Uh,» he said, and she remembered that she had a mundane's smoke-form. His sousedni-shape sharpened and, after what felt like forever, he glanced casually around.

«Sleet. It didn't roll far enough. I'll walk by it on my way out. Can you... indicate it for me somehow so I'm not kicking air?»

She sensed his focus snap off of her, back to his father.

Keeping her hand on the gas canister, Celka looked around. The storm-blessed Okhrana was the biggest threat. If Celka peeled back the sousednia shielding from Filip's ring, the concealment imbuement over the canister would glow bright as a spotlight to both Gerrit and the guard. But if she instead dropped part of the concealment imbuement, the Stormhawk himself or any of the three Okhrana could spot the canister in true-life.

«*Watch the ground in sousednia when you approach. I'll flash you the center of the cylinder, and we'll just have to hope the storm-blessed guard doesn't notice.*» It was a risk, but if Gerrit missed his kick or his angle was off, the canister might wind up somewhere even less useful and he'd have to risk another attempt.

Gerrit said nothing further, and Celka's nerves stretched as the minutes passed. This was supposed to be a quick conversation. What could Gerrit and his hail-eating father have to talk about? She tried to shake the thought. Focus. She glanced nervously up at the guards, worried one would walk this way and trip over the cylinder—she'd made it invisible, not insubstantial.

When she looked back at Gerrit, he was on his feet, almost to her.

She let out a startled *eep*, then panicked to realize she might have made the sound in sousednia. No time to check if the storm-blessed guard had noticed; Gerrit was almost to her. She opened the ring's imbuement like a flower, revealing a flash of the other concealment imbuement's blue glow. She slapped it quickly closed. «*Did you get that?*»

«*I did. Here goes.*» He swung his leg like an awkward step—and missed.

«*A little further forward.*»

Frustration rippled off him, a latrine stench that vanished almost as fast as she noticed it, then he kicked again, making contact.

The cylinder rolled faster this time, and she scrambled to keep up. A chill in her shoulder suggested she'd passed through something solid in true-life, then the cylinder torqued, twisting beneath her hand, and clunked to a stop. She thought.

Teeth gritted, she focused on the compressed gas—*coughing, lungs filling with fluid, choking to death while the doctors can do nothing*—searching for the cylinder in sousednia's abstract landscape. Her breath came quick by the time she rested her hand on the gray steel, confident she'd tracked its location.

Only then did she look up.

The guards and Gerrit were gone. She panicked before realizing the shape of her high wire platform had changed, the dust in the spotlights echoing a different room. She'd passed through the partition, Gerrit's kick perfectly angled roll the canister into the bedroom.

«*How'd I do?*» Gerrit asked, and she told him.

«*When you're out, could you describe the room for me?*» she asked.

«*I am out,*» he said.

Celka hunched over the canister with relief. «*Any problems?*»

«*No.*» His tone said otherwise. «*Nothing that affects you. Or the mission. How are you handling the dislocation?*»

Until he'd asked, she'd ignored the discomfort, but the question—and the release from the imminent danger of concealing the moving canister—brought her attention back to the pain knifing her temples. «*I'll manage.*»

«*You can do this, Celka,*» Filip said. «*You're strong. Just over an hour left.*»

She nodded, looking around sousednia, pushing through the true-life walls to spot the guards in the Stormhawk's sitting room. Despite her surprised *eep* and whatever true-life noise Gerrit's kick had made, they seemed relaxed.

«*So, the room,*» Gerrit said, and Celka let the echoes of true-life reshape sousednia so she could match her vague sense of her surroundings to Gerrit's glimpsed view of the bed and windows. Then she curled up to make her smoke-form as unremarkable as possible. To take some of the strain out of the dislocation, Celka echoed her sousedni-shape's hunched form in the true-life closet, and settled in to wait.

The strain of holding the sousedni-dislocation made time blur, worsened by the monotony of waiting, her true-form lulled by darkness while she struggled to keep her attention in sousednia sharp. The Stormhawk and his guards moved about, and she flinched when they neared the phosgene canister, but none of them tripped over it or reacted to her presence. Eventually, the Stormhawk settled into bed, one guard in the room with him, the two others in the adjoining sitting area.

«*Time.*» Filip's voice through their link startled her. «*Let's hope the scientists really did solve the dispersal problem.*»

Celka found herself holding her breath—as if she and the phosgene were physically in the same space—and forced herself to exhale. If all went well, she'd only need to hold the dislocation and concealment imbuements a little longer. The scientists had assured Lucie that fifteen minutes, if the canister opened in an enclosed room, would be plenty. Privately, Celka planned to hold the imbuements as long past that as she could: phosgene worked slow, so she wouldn't be able to gauge their success by the guards dropping to the floor. They'd have to trust that the timer worked, the valve opened, and the Stormhawk got his lethal dose. Celka didn't like it, but Filip had assured her it was better than the Okhrana turning the manor upside-down hunting an assassin.

«*Has anything changed?*» Gerrit asked after a few minutes, voice tense.

«*No,*» Celka said, wishing she had a way to tell whether the gas canister had really opened. If the release mechanism failed, all this would be for nothing and they would have tipped their hand with no way to discreetly extract the canister. «*Wait.*» The guard in the corner of the Stormhawk's bedroom had doubled over and seemed to be coughing. «*Should they be coughing?*» She focused, struggling to resolve the guard's heat-shimmer sousedni-shape. They'd put their hand over their mouth or nose, and strode quickly toward Celka.

She shifted to a crouch, as if they were closing to attack her, but they stopped in the doorway, and she could practically hear them cursing, hand waving the air as if... Oh, sleet. «*They smell something,*» she said. «*Filip, this was supposed to be undetectable!*»

«*What's happening?*» Gerrit demanded, even as Filip said, «*They shouldn't be coughing. It's too early. Phosgene takes hours to affect the lungs.*»

«*Well, they're coughing.*» Through the doorway that Gerrit had kicked the canister, Celka spotted the other two guards. The storm-blessed one waved the air like they smelled something foul, and the other, a mundane, doubled over. Then the guard in the Stormhawk's room rushed to the bed, shaking the Stormhawk. «*They're waking him.*» Celka's voice spiked high. «*Something's wrong!*» The mundane guard ran into the bedroom, hand over their face, headed for—«*Gerrit, were there windows in the bedroom?*»

«*I think so. There was one in the sitting room, but I don't think it opened. Celka, what's happening?*»

«*I don't know! Do the bedroom windows open?*»

«*Probably.*» Filip sounded like he clung to calm by his fingernails. «*The one in my room does.*»

«*Sleet.*» Celka leapt to her feet in sousednia. «*If they get the windows open, the gas will dissipate.*» She dropped the concealment imbuement—if they spotted the canister in true-life, too sleeting bad. She had bigger problems. In an effort of will, she snapped across the distance between herself and the mundane guard. Resolving their sousedni-shape was difficult, but they seemed to struggle with the window sash, giving Celka precious time. Bringing true-life and sousednia into contact, she kicked them in the backs of their knees. They stumbled, dropping to one knee, one hand up, gripping the sash, the other over their mouth and nose as they coughed. «Come on, stay down,» she muttered in sousednia, ignoring Gerrit's questions.

«*There's shouting,*» Filip said. «*Sleet, I think they've alerted the guards outside the room.*»

«*Can you delay them?*» Celka asked, horribly certain the answer was no. The Yestrab Okhrana would let every single person in the mansion die a horrible death before risking the Supreme-General.

The guard at the window dragged themself to their feet, and again Celka knocked them down, this time chancing a glance behind herself. «*Whatever was in that canister, it's affecting them* now, *not on some days-long delay.*»

«*Chlorine?*» Filip said. «*Did they give us the wrong gas?*»

«*Freezing sleet,*» Gerrit said, «*that'd be one storm-forsaken mistake.*»

But Celka was barely listening. The guard at the window had fallen to their hands and knees, coughing again, and didn't seem strong enough to rise, but the Stormhawk was no longer in his bed. As Celka swept aside the spotlit confines of the room, she discovered the two remaining guards propping the Stormhawk between them, all three nearing the door out of the suite.

Abandoning the guard at the window, Celka snapped over to the door. An imbuement glowed golden at the Stormhawk's throat—«*They've got some sort of healing imbuement on him,*» Celka said, panicked that she and Gerrit had been wrong, that it wouldn't matter that the gas was new, that the magic of past storm-cycles would combat it. But then the Stormhawk stumbled, doubling over to cough, leaning hard on the storm-touched guard who nearly crumpled beneath his weight. But the other guard lurched forward just as the door burst open, two storm-touched figures surging inside, swooping the Stormhawk up and dragging him out into the corridor and away. «*We've lost him!*» Celka said. «*The Okhrana got him out!*»

«*Get out of there,*» Gerrit snapped, and Celka didn't need to be told twice. She glanced over her shoulder, finding the window guard flat on the ground, then shattered the dislocation, her sousedni-shape snapping back into her true-form.

The return to the dark closet left her gasping, hands pressed into the rough floorboards. Her head spun, sparks of color behind her eyes, pain slicing her brain.

«*Filip, get into the corridor,*» Gerrit was saying. «*Give Celka the all-clear to get out of that closet. Celka, can you move?*»

«*I... don't know.*» Even breathing was a struggle, her body seeming to belong to someone else after so extended a dislocation.

«*You need to drop the imbuements,*» Gerrit was saying, «*get them back in the darkbag so they're not spotted on you. Get back to our room and get them to Lucie. She has to get out of here before the Okhrana lock the manor down.*»

Everything he said made sense, yet the world reeled, the darkness crushing her like a heavy, wet layer of snow. She fumbled in her pockets, fingers thick as sausages. She pulled out the jade carving, its bright blue glow illuminating nothing in true-life. Where was the darkbag? Right, around her throat, hung from her storm pendant. She struggled with the woolen pouch's ties, heart pounding in her ears, and slipped the carving inside. Its glow vanished from true-life and she reached into her other pocket for the iron ring's weaker glow.

«*Celka!*» Gerrit shouted through the link. «*Did you hear me? Get. Up.*»

«*The guards are scrambling,*» Filip said, calm but intense. «*They've already got people at the doors. Celka, the corridor's clear, but it won't last long. You need to listen to Gerrit. I'm coming down the hall. Get up and I'll meet you.*»

She got the ring out of her pocket and dropped it into the darkbag—except she missed, the ring cold where it slipped against her skin, caught in her breast band. She dug it out, still sausage-fingered, and finally got it into the bag. She yanked the ties closed.

Hands pressed against the floor, she wished desperately that she could rest. Instead, gritting her teeth, she shoved to her feet. Her knees buckled, but she caught herself on the closet door. She fumbled for the doorknob, finding only smooth wood. Searching blind in the darkness, she knocked into the handle of something—a broom, a mop—and it clattered against the shelves.

The door cracked open and she gasped, expecting red shoulders to drag her out, but it was only Filip. He caught her arm, and she fell into him, blinded by the light in the corridor, everything spinning as her headache spiked, and the time she'd spent separated from her true-form made it hard to control her limbs. He pulled her, stumbling, forward, then the door clicked closed and Filip turned her, one hand on her hips, pressing her back against the wall. She sagged against it for support and he leaned close, one hand slipping around the back of her head. «*We're not alone anymore,*» he said, voice through Nina warning. «*If I kiss you, this will look natural.*»

He shifted, broad shoulders blocking her view down the corridor—not that she could make anything focus anyway. «*Then kiss me,*» she said, heart hammering.

He did, his lips warm and soft, his hand on her waist a vital support. Back against the wall, the world still an agonizing blur of too-bright light, she closed her eyes, melting into his kiss as she had in Bludov before everything had gone to sleet.

"About sleeting time," a voice said, a little slurred but recognizably Hedvika.

Filip broke the kiss but drew back only enough to speak, not releasing Celka, his body still turned toward her, the tension barely visible in his jaw. "Do you mind?" The irritation in his voice could have been purely at the interruption.

"Not at all," Hedvika drawled. "Please go on. Though... I heard shouting. What happened?"

"Would you let go of my arm, please?" Another voice, smaller, deferential and a little afraid—but heart-stoppingly familiar. Lucie.

Filip's brown eyes met Celka's, and she saw the fear in them before he wiped it away. Now he did turn from Celka, hand around her waist to lock her hip to his—enough, barely, that she kept her feet.

Celka blinked the corridor into focus, discovering Hedvika, jacket missing, gripping Lucie's upper arm. Lucie wore a servant's uniform, but her hands were bound behind her back with satin rope that might have been a curtain tieback. Panic widened her eyes.

Shouts came from above, and the pounding of feet. Two Yestrab Okhrana burst into the corridor, another pair pounding down to the floor below, shouting gibberish that must have been code.

"Why are you dragging a servant around, Hedvika?" Filip's

voice hardened, acting as though a pair of Okhrana with rifles hadn't just stationed themselves a couple meters away, blocking their escape.

Hedvika jerked Lucie forward with a grip that blanched Lucie's brown skin. "Her? Found her in Celka's room."

"I was cleaning it," Lucie said, subservient voice quaking.

"Might have believed that if she hadn't tried to run," Hedvika said.

Lucie turned desperate eyes to them. "I turned her down, but she wouldn't let me go."

Hedvika's lips tightened, and Filip took a step forward, expression thunderous. Celka managed to stumble not too obviously at his side, slinging her arm around his waist. Cold, he demanded, "What is this, Hedvika?"

Hedvika glanced at Lucie, nostrils flaring, then back at Filip. "You recognize her?"

"I don't pay attention to the staff." An anger Celka didn't understand clipped his voice. "Let her go."

"I think not." Challenge edged Hedvika's slurred tone. Turning to the Okhrana, forcing Lucie to turn with her, she asked, "What's going on?"

"Have you seen any suspicious activity?" a storm-touched Okhrana corporal asked.

"No," Filip said, and Celka shook her head.

But Hedvika jerked her chin at Lucie. "Just her."

More Okhrana pounded up the stairs before she could say more. "Everyone out of your rooms," they shouted, going down the line and hammering their fists on doors with some variation of "Up. Now!" in a tone that left no room for dithering. More Okhrana ordered everyone to gather in the ballroom for questioning.

«Did you get Lucie out?» Gerrit asked, urgent through Nina.

«No,» Celka whispered. «*She's with us.*» Stomach churning, she cut Filip a glance. «*Maybe we can make a distraction, slip Lucie the concealment imbuements while the guards are questioning others. She could make a run for it.*»

«*Maybe.*» Filip didn't sound convinced.

Hedvika started for the stairs, jerking Lucie along. "Let's go."

Over her shoulder, Lucie caught Celka's gaze, whites too bright around her eyes.

How did this happen? Celka wanted to ask. *What went wrong?*

CHAPTER FORTY-FIVE

IN THE CHAOS of everything going wrong, Gerrit lost sight of Iveta. She'd been across the parlor from him, but must have slipped out while he'd focused on the link through Nina. Now the Yestrab Okhrana had ordered everyone out of the parlor, officers with more stars on their shoulders than him demanding answers and receiving only hard, suspicious stares.

Gerrit stepped out of the flow of people, catching a sergeant he recognized by sight. "What's happening? Is my father safe?"

"We'll handle it, sir," she said. "Go to the ballroom."

Gerrit wanted to protest—*to scream*—but the sergeant was just obeying orders. He needed to find Iveta or one of the Okhrana officers, get involved in the investigation so he could control the damage. He had to get Lucie out. Had to find out what had gone wrong.

In the ballroom, he scanned the milling uniforms for Okhrana officers, but they must have been with his father or securing the building. Sleet. He pushed through the crowd, headed for the main stairs leading to his father's rooms.

Lucie's in here somewhere. The thought crashed against his crumbling walls, threatening to choke him. He needed to get her out. He and Celka and Filip would be safe, but Lucie didn't belong. If anyone dug too closely into her story, he doubted it would hold up.

He spotted Filip in the crowd, taller than most of the guests, but stayed his course. Filip could handle himself and would take care of Celka—*kissing her, the sleet-licker*, but his mental walls dampened the jealousy, and he brushed it away.

"Gerrit, sir! Lieutenant Kladivo." Hedvika's shout deflected him, and he turned to find her pushing through the crowd. "There you are." A space opened between them, and Hedvika shoved someone forward.

Lucie fell to her knees on the marble floor, arms bound behind her back, cowering with the perfect subservience of terrified staff.

Gerrit's heart lodged in his throat, blood roaring in his ears. His mental walls cracked, but held enough for him to glower at Hedvika. "What is this?"

"Recognize her?" Hedvika asked.

Celka and Filip pushed to the edge of the crowd that now ringed Lucie. Celka caught her strazh's arm. "Hedvika, you're drunk. Stop making a scene."

Hedvika shook her hold without looking.

"I don't have time for this." Gerrit turned, hoping the snap in his voice sounded like impatience and that his walls would hold back his mounting panic.

"Then *make* time," Hedvika said. "I found her in your room."

"Cleaning it," Lucie murmured from the floor. "I was just doing my job."

"She cleans Usvit Hall," Hedvika said. Gerrit froze, flashing his attention to sousednia. The sun had risen too high in the sky, and the granite cliff face that was supposed to hold his emotions back was a mound of rubble. *They can't capture Lucie.* He focused, rebuilding the walls, shoving his panic down deep.

When he turned back to Hedvika, his calm barely quaked. "You're certain?"

Hedvika grabbed a fistful of Lucie's short black hair, jerking her face up toward Gerrit's. The terror in Lucie's eyes nearly undid him, but he clung to his control. "I've seen her in your rooms." When Gerrit didn't immediately reply, Hedvika glanced around. "I'm sure Corporal Shimunek would recognize her if you don't."

Gerrit took a measured step forward, scrambling to figure out what to say. Could he claim not to recognize Lucie? Claim Hedvika was mistaken, alcohol twisting a faint resemblance into recognition? But she was right, Corporal Shimunek was in the manor or its outbuildings, part of the bolt-hawk platoon that had accompanied them, and Shimunek had stood at his door often enough to identify Lucie.

"I have a sister," Lucie said, breathless and high. "Maybe you met her?"

"And your sister works in the Storm Guard Fortress, 'cleaning' Lieutenant Kladivo's rooms—just like *you* happen to do here?" Hedvika didn't release her hair.

Lucie squeezed her eyes shut, panting. "I... I don't know. I haven't talked to her in a while. Please... I didn't do anything wrong."

"She tried to run when the alarm sounded," Hedvika said. "That's why I tied her up."

Lucie tried to explain, but Gerrit spoke over her, cold and hard as if his shoulders were red. "Sub-Lieutenant Cizek"— he lifted his chin to Filip—"lead the investigation. See if you can verify her story."

A Yestrab Okhrana sub-lieutenant interrupted Filip's "Yes, sir."

"No need," the Okhrana said. "We'll take her from here." A quick gesture, and two other Okhrana dragged Lucie to her feet.

"This concerns me," Gerrit told the sub-lieutenant as the room erupted back into a babble of voices. "I'd rather my people conduct the interviews."

Two-headed Tayemstvoy hawks gleamed in the sub-lieutenant's ears, clutching bloody lightning bolts. "*We'll* conduct the interview, sir. You can have her when we're done."

Gerrit knew better than to argue. The Stormhawk had been attacked; the Okhrana would get answers. "Fine." He turned to Hedvika. "Good work, Bur. Cizek, go with the sub-lieutenant." To her, he said, "You won't mind if my strazh observes." He didn't make it a question, striding for the stairs without awaiting a reply. Ice coiled down his spine as he heard the sub-lieutenant order Hedvika to join them as well. She'd be debriefed, and whatever had led her to suspect Lucie—sleet-curse her interest in servants—the Okhrana would know.

Which meant what? Gerrit tried to think as he bounded up the stairs to find out what had happened to his father. He didn't know what sort of identification Lucie carried, but he bet it was forged. Had she made arrangements to be at the manor tonight as an actual servant, or was she inventing that alibi on the fly? Either way, he doubted it would hold up under investigation. If she was here officially, whoever had hired her would talk under Okhrana pressure, and Lucie's arrival at the manor on the same day as an attempt on the Stormhawk's life would be enough guilt by association for the Okhrana to tear her apart.

Worse, they would contact the Storm Guard Fortress's

Tayemstvoy to dig into Lucie's employment. They'd discover her missing—with what sort of alibi? That she was ill? A death in the family?—whatever it was, they'd unearth her trail, arrest anyone she'd so much as spoken to. How much of Captain Vrana's network would that unravel?

Sleet. Gerrit needed to warn Captain Vrana. But how? The telephone lines and telegraph cable out of the manor would be monitored, and the Yestrab Okhrana would have eyes on all the doors, guards on the gate. No one could get out—except possibly with a concealment imbuement.

Gerrit's only option, then, was to get Lucie herself out.

At that certainty, the pounding in his head eased. Beneath his mental walls, the goal focused him past his fear. Get Lucie out. Everything else was secondary.

Unfortunately, he had no time to plan, because the Yestrab Okhrana were challenging him, trying to send him back to the ballroom. If he lost authority here, allowed himself to be herded back amongst the masses, he'd become just another guest. To have any hope of giving Lucie an opening, he needed authority. He needed to be Lieutenant Kladivo, the Stormhawk's trusted son.

"Where is Iveta?" he demanded of the highest ranked Okhrana barring his way. "Is she with him? I need to see my father. This is *not* a discussion."

Finally they caved, a private showing him to a bedroom at the end of the hall, distant from the Stormhawk's room. Inside, Gerrit's father lay on the bed, undressed to the waist, the Okhrana doctor and her assistant blazing gold with healing imbuements, working over him while his breath rasped. Bandages covered his eyes.

Staff Sergeant Dolezal snapped a hand out, barring his way. Her storm-blessed sousedni-shape matched her true-form almost perfectly, only the shadows on her wrong.

"What happened?" Gerrit demanded. Several other Okhrana were stationed around the room, bright with active combat or protection imbuements, rifles in hand. He didn't see Iveta.

"Poison gas attack," she said. "We found a gas canister in his room."

"How did it get there?" He let worry sharpen his tone. "Shouldn't you have searched his room?"

The ice in her eyes could have shattered diamond. "We're looking into it. Do you know anything?"

"One of my people caught a servant she thinks is suspicious." He cursed himself the moment the words were out of his mouth, even as he knew he had to say them. "An Okhrana sub-lieutenant is questioning her downstairs."

Gerrit forced himself to turn back to his father, the staff sergeant's scrutiny making his skin crawl. "Will he live?" He tried to make his voice flat.

"One of the guards from his room is dead," the staff sergeant said with an edge that promised they'd be avenged. "He was trying to get the window open. The two other guards who were with him are in critical condition. One used a healing imbuement; it seems to have mitigated some of the effect of the gas, but it's too early to be certain."

"What was the gas?" Gerrit demanded, hoping the question would sound natural. "Why didn't he have protections?"

"Chlorine," the doctor said, not looking up.

Sleet. Gerrit felt his teeth grinding. Through Nina, he shared the information with Filip and Celka.

«*Stormy skies,*» Filip said, «*is that how they 'solved' the dispersal problem? It would work—*»

«*If it didn't sleet up the entire reason we were using phosgene to begin with,*» Gerrit said, reeling that the resistance could have made such a mistake.

"Son..." the Stormhawk rasped, and Gerrit pushed past Staff Sergeant Dolezal, dropping his connection with Filip and Celka.

"You shouldn't talk, sir," the doctor said. "You need to lie still. Stay calm." She cut a glance at Gerrit. "The gas is in his lungs, I can't tell if it's still doing damage, but exertion can only worsen it."

Gerrit nodded, but took his father's hand. "I'm here, sir."

"Find these hail-eaters." He erupted into a coughing fit, twisting to his side, the coughs wet and horrible.

Gerrit stood and snapped off a salute his father wouldn't be able to see. "Yes, sir!" He turned to the staff sergeant and, blessed by the Stormhawk's order, demanded to be brought to the Yestrab Okhrana captain.

FILIP SOMEHOW MADE it seem natural that he and Celka sat while the Yestrab Okhrana sub-lieutenant debriefed Hedvika. Celka was grateful for it, and grateful to have Filip at her side as her stomach twisted with fear. She shouldn't have been in this room—didn't *want* to be in this room with Lucie just next door, watched over by more Okhrana. Stomach churning, Celka kept expecting to hear screams.

She'd managed to slip Filip the concealment imbuements in their darkbag, but she was still wobbly on her feet, so Filip had used Celka's status as Gerrit's partner and Hedvika's tvoortse to keep them together. Celka clamped down on her fear and tried to focus as Hedvika described to the Yestrab Okhrana how she'd gone looking for Celka and, when no one answered the knock on her door, decided to wait in her and Gerrit's room. She'd found Lucie sweeping the floor. Lucie had apologized and tried to leave, but Hedvika had been drunk and horny and she'd told the girl to stay.

"She said she had duties and had to go." Hedvika kicked

back in her chair, relaxed despite reporting to the Stormhawk's terrifying guards. "She kept her face averted, trying to sidle past me. At the time, I thought she was playing coy, so I sweetened the deal. When she still claimed not to be interested, I..." Her gaze slipped to Celka, and she straightened, looking uncomfortable for the first time. But Hedvika focused back on the Okhrana officer, and her expression hardened. "Something felt off. I made her look at me. And that's when I recognized her."

"How certain are you that she's the same person?" the Okhrana asked.

"I propositioned her back at the Storm Guard Fortress." Hedvika made a moue of disgust. "She turned me down then, too. Probably trying not to be too memorable." She raised an eyebrow, like she and the sub-lieutenant were just discussing romance over drinks. "She must have been after something in our rooms. Are the Lieutenant and Captain Kladivo safe?"

"What happened next?" the Okhrana asked.

"I asked what she'd been doing at the Storm Guard Fortress, and she gave me that same line about a sister." She leaned forward over her knees. "She didn't say identical twin, and it would have to be. This is the *same* girl."

"And when the alarm sounded?" the Okhrana asked.

"I'd sat her on the bed to question her," Hedvika said. "She made a break for the door." She stretched her jaw. "Has a nasty right cross—especially for a servant. Put up a pretty good fight."

"This was *after* the alarm sounded, or before?" the Okhrana asked.

Celka's stomach churned, and she focused on Hedvika, expecting her strazh to take offense. Instead, Hedvika hesitated.

"After." Hedvika's gaze slipped again to Celka then back to the sub-lieutenant. "She turned me down. I respected that."

In sousednia, Celka breathed deep, chilled to find Hedvika's sousedni-cues muddy.

"How long did you question her?" the Okhrana asked.

Hedvika held the sub-lieutenant's gaze for a moment before saying, "Probably twenty minutes. I didn't like what she had to say."

Celka swallowed hard, the pieces clicking together—Filip's sudden anger in the corridor, Hedvika's cagy answers.

«*Breathe,*» Filip said through Nina but, from his tone, he might have been telling himself.

«*Was she planning to rape Lucie?*» Celka's voice shook. Hedvika was her *friend*. Sleet-storms, Celka was such an idiot to have ever trusted her—to have ever forgotten she was a regime toad. But that nausea tangled with memories of Hedvika braiding her hair and buying her honey cakes.

«*No,*» Filip said. «*But she has a tendency to push—and she's a hard person to turn down.*»

«*You're saying she's* justified?» Celka wanted to scream, wanted to cross the room right now and shake her strazh, demand to know what she was thinking keeping an innocent woman from leaving when Lucie had told her *no*.

«*I'm saying,*» Filip said, «*that we have to focus on saving Lucie's life.*»

The words felt like a slap, and Celka squeezed her eyes shut. He was right. They'd just tried to assassinate the Stormhawk, and Lucie had been captured. They had to stay smart. Celka couldn't let on her horror at Hedvika's actions because she shouldn't care that much about a stranger when Gerrit's father had just been attacked. The Yestrab Okhrana certainly wouldn't. They cared only about one thing: whether Lucie had been involved in a plot against the Stormhawk.

She made herself focus. She needed to know everything Hedvika told the Yestrab Okhrana, because information was their only weapon right now. If they could push suspicion off Lucie long enough, they might be able to get her out.

The Okhrana sub-lieutenant had Hedvika recount everything Lucie had told her, then thanked Hedvika for being so attentive.

Celka couldn't look at her strazh as they left the interview room, worried she'd fail to keep the disgust off her face. Out in the corridor, Filip said, "It's late. Celka, you should get some sleep." He called after the sub-lieutenant who'd started toward where the guards had taken Lucie. "I assume Specialist Prochazka is free to return to her room?"

At the sub-lieutenant's agreement, Hedvika took Celka's arm. "I'll go with you. We may not have caught all the resistance *dogs*."

Celka cast a desperate glance at Filip.

"You should go to bed, too, Hedvika," he said. "I'll send some bolt-hawks to guard Celka's door."

Hedvika didn't let go of Celka's arm, and the proprietary way her strazh hung onto her suddenly made Celka's skin crawl. "Good. I'm still not leaving her alone."

When Filip had to hurry after the sub-lieutenant or be shut out of Lucie's interrogation, Celka yanked her arm from Hedvika's grip. "I can walk on my own," she snapped, glad she'd recovered enough that it wasn't a lie.

Hedvika shrugged, strolling at her side like nothing was wrong, though her gaze darted about, watching for threats—or more servants she could intimidate into a tumble. Celka balled her hands into fists, her jaw so tight she thought it might crack.

At her room, she tried to close Hedvika out, but her strazh pushed in with a frown like she didn't understand why Celka was being unreasonable.

"What in *hailstorms* were you doing with her?" Celka demanded as soon as she got the door shut.

"What?" Hedvika said, dismissive. "The cleaning girl—or

whatever she is? Resistance dog." She turned away like Celka had asked about the weather, crossing to the windows, peering out before drawing the curtains. "You weren't here. She was cute. I didn't know she was a *traitor* when I propositioned her."

"When you *ignored* her refusal and wouldn't let her leave?"

Hedvika's expression hardened, and Celka became suddenly, deeply aware that she was alone in a room with a regime boot-licker who'd gleefully thrown a woman to the Yestrab Okhrana. "I would have let her go if she hadn't looked familiar," Hedvika said.

Celka's nails bit into her palms. "Would you have? You were drunk." Hedvika had been laughing and tipsy when Celka left the party to begin the assassination, and her words had been slurred when she'd first come out into the corridor dragging Lucie. Though she seemed to have mostly sobered by now.

Hedvika glanced to the side, uncomfortable like she'd been when talking to the Okhrana. "So maybe I kissed her." She met Celka's gaze again. "That's *how* I realized she was so familiar. After that, it's just what I said. I recognized her from Usvit, and she shouldn't have been here. But when I kissed her, I just thought she needed a little encouragement—and to know who she was turning down."

Celka's stomach twisted again. Maybe Hedvika just meant reminding Lucie she was a Storm Guard officer, but a coiling darkness like motorcar exhaust in Hedvika's sousedni-cues suggested a deeper evasion.

Struggling to make the question sound casual, Celka asked, "Who is your father?"

Hedvika rocked back on her heels, panic crossing her face before she was back to insouciance. "Dad's a doctor. He's my primary name."

Truth coiled with lies in sousednia, and Celka asked, "And your other father?"

"Doesn't matter."

"Then it won't matter if you tell me," Celka said.

Hedvika looked away, and Celka thought she was going to refuse to answer. But softly, Hedvika said, "Major Karel Rychtr."

Major Rychtr. The name struck like a blow across the face, like threats snarled into her ear. Memories of Major Rychtr still woke Celka drenched in sweat from nightmares.

Celka backed away from Hedvika until the door stopped her. Staring at the woman she'd called her friend, she groped for the doorknob, clutching it, but terrified to open it. Is this what Lucie had felt? After Lucie had refused to tumble her, had Hedvika casually mentioned that her father was a Tayemstvoy major before sitting Lucie down on the sleeting *bed* to 'question' her?

"Is *Rychtr* your primary name?" Celka managed barely a whisper. When she'd first joined her squad, she remembered people stumbling over Hedvika's family name, glancing at her nameplate and seeming to shake themselves. She'd dismissed it at the time, assuming they just didn't know her well, but they *did* know her, they'd all gone to the Storm Guard Academy together.

Hedvika shrugged, but Celka knew her well enough to read her tension. Sleet, knew her? She'd *never* known her. Hedvika *Rychtr*.

"Captain Kladivo thought it might damage our ability to work together," Hedvika said. "She ordered me to use my secondary name."

Celka grasped after her anger, blowing on its flames. If she was angry, she wasn't about to piss herself with fear. She'd slept in a bunk next to *Major Rychtr's daughter* for months. Celka had leaned on her shoulder, called her friend—and it was all a *lie*. "So you're disobeying orders now?"

Hedvika narrowed her eyes. "No. She ordered me not to tell you... until I thought you were ready."

"And when was that going to be?" Celka asked. "Never?"

"Obviously you're not ready now! So my father's Major Rychtr, so *what*? I'm sorry he questioned you, but you *weren't* innocent. He was doing his job—looking for Gerrit, who *you* were hiding. So yeah, I imagine it was unpleasant. Father can be sleeting scary if you cross him, but you were a *criminal*." Hedvika closed on her, and Celka realized she'd never seen her strazh with her claws out. She knew the Storm Guard twisted their cadets into regime-kissing monsters, but all these months, they'd treated her like one of their own. Monsters could be kind to other monsters. But as Hedvika stalked toward her, the same deep terror she'd felt before Major Rychtr made Celka want to cower.

The door pressed into her back, the metal knob cold beneath her grip. But Celka wasn't a civilian anymore, to be terrified into mute obedience. "What you did to that girl was wrong."

"She's a resistance dog."

"You don't know that!" Celka spat.

"She tried to run," Hedvika said, icy, like it proved Lucie's guilt.

"Because *you* refused to see her as a person, with rights to her own body."

Hedvika slammed her palm into the door by Celka's head. "That's not *why* she tried to run!"

Celka flinched but refused to break from Hedvika's gaze. "Look me in the eye, Hedvika, and tell me you're absolutely certain of that. Tell me you've *never* ignored someone's protests because you wanted to have sex with them and could terrify them into obeying." When Hedvika hesitated, Celka said, "Maybe it doesn't matter who your father is. But it matters who *you* are."

The cruel anger in Hedvika's face trembled, and Celka focused hard on true-life to ignore the sousedni-cues that didn't match a Tayemstvoy major's heartless daughter.

Finally, low, Hedvika said, "Get out of my way, Prochazka."

When Celka let go of the door handle, Hedvika shoulder-checked her aside and strode out without a backward glance.

Celka slammed the door behind her, leaning against it, trembling. She shoved a fist to her mouth, breathing hard, choking down both the sob and the scream that threatened to escape. When no one tried to open the door, Celka sunk down it to sit with her knees pulled tight to her chest. She pressed her head back against the wood until the ridges of its grain dug into her skull. Tears tracked down her cheeks.

Outside, she heard the occasional thump of boots, the shout of raised voices. She reached for Nina's link, desperate to feel less alone, but betrayal swirled up to choke her throat. Gerrit and Filip must have known who Hedvika was this entire time—and they'd said *nothing*.

She wanted to scream at both of them, and suddenly she was angry at herself for curling up on the floor. She paced the room, wishing she had something to smash, something to throw. She wished, stupidly, she could go to Hedvika's room and practice hand-to-hand fighting with her friend, see Hedvika grin and tell her she was getting better.

Grabbing a pillow from the bed, she slammed it against the wall. *She's not your friend! She's never been your friend!* But the pillow was too soft, useless. She needed a weapon.

A weapon—sleet.

Red haze darkened her vision, and Celka dropped the pillow, stumbling back. She was pulling on combat—of *course* she was sleeting pulling on combat. She needed to pound Hedvika Rychtr's face in and shoot the Okhrana so she could save Lucie!

Balling her hands into fists, she pressed her back against the wall and struggled to quell the raging nuzhda. She hadn't pulled on combat out of control in almost two months. She thought she was past this. But as sousednia blotted out true-life, the practice wire's steel cable dug ridges into her palm as Tayemstvoy surrounded Pa, beating him to the ground. Tayemstvoy, like Hedvika's father. Tayemstvoy, like the Yestrab Okhrana holding Lucie prisoner.

But as Vrana rounded on Celka in sousednia, Celka wasn't the child who'd cowered beneath the woman's blows. In her Storm Guard specialist uniform, she wore a pistol at her hip. True-life tracking sousednia, she dropped her hand to it, a practiced motion releasing the snap that held the pistol in its holster. Filip had the concealment imbuements. He was in the room where the Okhrana were interrogating Lucie, also armed. The bolt-hawks outside Celka's room wouldn't protest as she left—they trusted her; she was one of them now. She'd warn Filip through Nina on her way; he'd shoot the guards holding Lucie, and together they'd...

She faltered, rational thought edging through the combat haze. The concealment imbuement would only cover one person when they ran.

Celka's combat nuzhda shuddered, sousednia double-exposed. The high wire pressed into her feet beneath the big top even as she raised her pistol in the back lot to aim at the Tayemstvoy beating Pa.

If she strode into Lucie's cell and started shooting, she might be able to get Lucie out, but she and Filip would be captured, Gerrit would probably be implicated, and who even knew if Lucie would be able to get away? A tall iron fence surrounded the manor house, and the Yestrab Okhrana patrolled outside with dogs.

Pulse pounding in her ears, Celka managed to shred her

combat nuzhda. She locked her pistol back in its holster, gasping deep breaths of her core sousednia's sawdust and manure before dropping to her knees in front of Nina's crate and activating the snake's imbuement. As her true-life grounding sharpened, she closed her eyes, imagining Filip beside her, singing the Song of Calming. She made herself breathe, crossing the high wire in a sousedni-dislocation that sharpened her exhaustion. Hedvika had lied to her, had ignored Lucie's initial refusal—whether out of suspicion or an entitled lack of respect—but Celka could not dwell on it. Right now, Lucie needed help.

Celka couldn't win this fight head-on.

Returning to her true-form, Celka reached for Gerrit and Filip through Nina's link.

«*Lucie's sticking to her story,*» Filip said. «*They're almost done questioning her.*»

«*Which means we might have an opportunity while they're waiting to hear back from the fortress about her supposed sister,*» Gerrit said. «*I'm helping the Okhrana question the staff and guests. Let me know when they're done questioning Lucie. I might be able to arrange a distraction to draw some of the Okhrana away.*»

Not wanting to ask, but needing to know, Celka asked, «*Filip, have they hurt her?*»

His pause felt longer than could be needed to focus on whatever was happening in true-life. «*She should still be able to escape.*»

Celka squeezed her eyes shut, shuddering at the memory of Major Rychtr pinning her to the floor and growling threats. Lucie had warned that the Okhrana would be worse.

«*We'll get her out.*» Gerrit sounded like he believed it.

CHAPTER FORTY-SIX

BARELY HAD GERRIT dropped the link through Nina when Iveta entered the room where he was interviewing one of the kitchen staff with an Okhrana corporal. Iveta met his gaze and jerked her chin for him to join her. He told the corporal to continue without him.

Iveta strode down the service corridor. "We've got her."

Gerrit rushed to keep up, cold fear clambering down his spine. "Got who?"

"That servant Rychtr found, the one she recognized from Usvit Hall. We just got word from the Storm Guard Fortress. The servant matching her description used the exact same name and identification number. The Okhrana think her identity card is forged. She's the thread we need to unravel this entire conspiracy."

Iveta's words came to Gerrit from down a long tunnel. He didn't realize he'd stopped walking until Iveta turned, several meters down the corridor.

"Come on," she said. "I thought you'd want to help me question her."

"I do," Gerrit made himself say, but couldn't make himself move.

A frown flitted across Iveta's features before she caught his arm. "It's not your fault you didn't suspect her. Until tonight, she was just another servant. Sleet, she could have cleaned my room, too, I don't know." A flinty hardness settled over her expression. "The Storm Guard's Tayemstvoy will be making plenty of arrests tonight."

That shook Gerrit. What happened tonight affected more than the four of them. If Lucie gave the Okhrana the names of Storm Guard contacts, the Tayemstvoy could tear apart the resistance. Gerrit had to get her out. Which meant he needed to play out this interrogation flawlessly so he could go back in once Iveta had finished her questioning. Maybe he'd be able to slip Lucie the concealment imbuements and a handcuff key to use after he left. She'd need a weapon too, to kill the guards and escape. It was possible. If he could get through the initial questioning without revealing how much he cared about her.

"Good." Gerrit made his voice hard. "I just need to use the facilities. Don't start without me."

Seated on a closed toilet, Gerrit evaluated his mental walls. He wanted to wall off every last memory and emotion that had ever made him soft, but he needed to be able to communicate through Nina and keep sight of his resistance loyalties. Unfortunately, Lucie was deeply entwined with all their planning. Still, he'd stripped emotion from his memories before. He could do this. First, he completely buried the times Lucie had supported him through reintegrating his mind; of their assassination planning, he left only cold facts.

By the time he rejoined Iveta, his determination to free Lucie had become one of cold pragmatism.

Two enlisted Yestrab Okhrana guarded the door and followed them inside. The parlor's handsome furnishings had been pushed to the sides, leaving Lucie alone in the center of the ornate room. She sat on a plain wooden chair, curled over her knees, hands bound behind her and locked to the chair back. In her servant's costume, she looked small and plain.

Iveta took a handcuff key from one of the guards and released Lucie's arms. Lucie looked up at her, fearful-hopeful as Iveta helped her to her feet, expression falsely compassionate. Iveta flicked two fingers, and one of the guards leapt forward and pulled the chair away. "Now, Lucie," Iveta said gently, "how about you tell me the truth about what you're doing here."

Lucie started into a story about coming to the manor house looking for work, and Iveta tightened her grip warningly on Lucie's arm. "We know you were at the Storm Guard Fortress until three days ago," she said, still deceptively gentle. "You used the same identification card to start work on Usvit Hall's cleaning staff two months ago. We know you were part of a conspiracy to assassinate the Stormhawk—a conspiracy which has *failed*." Iveta clipped the word, her benign expression hardening into something every bit the Stormhawk's daughter. Lucie flinched away, but Iveta's hold stopped her retreat. When Iveta spoke again, the menace folded away, suggesting someone hard but fair. "You can tell me who else was involved and where you got the poison gas, and I can see that you're released. Or... this can go *very* badly for you."

Lucie swallowed visibly, eyes darting around, landing briefly on Gerrit. He kept his own expression hard—*no relief from this quarter*—and Lucie turned back to Iveta, jerking a frightened nod. Gerrit let out a breath, relieved Lucie hadn't revealed their connection.

Voice small, hesitant, Lucie said, "I was sent to the Storm Guard Fortress to get intelligence on imbuement mages and on the Stormhawk."

"Sent by whom?" Iveta asked.

"I don't know," Lucie said, eyes wide and trustworthy. "I got my orders through a dead drop. It had travel papers and instructions."

Iveta let that slide, but Gerrit suspected she'd have more questions. She'd circle back to it once they'd gotten Lucie's full story—it's what he'd do if he were leading the interrogation. Lucie explained that she'd searched the rooms she'd cleaned, but hadn't found much. She'd tried to listen in to conversations and had reported what she heard through another dead drop. When Iveta insisted, Lucie scuffed the floor but explained the details of where and how she left her messages. She was convincing enough that Gerrit feared it was true. But he knew Lucie—*did he?*—and she wouldn't break so easily. He questioned his read on her; their interactions had been coldly logical. Maybe he was a fool to expect her to hold up under questioning.

"And what?" Gerrit asked when Lucie said nothing about him. "You decided that overhearing conversations wasn't enough?" Lucie had been in and out of his room a handful of times while Corporal Shimunek was on duty at his door. If he didn't dig into why, it would look suspicious. He approached her, arms crossed, feeling nothing but cold disdain.

"They said I wasn't learning enough. I was..." Lucie glanced up at him, then dropped her eyes to his boots. "I was supposed to seduce you."

Iveta turned to Gerrit, brow raised.

Gerrit fixed his gaze on Lucie. "Not everyone has a penchant for the staff."

Iveta snorted. "What about tonight? Who did you work with?"

"No one," Lucie whispered. "It was just me."

"Walk me through it," Iveta said, a warning edge in her voice.

Lucie's tale was well-constructed, a series of dead drops and written instructions that she burned, leading her here, asking after a job just as the household staff was stretched thin by the Stormhawk's upcoming visit. She'd found the gas canister tucked in a storage closet, and her cleaning job gave her access to the Stormhawk's rooms. "We're taught never to meet anyone face-to-face." Lucie looked between Iveta and Gerrit with desperate eyes. "Please. I didn't even know what I was putting in his room. I just followed instructions. I *had* to."

"Had to?" Iveta asked.

Tears welled in Lucie's eyes, but she spoke through them. "My father was sick, and we couldn't afford the medicine to save him. But then I got a letter promising to get what he needed if I just took this job at the Storm Guard Fortress. My pa didn't want me to, but he's all the family I have, and I couldn't just let him die. After I got them some of the things they wanted, I tried to get out, but they threatened to expose me. Their notes kept saying I was a criminal now and if I didn't keep following orders, they'd expose me and my pa. I'm *sorry*." She burst into tears. "I didn't know what I was doing. I just wanted to save my pa."

"Shh." Iveta put an arm around Lucie's shoulders. "It sounds like you had no choice. But you do now. Tell us who really recruited you."

Lucie's breath caught, but only for an instant. She pulled away from Iveta and shook her head. "I never—"

"Come now." Iveta managed to sound both stern and compassionate. "You wouldn't have believed a letter. Who recruited you? If what you're saying is true, it's not your fault what you've done. Help me dig out the rotten grain before it spoils the whole bushel. Who recruited you?"

Lucie hesitated before finally answering, giving Iveta a name and a description. Iveta nodded, but again, in that same reasonable tone, pushed on Lucie's claims of a dead drop at the Storm Guard Fortress. Here, Lucie insisted. She hadn't met anyone. And again, digging back through her story about the manor house, Iveta pushed for details, but Lucie held firm. "I'd tell you if I could. I swear on the Storm Gods I didn't meet with anyone."

Iveta's face became a mask of disappointment. "I thought you could be reasonable."

"I'm telling the truth," Lucie said, desperate, pleading. "Please. Please, believe me."

Iveta turned away, calling for the Okhrana sergeant. "Find some hooks we can install in that ceiling beam"—she pointed overhead. "And fetch a length of rope." She turned a cold gaze back to Lucie. "Or you could start telling the truth."

"I am," Lucie whispered, terrified, gaze slipping to Gerrit.

Iveta waved the sergeant off, then turned to Gerrit, tipping her head. "You want to try your hand while we wait for supplies?"

Meeting Lucie's terrified gaze, he realized there was one detail Iveta hadn't pressed on—whether by mistake or design. Verifying his mental walls still held, he asked, "Why were you in my room tonight?"

"I was just doing my job. The instructions told me to keep doing my job."

"None of the other cleaning staff were in the guest quarters." He'd learned that from his interviews.

"I... but... that's what they told me to do."

Gerrit backhanded her across the face, startling himself, the motion coming seemingly from outside him. Low, he said, "Tell me the truth."

"I am," Lucie insisted. "I swear it."

Behind his mental walls, Gerrit heard screaming, but he found himself turning to Iveta, cold. "You're right. This is going nowhere." The Okhrana sergeant returned with a step ladder and dark metal eye-hooks. "Tie her up for the night. We can get some sleep, work her over in the morning."

Lucie edged backward, arms clutched tight to her chest, glancing between them and where the guards had begun installing the hooks.

Iveta raised a brow. "Sleep if you want, brother." She focused back on Lucie. "I have plenty of questions to get us through the night."

Gerrit's stomach lurched. Iveta torturing Lucie helped no one. He needed to get Lucie alone in order to—he shoved away the thought. The details didn't matter. "She's not going anywhere," he told Iveta. "Leave her to consider her options. We can contact the Tayemstvoy in her hometown, discover whether anything she's told us is true."

A cold smile curled Iveta's lips. "Oh, we will." She didn't turn to Gerrit, gaze focused on Lucie in a way that reminded him of Celka's python watching a rat. "But I think Lucie's smart enough to understand her options." The Okhrana finished installing the first eye-hook, and the sergeant asked Iveta where to place the second. She pointed, then returned her gaze to Lucie. "All you have to do is tell us the truth. You will eventually, anyway."

Lips pressed in a flat line, Lucie wrenched her gaze away from Iveta's. When she met Gerrit's eyes, her intensity shook something deep beneath his walls, a memory of sitting with her on his bed, knees touching, that fire in her eyes as they discussed—he slammed more stones into place, locking the moment away.

"You want to know why I was in your room?" Her voice shook, but its tenor had changed.

His stomach sunk. *No*, he wanted to say. Instead, he crossed his arms and lifted his chin, waiting.

"I was going to kill you."

"How?" Gerrit didn't know how he kept his voice cold. *Don't*, he wanted to tell her. *Don't say any more. Stick to your cover story. I can still get you out.* "You were unarmed."

"But you wouldn't have been." Hatred flared in her eyes. He nearly stumbled back, it felt so real. Slow so they wouldn't see her as a threat, Lucie raised a hand and drew a line across her throat. "One more Kladivo dead. And your storm-blessed partner—one more traitor who couldn't misuse the Storm Gods' gifts." Gone was the frightened girl blackmailed into supporting the resistance. In her place stood someone brilliant and beautiful and strong. *Stop talking!* Gerrit wanted to scream. *Don't do this.* "After you, I was going to kill your sister." She cut a glance at Iveta, back straight, head high. "It doesn't matter if you execute me. Someone else will come, and sooner or later we will *succeed*. Bourshkanya will be free!"

Gerrit punched her—hard, up under her solar plexus. She folded, unable to draw breath, and he slammed his fist down on where her shoulder muscle met her neck. Lucie collapsed on the floor.

Iveta toed Lucie in the side with her boot. "Such bravery. You think that if you shout in our faces, we'll believe your lies?"

Lucie pushed up to hands and knees, struggling for breath, diaphragm still spasming after Gerrit's blow. Trying to stand, she stumbled, but eventually got to her feet and spat on Iveta. The white glob landed on her jacket. "They're not lies, you monster."

Iveta raised her hand, and Gerrit expected her to strike Lucie. But she just pulled a handkerchief out of her pocket and wiped her jacket clean. "Oh, little dog," she said, falsely sweet, "you have no idea." To the Okhrana sergeant, she said, "Have her stripped and bound. I want her hanging from the rafters." A few steps from the door she paused, turning back to Lucie, who'd gone gray. "Make sure her feet can't touch the ground." She held Lucie's gaze a moment longer, a predator watching her prey, then tuned away. "Gerrit, join me outside."

Roaring sounded in Gerrit's ears as he made himself turn to follow his sister.

Motion flashed in the corner of his eye, and he reacted on reflex. Lucie's lunge closed the distance between them, and she grabbed the pistol at Gerrit's hip, agilely snapping the holster open even as Gerrit pinned her hand to the gun with his own. With his off hand, Gerrit punched her in the face. She stumbled, but kept her grip, yanking the pistol free. He caught her wrist and twisted, shifting her aim to the ceiling so the first shot shattered only plaster. But she'd trained at the Storm Guard Academy, too, and instead of trying to wrench free, she stepped inside his reach and drove her elbow into his face.

Her elbow smashed into his eye, and he lost his hold on the gun.

A shot cracked the air, and Gerrit failed to draw breath, hand pressed to his throbbing eye, struggling to see through pain-tears.

He blinked them aside in time to see two Okhrana tackle Lucie. His gun went flying from her hand. She fought, but blood spread bright from her thigh, and in heartbeats, she was face down on the floor, the guards on her back, handcuffs locking her wrists behind her back.

Stone-faced, Iveta holstered her pistol and crossed to Lucie, neatly avoiding the blood pooling on the rug. Impassive, she asked, "Who trained you?"

"Self-taught," Lucie choked out.

Iveta nodded to the sergeant. He wrenched Lucie's

bound hands up, tearing a cry from her throat. A flick of Iveta's fingers, and the guard relaxed his hold fractionally. "I've changed my mind," Iveta said with cool deliberation. "Sergeant, you have a specialist here?"

"Yes, sir," he said.

"Bind the wound so she doesn't bleed to death, then let your specialist work on her." She crouched next to Lucie's head, waiting until Lucie met her gaze. "As they make you scream, remember that you brought this on yourself. *I* would have been merciful."

Ignoring Lucie's choked sob, Iveta stood, waving for Gerrit to join her as she strode to the door. He made himself collect his fallen pistol, struggling to ignore Lucie's panicked breathing. As the door to the bloodied parlor closed behind them, his chest felt too tight, the edges of his vision gray.

Iveta looked him over. "You want to get a drink?"

Not with you, he nearly snarled. He squeezed his eyes briefly shut, focusing on the pain from Lucie's blow and the cold granite wall beneath his hands in sousednia. "I'm fine."

"Uh-huh." Iveta dropped her stone interrogator's face. "You look ready to pass out—and it's not just the eye. First assassination attempt messes with your head."

He flinched. How had she realized his part in it? Then his mind caught up, remembering Lucie's snarled *I was going to kill you.* "It's not my first." His vision grayed further, granite walls crumbling. "When they attacked Mother, they could have killed me too."

Iveta patted his arm, then her hands on his face made him flinch. Her fingers were cool as she turned him to look at his eye. "We should have Father's doctor look at this."

Suddenly desperate to get away, he said, "I'm sure she's busy."

"She's already done what she can for him." Iveta grabbed his arm, expression hardening as she glanced over her shoulder. "And we won't be needed in there for a while." She tugged him away from the door.

"I just need to lie down," he said.

"Doctor first." Her tone refused all arguments and, remembering the cruel edge to her voice as she handed Lucie to the Okhrana, he followed, struggling to keep his crumbling mental walls from crushing him.

CHAPTER FORTY-SEVEN

FILIP STRUGGLED TO contain his galloping panic as Gerrit paced the bedroom, suggesting increasingly outlandish plans for how they'd free Lucie from the parlor the Okhrana had turned into an interrogation cell. Her distant screams, echoing through the manor, weren't helping.

The flesh around Gerrit's right eye was swollen, purpled with a bruise that looked days old instead of hours, his eyes bloodshot. Filip had never seen Gerrit this close to breaking, even after the Tayemstvoy had driven Branislav storm-mad and Gerrit thought he was next.

«*We have to get her out,*» Gerrit repeated like he was saying it for the first time, like Filip and Celka hadn't both been struggling alongside him to come up with a functional plan. Filip needed to calm Gerrit down before he'd have any chance of getting him to see reason.

Unless he simply abandoned reason. Gerrit certainly had.

Desperation brightened Gerrit's eyes. «*We can't leave her with them.*»

When Gerrit had first admitted to walling off memories,

Filip had thought the idea reckless and dangerous. Now, he wondered how he could convince his best friend to rebuild whatever walls had allowed him to question Lucie at Iveta's side. If someone came to Gerrit's door now—and they could if Lucie broke, if she let even the slightest hint of their involvement slip—the entire charade could break down. *«I have a plan,»* Filip said before realizing he was going to speak.

When Gerrit and Celka both turned to him, hopeful, a cold lump formed in his stomach. Was this really the best solution? Filip swallowed hard, wishing he could believe otherwise. But Lucie had seen it too. Protecting the resistance was more important than her safety. That had to be why she'd claimed she'd been trying to kill Gerrit, why she'd attacked him.

«I can get her out.» Filip made his voice confident, left himself no room for doubt, no room to dwell on the lie of omission Celka might detect.

«How?» Gerrit asked.

«It's better you don't know,» Filip said. *«I'll use the concealment imbuements to get to her. You both need to stay here, be my alibi. I'll have to wait until I can get into the room where they're interrogating her. It might take a while. Get some sleep if you can.»* He pulled his storm pendant up from beneath his shirt, opening the second charging pouch that held the imbuements he'd taken from Celka.

Celka caught his wrist, and his chest squeezed. She stared up at him with her wide green eyes, desperate and searching. He made himself meet her gaze, trying not to let any hint of his plan show. Her fingers wrapping his wrist were cold. Her eyes dropped to the knife at his hip before she met his gaze with a determination that reminded him of their kiss in the corridor, their kisses in Bludov. Privately through Nina, the link connecting just the two of them, she said, *«You're going to save her.»* She made it a statement, but it felt like an absolution. She knew—or at least suspected. Her cold fingers squeezed his wrist in support.

Expanding their link to include Gerrit, she said, *«Good luck.»*

Filip nodded, relieved she understood, more relieved she hadn't let on to Gerrit.

«Are you sure you can do this alone?» Gerrit asked as Filip slipped the iron ring onto its familiar place on his thumb. *«You don't need us to make you a distraction?»*

Filip activated the ring to hide his sousedni-shape from any storm-blessed Okhrana, connecting with its weaves as easy as breathing after a month spent holding it active in the circus. Meticulously, he walled off its nuzhda before focusing on Gerrit. *«A distraction won't help. I need you to be my alibi.»* He gripped Gerrit's shoulder, struggling to look confident and calm as he held his best friend's bloodshot gaze.

Gerrit clasped his hand hard, and Filip was afraid he would demand details. If Gerrit pressed, all Filip would be able to give was the truth—the solution Gerrit should have seen well before now. What had happened between Gerrit and Lucie that he would risk himself and the entire resistance for her?

It didn't matter, not right now. He had to save Lucie—and the rest of them—while he still could. *«Trust me,»* Filip said. *«Let me handle this.»*

Finally, Gerrit gave him a solemn nod. *«Thank you.»*

Filip squeezed his best friend's shoulder, then dove into memory to activate the imbued jade carving. He draped its azure nuzhda fabric over himself, vanishing from true-life. Once he'd gotten the painful-desperate nuzhda locked behind mental walls, he cast one last glance at his best friend, wondering if their friendship would survive what he was about to do.

He couldn't linger on the question or he'd hesitate, and

every passing second risked all their lives. «*Celka, can you tell me when the corridor's clear?*»

Gerrit had dismissed the bolt-hawks guarding his door, ordering them to join the rest of the platoon searching for more rezistyenti, so Filip didn't have to worry about them wondering why the bedroom door opened when no one came out. Celka nodded, and Filip waited, tense, touching his knife's hilt.

Finally, Celka spotted an opening, and Filip slipped out, stealing down the corridor to wait outside Lucie's parlor-cum-cell, trying to let her screams wash over him and feel nothing while he waited for someone to go in or out. When that moment came, he dodged inside just ahead of the closing door.

Gerrit had told them Iveta's orders, but it still hit Filip to see Lucie hanging from her wrists, bruised and bloody. His stomach churned as the Yestrab Okhrana interrogator circled her. Drawing his knife, Filip made himself focus past Lucie's panicked breath, past her desperate insistence that she'd worked alone. Motionless, he watched for an opportunity. He had to make this appear an accident. Had to make it look like her interrogator had been sloppy, overenthusiastic—at least long enough for Filip to get out of the room and get the imbuements back to Gerrit.

This is mercy, he told himself. *It's necessary.*

The Storm Guard had trained him for this sort of mission. He'd just never thought his target would be a friend.

GERRIT PACED THE bedroom, eye throbbing in time with his heartbeat, trying to figure out what solution Filip had spotted and what would happen next.

Filip's voice through Nina startled him. «*Open the door. I'm on my way!*»

Celka had been resting, but she sat bolt upright as Gerrit ran to the door. «*It's clear,*» she said.

Gerrit flung wide the door, and air gusted over him as Filip charged invisibly inside. Gerrit shut the door behind him, holding the handle to close it as quietly as possible.

Filip blinked visible. «*You have to take these.*» Filip pulled the jade carving out of a pocket and the iron ring from his finger, fumbling at his collar to free his storm pendant and the second charging pouch that had been imbued as a darkbag. His hands were shaking.

«*Why doesn't Lucie have them?*» Gerrit took the two concealment imbuements while Filip got the darkbag's strings untied from his necklace. «*Where is she? Filip, answer me.*»

Voice rough, Filip said, «*She's free.*»

«*Free?*» Gerrit asked as Filip shoved the darkbag into his hands.

Celka came up beside them, laying a hand on Filip's back, but Gerrit barely saw her.

Icy water seemed to drag him under, his lungs failing to draw breath. Dropping the darkbag, he grabbed Filip's arms. «*What do you mean, free? Where's Lucie?*» He shouted through the link, fingers gripping hard. «*I trusted you. Where is she?*» He kept shouting even as Filip's grim expression gave all the answer he needed. How had he possibly believed that Filip had seen a solution where he hadn't? «*You killed her.*» He wished he could drop the link, wished he dared scream the words aloud. «*We were supposed to rescue her and instead you murdered her!*»

Low, Filip said, «*Either she was going to break—getting us killed and damaging the resistance further—or they were going to keep torturing her. This was the only way.*»

«*You don't know that,*» Gerrit snarled. «*I'm the Stormhawk's son. I could have—*»

«*You could have gotten yourself killed,*» Filip snapped. «*Could have gotten all of us killed! What's wrong with you, Gerrit? You know what we signed up for. What all of us signed up for. Lucie didn't want to—*»

Gerrit punched him in the face—or tried to.

Filip slapped his fist away. «*Why do you think she attacked you? She wanted you to end it.*»

«*You don't know her,*» Gerrit said.

«*I knew her well enough.*»

«*To murder her?*» Gerrit shoved Filip hard in the chest. «*To think I ever* trusted *you. Ever called you my friend.*»

Filip glanced at Celka, as if hoping she'd fly to his rescue.

Gerrit turned and found Celka grim-faced. «*We tried to come up with a better solution.*» Her voice was low, tight with grief, but she didn't seem surprised. «*I think Filip's right about why she attacked you.*»

Filip stooped, collecting the scattered imbuements and shoving them into the darkbag. He held it out to Gerrit. «*I tried to make it look like an accident, like her interrogator slushed up, but I don't know how long that will hold. You need to take these in case they start searching people.*»

A sound like screaming filled Gerrit's ears.

Filip grabbed his hand and closed it around the darkbag. «*I didn't want this. But you of all people, Gerrit, you have to understand?*» Filip's hands wrapped around his where he clutched the darkbag. «*If the Okhrana were to capture* me... *I'd hope you'd show me the same compassion.*»

Shaking, desperate for a gun or a knife, Gerrit glared at him. As if a weapon could make anything better; as if a weapon would let him change the past. «*Get out of my sight.*»

Filip opened his mouth, but Gerrit shoved him back toward the door.

«*Get out! Now. Or we might just get to find out what*

happens when they arrest you.»

Searching, Filip met his gaze, as if he expected something to change. Finally, after a lifetime, he nodded, jaw tight, and left.

Gerrit severed his connection with Filip. Blood pounded in his ears. His eye throbbed. He forced himself to hang the darkbag on his storm pendant's chain, tucking it beneath his undershirt with numb fingers.

Celka came up beside him, close but not touching.

«*You knew,*» he snarled through Nina, the connection private.

«*I suspected.*»

«*You could have told me.*»

She stared at the door, eyes filling with tears, but only shook her head.

Gerrit ground his teeth, wanting to scream at her, wanting to run from the room. Lucie couldn't be dead. They were going to escape into the resistance together, build an army together, destroy the regime *together*.

Celka touched Gerrit's hand, fingers curling tentatively around his. He wanted to strike her hand away, turn his back on her, but when she met his gaze, a dam seemed to break in Gerrit's chest. He pulled her to him, clinging to her as if she could keep him above water. Since Mrach, Celka had begun to feel like a stranger, Lucie the only person Gerrit could trust with all his secrets. Now Lucie was gone. Because Filip had murdered her.

They held each other for a long time before Celka whispered, «*What now?*» Her face pressed into his shoulder, her arms still tight around him. «*What happens next?*»

Next. The word echoed in his head, growing louder and louder. *Next. Next?* He tried to push away thoughts of the future, tried to focus on the warmth of Celka in his arms and not the yawning chasm in his chest.

They'd failed to assassinate his father. Lucie was dead. Where did they possibly go from here?

The Tayemstvoy would make arrests at the Storm Guard Fortress. He still had no way to warn Captain Vrana. The Yestrab Okhrana had the gas canister that had been filled with the wrong gas; could they use it to track down whoever had made it? Probably. More people would be arrested, though maybe they would know to run. The canister would have been discovered even if the assassination had succeeded. He could only hope those people got out. He had no way to help them.

No way to help. Just like he'd failed to help Lucie. Because he'd trusted Filip.

Choking, Gerrit pulled away from Celka, pacing to the window. But he didn't dare draw back the heavy drapes, didn't dare let the Okhrana in the yard see him pacing, see him panicking. But he couldn't sit, couldn't calm down. He wanted to run. He wanted to fight. But he had nowhere to go, no target at which to aim.

How soon until the Okhrana reported Lucie's death? Did Iveta already know? How soon until they came here, until someone with red shoulders knocked on his door and expected him to follow and snarl questions at the Okhrana interrogator, demanding whether one of Lucie's accomplices could have snuck in and silenced her?

Freezing sleet, how soon until he had to put back on his regime face and issue orders impassively at Iveta's side as they turned the country upside-down looking for 'resistance dogs?'

«*I can't do it,*» Gerrit said, pacing in a tighter and tighter circle, boxed in, jailed.

Celka caught his arms and he tore free, pacing again, moving, he couldn't stop moving or he'd *feel*—and he couldn't afford to feel. *Stormy skies, Lucie.* He'd finally found her again, found a friend, found someone who understood what he had to do, what he was doing, and now she was gone, murdered. By Filip. Freezing sleet, what was he supposed to do?

«Gerrit!» Celka caught his arms again, holding him when he tried to pull away. *«Gerrit, look at me. Please.»*

He looked at her and shook his head. When they eventually left Yinovatka Manor, after Iveta agreed to let the Okhrana handle tearing apart the resistance, he and Celka would have to go back to imbuing weapons—more emotional imbuements, and the only way he could do that was from behind his regime mask, memories locked away. Suddenly the thought was repulsive. Wearing that mask, he'd stood at Iveta's side as she'd threatened Lucie, as she'd shot her and handed her to the Okhrana's brutal sadists. Wearing that mask, Gerrit had stopped Lucie when she reached for his gun, stopped her when she'd had a chance to end it, to fight and somehow escape.

A small voice told him it wouldn't have worked. At best, Lucie would have ended up dead, but probably she would have just been strung up and tortured, just like she'd been tortured when he'd failed to rescue her and dithered until Filip decided she was better off dead.

He'd trusted Filip, and his strazh had betrayed him.

He'd trusted Captain Vrana and the resistance she'd built, and they'd sleeted up so badly that the Stormhawk was alive and Lucie was dead.

Over the past several months, he'd done horrible things to build his cover as the Stormhawk's loyal son, trusting that assassinating his father was critical to the resistance. He had played his role perfectly, and the assassination had failed because Captain Vrana's people had failed. Now, the Okhrana would start carrying gas masks, patching the one weakness he'd found in the Stormhawk's armor. The resistance had blown its only chance. After everything he'd done and endured to make this opportunity, the incompetence of others had slushed it up.

Maybe the problem was that he kept looking for others to find solutions. If he'd acted faster, he could have gotten Lucie out. If he hadn't been forced to trust Captain Vrana's people, the Stormhawk would be dead.

He wasn't just some nameless resistance fighter hiding out in a root cellar, waiting for orders. He'd been trained by the State's top bozhk military academy. He was the Stormhawk's son.

The resistance had failed. Captain Vrana had failed. But since returning to the Storm Guard, Gerrit had worked at Iveta's side, solidifying his powerbase, becoming someone the Stormhawk and his advisers would listen to.

Captain Vrana hadn't even organized the resistance to produce a suitable poison gas for the assassination. How could he trust her to overthrow the regime and install something better? But Gerrit had spent time with Iveta. Yes, she was ruthless, but maybe change required ruthlessness. She saw Bourshkanya's problems and cared about solving them. Iveta had already positioned herself and Gerrit as a team, his work in the imbuement platoon adding to her standing in the regime. Maybe his mistake was in agreeing to let Vrana pit Iveta's might against Artur's. If Gerrit stopped jumping at the end of Vrana's leash and instead focused on increasing his power alongside his sister's, they would have a real chance at changing Bourshkanya from the inside.

Instead of relying on others, maybe it was time he relied on himself.

«Gerrit, what is it?» Celka caught his hand, and he shook himself from his musing to focus on her. Where did Celka fit into this new vision?

He doubted she'd understand. Just like she hadn't

understood the necessity of the walls he'd built in his mind. Lucie understood. Lucie...

His throat closed off, his burgeoning plan crumpling into grief.

«*Gerrit.*» Celka caught his face in cold hands, and his gaze swam to hers. He couldn't make any progress if memories of Lucie continued to blindside him. «*I have an idea,*» Celka said, just as Gerrit realized what he needed to do. «*I think I know how we can win. How we can kill the Stormhawk.*»

Her words took a minute to make sense, and he frowned at her, irritated that she'd returned to their failures. «*It won't work,*» he said, voice raw with loss. He cleared his throat. He needed to rebuild his mental walls, but better this time. If he was going to stop waiting for others to tell him what to do, he needed to be certain he could depend on himself. That meant excising his weaknesses. This grief he felt for Lucie would tear a hole in his chest if he let it. He needed to cut it away, lock it behind mental walls so strong they ceased to be walls and became the new borders of his mind. «*The Stormhawk's unkillable,*» he told Celka. «*The Okhrana know his weakness now. We failed. It's time for a new plan.*» His plan. The one he needed to make sure he was strong enough to see through.

«*I know we can't use gas again,*» Celka said. «*I have a new idea. A better one.*»

He didn't want to hear it. An assassination now would be too soon. The Stormhawk had begun to favor Iveta, enough for her and Artur to smash their pet Tayemstvoy against each other, but to ensure that Iveta came out on top, they still had work to do. If they killed the Stormhawk now, Artur was too much of a risk.

Before Celka could elaborate, a fist pounded the bedroom door. "Lieutenant Kladivo, sir? There's been a development. You'll want to come with us."

Fear widened Celka's eyes, and she gripped Gerrit's hand. He shook off her hold. "I'll need a minute," he called and strode to the washbasin. There, he splashed water on his face and stared at his reflection. It was easy enough to snap walls into place around the memories he'd been hiding for weeks— his mother, Celka in the circus, their assassination plot, and more recently, his private conversations with Lucie. He buried all of them, not just the emotions—everything. He needed to do more, restructure his memory to permanently lock away his weaknesses. But for now, this would do.

Straightening the sleeves of his uniform jacket, he strode to the door, ready to control his own future.

CHAPTER FORTY-EIGHT

AFTER GERRIT'S ABRUPT departure, Celka laced her boots and headed for the door. There, she froze. Would the guards think it suspicious if she left her room? She scrubbed her hands over her face, trying to push away her exhaustion and think. If they questioned her, she'd tell them the truth: she didn't want to be alone right now. With Gerrit out, Filip was the only person she even remotely wanted to see.

Filip opened his door in shirtsleeves, his entire body vibrating tension. His gaze passed over her and beyond—looking for Gerrit—and the corners of his mouth tightened to find her alone.

"Can I come in?" she asked.

He stepped aside to admit her before closing them in together. His room was small, a single bed taking up most of the space. She looked around for Yanek, but he wasn't there. "Is something wrong?" Filip asked.

"Gerrit left. I... didn't want to be alone."

Filip's throat worked as though he was trying to swallow. He crossed his arms over his chest in a gesture that might have been defiant if it hadn't hunched his shoulders. He kicked at the rug, nodded.

"Where's Yanek?"

"Helping with the search." His voice managed to sound almost normal, but strain showed around his eyes. "Iveta lent the bolt-hawks to the Okhrana captain. Since I figured Gerrit would want me available, I suggested he join them."

Celka exhaled relief. Yanek could return at any time, but Filip's quick thinking had bought them space before they'd have to invent an innocuous cover. Picking up Nina's imbuement, Celka said, *«I have an idea for how we can finish the job. But I need help testing it.»*

Filip's attention sharpened. *«What is it?»* Desperation edged his voice.

She'd intended to just tell him—focus on the future, not the past—but when he reached for her hand, she recoiled and the words caught in her throat.

He froze. Everything but his breathing, which was too fast. Then he balled his hand into a fist and turned away, sitting on the bed, most of the small room between them. Elbows on his knees, he dropped his head into his hands.

She watched him for a minute, stomach churning, remembering Lucie's screams echoing down the corridor, remembering her friend's wide-eyed terror as Hedvika shoved her to the ballroom floor. Finally, Celka asked, *«Did she know it was you—at the end?»*

Filip shifted as though he might look up at her, but then shook his head. *«I couldn't risk the Okhrana noticing me.»*

«You really think it was the only way?» Celka certainly hadn't thought of any other solution, and when she'd realized what Filip was going to do... it fit with Lucie breaking her cover story to attack Gerrit. But she still reeled, struggling to understand the world where Lucie was dead and Filip been the one to do it.

When Filip spoke, his voice was barely a whisper. *«This place is locked down and she was their only lead. She would have been heavily guarded at all times. When the Okhrana moved out, they would have taken her somewhere more secure. Even if all three of us had concealment imbuements and guns, we probably couldn't have gotten her out without at least one of us being shot and arrested. And Gerrit's grand idea to get the resistance to ambush them on the road? Would have just cost more lives. If he'd gotten himself inside as part of her interrogation team, gotten her a weapon like he talked about—at best she could have turned it on herself. Even when I got to her, she was in no condition to run, not when they have dogs to track her. The only way Lucie could have gotten out alive was if we had left her until the Okhrana were done with her. If she survived that—if—maybe the resistance could have pulled her from a prison camp in a few years. Years, Celka. Do you think she could have kept silent about us and all her resistance contacts for years? Do you think she would have wanted to risk it?»*

Celka remembered Lucie bright-eyed in the Prochazka sleeper car, flopping back into her bunk, thrilled to have a bed to sleep in. Remembered her grabbing Celka's hand, fierce, saying that Pa was the real hero, that the Stormhawk was a monster. *«No.»* She settled on the bed next to Filip. *«She wouldn't have risked the resistance.»*

Filip turned to her, his eyes hollow. *«I wish there'd been another way.»*

«Me too.» She took his hand, and he squeezed back, hard. Then, though she didn't want to say it, didn't want to accept how all their plans had fallen apart, she whispered, *«Thank you—for giving her a way out.»*

His exhale shook his whole body. *«Did Gerrit...? Before he left...?»*

She shook her head. «*I think he was working through a plan.*» But that didn't explain how he'd strode to the washbasin and stared into the mirror, sousedni-shape sharpening, the scents of pine and wet stone howling around him. «*He did something to his sousednia before he left with the Okhrana— he must have put his mental walls in place, but he did it so fast. Maybe five minutes, and when he turned back from the mirror, he was the* other *Gerrit. And Lucie's death didn't matter anymore.*»

«*That's good.*» Filip grimaced. «*I never thought I would say that. But it means we'll make it through the night. After this, we need to talk to him, though. Or you should. I don't know if he'll listen to me. Lucie... I didn't realize he was so attached.*»

Celka swallowed hard but nodded, trying to shake both the knowledge that her friend was dead and the visceral wrongness she'd felt watching Gerrit transform. She had to focus on what she could change now. «*There was a guard in the Stormhawk's room who ran to the window, trying to open it. I stopped him. In sousednia, I kicked him in the backs of the knees and made him stumble. It was enough of a delay that the gas killed him.*» Gerrit had told them about the guard's death. «*And talking to Pa got me thinking about sousednia, about how people extend into it.*» She bit her lip, wondering if Filip would reach the same connections she had, wondering if she was just grasping at straws or if this really could work. «*A person breathes because their brain tells their lungs to move, right? Their blood flows because their heart knows it has to beat. What if... what if I can disrupt that?*»

Filip studied her, intent and focused, not immediately dismissing the idea. «*Show me.*»

She slipped into sousednia, stepping away from her physical form to come up behind him through the bed. Connecting true-life and sousednia, she placed her hands over his eyes.

"Sleet!" Filip jerked away, the motion startling her so much that she lost her dislocation, her sousedni-shape snapping back into her true-form.

«*Did it work?*» she asked.

«*For a second, it went dark.*» His jaw tightened, and his gaze slipped off her as he thought. «*The gas attack will have damaged his lungs. Can you smother me? Make a pillow in sousednia, press it over my face?*»

Celka frowned. She'd tickled Gerrit with an invented feather before she figured out how to wall off her concealment nuzhda's mischief. «*Maybe.*»

«*Try it.*» Filip lay back on his bed.

In sousednia, he rested on her high wire platform, a heat-shimmer. Her true-form still seated on the edge of the bed, she knelt over him in sousednia, trying to conjure a copy of the pillow that supported his head in true-life. It wouldn't come.

Exhaustion blurred her vision as she returned to true-life.

«*Try it without the dislocation,*» Filip said. «*We already know you can do that part; no reason to make it harder.*»

She nodded, climbing onto the bed. But when she moved to straddle him, she hesitated. Recalling his strong hands supporting her in the corridor, his lips soft against hers, her pulse thrummed. Even after all the horrors of the night, she fell too easily into the deep velvet of his eyes.

She shook herself. Stormhawk. Assassination. Focus. «*Close your eyes. Pretend you're asleep.*»

He did, and she hovered her hands over his face, trying to imagine not Filip, but the Stormhawk vulnerable before her. Concentrating on the object's purpose rather than its true-form, she imagined soft support and crushing suffocation. But the pillow refused to coalesce.

«*I don't understand why this is so hard,*» she finally said. «*When I'm imbuing, it's easy to pull an object into sousednia.*»

«*Maybe it's tied to the nuzhda,*» Filip said. «*You're not pulling against anything.*»

She tried pulling on combat, sousednia shifting to leave Filip lying in the back lot's weeds. She imagined him with red shoulders, just some hawk that Pa had briefly stunned. Celka needed to kill him before he could get back up and bring his truncheon arcing down.

This time, a pillow formed, slippery, twisting into other weapons—better weapons. When she pressed it over Filip's face, it shredded, a haze of red. She snarled, frustration enflaming the nuzhda.

Filip caught her wrist. The skin-to-skin contact startled her. «Release the nuzhda,» he said, and she heard him without Nina.

She wanted to strike his hand away, but she made herself breathe like she'd practiced with Hedvika. *Do not think about Hedvika.* Eventually, the combat nuzhda frayed, the back lot fading into the yawning darkness beneath the high wire, and she managed to reconnect with Nina's imbuement.

Filip shifted distractingly beneath her, crossing his arms behind his head, gazing up at her. «*What if we give up on having a weapon? Using both hands, you might be able to cover my nose and mouth.*»

It seemed worth a try. She started out in true-life, not sure what positioning she'd need. But as she placed her hand over his mouth, she hesitated. «*I don't want to kill you.*»

He smirked, lips warm against her palm. «*You won't. I can throw you off before you get close.*» His expression sobered. «*Hopefully that won't be a problem.*»

Using her other hand to pinch his nose closed, Celka leaned her weight onto her hand. Their eyes locked. For an instant, she thought she had it, then he turned his head to the side, twisting out of her grip, easily drawing a breath. «*Sleet,*» she said. «*This won't work if he can just turn his head.*»

«Grip down on my mouth, see if that helps.» His voice had gone rough, and when he touched her thigh, it sent sparks through her belly.

Focus, Celka. She clamped her hand down over his mouth, elbows bent, leaning her full weight on him as though to pin him to the bed. At first, when he started to struggle, she thought she had him, and triumph flared bright in her chest. Then Filip caught her wrists and twisted his hips, and they ended up on their sides in bed together, faces a handspan apart. He was breathing hard.

Celka couldn't look away from his mouth, his hands hot on her wrists. Her legs wrapped around his waist, and she felt every point of contact between them like a burning brand.

"That was good," he whispered.

She nodded, staring at his lips. Shaking herself, Celka retreated into sousednia and their link through Nina. *«I should try it as a dislocation.»*

He jolted, releasing her arms. *«Yeah, of course. Definitely.»*

She hesitated, not wanting to roll away. *Focus, Celka.*

She made herself sit on the edge of the bed, and Filip lay back, eyes raking her before he focused up at the ceiling. *«Ready whenever you are.»*

She straddled him on the high wire platform, sousednia smelling of old books and oiled steel as she pressed her hands over his mouth and nose. As she brought true-life and sousednia into contact, he tensed beneath her and his hand shot up—sousednia tracking true-life—catching her wrist as though to pull it away. But while Filip could out-muscle her in true-life, in sousednia, she had advantage. On the high wire platform, his grip tightened around her wrist, but when he pulled, she kept her weight over his mouth. On the bed, he made a strangled *mmurmph* that seemed more frustrated than actually panicked, so she held on.

Then he twisted on the bed, lashing his head to the side, sousedni-shape tracking. She tried to keep hold of him, but he twisted back the other way and tore free.

«*Hailstones.*» She abandoned the dislocation.

Filip propped himself up on one elbow, breathing hard. «*That was... disturbing. I really couldn't breathe.*»

Celka shook her head. «*And then you pulled away and you could.*»

He reached out and laid a hand on hers. «*Celka, this is incredible. I had no idea sousednia could be used like this—I don't think anyone did. You have a chance here. I wonder...*» He sat up in bed, legs crossed. «*What if he was sedated? Then he couldn't struggle.*»

Hope spiked Celka's chest, then flared out. «*How do we get him sedated?*»

Filip pulled a face. «*Right. Never mind. Sleet.*»

Celka flopped onto her back in the bed, staring at the ceiling. Stormy skies it felt good to lie down and close her eyes. Maybe if she could just sleep for a while... The memory of Lucie's screams jolted her, and she sat bolt upright, heart hammering, eyes darting to the closed door. She gripped handfuls of the comforter, trying to calm herself. *Sleet, Lucie...*

Filip touched her thigh, his shoulder pressing into hers. She tilted her head to lean against him, breathing in the scent of him. Yinovatka Manor had gone quiet, no more screams. Lucie was dead.

She squeezed her eyes shut. She needed to focus on the problem at hand. «*What if... Is there any way for me to attack him that he can't fight back?*»

«*I don't—*» Filip cocked his head, ideas clearly spinning together. «*You could choke him. With a carotid choke, you could drop him unconscious almost instantly. He'd hardly have any chance to fight.*»

«How hard is that to learn?»

He shrugged. *«You'll pick it up.»*

«Show me?»

They stood together next to the bed, and he touched her throat, explaining anatomy. Then he moved around behind her, his chest pressing against her back as he wrapped an arm around her throat. *«Ready?»* he asked.

Celka nodded, and his arm tightened. She had only the briefest moment of surprise before her vision tunneled in. Her limbs went slack, and a metallic taste filled her mouth.

Then light and sound burst and flickered around her, and she woke on the floor in his arms.

«Freezing sleet, that's fast,» she said.

«The timing varies person-to-person,» he explained. *«Angles matter, as does how well you position the choke. But a few seconds, maybe as much as half a minute, and he should pass out.»*

Hope flared Celka's chest. *«How long until it kills him?»*

«Several minutes. You'll have to keep holding the choke, but he won't be able to fight you.»

They could do this—salvage the resistance's plans, make Lucie's death mean something. The Stormhawk was already weak from the chlorine and phosgene. Celka gripped Filip's hands, hard. *«Teach me.»*

CHAPTER FORTY-NINE

GERRIT RETURNED TO his bedroom in the pre-dawn gray to find it empty. He struggled for long minutes before activating Nina, only to discover that Celka was with Filip. Once, the betrayal would have stung, but the sun would be rising soon and he was exhausted. He let them be, shredding his link with Nina, relieved to escape the imbuement's battering pressure against his walls.

He got his boots off and collapsed into bed. He didn't dream.

Gritty-eyed, Gerrit woke after too little sleep and met with his sister. Their father's condition hadn't changed, but a storm was brewing and Iveta wanted the imbuement platoon back in the field.

"Filip can command them," Gerrit said. "I'll stay here, of course." Iveta didn't dispute either statement, and Gerrit breathed a little easier. Both Celka and Filip had objected to his mental walls; having the pair of them out of the way would make what he had to do easier.

The Yestrab Okhrana balked at first at releasing the imbuement squads; they still hadn't found the accomplice who'd murdered Lucie, and any bozhk was a possible suspect. But Gerrit's platoon all had solid alibis, and imbuing weapons for the State remained a priority. Eventually, the Okhrana agreed to send them on their way.

Under the auspices of snatching a little more sleep, Gerrit retreated to his room while the imbuement platoon prepared to depart. Standing at the washbasin, he contemplated his options.

His mental walls had held overnight, allowing him to conduct more interviews alongside the Okhrana, but he felt uneasy, like a beast of fangs and claws watched him from the shadows. He'd never intended to wall off so many memories, and his mind had become a labyrinth of stone. He needed to start over.

The first step would be hardest, and he resisted, pacing to the window and staring out, wondering if maybe his current barriers would suffice. But that was cowardice, which proved how badly he needed to reshape himself. He couldn't afford cowardice as he shaped his own future, just as he couldn't afford excesses of sympathy or compassion. He had to cut away those weaknesses until the Gerrit Kladivo who remained was unflinching and strong.

He yanked the curtains closed. Sitting on the edge of his bed, he shattered his mental barriers.

Agony crashed over him, loss choking his throat and stealing his breath. His memories of Lucie bright and alive collided with the fresher memory of crouching beside her bruised and bloodied corpse, the Stormhawk's physician showing the cuts that had let her bleed out too fast for an imbuement to heal. On the edge of his bed, Gerrit bent double, breath ragged, tears stinging his eyes. He fought them, fought for control, but he had to reintegrate, had to endure every agony so he could wipe his mind clean and rebuild. He'd thought he'd escaped the pain of Lucie's death by building these walls, but grief raged through him like a fever, tangling with his memories of his mother's murder and rampaging through his mind.

He slipped from the bed to the floor, curling in on himself, panting shallow breaths.

For a time, he floated in memory, the world around him gray.

Slowly, other memories emerged. Moments of laughter, of supportive embraces. Celka stretched out in bed beside him, kisses and gasps of pleasure. He remembered when they'd first learned to joint-imbue, the ecstatic power he'd felt at her side; remembered pulling her toward him, kissing her lips, feeling the world right and full of possibility. He remembered Lucie, serious beside him, listening to everything he'd done, forgiving him, certain he wasn't a monster.

The pain in his chest swelled with those moments, even as the laughter and smiles were a comfort.

Celka's not gone, whispered a voice he hadn't listened to in a while. *You're pushing her away, but you could talk to her before she leaves. Tell her everything, ask for her help.*

Trust. The idea frightened him even as it sang a song so sweet he couldn't help but lean in. The song reminded him of Filip launching into fights to save him from older cadets. Filip, always at his back, supporting him, a sounding board for his ideas, their friendship so deep that Filip held Gerrit's life before his own.

Filip betrayed you, said a crueler voice, easier to listen to. It hurt less than the idea that Gerrit had failed to save Lucie— that he'd never had a chance. *Vrana betrayed you.* That, too, cut like a sharp, clean knife, the pain over quick so he could heal. Because the other option was that Gerrit had used the paranoia imbuement to turn prisoners and civilians against each other for nothing, and that pain sliced like a rusted shiv, a wound he couldn't face and that he knew would fester.

On the floor, he let himself listen to the cruel voice. It told him that compassion was weakness, and the only way out was through. Grief was weakness, too; it meant he'd cared too much about the wrong people. He was a diamond, strong and hard, but right now he was flawed. Celka had convinced him that those flaws were beautiful, but she was wrong. Bourshkanya didn't need someone who would crumble beneath grief, who would flinch away from necessary choices because the cost was too high. Bourshkanya needed a surgeon strong enough to cut away rotten flesh. Gerrit would become that surgeon, and his first patient would be himself.

The cruel voice echoing in his head, he pushed himself up from the floor. Straightening his uniform jacket, he made himself cross to the washbasin and face a reflection that looked painfully young. He splashed cold water on his face, washing away tears. Walling away memories one at a time had let him wear a mask of regime confidence, but a mask would no longer do.

A person's core sousednia echoed their personality, but the way his mountaintop had changed when he'd walled off memories proved that sousednia could be controlled just like any nuzhda. To imbue paranoid violence or paralyzing fear, he'd let nuanced, invented realities grow to fill his mind. He just needed to create a space that matched the Gerrit Kladivo who defined his own future and could rebuild the regime at Iveta's side.

That version of himself wouldn't hear his mother's last words or wallow in lonesome sunlight. Lieutenant Gerrit Kladivo would wear his Army uniform proudly—no, not an Army uniform. His father had built the Tayemstvoy to shape Bourshkanya and its citizens. To step into power, Gerrit needed to accept the transfer Major Blatnik had suggested after he'd demonstrated the paranoid violence imbuement.

Mouth dry, Gerrit met his gaze in the mirror and imagined his shoulders red.

By the time he finished, sousednia echoed his new strength. He stood on a narrow street, the city's sturdy stone walls rising on either side to meet an iron gray sky. The cobblestones beneath his black kneeboots were wet from a cold rain and, in the distance, he heard the stomp of soldiers marching in time. Distant, almost lost beneath the wind, came the sound of screams, and the air carried a gritty dampness, as if from a departing motorcade.

Grief would not touch him here, and neither would sentiment. His red shoulders would serve as armor and as warning. Gerrit Kladivo was not to be crossed. He would give the orders, not the other way around.

The weight of a truncheon on his belt felt momentarily wrong, but he pushed the discomfort aside and straightened the sleeves of his uniform jacket, his red epaulettes bright despite the thick clouds.

Facing his reflection in true-life's mirror, he felt a moment's disorientation. Fear flashed through his reflection's eyes, fear that belonged to the olive green epaulettes of his Army jacket. Lieutenant Kladivo made an impatient noise. He had no time for fear or uncertainty. He'd request the lateral transfer immediately, bringing his true-form in line with the person he needed to become.

Straightening from the washbasin, he turned for the door. The imbuement platoon would be departing soon. He'd see them off. Then he had work to do. Finally, he was strong enough to claim the power he'd always deserved.

CHAPTER FIFTY

A COLD WIND blew through Celka's Army overcoat while Captain Kladivo spoke about duty and vigilance on the steps to Yinovatka Manor. Gerrit stood at his sister's side, two steps above the rest of the platoon, and Celka tried again to contact him through Nina. He didn't even glance her way.

Filip stood at Celka's side, blocking some of the cold wind, failing just as utterly to reach Gerrit. «*I don't know if he can even sense the link.*»

Celka's already queasy stomach churned, too much coffee and too little sleep giving her fears an easy foothold. «*He always has before.*» Though suddenly, she wasn't so sure. He'd ignored her after the riot in Mrach, too. But today was worse. In sousednia, Gerrit looked like a stranger—like Tayemstvoy. «*How bad is his core nuzhda warped?*»

Filip's tension simmered through their link. «*We'll get him to reintegrate tonight. It's good that he built walls. It means we won't get arrested before you can work out the new technique.*» But Filip, always so good at showing a regime face, couldn't make the words convincing.

When Yanek had returned to his and Filip's room sometime before dawn, Celka had set aside her efforts to choke Filip from sousednia, forced to admit that she wouldn't figure it out before morning. The three of them had squeezed together in the narrow bed, and Celka had fallen asleep spooned against Filip's chest, glad not to be alone, glad not to be with Gerrit, fully expecting she'd have days more to practice. Yinovatka Manor was locked down, the Okhrana hunting the Stormhawk's assassins. She and Filip weren't going anywhere. She'd thought.

A brief train ride took them into a small industrial city, factory smoke darkening the close gray sky as thunder began to rumble overhead. Snow blew like stinging, icy rock chips. A single motorcar met them, the mayor apologizing for the lack of other suitable transport. The warehouse where they'd be imbuing wasn't far. Havel stepped forward, magnanimously offering that the rest of the platoon could walk.

Hedvika leaned in and muttered, "I'd call him a pretentious sleet-licker if I didn't want to stretch my legs."

Celka started to smile before realizing that Hedvika *Rychtr* had been the one to say it. Shooting her a glare, Celka crossed the train station to where a pair of bolt-hawks watched over Nina's crate. "I'll take her today," she said, wrapping the snake around her shoulders as a reptilian shield.

Not trusting it would deter her hail-eating strazh, Celka caught Filip's arm, putting a squad of bolt-hawks between them and Hedvika. Quietly, she asked, "Can you strazh for me today?"

He glanced back at Hedvika, jaw tightening. Pitching his voice to carry, he said, "Sub-Lieutenant Rychtr, as the hero of the hour, I'm giving you the day off. I'll strazh for Celka."

Hearing Hedvika lauded made Celka's blood curdle, but Filip was right—in the State's eyes, she'd discovered a resistance assassin. Celka would have to be very careful about how she avoided her strazh. Anger about Hedvika's lie might be excused, but only to a point.

Despite Celka's efforts to keep her distance, Hedvika joined the squad during their march, though she stayed behind Celka, which made it a little easier to pretend she wasn't there. As they walked, bolt-hawks circled the squad like carrion crows.

The city streets were nearly deserted, which would have been normal for a Storm Day, everyone gathered in temples for prayer and song. But Tayemstvoy guarded every corner, and Celka squinted against the icy snow, finding faces peeking from behind cracked shutters of the two- and three-story buildings they passed. Instead of curiosity or excitement, those faces stared back with hatred.

A few could have been a fluke, but every citizen wore the same loathing. Then the local Tayemstvoy detoured them up several blocks, and Celka craned to glimpse what the red shoulders wanted to hide. Painted red across a warehouse,

The State Cannot Silence Our Songs

Thunder crashed and, over the crunch of their hobnailed boots, distant voices rose in song. Celka's heart caught the Song of Fighting's hurried rhythm, then gunshots cracked the air. The bolt-hawks tightened around her squad, rifles slapping into palms, their focus outward.

"Minor disturbance," their local Tayemstvoy guide said. "Nothing to do with you."

Celka didn't believe them for an instant. She shifted into sousednia, breathing deep, but the local red shoulders' tension tangled with the bolt-hawks' edgy alertness and her own squad's expectant focus. Fingers itching, Celka smoothed her own sousednia into a featureless plain, escaping the storm's tug. Nina weighed heavy on her shoulders, the snowfall slowing the snake despite Celka's body heat.

«*Something's wrong,*» she told Filip. Pushing the words through the torpid snake felt like swimming through honey.

«*Stay close,*» he said, not disagreeing.

Movement in the corner of her eye made Celka turn. A bottle crashed to the cobblestones beside Private Navratil, flame leaping amongst splintering shards of glass. Celka raised an arm to protect her face as another bottle arced through the sky. It landed with a crack, and someone cried out, but the world spun out of true as Hedvika bowled into her, dragging her into the shelter of a doorway.

Olive uniforms shoved and elbowed her, crushing her back against unyielding stone. A rifle fired close by, deafening. More shouts. Pounding footsteps. Gunshots. Celka shifted, trying to see, but hands pressed her down.

Then, as quickly as it had started, silence overtook them. Celka heard only her ragged breath and the muted tap of icy snowfall. Hobnailed boots scuffed against snow and stone. Then voices clipped orders, distorted through the heartbeat hammering in her ears.

A hand clasped her wrist, and Celka flinched around to meet Masha's serious brown eyes. She exhaled and let Masha pull her from her crouch, stomach twisting to see her friend holding a pistol. *Friend?* Was Celka really so naïve to keep thinking of these regime officers as friends? Hedvika had shown her true face when she'd handed Lucie off to be tortured by the Okhrana.

Now Hedvika stood shoulder-to-shoulder with Filip and Yanek, a human wall between them and the street. Celka shuddered to think how easily they'd turn their weapons on her and Filip if they caught even the slightest hint of their involvement in the assassination attempt.

Shaking the thought, Celka asked, "What happened?"

"It's over," Hedvika said, though she didn't reholster her sidearm. Before last night, her cool competence would have reassured Celka. "The dogs scattered. Local hawks will chase them down."

"'Nothing to do with us,'" Filip quoted, wry.

"Any injuries?" Sergeant Mares asked.

Celka shook her head, though she'd have bruises from the wall.

At the others' all-clear, he ordered them out. "Two more blocks and we'll be in a defensible position."

Hedvika's shoulder brushed Celka's as they marched. "You'd think the hawks would do a better job cleaning up their city's filth."

Celka clamped her jaw shut and made herself face straight ahead. Nina lifted her head toward Hedvika and hissed.

Hedvika flinched away. "Sleet-storms. How can you stand that thing?"

"Well, Hedvika, one of the creatures with me is a cold-blooded reptile who might sneak silently up on me in the middle of the night and strangle me to death. The other is a python." She smiled, full of teeth. "I'll take the snake."

Hedvika kept her distance while Celka imbued, though Celka felt her scrutiny. Still, Celka managed to avoid her until they'd all piled into the wealthy factory owner's house that would serve as the night's barracks. Celka had expected they'd return to Yinovatka Manor, but when she asked Filip about it, he'd barely swallowed a grimace. *«I can't get anything out of Lieutenant Coufal about our itinerary—and neither can Havel. Either our next move isn't planned yet, she's been ordered not to tell us, or she's just a red-shouldered sleet-licker who enjoys stringing us along.»*

Celka laid a hand on his arm, wishing she had some reassurance to offer. It wasn't like Filip to criticize the

Tayemstvoy, even in the privacy of Nina's imbuement. *«Gerrit will be fine.»* She wished she could believe it.

The lack of travel left them time to kill, and when Filip recovered his calm, he suggested that Celka learn some ground fighting techniques—like choke holds. Masha and Yanek joined enthusiastically, and Celka managed to glare Hedvika out of the room. With Filip in charge, she practiced the carotid choke at different angles in true-life, and he even roped in the bolt-hawks who stood watch at the door. By the time they stopped for dinner, Celka felt almost confident in her technique—as well as a couple of moves that would get her victim into position.

Masha excused herself after the meal, but Yanek joined Celka and Filip back in the parlor.

"Why the sudden interest?" Yanek asked.

When Celka hesitated, not sure what story to spin, Filip said, "Rychtr."

Yanek narrowed his eyes, glancing to the door before laying a hand on Celka's shoulder. "I can only imagine what it must feel like that she lied to you about her name, but she's still an excellent strazh."

Celka flinched from his touch, hating that he sounded so sincere, hating that part of her still saw him as *friend* even when he was as much a boot-licker as the rest of them. Low, Celka said, "It's not just about her name." Memories of Filip's trembling hands after he'd killed Lucie left her wanting to vomit.

Yanek's expression hardened, and he glanced at Filip. At Filip's nod, he said, "You should talk to her about tumbling servants. Maybe she'll understand if it comes from you."

Celka crossed her arms tight over her chest. "Why would she listen to me?"

"Because she cares about you," Yanek said.

Celka shook her head, but sousednia smelled like fresh rye bread and laughter around him, and Celka couldn't make herself believe he spoke anything but the truth. Picking up Nina's link to Filip, Celka asked, «*If we manage to pull this off, what are you going to tell Yanek?*»

Filip recoiled visibly enough that Yanek reached out a hand with an *are you all right?* frown. "It's nothing," Filip said unconvincingly, and Celka felt like a sleet-licker for asking. Yanek wore a regime uniform as much as the rest of them, but she thought that of anyone, he might understand. "I'm just worried about Gerrit. Celka, you still want to practice?"

With only Yanek and Filip to witness, Celka decided to risk attempting the choke in sousednia. But whatever her feelings toward Yanek, she couldn't risk him suspecting what she was doing, so she still wrapped her arm around his throat. Instead of cranking down on the choke in true-life, however, she tightened her hold in a sousedni-disruption. Before dinner, she'd consistently managed the choke so long as she could maneuver her victim into the right position. Now, attempting it from sousednia, Yanek would grimace and occasionally get dizzy, but she couldn't take it all the way.

For what felt like the hundredth time, Yanek tapped out, rubbing his neck.

Celka spun away, pacing. "I don't know what I'm doing wrong." She wanted to sweep the rows of tiny glass birds off the shelves adorning the room, wanted to hear them shatter. Panic surged through her, a roaring in her ears too much like Lucie's screams. Maybe she couldn't make the choke work from sousednia because it wasn't possible. Maybe making an elephant poop and a guard stumble were fundamentally different. Maybe the body had defenses against the brain insisting that blood no longer flowed. Maybe she was wasting her time and Lucie had died for *nothing*.

"Slow down." Filip caught her arms lightly, drawing her to a stop. "Breathe. You'll get this."

Her chest was so tight that spots danced in her vision, but Filip held her gaze, his own calm slowly seeping into her. She wanted to fight it, jerk away and scream her frustration, flounder in grief, but Lucie deserved better. Lucie deserved Celka finishing what they'd started, and helpless rage would solve nothing.

As she started to breathe easier, Filip pulled her into an embrace. «*We'll figure this out,*» he said through Nina. «*We're just getting started. The Stormhawk will still be there when you're ready.*»

When Yanek suggested that she was struggling because she was tired, Celka grudgingly trudged up to her room. She wasn't just tired, she realized, she was *exhausted*, and a soft bed was suddenly the only thing she could think about. Someone had kindly left a light on in her room, and the back bricks of a hearth shared with the neighboring room kept it from being too cold. She shoved the door closed with her back and looked around for her pack.

Then she noticed Hedvika sitting on her bed and froze.

Hedvika held her hands up in surrender. "I just want to talk."

Celka glared at her, letting her strazh see exactly what she thought of that idea.

Hedvika swallowed visibly, but said, "I'm sorry."

Of everything Celka had expected to come out of her mouth, *sorry* had never made the list. It threw her off balance, and Hedvika took her hesitance as an indication that Celka was willing to listen.

"I'm sorry I lied to you." Hedvika picked at her fingernails. "I should have told you earlier, but I was scared. I like you. I like being your strazh, and I worried..." She glanced up at

Celka, then back down at her hands. "What you said last night? About that servant girl. It's not like that. When they say no, I respect them, I *do*."

"And how often does that happen?" Celka asked through gritted teeth. She wanted to turn and slam the door in Hedvika's face, but Yanek's insistence that she might be able to get through to Hedvika made her hesitate. Besides, where would she go? If they deployed beneath another bozhskyeh storm tomorrow, Lieutenant Coufal would expect Hedvika to strazh for her.

"Not often." Hedvika scowled at an ugly painting of a boat on a lake. "But when it does, sometimes they just want more from me—ration coupons or favors—I'm *sure* of it." She met Celka's gaze again, but couldn't seem to hold it. "I *like* that negotiation. I like to push. I like it when they pretend not to be interested, but they clearly *are*. Sometimes it makes them just as hot as it makes me... but I'm bad with words. You know that. And maybe I've sleeted it up and..." Her jaw muscles worked and she pulled at a loose thread on the comforter. "How do I know? I don't want a relationship, Celka. I just want a tumble and then to return to my duties. And they're getting something out of it—besides good sex. I'm trying to *help*, and you make it sound like I'm a monster."

"Leaving *Rychtr* out of the negotiation would be a good start." Celka twisted the family name, flinching from the memories it conjured.

Hedvika's gaze sharpened, like she was about to start arguing, but instead she scowled at the floor. "I know the name triggers you," she finally said. "But Father never questioned any of the servants. It's not the same."

"He's a Tayemstvoy *major*, Hedvika. It doesn't matter if they've *met* him."

Hedvika searched her, her pale blue eyes hard like they had been when she'd thrown Lucie to the Okhrana. Celka forced herself not to flinch away, though knowing who Hedvika's father was, she wanted to. How did you convince someone that the Tayemstvoy were terrifying when they believed the secret police's work was important and their brutality justified? If she tried, would Hedvika see her disloyalty—or assume it?

But Hedvika just made a frustrated noise and started picking at the comforter again. "You're one to talk."

"What?" Celka snapped.

"You're dating Gerrit *Kladivo*. I don't understand how you can condemn *me* using Father's regime status when you're barking up the same tree—no, an even higher tree. That analogy makes no sense." Hedvika scrubbed her hands through her hair. "You think it's wrong for me to make sure my tumbles know who I am and what I can do for them, but you're dating one of the most prestigious people in Bourshkanya. How is that different?"

Because I don't want him for his name, Celka almost said, but stopped herself. From Hedvika's perspective, maybe it did look the same. Celka couldn't *imagine* wanting someone because their father was a Tayemstvoy officer, but she tried to think past her resistance loyalties. A Tayemstvoy major had power, and power meant comfort—something Celka knew all too well from her time in uniform. Maybe some people would risk playing with fire if it could keep them warm through winter's bitter nights.

Celka made herself sit on the bed next to Hedvika. "Gerrit didn't tell me who he was when we first met."

Hedvika snorted. "But you're mad at me for doing the same?"

Celka grimaced. "I was mad at him too."

"So, what? I'm just supposed to pretend to be Hedvika Bur?" She pulled her jacket off the bed where she'd tossed it and tapped the nameplate. She'd replaced *Bur* with *Rychtr*. Celka tried not to shudder. "This is who I *am*, Celka. I'm not going to pretend to be someone else."

This was getting nowhere. "Have you ever thought," Celka said, "that some people might hear that your father's a Tayemstvoy major and think they *can't* turn you down? That if they do, you'll hurt them—or their families?"

"I wouldn't," Hedvika said.

"But do *they* know that?"

Hedvika eyed her. "The Tayemstvoy are only a threat if someone's disloyal." The edge to her voice suggested that Celka skated dangerously close to that line.

She swallowed hard, but kept going. If she could help Hedvika become a better person, maybe that was the best she could do for Lucie—besides killing the Stormhawk. "Who decides what constitutes 'loyal?' Can you look me in the eye and tell me that no Tayemstvoy has ever abused their power?"

Hedvika lifted her chin like she was about to do exactly that. Then she sighed and looked away.

"I'm a dirt-scrubber, right? We hear stories." Celka pushed down her revulsion to take her strazh's hand, twining their fingers together like she used to do without a second thought. It felt good, even as it felt terrifying and like a betrayal of Lucie. "Maybe some people will get excited by your standing in the regime; but others will be *terrified*. To them, you dropping your father's title isn't an incentive, it's a *threat*."

Hedvika tensed, and Celka could practically hear her next words—something about how those people were clearly disloyal and deserved to be afraid. But instead, Hedvika glared at the ugly painting. "So what do I do? Just never proposition anyone?"

"That's not what I'm saying. You're already impressive, Hedvika. You're a gold-bolt Storm Guard sub-lieutenant;

clearly you have regime connections—or you will. Let your tumble decide based on that—and if they say no, let them go. If they want a negotiation, let *them* bring it up."

Hedvika made a face, but Celka thought she was listening.

"If they're interested, you can play after that," Celka said. "You don't have to pretend not to be a tiger. Just... make sure you're with someone who *wants* to tumble a tiger."

"I guess that's reasonable." Hedvika finally met Celka's gaze. "I *am* sorry I lied to you. I just... I didn't want you to hate me because of something I couldn't control."

"You can control *this*," Celka said.

Hedvika nodded. "I will." She squeezed Celka's hand. "I guess you're pretty smart—for a dirt-scrubber."

Despite herself, Celka laughed.

CHAPTER FIFTY-ONE

"ALZBYETA PESEK?" GERRIT read the name off the report a courier had just brought from the Storm Guard Fortress.

"Does that mean something to you?" Iveta looked up from another report.

"She was at the academy with me." According to the write-up, when the Tayemstvoy started showing Lucie's photograph around, one of the Storm Guard Academy instructors had identified her as an old student. "She wasn't in my squad, but we were friendly." He glanced over at Iveta, the pieces coming together, though something about them seemed off. "That must have been why they thought she could seduce me. We kissed—back before Father had her expelled."

"Father?" Iveta leaned forward. He had her attention now.

"I did something stupid; he wanted me to understand 'consequences.'" Gerrit skimmed the rest of the report, which included details about Pesek from her time at the Academy. She'd been expelled just months before the resistance attack that had killed his mother. "What if it wasn't just Father and his brutal ideas of discipline? This doesn't have her transcripts, but I remember her being near the top of our class. Could the resistance have been recruiting mages that early? Could someone have suggested her dismissal?"

"You think the conspiracy could go that high up?" Iveta asked.

"Someone carried a strong enough concealment imbuement to execute Pesek in front of the Yestrab Okhrana. And that poison gas hit a gap in Father's magical protections." The details nearly formed into a coherent picture, but whenever Gerrit tried to look at it directly, understanding slipped away. What was he missing? "I think we need to look more closely at the Storm Guard. Dig through the lists of students who were dismissed—see if any look suspicious."

"That's smart. And maybe the Tayemstvoy will get something from the people on this list." Iveta passed him the report she'd been reading. They'd caught someone who had delivered letters for Pesek, and the courier had given a long list of names to their Tayemstvoy interrogators. Rather than make immediate arrests, the Tayemstvoy had placed the new suspects under surveillance. They'd capture them if they tried to run but, until then, would compile a list of everyone they met with. "I was planning to suggest we release the courier," Iveta said. "Have them watched. They didn't need too much convincing to cooperate, and if their contacts don't realize they've been turned, we might learn even more."

Interrogations of the other Storm Guard staff Pesek had worked with were still underway, and the Tayemstvoy had contacted their counterparts in Pesek's hometown and the city she'd been sent to after expulsion to see what they could dig up from former friends and family. "We should look through the records of other top bozhk academies," Gerrit said when he'd finished reading. "The rot might spread further than the Storm Guard."

Iveta nodded, her secretary in the corner busy taking notes. The Okhrana had widened their search for Pesek's collaborators into the nearby town, the local Tayemstvoy blocking off all access roads and shutting down rail travel, but they still hadn't caught Pesek's conspirators. They had, however, found a cellar full of homemade explosives and a handful of resistance leaflets tucked behind a loose brick. Gerrit and Iveta had joined the Okhrana for that interrogation, and the woman hadn't even tried to hide her anti-regime fervor. They'd gotten the names of the rest of her resistance cell, but she hadn't been involved in the gas attack.

"There's another thing," Gerrit said after they'd finished reviewing the reports. Once Iveta had sent her secretary out to stretch his legs, Gerrit strolled to one corner as if to inspect the painting there. Iveta joined him, sousedni-shape rippling as she pulled against a concealment nuzhda. The imbuement in her pocket flared, and she draped its magic over them.

Gerrit felt a little flash of pride. He'd made that imbuement a few storms ago, and it prevented any sound from escaping the imbuement's shroud. The pocket of silence wasn't large, but it made their private planning sessions that much more secure.

Something about the imbuement felt familiar, as though he'd based it off of a model, but the details escaped him. Probably just something he'd studied at the academy.

"I'd like to request a lateral transfer," he said once Iveta had walled off the nuzhda. This wasn't the only new imbuement she carried, and it felt good to know that his efforts would leave them both better prepared to run the country should something happen to their father. "It sends a certain message that I'm Army and not Tayemstvoy."

Iveta drew a sharp breath. "Gerrit—"

He cut into her objection. "Father could have been killed

in that attack, and we both know that part of Artur's agenda is to subject imbuement mages to more oversight. Few of my tvoortse are Tayemstvoy, and he'll flaunt that I'm merely Army. The hawks already consider us cannon fodder. But if my shoulders are as red as his—as red as *yours*—then no one can question our legitimacy in the regime."

"That's not the only consideration," Iveta said.

Gerrit lifted his chin, daring her to call him out as not being Tayemstvoy material.

She sighed. "I realize the events of the last two days have been... trying. And you've done well, you really have." She put a hand on his shoulder, expression softer than he'd seen since alarms had split the night and their father had nearly died. That compassion made something within him quail, a tremor shaking the foundations of sousednia.

He made himself hold her gaze and refused to let the quakes weaken him. "I can handle it."

"I know," she said. "You did well today while we questioned that rezistyent. And you handled the whole situation with Pesek better than I expected. But... you don't *have* to do this. You're right about Artur and the Tayemstvoy seeing the Army as inferior. But becoming Tayemstvoy is not just about wearing a new uniform. There will be... expectations. The Gerrit I knew from before the storms' return couldn't have handled them." She searched his face, her resemblance to Mother sharpening. "I'm just worried that you're driving yourself too hard." She squeezed his shoulder. "You're one of my most valuable assets, Gerrit, and you're my brother. I don't want you to put so much pressure on yourself that you break."

His throat felt tight, and the tremor in sousednia worsened, cracks radiating up one of the buildings. Then he thought about Artur ordering his paranoid violence imbuement deployed on innocent protestors and Filip returning to his room with news—*what news?*—that he'd gone behind Gerrit's back, *lied to him* after asking for Gerrit's trust.

The people Gerrit depended on had failed him, and Bourshkanyans were suffering. He had to ensure that he and Iveta gained their father's trust, and he couldn't do that if regime elites saw him as weak. Looking Iveta straight in the eyes, he said, "I'm stronger than you think. We need this."

She drew a deep breath, then nodded. "I'll put the transfer through."

They called her secretary back in, and a skittish servant brought steaming glasses of sbiten. Then Captain Kochevar, head of the Yestrab Okhrana detail, joined them in the parlor to discuss next steps. Kochevar nodded to Gerrit in casual greeting—as though she hadn't beaten him to the ground along with a squad of Artur's pet Tayemstvoy.

Barely had Gerrit lifted his glass of sbiten when an Okhrana private pounded into the room. "Come, now," they said, breathing hard. "It's the Stormhawk."

Gerrit sprinted behind Iveta up the stairs, finding his father's bedroom buzzing with activity. He shoved through, finding the Stormhawk supported by a nurse, violently retching yellow fluid. His face was ashen, tears streaming from his bloodshot eyes. He lay back on his pillows, breathing in shallow gasps.

"What happened?" Gerrit demanded.

The physician who'd originally treated the Stormhawk after the attack looked up, light brown skin pale with exhaustion. "We don't know, sir. He was showing improvement, but suddenly he worsened."

"Will he survive?" Iveta asked.

The physician hesitated, exchanging glances with an unfamiliar person listening to the Stormhawk's lungs through a stethoscope. The new physician shook their head minutely, and the Stormhawk's physician set her jaw and met Iveta's gaze. "We don't know."

Staff Sergeant Dolezal stormed in from the corridor, dragging someone by the arm. "She used an imbuement to try and heal him earlier today."

With surprise, Gerrit found himself facing Hana Ruzhishka, his old friend from the academy. Wide-eyed, Hana looked to the new doctor, her questions too steeped in medical jargon for Gerrit to follow. "This isn't because of my imbuement," Hana said.

Though Hana had trained at the Storm Guard Academy, her first imbuement had been healing. She'd gone on to lead a team of storm-blessed doctors out of Zolotoy Svyetlo, Bourshkanya's top bozhk medical academy. Hana turned to Gerrit and Iveta, snapping off a salute. "I came in earlier today after the nearby bozhskyeh storm. My team was contacted, told we had urgent chlorine gas poisoning. The imbuement I created wasn't strong—we don't have experience making anything to help these sorts of symptoms—but the Tayemstvoy provided us with"—her voice faltered—"test patients." Hana swallowed hard, betraying weakness unbecoming for an officer.

Their test patients would have been prisoners—criminals. Of course the Tayemstvoy would have deliberately poisoned them with chlorine gas; they couldn't risk an untested imbuement on the Stormhawk.

"The cases were acute," Hana continued, getting herself back under control, "so the situation was different, but my imbuement caused mild improvement." She glanced at the staff sergeant, then at the Stormhawk, who coughed more yellow bile from his lungs. "Nothing like this."

"Could it be a delayed side-effect?" the new doctor asked. "His lungs are *full* of fluid. Worse than when we arrived."

The comment tickled a memory, and Gerrit grasped after it. "What if it wasn't chlorine?"

"I know what chlorine smells like," the Stormhawk's physician snapped.

"I'm not disputing that, Doctor," Gerrit said smoothly. "But could it have been mixed with another gas? Something with a delayed effect?"

Staff Sergeant Dolezal pointed at one of her guards. "Get the gas canister to the capital for immediate testing." The corporal saluted, rushing out of the room.

Hana shot Gerrit a grateful look, which he ignored. He hadn't done it for her.

"Did your test patients die?" Gerrit asked her.

"Not all of them," she said, voice tight. "At least, not as of when I left."

"We need to find out," Gerrit said. "Monitor their progress."

Staff Sergeant Dolezal sent another Okhrana to do it.

"What about the Okhrana who were in the room with him?" Iveta asked the staff sergeant. "Did Sub-Lieutenant Ruzhishka treat them with her imbuement?"

"One of them," Dolezal said. "The other died in the night."

"Do they have similar symptoms?" Gerrit asked.

From the door, an Okhrana private said, "Yes, sir!" They stepped just inside the room to give their report. "I came to see the doctor on Specialist Madl's behalf. She's..." The private glanced at the Stormhawk, who was coughing again, hacking out more yellowish fluid into a bucket. Stormy skies, how could that much fluid come out of one person's lungs? How was he not already dead? "It's happening to her, too, sir."

Staff Sergeant Dolezal rounded on Hana. "If you use your imbuement again, will it help?"

"I don't know. Without a better understanding of—"

"Will it make it worse?" Iveta interrupted.

Hana spread her hands. "I can't say, sir."

"Try it on Specialist Madl." Gerrit looked to Iveta and Captain Kochevar for authorization. They nodded. As the staff sergeant marched Hana out, Gerrit added, "And keep Sub-Lieutenant Ruzhishka in custody." He didn't think these symptoms were Hana's fault, but you could never be too careful.

CHAPTER FIFTY-TWO

CHAPTER FIFTY-TWO

IN SOUSEDNIA, CELKA wrapped her arm around Filip's throat, the gossamer sleeve of her high wire costume cascading across his chest as she tightened the choke. In the humid circus tent, sweat dripped from her brow, but in true-life she shivered despite her heavy wool overcoat. She'd abandoned the true-life pretense she'd used with Yanek last night, her hands stuffed in her pockets against the cold. The tack shed smelled of leather and horseshoes, Filip's breath steaming where he knelt on the hardpacked dirt.

With focus, she held Filip's old books and oiled steel scents inside the space of his heat-shimmer. His sousedni-shape had faded overnight, brown skin and black hair melting into a heat-mirage, but already this morning, Celka had learned to sharpen her picture of him in sousednia. Whether it was her imagination or it really made him clearer didn't matter. Having a solid sense of him helped with the choke, Pa's advice needling at her, like the key to everything that she just didn't quite grasp. Objects didn't exist in sousednia, but intentions did. Filip's body *intended* to live, his blood *needed* to pump to his brain—and she needed the opposite.

Pressing her right fist against Filip's skull in the big top's summer humidity, Celka cranked her left arm tight about his neck, willing his sousedni-shape to remain solid. For a moment, she *had* it. She *squeezed*, and the air thickened with a pop she felt in her eardrums—a shift in something she'd started to think of as life-nuzhda.

In the freezing tack shed, Filip snapped one hand up to grab the arm that didn't encircle his throat.

Something in that movement—though it didn't change their positions in sousednia—damaged the strength of her hold. Filip's neck still seemed solid, but also... *slippery*.

The air thinned with a sigh.

No. Teeth gritted, Celka fought to tighten the choke, but the air rippled, smelling of mud and bloody noses. Celka struggled to adjust, to regain that perfect alignment, but it felt like trying to snatch a fish from a stream.

In true-life, Filip twisted away and stood. "Stop."

Out of spite or frustration, Celka made one last-ditch attempt to hold him beneath the big top.

Filip's sousedni-shape sharpened, and he caught her wrist. A twist of his shoulders and hips, and he threw her so she landed on her back on the high wire platform, gasping.

In true-life, she stumbled, disoriented from the sudden, uncontrolled sousedni-dislocation. She stared at him, not sure whether to be surprised or angry that he'd fight back in sousednia—that he could. Since he'd started seeing sousednia, his skill in the neighboring reality had increased, but it remained inconsistent.

"I need a break." His sousedni-shape shimmered back into a heat-mirage, as though she'd only imagined the khaki shirt and gold-bolt earing. He rolled his neck in the freezing shed. *«It's unpleasant, like a bad choke in true-life.»*

"Great," Celka said. *So I can make him grouchy. I'm sure that'll help.*

Filip pulled off one leather glove to rub his throat.

"Did I even make you dizzy?"

He adjusted his plum-dark scarf, tucking his chin against the cold. "No." He wriggled his fingers back into his glove. "Though it hurt. I don't think it hurt before."

Celka hunched her shoulders, pacing the tack shed as if it could make her warm. *Maybe this is hopeless.*

You don't believe that, Filip said, and she couldn't tell if he meant it as a statement or a question.

She shook her head, stomach churning. *Do you think Gerrit's—* all right? She couldn't finish the question. Of course he wasn't. He'd looked like a sleeting Tayemstvoy in sousednia. Celka sat on a stool and put a fist to her mouth. *We shouldn't have left him.*

That's not how orders work. The snap in Filip's tone startled her, and she drew a deep breath in sousednia, wondering if he was angry with her. She didn't think so. He was just worried.

He'll be all right, she said. But the thought of Gerrit spending days with only Iveta and the Yestrab Okhrana for company made her wonder who he'd be the next time she saw him.

He'd better be.

Despite the sharp-cold air, Celka forced herself to draw slow breaths, reaching for the calm to keep working on her murderous sousedni-disruptions. When she'd come up with this plan, it had seemed so natural—almost obvious. Now she worried that, even if she *could* make it work, it would take months or even years of practice. She doubted the resistance could afford that. She felt like she was trying to burn a pile of incriminating evidence while the Tayemstvoy banged on her door. Gerrit had been terrified that Lucie's arrest would cut deep into Vrana's network. If he was right, she didn't have *time* to fail.

Celka stood. She needed to stop worrying and get back to work. *«I felt like I almost had it last time,»* she told Filip. *«Let me try again?»*

He nodded and knelt. Kneeling wasn't important for the choke—now that Celka had gotten a good night's sleep, she didn't even need to be near him, much less have him on his knees, but it meant less chance of him injuring himself in the fall if she did make him pass out. *If.*

This time, she told herself.

But just like when she'd tried it before, the moment she felt the choke land, she lost it.

Yanking her hands out of her gloves, she rubbed them together and pressed them to her cheeks, trying and chase the chill. *«I feel like I'm closer this morning. What am I doing wrong?»* she asked, hoping Filip would have ideas.

«I need to see you work.» He glanced back in the direction of the darkened house, the rest of the squad still asleep.

«We can't wake Yanek,» Celka said, *«not without him wondering why this is so important.»*

Filip balled one hand into a fist but didn't argue. *«Show me on a horse.»*

She snatched up their oil lantern, making their long shadows swing. Inside the stables, horses snorted and shuffled in their sleep. She hung the lantern on a hook. *«I don't know if I can do it on a horse.»*

«You made elephants poop.»

She snorted. Fair enough. Turning to the nearest horse, an older roan mare, Celka gripped the stall's fence rail to anchor her true-form. Shifting into sousednia worsened her shivering, the heat from the illusory summer day making true-life feel colder.

Filip rested a hand on her shoulder. In sousednia, she caught it, glad for his support—and warmth. He hesitated, seeming to struggle with something, then stepped closer, his broad chest against her back, strong arms wrapping her waist.

She leaned into him, letting true-life and sousednia track, some of her chill easing. She gave herself a moment to rest—that's all it was, just rest, which she might have taken even if Filip hadn't wrapped her in his arms, sousednia bright with books and armor.

With effort, Celka focused, searching the darkness of her high wire platform for the sleeping mare.

If she concentrated hard enough on a mundane in sousednia, Celka could typically resolve a shape more-or-less matching the person's true-form—though the smoke-form's edges blurred and shifted. Touching a person for a sousedni-disruption became an effort of will, Celka's focus and knowledge of the person giving their sousedni-shape substance.

Resolving an animal's shape was trickier, but the disruption was actually easier. Animals appeared more faintly in sousednia—the simpler the creature, the fainter—and their sousedni-scents resembled the animal's true smells, tinted by dominant needs. A hungry horse smelled a little different from a cold horse or a sick horse but, fundamentally, they all smelled like horse.

Gathering up the smoky strands of horse felt like untangling threads from a tapestry. Celka envisioned the strands as opaque to her spotlight, holding them in her mind, constructing the mare in wisps. As the sleeping mare's form coalesced on her high wire platform, Celka stepped her sousedni-shape regretfully from Filip's embrace, approaching the horse-shaped shadow.

Inhaling deeply, Celka breathed the creature's needs. Sleeping, the mare rippled with basic life-nuzhda—the flow of blood and breath, the quieter rumblings of internal processes. Only since Celka had started practicing with Filip had she begun to identify these subtler scent-threads, and she'd never felt them in an animal before.

Surprisingly, Celka found it easier to trace the life-threads for the mare than for a person. Stepping close in sousednia, Celka ran her hand along the mare's smoky neck, fingertips skimming over where blood flowed from heart to brain.

Compared to Filip, the mare's neck was larger and higher, and Celka circled the animal, wondering how she'd wrap her arm around its throat to attempt the choke. Maybe envision herself on its back? She shook herself. True-life constrained her thinking, just like Pa had said. She didn't need to *physically* choke the horse. She needed to make the horse believe her blood flow had ceased. And the horse's sousedni-shape was smoke. Celka could pass through smoke.

Recalling the anatomy diagrams Filip had gotten Dbani to draw for her yesterday, Celka imagined arteries and veins sending and returning blood to the horse's brain, lines like rope running through the animal's neck. Leaning in, Celka let the scent of blood, of life, guide her hands.

She knew it the moment she gripped the arteries. The horse-smoke solidified, a terrified whinny echoing through the big top. Celka closed her eyes, gathered those slippery cords into one fist, and *squeezed*.

In fear, the mare's life-nuzhda strengthened, the rubbery strands in Celka's hands exploding into burning steel cables, strong and sharp-edged, searing her palm. The mare bucked, life-strands thrashing. Celka slipped, the motion so real she almost fell, Filip's true-life hold steadying her just enough that she gritted her teeth and kept her focus on the neighboring reality. Sousednia was mind. Her mind was stronger than a horse's.

The animal tried to throw her off, but Celka would not be thrown. Belief knotted her sousedni-shape to the horse's, a leech.

Yet the horse fought to live. Celka's hand trembled, her own ligaments screaming as the mare's life-threads sawed across her palm. Gripping hard, two-handed, Celka struggled to hold. Sweat slid beneath her arms and under her breasts. Her breath grew ragged. The mare thrashed, and Celka didn't know how much longer she could hold on.

Then the resistance vanished.

Steel cables of life-nuzhda flopped like wilted dandelion stems, and Celka fell against the animal's smokeform, a pillow of hay and warm breath in sousednia, the stems still clenched in her fist. Something struck her hard across the chest in true-life, the fence post knocking into her sternum before Filip slung her arm over his shoulders to keep her on her feet. Confused, Celka swam into true-life, frowning into the horse's stall.

The mare's knees buckled, and she collapsed to her forelegs. Celka gasped, sweat-slick skin icy as the mare fell onto her side on the straw.

Horrified, Celka lost her sousedni-dislocation. Snapping back in line with her true-form felt like falling from the practice wire. She gasped for breath even as she tried to surge out of Filip's grasp to go to the horse—*sleet*, she hadn't wanted to kill a horse! But she stumbled and had to catch the fence rail for support.

"You did it," Filip said.

Celka shoved out of his hold. She made it two steps toward the open back of the stall before the mare's legs twitched. The animal flung her head up, flailing to her feet. Celka sagged against the fence rail. "She's alive."

Filip nodded as though the fact weren't terribly relevant.

«*You dropped the disruption as she collapsed. Was that intentional?*» He shook his head, barking a laugh. «*Freezing sleet, this will work!*»

The mare's eyes rolled with too much white. Celka hugged her arms around herself, stomach roiling. She'd succeeded—partially, at least. This should feel like victory. Instead, she couldn't look away from the panicked animal.

"You can do this," Filip whispered.

Celka tried the words in her own mind and found herself turning from the mare, whose terror was already ebbing, to Filip whose expression had become intense and determined. *I can assassinate the Stormhawk. I can avenge Lucie.* She shivered. She was getting ahead of herself. She'd dropped a horse unconscious. She had no idea if the technique worked on people. But if it did...

«*It was different with the horse.*» The words sounded inane after she'd spoken them, but Filip's attention sparked.

«*Different how?*»

«*After I got the initial choke—that's where I keep losing it with you. But with the horse... She didn't go slippery quite the way you did.*»

He focused back on the mare, the corners of his eyes creasing the way they did when he was deep in thought—reviewing whatever he'd seen or felt, trying to match it to her description. «*What else happens when I go 'slippery'?*»

She shook her head, wishing she knew how to describe it. «*The air changes when I get you in the choke—when I have the choke. But then it shifts again, and I lose you.*»

«*You smell nuzhdi,*» he said. «*Does the air smell different?*»

«*I don't think...*» Except, maybe? She was always so concentrated on their physical positions—as if the physical meant anything in sousednia—that she hadn't really thought about the smells.

«*The moment the mare reacted to your hold,*» Filip said, nodding at the horse, who now nosed around in her feeding trough, «*her nuzhda shifted—I think. I'm not used to animal nuzhdi.*»

«*There's not much to them,*» Celka said before she realized what they were saying. «*Wait, a core nuzhda defines everything about a person's sousednia. If that shifts when I get you in a choke hold—*»

«*—then you could lose me.*»

Celka pulled a face. «*How do I use that?*»

«*When Gerrit's nuzhda-warped, he doesn't notice me if I pull on his core nuzhda. I have to guide his attention by first pulling against whatever nuzhda is warping him. Then I can shift, and he'll follow me instinctually back to his un-warped core.*»

Celka flexed and stretched her hands, trying to keep feeling in her fingertips. «*So if your core nuzhda warps because of the choke, I need to warp my hold to follow you. Maybe I managed to choke out the mare because her core nuzhda didn't change much? Because she's a horse.*»

«*It also means you need to practice on other people.*»

Celka frowned. «*And I have to basically learn how to become a strazh. How hard is it to pull against someone's core nuzhda? Sleet.*»

«*Wait,*» Filip said. «*What if we're making this too complicated? You still have your calming imbuement, right?*» They'd handed Celka's original imbuement over to the Yestrab Okhrana, but the storm pendant still hung around her neck. «*If you use it to make me calm, maybe my nuzhda won't shift.*»

Hope caught in her throat, and Celka grabbed the lantern, hurrying back into the tack shed so they wouldn't frighten the horses any more than they already had. In sousednia, she shot up out of the big top, fields and streams becoming a patchwork below her. Imbuement active, she bundled its nuzhda over Filip, just as she'd done with Pa, then returned to her big top. Leaving her true-form a few meters away, she crossed to where Filip knelt on the high wire platform, his back to her.

When she looped her arm around his neck, he touched her wrist lightly and smiled up at her. «*You've got this, Celka.*»

She drew a slow breath of distant fields and old books, and tightened her arm around his throat. The air thickened, and Filip tensed, but his hands came up only lazily to grasp her forearm. Before his fingers could really dig in, the thump of his body hitting the tack shed floor startled her back to true-life.

She rushed to his side as he flailed back to consciousness, her pulse pounding in her ears. She moved to help him sit, but he pushed up to hands and knees, grinning. He caught her face and kissed her on the lips.

Startled, Celka flinched back.

He released her, wide-eyed. "Sleet, I'm sorry, I—"

She caught his face in her own gloved hands, wishing the leather wasn't between them. "No, it's—you just startled me." A laugh escaped her throat, a little hysterical. Through Nina, she said, «*This is going to work. Filip, we can kill him. Bourshkanya can be free.*»

«*And we can get Gerrit back.*» The words sobered him.

«*Right.*» She dropped her hands from his face, cheeks heating as she realized how close she'd come to kissing him again. Filip's kiss had been impulsive, a release of tension after all the strain of the last two days. But she and Gerrit were exclusive—even if Filip and Yanek weren't. She stood, shoving her hands into her pockets. «*Can we practice again?*» At his nod, she asked, «*Can I try holding it for longer? Is that safe? Should we get you a pile of blankets to fall on?*»

Filip choked a laugh and started to stand. Then he hesitated. *«Actually, what if I lie down? We should attack the Stormhawk while he's asleep. If you get the choke fast enough, the guards might not even realize something's wrong.»*

«That's smart.» She reached out, catching his hand, so thoroughly grateful he'd chosen to help them. *«But I don't want to risk hurting you.»*

«Don't hold it for more than ten seconds,» he said, grimacing as he lay on his back on the frozen dirt. *«Sleet, it's cold out here.»*

She laughed. *«I could pile you up with horse blankets.»*

He made a face. *«Such a good friend.»*

She knelt at his side, his deep dark eyes snaring her in the lamplight. Laying a hand on his chest, she said, *«Thank you.»*

He gave her the private half smile that reminded her of learning to shoot, the warmth of his big hands over hers, his unflagging encouragement. Then he shivered, and the fog of his breath snapped Celka back to herself. Once the Stormhawk was dead, she could think about what it meant that looking at Filip could still make her forget how to breathe.

CHAPTER FIFTY-THREE

"Phosgene," Iveta read from the latest report. "Never heard of it."

Gerrit frowned. The name seemed familiar, though he couldn't recall from where. "Is that what's causing the fluid in his lungs?"

"Seems to match the symptoms," she said.

"Ruzhishka will be glad," Gerrit said, dry.

Iveta looked up from the report, brow raised. She studied him for a moment, then waved the rest of their staff out of the room. When they were alone, she said, "You've changed since the attack."

"Have I?" Gerrit supposed it was possible, though he didn't feel different. "I've finally started feeling like a part of our family. I guess I take exception to someone trying to kill Father."

Iveta's smile had a cold edge. Before she could speak, however, a sharp rap sounded on the door.

"Sorry to disturb you, Captain, Lieutenant," the young Okhrana private said, "but the Stormhawk requests your presence."

Gerrit hadn't known the Stormhawk was able to breathe well enough yet to make a request, but Iveta seemed unsurprised. She stood, handing Gerrit the report she'd been reading. "Let's not keep him waiting, then."

As they followed the private, Gerrit skimmed the report. He'd only just reached the notes about phosgene's origin when they entered the Stormhawk's rooms.

"Lesnikraj," the Stormhawk spat after they'd saluted. It sent him into another coughing fit, and he hacked something into the bucket at his side. His color was a little better, though, even from when Gerrit had visited him this morning. "Should have expected the stormless hail-chewers to find a way."

Gerrit glanced back down at the report. According to the scientists who'd analyzed the gas canister, phosgene had been developed and was exclusively manufactured in Lesnikraj. Whether or not the assassins had been Lesnikrayen, they'd certainly collaborated with the enemy.

"They made a mistake not finishing the job." The Stormhawk hacked and spat. "This means war."

Gerrit snapped his attention back to his father, but Iveta spoke first.

"You mean *preparing* for war." She kept her voice level. "Not an open declaration."

"No. I'm through appeasing the sleet-lickers. The storms have returned. We have weapons." He nodded at Gerrit, then doubled over, coughing.

When he'd finished, Iveta said, "Winter is closing in, Father."

The Stormhawk grimaced. "Then they won't expect an attack, will they?"

Gerrit felt the same tension he saw in Iveta's stance. Starting a war as winter iced the land would risk their own soldiers as well as the enemy's. Iveta's jaw muscles bunched, and he could practically see her trying to think of some argument that would convince their angry, despotic father not to throw away lives to get revenge. But he'd already shown his willingness to slaughter Bourshkanyans. The reports from Zbishov, where the Yestrab Okhrana had deployed the paranoid violence imbuement on a peaceful work strike, listed hundreds dead; Artur had gotten his desired carnage, and the Stormhawk hadn't blinked.

"Sir." Gerrit stepped forward. "I have an idea."

The Stormhawk narrowed his eyes but waved him to speak.

"The emotional imbuement I created to drive people to paranoid violence... what if you sent a strike team with it into Lesnikraj? A small team of bozhki with concealment imbuements could cross the border and infiltrate the enemy's heart. Strike them where they least expect it."

The Stormhawk coughed once, then relaxed back into his pillows. He studied Gerrit, seeming to consider the idea. "Where do you propose we strike?"

Gerrit frowned, thinking.

Iveta said, "Parliament—while it's in session."

Despite himself, Gerrit drew a sharp breath. His stomach roiled—a feeling like nascent horror—but he crushed it down.

The Stormhawk laughed, cut short as coughs wracked him. "That"—he spat more phlegm into the bucket and shook a finger at Iveta—"is perfect." Smiling, he leaned back and laced his fingers over his chest. "Why stop there, really?" He turned his grin on Gerrit, all teeth. "We could break their industrial and scientific spine before they realize what's happened."

"And while they scramble to rebuild," Iveta said, as much the predator as their father, "we use the winter to continue imbuing. Come spring, they'll be limping, and we'll be unstoppable."

CHAPTER FIFTY-FOUR

FILIP SAT BACK on his heels as he released the spark for his final prayer: *Let me reflect calm clarity in the heart of a storm.* The Song of Calming's final notes hung over the rocky cove, and his fingers burned from taking the spark in the absence of an altar. He knelt at the end of a dock, but it felt like the edge of the world as dawn shimmered orange through the mist. The air smelled of salt, and he let his overcoat hang open.

Footsteps behind him made Filip turn, but he kept his breathing slow, trying to maintain the calm of his morning prayers. Yanek emerged from the mist, bleary. He'd never liked mornings.

"I didn't mean to wake you," Filip said.

Yanek shrugged around a yawn, flopping to the planks beside Filip, dangling his feet just above the lapping waves.

Filip stared back out at the swirling mist, wishing he could relax. Nearly a month had passed since Gerrit sent them to imbue. Celka could achieve the sousedni-choke consistently now while using the calming imbuement, and she'd found a million small ways to practice subtle sousedni-disruptions on strangers to improve her control. They'd left word in a dead drop for Captain Vrana about their new assassination plan, and as soon as they got close to the Stormhawk, Celka was ready to finish what they'd started at Yinovatka Manor. Ready to make Lucie's death matter.

Yanek bumped his shoulder against Filip's. "Talk to me."

Filip made himself sit and dangle his feet off the dock at Yanek's side. "I shouldn't be out here." Yanek slung an arm around his shoulders, but Filip sat as if he stood at attention. The only word they'd gotten from Gerrit was a letter—a week ago—saying that he was proud of the platoon's progress. It had come by courier along with a velvet box for Celka—ruby lightning bolt earrings set in gold and a private note that said, *Thinking of you.* An expensive gift.

Gerrit had sent Filip nothing.

"I'm glad you're with us," Yanek said, serious in the brightening dawn. "You're a better leader than Gerrit."

Filip shook his head.

"It's true. You listen to the platoon. They're happy with their imbuements, proud. You've kept us from burning out despite the grueling itinerary." Yanek took his hand. "I like who you've become outside Gerrit's shadow."

The comment startled Filip, and he met Yanek's gaze. He hadn't thought of it that way. "I've... enjoyed leading the platoon." He was surprised to discover it was true. Worry for Gerrit gnawed at his stomach, but coordinating their travel and organizing the imbuement mages felt good.

"So tell me what's wrong," Yanek said.

"You know what's wrong." Filip glared back out at the mist that was already burning away. "I should be with Gerrit."

"He was the one who sent you away," Yanek said. "There's only so much you can do for someone who doesn't want your help."

The words felt like a knife, twisted in his gut. He wanted to argue, insist that wasn't what had happened. Instead, he said, "He's been walling off memories."

"Memories?" Yanek said, surprised. "Why? How?"

Filip searched for an answer that was true but covered their treason. He trusted Yanek, but not enough to risk all their lives—not enough to risk the mission. "He thinks it makes him stronger."

Yanek's snort was derisive. "How long's he been doing it?"

"Months," Filip said. "Since before Mrach."

"Sleeting Mrach. Is that why he...?" Yanek's jaw tightened, the horror of the riot washing over him, haunting his eyes. But even here, alone at the end of the world, they might be overheard. Yanek knew not to speak dangerous truths.

Filip didn't understand how that enforced silence had never bothered him before. If truths about the regime were so dangerous that you could be arrested for speaking them, how had he believed the regime deserved to rule? Casual conversation wasn't a threat. Armed Tayemstvoy silencing civilians and dragging them from their homes was a *threat*. Skilled bozhki using their magic to turn peaceful protests violent was a *threat*.

But he wasn't safe in the resistance yet. Struggling to turn his thoughts back to their conversation, Filip said, "The assassination attempt shook Gerrit. Before we left..." Part of Filip wished he'd never started seeing sousednia. Bad enough to feel the sounds and smells around Gerrit warped away from his best friend's alpine clearing. "He did more. His sousedni-shape... changed. He had red shoulders."

Yanek drew a sharp breath, hand tightening in Filip's. After a minute, he almost managed to sound casual as he said, "I suppose it was inevitable."

He's not Tayemstvoy, Filip wanted to protest. They'd talked about it before the storms' return, him and Gerrit, alone in the wilderness on a leisure day that seemed lifetimes ago. Iveta had just commissioned into the Tayemstvoy and Filip had asked if Gerrit planned to follow her. He'd probably sounded just like Yanek, trying to pretend it didn't matter. Failing. Gerrit had been adamant—vehement—that he never would. And that was when he'd still believed in the State.

"I'm worried he's been imbuing," Filip said instead. Even before Lucie's death, Gerrit had done a sleet-poor job reintegrating after erecting mental walls. With only Iveta and the Yestrab Okhrana for company, Filip could so easily imagine his friend convincing himself he had to keep the walls up. If Gerrit pulled down Gods' Breath with such a deeply warped core nuzhda, Filip feared the walls would become permanent.

"You think he deliberately pushed you away?" Yanek asked.

Throat tight, Filip jerked a nod. He hadn't talked about this, even with Celka, but the worry hung between them. Did Gerrit even support the resistance anymore? Or had he cleaved away that part of himself to hide from Lucie's death? Would they even get an opportunity for Celka to attempt another assassination?

The fog over the water thinned as they sat in silence.

Just as Filip started to think about heading back to the house, Yanek asked, "When are *you* going to try imbuing?"

Filip tensed. "I'm not an—"

Yanek squeezed his shoulders. "You're already leading this platoon while Gerrit's doing... whatever it is. Securing power. Becoming a Kladivo."

Filip wanted to protest that wasn't what Gerrit was doing; but he didn't know. He'd started down this path because of Gerrit. If Gerrit turned his back on the resistance, where did that leave Filip?

He shook the thought. Even if Gerrit's mental warping had pulled him away, Celka's assassination would succeed. They'd kill the Stormhawk. They'd get Gerrit back. Together, they'd join the resistance and lead an army to tear down the State.

"I'm not an imbuement mage." Filip stood and gave Yanek a hand up, stiff from sitting so long in the cold.

Yanek wrapped an arm around his waist as they headed up the rocky slope to the house. "I think you'd be good at it, if you change your mind."

Two days later, the conversation gnawed at him as Filip sat in the back of a Tayemstvoy motorcar winding through a town cratered with anti-regime sentiment. Broad faces of buildings had been painted over for their visit, but the paint ran in the freezing rain, resistance slogans struggling through. *The State Cannot Silence Our Songs.*

Bolt-hawks rode on the motorcar's running boards, alert and attentive so he didn't need to be. Yet something left Filip on edge.

He glanced at Celka, sandwiched between him and Hedvika, worrying one of her new earrings. Noticing his gaze, she stopped fiddling with the ruby lightning bolt, pressing her closed fist to her thigh. "What is it?"

He shook his head, glancing back out the window. Bells tolled in storm temples, the sky thick with clouds, and Filip fought the urge to rub the back of his neck. *I'm not an imbuement mage.* He repeated the words, as if that would make them true.

"They wouldn't attack a motorcade," Hedvika said, fingers drumming on her sidearm. But she didn't sound confident.

Unsure what had triggered him, Filip squinted into the falling snow. But that wariness felt wrong. Closing his eyes, he tried to understand. There, where a splinter had lodged deep in his chest, he found a spreading balm.

Surprised, he snatched up his link to Celka. *«Gerrit's here.»*

Celka's breath caught. *«You're sure?»* Her hand gripped his thigh, tense. After a moment, she said, *«I still can't reach him through Nina.»*

Filip kept the frown off his face as he pressed against Nina's pine and ice weaves, failing to establish the connection just as he had outside Yinovatka Manor. *«Maybe he's still too far away.»* He tried to believe it.

Celka's worry echoed through the python's magic. *«Can you tell if he's all right?»*

He couldn't. The strazh bond mostly let him sense Gerrit's location, though he'd learned to feel shifts in nuzhda through it. As far as he could tell, Gerrit wasn't pulling against any nuzhda. Filip tried to let that give him hope.

Outside a theatre, the motorcar slowed, waved in by a bolt-hawk from Lieutenant Raska's platoon, and Gerrit strode out into the sleet, uniform cap casting his face in shadow.

Filip flung the door open before the motorcar could stop. Leaping out, he slipped on icy cobblestones as he scrambled toward his best friend.

Gerrit's flinty gaze slammed him to a stop.

Filip nearly fell. But even if he'd mistaken the ice in his best friend's expression, there was no mistaking his uniform. Even in true-life, Gerrit's shoulders were red.

Struggling to crush down his panic, Filip straightened and snapped off a salute. "Sir." Roaring sounded in his ears, and Gods' Breath yanked on his spine, blurring true-life. Gerrit's sousedni-shape wavered in Filip's quiet library, Tayemstvoy uniform identical in both realities: black knee-boots, hawks on every shiny brass button, truncheon hanging casually from his belt. Instead of the banked pain of loss and glacial determination, Gerrit's core nuzhda tasted of iron and the stomp of an infantry parade. It echoed cell doors clanging closed and pistol rounds chambering. *You promised*, Filip wanted to say. *You're not Tayemstvoy.* But he choked down the words.

A captain's four stars glinted from Gerrit's shoulders. Voice wooden in his own ears, Filip said, "Congratulations on the promotion, sir."

He searched Gerrit for the faintest grimace, some acknowledgment that he'd been backed into a corner and donned red shoulders out of grim necessity. Instead, Gerrit dismissed Filip's salute with cold precision. In his eyes, Filip saw a stranger.

«*He still won't activate Nina.*» Celka's voice through the snake startled Filip, and he realized Gerrit had turned away from him, greeting the rest of the platoon.

«*He probably can't.*» Filip struggled to keep a soldierly face over his panic. Focusing on true-life, he waited until Gerrit started back inside, then fell in at his best friend's side. "Can we speak privately, sir?" He kept his voice neutral through sheer force of will. He needed to get Gerrit alone and force him to reintegrate. Gerrit couldn't imbue like this.

Gerrit didn't even glance at him. "After the storm, Sub-Lieutenant."

Filip pushed into sousednia, the transition easier—in the way that falling off a cliff was easy—beneath the bozhskyeh storm, and caught Gerrit's arm. «This can't wait.»

Gerrit met his gaze in sousednia's library, expression hard. «Change is necessary, Cizek.» Gerrit brushed imaginary dust from the captain's stars on his red shoulders. «I understand you've been taken by surprise and that your experience grounding me during storms is outdated. If you find it too difficult to adapt, I can remove you from duty until you're capable of doing your job.»

The words landed like blows. Filip opened his mouth to

protest, but Gerrit's eyes narrowed in subtle warning, and Filip realized they weren't alone in the neighboring reality—they weren't *ever* alone, but the ease of communicating through Nina had made him sloppy.

Gerrit's nod was almost imperceptible—one of their old signals—and Filip swallowed his protest, praying Gerrit knew what he was doing, that this warped and red-shouldered version of his friend was more illusion than it seemed.

When Gerrit wavered into nothingness, Filip flailed to return to true-life, his library too real until suddenly it wasn't, sousednia vanishing like it had never been. He realized he'd stopped walking and hurried to catch up as Gerrit strode down the long aisle between orchestra seats.

Gerrit's pace ate the distance toward the stage, stride whispering urgency distinct from the storm. Something more was afoot, and Filip needed to figure it out fast. Because no matter Gerrit's confidence, Filip didn't trust him to imbue while so badly warped.

"Have you imbued since I've been gone?" Filip tried to make the matter seem one of simple bookkeeping.

"Twice," Gerrit said, as if imbuing with a warped core nuzhda was unremarkable. "Sub-Lieutenant Bartos strazhed for me."

"Darina Bartos—Hana's strazh?" Filip failed to hide his surprise. "Are they here?" He struggled to put that new information into context. But at least Gerrit had imbued with a competent strazh.

Gerrit cut him an irritated glance, but said, "Yes." He leapt onto the stage, squinting into the dim audience seats.

Filip followed his gaze, frowning to see red shoulders guarding the exits to the theatre's balcony seats—seats inaccessible except through the theatre's lower doors. While Gerrit assessed their platoon, Filip made himself trace the lines of force flowing downward from those Tayemstvoy. They weren't Iveta's bolt-hawks. Squinting to dim true-life, he peered through his library's wavering stacks, grimly unsurprised to see bozhk heat-shimmers and even a few sharper sousedni-shapes. Active imbuements brightened the space like fireworks.

At the center of those imbuements, Filip discovered a small group in olive drab clustered in the frontmost balcony seats. Distance made it hard to be sure, but Gerrit had handed him the clues.

Stomach twisting, Filip reached through Nina's link to Celka. *«The Stormhawk is here.»*

AT FILIP'S WORDS, gunshots exploded through Celka's sousednia. Truncheons cracked. Pa screamed. Celka forced herself to breathe, plunging her hand into her pocket to grip the green silk square. Gerrit looked like the enemy, but he, apparently, was not the greatest threat here. As her high wire solidified, she asked Filip through Nina, *«Where is he?»*

«Front of the balcony. Too many storm-blessed are watching for you to try the choke here.»

She exhaled relief even as it rode on the worry that they wouldn't get another chance.

«We'll likely overnight in the same place,» Filip said, his calm close to cracking. *«Might even be Yinovatka Manor again; we're close enough.»*

She made herself keep breathing, finding the knot of olive drab at the front of the balcony. Shifting into sousednia left the bolt-hawks a heat-mirage tangle. Havel and Masha, plus the tvoortsei from Yellow Squad, appeared more vivid, but above—oh, above. Two of the Stormhawk's guards appeared razor-edged in sousednia, storm-blessed. One met her gaze with measured intensity, a tiger crouched in the underbrush. Most of the other Yestrab Ohkrana had bozhk heat-shimmers glowing with active imbuements.

"Is something wrong?" Hedvika asked.

Celka snapped back into true-life. "No." She tried to say it casually, making herself climb onto the stage as Gerrit ordered the imbuement squads forward. Looking at Gerrit in his Tayemstvoy uniform made her sick, so she gazed back out across the theatre. Iveta watched them from the front of the balcony, a little apart from the Stormhawk and his guards. The house lights caught her as she shifted to speak with someone, and Celka realized Iveta's insignia had changed, too—a major's five-pointed star above a bar. Iveta was now *Major* Kladivo.

Celka tried to think. Unless the Stormhawk had promoted Artur at the same time, Iveta's promotion meant she now matched him in rank. Maybe Gerrit's warping wasn't as bad as it seemed. Maybe he'd spent the last month preparing Iveta to split the regime's forces and was still himself, somehow, beneath those red shoulders.

But when Gerrit called their squads to attention, Celka couldn't make herself believe it. He moved and spoke like a different person. When Celka raised her voice in chorus with the rest of the platoon—"All hail the Stormhawk!"—her squadmates' righteous belief made her sick.

Gerrit started in on a patriotic speech, and Celka glanced at Filip. At the Storm Guard Fortress after Bludov, he'd looked so comfortable in uniform, so glad to be back. Alone amongst their platoon now, he wasn't comfortable or proud. He covered it well. She doubted she'd have seen it if not for breathing his core nuzhda in their clandestine practice sessions, her arm locked around his throat. It should have reassured her, but instead, it made her remember Lucie's screams. How had she ever felt safe amongst these people? Surrounded by Tayemstvoy and Yestrab Okhrana, Celka felt like a rabbit in a tiger's den. She'd been so stupid to see these people as friends. So stupid to believe she could hide her fluffy white tail.

Gerrit finished his speech, and the Stormhawk rose, vomiting propaganda and lauding their storm-blessings. His voice sounded hoarse, and Celka wondered whether his lungs still suffered from their gas attack. It didn't matter. Even if he was perfectly healthy, she'd be able to choke him to death—so long as no one spotted her sousedni-shape as she did it.

She might be surrounded by tigers, but no one had realized that her stripes were only painted on. If Filip was right, she could kill the Stormhawk tonight. She just needed to play the part a little longer.

To Filip, she said, «We need to get our imbuements back from Gerrit.»

«We'll get Gerrit back, too,» Filip said, like he was trying to convince himself.

Gerrit caught her gaze. "Specialist Prochazka." He gestured for the rest of the imbuement platoon and bolt-hawks to clear the stage. "We'll begin with a joint-imbuement." He held out his hand as if expecting her to take it. The hard lines of his face perfectly matched his red shoulders.

His stripes weren't false. Beneath his predator's stare, Celka couldn't move.

Hedvika kicked her in the ankle. "Yes, sir," Hedvika said, and her boot-licking snapped Celka out of her fear.

As Celka made her legs work, Filip stepped to Gerrit's side, leaning close, sousedni-shape brightening before he said, in the flat, green expanse of Celka's featureless field, «Joint-imbuing with a warped core nuzhda—»

«You want Darina to strazh for me?» Gerrit snapped.

Filip rocked back. One hand balled into a fist.

Before Filip could do something none of them could afford, Celka said, «Our joint imbuements were already becoming difficult before»—*the failed assassination*—«we spent a month apart. We don't know how your new core nuzhda will affect the process.» She wanted to catch Gerrit by the arms and scream at him until he listened. But rabbit instincts warned that if she so much as twitched wrong, he'd tear out her throat.

The air should have smelled like pine and glaciers around him, but instead it reminded her of being locked in a cell beneath the Storm Guard Fortress. She made herself hold his gaze, aiming for steady and calm—no challenge, just facts. When he spoke, the edge was tempered. «I have confidence in your weaves. You'll make this work.» He left no room for discussion.

Celka swallowed hard.

Before she could ask what they were imbuing, Gerrit said aloud, "Paranoid violence." He drew his belt knife from its sheath.

Celka barely stopped herself from recoiling, and horror crossed Filip's face before he locked his expression down. «We can't,» Celka said in sousednia, when what she wanted to say was, *We promised we'd never make one again.*

"I recommend a low-Category imbuement." Filip managed to make his voice almost impassive, like Gerrit hadn't blown past his earlier advice. "Verify that the *shift* in your core nuzhda isn't a problem."

Gerrit twisted his hand holding the knife, causing the sharpened steel edge to catch the spotlights. "Category Four." When he met Celka's gaze, his expression was as unyielding as any Tayemstvoy's.

At Celka's side, Hedvika radiated tension. She knew Gerrit's core nuzhda well enough to know this was a terrible idea. But she just laid her palm on the back of Celka's neck, her touch more shackles than support. From the corner of Celka's eye, she caught the glimmer of Hedvika's sousedni-shape shift and dodge, flaring red as she pulled against a combat nuzhda.

Past Gerrit, Filip hesitated. He'd lifted his hand as if to clasp the back of Gerrit's neck, but it was still balled into a fist like he couldn't quite make himself do it. A crease between his brows betrayed his racing thoughts.

Celka reached into their link through Nina, terrified Filip would turn away and leave her to imbue this horror alone. *«Just once more,»* she told him. *«Tonight, we kill the Stormhawk and get Gerrit back.»*

CHAPTER FIFTY-FIVE

WHEN GERRIT HAD asked whether Filip wanted Darina to strazh in his place, Filip had almost said *yes*. Joint-imbuing was dangerous under the best of conditions, and Filip had read plenty of journals by previous storm-cycles' imbuement mages that ended with a postscript written in another hand. They'd attempted to joint-imbue and gone storm-mad. Or died. Or pulled so much storm energy they triggered a madness cascade that left behind a field of corpses and fire.

That Gerrit and Celka could *usually* manage it was no guarantee. Having Filip and Hedvika to soak up failures shouldn't have given Gerrit license to be reckless.

I'm Gerrit's strazh, Filip told himself as Gerrit ignored his advice and insisted on a high-Category imbuement. But Yanek's words from months ago itched under his skin: *Is that all you are?*

Was it? Was his life worth nothing more than to throw himself into the fire whenever his best friend needed him? Was Filip worth so little that Gerrit could toss him aside again and again and Filip would keep crawling back to him, ready to fling himself between Gerrit and storm-madness even when this imbuement could kill them all?

What if he called Gerrit's bluff—was it a bluff? He didn't think so. What if Filip turned his back and let Gerrit call Darina down to take his place—Darina, who should sleeting well know better than to let Gerrit imbue this badly warped.

But Filip caught Hedvika's gaze as she laid her hand on the back of Celka's neck. Darina would do exactly what Hedvika was doing. She would follow orders. Hedvika didn't like it, but she didn't argue. Gerrit was their commanding officer—and a sleeting Kladivo. If he told them to throw themselves into fire, the stars on their shoulders and his meant they had to obey.

But Filip had already broken his oaths to the State.

«*Just once more,*» Celka said. But would it be? If they killed the Stormhawk tonight, if they brought Gerrit back to himself, would this really be the end? All his life, Filip had protected Gerrit, but when it really mattered—when their lives and the entire cause they'd been fighting for were on the line—he couldn't make Gerrit listen. Did Gerrit have so little faith in him? So little trust?

There's only so much you can do for someone who doesn't want your help.

Yanek's words had cut. But maybe that blade was what Filip needed—to cut old ties to make room for new. Bourshkanyans were suffering under the Stormhawk's regime, their Songs silenced by a paranoid despot. Celka had a chance to end his rule, to make space for Captain Vrana and the resistance to build something better. But only if Gerrit didn't shatter her core grounding the way he'd deliberately twisted his own.

Turning his back wasn't the answer. Filip kept looking for someone else to give the orders and solve the problems, but maybe Yanek was right. Maybe he *could* lead. He could at least sleeting well try.

Reaching out, Filip gripped the back of Gerrit's neck. The position was the same as it had always been, but everything had changed. Gerrit no longer sounded like the shush of blowing snow or the glint of pine needles sheathed in ice, and as Filip edged sideways to resolve sousednia's library, he relinquished the idea that he was no more than Gerrit's strazh.

Celka dropped their link through Nina, and Filip let it go, too, knowing he'd need all his focus to pull this off. Because if he wasn't just following orders, he had to choose his own path.

All his life, he'd prayed to the Storm Gods and trained to understand imbuements. Maybe Yanek was right that he could imbue. He'd done it in Bludov, had protected Gerrit on instinct. Now, with a few moments to prepare, he could do better than instinct. He could fight for Celka. He could fight for the resistance.

When Filip touched Gerrit's neck, Celka forced herself to lay her own hand over Gerrit's—the two of them, together, clutching the knife. She was a performer. She could do this.

At the contact of skin on skin, Celka expected true-life to brighten. During their nights together, she'd grown used to the buzz like storm energy the moment they touched, true-life and sousednia sharpening. Instead, contact screeched like metal grating on metal, an enraged nerve-jangling that shot electric up her arm. She gasped.

Fighting the urge to pull away, Celka made herself tighten her grip on his hand. *It's just our weeks apart.* She tried to believe it, expecting the burn to ebb.

Instead, the pain worsened, an edged agony like broken glass slicing up her arm to her shoulder. She held for a second, teeth gritted. Gods' Breath burned at first, too, the agony transmuting beneath the strength of her weaves. But this pain didn't fade.

She blinked through tears to see true-life, expecting, still, the realities to be balanced like a trapeze artist's perfectly timed jump-and-catch. All she needed was to push past this pain and she'd reach true-life and sousednia, a trivial shift of focus transitioning her one to the other, that clarity making joint-imbuing natural.

But the realities tangled. The theatre's old sweat and mildewing wood thrashed against the circus's sweetness of hay and sawdust before twisting into the burnt dust smell of a furnace fighting the cold. Celka squinted to see sousednia, but the high wire hung too close to the ground, bleachers smearing into theatre seats, every member of the audience red-shouldered.

Gasping, she opened her hand to snatch it away. «We can't joint-imbue.»

Gerrit clapped his free hand down on hers, pinning her hand between his just as he had the first time they'd imbued this horror. Eyes wide, he met her gaze, some of his icy command crumbling. He felt it, too, the wrongness.

«Something's wrong,» she said as pain knifed her spine. Except she knew what was wrong—just as she knew how he would respond.

«Make it work.» He spoke through gritted teeth, but spotlights—from true-life or sousednia?—glinted off his red shoulders and made it an order.

The big top's tent canvas dripped with blood, hung with starved bodies screaming beneath the blades of monsters who dressed just like him. Beyond them, in the bleacher seats— *theatre seats*—the Stormhawk watched from beneath a glowing shroud of imbuements.

Supreme-General Kladivo had come for his theatre. She could not bow out of her act.

Panting through the pain, Celka focused on her past, hoping a combat nuzhda would wash away sousednia's tangled chaos, allow her to make sense of the world. Tayemstvoy strode around the cook tent, Vrana at their head, and blood flew from truncheons just like the one on Gerrit's belt.

The pain of Gerrit's grip eased as blood and mud mingled with gun oil. Standing in the back lot's weeds, Celka gripped Gerrit's hand, the knife as clear in sousednia as true-life. Something still sliced against her thoughts, a tug and pull like a razor blade in her boot, but she ignored it. She'd kill the red shoulders, save her pa.

Then Gerrit pulled against the paranoid violence nuzhda and—

—at the high table, Filip stands and points. "Celka's a traitor."

All the bozhk officers and red-shouldered servers turn. Celka's squadmates follow Filip's accusing finger.

"Resistance dog." Hedvika whips her belt knife into her hand and reaches for Celka's wrist—

—but Celka twists away. She yanks the pistol from Hedvika's belt, and the first bullet punches through her strazh's heart. Before Hedvika can fall, Celka fires again and Yanek's head snaps back, a bullet hole in his forehead. Then Masha, Havel, Dbani. Dead before they can betray her.

At her side, Gerrit raises his own pistol, sighting casually across the mess hall. His shot takes Filip between the eyes.

FILIP FELT THE wrongness the moment Celka and Gerrit touched. He didn't wait for her protests or Gerrit's inevitable dismissal. Hedvika was already pulling against a suite of nuzhdi that came close to paranoid violence without quite achieving it and, if Filip was doing his job as Gerrit's strazh, he should do the same. But he'd worked with Celka as she developed her calming nuzhda, and he'd scrambled to create the paranoid violence and paralyzing fright nuzhdi after Gerrit invented them. Getting the right mixture of pure nuzhdi wasn't enough. Like with a person's core nuzhda, the elements that shaped an emotional imbuement had to harmonize, resonating to create more than the sum of their parts. That's why Hedvika's strazh weaves couldn't catch all the overflow, why, Filip realized, even his own had failed. Those failures hadn't mattered as much before, when Gerrit and Celka were in control, when *they* harmonized in the same way as the elements of their complex nuzhdi.

But they didn't anymore.

A strazh's weaves worked because, at the interface between imbuement mage and strazh, the strazh's nuzhda matched their tvoortse's, creating a bridge from one to the other. As the strazh siphoned out excess storm energy, they shifted it from its original, destructive-creative form to embrace the ground's inert safety.

The imbuement mage formed their own bridge—from Gods' Breath to imbued object—shifting raw storm energy into a crystalized form that could power their weaves' magic.

Joint-imbuing, then—with energy flowing through both Gerrit and Celka into the knife—required its own bridge, its own matching. And their bridge was broken. If they joint-imbued like this, the storm energy wouldn't flow smoothly between them, funneled into their weaves. Instead, it would hit that broken bridge and explode, raw storm energy twisted by the paranoia nuzhda, refusing to be contained by the complex weaves Celka was already shaping.

Hedvika's strazh weaves were an imperfect bridge to Celka. They wouldn't absorb enough of the overflow. Even if Filip used his own strazh weaves on Celka, it might not be enough—and he'd lose Gerrit for certain.

But if Filip patched their bridge, it might save them both.

He didn't know what it would do to the imbuement, didn't have time to figure it out or to care. Gerrit's paranoid violence nuzhda and whatever connection still remained between him and Celka had enflamed Celka's own, and she shaped it with a speed that spoke of desperation and fraying control.

Mind racing, Filip had already begun pulling against Celka's core nuzhda, and now he made himself pull against Gerrit's—not the nuzhda he knew, the pine and lonesome wind that was as familiar as breathing, but the infantry stomp, bullet-chambering, wet stone of Gerrit's twisted core. He wouldn't get it perfect—he didn't have the time or the experience, and worse, he didn't *want* to get it. So into the crunch of hobnailed boots marching on parade, he added icy wind and the crump of snow, sun warming his face. It was stupid maybe, or maybe it was brilliant. It felt right, or at least *better*, and Filip didn't have time to question his intuition.

Splitting his focus, Filip wove their nuzhdi together with the Song of Fighting, even as he used the Song of Calming to strengthen the weaves into something that could hold—and not leave them all combat-warped. Because he didn't know how to build weaves—not real ones. He was guessing, his sousednia a tangle.

Truncheons crack on wretched prisoners cowering on the high wire platform, and rich, moist garden soil falls through Filip's fingers as he struggles to balance. The wind whips around him, smelling of ice and summer humidity, and his boots slip on wet cobblestones twisting into steel cable. The circus band fades beneath the crack of a gunshot, but his library's silence nearly drowns it all out.

Stepping out from behind Gerrit, Filip clasped both hands around Celka and Gerrit's, around the knife they had no business imbuing.

Celka's gaze snapped to his and—for an instant—he saw and believed her betrayal, saw Gerrit raising a pistol and aiming it between his eyes. Then she snapped her attention back to their clasped hands and *reached*.

Gods' Breath struck them—all three of them—the copper bolt splitting as it met them, or they met it. Agony flared down Filip's spine, and the theatre's stage burned white. Filip threw all the force of his belief into the high wire under his boots that marched in time with a thousand other soldiers that struck a prisoner with his truncheon that flinched away onto a sunny mountain clearing sighing with wind and fresh air that smelled faintly of old books and the silence of thick walls and scholarship.

He held the Song of Calming and the Song of Fighting, twisting them into a new rhythm as he believed with all his heart that the three of them had *chosen* to be here, gripping this knife—had *chosen* to trust each other and watch each other's backs.

CHAPTER FIFTY-SIX

Captain Gerrit Kladivo realized he'd made a horrible mistake. But he realized it too late.

He'd thought he could ignore the pain up his arms where his hands touched Celka's. Thought he could ignore Filip's warning and compensate with skill and determination for a connection that had once seemed effortless and now cut like a rusty blade. His core nuzhda had *changed*, he knew that, but change could be good—could be *necessary*. He didn't remember what it had been before, but he knew that he'd been weak.

Being *strong* would make this imbuement easier, not harder.

He was wrong.

That understanding hit him as Celka's weaves coalesced and she reached for her storm-thread. She'd pull Gods' Breath and it would strike him, too, and he wasn't ready. The weaves she'd built felt right but *he* felt wrong—and their connection, all *wrong*. He whipped his head around, seeking Filip at his back. But Filip was gone.

Filip, who'd claimed he'd always have Gerrit's back, had abandoned him.

Gerrit had been a fool.

He'd known he couldn't rely on others. Known he could depend only on himself, on his own strength. But he'd forgotten. He'd been lulled by the remembered ease of imbuing with Celka and forgotten that it had been before—before... *what?* His memory wavered in those fractured moments before she reached for Gods' Breath.

It didn't matter.

He thought desperately for a solution—some way to salvage the imbuement or at least survive it—but he was too late. He'd trusted others, and that mistake would destroy him.

Then Filip slapped his hand down atop Gerrit's, his other hand swooping around their clutched grip to crush his and Celka's hands between his, against the knife, and everything stopped.

Icy wind whipped past Gerrit out of the tangle of true-life and sousednia, and a thought rose out of nowhere in a voice like Celka's, like Filip's, like his mother's—*compassion isn't weakness.*

Then Celka dragged against her storm-thread and Gods' Breath lashed down through the theatre's ceiling and the stage went *red*, washed in his friends' blood as he stabbed and shot and screamed—killing them before they could turn against him.

Pain rode on every snarl and grimace, on every slash of his knife, every shot from his pistol. The agony drove him to his knees, pouring into the knife, pouring into Celka, into Filip, lashing between them and through them—building, growing like the desperate certainty that everyone he'd ever trusted would turn against him and knife him in the back.

Celka had pulled too hard on the storm, frenzied by the violence *he*'d driven, the pain *he*'d caused—gripping too hard, forcing rather than asking—and the gust of alpine air, of sunlight on fresh snow was so *distant*: a memory, a haze through combat reds and concealment's terrible lies. Storm energy ricocheted and rebounded, growing with each circuit between them when it found no release into their fractured weaves.

Gerrit screamed.

He struggled to contain the storm energy, to endure, seeing no solution but refusing to give in. Just as his mind and will began to crumble, the storm energy lashed into the knife. Before it could tear itself free again, Filip wrenched the knife from his and Celka's hands and threw it.

The knife spun away, the silver of its cutting edge glinting in the spotlights. It landed with a *thunk* in the wall, driving in halfway up its blade from the force of Filip's throw.

"Down!" Filip shouted as he tackled Celka.

Gerrit threw himself to the floor without thought, and the knife exploded, steel shrapnel cutting through the air. In the audience, someone cried out.

Gerrit's ears rang from the explosion, his mind scoured but free of the exploding storm energy. He lay panting on the stage. Pain chased up and down his spine, and his hands and forearms burned like he'd plunged them into boiling water. His breath rasped in his throat, sore from screaming. He wanted to lay his cheek on the scuffed floorboards and close his eyes.

But he was Captain Gerrit *Kladivo*, and no matter how much he hurt, no matter how hard exhaustion pressed him down, he couldn't afford to collapse. Especially not after he'd failed—in front of his father.

That realization drove him to his feet, and he forced himself to think through the molasses creep of his mind. His father had seen him ignore his subordinates' advice only to fail. He had to minimize the damage. "Quick thinking, Cizek." He offered Filip a hand up.

Wariness nearly hidden, Filip took his hand and stood. Storm-scars covered their clasped hands and wrists, angry and red. At their feet, Celka was pushing herself shakily up, Hedvika catching her shoulder, eyes bright with worry.

"Specialist Prochazka," Gerrit made his voice stern. "I expect you to practice these weaves and figure out what you did wrong."

Her gaze flashed to his and, for an instant, he saw murder in her eyes. But she ducked her head to face the floor, shoulders hunching in a passable imitation of submission.

It would have to do.

"Clear the stage," he ordered, leading the way. Filip, instead of falling in at his side, hung back to help Celka to her feet. Gerrit tried not to let his irritation show. Filip was *his* strazh. Seeing him turn his back and reach to help Celka felt too close to a betrayal, too close to the memory-hallucination of Filip stabbing him in the back.

Gerrit balled one burning hand into a fist at his side and, after Filip got Celka seated, motioned his strazh over. "I need you to verify my grounding." The words were hard to get out. "My *current* grounding," he clarified, low, in case Filip thought that gave him license to push Gerrit back toward his old weaknesses.

Filip met his gaze and held it a little too long. "You should have Darina do it. She knows your *current* grounding better than I do." He snarled the word, just a little. Not quite insubordinate, but close.

Gerrit narrowed his eyes, ready to call him on it and remind Filip that he was not *just* Gerrit's strazh, that Gerrit was also his commanding officer—but he noticed that Filip gripped the orchestra pit's railing. He managed to make it look casual, but Filip's storm-scars showed angry red against his knuckles' too pale skin. He had a death-grip on the rail, as if it barely kept him on his feet. Swallowing his irritation, Gerrit tipped his attention into sousednia.

He was starting to grow used to Filip appearing clearly in his sousednia, but even still, Filip generally had to struggle to meet him in the neighboring reality. Today, Filip's attention snapped to him. In true-life, Filip stood with a soldier's straight posture, expression blank but for that hint of insubordination. In sousednia, his lips were drawn in a tight line and he hunched in on himself.

Gerrit and Celka weren't the only ones who'd imbued on that stage.

A frisson passed through Gerrit, carried on an alpine breeze, and he clapped a hand to Filip's shoulder in sousednia. He almost asked whether Filip was all right, but something stopped the words in his throat. With them, worry clawed at his esophagus along with a warmth of friendship that felt strangely apart from him. He grasped at it, but it slipped through his fingers, crushed by the stone walls hemming in his sousednia's narrow street.

Disconcerted, he returned to true-life. "Have Yanek verify your grounding," he said, though they weren't the words he needed. "After Masha imbues, I'll send all of you back to the manor house where you can get some rest." It might look like favoritism or weakness, but compared to sleeting up an emotional imbuement in front of the Stormhawk, it would hurt no more than a wasp's sting. "We'll speak later tonight."

Filip's gaze sharpened, and Gerrit wanted to call the words back. Why had he said that? Why had it sounded so important? He struggled to tamp down a rising panic. Filip had commanded the imbuement squads for the past month, of course they needed to speak. That was all. Just normal business, coordinating with his second-in-command.

Gerrit made himself turn away, waving over a bolt-hawk and sending him to fetch Darina. He still needed to verify his grounding, though the itch of betrayal between his shoulder blades had waned, a new, formless fear settling in its place. Something was wrong, and Filip was at the heart of it.

THE REST OF Gerrit's mages completed their imbuements with no difficulties. They'd improved in the month since he'd imbued alongside them, and Masha's work on new artillery designs had proven especially fruitful. He wished he could stand at his father's side, see whether the Stormhawk appreciated his work—and whether it could make up for his own, public failure.

After he dismissed his platoon, Hana Ruzhishka descended from the balcony with an Okhrana escort. The Stormhawk followed, wheezing, supported by his guards. His damaged lungs made him speak in a thready whisper, nothing like the rough but commanding voice that imbuements had given him for his speech. Still, Gerrit's platoon seemed not to have suspected anything amiss, and they would write their well-connected families about the honor of the Stormhawk attending their imbuement, dispelling growing rumors that the Stormhawk had been gravely wounded in a resistance attack.

With even Iveta's bolt-hawks cleared out and Yestrab Okhrana standing guard at every door, the Stormhawk lay down on the stage. Hana had been working on an imbuement to repair his lungs—using test subjects—and had made reasonable progress. Unfortunately, the imbuement needed to be directly inhaled and couldn't be stabilized for multiple imbuements. Captain Kochevar had snarled that it was a trap and they couldn't risk it, but Gerrit had vouched for Hana. The Stormhawk, desperate to regain his old vigor, had agreed.

In a storm two days ago, Gerrit had observed while Hana imbued to save a test patient's life. Throughout, he'd scrutinized her weaves. If she modified them today—deliberately or by accident—he would stop the imbuement and alert the Okhrana. Hana knew it. She met Gerrit's gaze with a deliberate nod before pulling against a healing nuzhda.

By the time Gerrit and his father returned to Yinovatka Manor, the Stormhawk was breathing easier. His lungs were not fully repaired, but his voice was stronger, and he climbed out of the motorcar and up the manor's steps without assistance. In the foyer, he clasped Gerrit's shoulder. "Good work, Captain. You should be proud."

The praise buoyed Gerrit all the way back to his room, where he hoped Celka would be waiting for him.

Though their imbuement today had failed, she was his partner, and they'd been apart for a whole month. He imagined coming back to his room to find her in bed wearing the lacy nightgown he'd had set out for her, a fire blazing in the hearth. He imagined her congratulating him on his promotion, kissing him, peeling away his new uniform with hands and lips hungry after their weeks apart. *I've missed you,* he'd say, sliding his hands up along her sides, slipping the nightgown off.

A fire crackled in his hearth, but Celka paced, still in uniform.

She froze when he entered, watching him, wary, and didn't relax when he shut the door.

"I've missed you," he said, coming towards her. He touched her cheek, intending to kiss her—but she flinched back.

"What have you been doing while we've been away?" Her suspicion was a far cry from the admiration he'd expected. "What is this?" She swept a hand to indicate his new uniform.

"It seemed the appropriate move." He smiled a little to dismiss the subject. Celka had unpleasant history with the Tayemstvoy, he shouldn't have been surprised to see her flinch at his transfer. "But I'm a captain now." He thumbed the fourth star on one shoulder, only a week old. "I thought you'd be impressed."

Her expression twisted. "Impressed." It sounded like an accusation.

Gerrit tipped his head, studying her, and unbuttoned his jacket. He tossed it over a chair, unbuckling his weapons belt and dropping it on a side table. He hadn't expected the weight of a truncheon to matter, but it added up across the day. Lighter, he reached for her, catching her hips. "Imbue anything good while you were travelling?"

She resisted as he tried to draw her in. "You had reports."

"I'd still rather hear it from you." He started to unbutton her jacket, and she tensed. He stopped, searching her face with narrowed eyes. "Is there a problem?" He let his tone take on an edge, tiring of whatever game she played. Her breathing had quickened, and it made him want her.

"What have *you* been doing?" Again that accusatory tone. She hadn't been so insolent before.

He finished unbuttoning her jacket. "Are you angry I didn't write?"

"We didn't know where you were! Or what was happening. What—?" She searched his face, wide green eyes bright with some of the spark he remembered.

"You were worried." It made him smile. Slipping a hand into her short hair, he kissed her lips.

She jerked away. "Gerrit—" She struck his hand away when he reached for her again. "Would you *stop*? I haven't seen you in weeks and your core nuzhda is *warped*. That imbuement— what happened?" She unbuttoned her cuff and shoved up the sleeve, revealing angry red lines like a bramble thicket up her forearm. "*You* did this because you wouldn't listen to me or Filip. Because you're nuzhda-warped."

Anger coursed like a machinegun burst through him. "You're tumbling Filip, aren't you."

"*What?* No! What? That doesn't even... even if I *were*. Are you *listening* to me?"

Gerrit caught her wrist, preventing her from retreating while he tried to read whether she was telling the truth. The doorknob rattled like someone was trying to get in, but he'd locked it.

Someone knocked. "It's Filip. Can I come in?"

Not taking his eyes off Celka, he asked, "You arranged this?"

"I didn't need to *arrange* anything. He's your strazh. He cares about you. And so do I."

He stepped a little closer, grip on her wrist preventing her retreat. "You're not acting like it."

She narrowed her eyes, not cowed or respectful the way she'd been at the theatre today. Her sousedni-shape shifted, flinching away from her true-form, fighting and then cowering, beginning to ripple with color. Recognizing the flicker of his old, weak core nuzhda, he dropped her wrist in disgust.

"It won't change anything," he said as he unlocked the door to admit Filip.

Filip bowled through, catching Gerrit's arms and shoving him back, his sousedni-shape a riot of color, echoing a lonesome wind, smelling of ice and pine. The assault from sousednia tore his focus from true-life, and Filip punched him hard just beneath the sternum, the blow stunning his diaphragm. Filip used the shock to slam Gerrit to the ground.

As Gerrit gasped for air, Filip tore open his collar, grabbing his storm pendant—no, not his storm pendant, but the second charging pouch that hung off it. Why did Gerrit have a second charging pouch? He dismissed the question, pushing past his confusion and surprise.

He was through being a target. He bucked his hips to throw Filip off him, and his strazh rolled away, not even trying to fight. Gerrit leapt to his feet, but not fast enough to stop Filip from tossing the charging pouch to Celka—but Gerrit wasn't worried about her. Filip was the bigger threat, his sousedni-shape still rippling with the colors of Gerrit's old, weak core nuzhda.

"Remember the howl of wind over boulders," Filip said as they circled each other, searching for an opening to take the other down. "It sighs in your mother's voice through the trees."

Blue flared in Gerrit's peripheral vision and, faint in true-life, a dome unfurled over them, the air in the room growing still even as icy wind screamed past him in sousednia. He tried to ignore Filip's words, looking for an opening, angry that Filip would dare attack him, would think to twist Gerrit's newfound strength back to weakness.

Celka slunk around behind him, but he refused to turn and give Filip another opportunity to attack. "I've figured out how to finish what we started here," Celka said.

Gerrit tried to ignore her, telling himself he didn't understand. But understanding gnawed at him, slicing against his mind like the alpine wind, like sunlight that was wrong for his sousednia of cobblestones and close walls.

In his disorientation, Filip closed, catching his arms, stepping close in a way that shouldn't have been threatening, but created a wrenching pain in his chest. He wanted to fight free, but Filip glowed so bright in sousednia that Gerrit couldn't look away.

"Tonight, we'll finish what we started with Lucie," Celka whispered.

The name landed like a punch. A *crack* sounded in sousednia, a shattering of granite. Cracks shot through the walls surrounding sousednia's cobblestone street, widening, the facades of entire buildings sheering off. As they crashed to the ground, granite crumbled into snow. Sunlight pierced the sky's thick clouds, blinding.

No! Tearing free of Filip's grasp, he spun on Celka. They thought to fight him; but he could fight back. "We learned where the resistance dogs got the gas canister," he said, low and fast. "It was Lesnikrayen. The gas they used gave them away. Not just chlorine, but something called phosgene."

Celka's eyes widened, like she knew of it—which he'd expected, but didn't know why.

Pressing his advantage, he caught her arm, fingers digging bruises. She glared at him, teeth bared. Too much to hope that a little pain would distract her from her nuzhda. Never mind. He had something better than physical discomfort. "It was the perfect opportunity to use our paranoid violence imbuement."

She tried to wrench free, but he held her. "What are you talking about?"

"I sent a strike team with it into Lesnikraj."

Her mouth dropped open and she froze. She didn't lose the nuzhda, but it stopped battering him. Quietly, he began to repair the cracks in his walls, locking away the sunlight.

As if this was an interrogation, he said, "It was marvelously effective. The Lesnikrayen Parliament tore themselves apart."

She shook her head, trying to retreat. He let her go, and she stumbled back.

"The team's next stop was a weapons laboratory." He prowled forward. "A place where the Lesnikrayens experiment with phosgene." He smiled despite the part of him that cringed at the knowledge. "Perhaps they'll dismiss it as an industrial accident—some side effect of experimental chemicals. Though presumably even the Lesnikrayens will put it together eventually." He closed on her, running the pad of his thumb across her cheekbone, catching her arm when she tried to flinch away. "How many attacks will it take, do you think? Five? A dozen? We don't have many concealment imbuements left from the war, but we have enough. Our people are ghosts."

Her nuzhda shattered. "Listen to yourself, Gerrit," she whispered. "Do you even hear what you're saying?"

"I think what you meant to say was, 'Brilliant strategy, Captain Kladivo. No wonder your father promoted you.'" He glanced back over his shoulder at where Filip no longer glowed. "I averted a war. The Stormhawk was prepared to attack—despite the onset of winter. The cost to our own soldiers would have been terrible. I bought us time."

"You ordered civilians slaughtered," Celka said.

"Lesnikrayens," he snapped. "Not *our* people."

"They're still people," she whispered. "You used to care about people."

Angry, he tightened his grip. "I still do. Why do you think I ordered the attack?"

She shook her head, staring at him like he was a monster, and something inside him quailed. He tried to ignore it, shoving it beneath the walls he'd rebuilt.

"Are you proud of what Artur did with that imbuement in Zbishov, too?" she asked, voice shaking. "Do you have a nice justification for murdering peaceful protestors?"

"No!" He shoved her back, wanting to scream at her, hit her—anything to make her stop talking. He'd done *great* work here. He'd strengthened his father's trust, delayed a war until they could win it. She should be *impressed*, not trying to paint him as the villain. "We developed that imbuement for war—that's what *I'm* using it for. It can't hurt Bourshkanyans while it's in Lesnikraj."

"Then why try to make another one today?" Celka asked.

Gerrit rubbed the burning lines of pain on his arm before catching himself. "They're useful."

"Useful?" She shook her head like she couldn't believe he was so naïve. Stepping close, she laid her hands on his cheeks, staring into his eyes. The sorrow in hers made him want to look away. "Gerrit, we promised each other we would never make another one. Do you remember? Or have you hidden that memory away, too?" As she spoke, her voice sighed like the wind, her hands warm on his cheeks like sunlight in the brittle air.

Something in his chest shuddered.

"The Gerrit I know," she continued before he could form words, "the Gerrit I *love* would never cheer civilian casualties—even if those people weren't our own. I know it must have been hard being here in the wake of Lucie's death. You did what you thought you had to, warped your own sousednia. Did you tell yourself it made you strong?" The question shook him, but she kept speaking, giving him no space to fight free. "*I* did. When I was combat-warped, I thought it made me powerful. Safe. But hiding from yourself isn't safety or strength. Help us break through, Gerrit. Show us your mountain clearing, the sunlight bright and scouring."

His chest tightened. He shook his head, struggling to draw breath.

"You've survived grief before, Gerrit," she said. "It brought you here. You built this mountaintop not to forget, but to let your mother's strength bolster yours."

He stumbled back, but she followed him, the scent of pine and ice filling the air as she cupped his cheeks. Her emerald eyes held a warmth and understanding that terrified him, but he couldn't make himself look away. He wanted to shout that she was wrong, that he was *strong*. He'd been weak before, he was certain of it. But when granite shattered, he stared up at the sky's bright cerulean; and even as he felt himself drowning, he could finally breathe.

"No," Gerrit whispered, but the cobblestones beneath him crumbled into snow.

Celka had guided him back toward the bed, and it bumped against his knees. He sat, and Celka pulled him into an embrace. He pressed his face into her neck, chest shaking as more walls fell. Filip sat on his other side, glowing fierce with violet and crimson, his strong arm encircling Gerrit, supporting him as he shattered.

Lucie dead and lifeless, her body broken and crusted with blood.

Lucie alive and smiling, bumping his shoulder with hers, assuring him he isn't a monster. The memories crashed in, faster and faster, and a sob tore from his throat.

"I can't," he choked. "Please stop. I can't."

"You're strong enough for this, Gerrit," Celka said. "And it won't be much longer. After tonight, we'll get out."

He grasped after that hope as pressure built in his chest, the air rarifying like he'd climbed an immense mountain. Agony split his sinuses before his ears popped and sousednia opened wide around him—his mountain clearing, icy yet warmed by sunlight, the forest shadowed in the valley below.

And a voice. *«There you are, Gerrit. I've missed you.»*

«Mother?» He knew the instant he said it that he was wrong. *«Nina.»*

«Welcome back,» the python said, and his alpine clearing stabilized.

Gerrit exhaled, shuddering. But something about the clearing seemed wrong, the light too harsh, the wind too sorrowful. Celka and Filip appeared at his sides, Celka radiant in her high wire costume, but also out of place; Filip still rippling with color. «*This isn't right,*» he said, the link through Nina grating like sand in his eye. «*This isn't me.*»

Celka gripped his hand. «*It is.*» Emotion tightened her voice. «*It's finally you.*»

«*She's right,*» Filip said, nuzhda draining until he sat at Gerrit's side on the granite rock outcrop, khaki shirtsleeves rolled to mid-forearm, gold-bolt earring gleaming faintly in light too subdued for Gerrit's alpine sun. «*This is your core nuzhda.*»

Gerrit made himself sit there, breathing the pine-fresh air, the ragged edges of grief tearing at his chest. Was it just pain that made this place feel wrong? He could breathe easier here, the air fresh instead of damp and clogged with diesel smoke. Yet that feeling of naïveté remained. This mountain felt like a refuge—but the refuge of a lonely, desperate child.

Leaving his true-form sitting with his friends, Gerrit crossed the clearing, boots crunching through a thin layer of ice into the soft powder beneath. At the clearing's edge, he peered down into the shadowed forest. Memory called to him from the darkness, memories he wanted to flinch from in this sunlit space.

Was he wrong to have ordered that attack on Lesnikraj? Standing in this sunlit clearing, he didn't think he could have done it. But it had averted a war. True, civilians had bought that abeyance with their lives, but were rich Lesnikrayen politicians more precious than conscripted Bourshkanyan soldiers? He didn't think so.

He turned back to his friends. Both Celka and Filip watched him.

Celka would tell him that no one deserved to die. She was right, but that wasn't how the world worked. Every choice was a trade-off. Lucie had understood.

Pain spiked his chest just thinking about her. But Celka was right that he'd survived grief before. The thought of clawing through that abyss again made him want to crumple, but he forced himself to breathe. Lucie was gone, but he'd carry her with him. She'd understood that sometimes hard choices were necessary. She'd understood sacrifice.

He'd been wrong, before, wanting to risk all their lives to free her. Lucie wouldn't have asked that. Filip had done the right thing—even if part of Gerrit still hated him for it.

Dropping his dislocation, Gerrit let his attention bleed back into the bedroom. There, he stood. Filip rose to meet him, and Gerrit clasped his shoulder. "You were right," he told his best friend. "You saved Lucie when I couldn't. I forgive you."

Filip searched his expression, filled with hope and yearning.

"Thank you for pulling me back," Gerrit said, because Filip needed to hear it—and maybe Gerrit was glad. He glanced at Celka, too, who'd stood, hopeful but still wary. "Both of you."

Filip nodded, then pulled Gerrit into an embrace. Gerrit returned it, feeling like a vice unclenched in his chest. But the tension in his shoulders remained. They weren't the friends they'd been at the academy; they'd never be able to recapture that simplicity. Like sousednia's too bright sunlight, Filip's embrace felt restrictive in a way Gerrit hadn't noticed before. Something had changed—or was changing—but Gerrit wasn't confident his friends would understand.

To distract them from it, he dredged back through their conversation, pulling out words that echoed with the crack of shattering granite. Forcing himself to ignore the way Nina's link grated, he said, *«You said that after tonight, we'd get out. What did you mean?»*

Celka bit her lip and glanced at Filip, who nodded. *«I have a new assassination plan,»* she said. *«I'll do it tonight.»*

Gerrit forgot to breathe. The memory of his father clapping him on the shoulder welled up, choking him. *Assassination.*

The Gerrit who'd worn his new Tayemstvoy uniform with pride screamed that he couldn't allow Celka to succeed. If the Stormhawk died, Artur would leap into his place, slitting the throats of anyone who stood in his way. Except—

Drawing a slow breath, Gerrit made himself think. The Stormhawk had promoted Iveta to major when he'd given Gerrit his fourth star. The line of succession from the Stormhawk to Artur was no longer clear. If the Stormhawk died here, tonight, then Gerrit and Iveta could control the information. Artur need not learn of their father's death until he and Iveta were already positioned to take control.

He and Iveta? The idea had risen naturally, but as Gerrit focused on his friends, he doubted himself. Captain Vrana planned to extract all three of them, turning them into figureheads and imbuement mages to lead the resistance army.

Thoughts spinning, Gerrit focused back on Celka. *«How?»*

She shook her head. *«You don't need to know details. I'll handle it.»*

The words cut like a knife, recalling Filip's claim in this very room that he'd found a way to save Lucie and Gerrit didn't need to know details. But he'd learned something from his time in this uniform. The best way to get answers was not always the direct path. So he made himself breathe through the fear of betrayal, and when he was sure his voice would stay calm, asked, *«How soon will the resistance get us out afterwards?»*

«We don't know,» Filip said. *«We left word through a dead drop, but haven't been contacted. What's happened to the Wolf's network since we left?»*

Gerrit sorted back through memories that tasted of steel and infantry parades. *«She hasn't been captured. But the Tayemstvoy made a lot of arrests in the fortress and Solnitse. I haven't heard anything from Vrana. I don't know how bad the damage is.»*

Celka shook her head. «*If she's still free, she'll be able to get us out. It might just take time.*» She scrutinized Gerrit. «*Will that be a problem?*»

Gerrit scrubbed a hand through his hair, playing out possible scenarios. «*If he dies tonight, they'll blame Hana.*»

«*Who's Hana?*» Celka asked even as Filip said, «*Why?*»

«*A friend of ours from the academy,*» Gerrit said, then to Filip, «*She imbued today to heal Father's lungs. At the very least, they'll suspect her. The timing's too close.*» Not only that, but Iveta's promotion to major was fresh. She'd been gaining regime favor, but how many of her new supporters would equate the timing of her promotion and assume she'd arranged the Stormhawk's murder? To Celka, he asked, «*Can you wait?*»

«*And lose him? If his lungs are healed, how long will he stay here?*»

Gerrit didn't know.

«*So we have to recruit Hana,*» Filip said. «*And Darina.*»

Gerrit shook his head. «*Hana's been leading a medical imbuement team. I don't think she or Darina will want to go.*»

«*If it's that or have the Okhrana torture them to death?*» Celka asked.

«*They're innocent,*» Gerrit said.

«*You think that'll matter?*» Celka asked.

«*No, but Hana will.*» Gerrit grimaced, a plan starting to take shape. He wouldn't be able to delay this assassination; he'd just have to make the best of it. «*I might be able to throw suspicion off of her.*»

«*And onto us?*» Filip asked.

«*No.*» Gerrit drew a steadying breath. «*But I need to know what you're planning.*»

Celka hesitated, and when Gerrit looked to Filip, his best friend crossed his arms and turned to Celka. Her decision.

Gerrit reached out a hand, offering it to her to take or not. *«Please,»* he said. *«Trust me?»*

«You're wearing a Tayemstvoy uniform, Gerrit,» she said. *«You nearly killed all three of us imbuing today. How am I supposed to look past that?»*

«You broke through my warping,» he said, low, like speaking to a skittish cat. *«It's me. I have your back. All we've gone through is for nothing if you won't trust me.»*

She studied him for a long time, weighing his conviction. *«Promise you won't try to stop me.»*

«I won't stop you from assassinating my father tonight.» He said it plainly. Let her read his sincerity. Bourshkanya would be better without a lying, murderous dictator in command. What happened after that assassination still remained to be seen.

Finally, she nodded. *«Let me show you.»*

CHAPTER FIFTY-SEVEN

CELKA CLAIMED A headache to excuse herself from post-dinner conversation, returning to the bedroom she would share with Gerrit. Though she'd left Gerrit in a dark, wood-paneled parlor in deep discussion with Masha about her new artillery imbuements, her stomach still twisted as she neared their room. Things hadn't been great between them since Mrach, but today, for all she'd glared him down and refused to cower, he'd been terrifying. Unable to help glancing down the empty corridor, she rubbed the bruises on her arm from where he'd grabbed her while clinging to his warped core nuzhda.

The bedroom was empty—of *course* it was empty—and she pressed her back to the door, wrapping her arms around her stomach and curling over them to shake with all the fear she'd refused to show. When the shakes had passed, she lay down fully dressed in bed. She needed to rest. They'd wait until midnight to strike, giving the Stormhawk time to fall asleep. With luck, she'd tighten the choke fast enough that his guards would think he'd just flailed out during a nightmare and fallen back asleep. Unconscious and sleeping looked similar enough. Maybe the guards wouldn't even check his breathing or sense his life nuzhda through imbuements, not discovering their mistake until the Stormhawk failed to wake in the morning. They might even think he'd died naturally, his lungs too damaged from the gas. The sousednia choke would leave no evidence of murder.

She shuddered. Murder. Assassination. The gas attack had been no different, she tried to tell herself, but it *was* different. Tonight, she'd murder the Stormhawk with her bare hands. No neat poison to do the final deed, no illusions that anyone else shared the responsibility.

A knock woke her from a light dose, and she shot bolt upright in bed. But it was just Filip.

«The Wolf got our message,» he said through Nina. *«They'll get us out tonight.»*

Relief crashed over her as he explained details. Jolana Kohout, Branislav's strazh and Filip's friend from the Storm Guard Academy, would meet them out past the ornamental gardens. They'd snowshoe to a safehouse, and the resistance had arranged transportation from there. The news loosened a knot in her chest. No more imbuing for the State. No more suppressing her flinch when Hedvika cheered the Tayemstvoy for arresting resistance dogs. Gerrit would stop convincing himself he needed to warp his mind to survive, and they'd go back to the way things had been before Bludov—except better, because Filip would be with them.

«There's bad news, too,» Filip said. *«I scouted around, and it looks like your best hiding place will be the closet Lucie found on the top floor. It's across the hall and two doors down from the Stormhawk's new rooms, which puts it inside your range, but it's in easy view and an obvious place for the Okhrana to search.»*

Celka's pulse sped. She did *not* want to be anywhere the

Okhrana could easily search. *«There has to be something on the floor below?»* The closet she'd used for the gas attack wouldn't work. To hold the choke's intense sousedni-disruption and the massive calming imbuement active over the Stormhawk, she needed to be close.

Filip shook his head. *«Not unless you want to sneak into Captain Kochevar's bedroom.»*

«I'll pass.» Celka rubbed her hands over her arms, trying to chase a phantom chill. *«If they look in and see the closet empty, will they go in? The concealment imbuement should hide me from a casual glance.»*

«I don't know,» Filip said. *«But I'll go with you.»*

That warmed her a little. *«You just want an excuse to kiss me again.»*

«No, it's—» A smile tugged at his lips as he realized she was teasing. *«I mean, I wouldn't mind.»*

Realizing she wouldn't either, Celka leaned toward where he sat on the edge of the bed. Apart from that time in the tack shed, they'd come close to kissing a handful of times while on the road, but something had always interrupted or one of them found an excuse to turn away. That she and Gerrit had agreed to be exclusive should have stopped her from even thinking about it, but that mattered less and less with each passing day. After today... She shuddered.

Filip's gaze dropped to her lips, and he leaned a little towards her. Like she was a magnet whose pull he couldn't escape.

"You and Yanek still aren't exclusive, right?" she asked.

Filip froze, a catch in his breath. His gaze flicked from her lips to her eyes, and he pulled away. Standing, he paced one way and then another before crossing to the hearth and stabbing the fire with a poker. Beneath his jabs, the logs sprayed sparks.

Struggling past her internal monologue of *stupid, stupid,*

why did you say that? Celka picked Nina up to ask, «*What is it?*»

He hesitated before stabbing the poker violently into a log. «*Yanek still doesn't know.*»

«*Of course not,*» she said, before realizing what that meant. They were leaving *tonight.* «*Sleet-storms. Are you going to ask him to come?*»

Filip stabbed the fire again. «*Do you think I should? What if he says no? Then what?*»

«*Would he stop us from leaving? Would he call the Okhrana?*»

«*I don't think so.*» He slumped cross-legged before the enraged blaze. «*But... if I tell him and he raises the alarm? We can't fight our way out of here.*»

«*He can't want to hand you to the Okhrana.*»

«*Want might not be enough,*» he said.

«*You didn't betray me and Gerrit,*» Celka said, but she didn't know how closely the parallel ran. She *liked* Yanek. Would she trust him with her life and freedom? No. But Yanek was more to Filip than just a friend. She wrapped her arms around herself, cold once more. «*Yanek's not Hedvika.*»

Filip's sigh seemed to deflate him. He shook his head and racked the fire poker beside the hearth, dusting ash off his hands before returning to the bed. «*We don't need to solve this now. I'll come with you—I can hold the concealment imbuement active so you can focus on the choke.*»

She shook herself. Filip was right; they needed a plan. «*Will the imbuement cover us both?*»

«*Not easily, but it can if we stay close. Though you'll have to hold the ring active to mute your sousedni-shape.*»

She nodded. «*And if anyone finds us and questions what we're doing?*»

Filip leaned down, sweeping a lock of hair out of her eyes.

«*We give them the expected answer.*» Holding her gaze, giving her plenty of space to refuse and say they needed a different alibi, Filip kissed her lips.

Celka caught his neck lightly, holding him, but only if he wanted to be held.

Filip drew back enough to break their kiss, but didn't pull away. Her insides felt watery, her lips aching for more. "What about Gerrit?" He sounded regretful.

"We're through." Celka only realized the truth as she spoke it, hard-edged. "After today..." She shook her head, cupping Filip's jaw, staring into his rich, mahogany eyes, hoping he'd understand. "I can't—" The words caught in her throat, too dangerous to speak aloud. «*I don't trust him enough.*»

Filip's jaw muscles tensed, but he nodded. «*I feel like something's still wrong.*»

«*He's changed,*» Celka whispered.

He searched her face, then pulled away.

She caught his hand.

«*Get some sleep if you can.*» He squeezed her hand. «*I'll wake you when it's time.*» Then he was gone.

Celka pulled a pillow to her chest, staring at the door long after it had closed. Had she meant what she'd said about Gerrit? She tried to imagine snuggling against him, bare skin on skin. She'd just as well cuddle Major Rychtr. The storm-scars snaking her forearms burned. She rubbed them, uneasy, before tossing the pillow aside and going to make sure her pack was ready. She'd sort things out with Gerrit somehow—at least enough that they could work together in the resistance. What mattered was they were getting out.

Tonight, she'd leave the Army and Tayemstvoy behind. Forever.

CHAPTER FIFTY-EIGHT

INVISIBLE BUT VULNERABLE in the corridor outside the Stormhawk's rooms, Celka gripped the closet doorknob. They needed to get inside, but first they needed the pair of Yestrab Okhrana guarding the Stormhawk's bedroom to look away. Filip stood close at Celka's back, holding the concealment imbuement active over their true-forms while Celka used the iron ring's imbuement to hide the magic's blue glow and minimize their sousedni-shapes. To keep close enough for both to work, Filip's hand rested on her hip. In other circumstances, it would have been distracting.

Celka's heart beat so loud in her ears it was hard to imagine the Okhrana couldn't hear it, but they stood motionless at their posts, only their eyes darting as they scanned the hallway. Celka bit her lip, glancing down the corridor to the servant's stair that Filip had discovered on his earlier scouting mission. Gerrit had 'gone to get a midnight snack' and cause a ruckus. She hoped it would draw the guards' attention away. If she and Filip tried to slip inside the closet now, the Okhrana would see the door open and investigate.

Filip's other hand touched her shoulder. «*Patience,*» he said through Nina. «*He'll get it.*»

A crash sounded, followed by shouting. The two Okhrana dropped their rifles into their hands, shifting to stand back-to-back in front of the Stormhawk's door.

Celka gripped the doorknob tighter. *Go investigate,* she urged them silently.

Through Nina's link, Filip told Gerrit, «*Not enough.*»

The shouts turned to swearing, and something shattered like glass.

"Go," one of the Okhrana said, and the other jogged down the hall to the head of the stair. The other kept their gaze pointed the opposite direction down the corridor—in Celka and Filip's direction.

Sleet. Look away. Much longer, and she'd have to risk a sousedni-disruption to distract the remaining guard, or they'd lose their opening.

Finally, the guard glanced back at their companion, and Celka yanked the door open and dashed inside, not worrying whether Filip could keep the imbuement over her. He slipped in behind her, catching the door and pulling it shut. The latch clicked into place with the faintest scrape.

Celka's breath sounded loud in the close-dark space.

Her true-life eyes useless, Celka shifted into sousednia and groped to find Filip. When she brushed the soft wool of his jacket, he turned, finding her arm, stepping cautiously close. He hadn't been able to scout inside the closet to tell how spacious it would be, and they couldn't risk lighting a match for fear a too-attentive guard would notice the glow beneath the door. But sousednia let Celka intuit a vague sense of the space, and she pulled Filip close, careful not to brush the closet's sides where something might be precariously propped.

She moved to step in front of him, a little closer to her

target, but Filip stopped her with a hand on her hip. *«Let me stay between you and the door. If they shoot, they'll hit me first.»* He said it calmly, like the possibility didn't worry him, like a bullet wound was just another day's work.

Celka swallowed hard. How bad an idea was this hiding place? She shook her head. She didn't want to know. A few centimeters wouldn't make much difference in her dislocation. So she turned, putting her back against the solid warmth of Filip's chest. His hands landed on her hips and, trusting him to handle true-life, she dropped into sousednia.

Beneath her darkened big top, Celka swept away the closet's walls, revealing the heat-shimmer from of the Okhrana guarding the Stormhawk's door. The other guard was a mundane, already returning from investigating Gerrit's distraction. Their voices filtered in vaguely from true-life, but she didn't try to catch details, ghosting between them into the Stormhawk's rooms.

Inside, she took a moment to orient herself. The Stormhawk had moved across the mansion—maybe the Okhrana had worried about lingering gas. Celka didn't know, and it didn't matter. What mattered was that a mundane stood just a meter from her, sousedni-shape hazy. Celka's throat tightened, worried the Stormhawk wasn't in bed.

She glanced around, but walls blocked her view of anyone else, so she risked edging closer to the mundane. In sousednia, she inhaled. When she'd faced the Stormhawk before their first assassination attempt, he'd smelled of swamp and battle. This mundane carried the sweetness of a candy shop. Not the Stormhawk.

Releasing a shaky breath, she swept aside more walls, discovering another heat-shimmer standing near the manor's outer wall, glowing lines of violet and gold nuzhda flowing out from them to the prone form of another mundane. The imbuements cocooned him, bright enough that she almost missed the second heat-shimmer on the other side of the room.

She bit her lip, trying not to feel triumphant. *«Two storm-touched guards inside,»* Celka told Filip and Gerrit through Nina. *«No one storm-blessed.»* Which meant no one who could see her or disrupt her choke.

«No one you can see,» Gerrit corrected. *«They could have imbuements too. Be careful.»*

Celka wanted to snap at him—*you're not the one doing the hard work, so shut up*—but she made herself breathe. Gerrit was trying to help. He was on their side. And Celka needed to focus.

Placing her high wire platform beneath the prone figure, Celka crept forward, ducking lines of active nuzhda. She stopped just outside the imbued cocoon and crouched to put herself on a level with the Stormhawk. A deep inhale made her nearly cough. She put a fist to her mouth, rearing back, feeling an echo of true-life as she pressed against Filip's chest, barely swallowing the cough before it could give them away to the Okhrana. Filip's hands tightened protectively on her waist.

Shaking herself, Celka leaned forward again, inhaling more cautiously. Their month on the road had given her a chance to practice small sousedni-disruptions on mundanes, and she'd learned that they worked better the clearer the picture she had of the person—not physically, Pa was right that the physical wasn't important in sousednia, but mentally. So, pressing through the gossamer strands of violet and gold, Celka breathed in the Stormhawk's swampy smell of rot tangling with the incense of storm temples.

Squeezing her eyes closed, Celka tried to come up with a way to capture the Stormhawk's stomach-twisting, fetid, choking, angry humidity—and something clicked. She'd read a State-sanctioned biography during the long hours on the train this last week, and his earlier comment about humble origins and exceptional abilities slotted into place.

The biography had mentioned an episode in which self-important Army officers from Bourshkanya's old nobility had allowed their supply chain to be cut off. In their arrogance and fear, they'd hoarded the imbuements that could have saved the battalion. The book's discussion had centered around the importance of clean water and sanitary facilities, things the Stormhawk had championed since taking control—but the incident had seemed a strange aside. Breathing the undercurrent of shit and vomit around the Stormhawk now, Celka realized that the biography hadn't mentioned whether the Stormhawk had been involved in the incident. As a youth, he'd traveled extensively with his mother, an Army NCO, and his storm speaker father; could he have been present for the disaster? Taken ill? Lost someone he cared about?

The details didn't matter; the idea alone was enough for Celka to sink into her own memory of a humid summer day, boards laid on boggy ground to keep some of the black mud out of the performers' tents. The elephants had labored to pull wagons through the muck, and mosquitoes buzzed and stung. The circus quartermaster had stoked huge fires to boil water, but Celka forced a departure from memory, recalling instead the scent of sickness in the hospital where Ma had been taken after her catastrophic fall from the high wire after Pa's arrest. The Prochazkas weren't rich enough to afford a private room, so Ma had lain on a narrow bed in a crowded space, people moaning and vomiting and shitting nearby.

Stoking those memories like fire, Celka felt an answering resonance in the sleeping Stormhawk—just a frisson, far weaker than the buzz from connecting a nuzhda to an imbuement, but enough.

Erecting tent canvas around the memory-hallucination so she wouldn't lose it, Celka drew a deep, slow breath of hay and sawdust, then touched her true-life hand to the imbued storm pendant about her throat. In sousednia, she left the big top behind, floating up into the sky, letting her concerns dwindle and a deep calm settle over her. Pressing that calm into her storm pendant, she activated the imbuement then brought its shimmering nuzhda down around the sleeping Stormhawk.

He shifted on the bed, rolling onto his side with a sigh that eased through sousednia. Celka smiled, too, relaxed for the first time that evening. Shaking herself, she walled off the calming nuzhda, centering herself back on the high wire platform and ensuring that the entirety of the calming imbuement wrapped the Stormhawk.

Her own calm faded into determination, and she edged her focus back into the swampy memory-hallucination, feeling again that resonance with the Stormhawk's core.

Mind fractured with tent canvas, Celka pressed her senses into true-life, trying to see the murderous Supreme-General in his nightclothes, asleep and dreaming of power. Abandoning the strictures of true-life, Celka shifted sousednia, snapping herself around behind him—laying on her side on what would have been true-life's plush mattress—and hooked an arm around his throat. She pressed her forearm to the back of his head, and squeezed.

Nothing happened.

Gritting her teeth, she concentrated harder, willing true-life and sousednia to touch, to merge. «I'm going to kill you, you hail-eater,» she whispered in the neighboring reality, hoping he'd feel the sentiment though he couldn't hear the words, hoping it would infiltrate his dreams.

Just as she started to doubt herself, Supreme-General Kladivo lurched, smoke-form hands grasping at his throat. He sat up in bed, the swamp-rot of his core nuzhda shifting into the smooth, oiled action of a pistol. Celka's disruption nearly shattered, but the calming imbuement soothed his fear, his nuzhda settling, and Celka strengthened her hold on his throat.

The Stormhawk twisted to the side, but she locked herself in place against his back. A fight, she could handle. For weeks, Filip hadn't let her choke him passively; he'd tried everything, including his own sousedni-dislocations, to free himself. He'd failed.

«You call yourself the Stormhawk,» she snarled in sousednia. «Did you think the Storm Gods wouldn't take offense?» She held the choke as he fought for his life, his desperation battering against the calming imbuement's lullaby. He lurched as though to rise, but fell back into bed when she twisted her sousedni-weight against his back. «You're no mythical being, no divine hawk—just a cruel, greedy man stealing from your people.»

After one last surge, he went limp.

His collapse startled her. She almost loosened her grip, accustomed to releasing Filip shortly after he passed out. She caught herself before she could, renewing her focus, arms tight around his throat where he lay in bed.

A glance showed a pair of storm-touched figures leaning over the bed.

«Just a nightmare,» she whispered, pretty sure they wouldn't be able to hear her, but hoping they'd catch a flavor of the idea. «He's sleeping peacefully now. Don't disturb him.»

Tight in the crook of her arm, she could feel the threads of the Stormhawk's life nuzhda, squeezed tight, blocked. They strained against her, a slicing burn, but she gritted her teeth and endured. *«He's down,»* she told Filip and Gerrit, so they could begin a count.

Six minutes to ensure brain death. She just had to hold on.

Focused on clinging to the Stormhawk, on gripping his throat and not letting a single drop of blood or life nuzhda slip through her grasp, she thought at first she'd imagined the jolt. Then it happened again, shaking her hold on him. She gripped harder, refusing to lose the choke now that she had it, but opened her focus back up to find one of the storm-touched Okhrana shaking him.

Worry leeched off the guard, tasting like the shout of an angry commander. The other guard tried their hand, more imbuements flaring gold around Celka, crawling over her skin like hornets. She struggled to ignore the prickling pain, concentrating on the burning life-threads gripped in the crook of her elbow. Then the jolt became a lurch, and sousednia shifted.

«They've noticed something,» Filip said, tense but controlled. «I'm hearing shouts. The hallway guards just entered his room.»

Her sense of space shifted again, as if the Stormhawk had gotten to his feet. But that shouldn't have been possible. Was one of the healing imbuements compensating for the choke hold? She struggled to understand while not releasing her grip.

Two heat-shimmers, now both blazing gold with healing nuzhda, stood on either side of the Stormhawk, who seemed to be standing. Celka stayed leeched to his back, choke hold locked while her feet floated above the ground. Okhrana and Stormhawk moved forward together with a stumbling gait, and Celka figured it out. «They've pulled him out of bed.»

«One of them is shouting for a doctor—footsteps just ran by the closet,» Filip said.

«We're moving toward the door,» Celka said. «I... think.» Pain sliced her temples as she tried to understand true-life without losing her choke or releasing the massive calming nuzhda that made it possible. «*What are they doing?*»

«*Gas,*» Gerrit said, as if in sudden understanding. «*They're worried it's another gas attack. They're moving him.*»

«*Moving him where?*» Celka's voice squeaked as she nearly lost her hold on the Stormhawk's throat. «*If they move him too far—*»

«*—you won't be able to hold the dislocation,*» Filip filled in when she needed all her attention for the choke.

«*I'm coming up,*» Gerrit said. «*There's been enough noise I can claim to have heard something.*»

«*How does that help?*» Celka asked, the Stormhawk's throat slippery in sousednia with all the people and imbuements pressing around him. Or was it one of the imbuements, interfering with her hold? She couldn't tell. All she could do was try to compensate.

«*I can... slow them down?*» Gerrit said. «*Try to get them to stop just outside his room.*»

«*That'll look suspicious.*» Filip's voice was an anchor, a tiny pool of calm that Celka desperately needed. She'd lost true-life completely, but his voice told her that everything would be all right—somehow. «*I'll help Celka move in true-life if we need to follow him. Gerrit, figure out where they're going— and try to keep any storm-blessed away.*»

Gerrit and Filip might have said more, but Celka couldn't spare the attention. Filip would take care of true-life. She needed to concentrate on keeping her arm latched around the Stormhawk's throat.

CHAPTER FIFTY-NINE

Boots pounded the corridor outside the closet, making it hard for Filip to tell what was going on. Celka stood rigid before him, every muscle taut, and when he touched her shoulder to figure out if she'd be able to walk when he moved them out, he discovered her arms up, encircling the air like she choked the Stormhawk right there in the closet. Tense voices snapped questions and orders too low for Filip to make out, and he risked edging away from Celka, keeping a grip on her jacket so as not to lose her in the dark, pressing his ear to the door, able to catch snatches.

—gas attack—don't smell—phosgene—doctor—

And other words that had to be code for specific imbuements or guard movements.

—wake the captain—

Then, loud enough he could hear it clearly, Gerrit demanded to know what was happening. A pause, then he said, "Then move him next door, stop standing around out here."

"If it's gas, it could have leeched into neighboring rooms," someone said, voice growing fainter until Filip could barely make out the last word.

«*We're moving,*» Gerrit said. «*Toward the main staircase.*»

How far? How fast? Sleet, Filip needed more information. Needed to know when everyone's back was turned—but how could Gerrit give him that information without lagging behind, looking suspicious? Maybe Gerrit could tell from sousednia—Celka would have been able to; but Celka had bigger problems and Filip had said he'd handle it. «*Can you tell me when I have an opening to get out?*» Filip asked.

«*They've posted a rear guard on the group in case of a linked attack,*» Gerrit said. «*They'll have eyes on your location until we get to the staircase.*»

Sleet. The staircase was halfway down the corridor. Too far for Celka to hold the choke reliably, even if her target wasn't moving. Filip needed another solution, fast. «*Gerrit, can you take the rear guard?*» He knew the answer even as the words passed through the link; the Stormhawk's son wouldn't guard the rear with enlisted Okhrana to do the job. Gerrit didn't bother answering.

Think, Filip. He had to come up with a solution before Celka lost the choke.

Whatever the answer, he'd need to be agile. «*I'm going to carry you,*» he told her. Even if she could walk, she wouldn't be able to move fast or reliably with all her focus on sousednia. Besides, if they moved independently, he wouldn't be able keep their true-forms concealed. «*This'll be a little uncomfortable. Just try to relax.*»

«*Do it.*» Her words sounded forced through gritted teeth.

His hand on Celka's hip gave Filip enough of a sense of her position that he got his leg between hers and ducked under her locked arms, which still tracked her sousednia grip on the Stormhawk's throat. It made the fireman carry awkward, her elbow jabbing into his back, but he'd had enough practice carrying wounded cadets out of training exercises that he got her settled across his shoulders. She muttered a curse when he stood, but didn't fight the hold.

«We're headed to Iveta's room,» Gerrit said. «It's down one floor and across to the adjoining hall.» He gave a room number, which Filip was pretty sure he wouldn't need. By the time they got close, it'd be teeming with Okhrana. Getting there, though—hailstones, they'd need to follow the guard the whole way and pray the corridor didn't get too clogged with Okhrana to invisibly dodge.

But first, he had to get them out of the closet—and soon.

Filip grabbed the doorknob with his free hand, turning it slowly so he could surge out as soon as he had an opening—but he still had no idea how to make that opening. If he just burst out, the rear guard would shoot the moment the closet door opened.

«We're halfway to the staircase,» Gerrit said, which meant Filip needed to stop thinking and *act* or Celka would lose the choke. If she lost her hold even briefly, they'd have to restart the count and it was possible that one of the Yestrab Okrana's healing imbuements—now that they were all active—would prevent her from landing it again.

Could he use the concealment imbuement to hide the door's opening? No, that would just make the door suspiciously disappear.

«Filip, I'm losing him!» Celka cried.

Sleet. He had to risk leaping out and hope they didn't get shot. At least the bulk of Celka's body would be hidden behind his shoulders—so *he*'d be more likely to take the bullet—but he couldn't edge out sideways to minimize his target area; the doorway wasn't wide enough.

«Here we go.» With a firm hold around Celka's leg to keep

her over his shoulders, he yanked the door open and lunged through.

A rifle cracked, the gunshot loud in the enclosed corridor, splitting the wood just behind his head. Filip kept moving, momentum slamming him into the opposite wall. He checked their motion with his free arm, smacking into a gilt picture frame and bruising his forearm. More gunshots sounded. The guards were shouting, but Filip couldn't spare the attention to understand, his only thought to *keep moving*. If he'd been shot, he might not have noticed yet, but he could be bleeding, phantom bloodspots providing a target for the Okhrana accustomed to training with bozhki.

He ran, staggering beneath Celka's weight, twisting to the side as two figures in olive drab sprinted past him toward the open closet. His breath came hard in his chest as he slid to a stop near the Stormhawk's entourage and pressed Celka's hip against the wall, trying to minimize their silhouette to gunfire.

The gunshots had accelerated the Okhrana's retreat. Before, they'd been moving cautiously down the corridor, but now a big guard hefted the Stormhawk over their shoulders in the same way Filip now held Celka, and the whole group ran for the stairs.

Whether from the gunshots or the original alarm, more Okhrana came pounding up past the Stormhawk's retreating entourage, and a quick glance showed more converging from down the corridor where they must have come up the servant's stair. Filip heard a shout along the lines of "Search for someone with a concealment imbuement!" and swallowed a curse. Even if these soldiers weren't storm-blessed, they could well be carrying imbuements that would reveal him. "Get the dogs!" another shouted, which would be as much of a problem: his concealment imbuement didn't cover smell. All problems he had no time to worry about.

Carried by his guard, the Stormhawk was quickly retreating down the stairwell, and Filip had to keep Celka close enough to hold her choke.

But three armed Okhrana now barricaded the stairs. Rifles in hand, they would ensure that no one from this floor—invisible or not—could follow the retreating Stormhawk. Right now, the Okhrana had only suspicions that someone had been in that closet; if Filip attacked the guards, they'd know for certain. If he waited, hoping for them to move aside enough that he could slip past, Celka would lose the choke.

Nothing for it.

Circling around to avoid getting shredded by cross-fire, Filip warned, *«Celka, this might hurt.»* He couldn't wait for her answer. With Celka's hip, he body-checked the guard nearest the wall, sending them stumbling, then punched them hard in the jaw with his free hand.

Not waiting to see if his blow had dropped them, Filip bowled past, racing down the stairs, desperate to round the corner before the other guards could open fire. The first rifle report cracked the air as he reached the landing, and Filip stumbled, biting back a cry as the bullet buried itself in the back of his thigh.

He kept running, pain blazing in his leg with every step—but pain, he could ignore. He stumbled again, nearly taking a nose-dive down the second half of the staircase, realizing he'd gotten too close to the wall and Celka's invisible feet had caught on a picture frame.

Shouts came too close behind him, and more gunshots.

Refusing to look back, Filip trusted that Gerrit's instructions were correct and made a left when he reached the second floor landing, running for all he was worth toward the Stormhawk and far too many armed guards. At least if he got close to the Stormhawk, the Okhrana behind him would hesitate to shoot, not wanting to risk friendly fire.

More shouts, and Filip's stomach tried to crawl up through his throat. The guards on his tail were checking that the Stormhawk's defensive imbuements were active. If Gerrit was right about those imbuements, the Okhrana could probably fire a shrapnel shell from a howitzer and not ruffle a hair on the Stormhawk's head.

Freezing sleet, he was going to die.

Even as the first gunshot sounded, he ran. If Filip could get close enough to the Okhrana protecting the Stormhawk, he might be able to get inside the range of their defensive imbuements. If they suspected his presence, he'd have new problems—he could hardly fight hand-to-hand with Celka slumped across his shoulders. But one deadly threat at a time.

Another bullet clipped his back, the pain sharp like it might have cracked a rib—but at least it missed Celka. Filip jinked to the side, stumbling as his wounded leg tried to give out, but if there'd been a spray of blood when he'd been hit, he couldn't let the Okhrana use that to aim another shot.

A few meters ahead, retreating with the Stormhawk's entourage, bullets burst like violet starbursts on an invisible barrier. The bozhk Okhrana now guarding the Stormhawk's rear scuttled backwards to keep within the barrier's protection, rifles facing outward toward Filip and Celka. Two had fixed bayonets, sharpened steel sweeping in deadly arcs. At least they couldn't fire without the risk of hitting their colleagues—Filip could only hope they cared.

"Watch the floor!" someone shouted, and Filip realized the thick rug probably showed the impression of his boots—especially with Celka's added weight on his back.

Filip wanted to ask Gerrit how much time they had left, but it wouldn't matter. Even if the Stormhawk died right now, he and Celka would still be trapped between too many armed Yestrab Okhrana to survive.

He had to get inside the barrier. He could worry about next steps if he was still alive.

"Quick," Gerrit called, "get inside!" *«Filip, I'll hold the door, give you space to squeeze in.»* The Stormhawk's guard must have reached Iveta's room—either that or they'd decided to pull out of the corridor early.

«Inside?» Filip said, incredulous, glad that speaking through Nina didn't waste breath he didn't have. Getting locked in a room with a bunch of Okhrana while bleeding from multiple bullet wounds sounded like a terrible idea.

«You have a better plan?» Gerrit snapped.

He didn't.

Gunshots splintered wood and cracked plaster up and down the corridor. Despite the Okhrana's efforts to look for his footfalls in the rug, they didn't seem to have narrowed down on his position, but it wouldn't be long before they got a lucky—luckier—shot.

Filip pushed inside the protection imbuement's violet barrier as the Okhrana were bottlenecked by the doorway. A lucky swipe of a bayonet sliced through his jacket, but he curled away before it did more than cut a line of pain across his ribs. He was breathing so hard, he expected the Okhrana with the bayonet to sweep it back around and fire, but Gerrit was shouting "Get inside, get inside!" as others shouted something about a concealed bozhk.

The blockage at the door cleared out, but the protection nuzhda's bubble of safety went with it, leaving Filip exposed again. *«Gerrit,»* he called warningly, desperately, as the Okhrana down the hall pounded closer, a brief pause in their firing that wouldn't last long.

Then Gerrit was at the door, scanning the corridor, pistol

in hand, his back pressed against the door to prop it foolishly open—just wide enough for Filip to squeeze himself and Celka through.

"They're trying to escape!" Gerrit cried, opening fire down the corridor in the direction Filip had been running. Filip heard bullets crack into wood, then he was through.

CHAPTER SIXTY

GERRIT SHOUTED ORDERS to the Okhrana in the corridor, then slammed the door closed, pistol still in hand. One of the Okhrana who'd been part of the rear guard turned a key to lock them inside, and Gerrit put his back to the wall to take stock.

Iveta's bedroom was not dissimilar to his own, though it seemed smaller when crowded with a dozen Yestrab Okhrana. Most ringed the four-poster bed where they'd laid his father, rifles in hand, facing outward to deal with threat from any direction. The protection imbuement that had kept them from getting hit by friendly fire hung like a violet curtain, visible as Gerrit held his focus slightly in sousednia; rifle barrels stuck out from it like venomous spines.

The rear guard that Gerrit had shoved out of the way to make room for Filip and Celka to get inside guarded the door from inside the room, and Gerrit moved deeper into Iveta's room. He stopped next to Filip and Celka, who rippled cobalt from the concealment imbuement. They were sleeting lucky that none of the Okhrana in the hallway had been storm-

620

blessed, or they'd be dead. As it was, *«How badly are you wounded?»* Gerrit asked Filip through the snake.

«I don't know,» Filip ground out. *«Shot in the leg and the back.»* He edged up to a dresser, shifting to lower Celka onto its top, leaving her in a seated position with her back to the wall. She barely reacted, her arms still locked in a choke-hold around the empty air. Even without having to crouch, Filip's pain echoed through Nina.

Gerrit wished he could bandage his friend's wounds, but with a dozen watching Okhrana, he couldn't risk a suspicious move. Instead, he glanced at the ground. At least Filip wasn't dripping blood—yet.

Across the room was a washbasin with a few small towels, which could help staunch Filip's bleeding before it made him pass out or revealed them to the Okhrana. Gerrit just had to grab the towels casually, without anyone noticing.

Time to act like the concerned son. "What's his status?" he demanded, crossing the room to put himself near the washbasin.

The Stormhawk's personal physician bent over him, rippling gold with healing imbuements. She'd torn open his nightshirt and had a stethoscope pressed to his chest.

"Was it poison gas? Poison?" Gerrit asked.

"I can't tell. I've done what I can if it is." She jerked her chin toward a messy pile of vomit on the floor. "Though he doesn't show the right symptoms—and shouldn't be susceptible to natural poisons." Picking up one of the Stormhawk's hands, she pressed on a fingernail in some medical inspection.

"An imbuement?" Gerrit asked, stopping with his back to the washbasin. "Something new?"

"You saw concealed bozhki in the corridor," Iveta said, looking like she barely stopped herself from pacing. "Could you tell if they were holding other nuzhdi?"

"Nothing I saw," Gerrit said, "but they could have had it

walled off. There were two of them." He'd said as much to the guards in the corridor, ordering them to send the storm-blessed Okhrana out to search. He hoped they obeyed—he wasn't actually in their chain of command. He'd shouted that he'd keep an eye on sousednia from inside the room, and Storm Gods grant that Staff Sergeant Dolezal or one of the other storm-blessed wouldn't get sent in as backup. Until the six minutes of Celka's choke had elapsed, she and Filip were too vulnerable to anyone who could see sousednia.

Six minutes had never felt so long.

Iveta turned to one of the guards who'd pulled the Stormhawk from his bed, and Gerrit took the opportunity to stuff a hand towel into one of his back pockets. "What about you?" Iveta asked the guard. "Sense any imbuements?"

"No sir," the sergeant said. "I'm not storm-blessed."

Iveta slashed a hand in an impatient gesture that made her look like their father. She sleeting well knew he wasn't storm-blessed.

"Sir," one of the other original guards said. "Something else seemed... off. The Stormhawk sat up in bed, clawing at his throat. I would have said he was fighting someone, but it was just us in there." The corporal gestured between themself and the sergeant.

A guard at the door, not taking their eyes from the doorknob, said, "I came in from outside his room when they called, sir. It felt like someone was in there with us."

"So the resistance has imbuements," Iveta said.

"Or Lesnikrayen assassins do," Gerrit said, crossing his arms to hide a washcloth. He paced back over to where Filip leaned heavily against the wall beside Celka.

A knock on the door startled them all.

"It's Captain Kochevar," the Okhrana captain called. One of the door guards reached for the knob.

"Hold," Iveta ordered. "Gerrit, can you verify?"

Gerrit leaned a hip against the dresser, tilted so Filip would be able to see the towel bulging his back pocket. He slipped deeper into sousednia and swept the wall aside to see out into the corridor.

Iveta raised her voice and asked, "Kochevar, are you alone?"

"Yes," the captain said.

Gerrit nodded, focusing back on true-life. "It's her." A tug on his trousers, then Filip got the towel free.

"Keep an eye on sousednia," Iveta ordered.

Gerrit couldn't risk glancing back to make sure Filip had wrapped the concealment imbuement around the towel, but Filip was no amateur. As soon as Iveta had focused back on the door, Gerrit pulled the washcloth from the crook of his elbow and held it behind him for Filip. Then, drawing his pistol, Gerrit focused back on the corridor as if he believed another attack possible.

At Iveta's order, the guards just inside the door unlocked it and, rifles ready, let their captain inside. Kochevar scanned the scene, stone-faced.

As she demanded a situation report, Gerrit dared pull out his pocket watch. *«We're at five minutes,»* he told his friends. Any second now, the Stormhawk would die and they could figure out how in sleet-storms to get Filip and Celka out without anyone noticing. *«Filip, how are you doing?»*

«I think my rib stopped the bullet in my back. But the blood's soaked through my jacket.»

«And your leg?» Gerrit tried to calm his fears by telling himself that if the bullet had clipped Filip's femoral artery, he'd already be dead. It wasn't as reassuring as he'd hoped.

«Bleeding pretty bad.» A low, pained noise escaped Filip in true-life.

Gerrit's breath caught, expecting the Okhrana to turn, rifles aimed at the spot where Filip glowed blue in sousednia. But the guards didn't react. Gerrit released a shaky breath.

«I tied it off with my trouser leg and your towel.» Filip's breath came quick, even though the link. *«Should hold for a little while. Though not if I have to run.»*

Whatever escape Jolana had planned for them tonight, Filip's wounds would not make easy. Gerrit shoved the thought aside. First things first. Finish the assassination. Get out of this Okhrana stronghold. Prevent Filip from bleeding to death.

"No!" the doctor's urgency broke through Iveta and Captain Kochevar discussion about organizing a search. "No, no, no..." The doctor snapped something at one of the Okhrana, and another imbuement flared to life even as she started pressing on the Stormhawk's chest—hard, angry thumps that Gerrit expected the Okhrana to take offense to, but the doctor just snapped out, "I'm trying to restart his heart, give me space." Then she leaned down as though to kiss him, breathing into his lungs.

It won't work, Gerrit told himself, but he couldn't help glancing at the dresser, where Celka still sat, invisible, arms locked around nothing. *It won't work, right?* He forced himself not to ask it through Nina, unwilling to distract Celka.

Iveta glanced at him, jaw tight. Her hand dropped to the pistol at her hip, where she very quietly unsnapped its holster.

Gerrit barely kept the frown off his face. If only he could speak as easily with his sister as he could with Filip and Celka. Was she planning to shoot the doctor if she didn't save their father? He dismissed the thought. Iveta wouldn't be so petty or shortsighted. What, then? Had she realized Filip and Celka's presence? No, she would have shot them immediately. Gerrit's complicity? She might hesitate to call him out if the Stormhawk survived, might make the issue private, but if their father died, and she thought him part of the conspiracy...

Gerrit closed his own hand around the butt of his pistol. Iveta gave him an almost imperceptible nod, then glanced toward the door.

What in sleet-storms did that mean? Her nod made no sense if she suspected him of treason. Did she want him to go? Join the hunt for their father's supposed assassins? That, she could simply say aloud.

As if confident she'd communicated her message, Iveta turned back to the Stormhawk's physician, still fighting to save their father's life. In true-life, Iveta was impassive, but her sousedni-shape moved abruptly, heat-shimmer rippling in the air. Gerrit snapped his attention deeper into sousednia, searching for a threat that might have caused Iveta to react. Her movements were aggressive, as if... Suddenly, he understood. Iveta was pulling against a nuzhda—probably combat or protection. Barely had he realized it when one of the imbuements he'd made recently flared, coating her with an aubergine glow; she'd activated a protection imbuement. Why now?

"Well?" Captain Kochevar finally asked after the doctor's efforts to revive the Stormhawk seemed to have gone on for too long.

The doctor sat back on her heels and wiped sweat from her eyes. She looked sick. Lips pressed tight, she pulled out her stethoscope, but her expression said she didn't need it. Still, she listened for a minute before she shook her head. "He's dead."

«He's dead,» Gerrit repeated through Nina, doubtful Celka could hear true-life right now. He could hardly believe it. Even speaking it, the words seemed to belong to someone else. His father was dead. The Stormhawk was dead. They'd done it. They'd won.

It didn't feel like victory. He felt... ill.

Captain Kochevar barked the names of two of the Okhrana. "Red Hawk Ten." Her tone made it an order, and they yes-sirred before hurrying to the door.

"Hold," Iveta snapped. "No one leaves this room without my order. In light of my father's death, I'm assuming command of the Yestrab Okhrana." Her hand rested almost casually on her pistol.

Captain Kochevar stiffened. "With all due respect... Major"— the hesitation before her rank seemed deliberate, almost a challenge—"our orders are to report to your brother, Artur."

Iveta locked gazes with Kochevar. "Your orders have changed. Captain."

Captain Kochevar narrowed her eyes, her own hand on her sidearm.

Suddenly, Iveta's silent communication made sense. She'd been warning Gerrit to expect a fight if their father died. Artur had Captain Kochevar in his pocket; how many of the other Okhrana were his? Iveta had identified a few of Artur's spies, but they couldn't trust that she'd found them all. And Artur had been the Stormhawk's favored heir for years. Even if he hadn't recruited these Okhrana to his personal agenda, they might still support him; at the very least, most would follow their captain's orders.

Iveta's nod to the door must have meant she wanted him to ensure that no word of their father's death left this room until they were ready. Sleet, if only Gerrit had his own protection imbuement.

He shoved aside his fear, hoping the Okhrana would hesitate to shoot the Stormhawk's child even in a succession war, and forced himself to think. Once the Okhrana in this room accepted Iveta's rule, they had to secure their power base in the manor. Iveta had hand-picked the Tayemstvoy in the imbuement company, so most would be loyal to her—

though Artur would have done his best to plant spies—which meant Gerrit could trust the bolt-hawks, but not completely.

First, they had to win this fight. Then they had to secure the manor. Throughout it, they had to ensure that news of the Stormhawk's death did not spread before they were ready. They couldn't give Artur any warning, or he'd consolidate his own power before they could remove him.

Stepping forward, Gerrit said, "The Stormhawk favored Iveta. You saw this, Captain Kochevar." He made his voice commanding yet calm, simple statements of fact. "He followed our recommendation on the Lesnikrayen front and promoted us as a show of his trust in our judgement. His untimely death puts Bourshkanya at great risk—both from internal and external forces. Supreme-General Kladivo created the Yestrab Okhrana to protect his person as the Stormhawk, but also to ensure the safety of the regime and the State. With the bozhskyeh storms' return, the new Stormhawk must have the Storm Gods' blessings. *Iveta* Kladivo, not Artur, must be the new Stormhawk." He let that soak in for a moment then, before anyone could speak into his silence, he clicked his heels and saluted his sister. "All hail the Stormhawk!"

Several Okhrana shifted as though to follow his salute, but before they could, Captain Kochevar snapped, "That is not for you to decide, *Captain*." She made a two-fingered gesture toward the door and, not missing a beat, strode toward Iveta. "The Okhrana have a procedure in the event of—"

Gerrit stopped listening as two Okhrana exploded into motion, one flinging the door wide, the other moving to cover their colleague's escape, rifle snapping into their hands— pointing into the room.

Pistol already in hand, Gerrit moved before he could think, certain that rifle would be aimed at Iveta. At this close range, his shot easily took the guard in the head.

Another gunshot sounded half a heartbeat after his—a pistol, not a rifle. Gerrit didn't try to track the shot, aiming to take out the second Okhrana as they surged out of the room. He fired, only realizing as he did that the guard was falling, not running—already dead or badly wounded. Iveta's shot, he'd bet, but Gerrit couldn't stop to assess. The Okhrana would react to two of their number being shot, and he'd bet that the captain wasn't the only one who thought they should be saluting Artur.

Diving for corridor, Gerrit got the door between him and the main Okhrana force, stumbling over one of the corpses. A bullet splintered the wood beside him, low, as though whoever had fired had shot to wound. Good, they weren't trying to kill him—though with a firefight in an enclosed room, it'd be easy for a shot to go astray... or to claim later that his death had been an accident.

«Filip and Celka, I'll cover you. Go!» Invisibility wouldn't be much protection from bullets, but the door was open, and they might not get a better chance. Crouched, Gerrit ducked out from behind the door, trying to assess the situation fast enough to provide cover, not get himself shot, and not shoot any Okhrana who'd taken their side.

A bullet clipped his shoulder, and he returned fire, hitting his attacker in the chest. As the guard fell, Captain Kochevar dove behind the bed, ruining Gerrit's shot. He was pretty sure she wasn't the only one back there, but at this angle he couldn't tell for certain. No one else was aiming at him, so Gerrit fired twice, punching holes in the wainscoting, deliberately missing anyone else. He wanted to keep enemy heads down but avoid friendly casualties. They'd need Okhrana allies.

Behind him, Filip and Celka limped into the corridor, their blue sousedni-glow making it impossible to say who was supporting whom.

«*Celka, get to the rendezvous if you can,*» Gerrit said. «*Warn Jolana about the coup so she doesn't get caught in the crossfire. Filip, get some of the bolt-hawks—you can probably trust them, but watch your back—and secure the house's telephone and telegraph lines. We can't let word get out. Not yet.*»

«*He's wounded,*» Celka said. «*He can't—*»

«*Filip, you* have *to do this,*» Gerrit said. «*Expect Okhrana fire.*»

Celka started to protest again, but Filip interrupted, voice tight around pain. «*It'll explain my injuries.*»

«*And once we* win *this fight,*» Gerrit said, ducking back around the door, thinking to fire again—but the room had become a melee. He couldn't spot Iveta or the Okhrana captain; the room was a churning sea of olive drab, people fighting with truncheons and fists. «*We'll get the doctor to heal Filip.*»

«*Unless he's dead,*» Celka snapped, but Gerrit could spare no more attention for the conversation and cut the link.

Taking advantage of his distraction, someone tackled him, bowling Gerrit over onto his back. A punch in the face snapped his head to the side, smearing his vision before he could even see who'd tackled him. He fought back automatically, blocking and trying to dislodge his attacker, his shoulder burning from where the bullet had torn through muscle. The distraction was enough he almost didn't notice the other Okhrana surge past, leaping over him to escape into the corridor, shouting "Red Hawk Ten! Red Hawk Ten!"

Snarling, Gerrit managed to punch his attacker in the face with his pistol, throwing them back enough that he could twist to fire down the corridor. But the Okhrana he'd been fighting grabbed his wrist, and Gerrit's shot missed. His attacker tried to twist the gun from his grasp, but Gerrit fought, getting a knee between them and managing to kick out—by pure chance, he outmassed his attacker.

He twisted up to a crouch and fired again, missing again as the Okhrana tackled him, shouting something he couldn't hear over the gunshots ringing in his ears and the retreating guard's cry of *Red Hawk Ten*.

As Gerrit fell, he managed to throw the Okhrana from his back, flipping them over his shoulder and twisting around to try and elbow them in the head to keep them down. They landed on their back, somehow having drawn their truncheon in the fall, and his elbow connected with the heavy wood. Pain flashed up his arm, but he managed to keep his momentum, rolling up onto one knee and hook-punching them in the face with his empty pistol.

The blow stunned them enough that he managed to wrench the truncheon from their grasp, tossing it aside. Lurching to his feet, Gerrit grabbed a spare magazine from his belt, dropping his pistol's spent magazine to the floor and slapping the fresh one in place as he looked around.

He found himself facing the dark maw of a pistol—just far enough back that he couldn't strike the gun away, too close to risk trying to dodge.

But they hadn't fired yet.

He snapped his attention to the person holding the gun, and met Staff Sergeant Dolezal's granite gaze. "Who are you supporting?" she demanded.

Gerrit swallowed hard. If he gave the wrong answer, he had no doubt she'd shoot. Whether the shot would be to disable or kill, he wasn't sure.

"Now!" The snap to her voice was an almost physical blow, and he saw her finger tighten on the trigger. Delay any more, and she'd shoot anyway.

"Iveta," he said, pleased at how confident his voice sounded.

She gave the smallest nod, and her aim swung off him before she fired.

Gerrit turned, discovering that she'd shot the Okhrana he'd been fighting moments before.

"He was Artur's," the staff sergeant said, voice tight. With one hand, she reached up and tore the red epaulette from her right shoulder, leaving her uniform lopsided. She reached out, serpent-fast, and did the same to him. "Secure communication lines," she told him, already striding toward the room where the Stormhawk lay dead. "I'll—"

But Gerrit didn't trust her enough to risk Iveta's life. "I contacted my people," he caught up, reaching the bedroom door at the same time. Another door down the corridor banged open and Dolezal's head snapped up. Gerrit barely had time to register another Okhrana before Dolezal fired. The Okhrana leaving their room staggered up against the wall, red blooming beneath their open jacket, and Gerrit recognized one of Kochevar's lieutenants. His throat tightened, a screaming panic threatening to overwhelm him.

Dolezal caught his arm with one hand, shoving him behind her. "Then come in with me, but don't shoot anyone unless I shoot first. *Sir*." That last was added as afterthought once she was already moving. She kicked the door open with a muted bang, calling out names he didn't know, ordering some of her people to protect Iveta, others to stand down.

By the time Gerrit got into the room, the fight was mostly over. Three Okhrana formed a wall before Iveta, two holding their rifles like they'd used them as clubs, another gripping a truncheon. Several Okhrana had surrendered, hands up, including the doctor, and what fights were still ongoing seemed nearly over. Dolezal's unconcern suggested that the right people were winning.

In the corner, Captain Kochevar pushed herself up to one

knee, breathing hard, one hand pressed to a bloody wound just beneath her collarbone. "You're making a mistake, Staff Sergeant. Iveta won't last a week."

Staff Sergeant Dolezal ordered one of her people to disarm the captain. The others who'd surrendered were undergoing the same process, hands being cuffed behind their backs.

Iveta stepped around her wall of guards, sparing a nod for Gerrit, who nodded back, relieved to see her well, though her face was covered in blood, and it looked like her nose had been broken.

Through gritted teeth, Captain Kochevar said, "Don't be a fool, Major. The Tayemstvoy won't follow you. Insist on this coup, and you'll end up dead."

"Will you pull the trigger?" Iveta's swelling nose muffled her hard voice. She'd lost her own pistol during the fight, and blood dripped from her truncheon.

Captain Kochevar's jaw worked, but she finally shook her head. "No."

Gerrit caught movement from the corner of his eye and jerked his attention off Iveta in time to see a rifle barrel edge around the bathroom door. "Iveta, down!" he shouted—too late.

The rifle report split the air. The bullet burst violet a handspan from Iveta, stopped by her protection imbuement.

The shooter fired again, but Iveta dropped to the ground, and they missed.

Gerrit's return shot missed, too, but forced the shooter to duck back enough that they didn't fire a third time; his second shot took them in the head. Their body slumped to the side, leaving a reddish stain on the gold leaf wallpaper. Gerrit's stomach tried to empty itself, but he fought the reflex, jerking his attention away from the stain as he heard the staff sergeant ordering two of her people to search the bathroom.

They should have searched it earlier, he thought helpfully, his hands shaking with adrenaline from the fight.

He turned to see Iveta picking herself up from the floor and two Okhrana menacing Captain Kochevar with their rifles. Iveta stooped to grab a pistol that looked suspiciously like it had been struck from Kochevar's hand.

"Pity you chose the wrong Kladivo," Iveta said, turning the pistol on Captain Kochevar.

The captain, to her credit, said nothing.

Iveta fired, and the bullet punched a neat hole in Kochevar's forehead. Her body slumped to the ground, and Iveta swept the room with a hard gaze.

Gerrit's throat tasted of bile, but Iveta was right not to leave a traitor of rank alive in their midst. He clicked his heels and saluted his sister. "All hail the Stormhawk!"

This time, the surviving Yestrab Okhrana echoed his salute.

Now, they had to finish securing the manor—or all this would be for nothing.

CHAPTER SIXTY-ONE

FILIP LIMPED INTO his room, and Yanek spun from the window, hand going to his sidearm. Good, he was fully dressed, roused by the shouting and gunshots. "Filip, what—? Stormy skies." He swooped under Filip's arm, half dragging him over to sit on the bed.

Filip hissed air through gritted teeth as Yanek's hold pulled against the bullet wound in his back. More gunshots sounded down the corridor.

"What's happening? What happened to *you*?" Yanek had found the gunshot wound on his back, was pulling off Filip's jacket even as he spoke.

"The Stormhawk's dead," Filip said.

"You're sleeting bleeding *everywhere*," Yanek said. "Don't move." He ran to get towels, then started slicing strips from the bedlinen to use as bandages.

"We have to secure the manor, make sure no one gets word out. Iveta's staging a coup. If Artur learns of it, she won't have time to solidify her power base."

"And the Okhrana?" Yanek asked as he lifted Filip's blood-soaked shirt and pressed a towel against the bullet wound. He gave Filip one edge of the bandage to hold and wound the sheet tightly around his ribs to hold the towel in place. He tied it off, tight, and Filip had to pant around the pain before he could speak again.

"Divided," Filip said. "They shot me, but they can't all be on Artur's side, or Gerrit wouldn't have been able to reach me."

"Reach you?" Yanek wound more layers of sheet around Filip's chest.

"Through sousednia." He hated the lie, but he could explain the larger, treasonous details and ask Yanek to join him when they weren't in the middle of a fight. "He's with Iveta. They're pinned down. We need to get the rest of the squad and the bolt-hawks, secure the manor before Artur's Okhrana can warn him."

Yanek made Filip lay on his stomach on the bed and untied the trouser leg Filip had cut off to bandage his thigh wound. The blood-soaked towel hit the floor with a sloppy wet sound and Filip was almost glad he couldn't see the blood welling around the bullet wound. "Do we trust the bolt-hawks?" Yanek asked as he wrapped more sheet-bandage around Filip's leg.

"Mostly."

"Great." Yanek almost managed dry humor, but worry left his voice brittle. "All right, I'm almost done. You stay here, I'll get the squad, then rally the bolt-hawks." Since their squadmates were officers, their rooms were nearby, but most of the bolt-hawks had been quartered with the household guard and staff in an outbuilding.

"No." Filip sat up once Yanek had tied the last layer of bedsheet. "I can still shoot. We have to cover the telephone and the telegraph. We need the bodies."

"I need you to *not* be a body," Yanek said, but he slung Filip's arm over his shoulder when Filip struggled to stand on his own.

Filip met Yanek's gaze, leaning hard on him. "I won't be. Now that I'm not bleeding out."

Yanek blew out a frustrated breath but didn't argue. He could count as well as Filip. "Come on." He helped him to the corridor, then left Filip propped against the doorframe while he gathered the others. More gunshots sounded from the direction they'd taken the Stormhawk, and Filip leaned against the wall to limp toward the stairs. The manor's telephone was in one of the front parlors. He wasn't sure about the telegraph.

He'd nearly reached the stairs when Dbani flung Filip's arm over their shoulder, taking his weight so they could move faster. Yanek took off at a dead run to alert the bolthawks, and Hedvika took point, pistol in hand. Masha took rear guard and Havel strode just ahead of Filip and Dbani. Filip made sure they knew where they were headed, then concentrated on moving without passing out.

Rounding a corner on the ground floor, Hedvika signaled for them to hold. Dbani eased out from under Filip's arm, and Filip told his leg to sleeting hold his weight while he drew his own sidearm. The squad eased forward, and Hedvika gestured to warn them of two Okhrana about ten meters down the corridor. That likely put them outside the parlor with the telephone.

"Shoot to kill," Filip whispered, and gestured haste.

Hedvika and Dbani took the lead, bursting around the corner already firing, Masha quick on their heels. Havel matched Filip's slower pace, covering their rear in case their gunfire drew more Okhrana.

Filip limped into the parlor just as the Okhrana who'd been holding the telephone receiver crumpled to the floor, shot in the back of the head.

Reholstering his pistol, Filip let the rest of his squad deal with securing the room and hurried to the telephone. He pressed the receiver to his ear. "Hello?" Silence during which Filip leaned hard on the table, terrified he was already too late, that the delay caused by his injuries had cost Iveta her chance at splitting regime loyalties. If Artur swept into his father's role without challenge, the resistance would lose a critical diversion, and their coup would be that much harder fought.

Then the operator spoke, concerned. "Please repeat. There was noise on the line. Where should I direct the call?"

Relief made Filip sink into a chair. "Nowhere," he said. "My mistake. Sorry to have disturbed you." He replaced the receiver in its cradle. At Havel's raised eyebrow, he said, "We made it in time."

"Good," Havel said in a voice of calm command. Hedvika and Dbani finished dragging the second Okhrana corpse out of the corridor, dropping the body unceremoniously behind a sofa. "Rychtr, stay with Cizek in case they try again. We"— he gestured at himself, Masha, and Dbani—"will secure the telegraph and make sure there isn't a second telephone somewhere." He made it sound unlikely, and Havel was better placed than Filip to know; he had some family connection to the estate.

Without waiting for agreement, Havel moved them out.

Filip shoved his chair back, starting to reach under the desk to yank the telephone out of its connection in the wall. Shooting pain up his back stopped him, and the edges of his vision tunneled in.

"Let me do it." Hedvika placed her pistol on the table, getting down on hands and knees to do the deed. "There." She reclaimed her gun and moved toward the door, peering both ways down the corridor.

Filip held his breath, listening for gunshots, hoping Gerrit was safe and Celka well on her way out of the manor. For a moment, everything seemed eerily calm.

Hedvika reholstered her pistol and pulled a padded wooden chair over to the wall by the door. One eye on the corridor, she angled it to see out, and Filip forced his body to move. He tried not to limp as he crossed the room to Hedvika's chair, but it seemed like each time he stopped moving, the pain was worse again when he started. He nearly cried out when he tried to sit, and Hedvika caught his elbow, helping lower him.

She took up a post on the other side of the door. "I hope Gerrit appreciates what you've done for him." She kept her voice low.

Filip had no idea how to respond.

"Is that why you're doing it, the coup? For him?" She didn't look at him, pistol in hand as she scanned the corridor.

"No." Filip's answer surprised him. Until recently, almost everything in his life had been for Gerrit. But this... no. Gerrit was a part of it; but even if he hadn't been, Filip would make the same choices. The realization was like a gust of cold air—a shock, but refreshing.

"Hey," Hedvika said, and he caught her worried glance. "You still with me?"

Filip blinked, wondering how long he'd been silent. His pistol rested on his lap, and he forced his attention to the empty corridor. "Yeah."

"So why, then?" Hedvika asked.

"Because it's the right thing to do," Filip said.

Voice tight, she asked, "Since when does doing the right thing come before following orders?"

Filip narrowed his eyes, but kept his focus on the corridor. "I *am* following orders."

"Shooting a bunch of Okhrana so *Iveta* Kladivo can become Stormhawk?" She lowered her voice. "Did she kill her father?"

"No." Filip realized that sounded too certain. "I mean, I don't think so. Gerrit said something about concealed attackers. And why would she? He was showing her favor. A year or two, she might have been the obvious heir."

"But she's not right now." Hedvika's voice gained an edge. "We're committing treason."

"Only if we fail," Filip said.

Hedvika cut him a glance, and Filip realized that in his blood loss and self-revelation, he'd missed her growing tension. Hedvika's stance shifted, and she glanced back inside the room. At the telephone. Her father was Tayemstvoy, a mundane like Artur. Hedvika's personal loyalties burrowed deep into the regime, and Iveta, for all she was a red-shouldered Kladivo, might seem like a wild card.

Filip couldn't give Hedvika time to think through the hero she'd become if she warned Artur of a coup in time to crush it. "Artur sees the Storm Guard—all of us—as a threat. If he wins, he'll put Tayemstvoy boots on all our necks."

Hedvika's attention snapped back to him, then out into the corridor, assessing. But she wasn't just a soldier following orders anymore. He could tell she was thinking. And if she decided to run for the telephone, Filip wasn't sure he could stop her without shooting her in the back. And she'd think of that. She'd disarm him first, and it would hardly be a fight. He'd lost too much blood.

More gunshots sounded, and boots pounded the floorboards overhead. Hedvika tensed. If she was going to betray her company commander, she was running out of time.

Filip couldn't give her the space to betray them. But what argument would sway her? "Iveta's smart. She's ruthless enough to win but compassionate enough to be a good leader. Artur wouldn't be."

Hedvika's grip on her pistol tightened, her pale knuckles

whitening, and he could practically feel her assessing him.

"She took the same oaths we did," Filip said. "Protect Bourshkanyan citizens. *She* believes them." In a rush, he told her about Zbishov, about Artur ordering the paranoid violence imbuement turned against peaceful protestors. Hedvika scoffed at first—were they really peaceful? She'd seen the graffiti. The workers were lazy, grasping above their station. But he refused to let her turn him from the facts. It didn't matter what she thought of workers' rights. The protest had been *peaceful*, and Artur had ordered the square blanketed in magic, turning friends and family against each other so he could march the Tayemstvoy in and call their brutality justice.

Little by little, Hedvika's objections died, and the horror sunk in.

"Major *Iveta* Kladivo is our commanding officer," Filip said. "She's led the imbuement company well. We owe her our loyalty."

When boots pounded down the corridor, Hedvika snapped her pistol up, a determined set to her jaw—though by the sound of it, they were badly outnumbered. Filip levered himself up, leaning against the door to keep weight off his bad leg. If these were Artur's Okhrana, they'd probably die here.

Yanek, I'm sorry, he thought. At the same time, he hoped Celka and Gerrit would get out.

Rifle barrels nosed out around the corner that he and the squad had rounded just minutes before, and Filip pressed right up to his pistol's trigger break. A hair more pressure, and he'd fire. But first, he needed to make sure they were facing the enemy.

"Hedvika?" Yanek called from down the corridor. "Filip?"

Filip almost blacked out with relief. Hedvika called back that they'd secured the telephone, and Yanek appeared around the corner flanked by a dozen bolt-hawks.

He caught Filip's arm as he wavered. "Sit before you fall down. We've got this."

Filip didn't want to release his hand, but he did. The room shifted between each blink, like flipping through photographs. He heard voices, sometimes distant and sometimes close, then Gerrit was there, crouched beside him—when had Filip lain down?—concerned, saying words Filip couldn't quite make out. The room spun, and Filip found himself on his stomach on the floor. When he tried to push himself up, a hand pressed him down.

Then a face he recognized only belatedly as the Stormhawk's physician. "This is going to hurt," she said, and Filip's world turned red with pain.

CHAPTER SIXTY-TWO

CELKA HAD LAIN down for just a minute, reintegrating her mind and closing her eyes just briefly, just to recover her strength before climbing out the window to meet Jolana and warn her about the coup. She woke to someone shaking her shoulder and sat bolt upright in bed.

"It's just me," Masha said. She'd lit the bedside lamp, and it gleamed dark on a dried smear of blood across her cheek.

"Wha—?" Celka floundered, her limbs too heavy, tongue thick with sleep.

"I can't believe you slept through that," Masha said, gentle, and Celka glanced at the window in panic—the curtains were still open, the signal to Jolana that the Stormhawk was dead. Sleet, the Stormhawk was *dead*. She'd *done* it. She was a resistance assassin.

Celka snapped her attention back to Masha. She was a resistance assassin and she should be long gone from here. At least it was still dark outside. How long had she been asleep?

"We won," Masha said in answer to her unasked question. "The doctor was about to treat Filip. I thought maybe you'd...

want to see him. I thought..." Her light brown skin reddened. "I figured you'd be worried, locked up in here. Sorry I woke you."

"No, no, you did great. I want to—" She was on her feet before Masha's words really registered. "Is Filip...?"

"He lost a lot of blood." Masha headed for the door. Celka followed, leaving behind Nina in her crate and their full packs. She glanced back at the curtains, hoping dawn wasn't too close or they'd lose their window to escape tonight. "But fortunately, the... Stormhawk's physician"— Masha stumbled over the title but recovered—"has plenty of imbuements."

"He's really dead?" Celka asked as they emerged cautiously into the corridor, Masha scanning both ways, hand on her sidearm, before leading them toward the stairs.

"That's what they say."

«Gerrit? Filip?» Celka reached out through Nina, finding both of them easily through the link, though Filip's threads felt too heavy. She repeated what Masha had said, and Gerrit confirmed he was with Filip and the doctor. *«I fell asleep,»* she said at his question, but he didn't snap at her.

Instead, Gerrit said, *«Might be best.»*

«What might be best?» Celka asked, but by then Masha had led her into a parlor, and Filip lay on the floor, uniform dark with blood.

As Celka neared, a sunshine glow around the Stormhawk's physician brightened, and a pained cry tore from Filip's throat. Celka lunged forward, but Masha caught her arm. The doctor pulled a bloody lump of metal from Filip's back and tossed it on the floor. With a lurch, Celka realized it was a bullet.

The doctor wiped her hands on a towel and pulled a different imbuement out of a case. Celka gripped Masha's hand as that one did its work, knitting together the muscles of Filip's back.

One more imbuement, then he sat up, woozy.

Celka ran to him, crouching at his side, gripping his shoulder. "You're all right?"

Distantly, she heard the doctor saying that he needed to sleep and drink plenty of fluids. She'd restored some of his lost blood, but he'd have to rebuild the rest himself. Then she was gone, and Yanek was helping Filip over to a couch. Celka swooped in to support his other side, nearly colliding with Gerrit, who apparently had the same idea.

Once Filip was seated and able to assure them that he'd be fine, Gerrit ordered everyone else out. Yanek, who'd settled next to Filip, hesitated. Celka expected Gerrit to snap at him, but Gerrit's voice gentled. "I'll just be a minute."

Filip squeezed Yanek's hand reassuringly, though his attempted smile failed.

Before Yanek had even reached the door, Gerrit asked Celka, «*Can you activate the silencing imbuement?*»

She pulled the darkbag from around her neck, slipping the imbuement free. It took her longer than usual to pull against concealment, exhausted even with her accidental nap, but she activated it and walled it off.

"Good," Gerrit said, once the imbuement covered them. "I need your help."

Celka's chest tightened, and she realized what he was about to say. "You're not coming with us."

He straightened, surprised but not denying it. She expected it to feel like a betrayal; instead, it was almost a relief.

"You're *what?*" Filip started to rise from the couch, but Celka pulled him back down. He needed to save his strength.

Gerrit nodded. "She's right. That's why I need your help. I want you both to stay."

* * *

GERRIT HAD EXPECTED the request to be easy—not for Celka, but for Filip.

Instead, Filip's expression closed off. "The resistance needs us."

Gerrit crouched and took Filip's hands. "Maybe. But do *we* need the resistance? Look at everything we've accomplished tonight. Iveta and I will take command, and we'll do it right. We'll make Bourshkanya better. You said it yourself when we returned to the Storm Guard: whatever the resistance has, it doesn't compare to the State. We'll stop Artur, and we'll return the Storm Gods' blessings to the people."

Filip's gaze defocused, his sousedni-shape sharpening. "Are you walling off memories again?"

Gerrit met his gaze in sousednia, still marveling that he could. "No." He looked to Celka, knowing she'd be able to read the truth behind his words. "I remember everything. Vrana's plans; my father ordering my mother's death; Lucie." His voice caught and he gave himself a moment to feel that loss before reaching a hand out to Celka. "I remember our time together, trusting each other." She didn't take his hand, and he sighed, letting it drop. "And I remember asking for this uniform."

He stood and thumbed the torn red epaulette. "I made cold, hard decisions after I sent the two of you away—and I shouldn't have sent you away. That was a mistake. But the rest of what I did—" He focused on Filip, willing his best friend to understand.

Filip still looked closed off, his face the mask he'd worn during their cruelest Storm Guard training. Gerrit grabbed a chair and pulled it around so he could sit facing them, not wanting to tire Filip. He needed his best friend's help. Because he'd been wrong before that he couldn't rely on anyone else. He could rely on Filip. He'd always been able to.

Sitting, he reached for Filip's hands, and his best friend took them. "I believe I made the right calls, despite their consequences. The attacks on Lesnikraj..." He shook his head. "We stopped my father from going to war and did it in a way that positioned Iveta to succeed in this coup. With me and Iveta in power, we can prevent the war entirely. People died, but we saved more lives than we sacrificed."

"And Mrach?" Celka asked, voice clipped. "Or today's imbuement? Do you stand by those, too?"

Gerrit grimaced, not bothering to hide the reaction. "You broke me from my nuzhda-warping. I'm not walling off memories anymore. I won't make the same mistakes."

"Until you have to do something you don't like," Celka said.

He gripped Filip's hands a little harder, wishing he'd been smart enough to have this conversation alone with Filip. He should have known he'd never convince Celka to stay; but this was his and Filip's world—Filip had said as much when trying to turn Gerrit from the resistance.

But Celka was here, and Gerrit couldn't ignore her. "You were right," he told her, "what you said tonight. I *am* strong enough to handle this. I thought I wasn't. And maybe when I first returned to the Storm Guard that was true. But I'm strong now—even as Lucie's death and all the lives we lost at Mrach and Zbishov cut me apart. I won't lose myself." He turned to Filip again. "You trusted me before. You had my back. I'm asking you to trust me now. Help me change Bourshkanya from the inside, just like you wanted."

Filip opened his mouth to argue.

Gerrit didn't let him. "I didn't listen to you before, but I'm listening *now*. I was scared and blinded by anger at my father. He was a despot, and either I agreed to kill him or Captain Vrana would have shoved me off a cliff."

Filip straightened at that, surprised.

Gerrit nodded. "But Vrana's not here right now, and the Tayemstvoy sweeps after Lucie's arrest have torn apart her network. The resistance is in tatters, but my father is dead. He was the one whose ego wouldn't allow civilians to imbue and threaten his tale of might and the Storm Gods' favor. But he's *dead*. Iveta won't be so foolish."

"You're certain?" Filip asked.

Gerrit kept his expression confident, even though he wasn't, and managed to avoid glancing at Celka. Still, if he lied, she'd sense it—and maybe Filip would too—and Gerrit would lose him. "I know she listens to me. And *I* am not so foolish."

Filip's jaw tightened, the crease between his brows showing that his thoughts raced ahead. "She won't risk looking weak as she consolidates power."

"She already pushed Father to negotiate with factory workers—" Gerrit started.

"Alienating wealthy, powerful regime supporters," Filip said. "If she repeals the interdiction on Songs, Artur can spin that as proof of her proletarian sympathies. She might gain a popular following, but the people with power and guns will turn their backs on her."

"We can find a way," Gerrit said. "And maybe it won't be immediate, but—"

"Captain Vrana has a plan," Filip said, obstinate.

"Vrana will be running for her life," Gerrit snapped, irritated that Filip refused to listen to him. "If she isn't already."

"Because you'll betray her?" Celka asked.

Gerrit cut her an angry glance. "No. But with her network compromised and—" He bit off the words before he could give them more fodder against him.

But Filip figured it out. "With you turning your back on the resistance, she can't risk that you'll keep her identity secret." He released Gerrit's hands, leaning away from him. "By staying, you sabotage the resistance—even if you don't *directly* betray us."

Gerrit shook his head, but it was true. *Us*, Filip had said. Like he'd already decided. Gerrit felt the ground crumbling beneath him.

"Come with us," Celka said, but the edged invitation reminded Gerrit too much of Vrana walking him to a cliff face and putting her gun to his back.

"Vrana probably won't be able to stay in the Storm Guard even if I do," he said, wishing he had a better sense for the damage the Okhrana and Tayemstvoy had done to her network so he could say it with certainty.

Filip just crossed his arms.

Gerrit needed to try a different tack. "Celka, I know you've supported the resistance your whole life, but think about the good you could do *here*. This is no longer my father's regime. Be my adviser. Help me know what to change so Iveta and I get it *right*." He wanted to reach out, but stopped himself, smart enough not to give her another chance to reject his touch. "Your calming imbuements could make an enormous difference to our rule. I promise I won't force your imbuements. If you stay, you'll control your magic. And when Iveta needs to negotiate with entrenched power, when she needs to get factories producing so people see it's possible to be a strong leader without Tayemstvoy oppressions, *your* imbuements could help."

Her lips pressed together as if she tasted something bitter. "And when you need weapons?"

"We *have* people who can imbue weapons," Gerrit said. "*I* can imbue weapons. No one but you can imbue calming."

"And if you can't prevent a war?" Celka asked. "If Iveta doesn't want to?"

"She does." But doubt needled him. War would turn attention on an outside enemy. If Iveta undercut most of Artur's support, a war might make the stragglers fall into line.

Celka lifted her chin as if he'd made her point for her.

Gerrit shook his head. "We can't know. But *I* don't want war, and Iveta listens to me."

"Captain Vrana never intended your sister to become the next Stormhawk, not permanently," Filip said.

"Vrana is *wrong*," Gerrit snapped, surging up out of his chair to loom over them both. "Her mistakes got Lucie killed and loosed the Tayemstvoy to tear apart the resistance. I'm asking you to turn your back on her. I'm asking you to *listen* to me. Follow *me*. Vrana's plan is flawed. Her revolution will tear Bourshkanya apart and will probably *fail*. Iveta is a guaranteed solution that will make Bourshkanya better." He turned all his attention on Filip, willing him to understand. "You promised me you'd have my back. This is your chance to prove yourself. Your chance to stand beside me like we always dreamed. It's your chance to *matter*." He held out his hand. "Come with me. Help me give the people back their Songs."

Filip stared at his hand, the struggle apparent in his face. But finally, he shook his head. "I believe the resistance has a chance." He met Gerrit's gaze, regret in his dark eyes. "You claim you want advisors, but you've never listened to me. Just like you're not listening now. Iveta won't change the regime— not enough. The rot goes too deep to heal it by changing the bandage."

Gerrit dropped his hand back to his side, the knife of betrayal in his gut.

Filip levered himself up, clasping Gerrit's shoulder as he wavered. "I'm sorry, Gerrit. But I've made my choice."

Gerrit wanted to strike Filip's hand away even as he wanted to shake his best friend and scream, *Don't go. I can't do this without you!* But he could. He'd managed without Filip this past month, and he hadn't even been his whole self. For the first time in months, Gerrit's thoughts were clear, his memory no longer fogged by walls. Filip was making a mistake, but it was his to make.

Stiff, Gerrit nodded, throat too tight to speak. Instead, he forced himself to think. He couldn't allow Filip and Celka's disappearance to weaken his and Iveta's chance at coming out on top of this coup. That meant that everyone had to believe them dead—even Iveta—so there'd be no chance of them being associated with the assassination.

When Gerrit could make his voice work again, he said, "Leave your uniform jackets and insignia. Celka, can you leave your storm pendant?"

She recoiled, clutching at where it hung about her throat.

"It wouldn't surprise me if there are a few Okhrana who've claimed loyalty but might be out for blood," he said, laying out the alibi he'd use. "Plenty of people have died tonight; I should be able to find a couple of corpses that we can damage enough to make stand in for you. If we find your storm pendant on one, it could sell it—and I meant what I said. I think that imbuement could make a big difference."

Celka flinched at the mention of corpses, but she stood and caught Filip's hand. Gerrit tried to ignore the flare of jealousy that they'd turned their backs on him for each other.

"What about our earrings?" Filip asked.

"Our attackers could have stolen them," Celka said. "My storm pendant doesn't look like it's worth anything, but our earrings would be worth a lot of money."

Gerrit nodded. The alibi held up. "But Nina—"

"Could have slithered away," Filip said. "Or been taken by the people who killed us."

"She comes with us." Celka's tone brooked no argument.

Gerrit sighed. "Fine." Compared to faking their corpses, eliding over the snake's disappearance wouldn't be that difficult.

He looked between them, forcing himself to feel the ache in his chest even as he wanted to shrug it behind walls. He wanted to beg them to reconsider, but it was too late for second thoughts. Swallowing a lump in his throat, Gerrit pulled out his pocket watch. "You have a few hours before sunrise. It'll be easiest to cover your disappearance if you leave tonight."

Filip nodded then, voice rough, said, "Take care of yourself, Gerrit."

Gerrit hesitated, but compassion wasn't weakness. He flung his arms around his best friend, gripping tight one last time. "You too. Don't get yourself killed."

Returning the embrace, Filip said, "Don't turn into your father."

When they parted, Gerrit turned away before the loss could swallow him. His gaze snagged on Celka, who stood stiffly. Was she glad to turn her back on him? The idea that she might be—and that it was his fault—hurt. Awkward, he held his hand out to shake, hoping she'd take it. "Stay safe, Celka."

She searched his face, not taking his hand. "What happened, Gerrit? Were we always just lying to each other?"

He let his hand drop. He wanted to kiss her again; already he missed the warmth they'd shared and the bright explosion of her laugh. Maybe they had always been lying—about who they were and what they wanted. He hadn't thought so, but he'd also been certain he was too weak to face the world as himself. "I'll miss you," he finally said, because it was true. She'd pulled him out of a dark place and helped him imagine a better world. He wished she would see that he was going to go build it, but Filip had been right, months ago, when he said that Celka couldn't understand.

Regret tightened the corners of her mouth. "Yeah. I guess I'll miss you too." She started to turn away, but hesitated. Turning back, she wrapped him in a powerful embrace. "Hold onto yourself, Gerrit," she whispered. "You *are* strong enough."

He held her for a long time, her familiar warmth echoing a keening wind across his sousednia. But true-life and sousednia didn't balance perfectly at her touch anymore, and he knew this comfort would be fleeting. When she pulled away, he touched her cheek gently and saw the faintest glimmer of tears in her eyes. "Goodbye," he whispered, and turned away.

CHAPTER SIXTY-THREE

WHEN THE DOOR shut behind Gerrit, Filip lowered himself heavily onto the sofa, feeling like he'd torn a hole in his chest. That the strazh bond remained, a rope still tethering him to Gerrit, made it worse, not better.

Celka sat at his side, clasping his hands in her smaller ones. "Thank you," she said.

He made himself focus on her—on the future instead of the past—and nodded.

"Do you think we can risk taking our packs?" she asked, and Filip forced himself to think.

Already it would be suspicious that their outwear disappeared, but in no world would he snowshoe into winter in the resistance without his warm furs. "Gerrit will find a way to explain it—or just pretend they got lost during an equipment transfer." Compared to finding appropriate corpses, losing a couple of packs would be no challenge. "Gerrit's right that we don't know what state the resistance is in. We need our gear."

Celka fiddled with one ruby and gold earring before forcing

her hand down. She nodded once, decisive. "Want me to get Yanek?"

Filip's throat closed off. What if Yanek turned his back on him too? But he made himself nod. Celka handed him the silencing imbuement and reintegrated while he activated it in her stead.

A pained smile tugged at her lips as she stood. "I hope he'll join us."

When Yanek sat at Filip's side with his burnished brass eyes, Filip managed to keep breathing. All these years, he'd believed that a relationship would distract him from what mattered. And maybe that was because the only relationship he'd allowed himself was with Gerrit—and Gerrit took everything from him. But with Yanek, it had been different. Their relationship had meant support and understanding, had meant a partner who listened and who helped him grow—even when, *especially* when, that change was terrifying. Filip didn't want what they had to end.

"I'm leaving," Filip said, wishing there were some way he could break the news gently.

"Like, reassigned?" Yanek glanced over his shoulder at the closed door. "Is that why Gerrit wanted to talk to you?"

"No," Filip said. Then, "Yes. Sort of." He shook his head. "I'm joining the resistance. I'd like you to come with me."

Yanek pulled back. Filip's stomach tensed, but mostly, Yanek looked confused. "You're *what?*"

"I wish I could have risked telling you earlier. But we have to leave tonight." Filip took his hands, willing him to understand. "The resistance has a plan, and more powerful leadership than I would have expected. The chaos of the assassination—"

"*Sleet*," Yanek interrupted, his gaze skipping across Filip's face as he put the pieces together. "The Stormhawk. Your... *freezing sleet*, your bullet wounds. That wasn't from trying to get to me, it was from trying to escape after you—what? *Assassinated him?*" His voice dropped to a whisper, and he glanced over his shoulder, panic widening his eyes. "Did they *plan* tonight's coup? And what, Gerrit's throwing you to the dogs now that you've opened the way for him?"

"No. Yanek, stop." Yanek's hands had gone cold with fear-sweat. "No. It's..." But he wasn't entirely wrong, either.

"Tell me," Yanek said, and it wasn't a request. "Tell me *everything.*"

Filip swallowed hard. But if he wanted Yanek to come with him, he needed to know. So he told him what he could without risking the resistance further. Lucie and phosgene; the Wolf who was Celka's father. The mental walls Gerrit had built to become a Kladivo and hide from his grief. Celka's sousedni-choke. And tonight. Bursting out of the closet, invisible, getting shot to keep Celka close to the Stormhawk.

When he finished, Yanek stared at him, expression a book Filip couldn't read.

"Gerrit's staying behind," Filip said, the words still a gut-punch. "He's thrown in with Iveta and refuses to see that the changes she'll make won't be enough. She's still Tayemstvoy, still a Kladivo. She might loosen the State's death-grip on the people, but she won't release it. She might claim she will, but by the time she's solidified her powerbase, she'll be nearly as bad as her father."

"So you'll start a civil war," Yanek said, voice flat and hard. "Try to depose her—or Artur—whoever comes out on top."

Of course Yanek would see through to that conclusion. Filip wasn't dating him just because he was hot. "We will," Filip admitted. "And innocent people will die. But they're already dying. Beneath Tayemstvoy truncheons and harsh rationing and the indifference of regime elites who care only about their own wealth and power. I've done the math. This revolution will cost fewer lives than will be lost continuing to live under the Stormhawk's regime—even if Iveta makes it better. And on the other side of revolution, we have a chance to build something better. People shouldn't be afraid to speak their minds, Yanek. They shouldn't be afraid to sing in prayer or protest peacefully.

"My Storm Guard oaths were to protect Bourshkanya," Filip continued. "That's what I'm doing. I'm protecting Bourshkanyans who can't fight alone. I'd like to do it at your side."

Low, Yanek said, "Maybe you should have thought of that a week ago. A month ago. How long have you been planning this? The whole time we've been together? Have you *always* been planning to leave?"

Filip shook his head. "I tried to convince Gerrit to stay." The irony of it didn't make the pain any easier to bear. "I thought for a long time we could change the regime from within. I was wrong."

"What about your family?" Yanek asked, pained, and Filip could see him thinking about his own.

"Gerrit plans to make it look like we died in the aftermath. It wouldn't be that hard for him to do the same for you. Your family would be safe."

Yanek shook his head but didn't argue.

"Come with me," Filip said. "You've been as disturbed by civilian oppressions as I have. Help me end them."

Yanek slumped back against the couch and covered his face with his hands. "*Sleet.*"

Tentative, Filip laid a hand on Yanek's thigh. Yanek tensed, but didn't pull away. "I'm sorry I couldn't tell you earlier. I couldn't risk our mission. Though I wanted to—a million times I wanted to ask you. And I'm asking *now*. Please."

He felt it the moment Yanek decided. After all the time

they'd spent exploring each other's bodies, he knew the way Yanek's breath slowed when he'd made a decision, worked through some problem. Yanek's tension eased—just a little—and his hands slipped from his face. One hand landed on Filip's, and Yanek squeezed in familiar comfort.

Filip struggled to keep breathing. He knew Yanek had decided—but he didn't know what choice he'd made.

"You're right," Yanek whispered, "that the regime is corrupt, that the Tayemstvoy take too many liberties. The Storm Gods' blessings are for everyone. But..." He shook his head, and Filip felt himself falling. "We can't tear it all down. The major—Iveta—she's been a good commander. She understands people and magic. She has a chance to make it better without first making everything worse."

"She *will* make it worse," Filip said, even as he knew that arguing would do him no good.

Yanek shook his head. "You know I hate agreeing with the baby-hawk, but I think Gerrit's right. Iveta has a chance—if we back her. You're brilliant, but you've calculated wrong." Yanek cupped his face in one big hand, and Filip couldn't help but lean into his touch. "Starting a civil war isn't the answer, my love."

Those last words choked Filip's throat, but he shook his head.

Yanek searched his face. "I know you care about people. A civil war will kill so many. Stay with me. Stay with Gerrit—he asked you to, didn't he? Imbue. You can lead the imbuement platoon while Gerrit and Iveta consolidate power. Your people are *here*, Filip, in the platoon. *We* need your leadership too. Don't abandon the real people and real change you can make here for some lightning-strike chance that could as easily burn the countryside as save it." He brought his other hand up, cupping Filip's face. "Stay with me."

Yanek's imagined future drew Filip in a way that all Gerrit's self-important arguments had not. This last month, when he hadn't been worrying about Gerrit warping or Celka's assassination, Filip had finally found his place. He'd liked leading the imbuement platoon, loved waking up next to Yanek every morning. But he couldn't bury his head in a snowdrift and pretend winter hadn't come.

Leaning in, Filip kissed Yanek lightly on his lips. When he drew back, he whispered, "I'll miss you."

Yanek caught his cheeks, arresting his retreat. "Don't."

But his hold only caught Filip for a second, a spear of regret in his chest before he pulled free. Touching his partner's face, he said, "Take care of yourself, Yanek. I hope we'll meet again in a better Bourshkanya."

CHAPTER SIXTY-FOUR

Dawn lightened the sky as Celka climbed out of a ravine, following the trail Jolana had broken in the snow. They'd hiked for several hours in darkness, snowfall muffling the creak of wind through the trees. At first, Jolana had taken rear guard, watching for pursuit as Celka and Filip traded off breaking the trail, Celka awkward in the unaccustomed snowshoes, Nina and a full pack weighing her down.

More than scanning for pursuit, Jolana had covered their tracks, a concealment imbuement wiping the snow free of any sign of their passing. She'd abandoned the imbuement after the first hour and moved to the head of their group, taking Nina from Celka and breaking the trail as easily as if they hiked on solid ground. Celka had been relieved to fall back, her breath coming hard at the exertion—though at least the Army's obsession with running was finally paying off.

As dawn revealed colors, Celka found that Filip had fallen further behind, his face ashen. Though they'd transferred what they could from his pack, he barely kept pace. She wished they could afford to let him rest, wished the Okhrana doctor could have restored more of his lost blood. But Celka didn't know whether Gerrit's charade of discovering them 'dead' would hold and, despite the precarious nature of her coup, Iveta might still send the Okhrana out hunting the Stormhawk's assassins.

Celka stepped off the packed trail, waiting for Filip to catch up as bare larch branches blazed orange in the rising sun. She expected Filip to pause when he reached her, but he trudged on, gaze on the snow at his feet.

Floundering through the unbroken snow, Celka fell in at his side and reached out, catching his fur-lined mitten.

Filip's stride faltered but resumed. After a moment, he returned her grip weakly before slipping free.

They'd had no time to discuss Gerrit's betrayal, and Filip had said no more about Yanek than "He's not coming." Filip had lost a lot of blood, but she suspected that some of what dragged him down was heartbreak.

She fell in behind him on Jolana's trail, part of her still amazed that Filip had come. But if she'd learned anything from their time together, it was Filip's strength—a strength drawn from how deeply he cared about people. Losing Gerrit and Yanek would shake him, but he wouldn't shatter. He'd chosen the resistance. He'd chosen her.

He'd regain his strength, and together, they'd imbue the sky.

At the top of the ridge, Celka paused. The sun formed a burning ball on the horizon, the mountains glowing like they'd been imbued. Shadows still cloaked the valley they'd climbed out of and, somewhere beyond it, the glittering opulence of Yinovatka Manor.

Breathing deep lungfuls of crisp, cold air, Celka faced the rising sun, reveling in a feeling of lightness. Despite her heavy pack, weight eased from her shoulders with each kilometer they put between themselves and State control.

No longer would she imbue what the Tayemstvoy ordered. From now on, her imbuements would be her own. She was free to help people—and to fight.

Thinking of Gerrit locked inside the regime's long shadow made that victory colder, though the ache of losing him wasn't as sharp as she'd expected. Joint-imbuing paranoid violence and the riot in Mrach had driven a wedge between them. With a cold creep like frostbite, Celka realized that ever since Gerrit had sent them to imbue without him, she'd been waiting for him to turn his back.

She expected to be angry at him, but staring down into a world slowly brightening with dawn, what squeezed her chest was sadness. She'd miss him.

Gerrit had come into her life when she'd desperately needed a friend who understood the bozhskyeh storms' pull. He'd been that and so much more.

Had the resistance asked too much of him? Had she? Could she look back and find some mistake that had shattered their trust, or had losing him been inevitable? They'd come from such different worlds. But even knowing he'd turned his back—on her, on the resistance—she couldn't hate him. She didn't want his coup to succeed, didn't want another Stormhawk to crush Bourshkanya, even if Iveta would be a gentler dictator. But she also didn't want to see Gerrit hurt.

Because Celka couldn't kid herself that what was coming would be easy. Even if Captain Vrana's plan worked perfectly— if Gerrit and Iveta wrested enough regime control from Artur to break the regime's spine with infighting—the State was strong. They had trained soldiers and ruthless Tayemstvoy and wealth beyond Celka's childhood imaginings.

But Celka still believed the resistance could win.

All across Bourshkanya, people had begun to stand together against the State. Despite Tayemstvoy violence, they refused to cower, refused to fall silent. Soon, Celka would add her voice to theirs, bringing the Storm Gods' blessings to the people who deserved them.

In the shadows below, the Stormhawk was dead. Turning her back on the shrinking darkness, Celka returned to the path Jolana had beaten into the snow. The resistance may not have the State's wealth, but they had their own strength. Celka had done and seen terrible things to reach this moment, but now she strode forward into the light.

The revolution had begun.

GLOSSARY

Bourshkanyan is derived largely from Czech and
Russian and, as such, some words may have other meanings.
For more detailed world notes and bonus content,
visit: *www.corrylee.com*

Bourshkanya (n), **Bourshkanyan** (adj): Country with a high
rate of storm magic, currently ruled by the fascist leader
styling himself The Stormhawk.

bozhk (pl. **bozhki**): Someone with a storm-affinity; a storm
mage. Typically used for a State-trained mage who has
demonstrated control of their storm-affinity (at least a
copper-bolt).

bozhskyeh storms: Thunderstorms in which (some of) the
lightning is actually Gods' Breath, which can be used by
an imbuement mage to create new magical objects.

cizii (adj), **cizli** (n): Imprudent in storms, not respecting the
Storm Gods, foreign.

cizii myesto: "Imprudent city," a game played by throwing
a lightning bolt (a wooden bat) at a group of cylindrical

wooden "houses" that are arranged inside a box drawn on the ground (the bounds of the city). The goal is to knock all the cizii domu (imprudent houses) out of the city in the fewest throws possible.

Gods' Breath: Magical lightning from bozhskyeh storms. See *storm energy*. Color appears red-gold to someone with a strong enough storm-affinity.

kosovorotka: A long-sleeved shirt reaching down to mid-thigh, which buttons half-way down the chest, with the opening off to one side of the collar, giving it an asymmetric look. Collar and cuffs are often colorfully embroidered.

kvass: Carbonated drink made by fermenting bread (typically rye); sometimes flavored with fruit, berries, or birch sap. Non-alcoholic (or very low alcohol). Can be sweet or sour. Served cold.

loupak: Sweet, cardamom-filled crescent rolls coated with poppy seeds.

Lesnikraj (n), Lesnikrayen (adj): Country with which Bourshkanya fought a devastating war two decades ago.

medovnik: Spongey, multi-layered honey cake.

mundane: Colloquial term for someone with no storm-affinity.

nuzhda (pl. nuzhdi): The intense, desperate need used to activate an existing imbuement or create a new one.

plodnosti (n): Medical procedure using a healing imbuement that stops a person's menstrual cycle and prevents them from becoming pregnant until the treatment is reversed. Under the Stormhawk's regime, this treatment is only available to those of "high potential," typically meaning the wealthy, in a program to repopulate Bourshkanya after the losses in the Lesnikrayen war.

ponchiki: Round balls of fried dough usually dusted with powdered sugar.

red shoulders (n): Derogatory term for the Tayemstvoy, based on the red epaulettes of their uniforms (and perhaps their penchant for violence, often resulting in blood).

Adj form is hyphenated (e.g., "he's a red-shouldered hail-eater!")

rezistyent (pl. **rezistyenti**): A member (or presumed member) of the resistance, acting against the Stormhawk's regime. A traitor to the State.

sarafan: A long dress.

sbiten: A hot, dark purple drink made with honey mixed with water, spices, and jam. Can be very spicy or very sweet, depending on the recipe.

Slavni Cirkus: Traveling circus in which Celka's family, "The Amazing Prochazkas," perform.

smoke-form: Colloquial description of the sousedni-shape of a person with no storm-affinity.

sousednia: The neighboring reality of needs and ideas, which has tenuous connections to physical objects/space. Storm-blessed bozhki can see sousednia and, during bozhskyeh storms, build from within it the magical weaves necessary to imbue.

sousedni-cues (n): Synesthetic bleed-through from sousednia into true-life; used by some to read emotional state, lies vs. truth, etc.

sousedni-dislocation: Separating one's true-form and sousedni-shape in 'physical' distance

sousedni-shape: How a person appears in sousednia. (Often in contrast to their true-form.)

Stanek pistol (n): Side-arm carried by Bourshkanyan Army and Tayemstvoy officers. Similar to a Colt 1911 pistol.

storm-affinity: Magical ability; sensitivity to storm magic.

storm-blessed: A bozhk able to see and interact with sousednia. During a bozhskyeh storm, they may be able to create new magical imbuements.

storm blood (n): Colloquially, someone with a storm-affinity has "storm blood" in their veins.

storm energy (n): The raw energy from Gods' Breath (lightning in a bozhskyeh storm), which is necessary to crystalize nuzhda weaves to create an imbuement. A bozhk channels storm energy through themself and into their weaves in order to imbue.

storm temple: Religious gathering place for Bourshkanya's dominant religion, which worships the Storm Gods and their Miracles. Typically, an asymmetric building with one wall that opens up on a square containing a storm tower (lightning rod).

Storm Gods: The primary gods revered in Bourshkanya; always referenced in plural.

Stormhawk: (1) The popular name used by Bourshkanya's dictator, Supreme-General Kladivo; (2) a hawk said to herald bozhskyeh storms, which rides the wild currents of such storms; (3) a 2-headed stormhawk is used as a symbol for the Tayemstvoy.

storm-mad (adj): A person who loses true-life (often a storm-blessed mage who overflowed storm energy into themself from too large or uncontrolled an imbuement) is considered storm-mad.

storm-mark: The lightning strike filigree left behind on physical objects where an imbuement mage called down Gods' breath. The equivalent mark left on a person is called a storm-scar. Similar in appearance to a Lichtenberg figure.

storm pendant: Common religious item in Bourshkanya. Typically made of a conducting metal that can be charged by rubbing with a 'charging cloth' to produce a spark, used in prayer to the Storm Gods.

storm-scar (n): The lightning strike filigree burned into a mage's flesh as the result of an imbuement. For an imbuement mage, it begins at the base of their skull, extending in a roughly radial pattern across back and shoulders and down to the arm(s) holding the imbued object. Strazh mages can also end up storm-scarred, their scars growing from their point-of-contact with the imbuement mage.

storm-thread (n): The connection an imbuement mage feels to a bozhskyeh storm, which manifests physically in sousednia during a storm.

storm-touched (adj): A bozhk capable of controlling nuzhdi enough to activate imbuements, but incapable of seeing sousednia.

strazh (pl. **strazhi**): A bozhk who works with an imbuement mage during imbuements to ground them and control overflowed storm energy, thereby making it safer to imbue. Typically, a strong storm-touched bozhk with a high bolt-level and an affinity to protection nuzhda.

Tayemstvoy: The Bourshkanyan regime's secret police. Colloquially called: "hawks" (respectful); "red shoulders" (derogatory)

true-life: The reality visible to everyone (in contrast to sousednia, visible only to storm-blessed bozhki).

true-form: A person's physical appearance (in contrast to sousedni-shape).

tvoortse (pl. **tvoortsei**): Imbuement mage (implication that they have imbued at least once, in control). All tvoortse are storm-blessed; not all storm-blessed are tvoortse (e.g., a storm-blessed bozhk in the off-cycle would have no opportunity to become a tvoortse).

Uhersky rifle: Bourshkanyan bolt-action rifle; standard issue to modern infantry.

Wolf, the: The resistance leader, from the design of a running wolf that signs resistance leaflets.

Yestrab Okhrana: The Stormhawk's personal guard.

ACKNOWLEDGEMENTS

So MUCH CAN change while writing a single book. When I started *The Storm's Betrayal* in 2019, *Weave the Lightning* had not been published, my little brother was still alive, and 2020 seemed full of promise. Whew. But we're here. We're pushing forward.

I owe so much of this book's excellence to my husband, Dr. Josh Boehm. My staunchest ally, stalwart parenting support, inventive brainstormer, and critical fiction-reader—you, my love, have made so much possible.

Many others helped me make this book enormously better. Thanks to... The No Name Writing Group—Rhiannon Held, Kate Alice Marshall, Susan J. Morris, Erin M. Evans, and Shanna Germain—for telling me hard truths in early drafts and supporting me as I figured out how to fix those problems. My agent, Lisa Rodgers, who saw straight to the heart of several problems no one else had noticed. My editor, David Thomas Moore, for sharpening the language. All the wonderful folks at Rebellion for believing in this book; and Sam Gretton for another beautiful cover.

Special thanks to my daughter, Alarice, who gives the best hugs, asks questions about my writing that inspire challenging discussions to have with a 6-year-old, and calls me a "famous author."

I came out as pansexual while writing this book. Thank you to all the wonderful people, including my parents, who've supported me as I embrace my whole self.

To people working to destigmatize and make treatment available for mental health issues, thank you. For people struggling with mental health, you are brave and valued—and you are not alone.

Finally, as I revised this book in the midst of a global pandemic, thousands of people were out protesting police brutality and demanding racial justice. For all the courageous people who stood up, spoke up, and demanded equality, thank you. #BlackLivesMatter. Let's keep fighting until justice is real.

FIND US ONLINE!

www.rebellionpublishing.com

/rebellionpub   /rebellionpublishing /rebellionpublishing

SIGN UP TO OUR NEWSLETTER!

rebellionpublishing.com/newsletter

YOUR REVIEWS MATTER!

Enjoy this book? Got something to say?

Leave a review on Amazon, GoodReads or with your
favourite bookseller and let the world know!